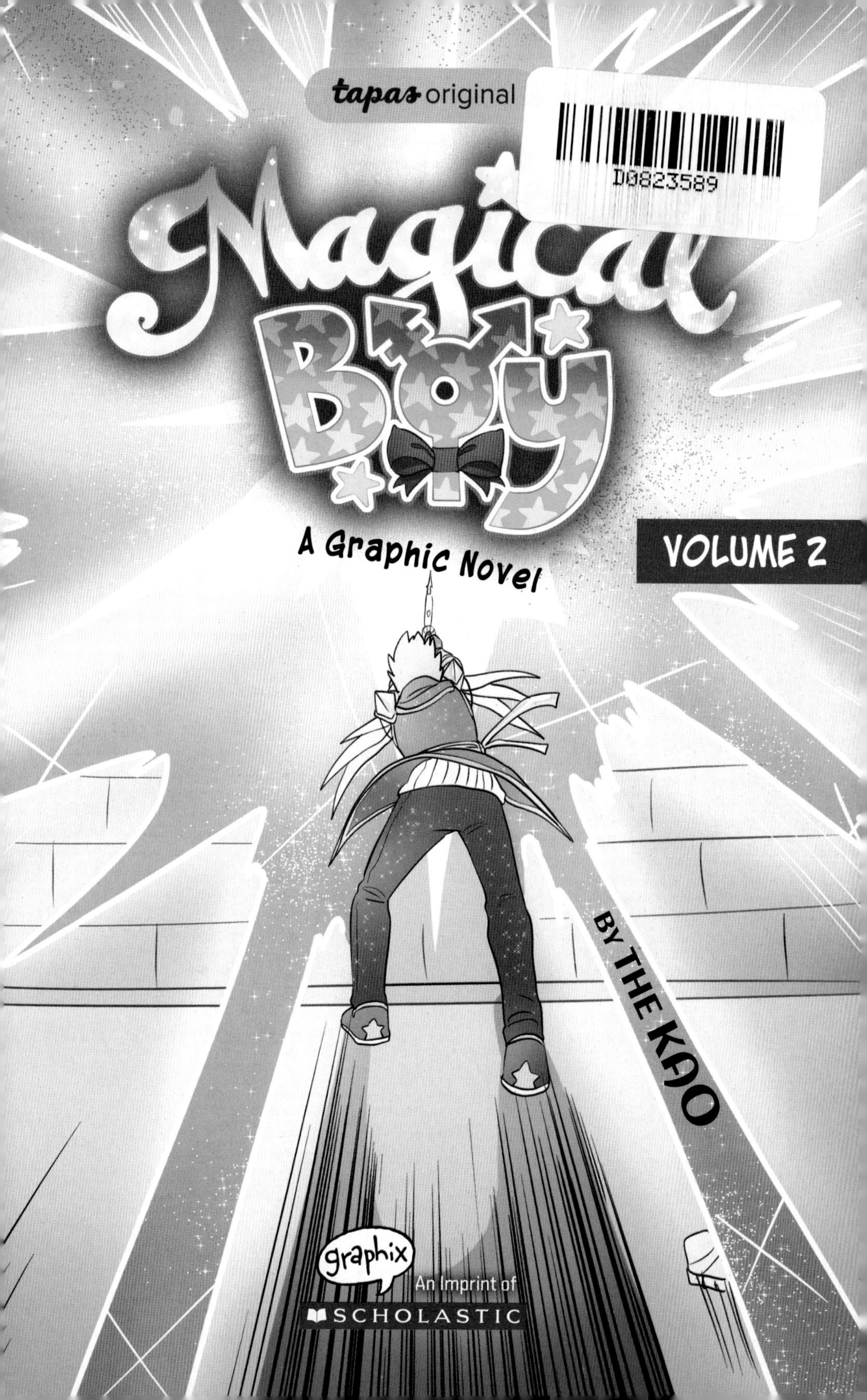
tapas original
Magical Boy
A Graphic Novel
VOLUME 2
BY THE KAO
graphix
An Imprint of
SCHOLASTIC

CONTENT ADVISORY:
THIS GRAPHIC NOVEL CONTAINS INSTANCES
OF DEAD NAMING, HOMOPHOBIA, TRANSPHOBIA,
MISGENDERING, AND FORCED GENDER EXPRESSION
THAT MAY BE DISTRESSING TO SOME.

Copyright © 2022 by The Kao and Tapas Media, Inc. All rights reserved.

First published online in 2018 by Tapas. All rights reserved. Published by Graphix, an imprint of Scholastic Inc., *Publishers since 1920*. SCHOLASTIC, GRAPHIX, and associated logos are trademarks and/or registered trademarks of Scholastic Inc.

The publisher does not have any control over and does not assume any responsibility for author or third-party websites or their content.

No part of this publication may be reproduced, stored in a retrieval system, or transmitted in any form or by any means, electronic, mechanical, photocopying, recording, or otherwise, without written permission of the publisher. For information regarding permission, write to Scholastic Inc., Attention: Permissions Department, 557 Broadway, New York, NY 10012.

This book is a work of fiction. Names, characters, places, and incidents are either the product of the author's imagination or are used fictitiously, and any resemblance to actual persons, living or dead, business establishments, events, or locales is entirely coincidental.

ISBN 978-1-338-81592-4 (PB)

ISBN 978-1-338-81597-9 (HC)

10 9 8 7 6 5 4 3 2 1   22 23 24 25 26

Printed in China   62

First edition, September 2022

Edited by Michael Petranek and Lori Wieczorek

Book design by Jeff Shake and Salena Mahina

Lettering by Dezi Sienty

For Tapas:

Edited by Brooke Huang

Colored by Dojo Gubser

Art assistance by Sera Swati

Additional assistance by Selena Ahmed

Editor in Chief Jamie S. Rich

Dear Reader,

Magical Boy is a story I've been wanting to tell for a long time. I wanted to create a story about a hero who embarks on a messy, funny, difficult, outrageous, and ultimately rewarding journey, and I wanted that hero to be someone who all readers—but especially transmen—can cheer on and relate to.

Like any good story, there will be conflict. There will be times when Max faces hardships and obstacles to his transition, and some of those will be from Max's own internal struggles as well. He's a teen who's still going through the messy process of figuring out who he is as a person in many aspects. There are people in his life who won't understand him, and there will be times when he doubts himself.

I know that *Magical Boy* will be tough for some to read at times. I wanted to create a story that is authentic and true to experiences that many transmen have faced, but please don't doubt that I have the best intentions for Max. I know that *Magical Boy* can't be representative of every transman's experience, but I hope that you'll find his journey of self-discovery and overcoming the fictional obstacle of his Magical Girl lineage to be fun, compelling, and genuine.

Max is a character that I hold close to my heart, and I hope that you'll hold him close to yours, too.

—The Kao

EPISODE 16:
SELF-DOUBT

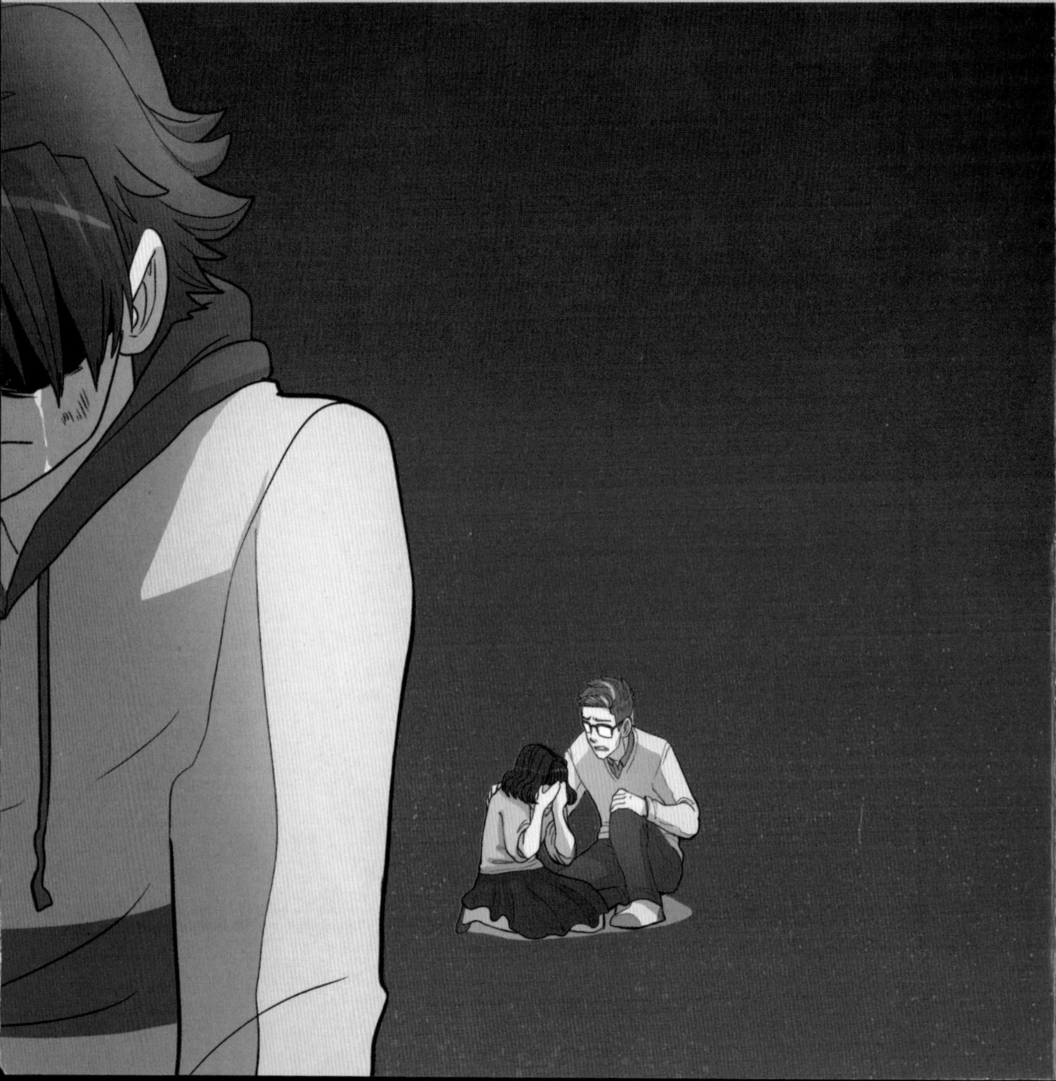

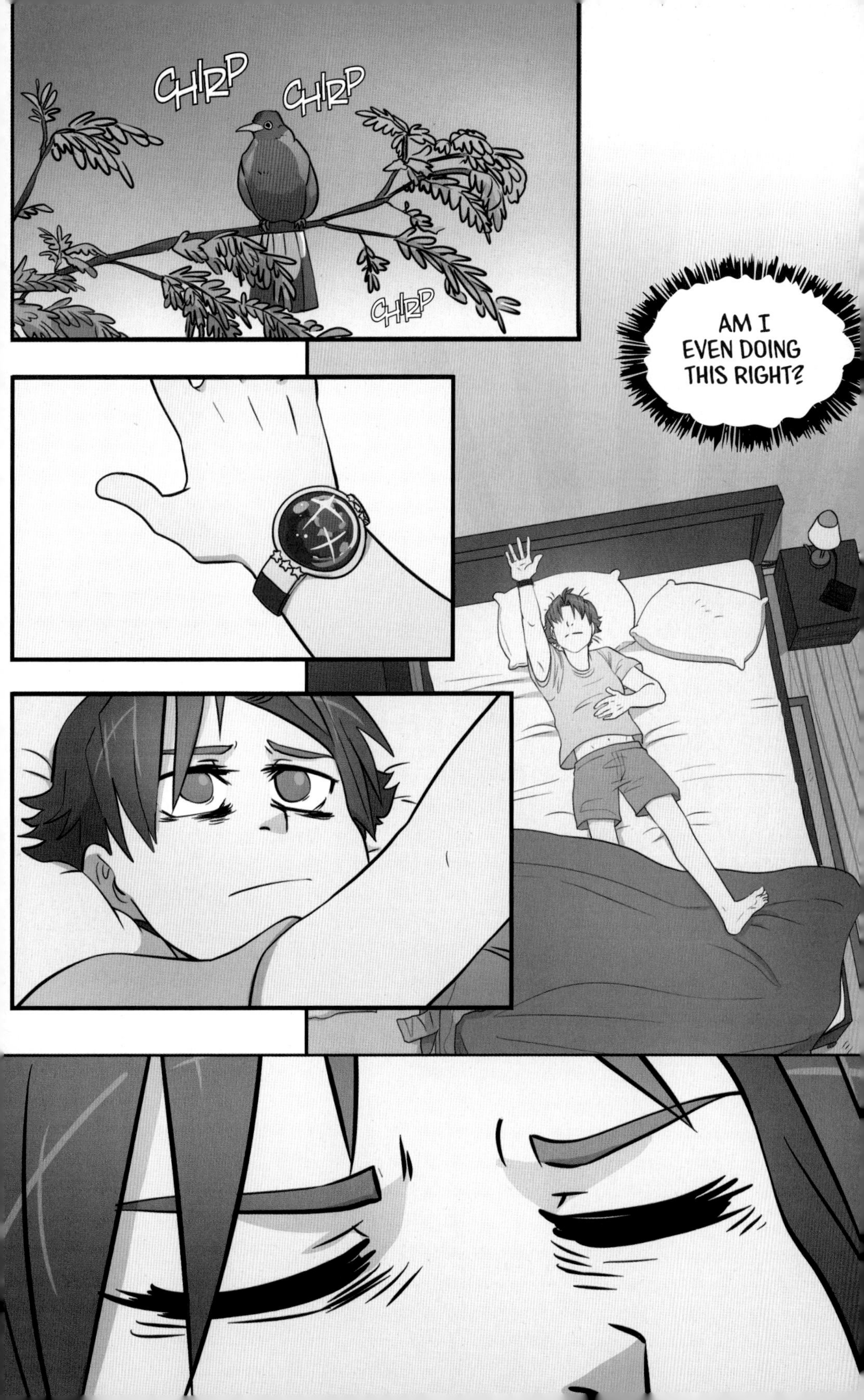
CHIRP
CHIRP
CHIRP
AM I EVEN DOING THIS RIGHT?

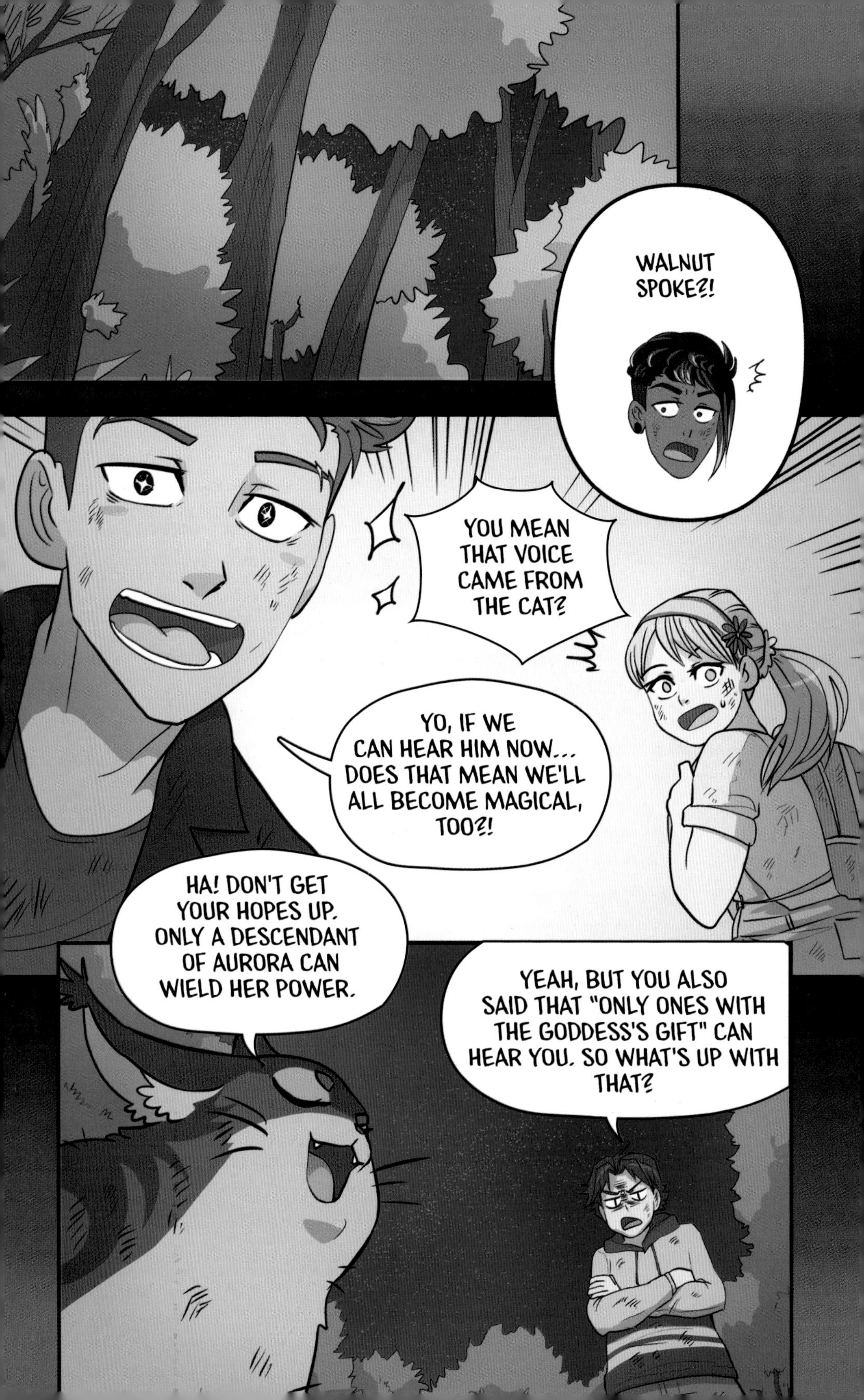
WALNUT SPOKE?!
YOU MEAN THAT VOICE CAME FROM THE CAT?
YO, IF WE CAN HEAR HIM NOW... DOES THAT MEAN WE'LL ALL BECOME MAGICAL, TOO?!
HA! DON'T GET YOUR HOPES UP. ONLY A DESCENDANT OF AURORA CAN WIELD HER POWER.
YEAH, BUT YOU ALSO SAID THAT "ONLY ONES WITH THE GODDESS'S GIFT" CAN HEAR YOU. SO WHAT'S UP WITH THAT?

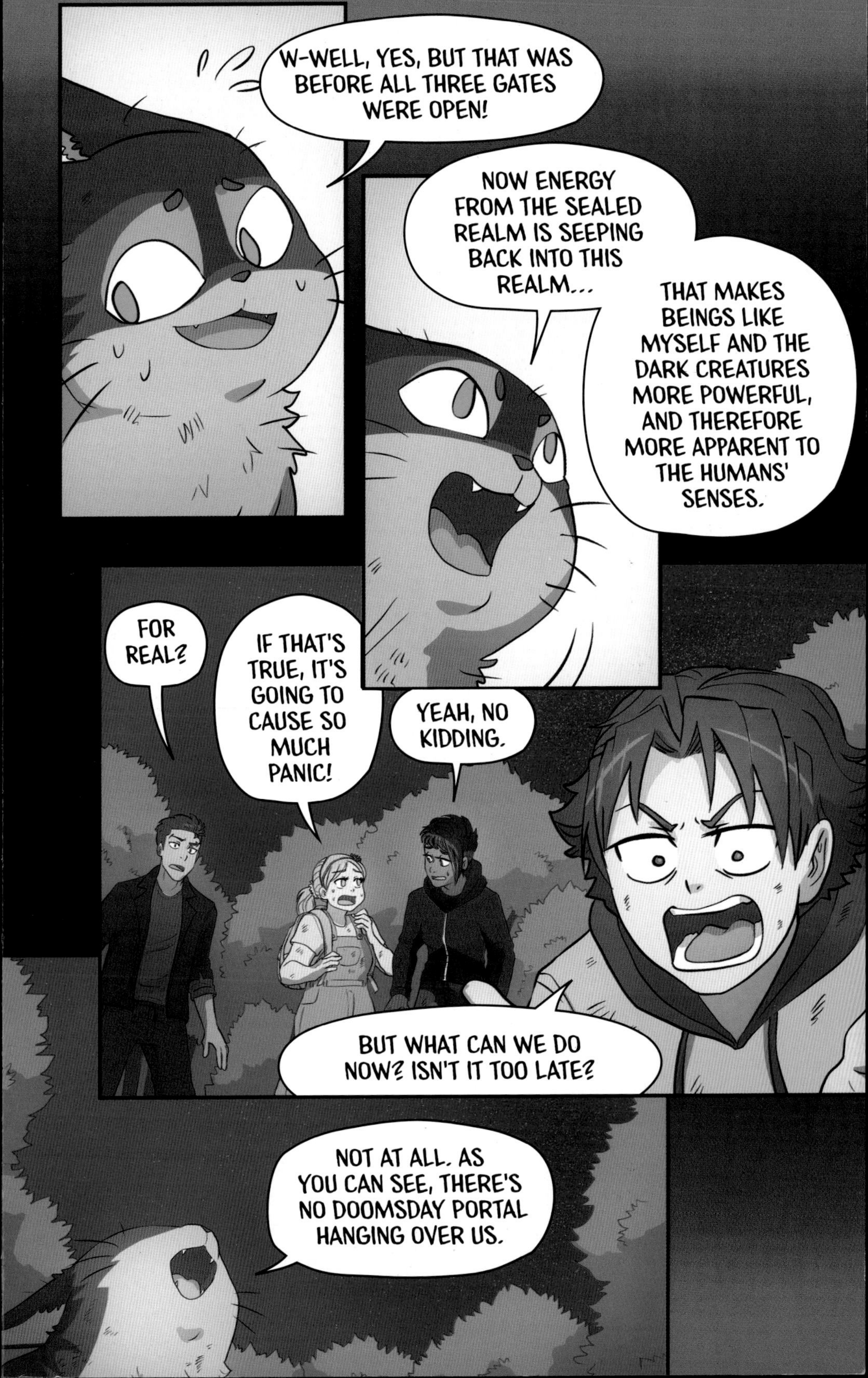
W-WELL, YES, BUT THAT WAS BEFORE ALL THREE GATES WERE OPEN!
NOW ENERGY FROM THE SEALED REALM IS SEEPING BACK INTO THIS REALM...
THAT MAKES BEINGS LIKE MYSELF AND THE DARK CREATURES MORE POWERFUL, AND THEREFORE MORE APPARENT TO THE HUMANS' SENSES.
FOR REAL?
IF THAT'S TRUE, IT'S GOING TO CAUSE SO MUCH PANIC!
YEAH, NO KIDDING.
BUT WHAT CAN WE DO NOW? ISN'T IT TOO LATE?
NOT AT ALL. AS YOU CAN SEE, THERE'S NO DOOMSDAY PORTAL HANGING OVER US.

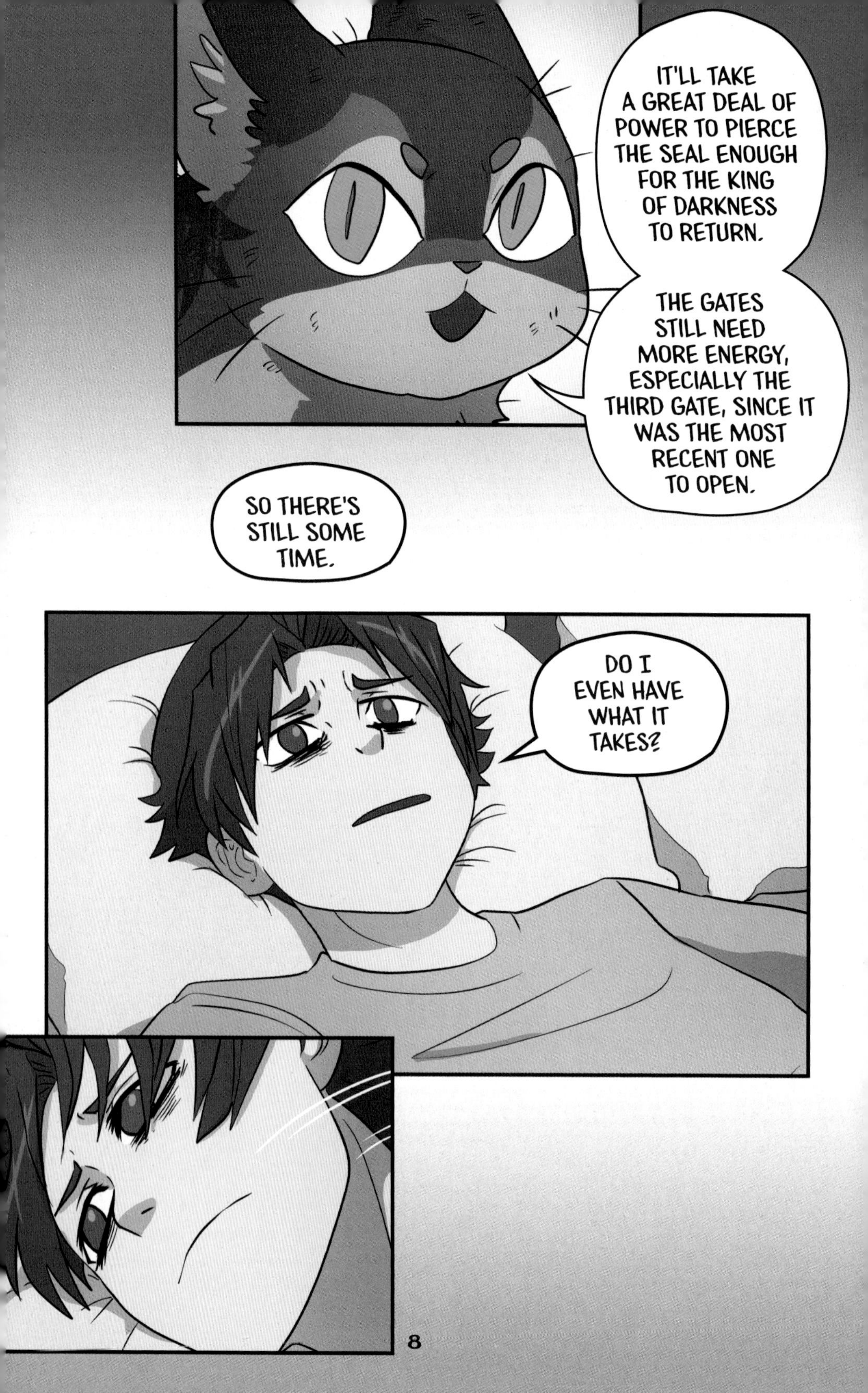
IT'LL TAKE A GREAT DEAL OF POWER TO PIERCE THE SEAL ENOUGH FOR THE KING OF DARKNESS TO RETURN.
THE GATES STILL NEED MORE ENERGY, ESPECIALLY THE THIRD GATE, SINCE IT WAS THE MOST RECENT ONE TO OPEN.
SO THERE'S STILL SOME TIME.
DO I EVEN HAVE WHAT IT TAKES?

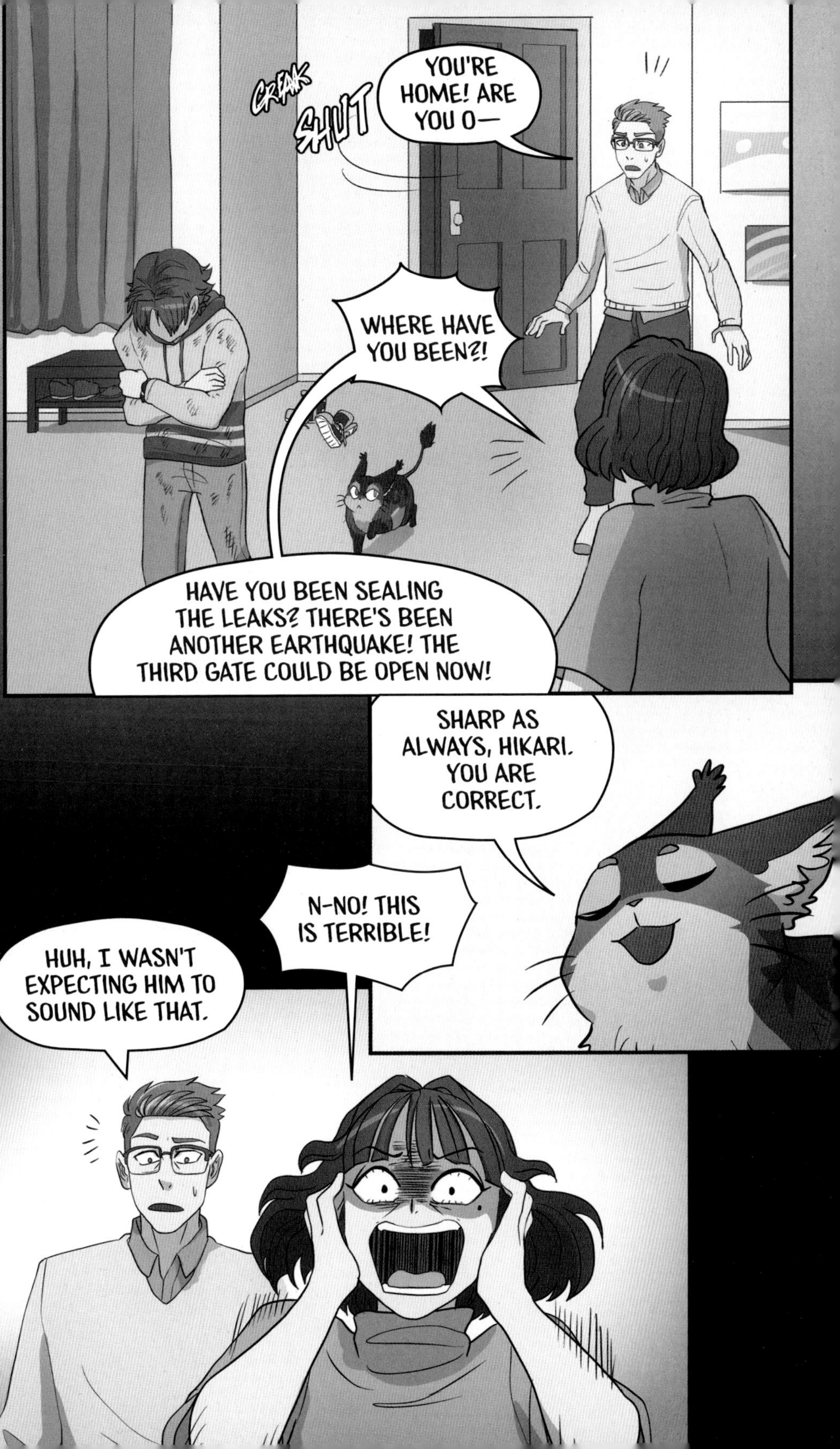
CREAK
SHUT
YOU'RE HOME! ARE YOU O—
WHERE HAVE YOU BEEN?!
HAVE YOU BEEN SEALING THE LEAKS? THERE'S BEEN ANOTHER EARTHQUAKE! THE THIRD GATE COULD BE OPEN NOW!
SHARP AS ALWAYS, HIKARI. YOU ARE CORRECT.
N-NO! THIS IS TERRIBLE!
HUH, I WASN'T EXPECTING HIM TO SOUND LIKE THAT.

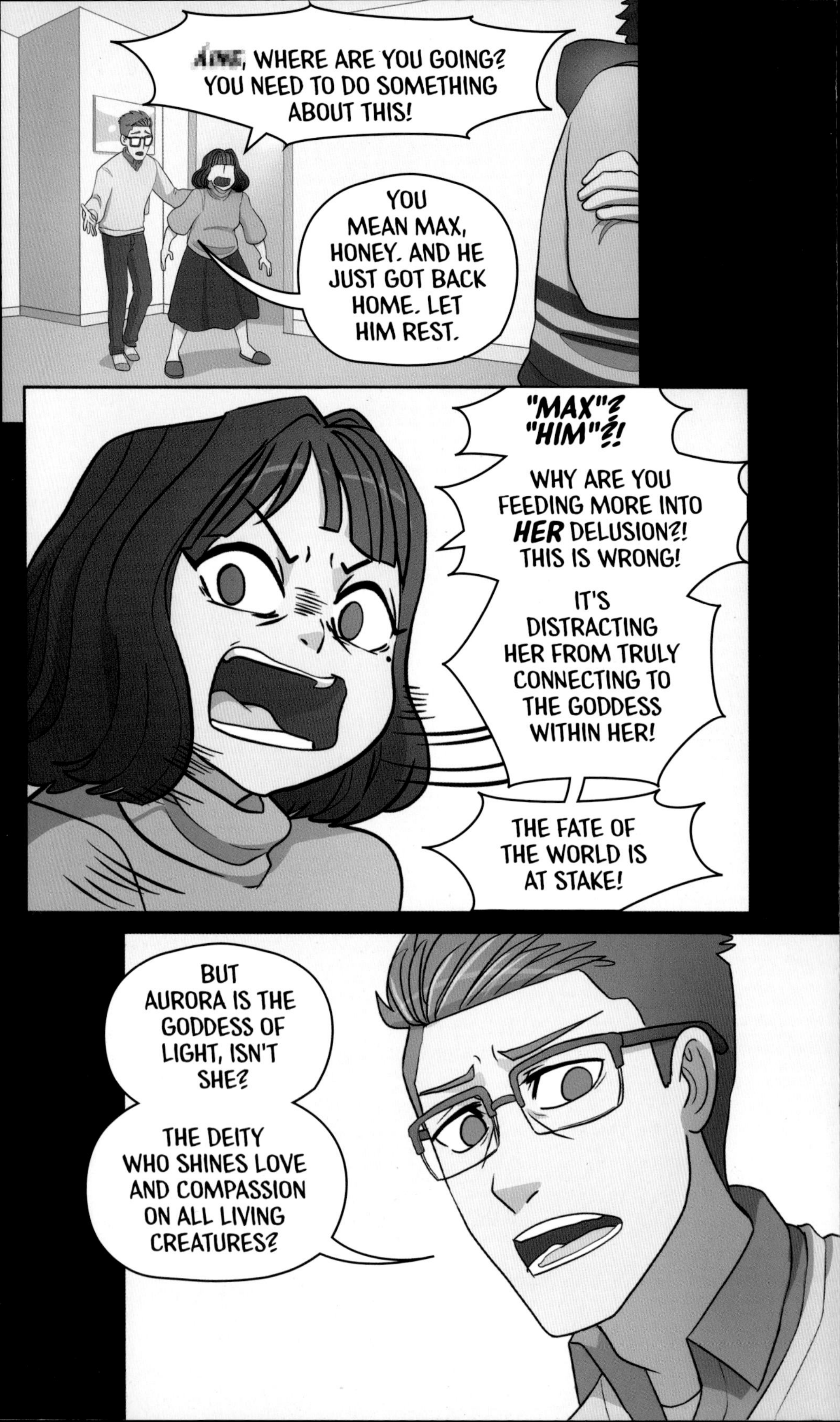
[redacted], WHERE ARE YOU GOING? YOU NEED TO DO SOMETHING ABOUT THIS!
YOU MEAN MAX, HONEY. AND HE JUST GOT BACK HOME. LET HIM REST.
"MAX"? "HIM"?!
WHY ARE YOU FEEDING MORE INTO HER DELUSION?! THIS IS WRONG!
IT'S DISTRACTING HER FROM TRULY CONNECTING TO THE GODDESS WITHIN HER!
THE FATE OF THE WORLD IS AT STAKE!
BUT AURORA IS THE GODDESS OF LIGHT, ISN'T SHE?
THE DEITY WHO SHINES LOVE AND COMPASSION ON ALL LIVING CREATURES?

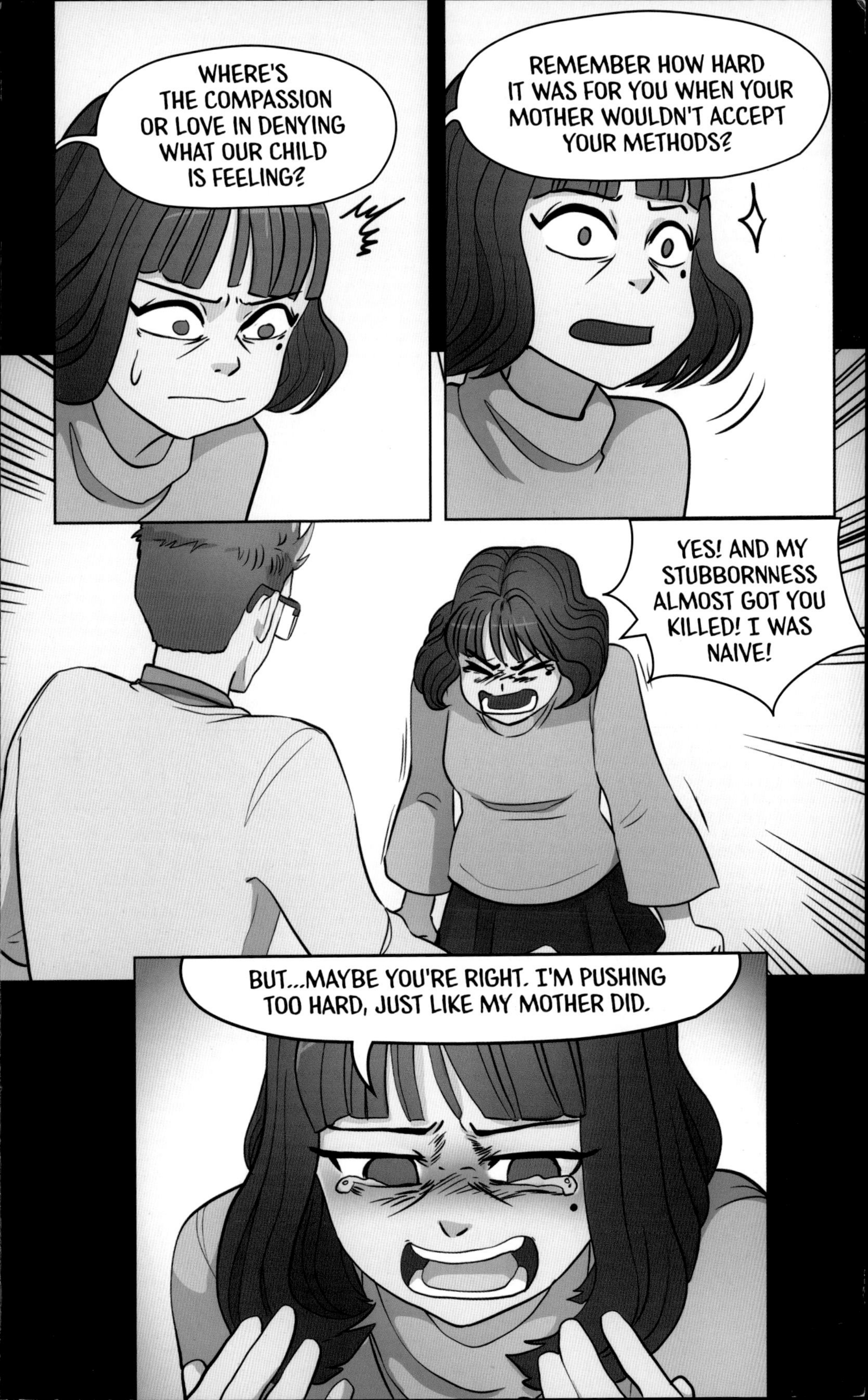
WHERE'S THE COMPASSION OR LOVE IN DENYING WHAT OUR CHILD IS FEELING?
REMEMBER HOW HARD IT WAS FOR YOU WHEN YOUR MOTHER WOULDN'T ACCEPT YOUR METHODS?
YES! AND MY STUBBORNNESS ALMOST GOT YOU KILLED! I WAS NAIVE!
BUT...MAYBE YOU'RE RIGHT. I'M PUSHING TOO HARD, JUST LIKE MY MOTHER DID.

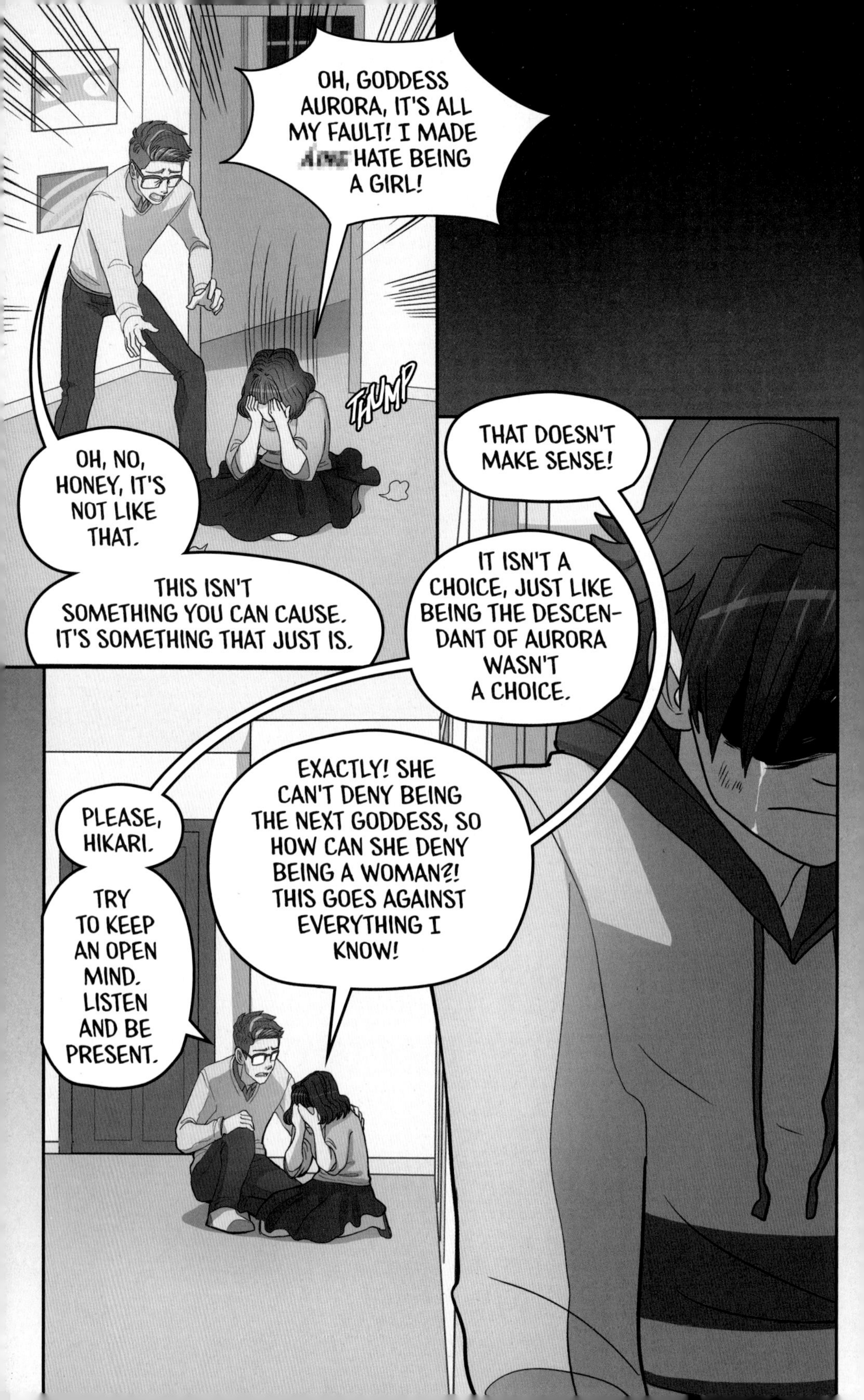
OH, GODDESS AURORA, IT'S ALL MY FAULT! I MADE [redacted] HATE BEING A GIRL!
THUMP
OH, NO, HONEY, IT'S NOT LIKE THAT.
THIS ISN'T SOMETHING YOU CAN CAUSE. IT'S SOMETHING THAT JUST IS.
THAT DOESN'T MAKE SENSE!
IT ISN'T A CHOICE, JUST LIKE BEING THE DESCEN-DANT OF AURORA WASN'T A CHOICE.
PLEASE, HIKARI.
TRY TO KEEP AN OPEN MIND. LISTEN AND BE PRESENT.
EXACTLY! SHE CAN'T DENY BEING THE NEXT GODDESS, SO HOW CAN SHE DENY BEING A WOMAN?! THIS GOES AGAINST EVERYTHING I KNOW!

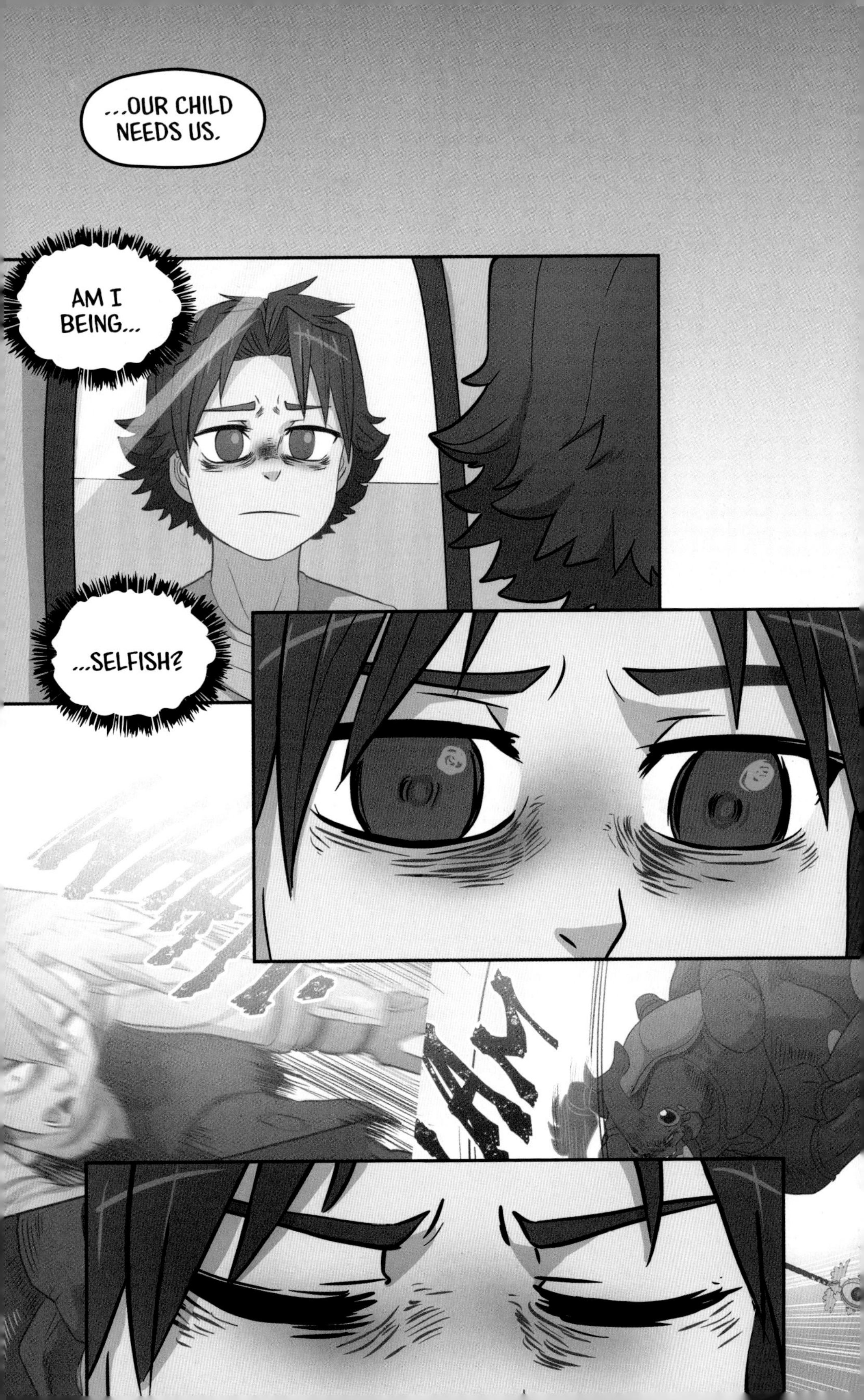
...OUR CHILD NEEDS US.
AM I BEING...
...SELFISH?

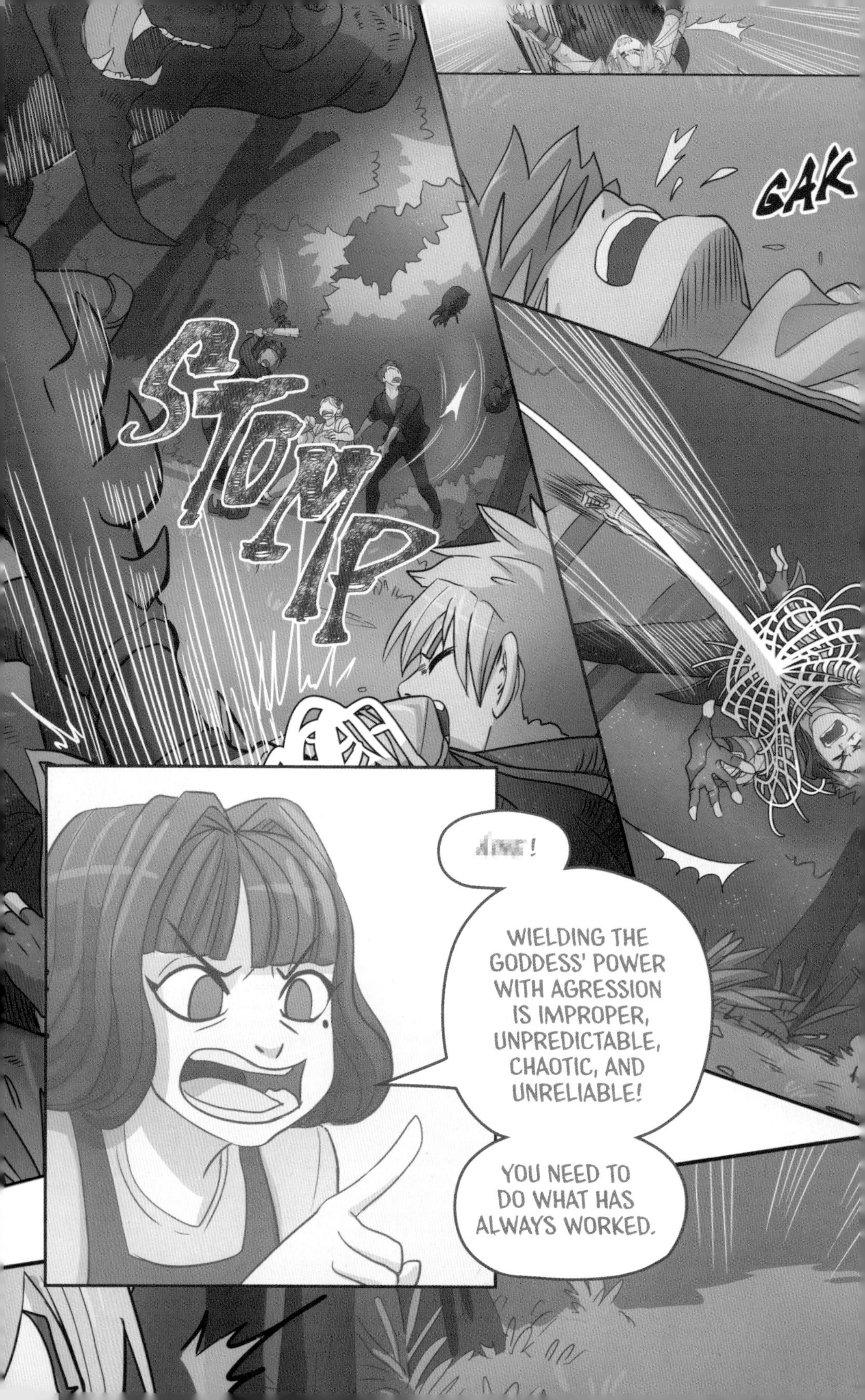
GAK
STOMP
WIELDING THE GODDESS' POWER WITH AGRESSION IS IMPROPER, UNPREDICTABLE, CHAOTIC, AND UNRELIABLE!
YOU NEED TO DO WHAT HAS ALWAYS WORKED.

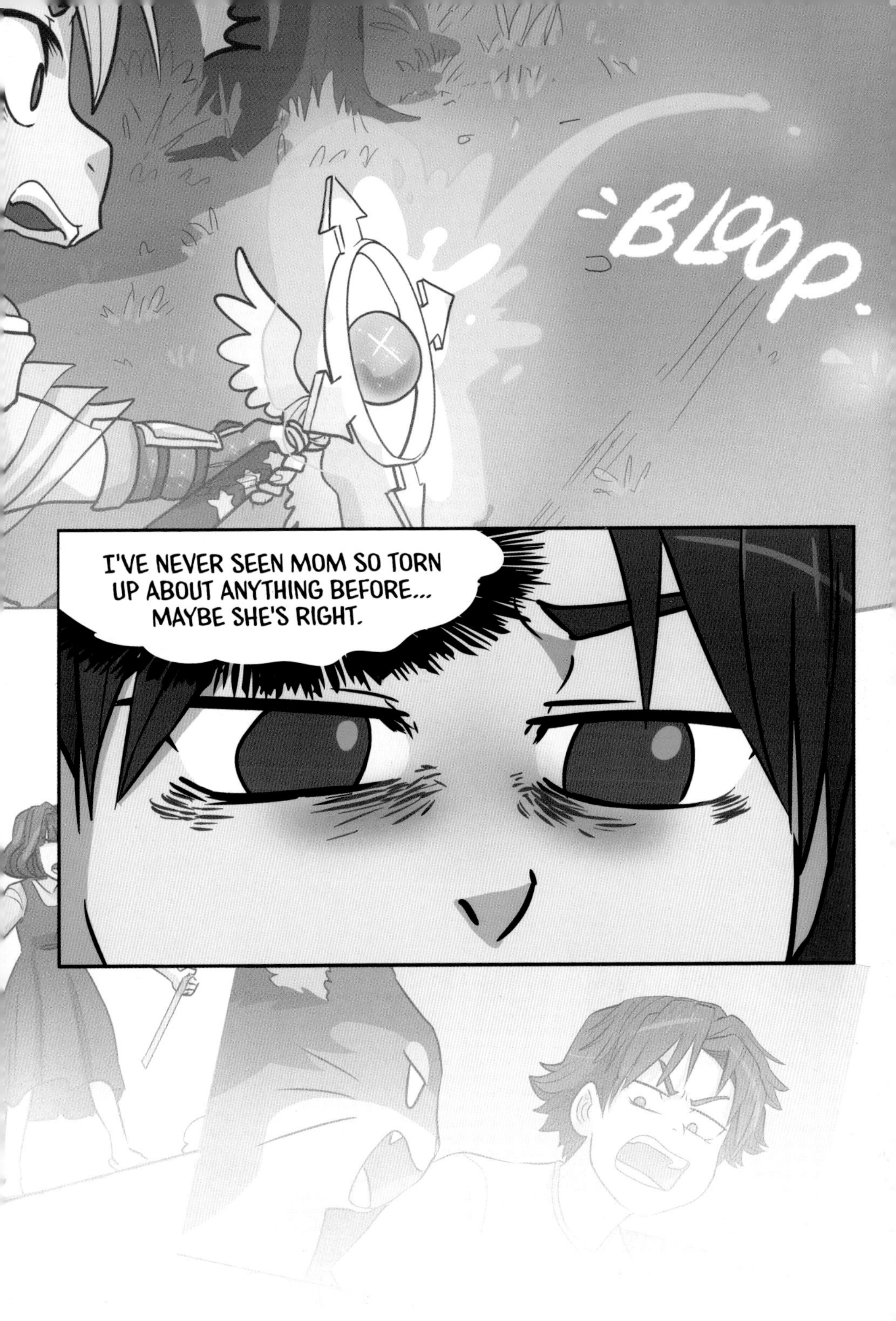
BLOOP
I'VE NEVER SEEN MOM SO TORN UP ABOUT ANYTHING BEFORE... MAYBE SHE'S RIGHT.

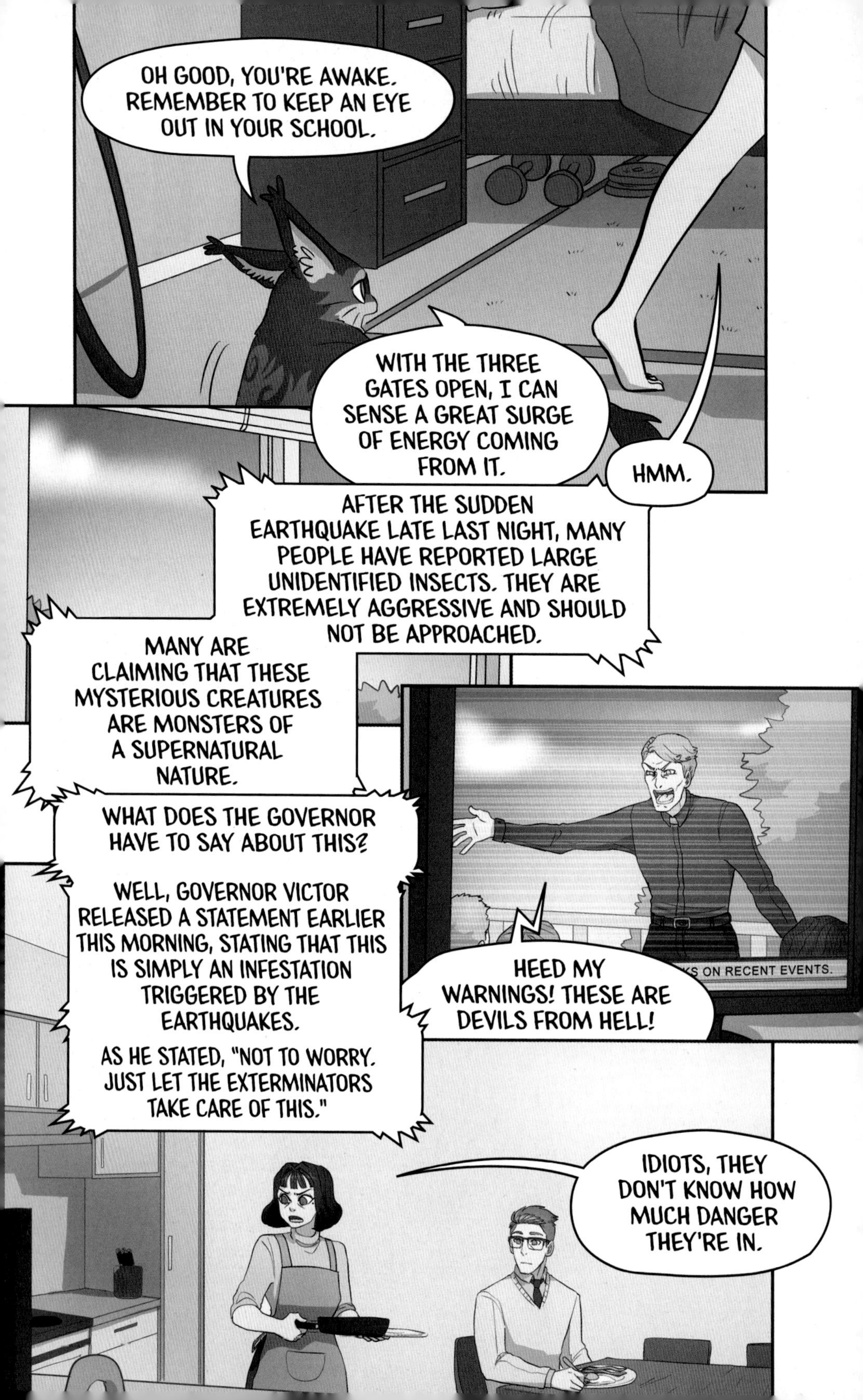
OH GOOD, YOU'RE AWAKE. REMEMBER TO KEEP AN EYE OUT IN YOUR SCHOOL.
WITH THE THREE GATES OPEN, I CAN SENSE A GREAT SURGE OF ENERGY COMING FROM IT.
HMM.
AFTER THE SUDDEN EARTHQUAKE LATE LAST NIGHT, MANY PEOPLE HAVE REPORTED LARGE UNIDENTIFIED INSECTS. THEY ARE EXTREMELY AGGRESSIVE AND SHOULD NOT BE APPROACHED.
MANY ARE CLAIMING THAT THESE MYSTERIOUS CREATURES ARE MONSTERS OF A SUPERNATURAL NATURE.
WHAT DOES THE GOVERNOR HAVE TO SAY ABOUT THIS?
WELL, GOVERNOR VICTOR RELEASED A STATEMENT EARLIER THIS MORNING, STATING THAT THIS IS SIMPLY AN INFESTATION TRIGGERED BY THE EARTHQUAKES.
AS HE STATED, "NOT TO WORRY. JUST LET THE EXTERMINATORS TAKE CARE OF THIS."
HEED MY WARNINGS! THESE ARE DEVILS FROM HELL!
IDIOTS, THEY DON'T KNOW HOW MUCH DANGER THEY'RE IN.

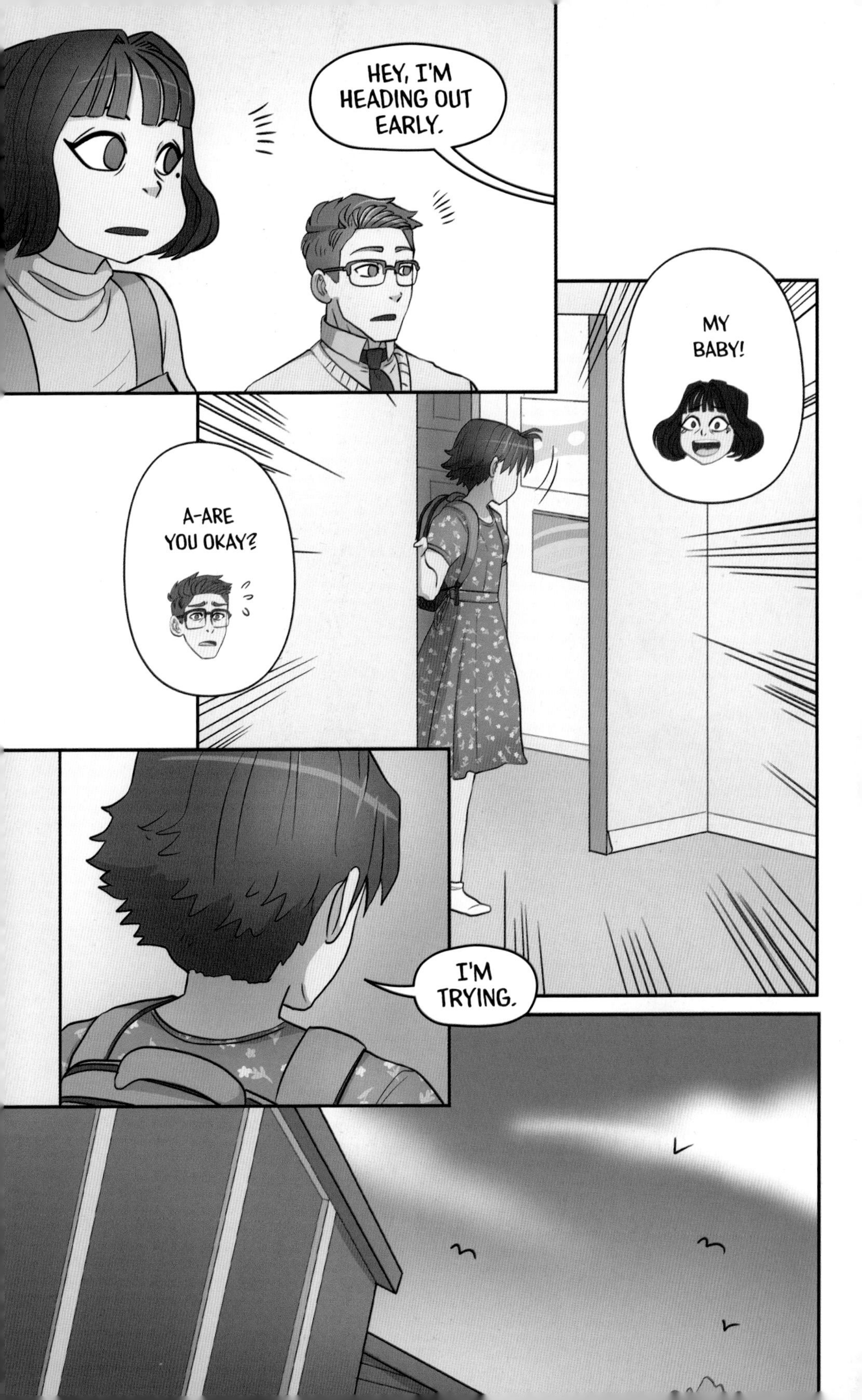
HEY, I'M HEADING OUT EARLY.
MY BABY!
A-ARE YOU OKAY?
I'M TRYING.

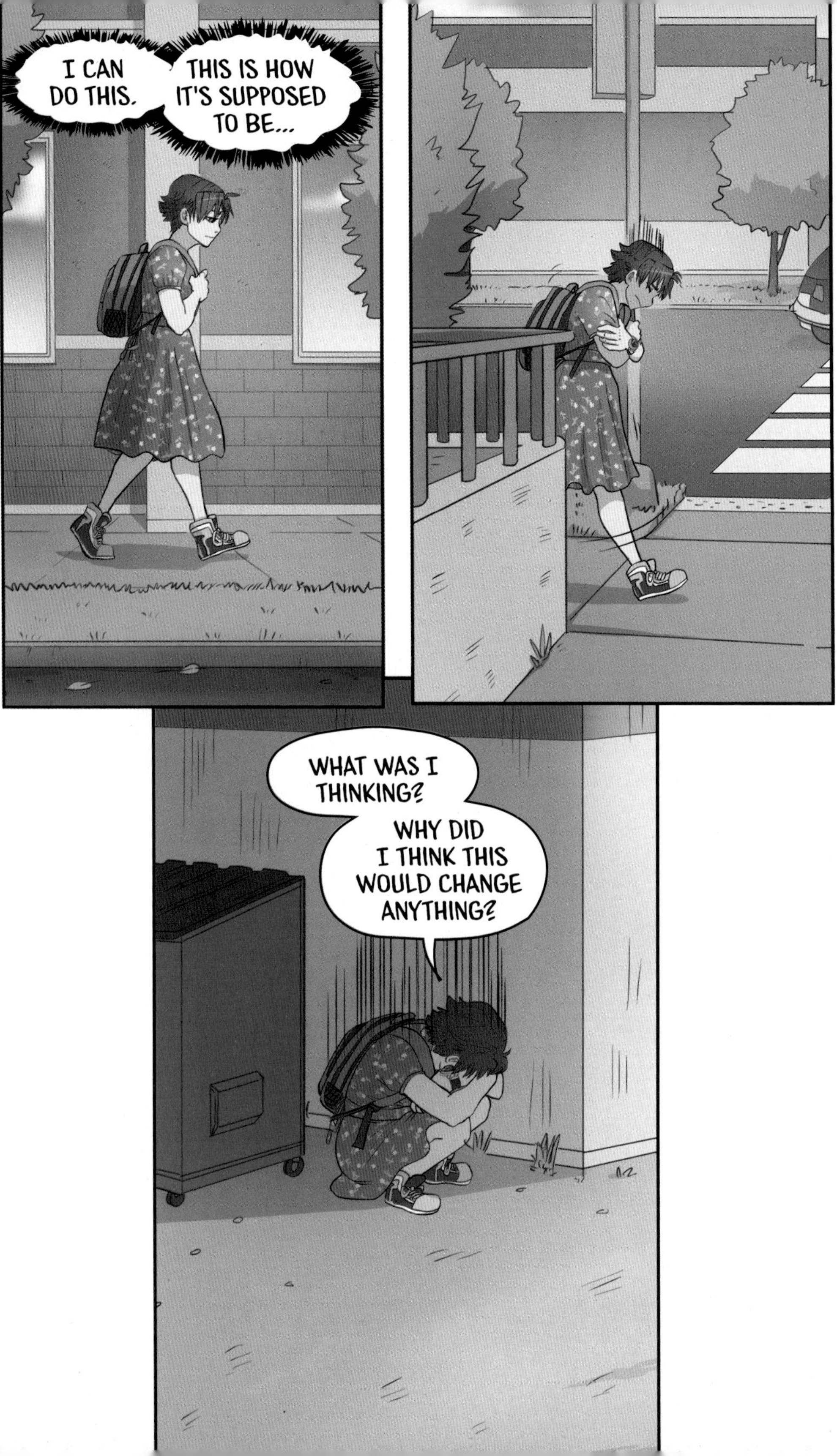
I CAN DO THIS.
THIS IS HOW IT'S SUPPOSED TO BE...
WHAT WAS I THINKING?
WHY DID I THINK THIS WOULD CHANGE ANYTHING?

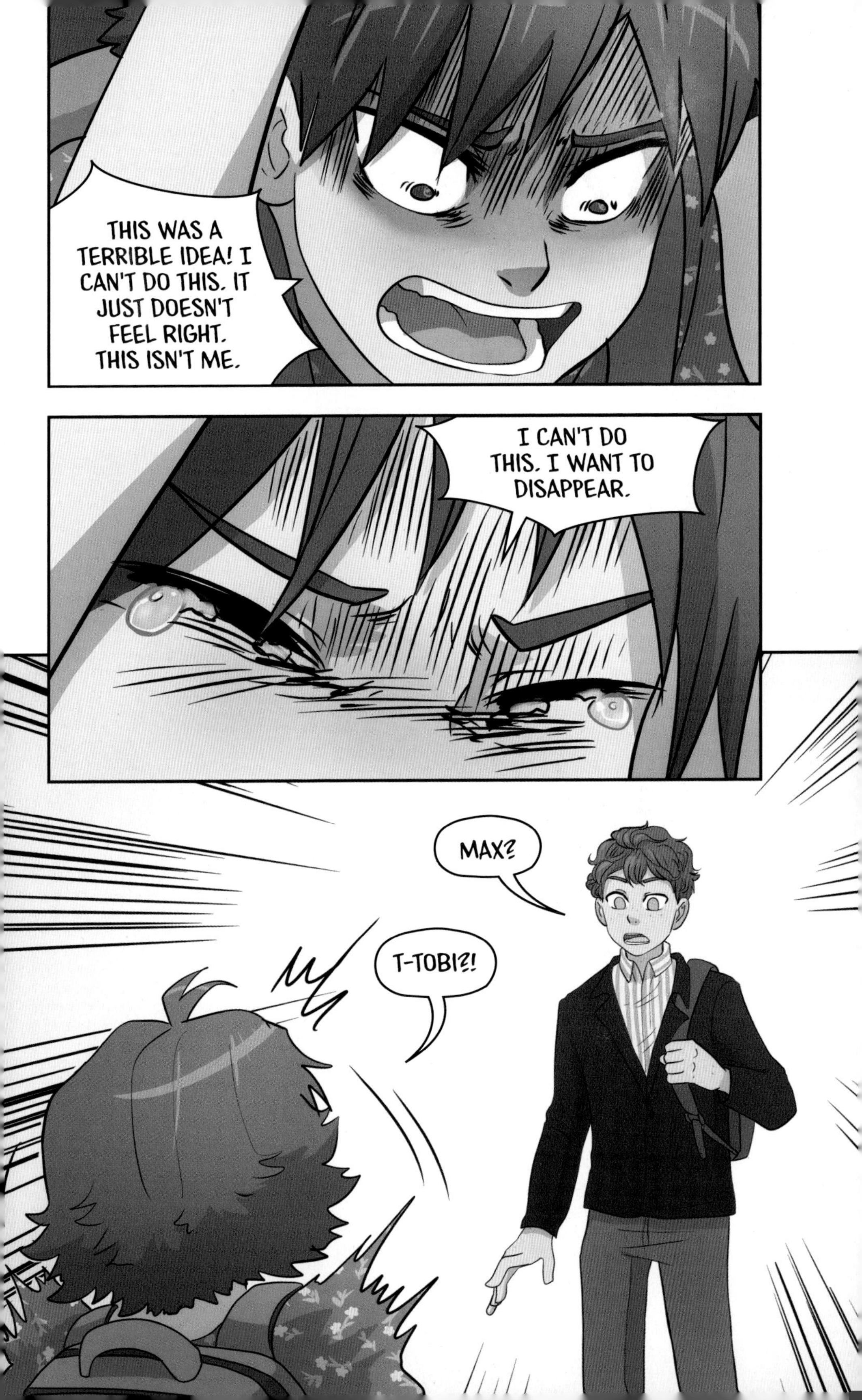
THIS WAS A TERRIBLE IDEA! I CAN'T DO THIS. IT JUST DOESN'T FEEL RIGHT. THIS ISN'T ME.
I CAN'T DO THIS. I WANT TO DISAPPEAR.
MAX?
T-TOBI?!

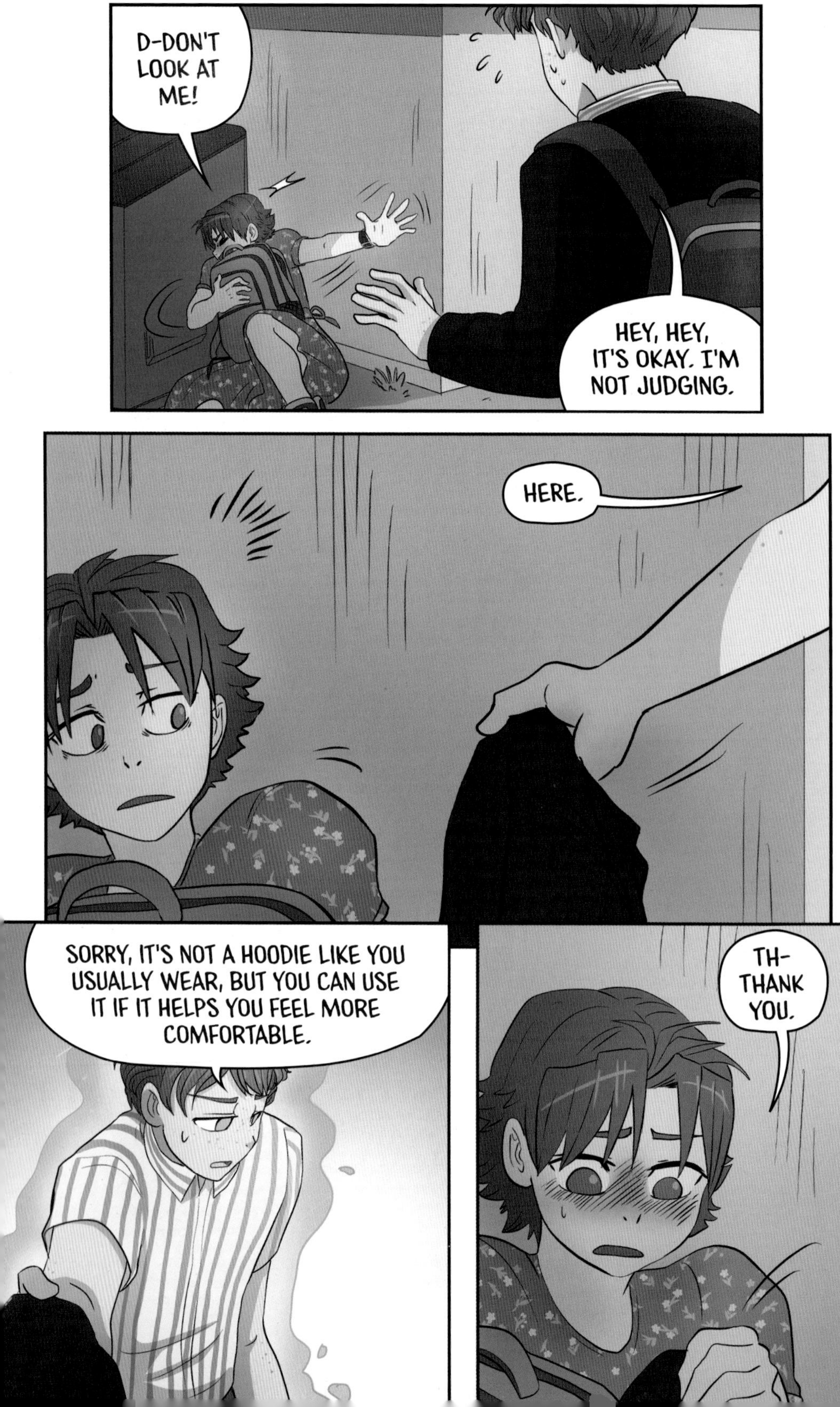
D-DON'T LOOK AT ME!
HEY, HEY, IT'S OKAY. I'M NOT JUDGING.
HERE.
SORRY, IT'S NOT A HOODIE LIKE YOU USUALLY WEAR, BUT YOU CAN USE IT IF IT HELPS YOU FEEL MORE COMFORTABLE.
TH- THANK YOU.

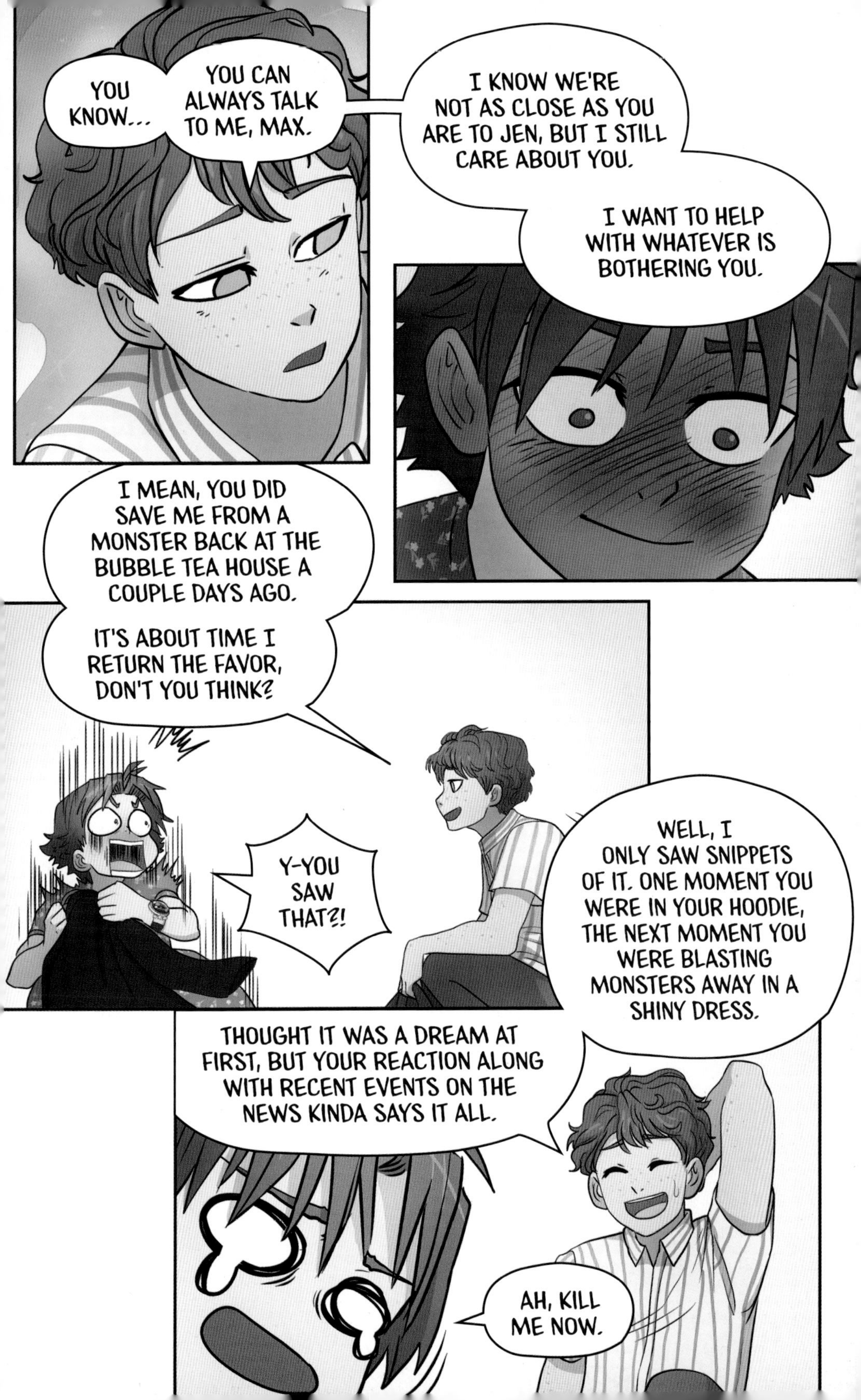
YOU KNOW...
YOU CAN ALWAYS TALK TO ME, MAX.
I KNOW WE'RE NOT AS CLOSE AS YOU ARE TO JEN, BUT I STILL CARE ABOUT YOU.
I WANT TO HELP WITH WHATEVER IS BOTHERING YOU.
I MEAN, YOU DID SAVE ME FROM A MONSTER BACK AT THE BUBBLE TEA HOUSE A COUPLE DAYS AGO.
IT'S ABOUT TIME I RETURN THE FAVOR, DON'T YOU THINK?
Y-YOU SAW THAT?!
WELL, I ONLY SAW SNIPPETS OF IT. ONE MOMENT YOU WERE IN YOUR HOODIE, THE NEXT MOMENT YOU WERE BLASTING MONSTERS AWAY IN A SHINY DRESS.
THOUGHT IT WAS A DREAM AT FIRST, BUT YOUR REACTION ALONG WITH RECENT EVENTS ON THE NEWS KINDA SAYS IT ALL.
AH, KILL ME NOW.

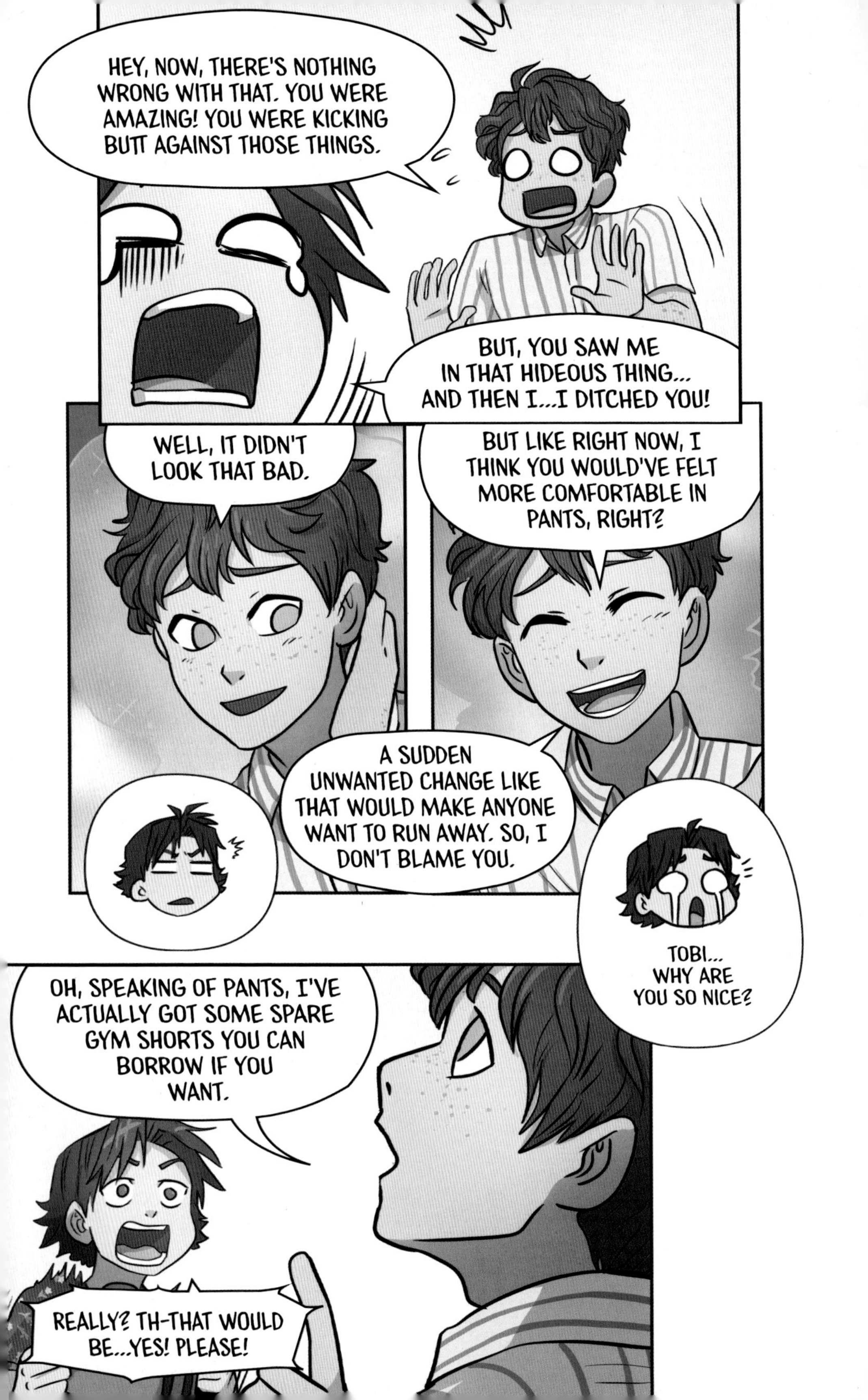
HEY, NOW, THERE'S NOTHING WRONG WITH THAT. YOU WERE AMAZING! YOU WERE KICKING BUTT AGAINST THOSE THINGS.
BUT, YOU SAW ME IN THAT HIDEOUS THING... AND THEN I...I DITCHED YOU!
WELL, IT DIDN'T LOOK THAT BAD.
BUT LIKE RIGHT NOW, I THINK YOU WOULD'VE FELT MORE COMFORTABLE IN PANTS, RIGHT?
A SUDDEN UNWANTED CHANGE LIKE THAT WOULD MAKE ANYONE WANT TO RUN AWAY. SO, I DON'T BLAME YOU.
TOBI... WHY ARE YOU SO NICE?
OH, SPEAKING OF PANTS, I'VE ACTUALLY GOT SOME SPARE GYM SHORTS YOU CAN BORROW IF YOU WANT.
REALLY? TH-THAT WOULD BE...YES! PLEASE!

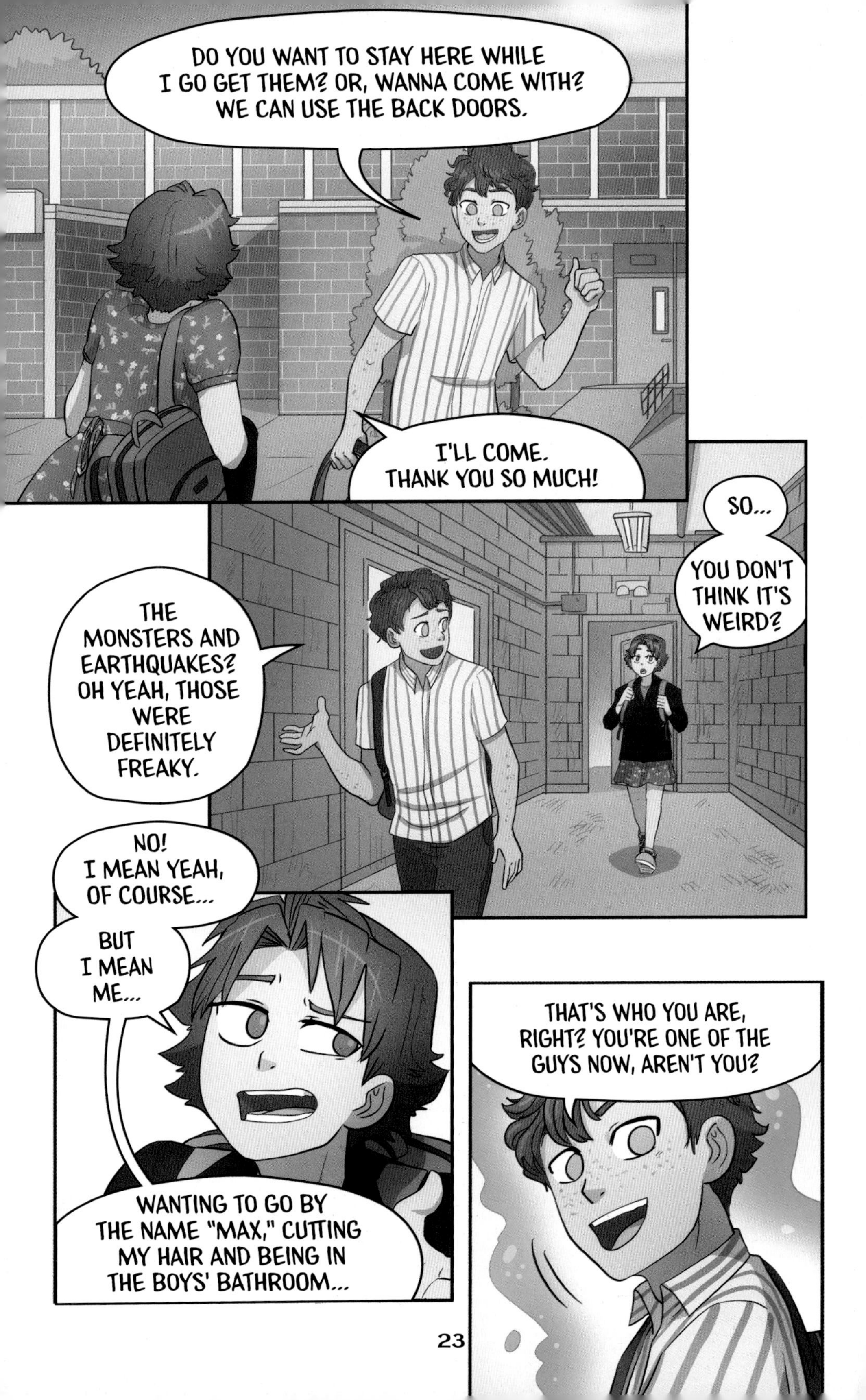
DO YOU WANT TO STAY HERE WHILE I GO GET THEM? OR, WANNA COME WITH? WE CAN USE THE BACK DOORS.
I'LL COME. THANK YOU SO MUCH!
SO...
YOU DON'T THINK IT'S WEIRD?
THE MONSTERS AND EARTHQUAKES? OH YEAH, THOSE WERE DEFINITELY FREAKY.
NO! I MEAN YEAH, OF COURSE...
BUT I MEAN ME...
WANTING TO GO BY THE NAME "MAX," CUTTING MY HAIR AND BEING IN THE BOYS' BATHROOM...
THAT'S WHO YOU ARE, RIGHT? YOU'RE ONE OF THE GUYS NOW, AREN'T YOU?

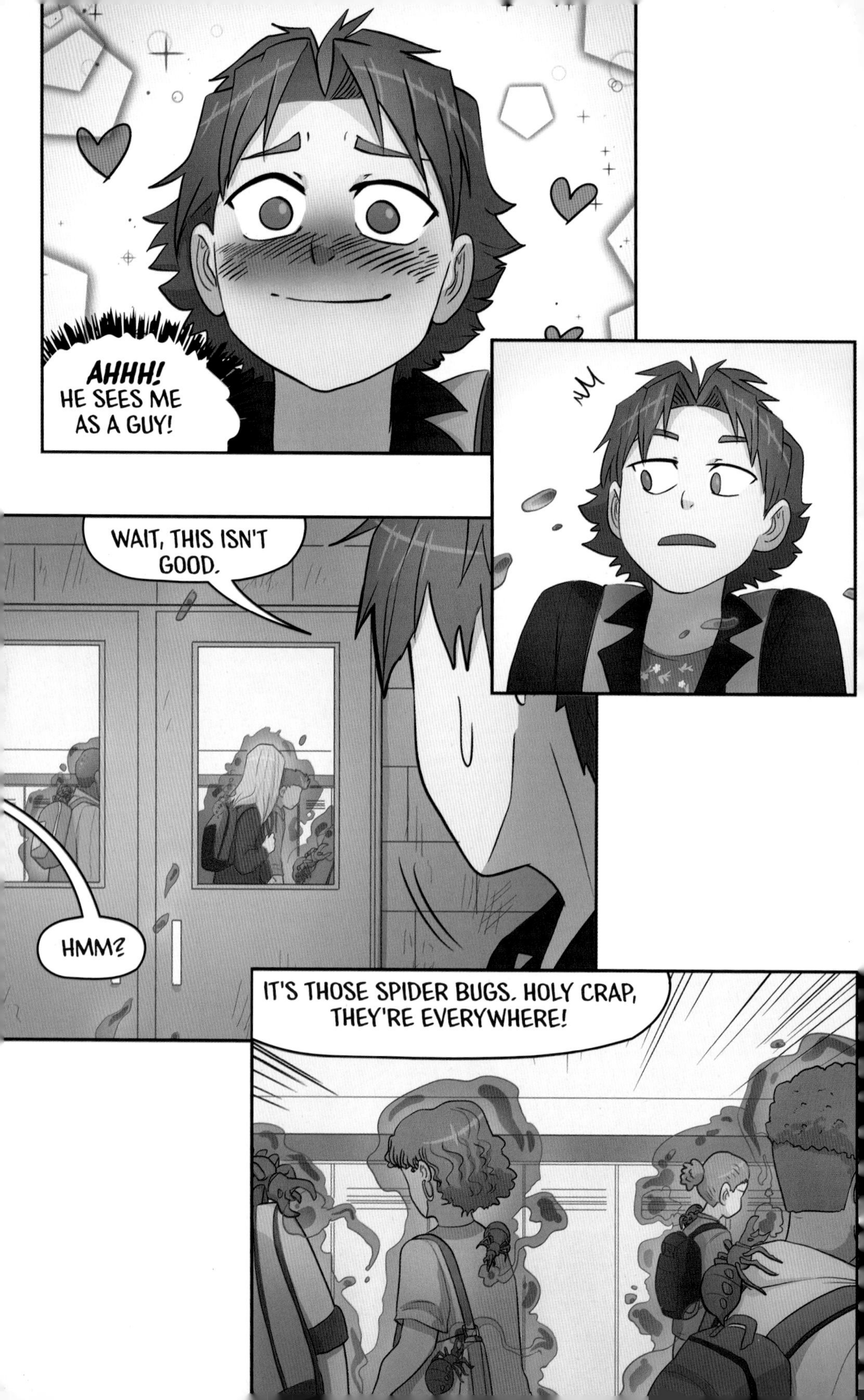
AHHH! HE SEES ME AS A GUY!
WAIT, THIS ISN'T GOOD.
HMM?
IT'S THOSE SPIDER BUGS. HOLY CRAP, THEY'RE EVERYWHERE!

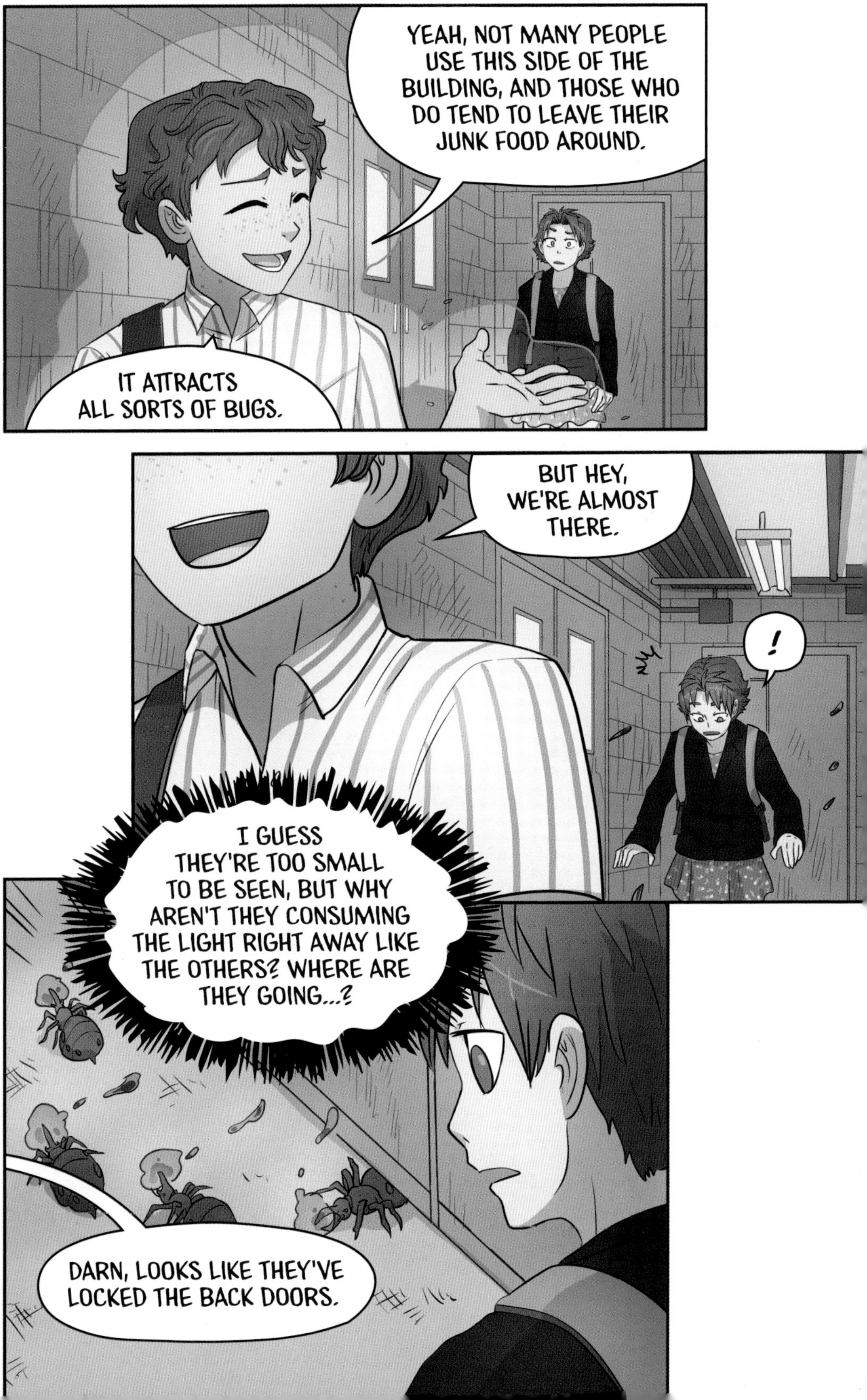
YEAH, NOT MANY PEOPLE USE THIS SIDE OF THE BUILDING, AND THOSE WHO DO TEND TO LEAVE THEIR JUNK FOOD AROUND.
IT ATTRACTS ALL SORTS OF BUGS.
BUT HEY, WE'RE ALMOST THERE.
!
I GUESS THEY'RE TOO SMALL TO BE SEEN, BUT WHY AREN'T THEY CONSUMING THE LIGHT RIGHT AWAY LIKE THE OTHERS? WHERE ARE THEY GOING...?
DARN, LOOKS LIKE THEY'VE LOCKED THE BACK DOORS.

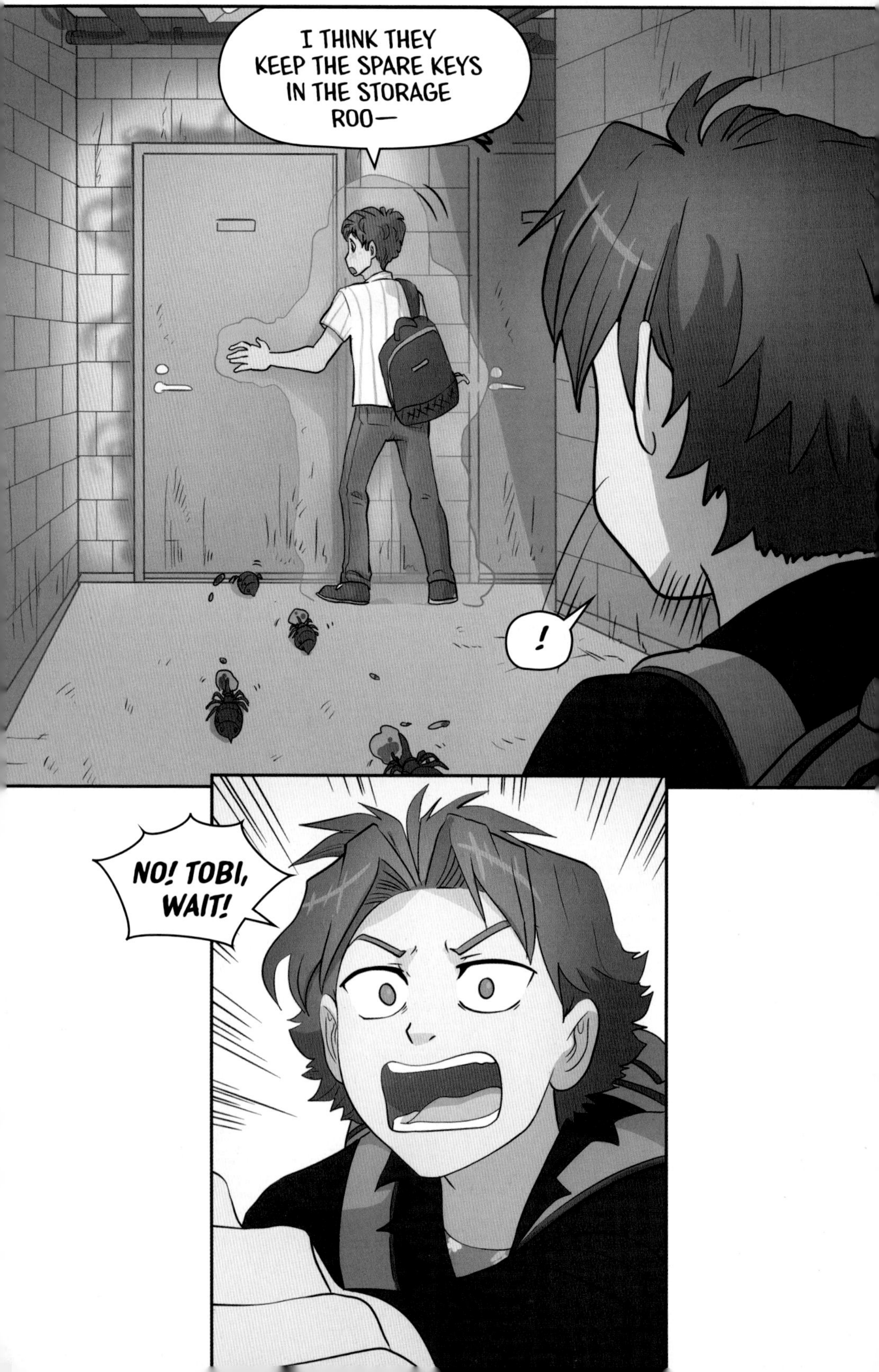
I THINK THEY KEEP THE SPARE KEYS IN THE STORAGE ROO—
!
NO! TOBI, WAIT!

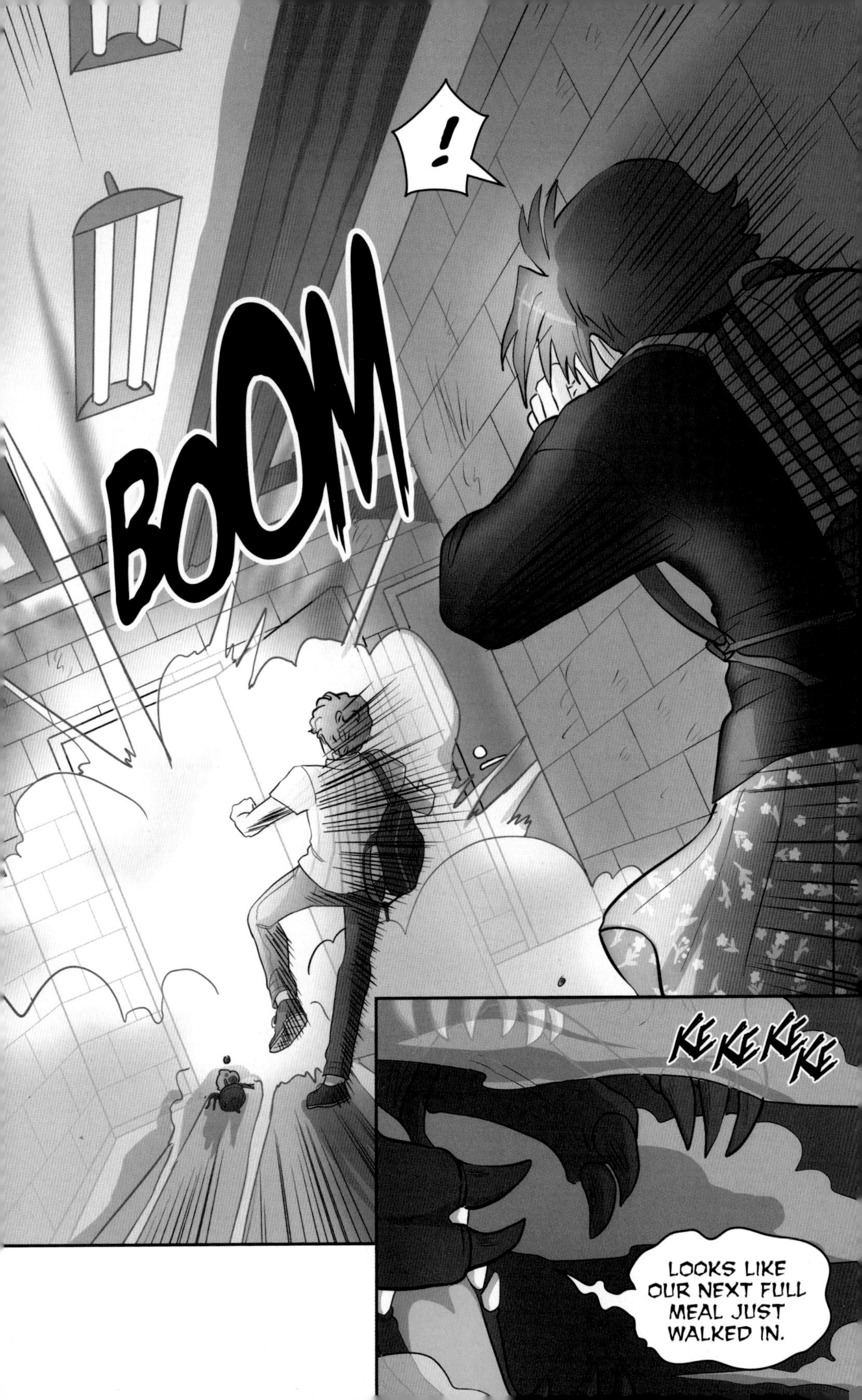
!
BOOM
KEKEKEKE
LOOKS LIKE OUR NEXT FULL MEAL JUST WALKED IN.

EPISODE 17:
THE RISE

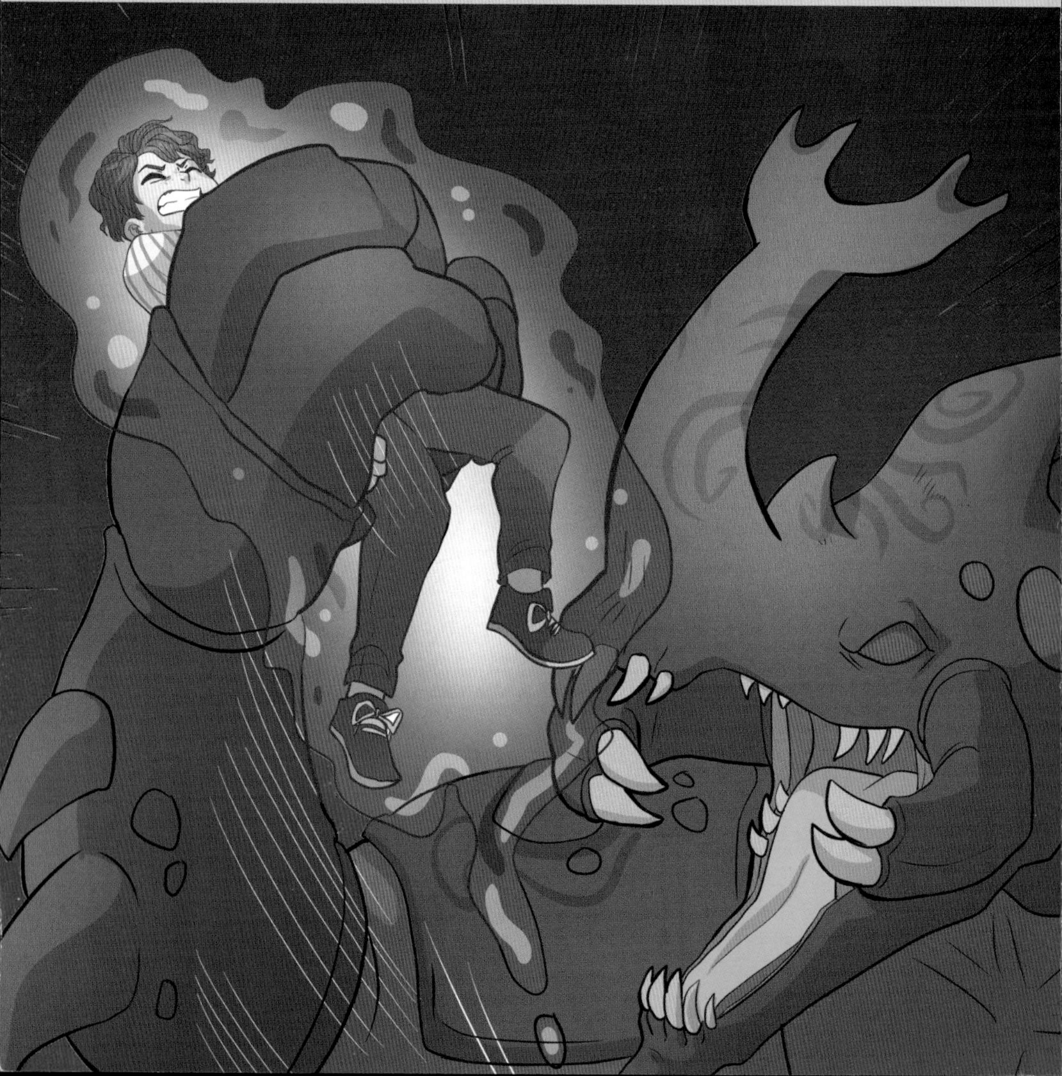

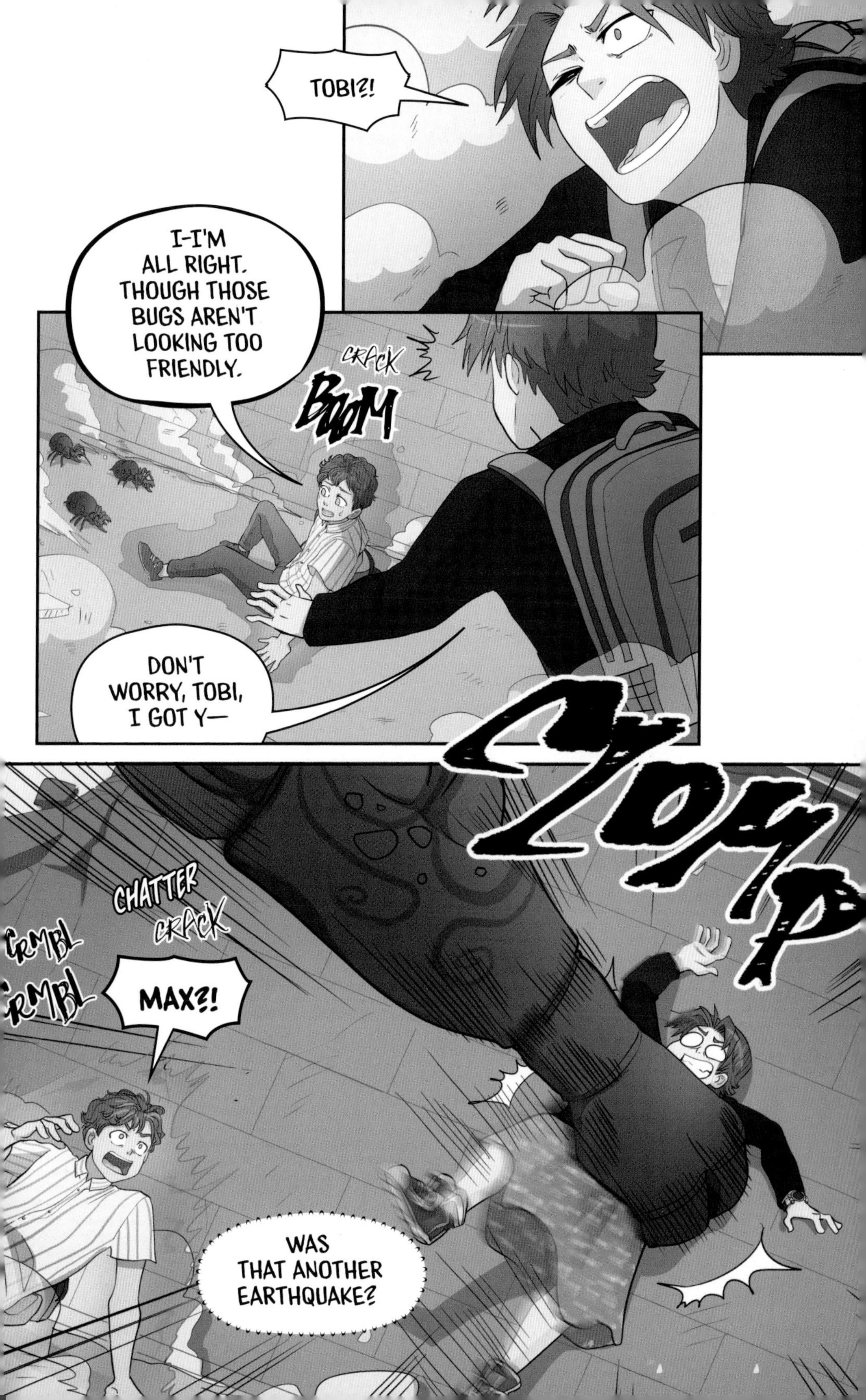
TOBI?!
I-I'M ALL RIGHT. THOUGH THOSE BUGS AREN'T LOOKING TOO FRIENDLY.
CRACK
BOOM
DON'T WORRY, TOBI, I GOT Y—
CHATTER
CRACK
GRMBL
GRMBL
MAX?!
WAS THAT ANOTHER EARTHQUAKE?

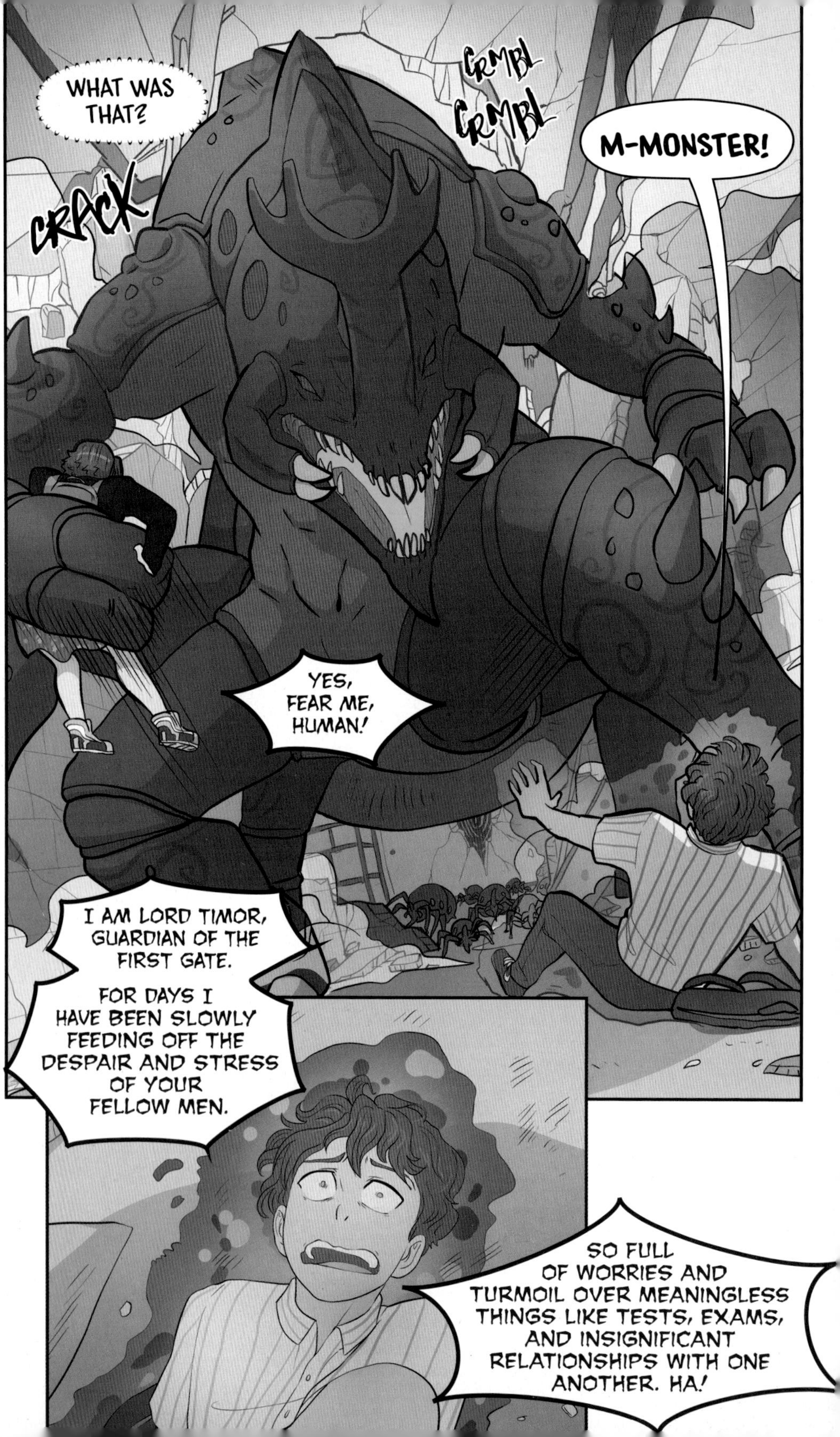
WHAT WAS THAT?
CRACK
GRMBL GRMBL
M-MONSTER!
YES, FEAR ME, HUMAN!
I AM LORD TIMOR, GUARDIAN OF THE FIRST GATE.
FOR DAYS I HAVE BEEN SLOWLY FEEDING OFF THE DESPAIR AND STRESS OF YOUR FELLOW MEN.
SO FULL OF WORRIES AND TURMOIL OVER MEANINGLESS THINGS LIKE TESTS, EXAMS, AND INSIGNIFICANT RELATIONSHIPS WITH ONE ANOTHER. HA!

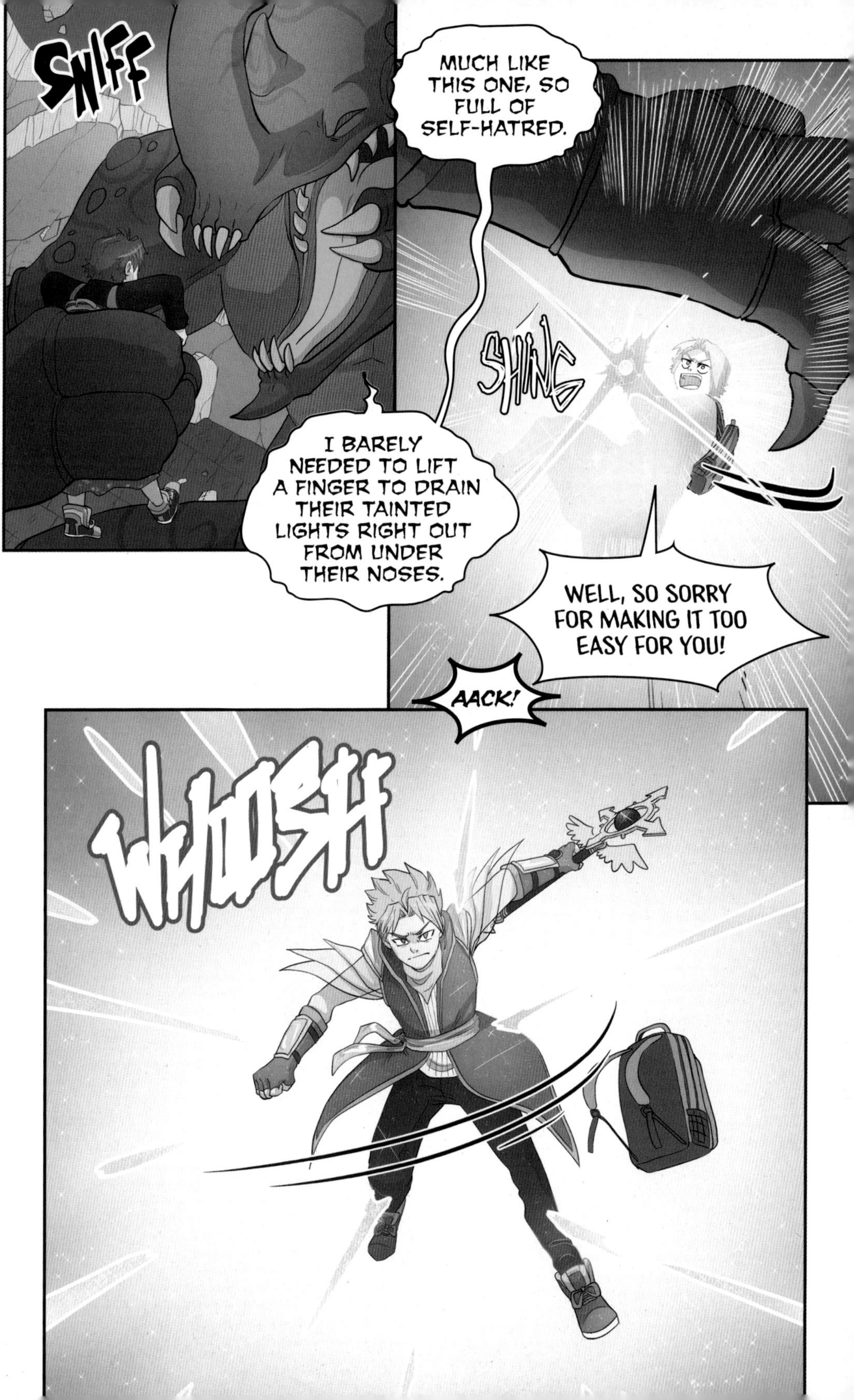
SNIFF
MUCH LIKE THIS ONE, SO FULL OF SELF-HATRED.
I BARELY NEEDED TO LIFT A FINGER TO DRAIN THEIR TAINTED LIGHTS RIGHT OUT FROM UNDER THEIR NOSES.
SHING
WELL, SO SORRY FOR MAKING IT TOO EASY FOR YOU!
AACK!
WHOOSH

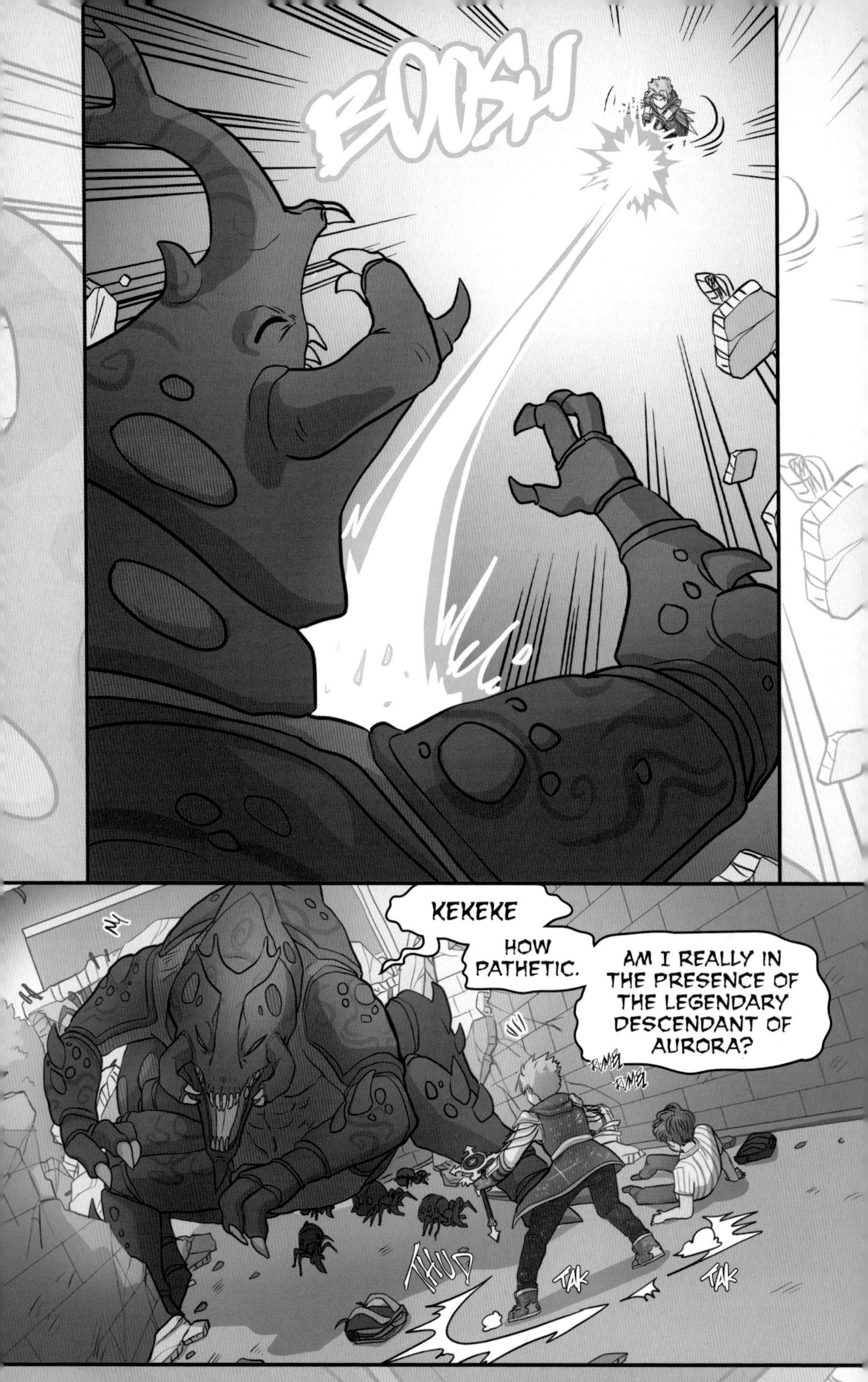
BOOSH
KEKEKE
HOW PATHETIC.
AM I REALLY IN THE PRESENCE OF THE LEGENDARY DESCENDANT OF AURORA?
THUD
TAK
TAK

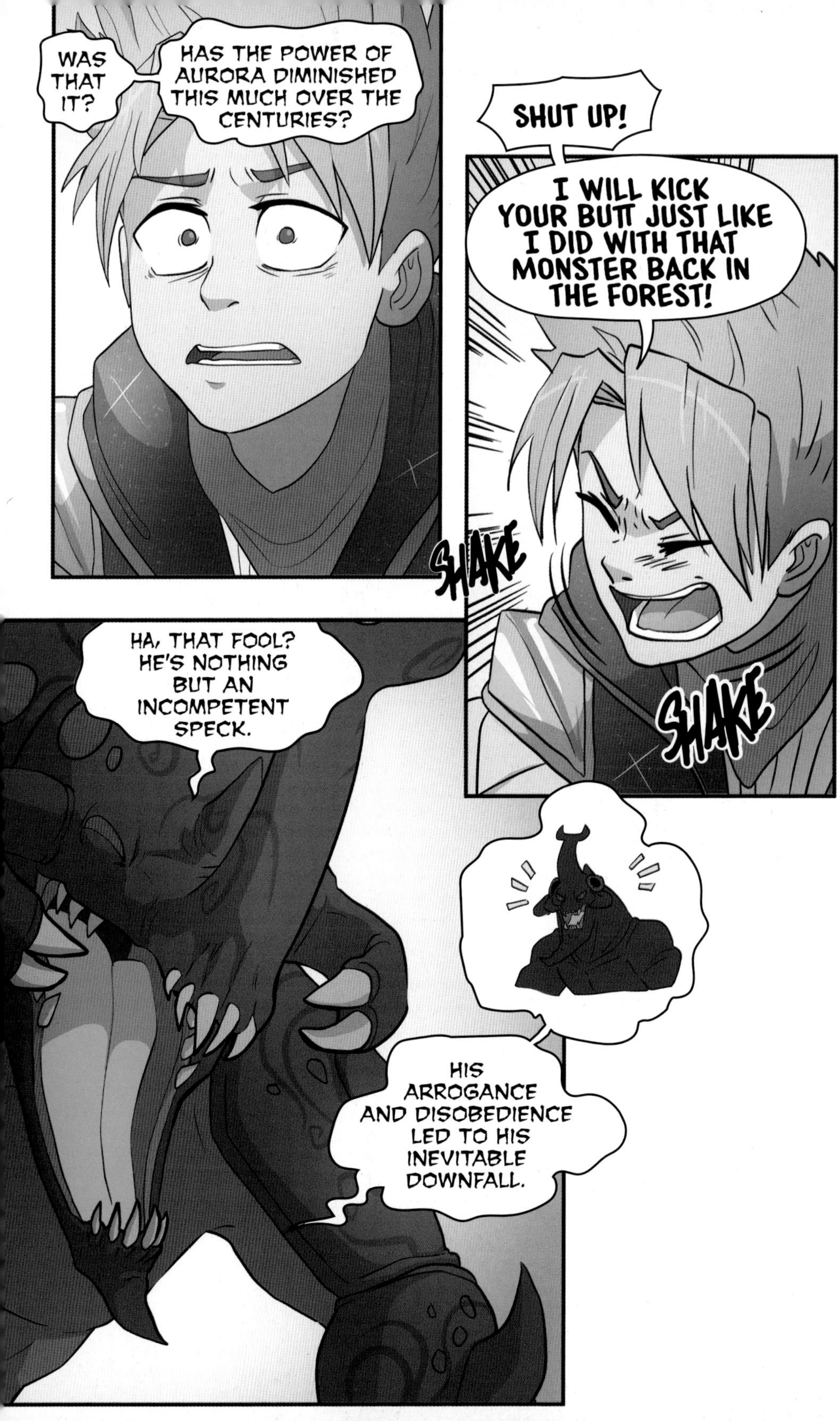
WAS THAT IT?
HAS THE POWER OF AURORA DIMINISHED THIS MUCH OVER THE CENTURIES?
SHUT UP!
I WILL KICK YOUR BUTT JUST LIKE I DID WITH THAT MONSTER BACK IN THE FOREST!
SHAKE
SHAKE
HA, THAT FOOL? HE'S NOTHING BUT AN INCOMPETENT SPECK.
HIS ARROGANCE AND DISOBEDIENCE LED TO HIS INEVITABLE DOWNFALL.

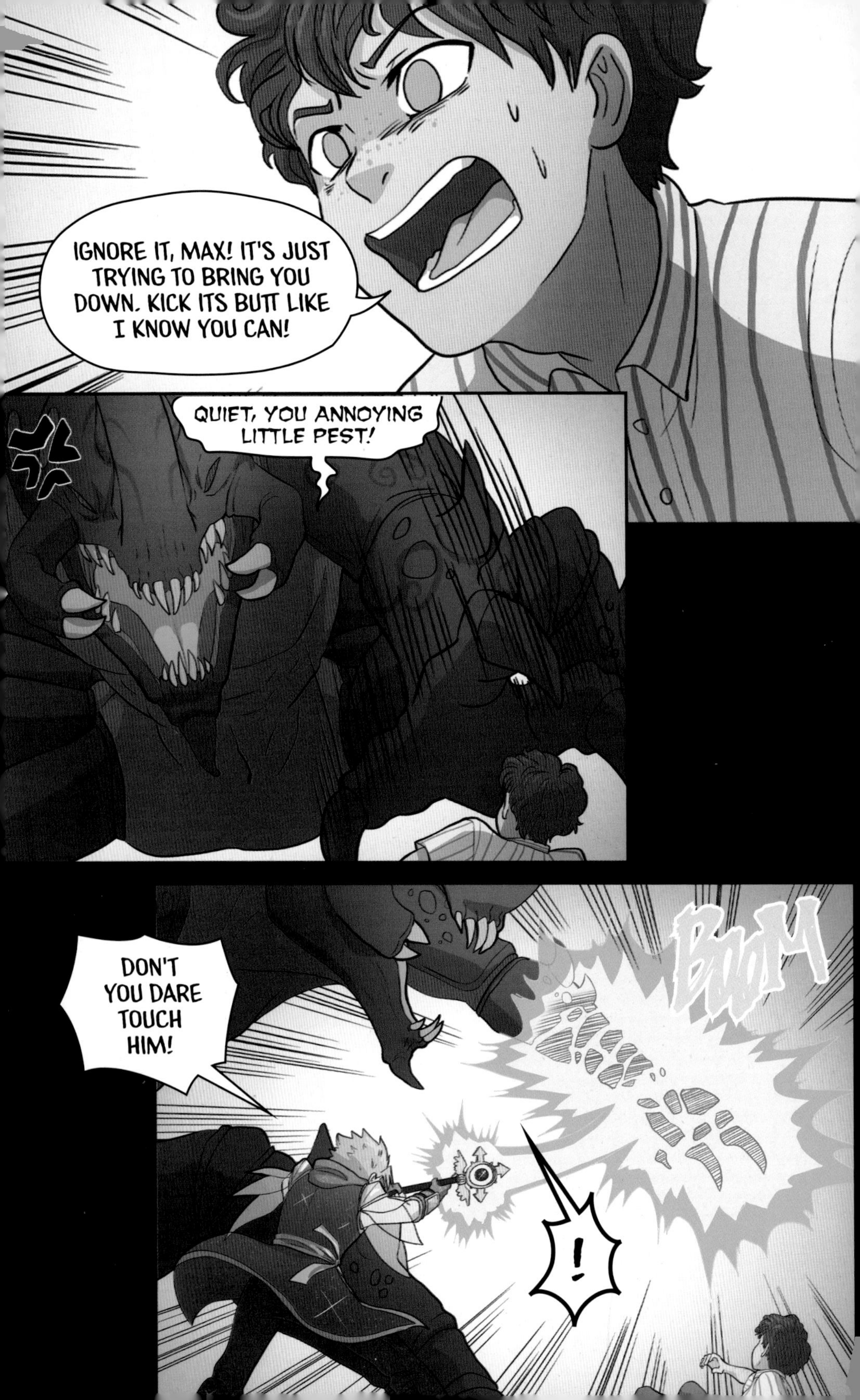
IGNORE IT, MAX! IT'S JUST TRYING TO BRING YOU DOWN. KICK ITS BUTT LIKE I KNOW YOU CAN!
QUIET, YOU ANNOYING LITTLE PEST!
DON'T YOU DARE TOUCH HIM!
BOOM
!

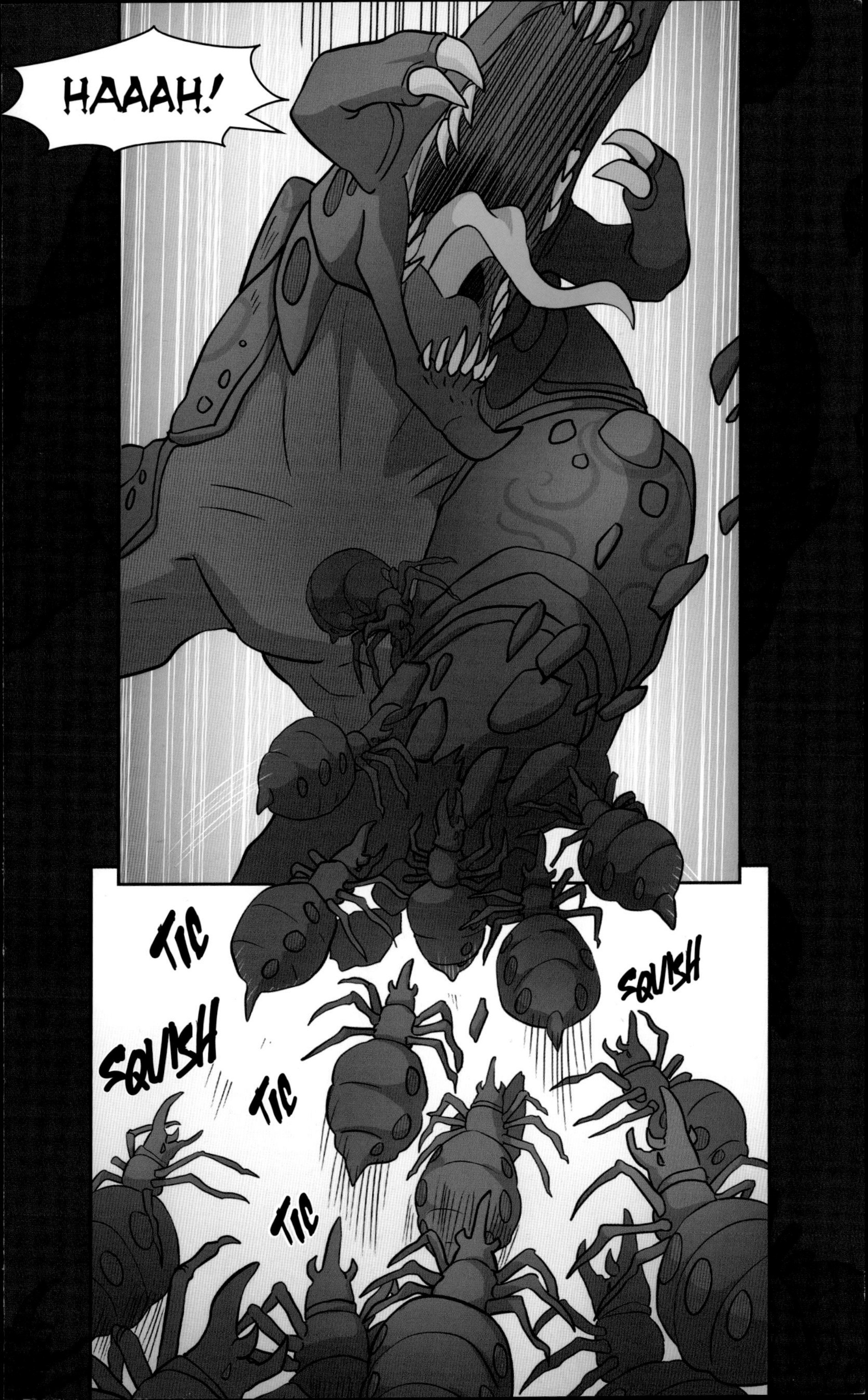
HAAAH!
TIC
SQUISH
SQUISH
TIC
TIC

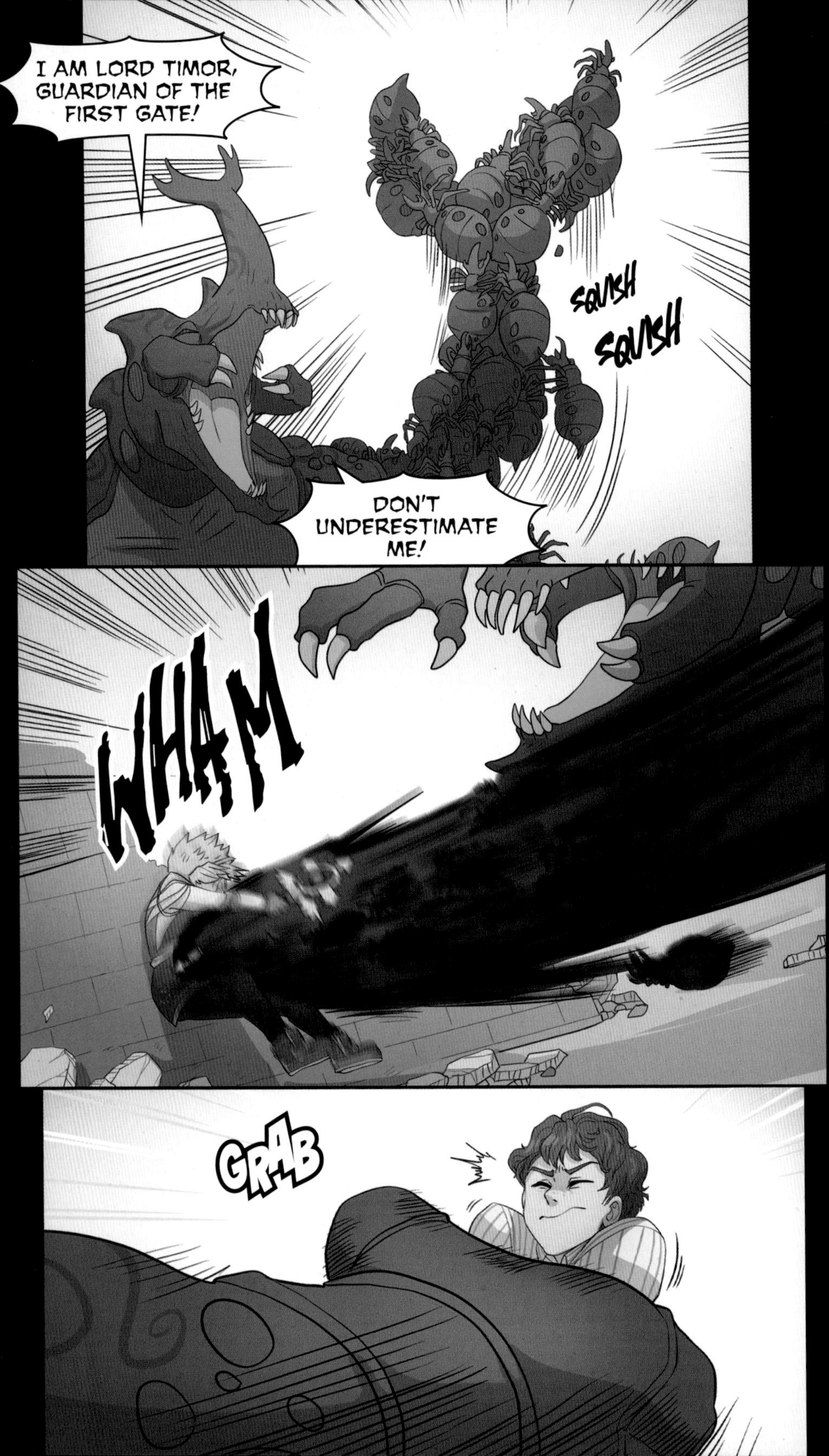
I AM LORD TIMOR, GUARDIAN OF THE FIRST GATE!
SQUISH
SQUISH
DON'T UNDERESTIMATE ME!
WHAM
GRAB

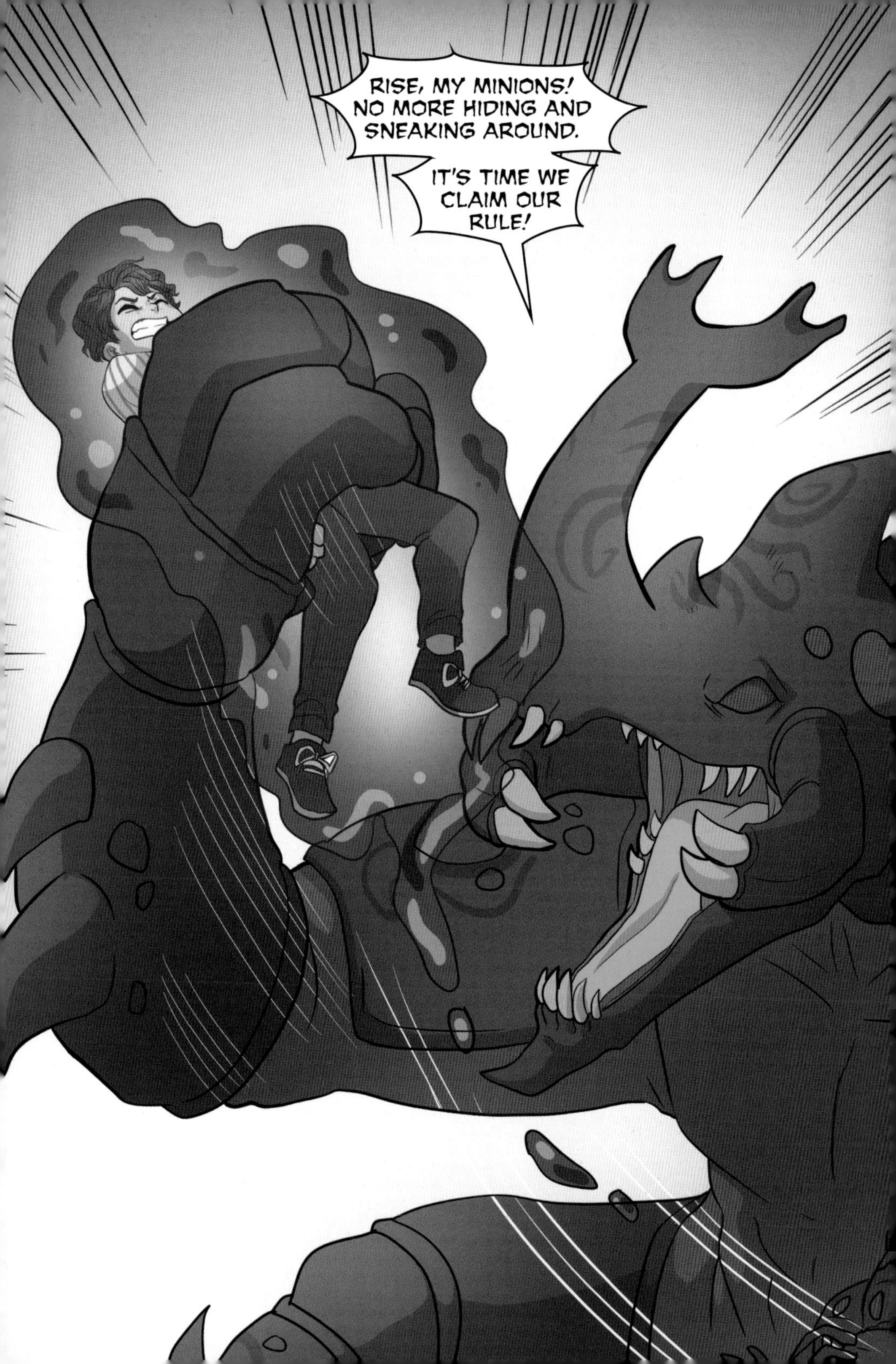
RISE, MY MINIONS! NO MORE HIDING AND SNEAKING AROUND.
IT'S TIME WE CLAIM OUR RULE!

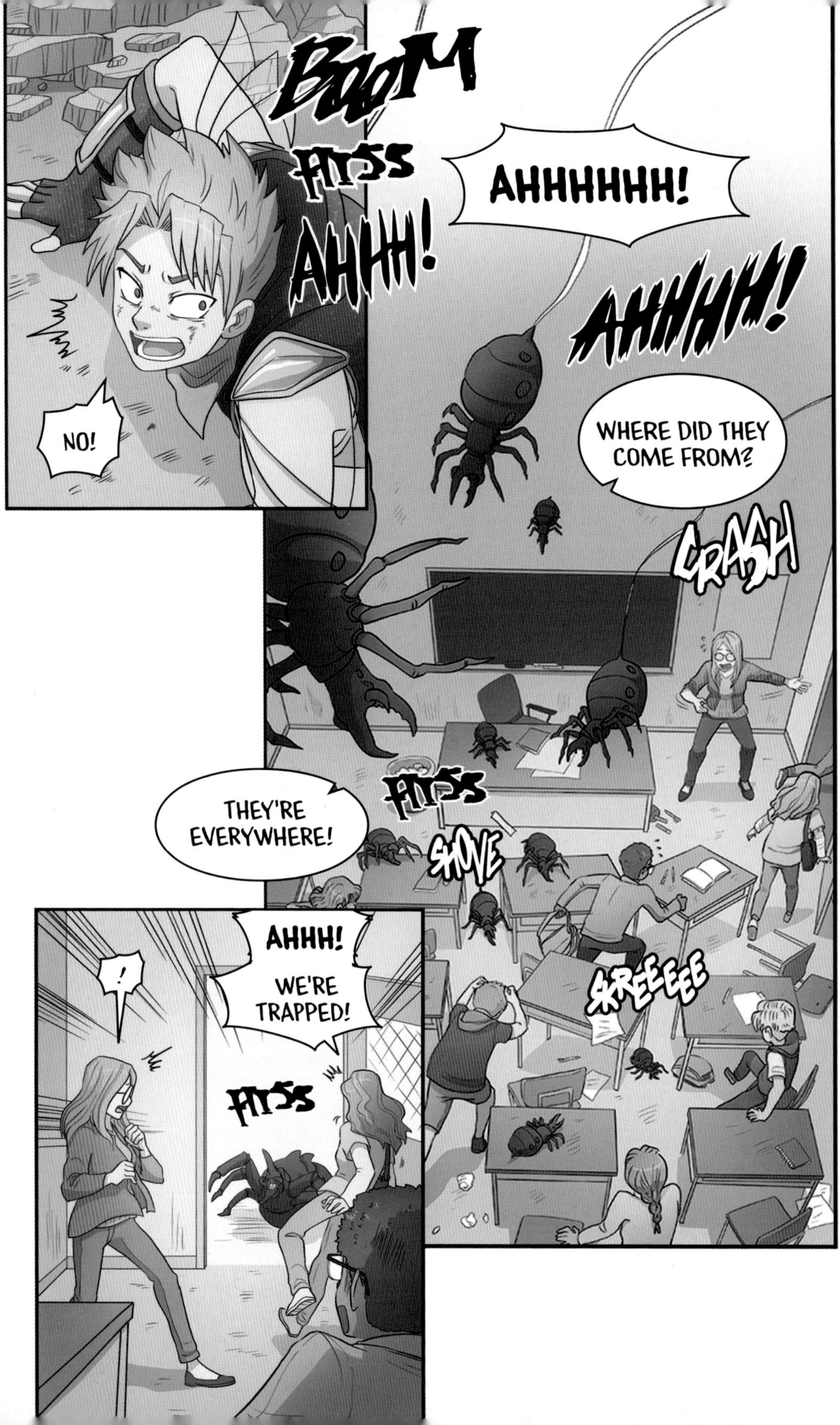
BOOM
FITSS
AHHH!
NO!
AHHHHHH!
AHHHHH!
WHERE DID THEY COME FROM?
CRASH
FITSS
THEY'RE EVERYWHERE!
SHOVE
AHHH!
WE'RE TRAPPED!
!
FITSS
SKREEEEE

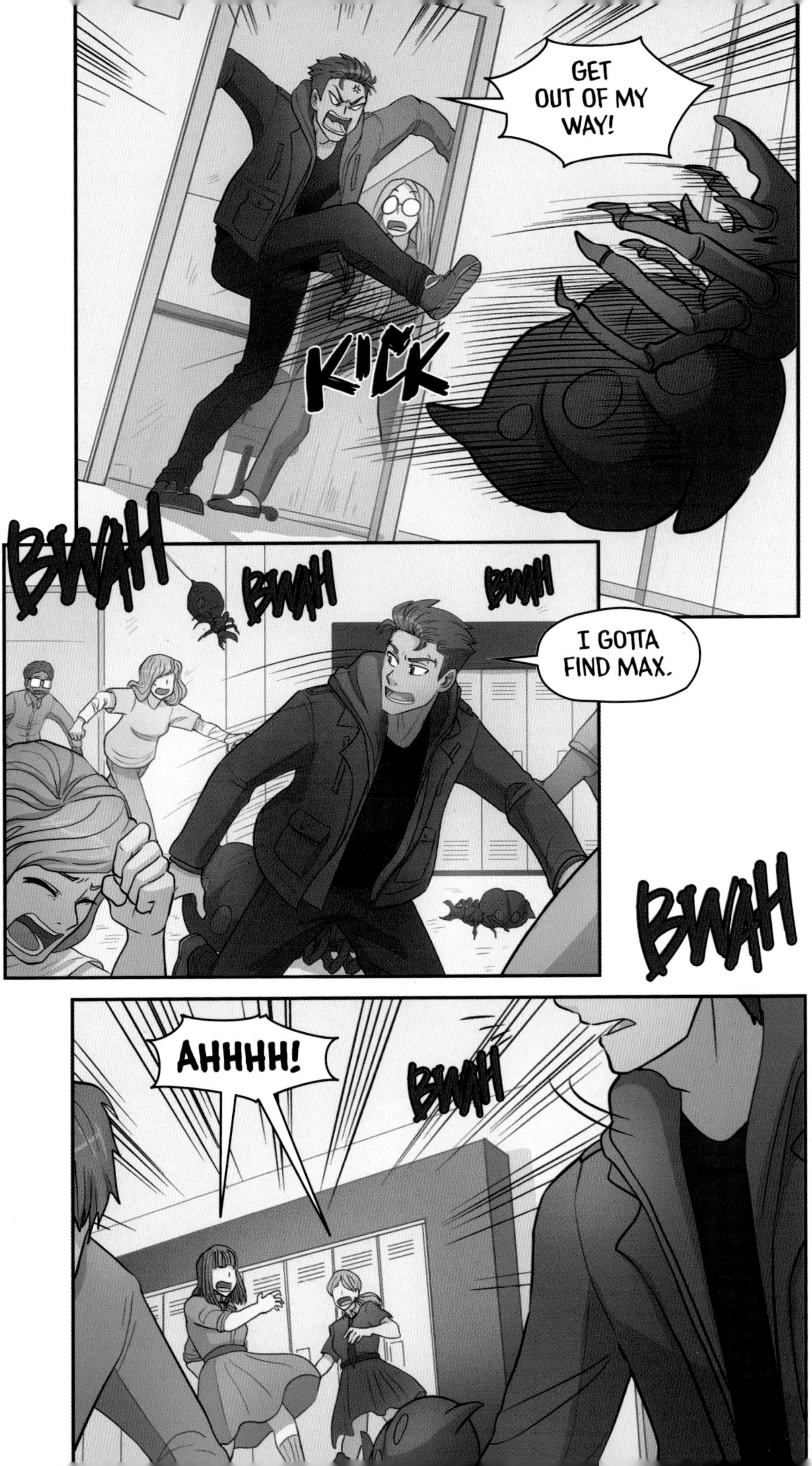
GET OUT OF MY WAY!
KICK
BWAH
BWAH
BWAH
I GOTTA FIND MAX.
BWAH
AHHHH!
BWAH

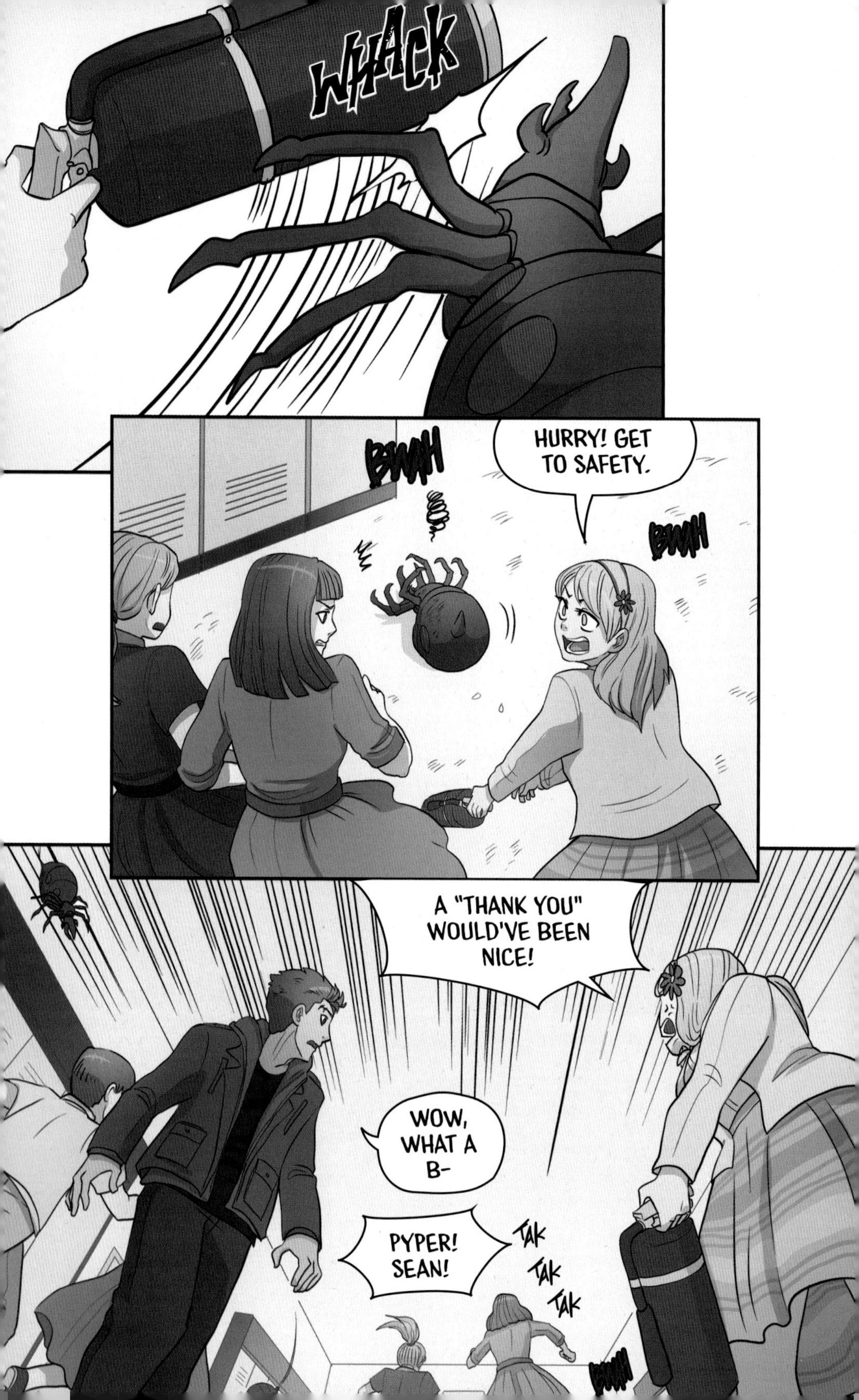
WHACK
BWAH
HURRY! GET TO SAFETY.
BWAH
A "THANK YOU" WOULD'VE BEEN NICE!
WOW, WHAT A B-
PYPER! SEAN!
TAK
TAK
TAK

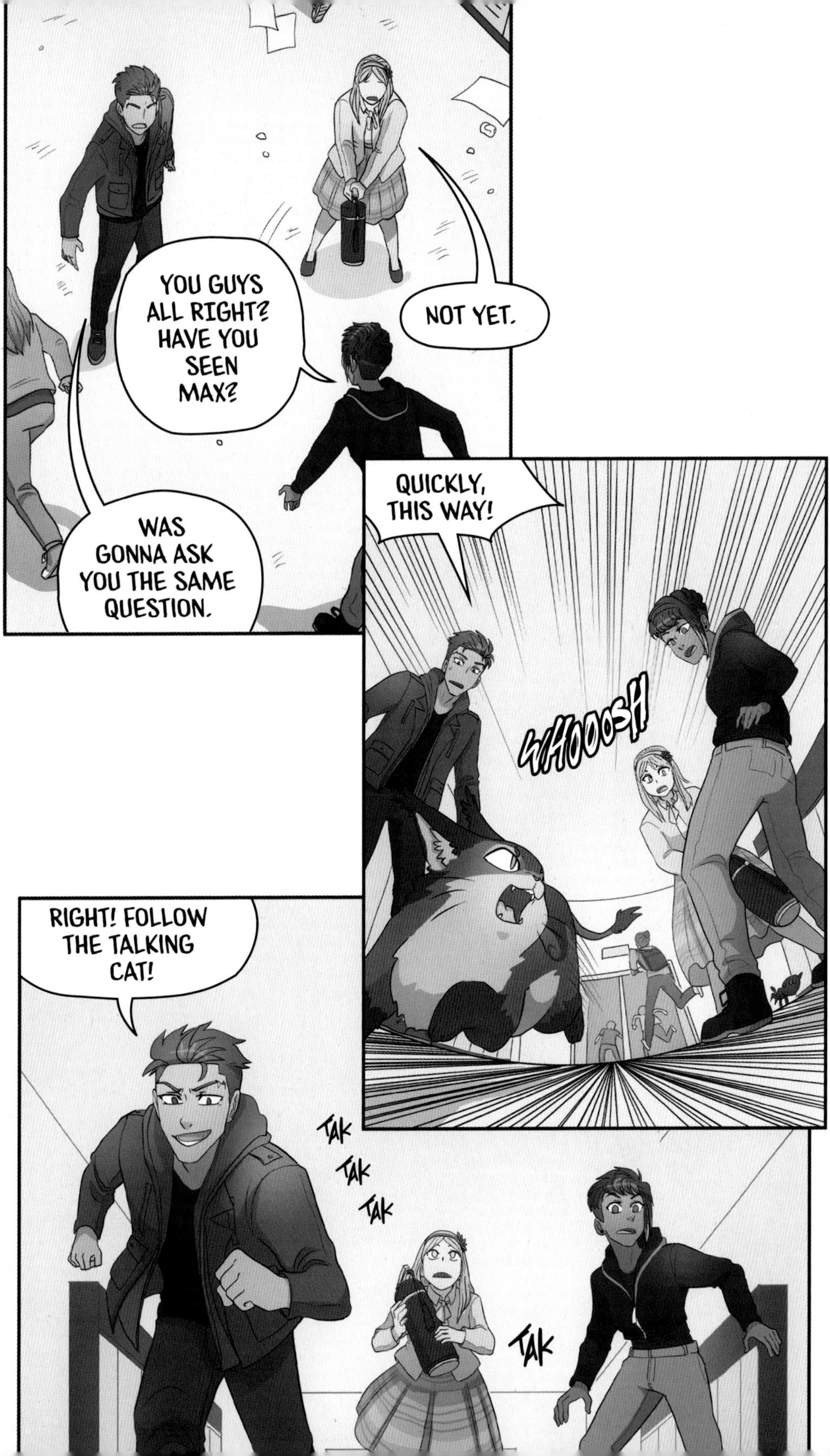
YOU GUYS ALL RIGHT? HAVE YOU SEEN MAX?
NOT YET.
WAS GONNA ASK YOU THE SAME QUESTION.
QUICKLY, THIS WAY!
WHOOOSH
RIGHT! FOLLOW THE TALKING CAT!
TAK
TAK
TAK
TAK

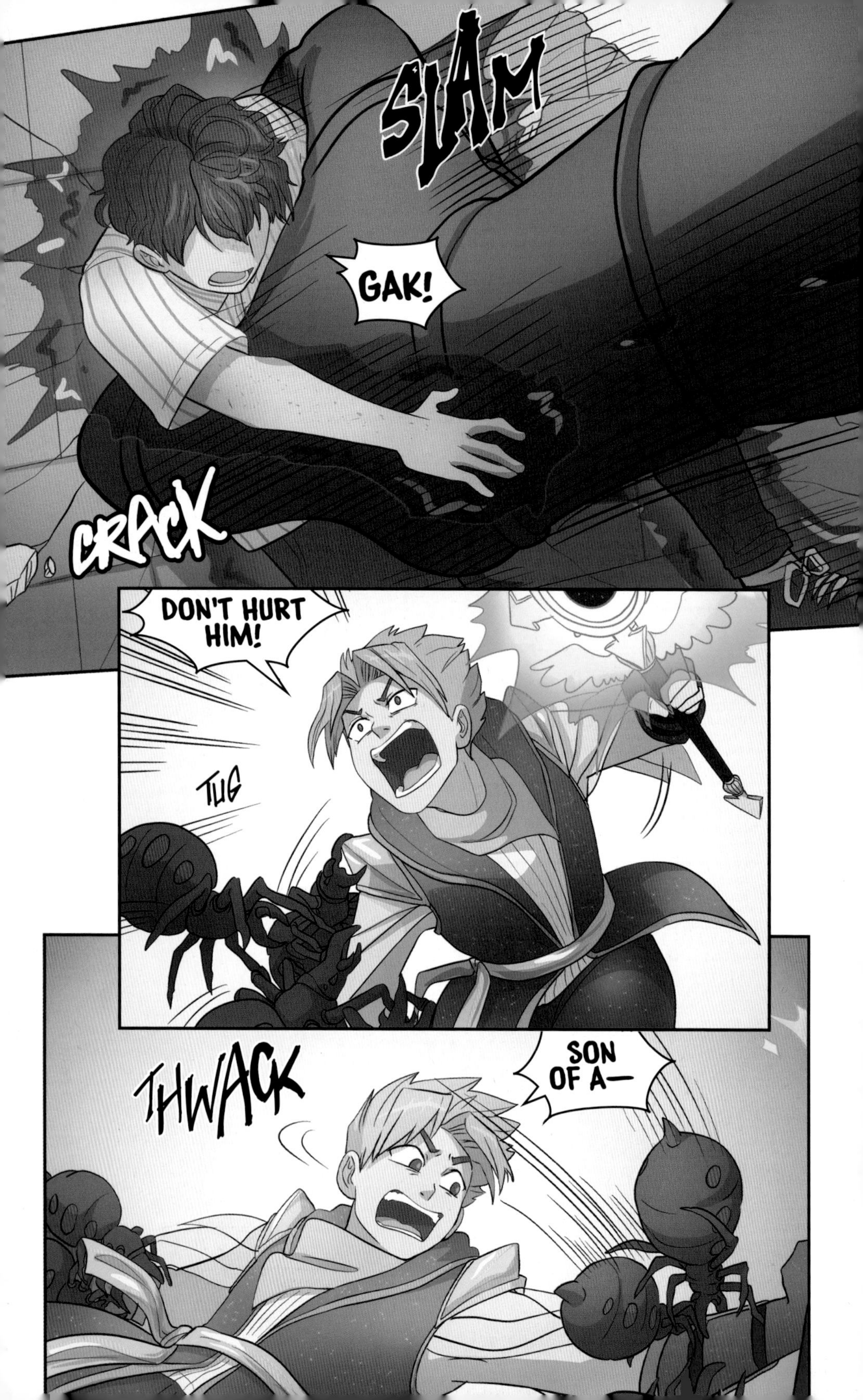
SLAM
GAK!
CRACK
DON'T HURT HIM!
TUG
THWACK
SON OF A—

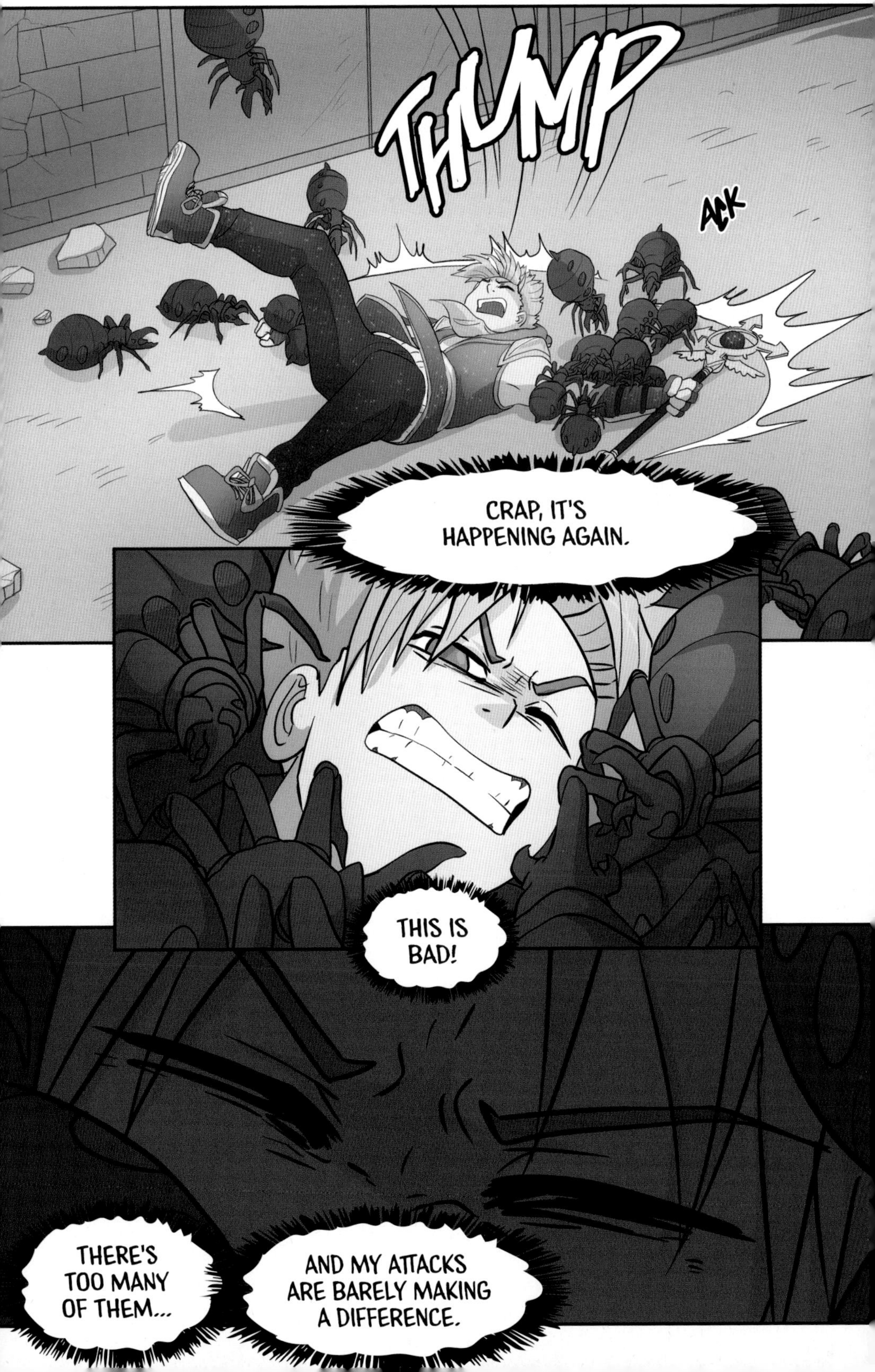
THUMP
ACK
CRAP, IT'S HAPPENING AGAIN.
THIS IS BAD!
THERE'S TOO MANY OF THEM...
AND MY ATTACKS ARE BARELY MAKING A DIFFERENCE.

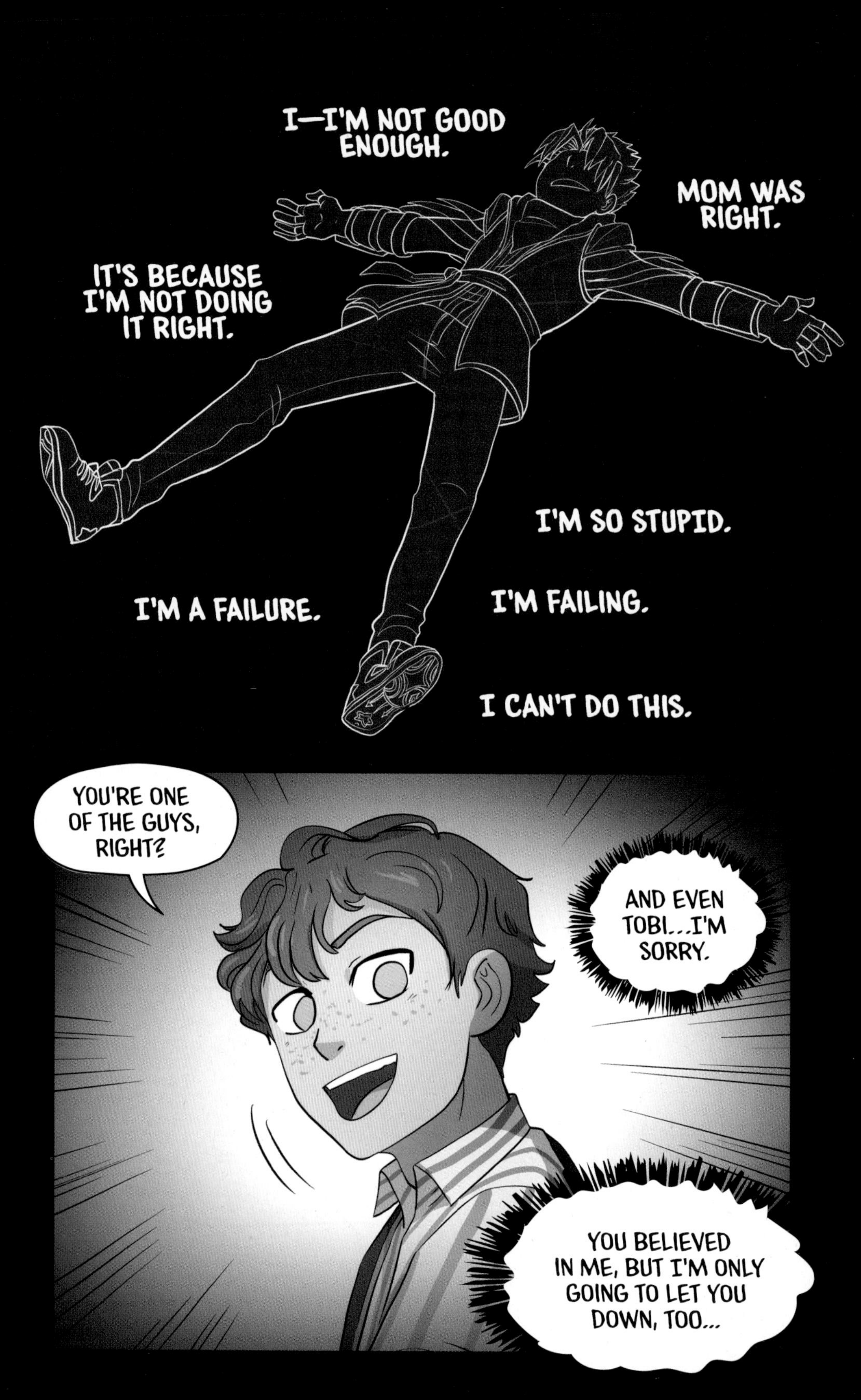
I—I'M NOT GOOD ENOUGH.
MOM WAS RIGHT.
IT'S BECAUSE I'M NOT DOING IT RIGHT.
I'M SO STUPID.
I'M A FAILURE.
I'M FAILING.
I CAN'T DO THIS.
YOU'RE ONE OF THE GUYS, RIGHT?
AND EVEN TOBI...I'M SORRY.
YOU BELIEVED IN ME, BUT I'M ONLY GOING TO LET YOU DOWN, TOO...

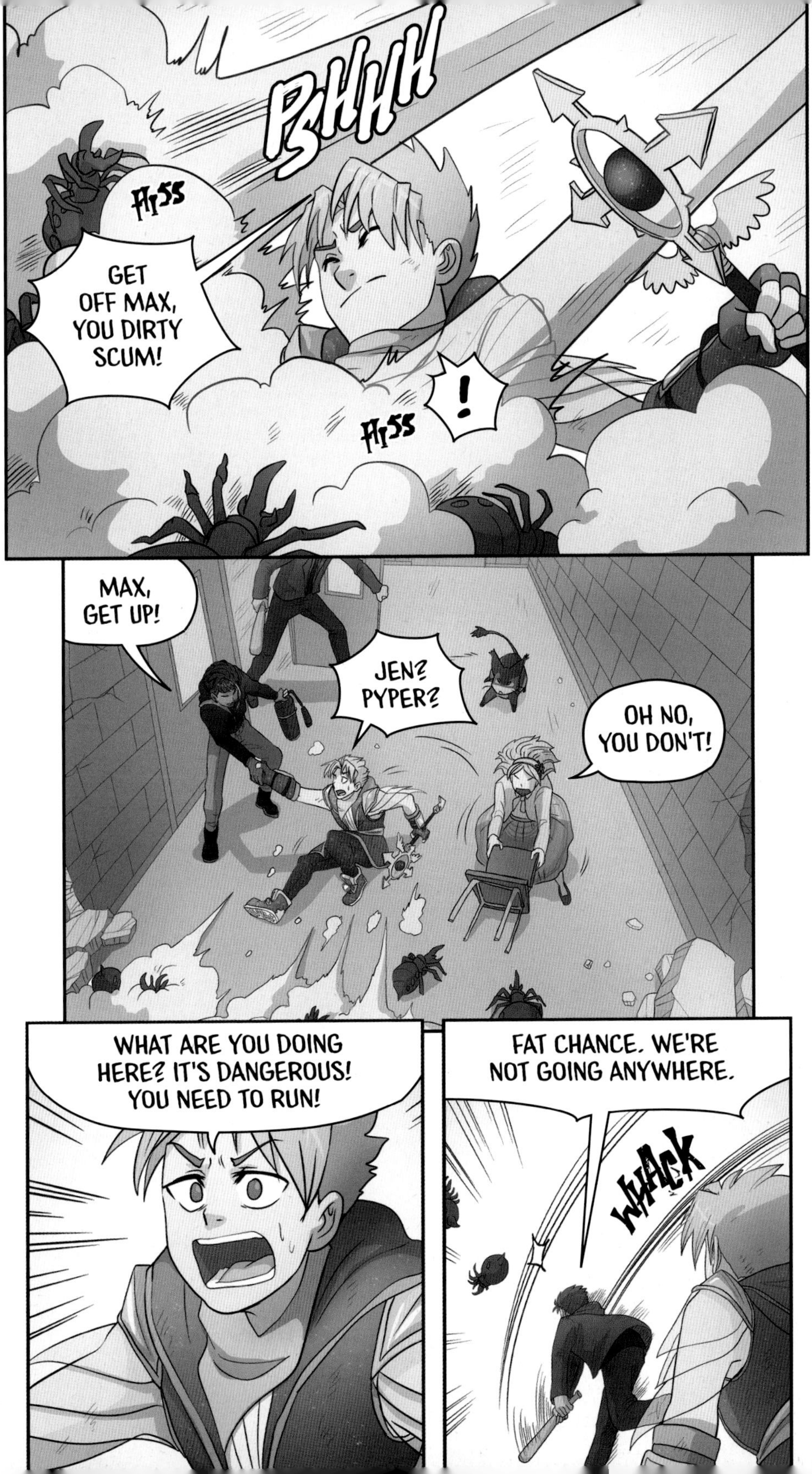
PSHHH
HISS
GET OFF MAX, YOU DIRTY SCUM!
!
HISS
MAX, GET UP!
JEN? PYPER?
OH NO, YOU DON'T!
WHAT ARE YOU DOING HERE? IT'S DANGEROUS! YOU NEED TO RUN!
FAT CHANCE. WE'RE NOT GOING ANYWHERE.
WHACK

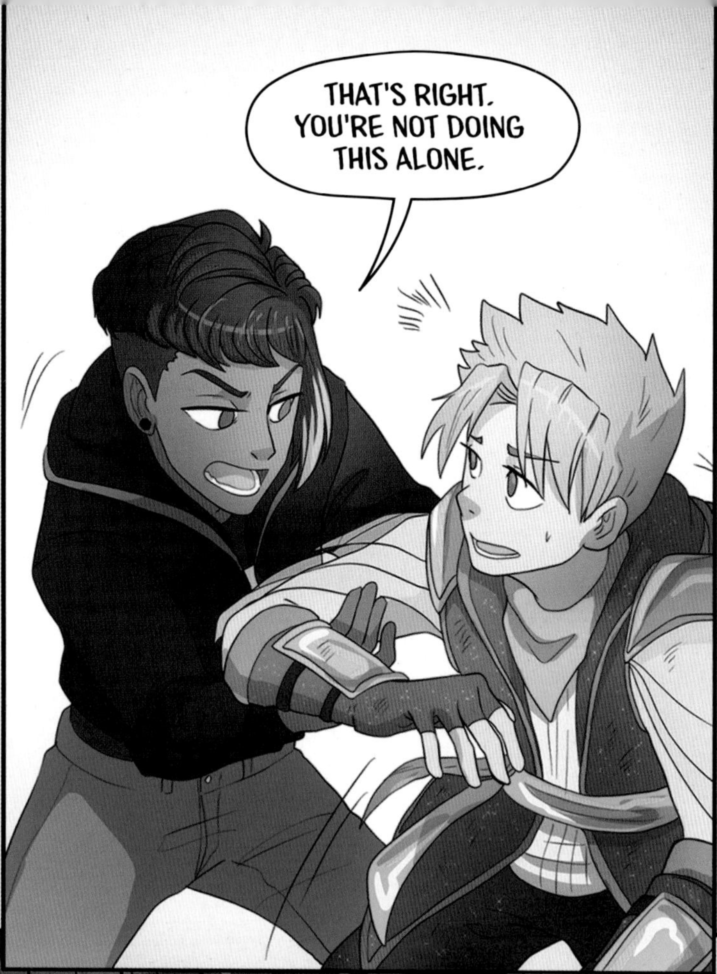
THAT'S RIGHT.
YOU'RE NOT DOING THIS ALONE.

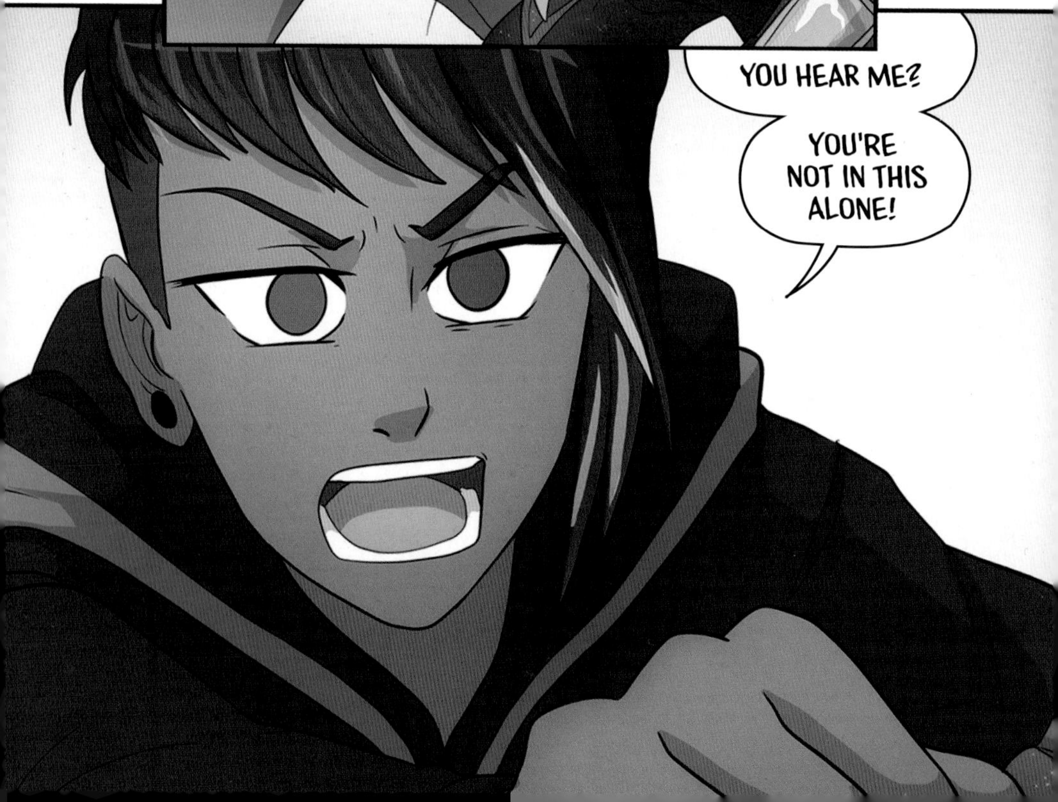
YOU HEAR ME?
YOU'RE NOT IN THIS ALONE!

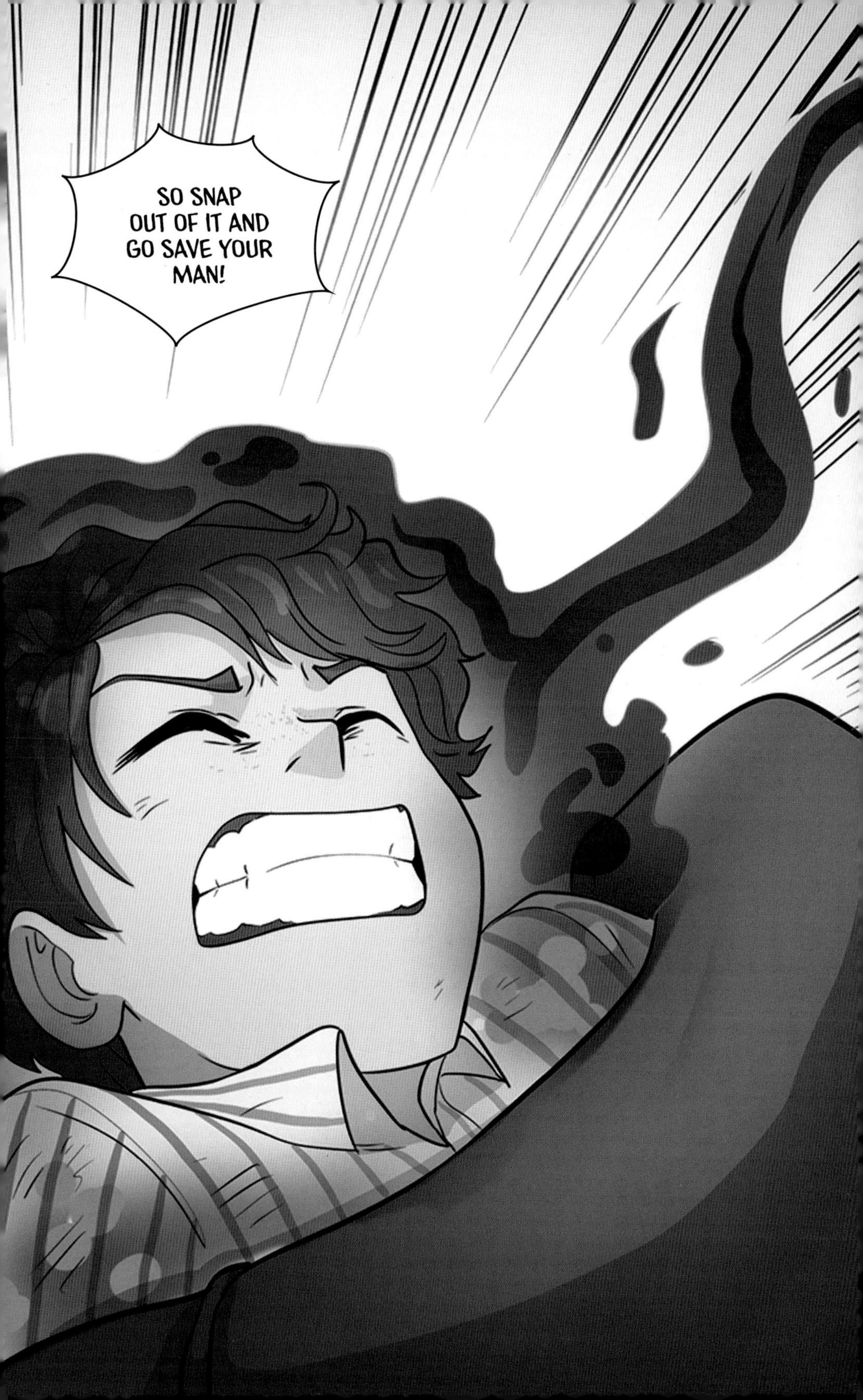
SO SNAP OUT OF IT AND GO SAVE YOUR MAN!

EPISODE 18:
SHUT DOWN

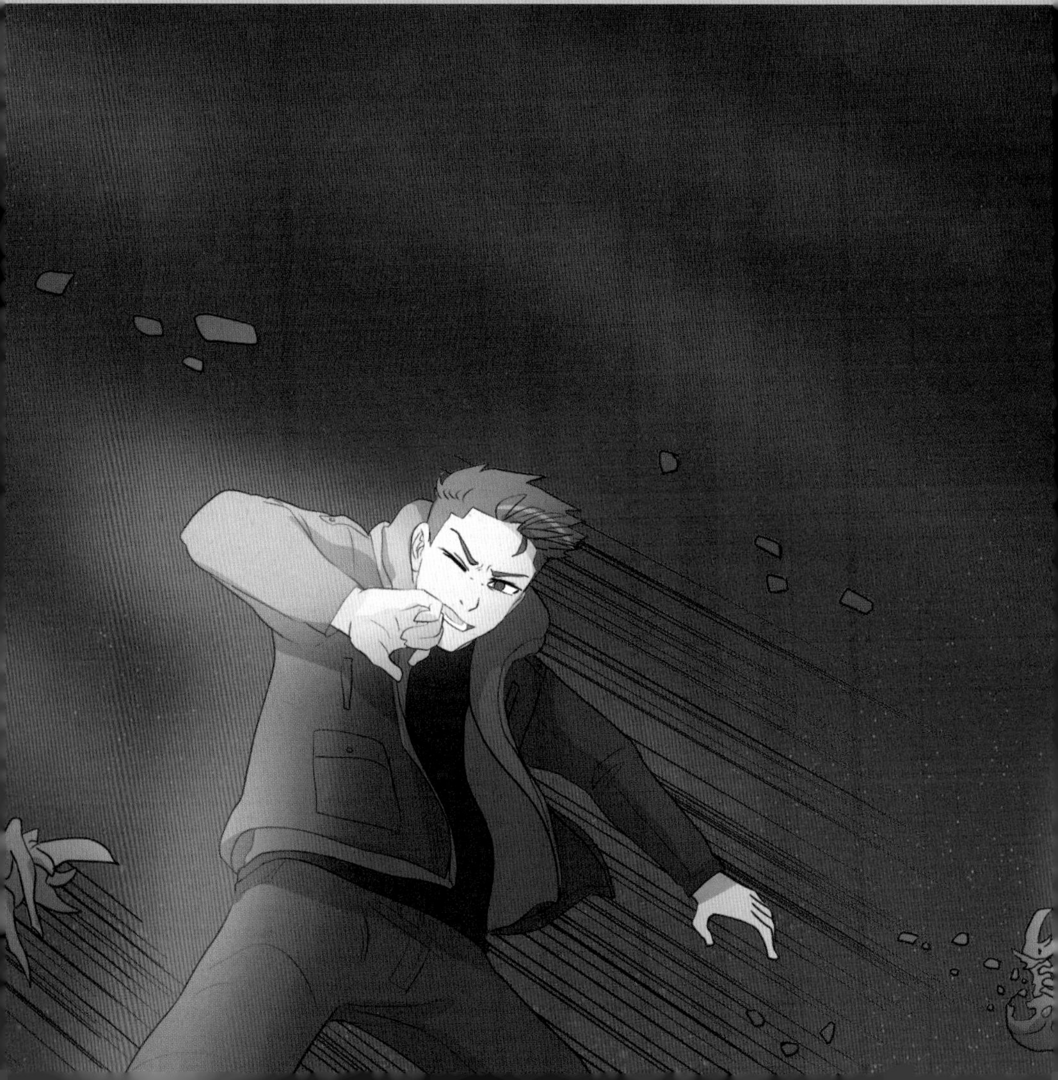

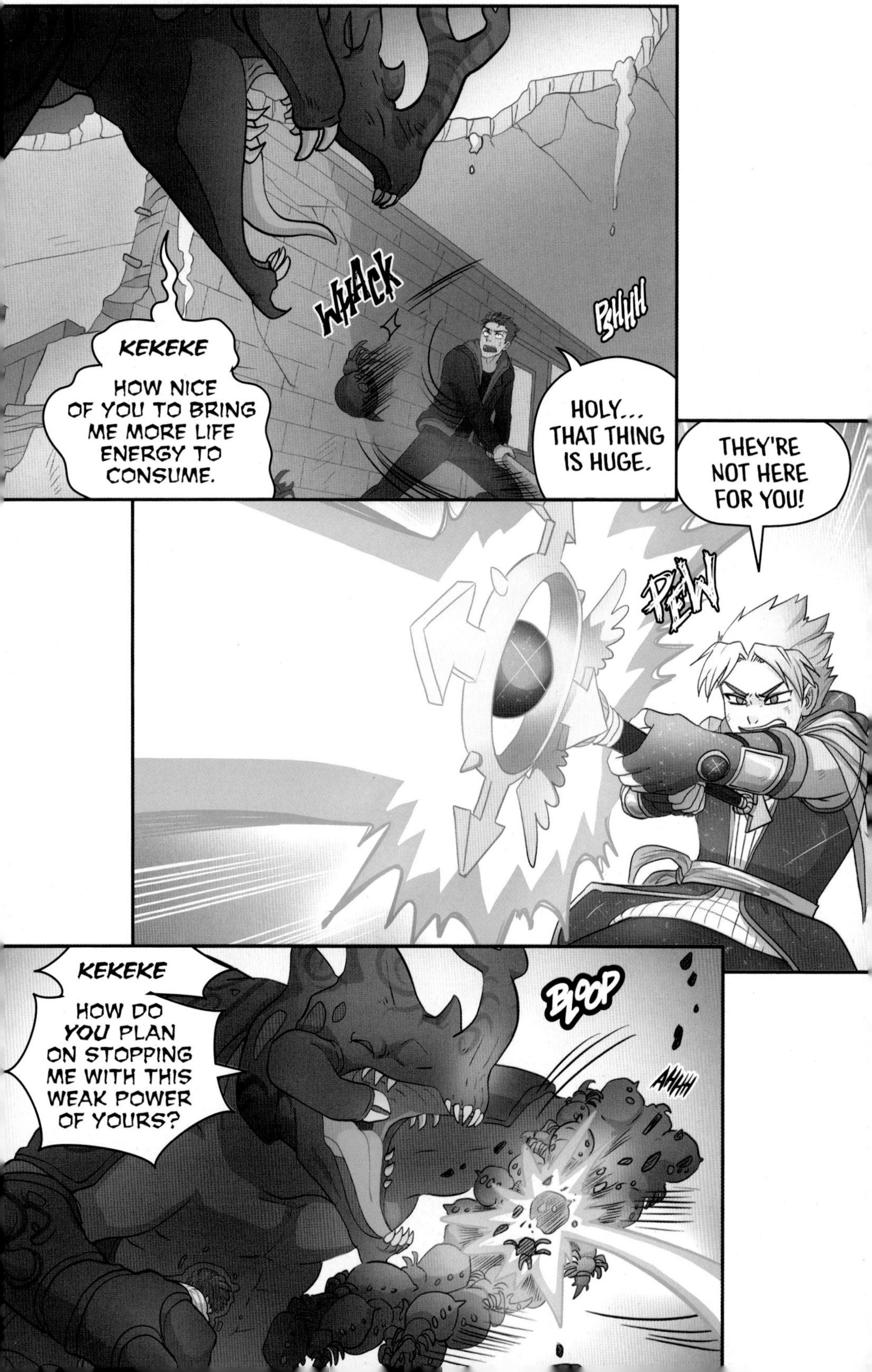
WHACK
KEKEKE
HOW NICE OF YOU TO BRING ME MORE LIFE ENERGY TO CONSUME.
PSHHH
HOLY... THAT THING IS HUGE.
THEY'RE NOT HERE FOR YOU!
PEW
KEKEKE
HOW DO *YOU* PLAN ON STOPPING ME WITH THIS WEAK POWER OF YOURS?
BLOOP
AHHH

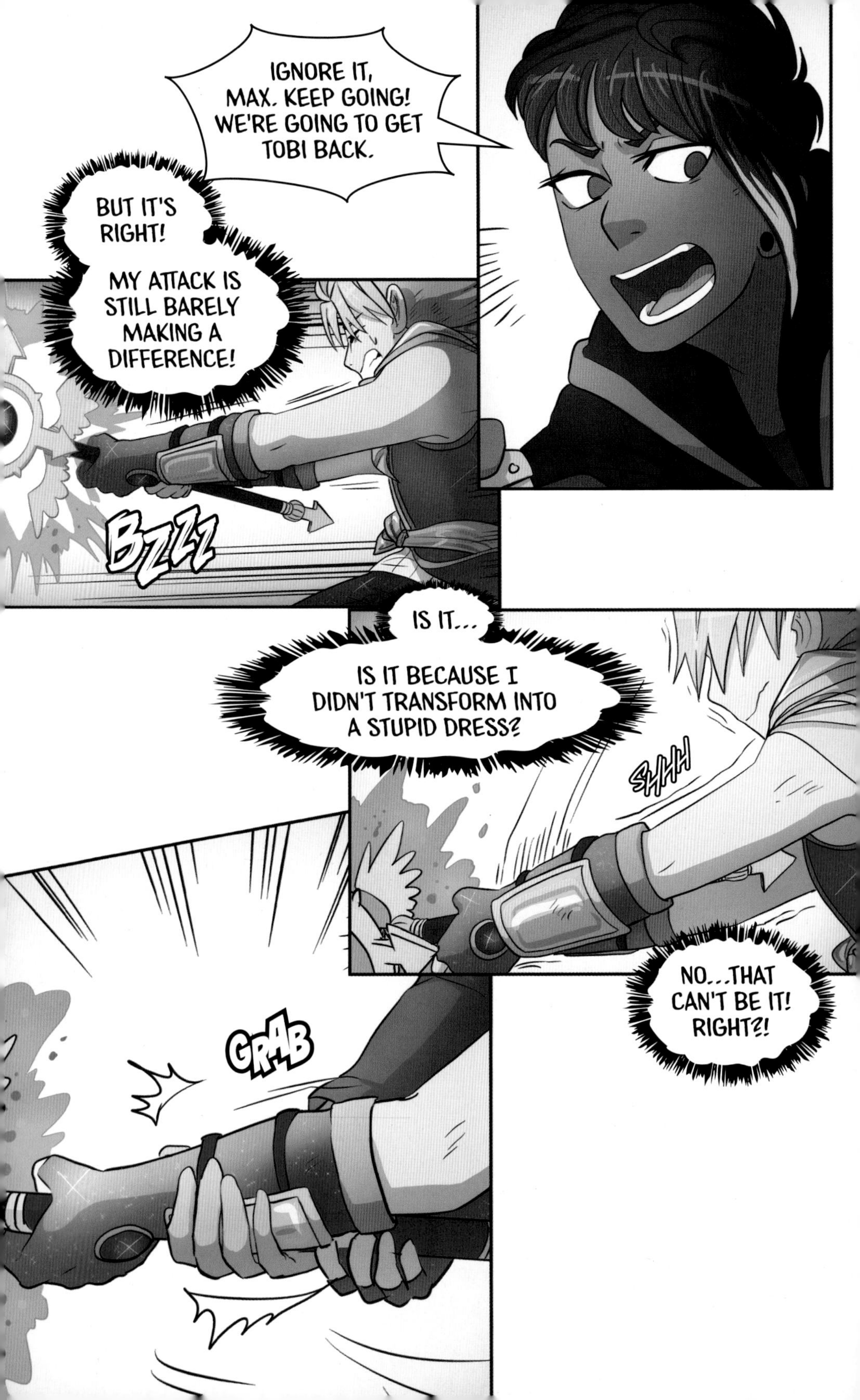
IGNORE IT, MAX. KEEP GOING! WE'RE GOING TO GET TOBI BACK.
BUT IT'S RIGHT!
MY ATTACK IS STILL BARELY MAKING A DIFFERENCE!
BZZZ
IS IT...
IS IT BECAUSE I DIDN'T TRANSFORM INTO A STUPID DRESS?
SHHH
NO...THAT CAN'T BE IT! RIGHT?!
GRAB

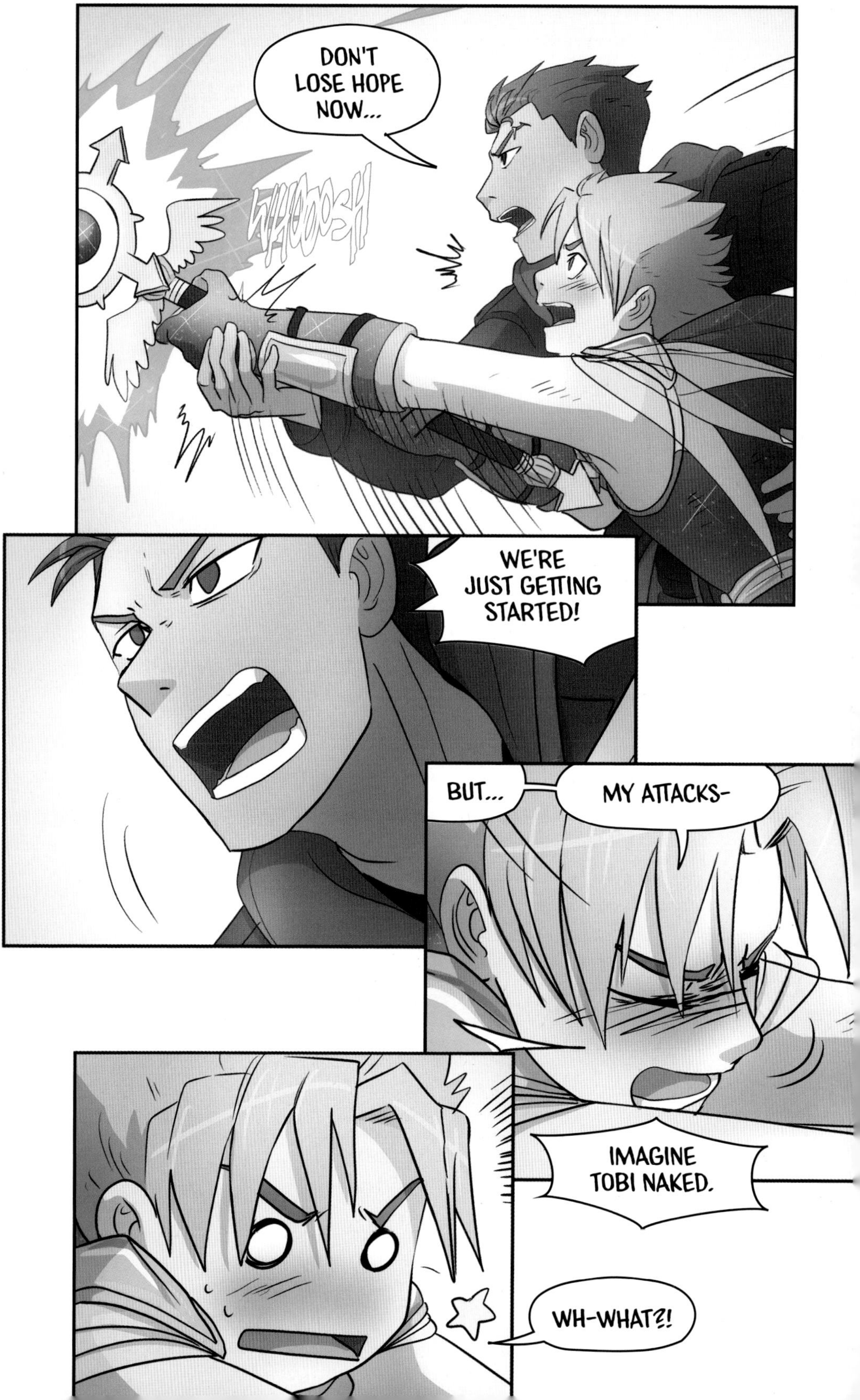
DON'T LOSE HOPE NOW...
WHOOOSH
WE'RE JUST GETTING STARTED!
BUT...
MY ATTACKS-
IMAGINE TOBI NAKED.
WH-WHAT?!

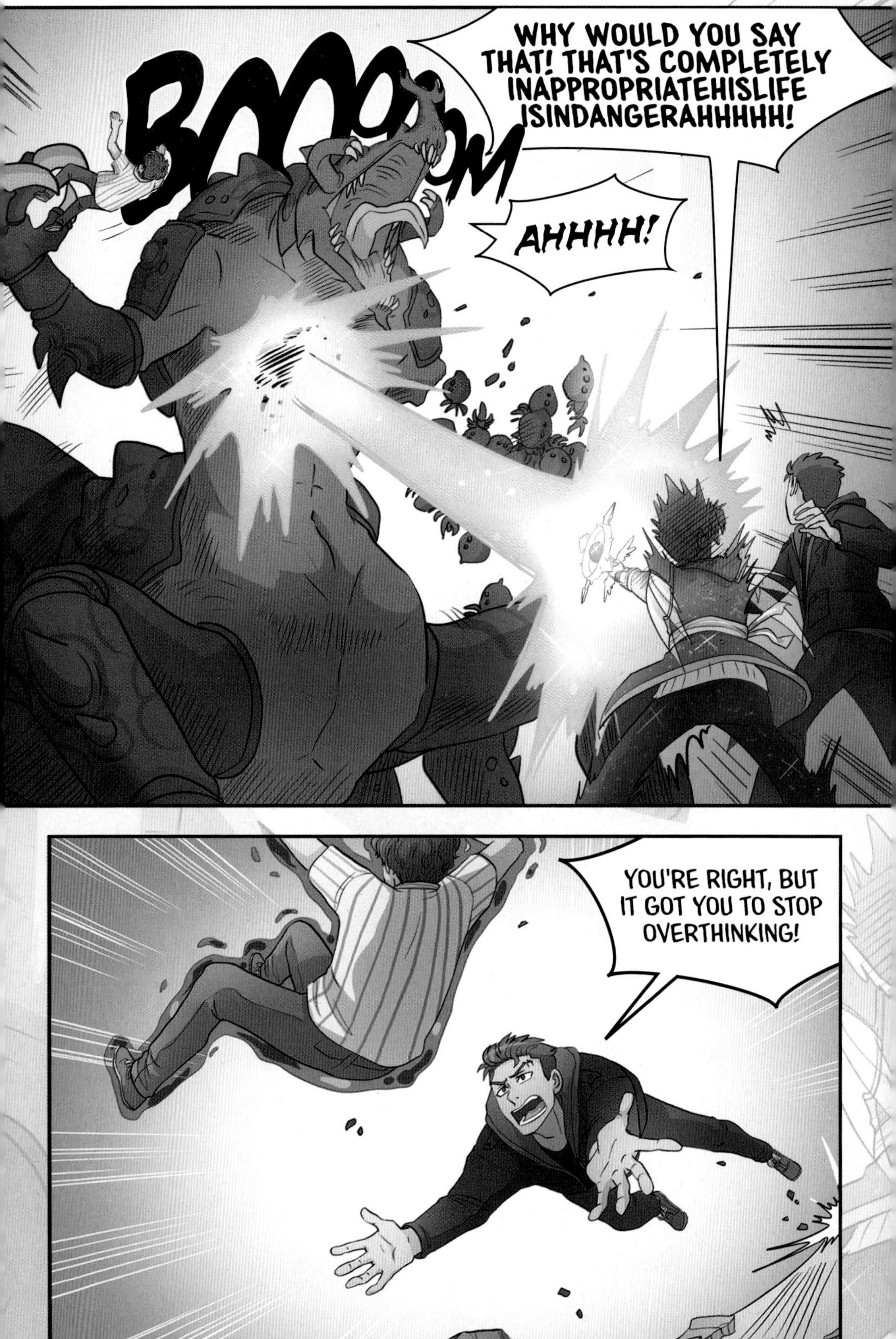
BOOOOOM
WHY WOULD YOU SAY THAT! THAT'S COMPLETELY INAPPROPRIATEHISLIFE ISINDANGERAHHHHH!
AHHHH!
YOU'RE RIGHT, BUT IT GOT YOU TO STOP OVERTHINKING!

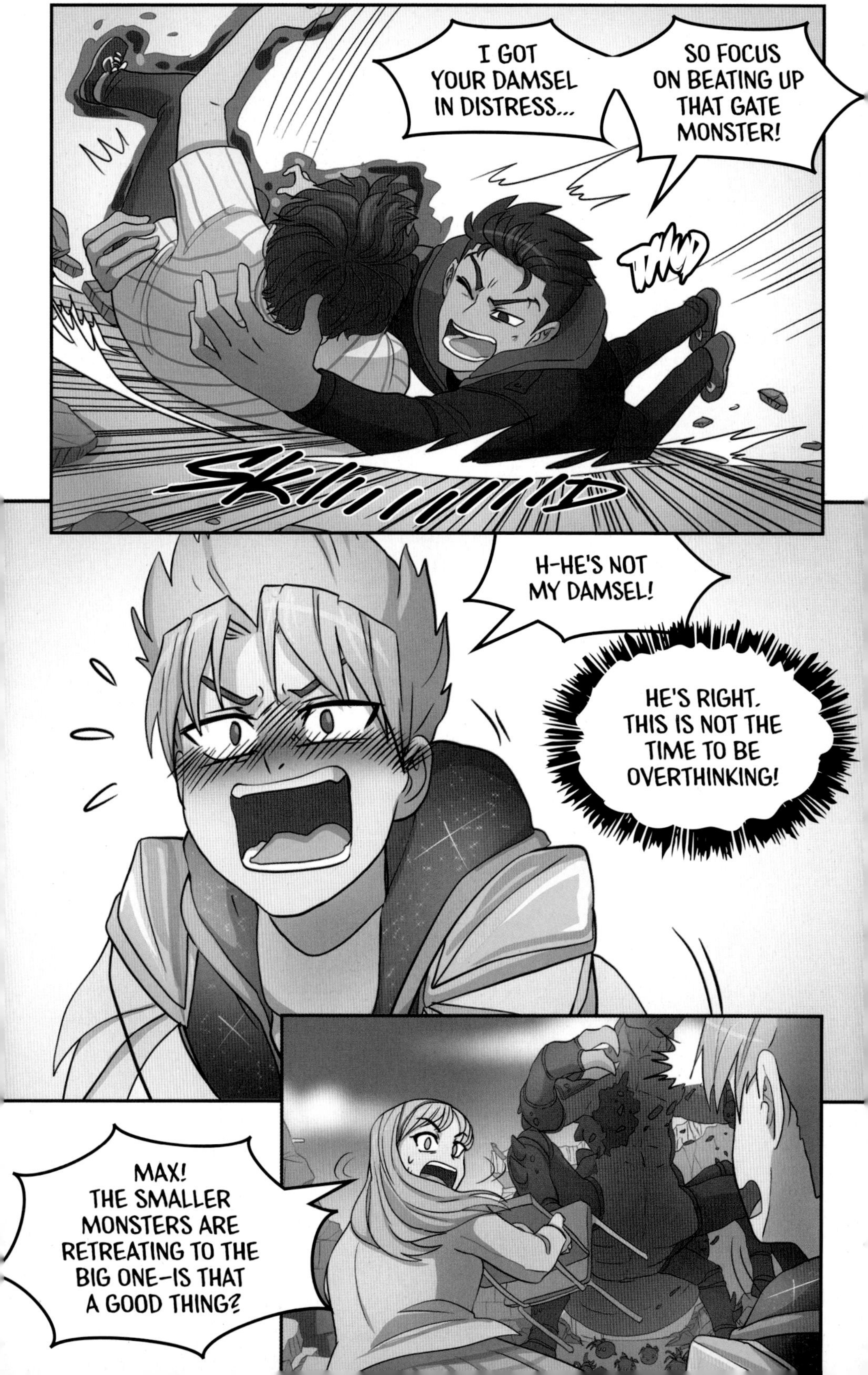
I GOT YOUR DAMSEL IN DISTRESS...
SO FOCUS ON BEATING UP THAT GATE MONSTER!
THUD
SKIIIIIIIIID
H-HE'S NOT MY DAMSEL!
HE'S RIGHT. THIS IS NOT THE TIME TO BE OVERTHINKING!
MAX! THE SMALLER MONSTERS ARE RETREATING TO THE BIG ONE—IS THAT A GOOD THING?

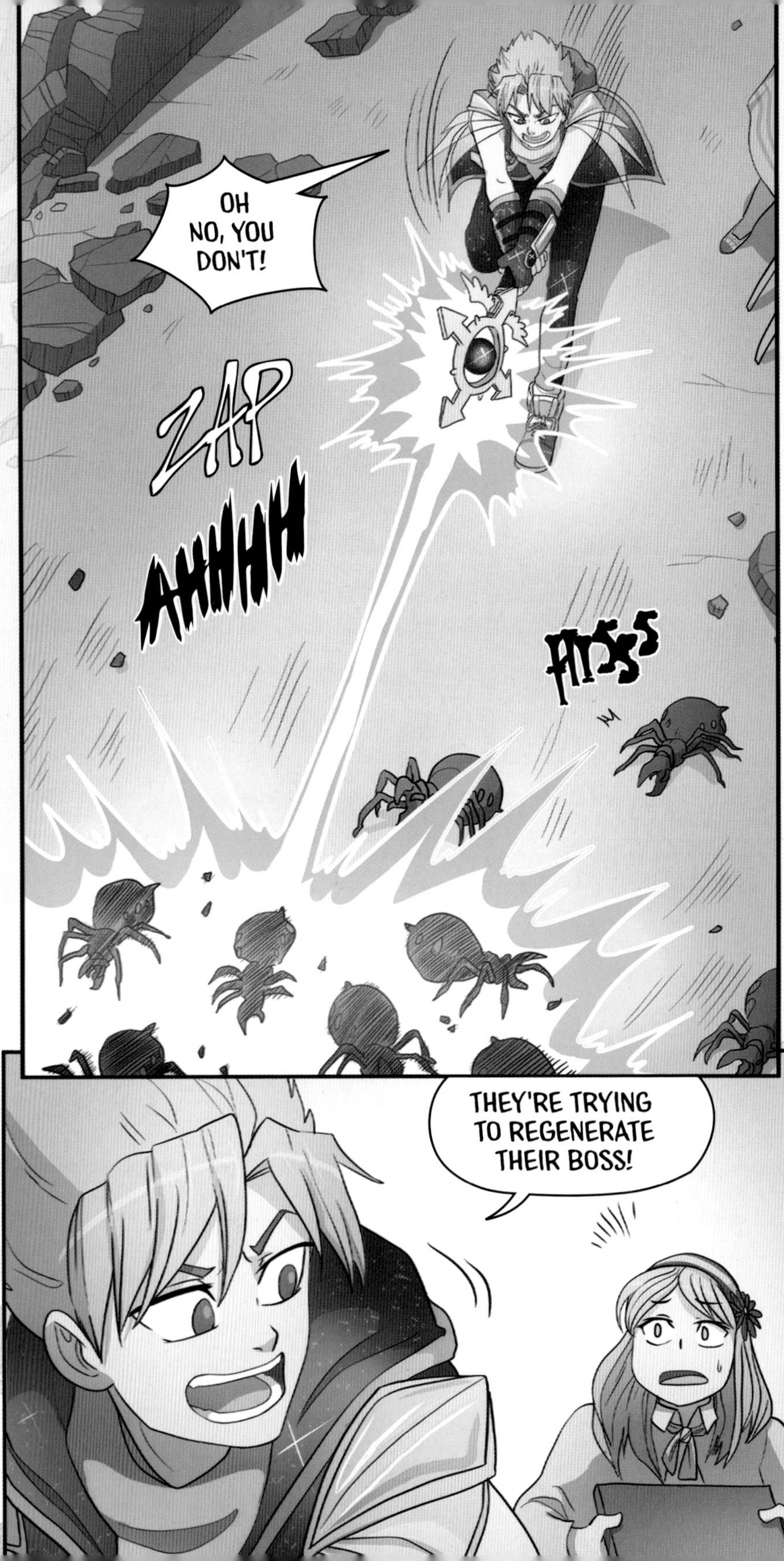
OH NO, YOU DON'T!
ZAP
AHHHH
HISSS
THEY'RE TRYING TO REGENERATE THEIR BOSS!

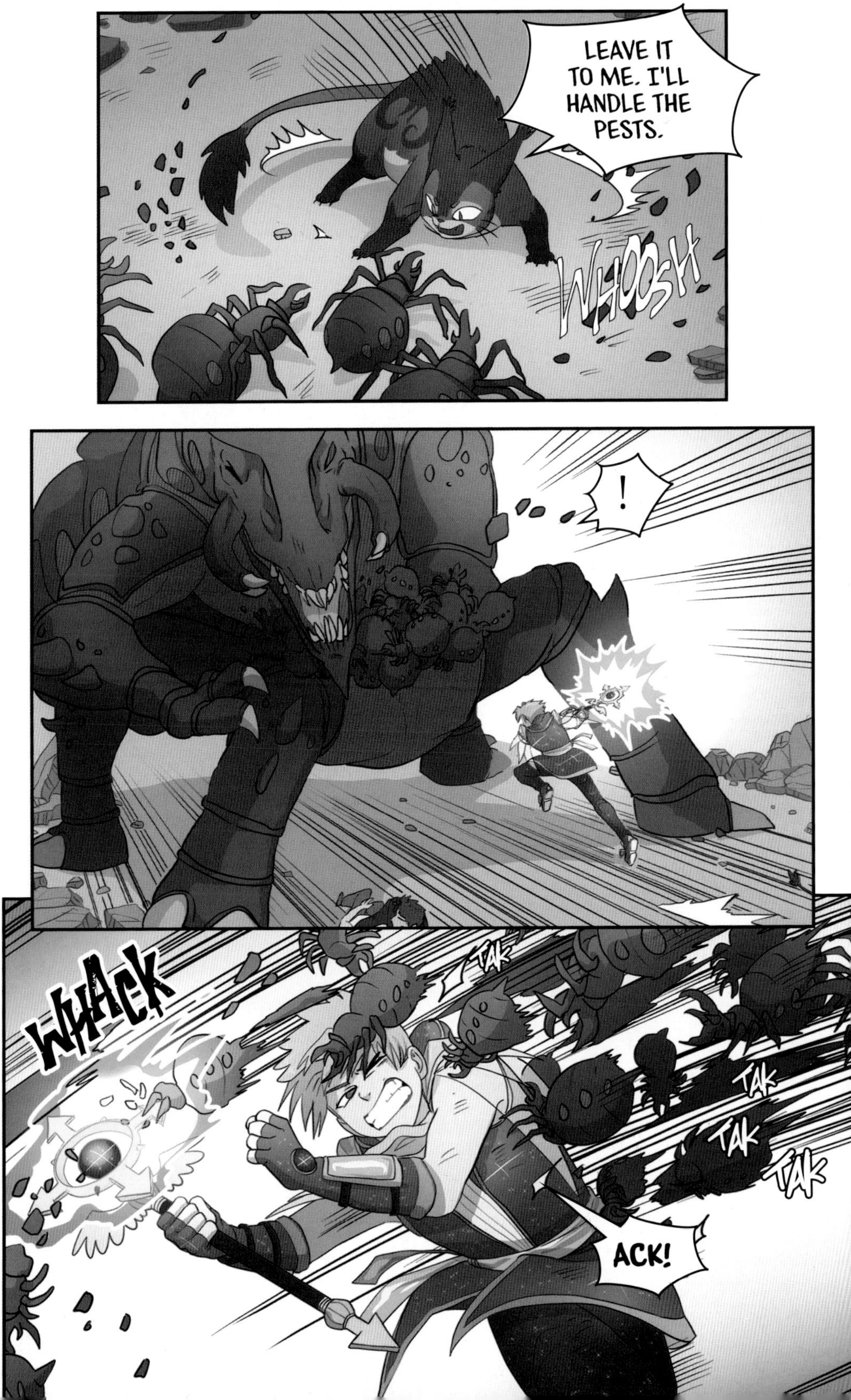
LEAVE IT TO ME. I'LL HANDLE THE PESTS.
WHOOSH
!
WHACK
TAK
TAK
TAK
TAK
ACK!

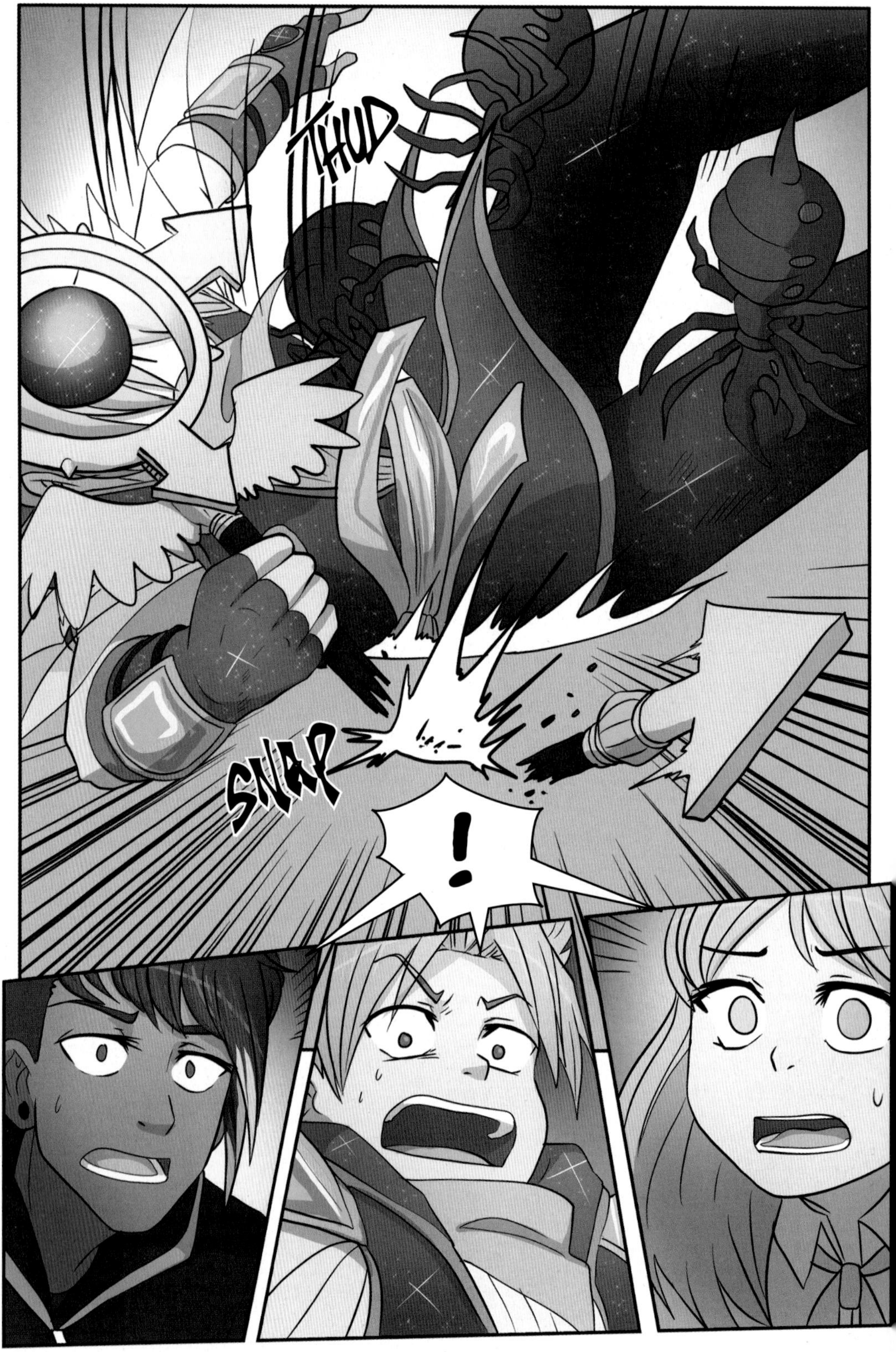
THUD
SNAP
!

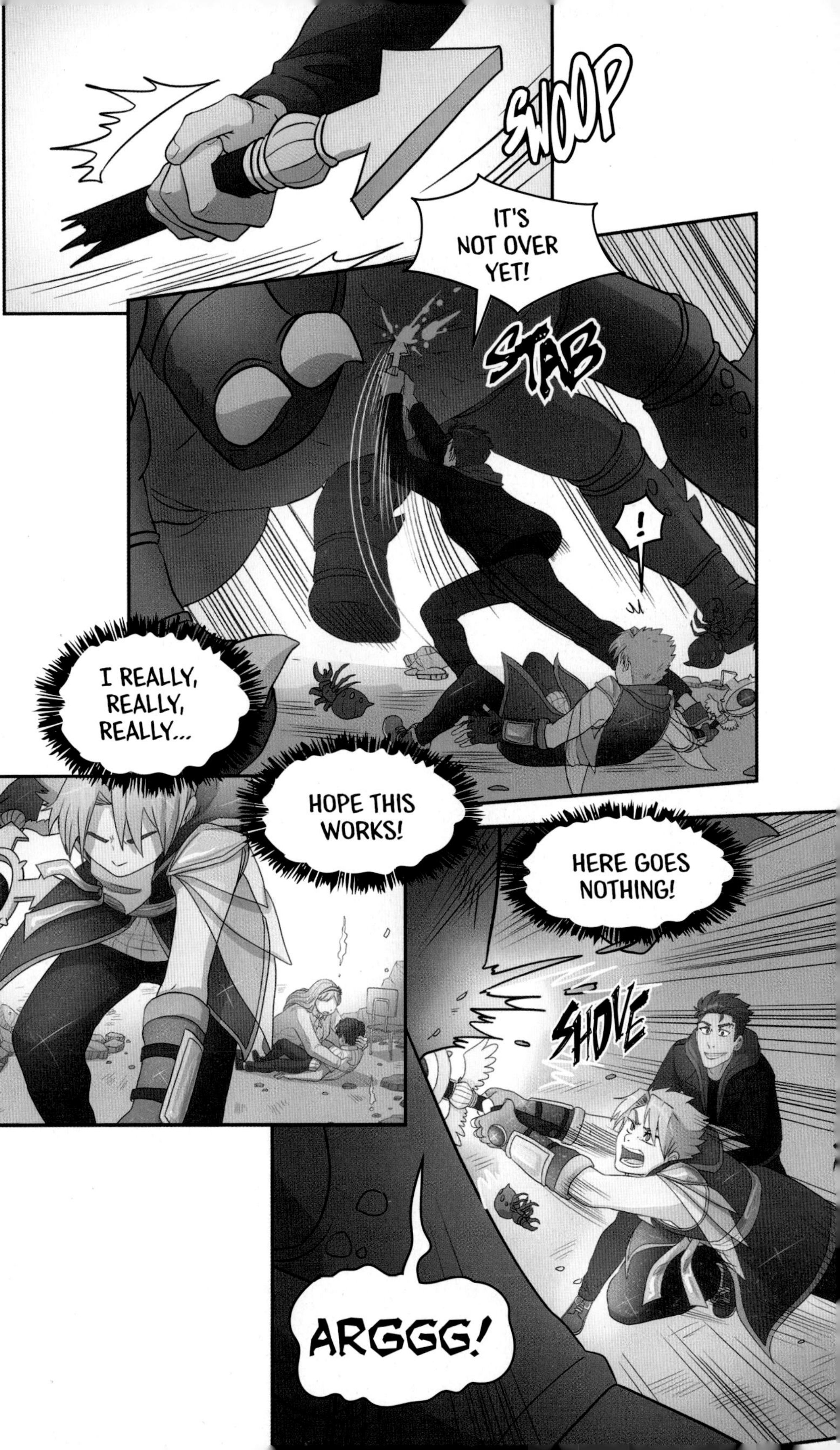
SWOOP
IT'S NOT OVER YET!
STAB
!
I REALLY, REALLY, REALLY...
HOPE THIS WORKS!
HERE GOES NOTHING!
SHOVE
ARGGG!

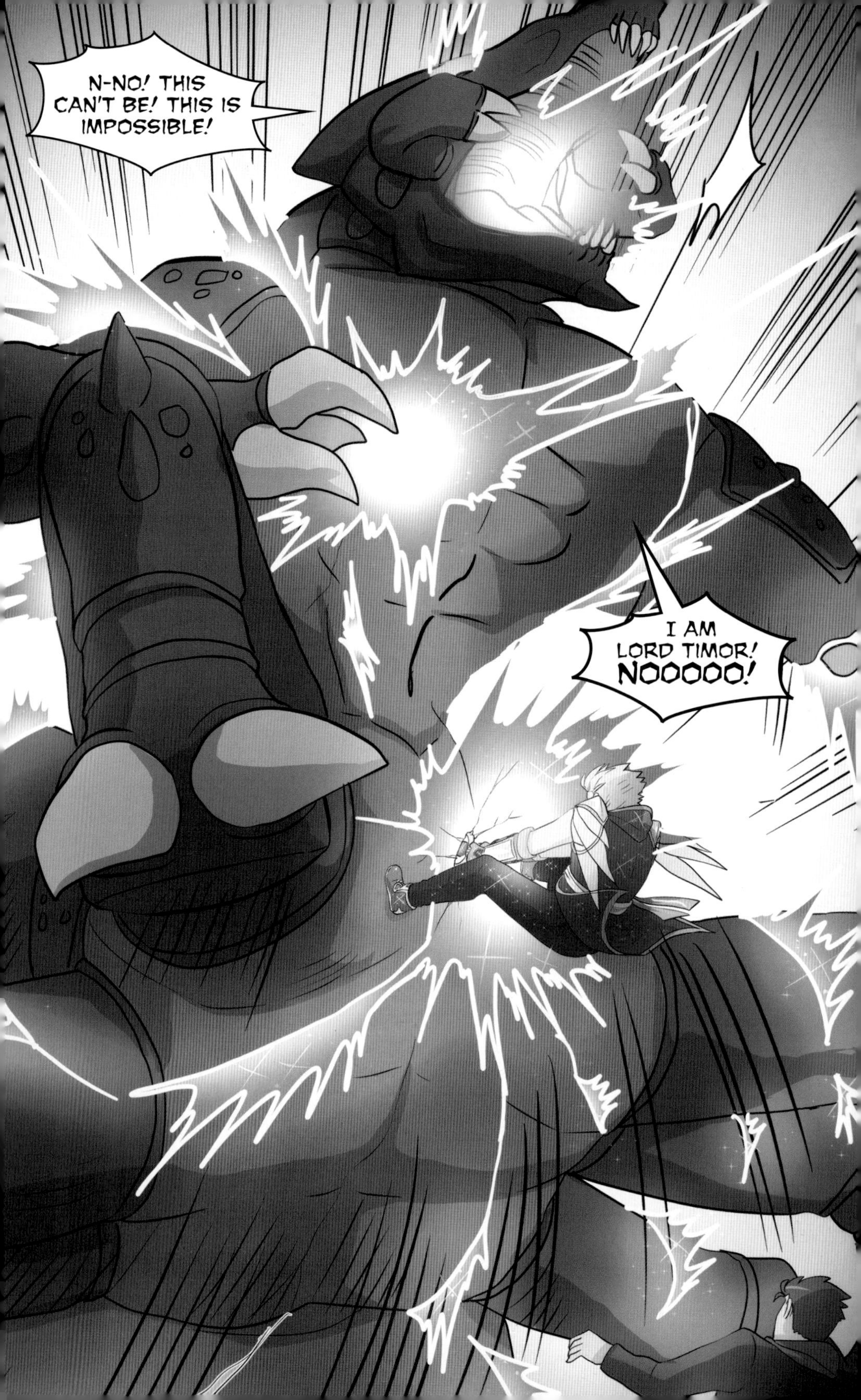
N-NO! THIS CAN'T BE! THIS IS IMPOSSIBLE!
I AM LORD TIMOR! NOOOOO!

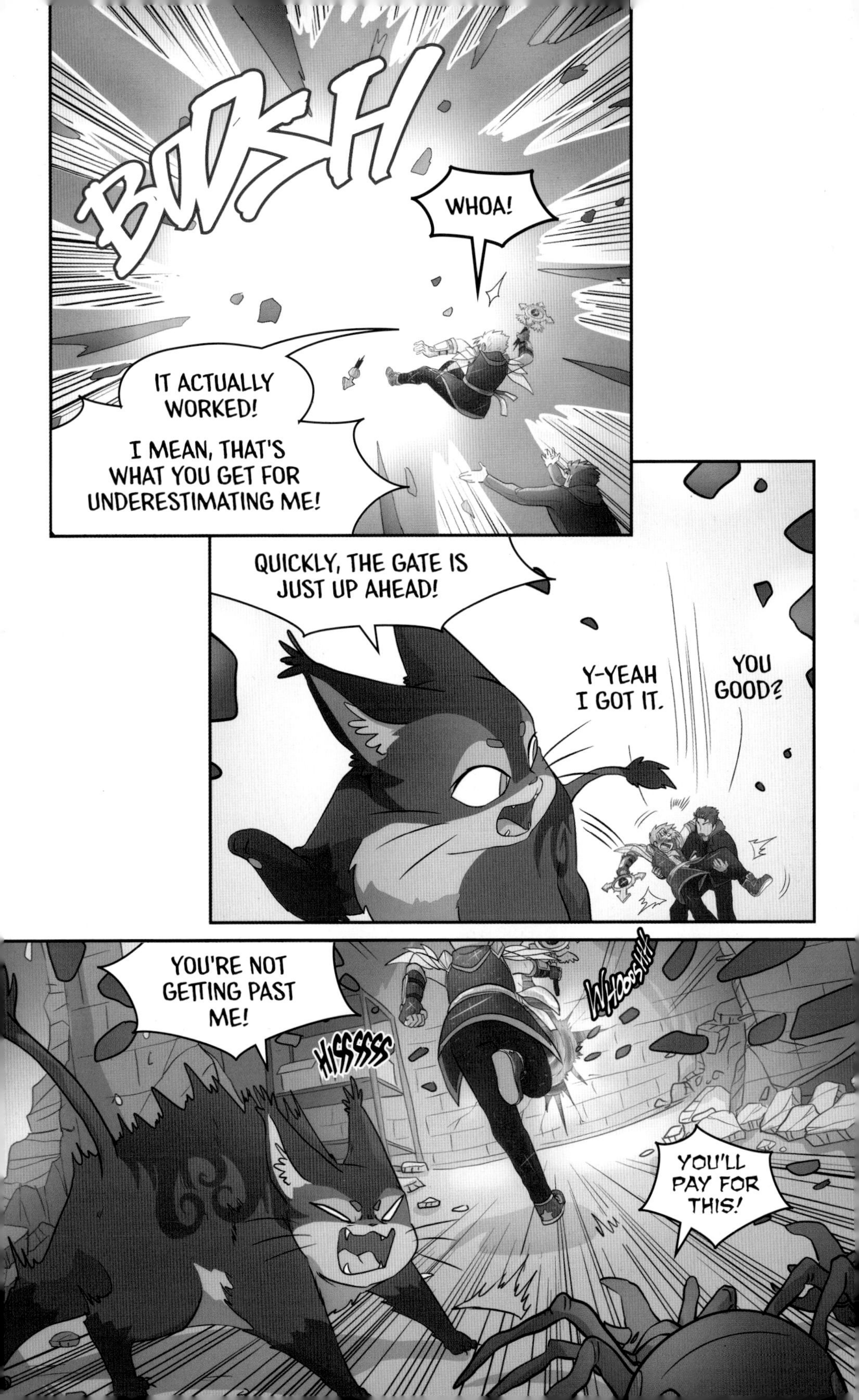
BOOSH
WHOA!
IT ACTUALLY WORKED!
I MEAN, THAT'S WHAT YOU GET FOR UNDERESTIMATING ME!
QUICKLY, THE GATE IS JUST UP AHEAD!
YOU GOOD?
Y-YEAH I GOT IT.
YOU'RE NOT GETTING PAST ME!
HISSSSS
WHOOOSH
YOU'LL PAY FOR THIS!

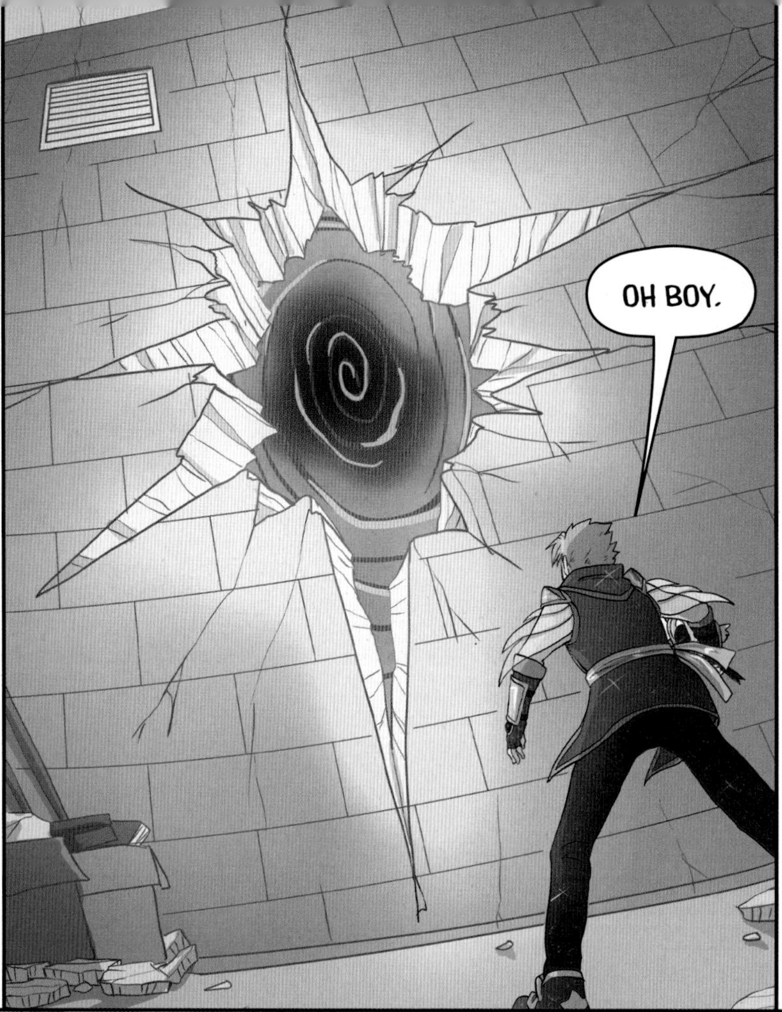
OH BOY.

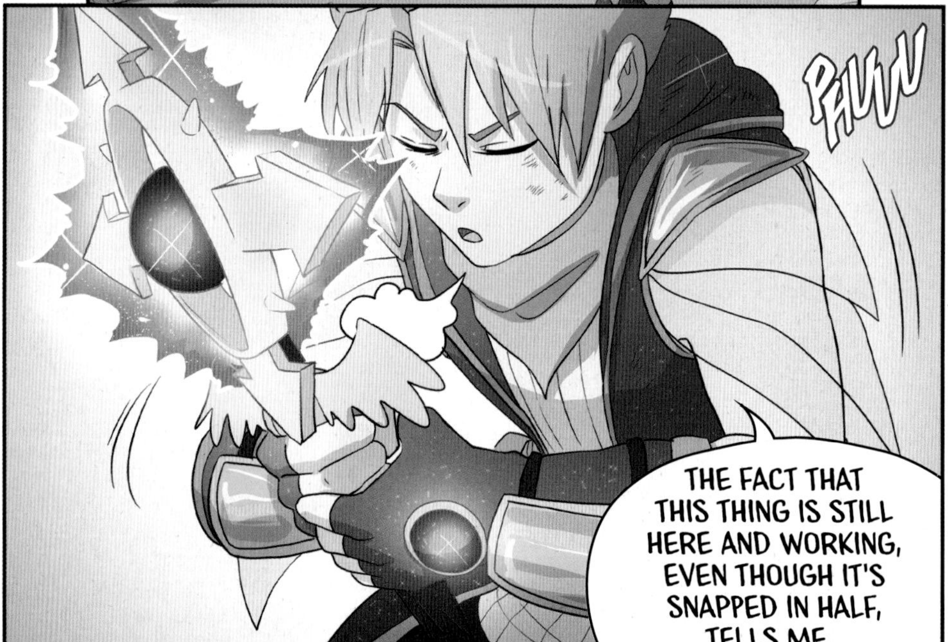
PHWW
THE FACT THAT THIS THING IS STILL HERE AND WORKING, EVEN THOUGH IT'S SNAPPED IN HALF, TELLS ME...

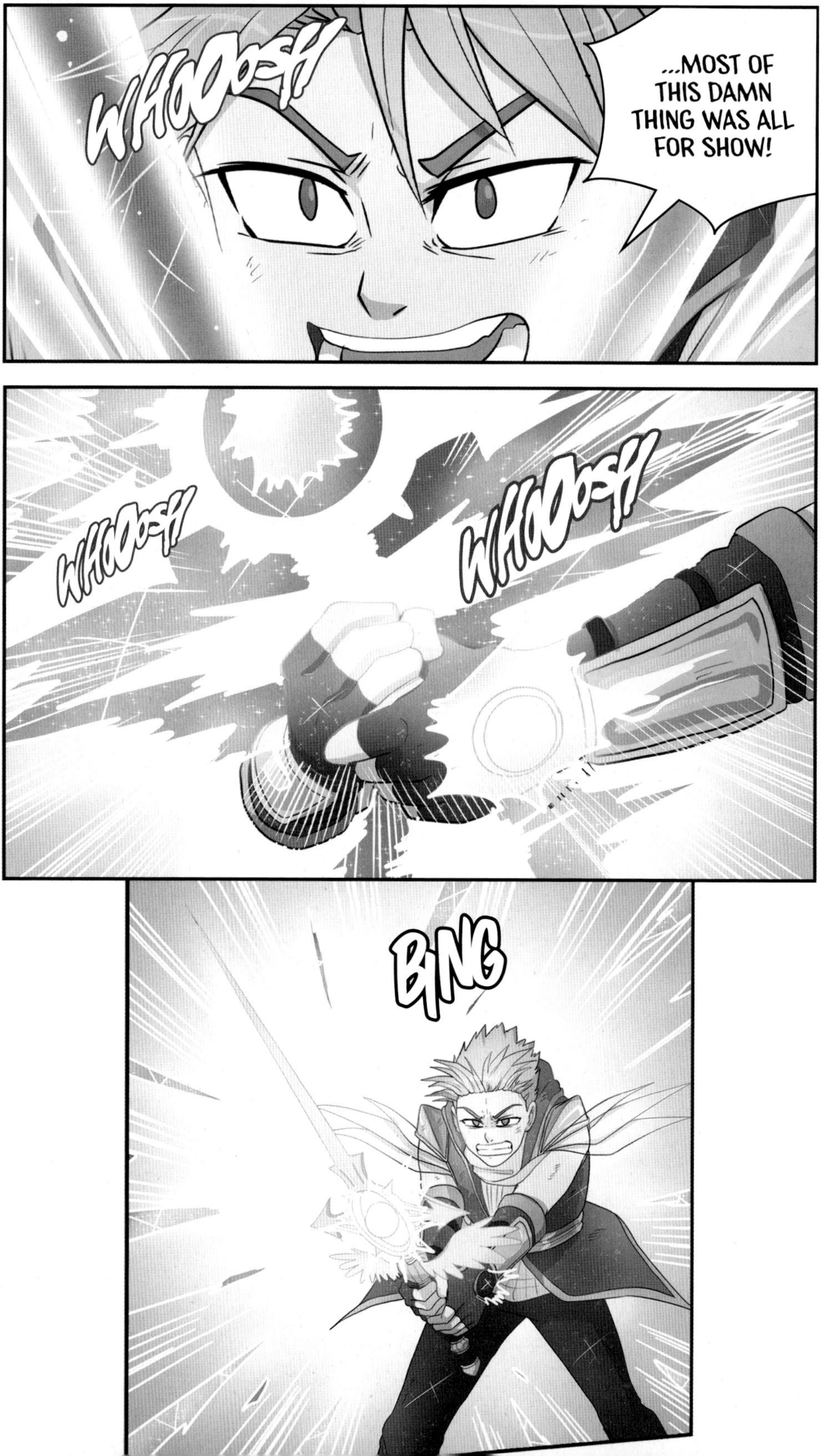
WHOOOSH!
...MOST OF THIS DAMN THING WAS ALL FOR SHOW!
WHOOOSH!
WHOOOSH!
BING

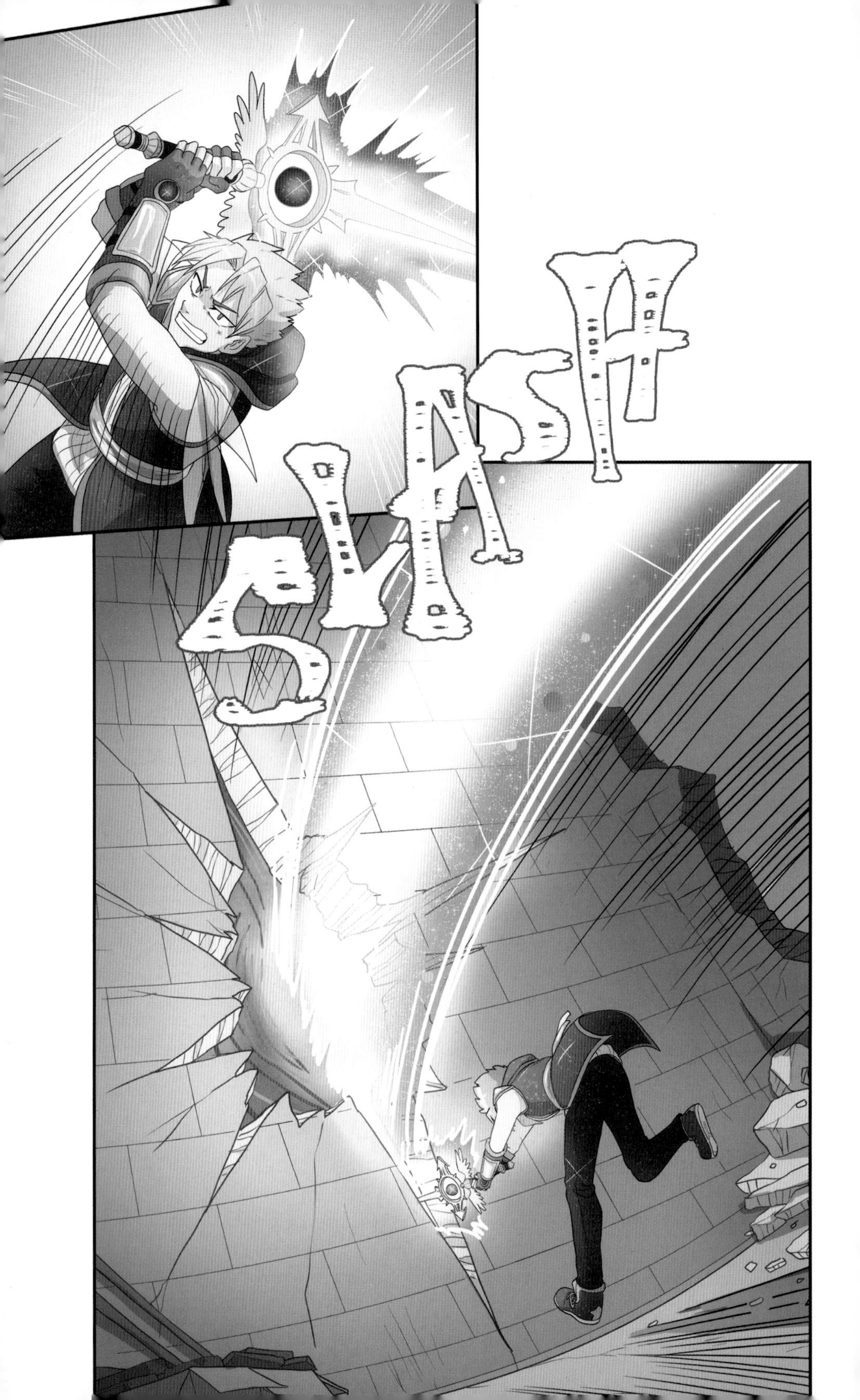
SLASH

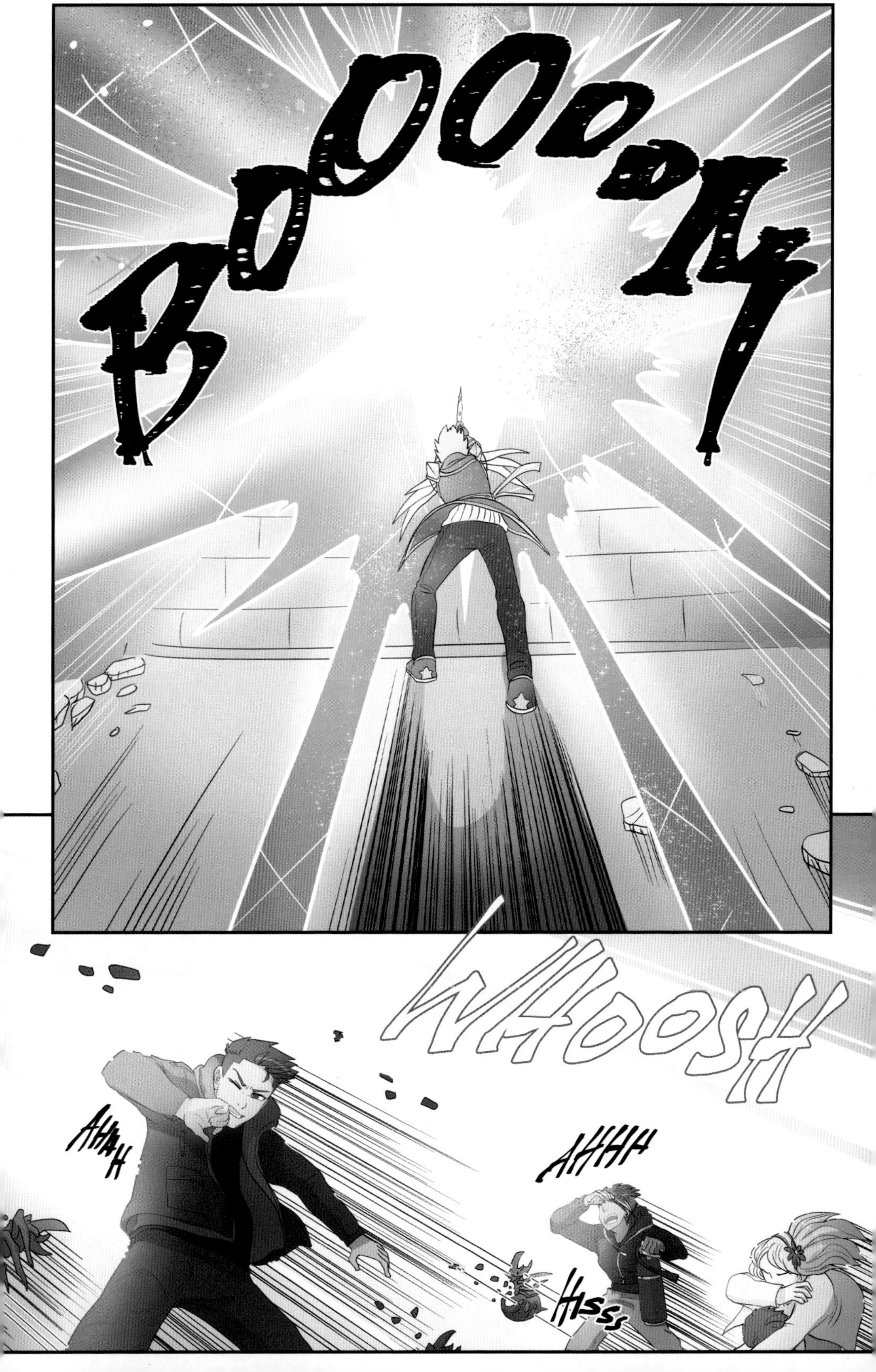
BOOOOOOM!
WHOOSH
AHHH
AHHH
HISSS

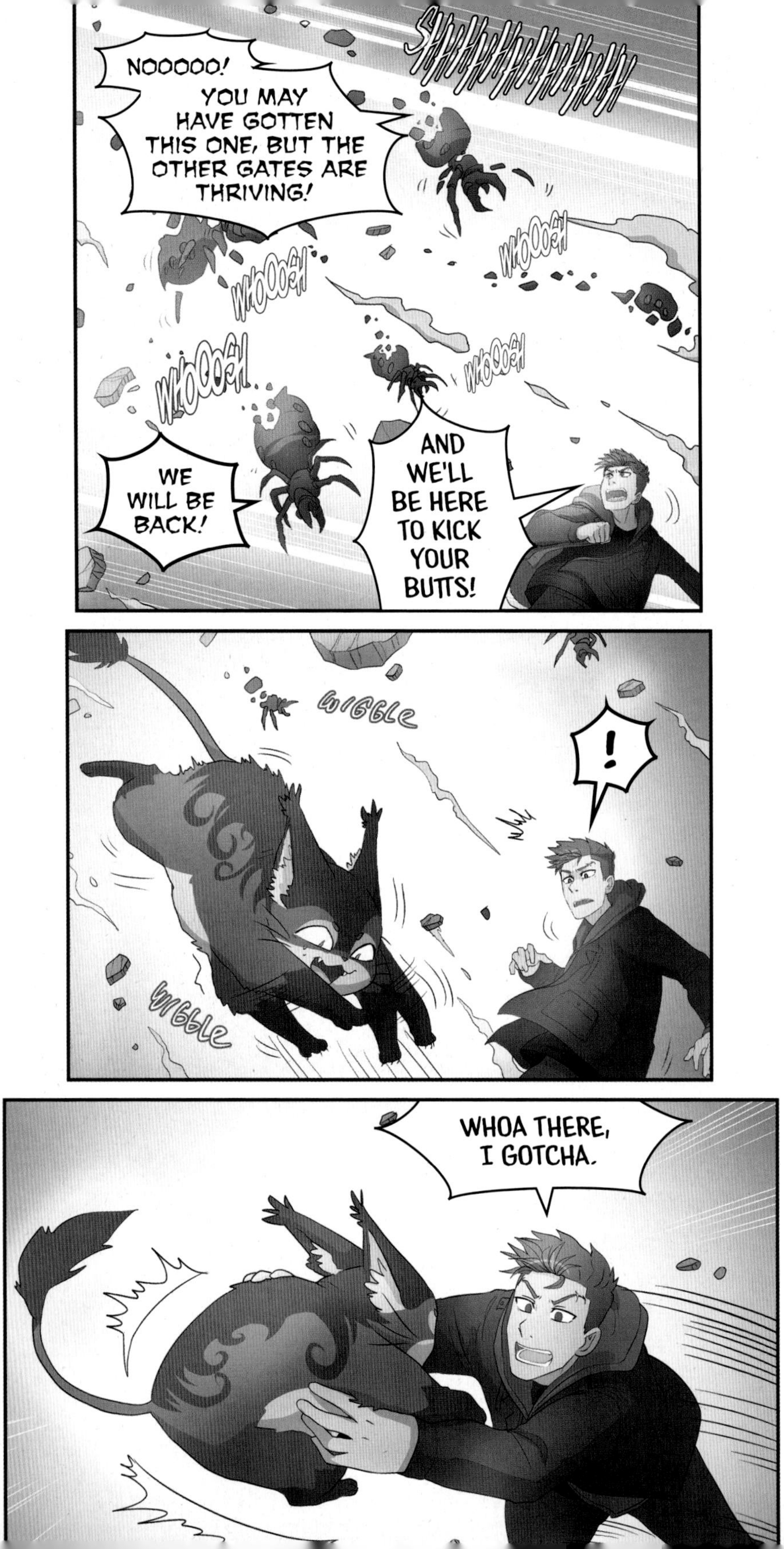
SHHHHHHHHHHHHHHH
NOOOOO! YOU MAY HAVE GOTTEN THIS ONE, BUT THE OTHER GATES ARE THRIVING!
WHOOOSH
WHOOOSH
WHOOOSH
WHOOOSH
WE WILL BE BACK!
AND WE'LL BE HERE TO KICK YOUR BUTTS!
WIGGLE
!
WIGGLE
WHOA THERE, I GOTCHA.

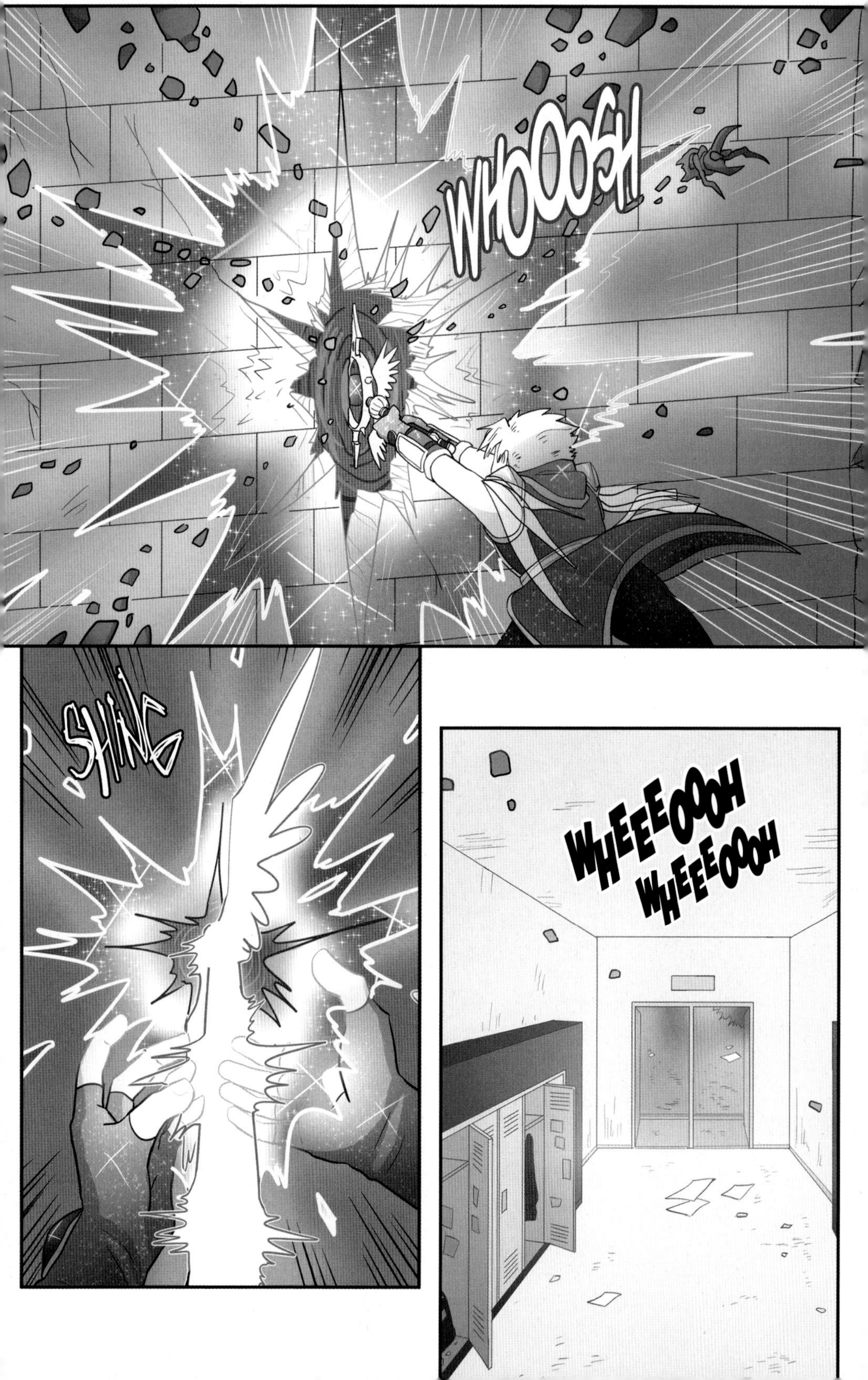
WHOOOSH
SHING
WHEEEOOOH
WHEEEOOOH

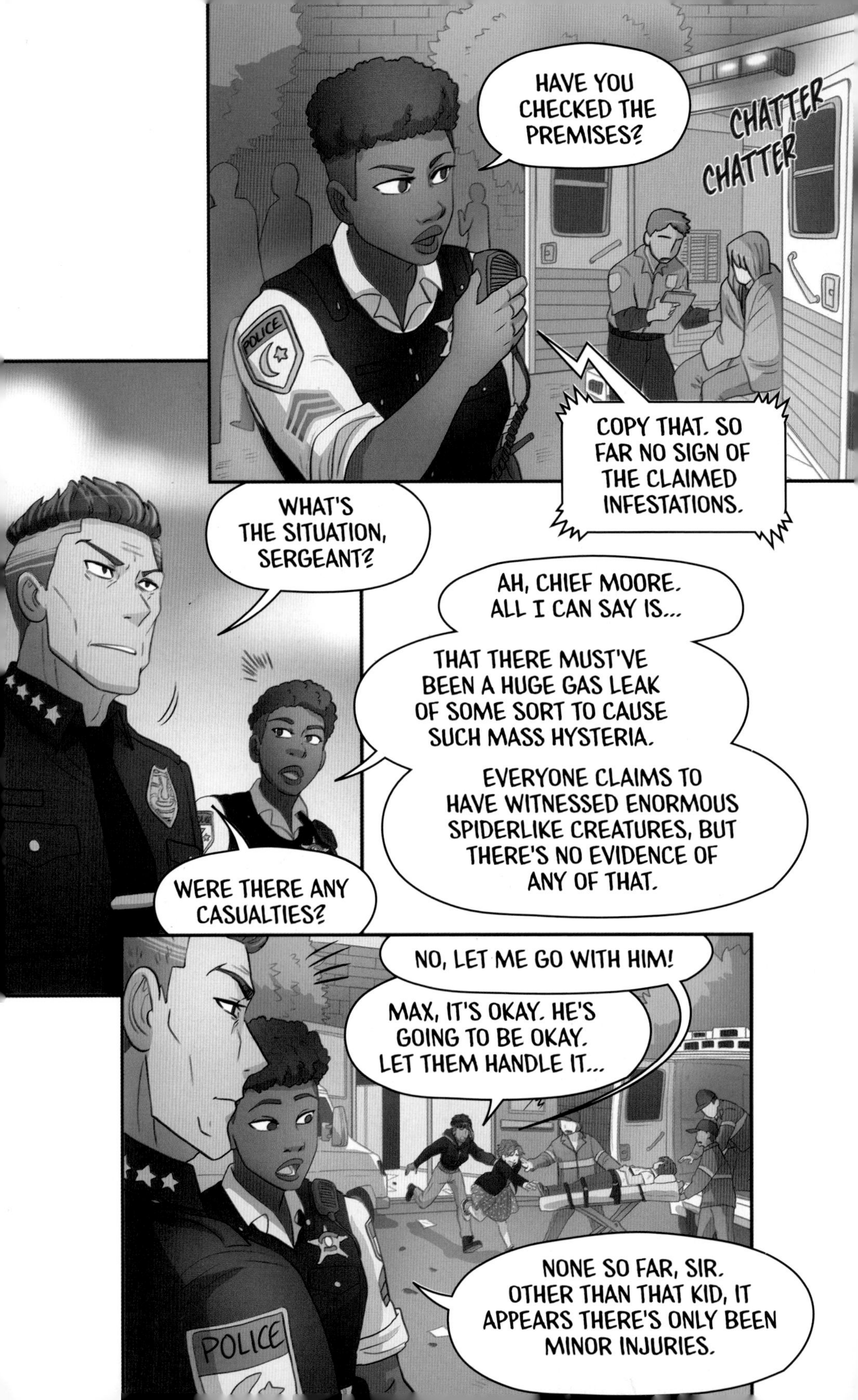
HAVE YOU CHECKED THE PREMISES?
CHATTER CHATTER
COPY THAT. SO FAR NO SIGN OF THE CLAIMED INFESTATIONS.
WHAT'S THE SITUATION, SERGEANT?
AH, CHIEF MOORE. ALL I CAN SAY IS...
THAT THERE MUST'VE BEEN A HUGE GAS LEAK OF SOME SORT TO CAUSE SUCH MASS HYSTERIA.
EVERYONE CLAIMS TO HAVE WITNESSED ENORMOUS SPIDERLIKE CREATURES, BUT THERE'S NO EVIDENCE OF ANY OF THAT.
WERE THERE ANY CASUALTIES?
NO, LET ME GO WITH HIM!
MAX, IT'S OKAY. HE'S GOING TO BE OKAY. LET THEM HANDLE IT...
NONE SO FAR, SIR. OTHER THAN THAT KID, IT APPEARS THERE'S ONLY BEEN MINOR INJURIES.
POLICE

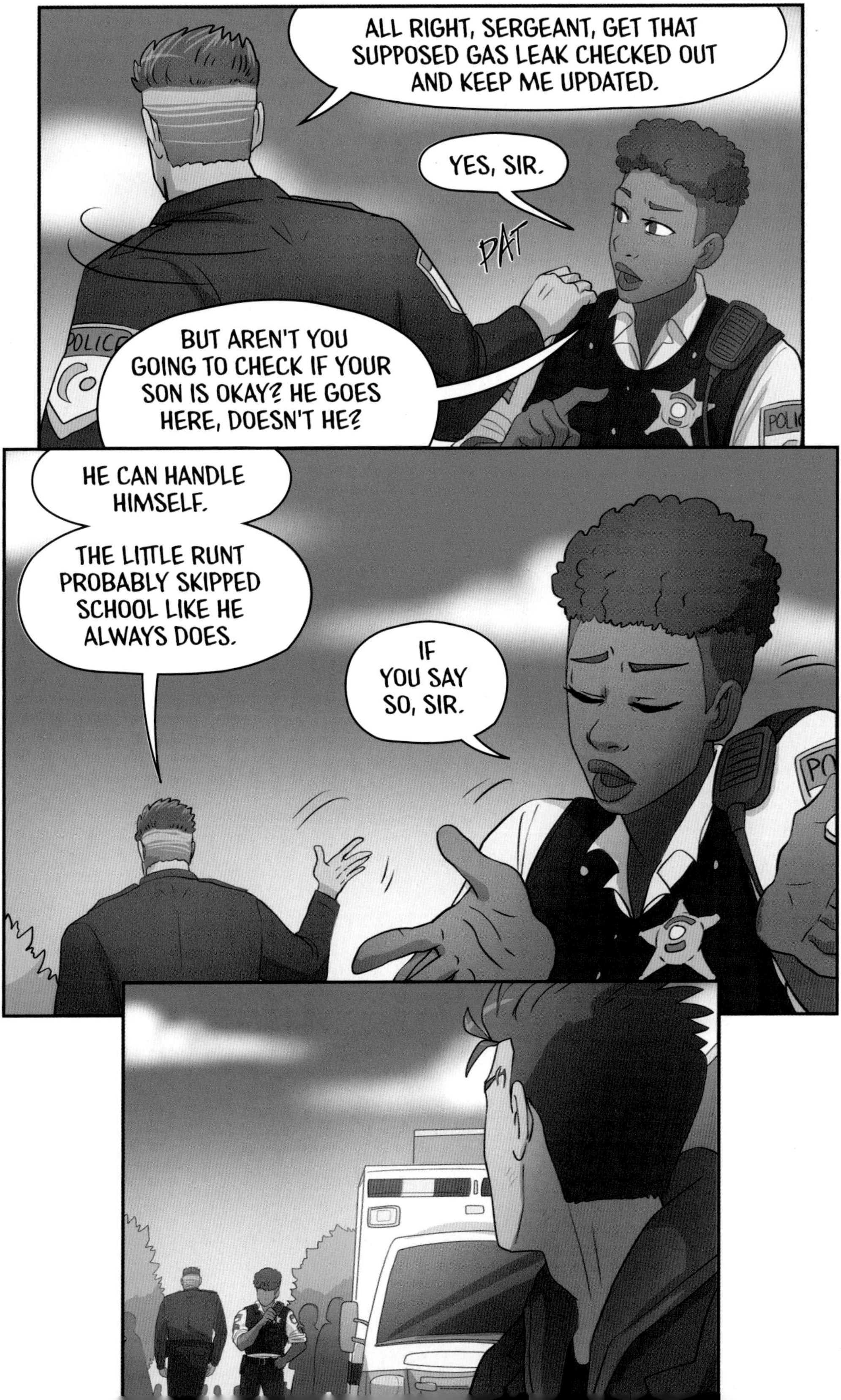
ALL RIGHT, SERGEANT, GET THAT SUPPOSED GAS LEAK CHECKED OUT AND KEEP ME UPDATED.
YES, SIR.
PAT
BUT AREN'T YOU GOING TO CHECK IF YOUR SON IS OKAY? HE GOES HERE, DOESN'T HE?
HE CAN HANDLE HIMSELF.
THE LITTLE RUNT PROBABLY SKIPPED SCHOOL LIKE HE ALWAYS DOES.
IF YOU SAY SO, SIR.

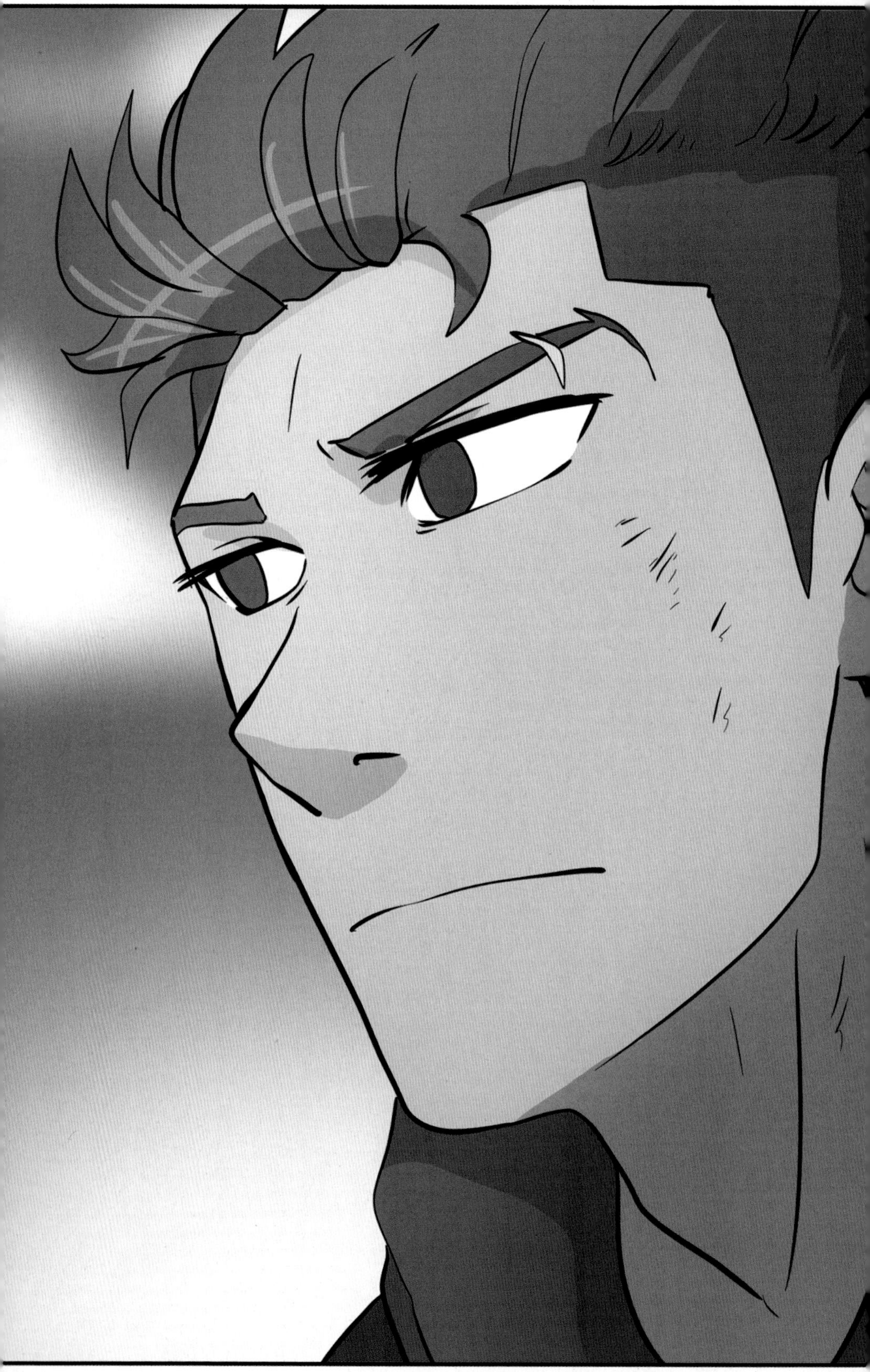

EPISODE 19:
PIZZA DELIVERY

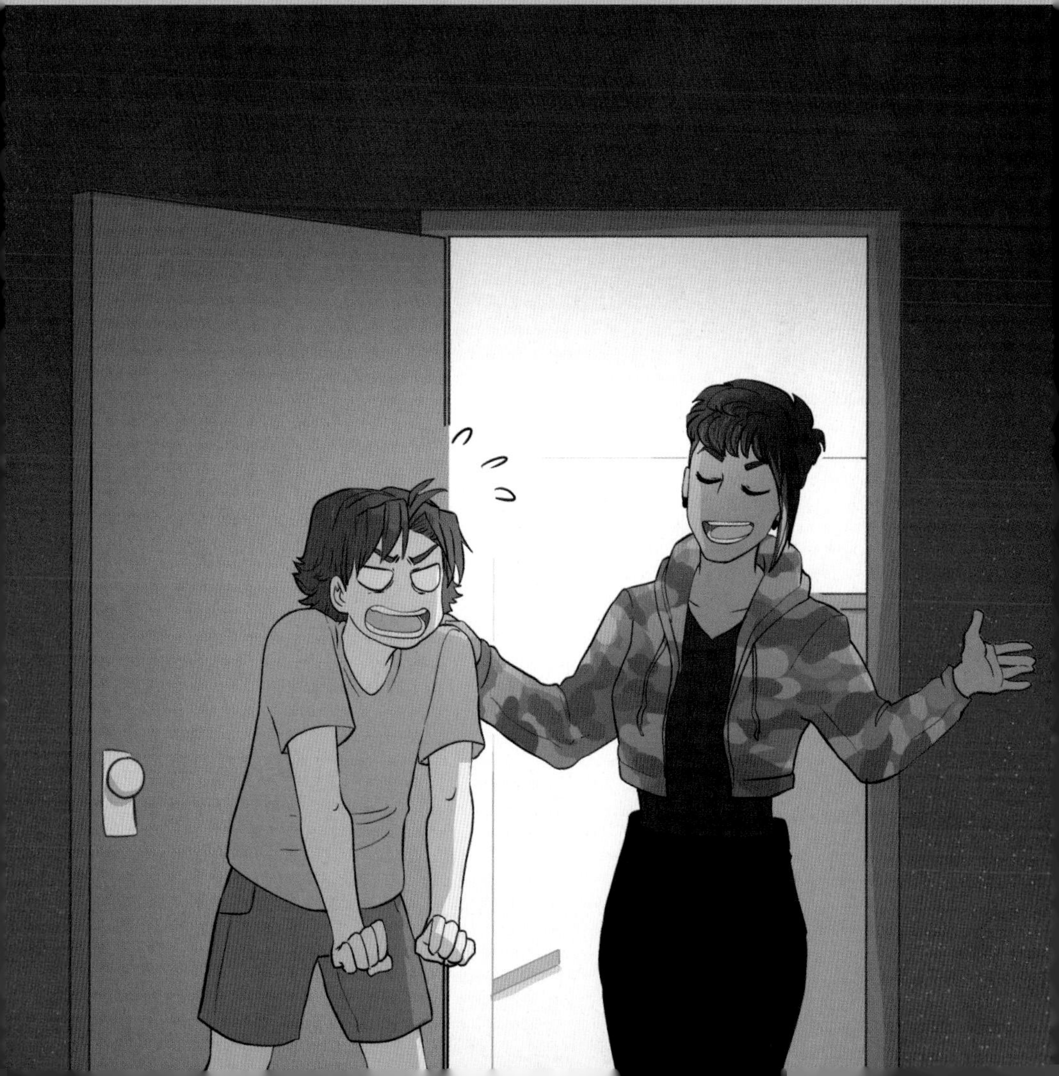

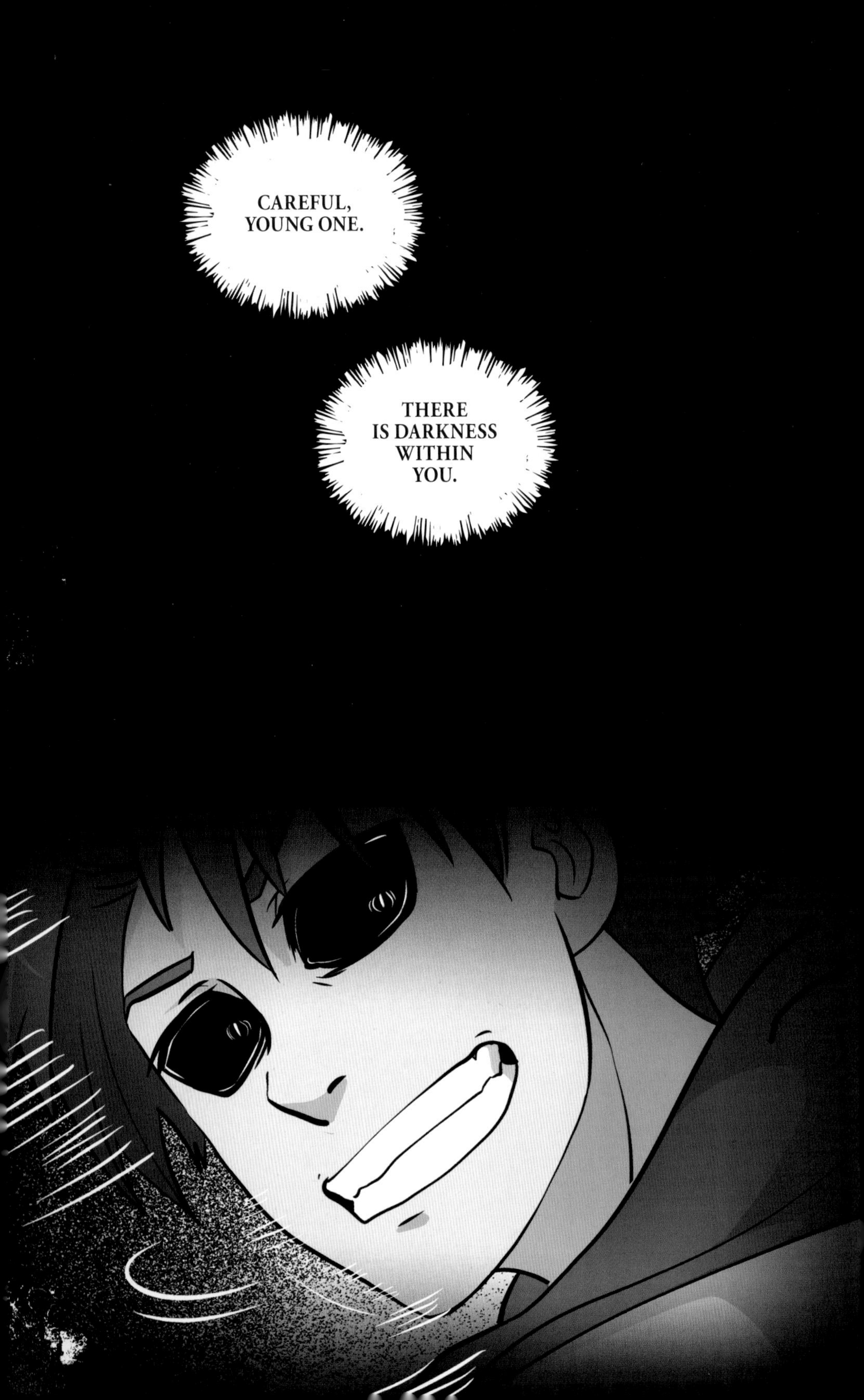
CAREFUL, YOUNG ONE.
THERE IS DARKNESS WITHIN YOU.

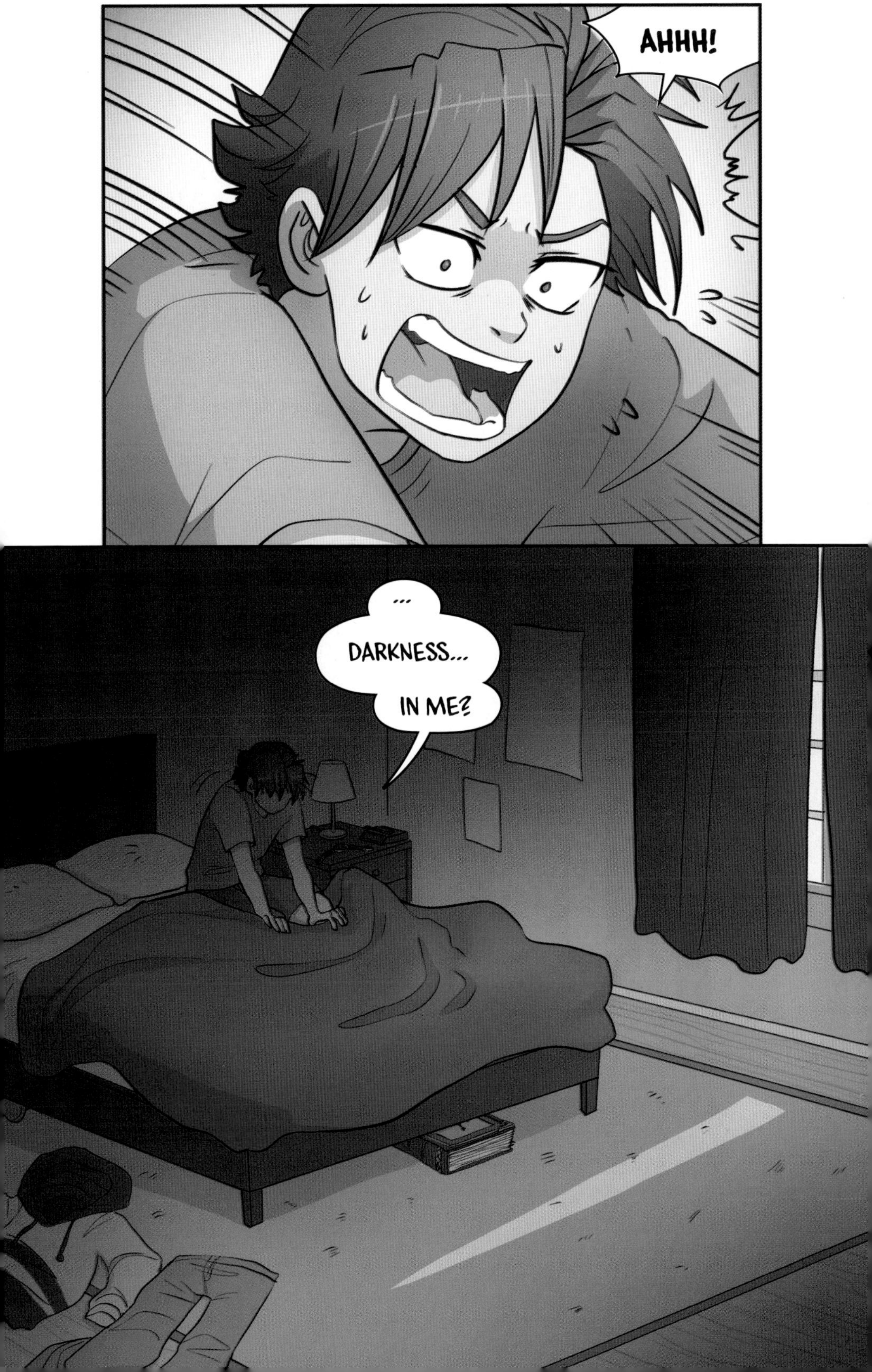
AHHH!
...
DARKNESS...
IN ME?

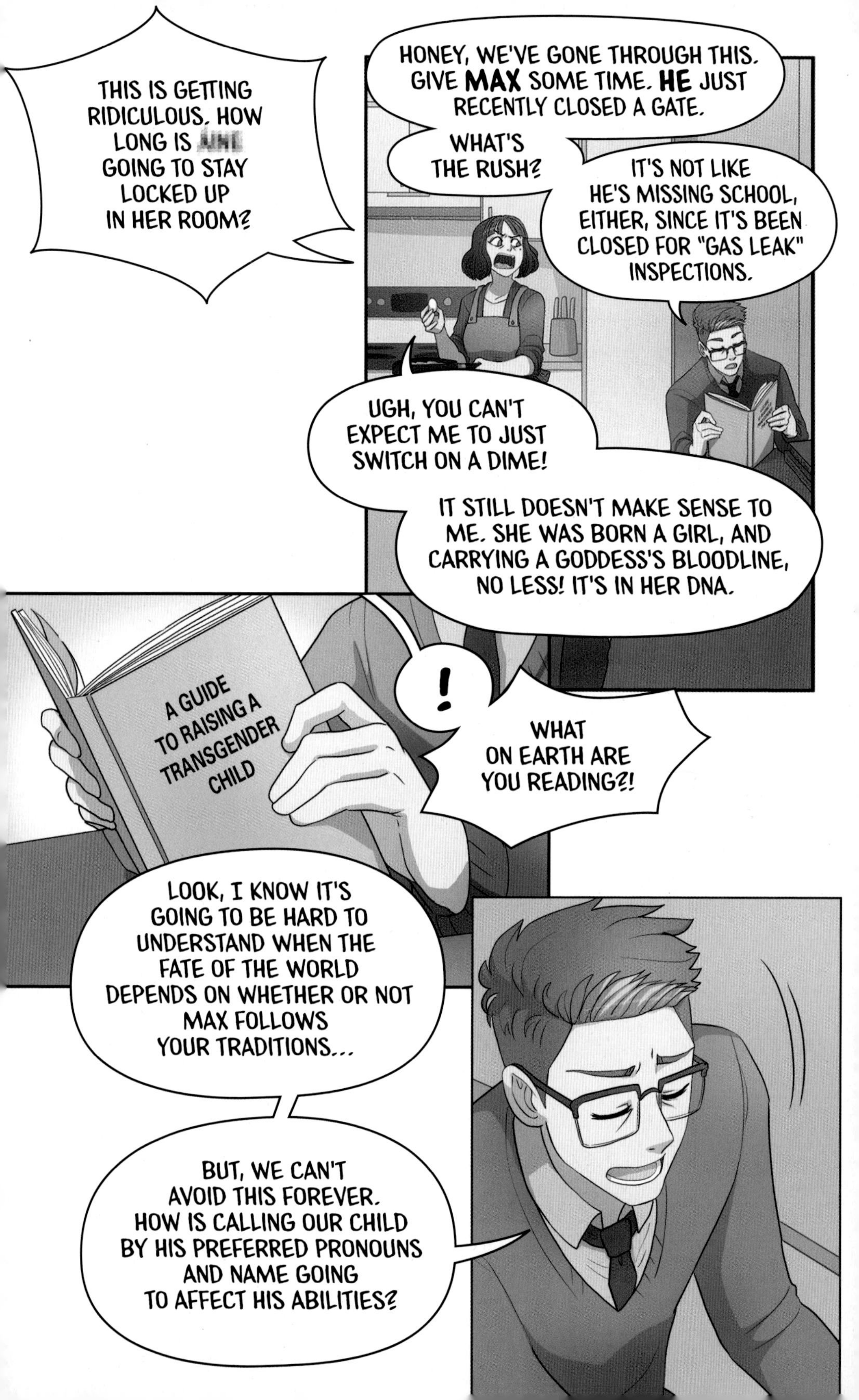

THIS IS GETTING RIDICULOUS. HOW LONG IS GOING TO STAY LOCKED UP IN HER ROOM?
HONEY, WE'VE GONE THROUGH THIS. GIVE **MAX** SOME TIME. **HE** JUST RECENTLY CLOSED A GATE.
WHAT'S THE RUSH?
IT'S NOT LIKE HE'S MISSING SCHOOL, EITHER, SINCE IT'S BEEN CLOSED FOR "GAS LEAK" INSPECTIONS.
UGH, YOU CAN'T EXPECT ME TO JUST SWITCH ON A DIME!
IT STILL DOESN'T MAKE SENSE TO ME. SHE WAS BORN A GIRL, AND CARRYING A GODDESS'S BLOODLINE, NO LESS! IT'S IN HER DNA.
A GUIDE TO RAISING A TRANSGENDER CHILD
!
WHAT ON EARTH ARE YOU READING?!
LOOK, I KNOW IT'S GOING TO BE HARD TO UNDERSTAND WHEN THE FATE OF THE WORLD DEPENDS ON WHETHER OR NOT MAX FOLLOWS YOUR TRADITIONS...
BUT, WE CAN'T AVOID THIS FOREVER. HOW IS CALLING OUR CHILD BY HIS PREFERRED PRONOUNS AND NAME GOING TO AFFECT HIS ABILITIES?

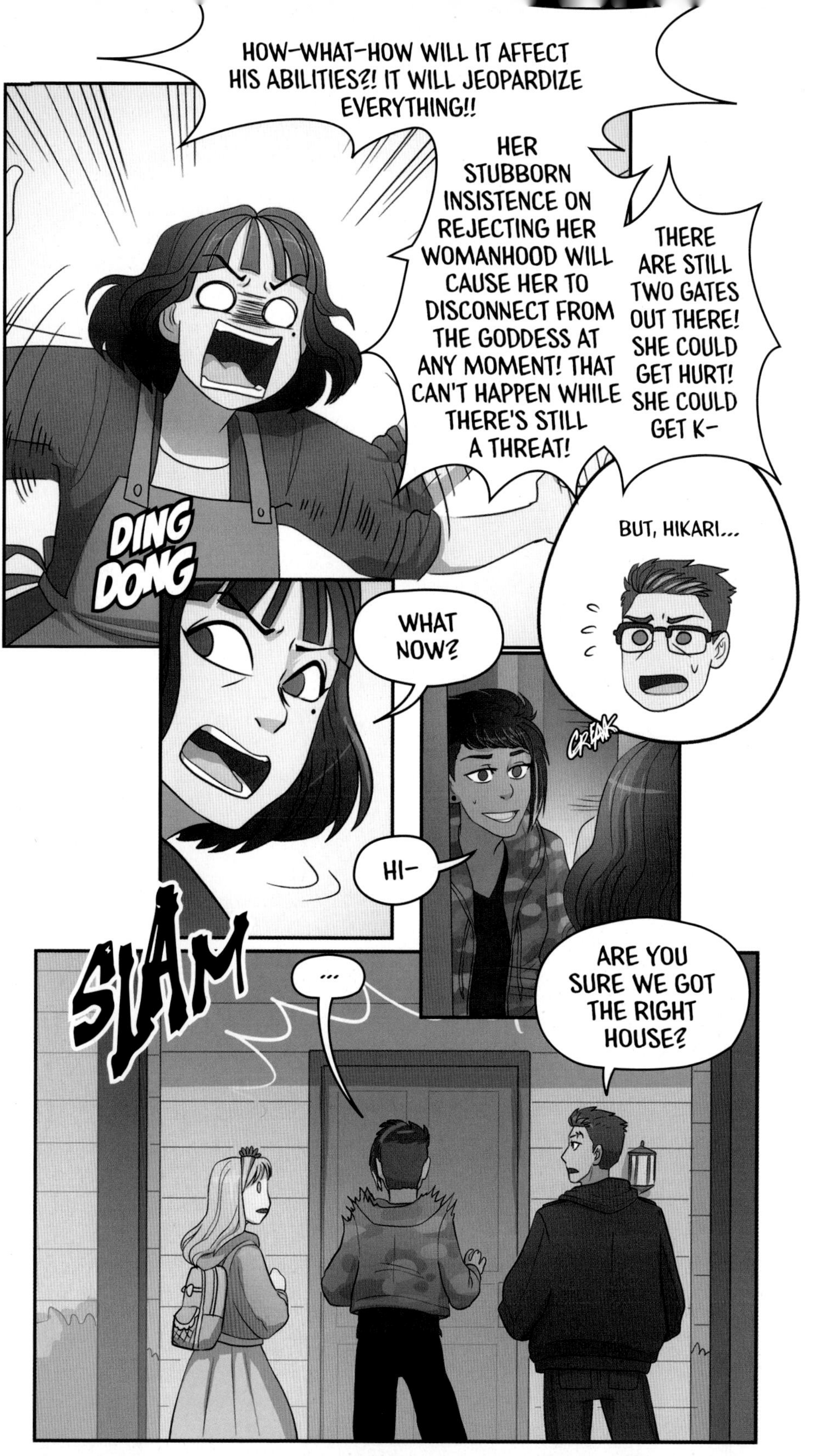
HOW-WHAT-HOW WILL IT AFFECT HIS ABILITIES?! IT WILL JEOPARDIZE EVERYTHING!!
HER STUBBORN INSISTENCE ON REJECTING HER WOMANHOOD WILL CAUSE HER TO DISCONNECT FROM THE GODDESS AT ANY MOMENT! THAT CAN'T HAPPEN WHILE THERE'S STILL A THREAT!
THERE ARE STILL TWO GATES OUT THERE! SHE COULD GET HURT! SHE COULD GET K-
BUT, HIKARI...
DING DONG
WHAT NOW?
CREAK
HI-
SLAM
...
ARE YOU SURE WE GOT THE RIGHT HOUSE?

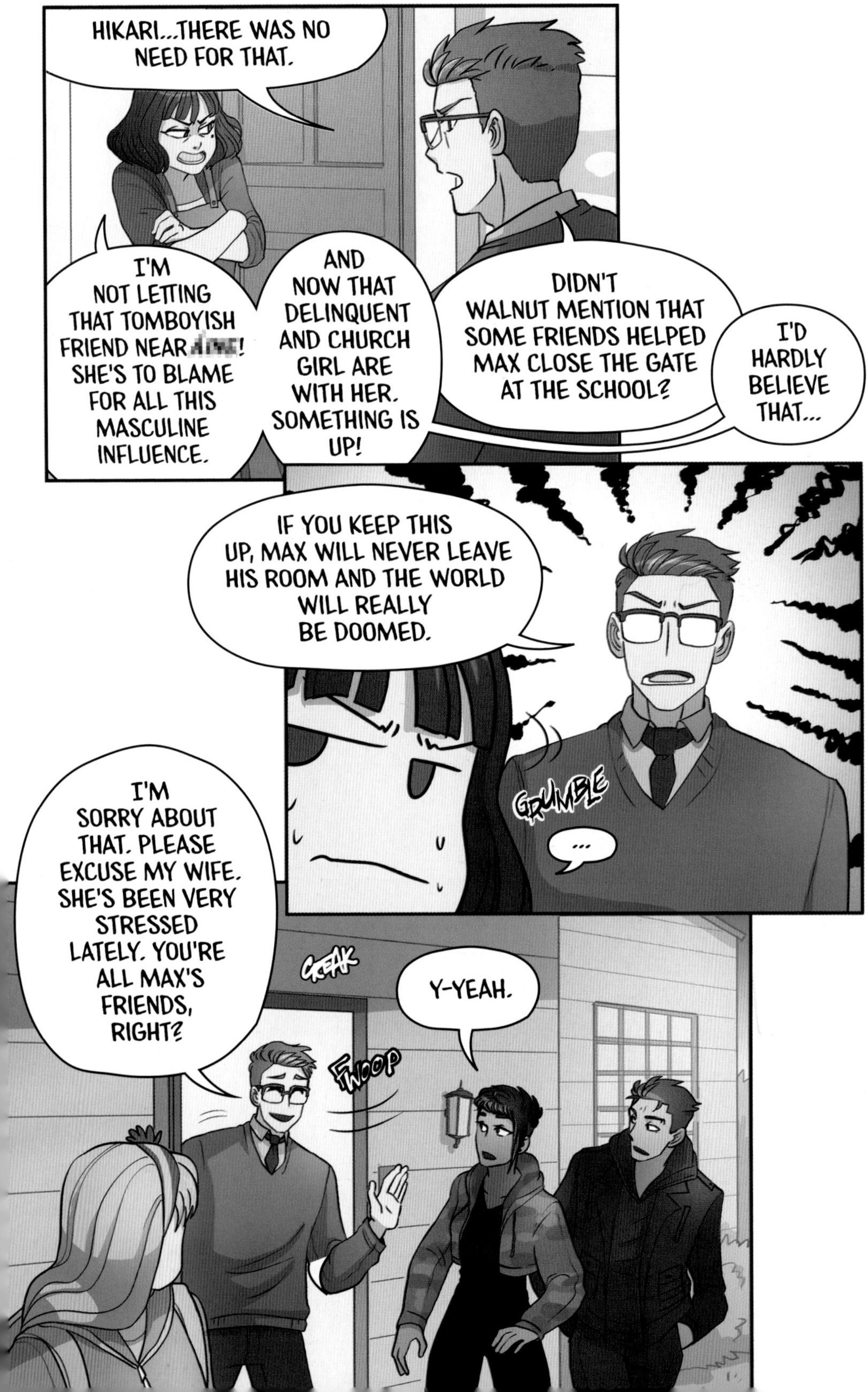
HIKARI...THERE WAS NO NEED FOR THAT.
I'M NOT LETTING THAT TOMBOYISH FRIEND NEAR! SHE'S TO BLAME FOR ALL THIS MASCULINE INFLUENCE.
AND NOW THAT DELINQUENT AND CHURCH GIRL ARE WITH HER. SOMETHING IS UP!
DIDN'T WALNUT MENTION THAT SOME FRIENDS HELPED MAX CLOSE THE GATE AT THE SCHOOL?
I'D HARDLY BELIEVE THAT...
IF YOU KEEP THIS UP, MAX WILL NEVER LEAVE HIS ROOM AND THE WORLD WILL REALLY BE DOOMED.
GRUMBLE
...
I'M SORRY ABOUT THAT. PLEASE EXCUSE MY WIFE. SHE'S BEEN VERY STRESSED LATELY. YOU'RE ALL MAX'S FRIENDS, RIGHT?
CREAK
Y-YEAH.
FWOOP

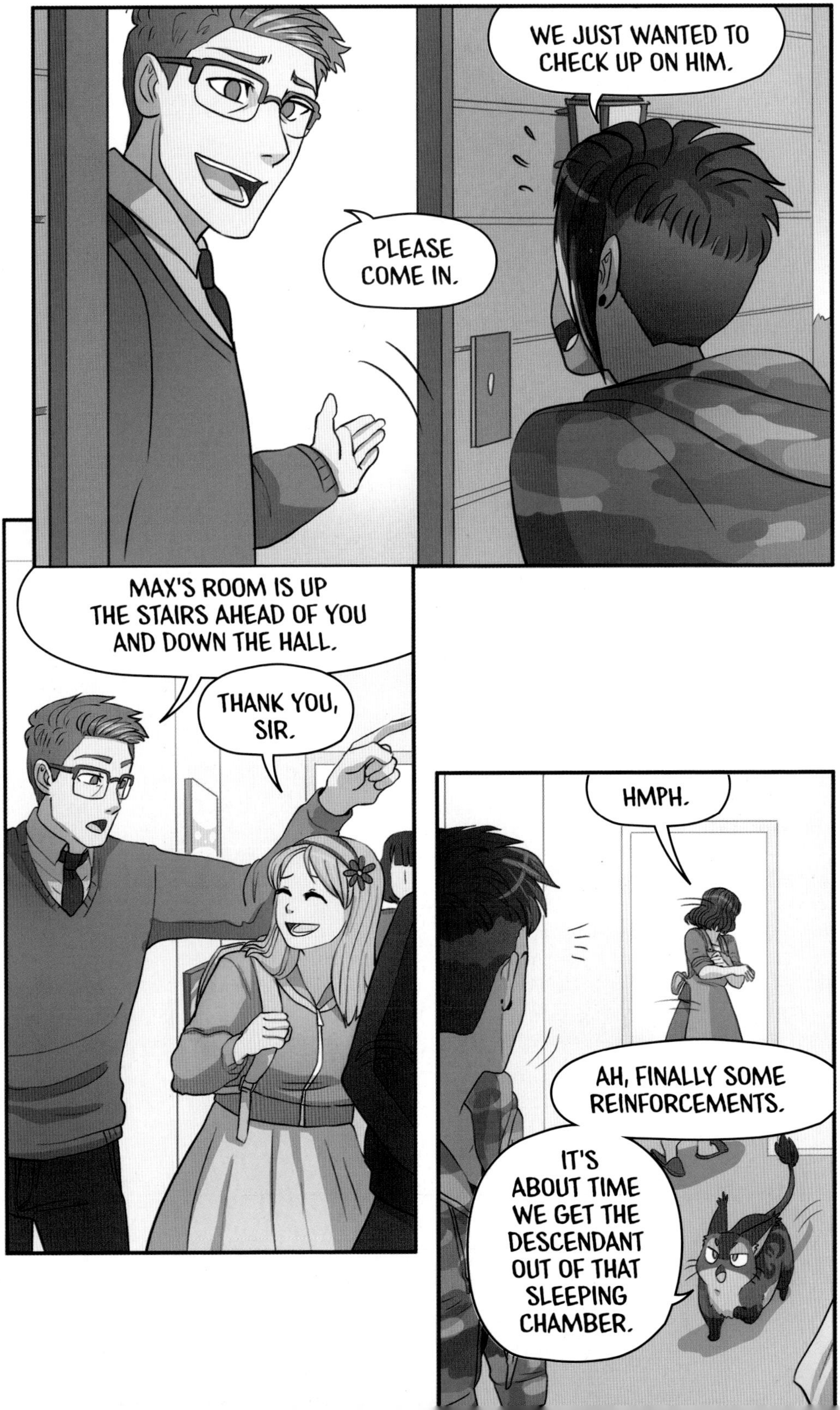
WE JUST WANTED TO CHECK UP ON HIM.
PLEASE COME IN.
MAX'S ROOM IS UP THE STAIRS AHEAD OF YOU AND DOWN THE HALL.
THANK YOU, SIR.
HMPH.
AH, FINALLY SOME REINFORCEMENTS.
IT'S ABOUT TIME WE GET THE DESCENDANT OUT OF THAT SLEEPING CHAMBER.

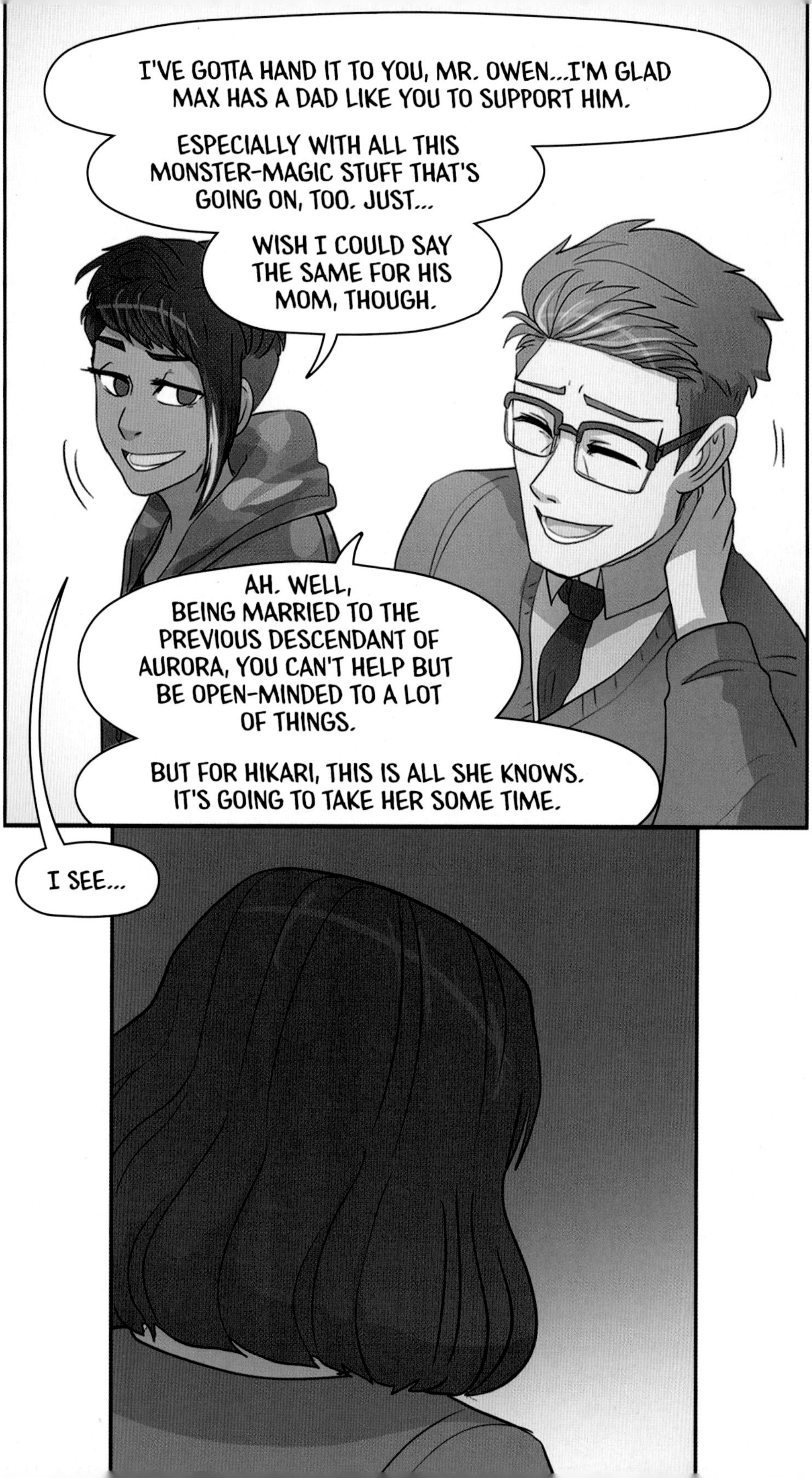
I'VE GOTTA HAND IT TO YOU, MR. OWEN...I'M GLAD MAX HAS A DAD LIKE YOU TO SUPPORT HIM.
ESPECIALLY WITH ALL THIS MONSTER-MAGIC STUFF THAT'S GOING ON, TOO. JUST...
WISH I COULD SAY THE SAME FOR HIS MOM, THOUGH.
AH. WELL, BEING MARRIED TO THE PREVIOUS DESCENDANT OF AURORA, YOU CAN'T HELP BUT BE OPEN-MINDED TO A LOT OF THINGS.
BUT FOR HIKARI, THIS IS ALL SHE KNOWS. IT'S GOING TO TAKE HER SOME TIME.
I SEE...

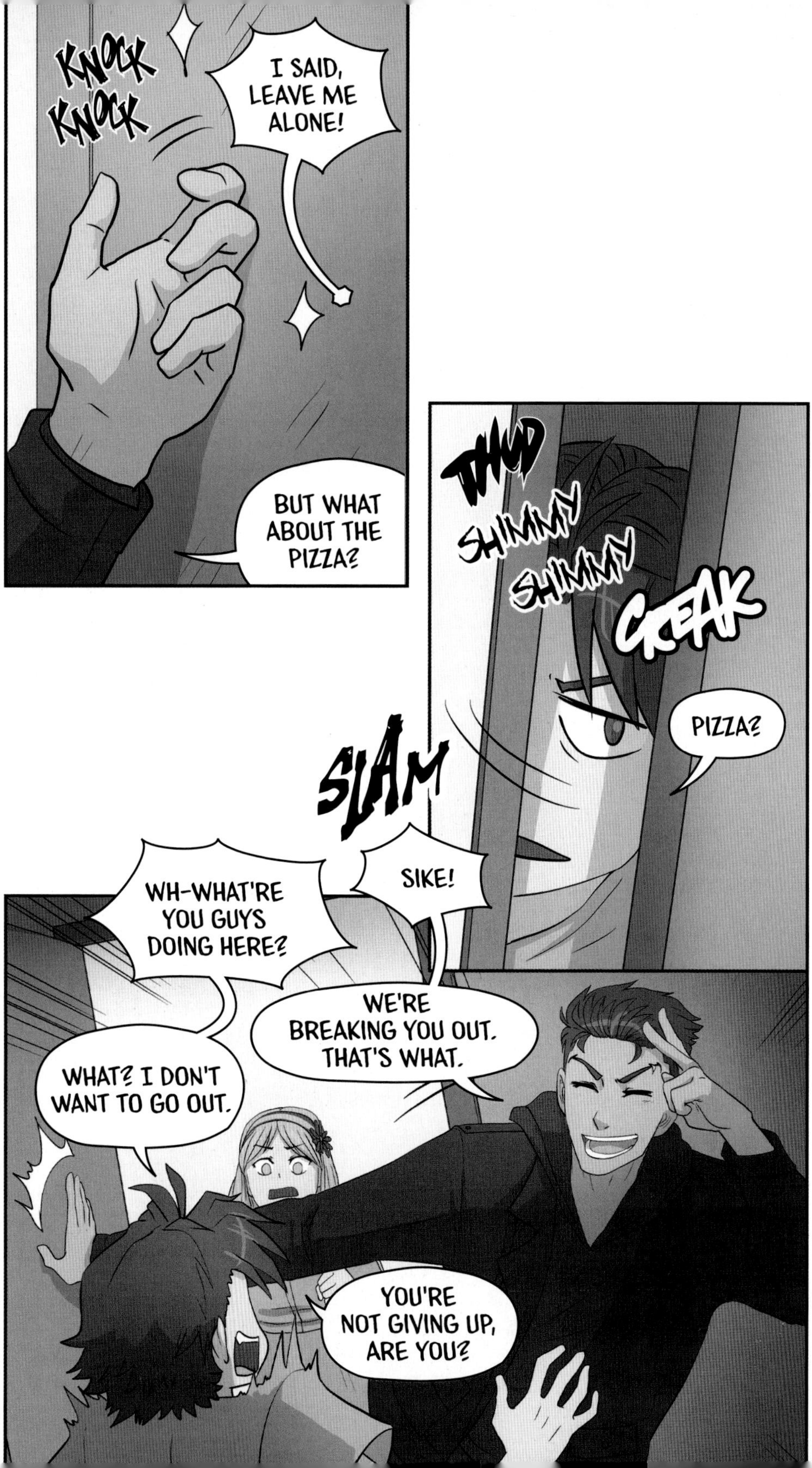
KNOCK KNOCK
I SAID, LEAVE ME ALONE!
BUT WHAT ABOUT THE PIZZA?
THUD
SHIMMY SHIMMY
CREAK
PIZZA?
SLAM
SIKE!
WH-WHAT'RE YOU GUYS DOING HERE?
WE'RE BREAKING YOU OUT. THAT'S WHAT.
WHAT? I DON'T WANT TO GO OUT.
YOU'RE NOT GIVING UP, ARE YOU?

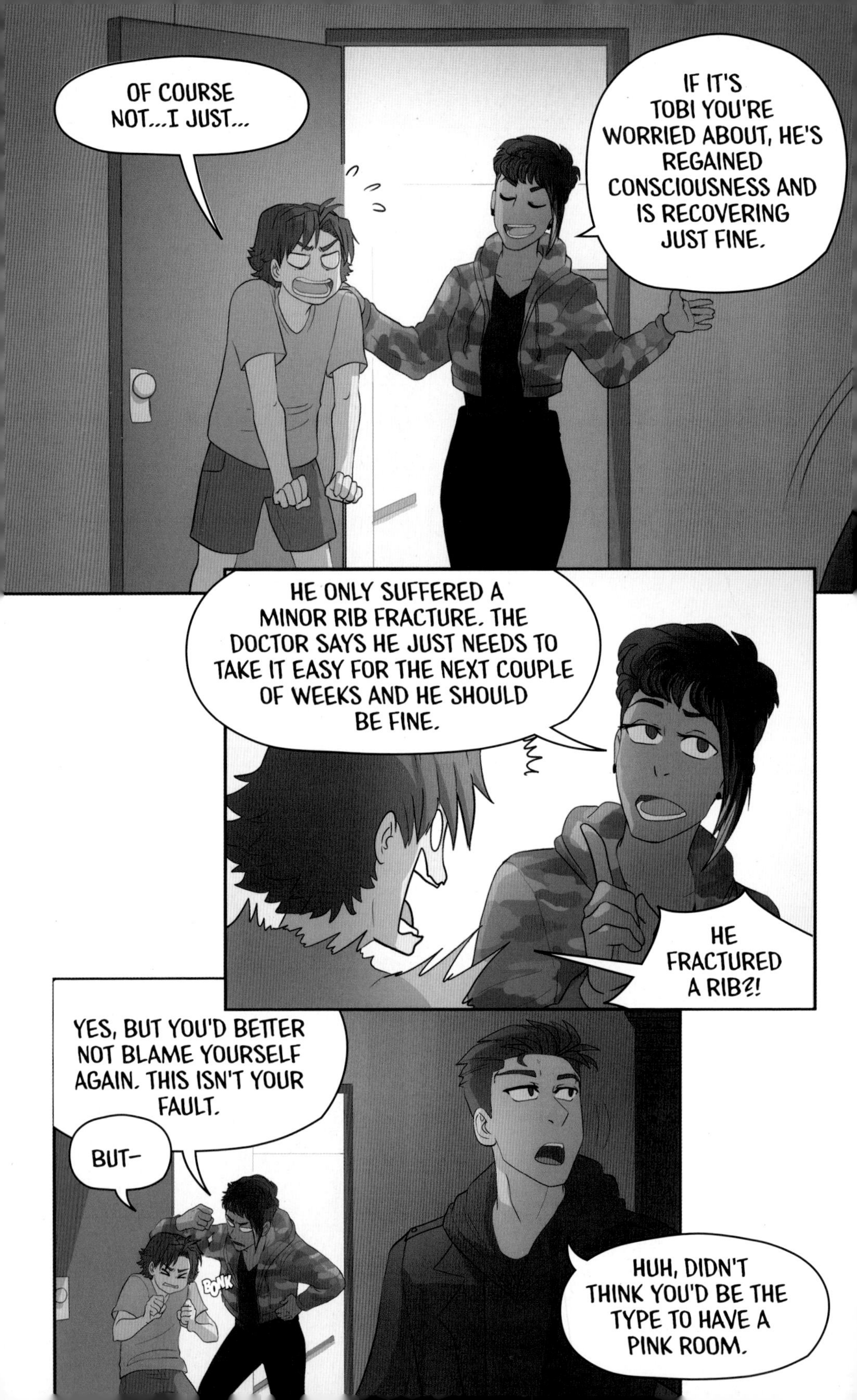
OF COURSE NOT...I JUST...
IF IT'S TOBI YOU'RE WORRIED ABOUT, HE'S REGAINED CONSCIOUSNESS AND IS RECOVERING JUST FINE.
HE ONLY SUFFERED A MINOR RIB FRACTURE. THE DOCTOR SAYS HE JUST NEEDS TO TAKE IT EASY FOR THE NEXT COUPLE OF WEEKS AND HE SHOULD BE FINE.
HE FRACTURED A RIB?!
YES, BUT YOU'D BETTER NOT BLAME YOURSELF AGAIN. THIS ISN'T YOUR FAULT.
BUT-
BONK
HUH, DIDN'T THINK YOU'D BE THE TYPE TO HAVE A PINK ROOM.

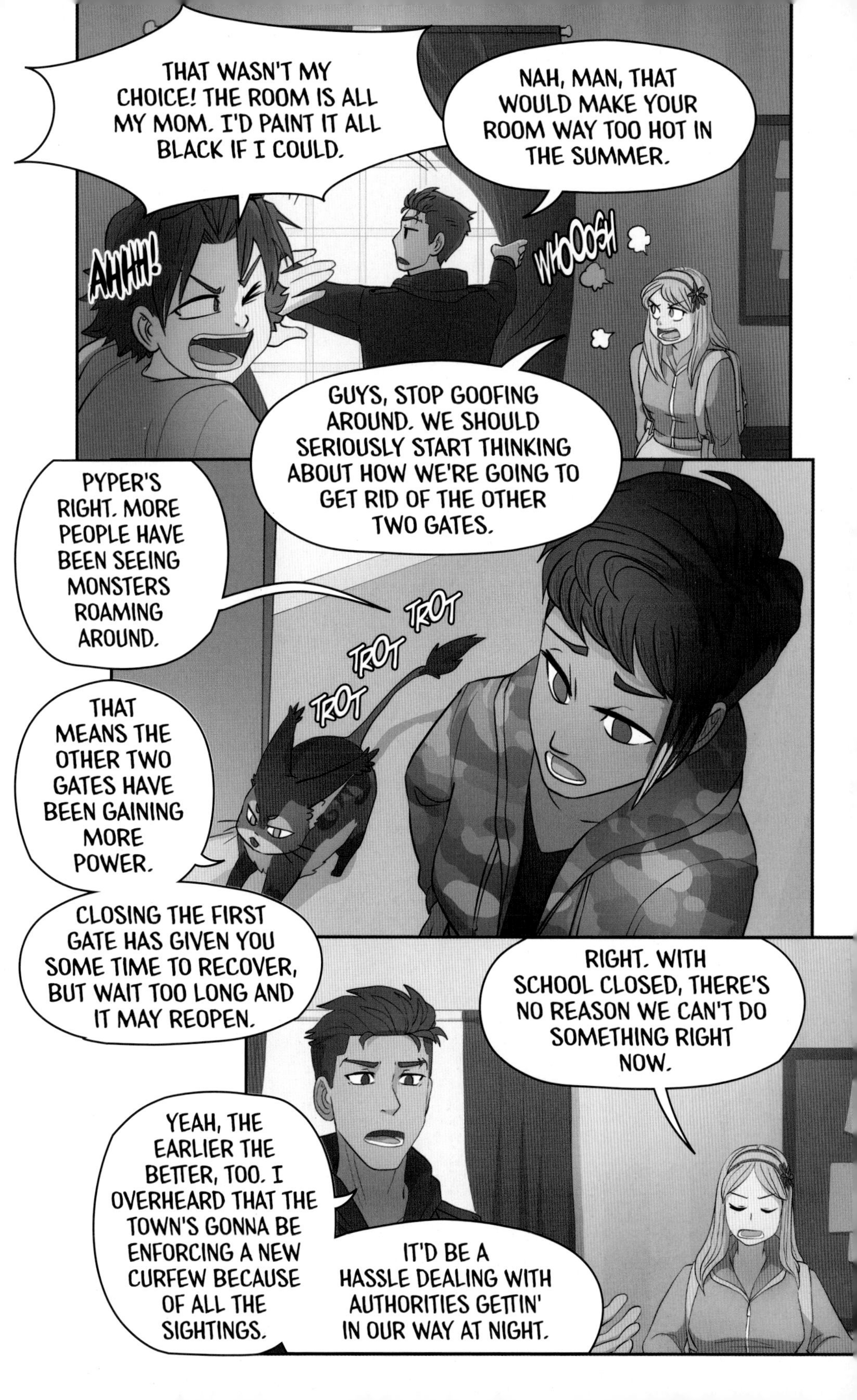
THAT WASN'T MY CHOICE! THE ROOM IS ALL MY MOM. I'D PAINT IT ALL BLACK IF I COULD.
NAH, MAN, THAT WOULD MAKE YOUR ROOM WAY TOO HOT IN THE SUMMER.
AHHH!
WHOOOSH
GUYS, STOP GOOFING AROUND. WE SHOULD SERIOUSLY START THINKING ABOUT HOW WE'RE GOING TO GET RID OF THE OTHER TWO GATES.
PYPER'S RIGHT. MORE PEOPLE HAVE BEEN SEEING MONSTERS ROAMING AROUND.
TROT TROT TROT
THAT MEANS THE OTHER TWO GATES HAVE BEEN GAINING MORE POWER.
CLOSING THE FIRST GATE HAS GIVEN YOU SOME TIME TO RECOVER, BUT WAIT TOO LONG AND IT MAY REOPEN.
RIGHT. WITH SCHOOL CLOSED, THERE'S NO REASON WE CAN'T DO SOMETHING RIGHT NOW.
YEAH, THE EARLIER THE BETTER, TOO. I OVERHEARD THAT THE TOWN'S GONNA BE ENFORCING A NEW CURFEW BECAUSE OF ALL THE SIGHTINGS.
IT'D BE A HASSLE DEALING WITH AUTHORITIES GETTIN' IN OUR WAY AT NIGHT.

BUT...
I DUNNO IF I'M
READY, YOU GUYS.
I HAD TROUBLE
CONTROLLING MY
POWERS IN THE LAST
TWO FIGHTS.

WHAT'RE YOU TALKIN'
ABOUT? YOU DID GREAT! AND
YOU EVEN TURNED YOUR
BROKEN WAND THING INTO A
FREAKIN' SWORD!

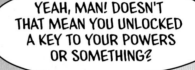

YEAH, MAN! DOESN'T
THAT MEAN YOU UNLOCKED
A KEY TO YOUR POWERS
OR SOMETHING?

I DON'T KNOW!
I WASN'T EVEN SURE IF IT
WAS GOING TO WORK.

I NEVER KNOW
HALF THE TIME...
AND IT GOT TOBI HURT
WHEN IT DIDN'T.

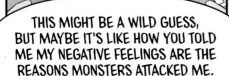

THIS MIGHT BE A WILD GUESS,
BUT MAYBE IT'S LIKE HOW YOU TOLD
ME MY NEGATIVE FEELINGS ARE THE
REASONS MONSTERS ATTACKED ME.

WHAT IF DOUBT
AND FEAR MAKE YOUR
POWER WEAKER?

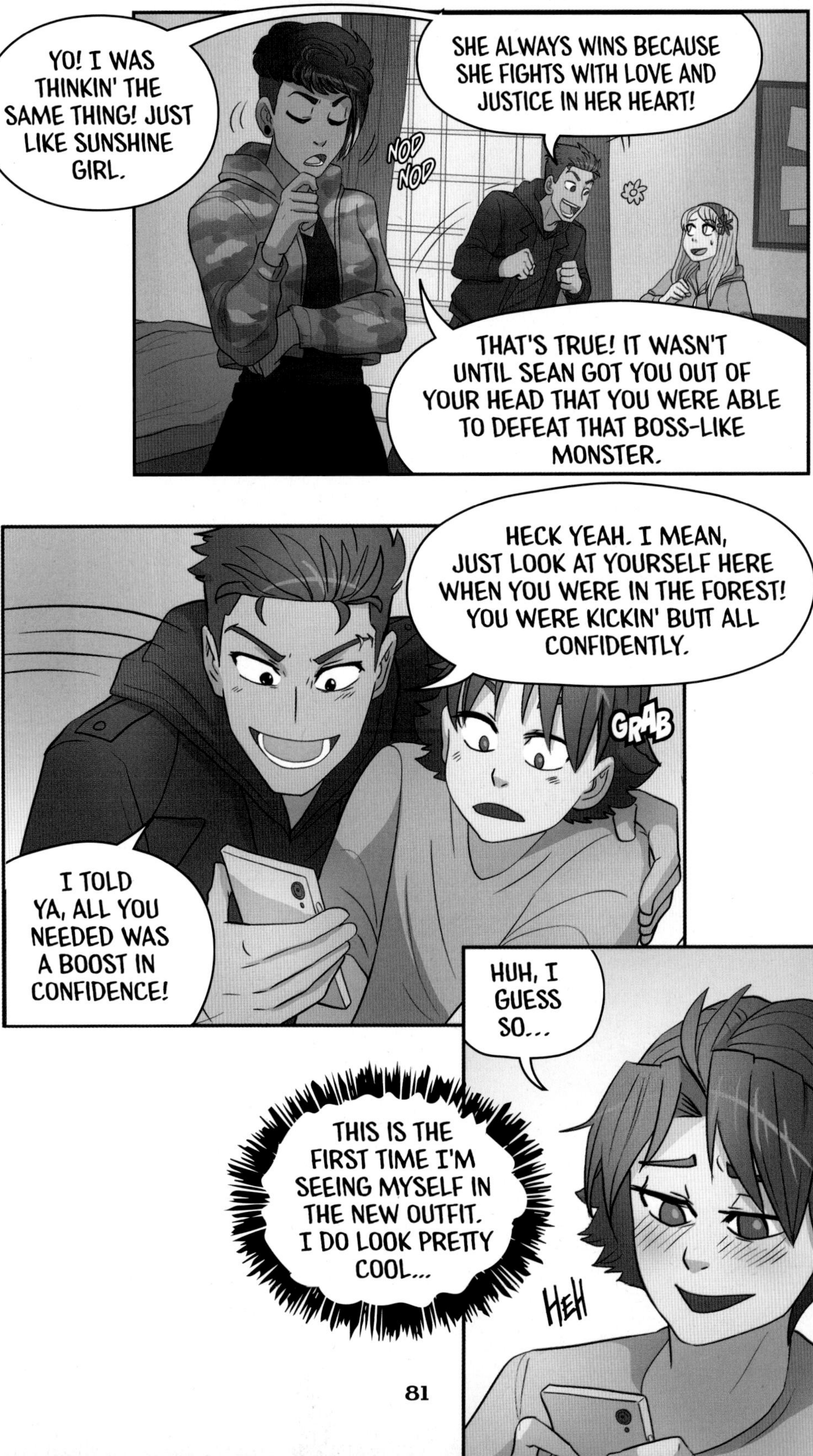
YO! I WAS THINKIN' THE SAME THING! JUST LIKE SUNSHINE GIRL.
SHE ALWAYS WINS BECAUSE SHE FIGHTS WITH LOVE AND JUSTICE IN HER HEART!
NOD NOD
THAT'S TRUE! IT WASN'T UNTIL SEAN GOT YOU OUT OF YOUR HEAD THAT YOU WERE ABLE TO DEFEAT THAT BOSS-LIKE MONSTER.
HECK YEAH. I MEAN, JUST LOOK AT YOURSELF HERE WHEN YOU WERE IN THE FOREST! YOU WERE KICKIN' BUTT ALL CONFIDENTLY.
GRAB
I TOLD YA, ALL YOU NEEDED WAS A BOOST IN CONFIDENCE!
HUH, I GUESS SO...
THIS IS THE FIRST TIME I'M SEEING MYSELF IN THE NEW OUTFIT. I DO LOOK PRETTY COOL...
HEH

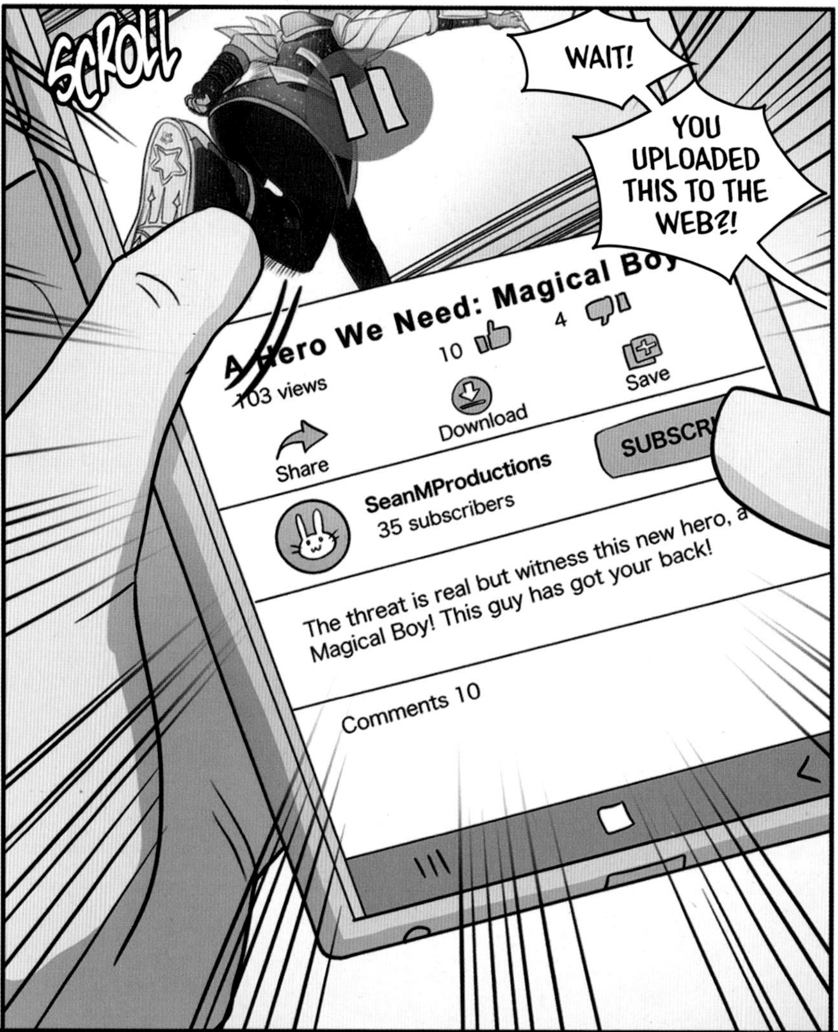
SCROLL
WAIT!
YOU UPLOADED THIS TO THE WEB?!
A Hero We Need: Magical Boy
10
4
103 views
Save
Download
Share
SUBSCR
SeanMProductions
35 subscribers
The threat is real but witness this new hero, a Magical Boy! This guy has got your back!
Comments 10

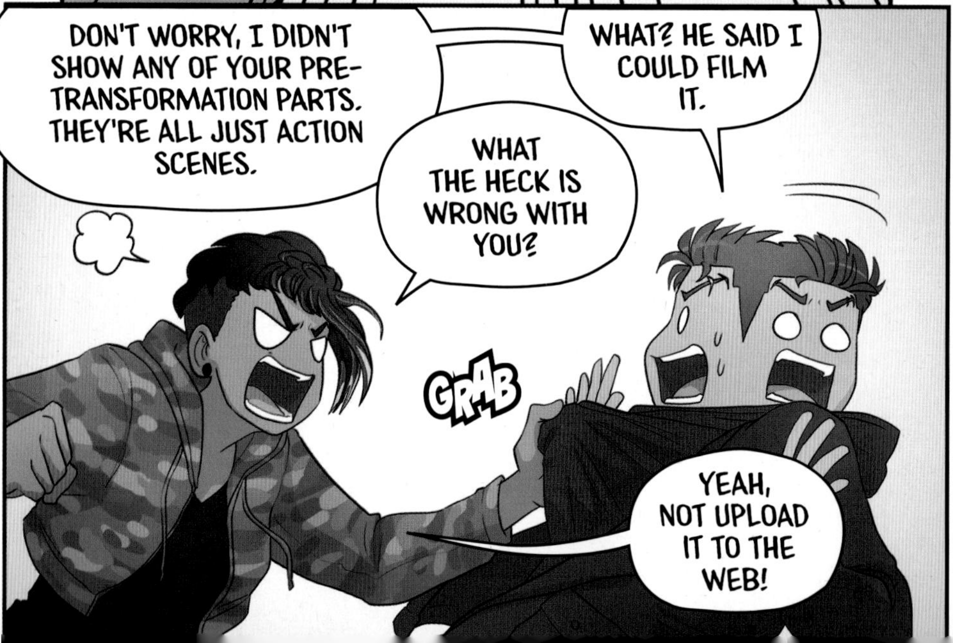
DON'T WORRY, I DIDN'T SHOW ANY OF YOUR PRE-TRANSFORMATION PARTS. THEY'RE ALL JUST ACTION SCENES.
WHAT? HE SAID I COULD FILM IT.
WHAT THE HECK IS WRONG WITH YOU?
GRAB
YEAH, NOT UPLOAD IT TO THE WEB!

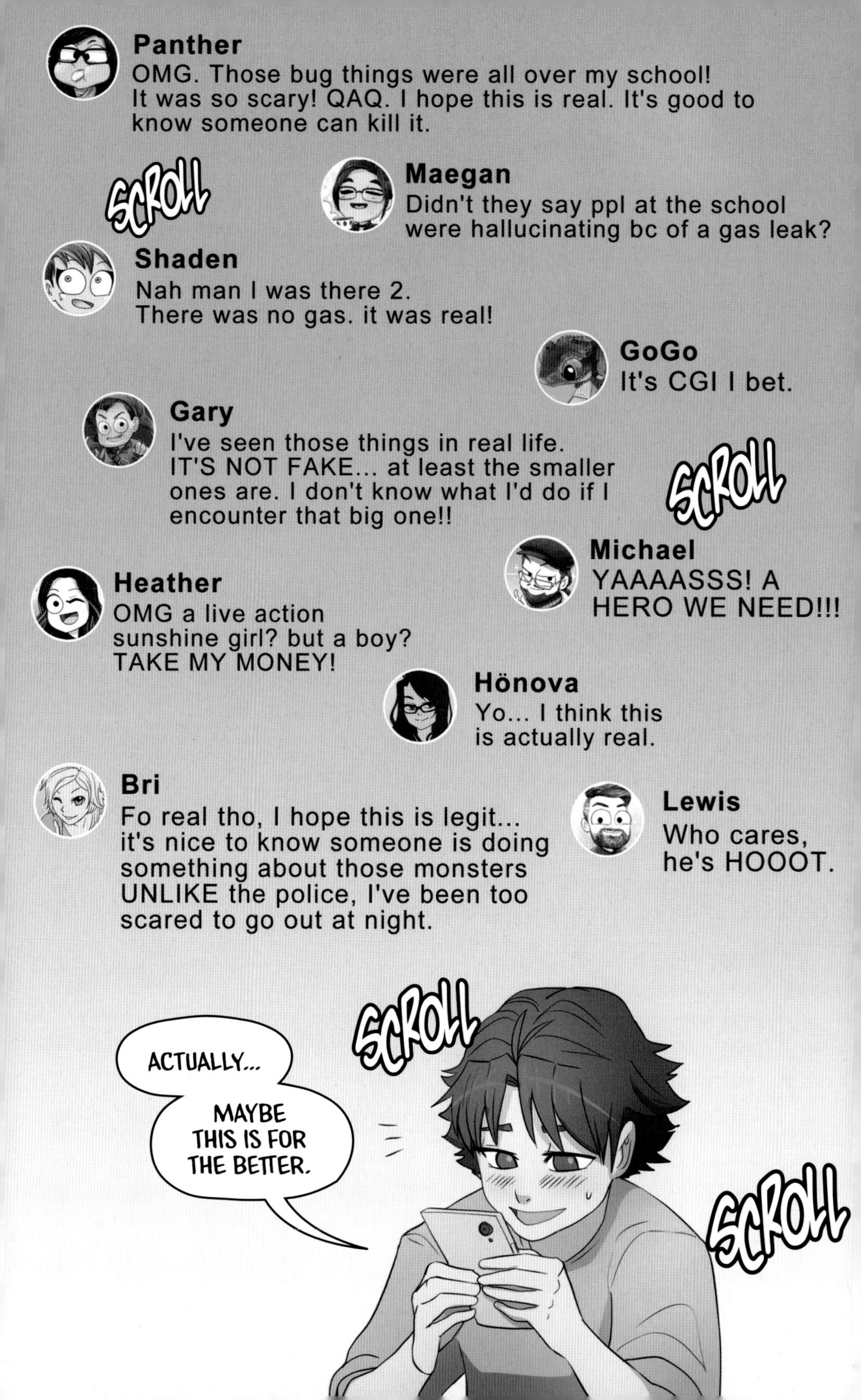
Panther
OMG. Those bug things were all over my school! It was so scary! QAQ. I hope this is real. It's good to know someone can kill it.
SCROLL
Maegan
Didn't they say ppl at the school were hallucinating bc of a gas leak?
Shaden
Nah man I was there 2. There was no gas. it was real!
GoGo
It's CGI I bet.
Gary
I've seen those things in real life. IT'S NOT FAKE... at least the smaller ones are. I don't know what I'd do if I encounter that big one!!
SCROLL
Michael
YAAAASSS! A HERO WE NEED!!!
Heather
OMG a live action sunshine girl? but a boy? TAKE MY MONEY!
Hönova
Yo... I think this is actually real.
Bri
Fo real tho, I hope this is legit... it's nice to know someone is doing something about those monsters UNLIKE the police, I've been too scared to go out at night.
Lewis
Who cares, he's HOOOT.
SCROLL
ACTUALLY...
MAYBE THIS IS FOR THE BETTER.
SCROLL

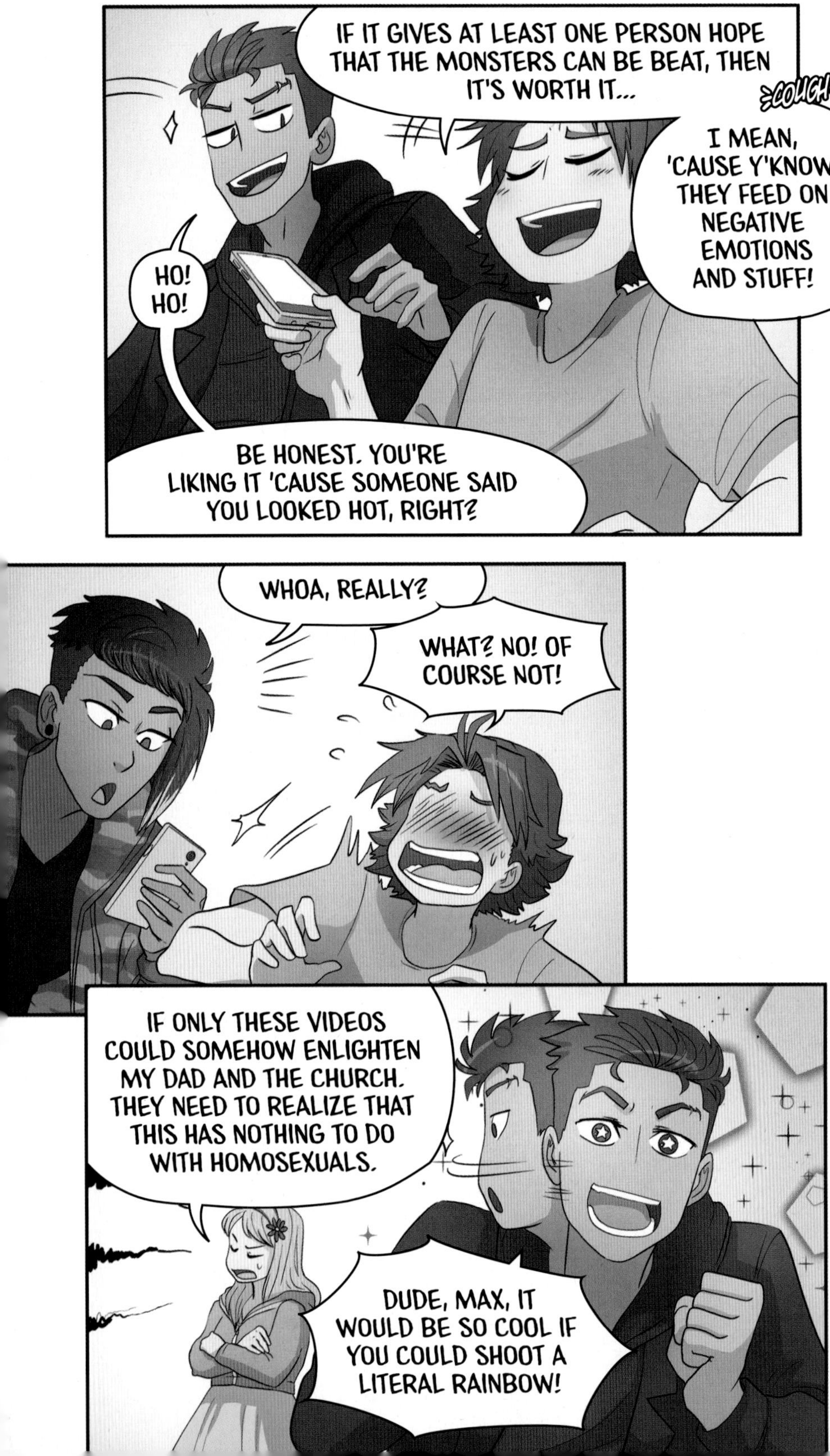
IF IT GIVES AT LEAST ONE PERSON HOPE THAT THE MONSTERS CAN BE BEAT, THEN IT'S WORTH IT...
COUGH
I MEAN, 'CAUSE Y'KNOW, THEY FEED ON NEGATIVE EMOTIONS AND STUFF!
HO! HO!
BE HONEST. YOU'RE LIKING IT 'CAUSE SOMEONE SAID YOU LOOKED HOT, RIGHT?
WHOA, REALLY?
WHAT? NO! OF COURSE NOT!
IF ONLY THESE VIDEOS COULD SOMEHOW ENLIGHTEN MY DAD AND THE CHURCH. THEY NEED TO REALIZE THAT THIS HAS NOTHING TO DO WITH HOMOSEXUALS.
DUDE, MAX, IT WOULD BE SO COOL IF YOU COULD SHOOT A LITERAL RAINBOW!

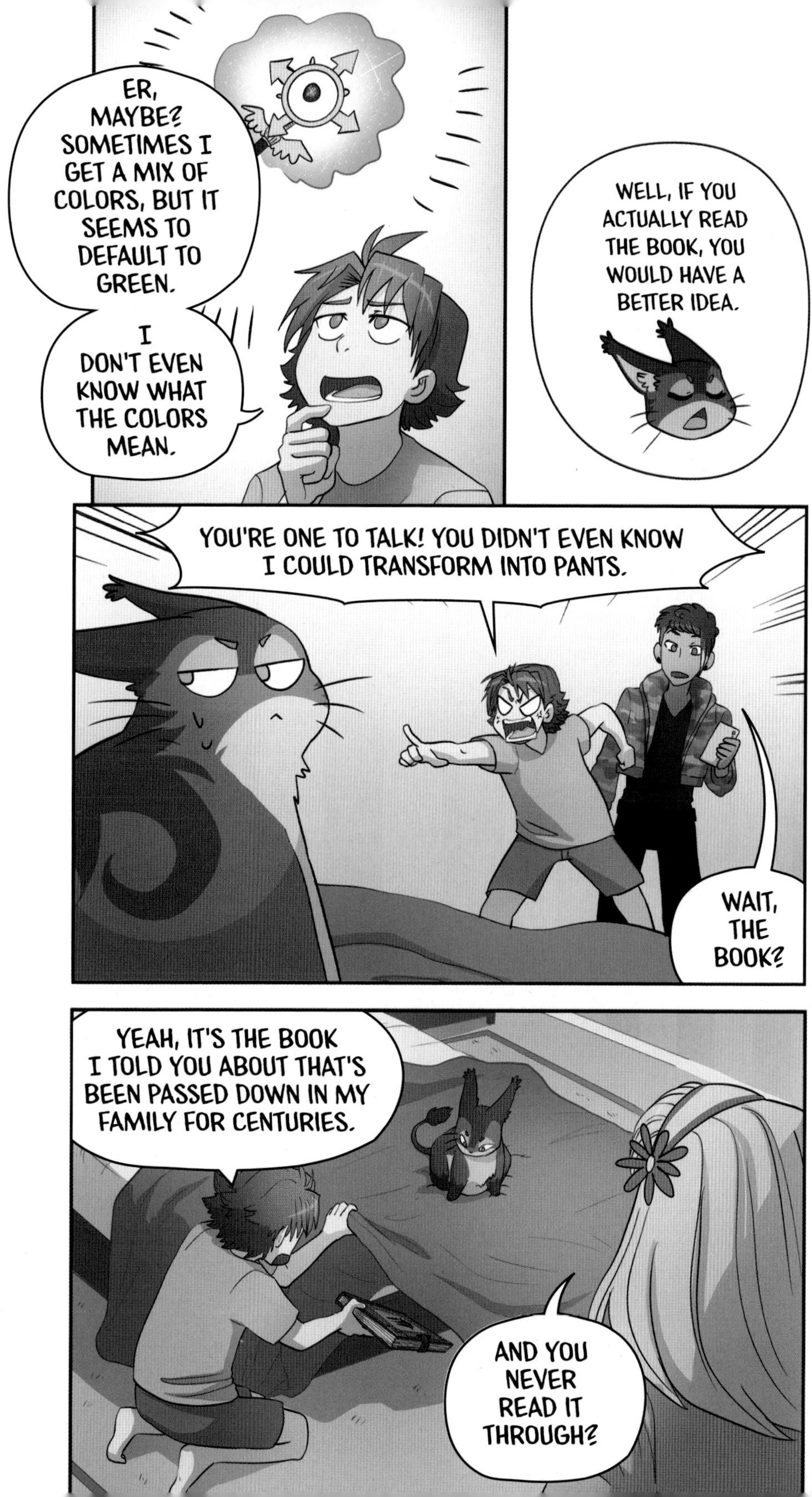
ER, MAYBE? SOMETIMES I GET A MIX OF COLORS, BUT IT SEEMS TO DEFAULT TO GREEN.
I DON'T EVEN KNOW WHAT THE COLORS MEAN.
WELL, IF YOU ACTUALLY READ THE BOOK, YOU WOULD HAVE A BETTER IDEA.
YOU'RE ONE TO TALK! YOU DIDN'T EVEN KNOW I COULD TRANSFORM INTO PANTS.
WAIT, THE BOOK?
YEAH, IT'S THE BOOK I TOLD YOU ABOUT THAT'S BEEN PASSED DOWN IN MY FAMILY FOR CENTURIES.
AND YOU NEVER READ IT THROUGH?

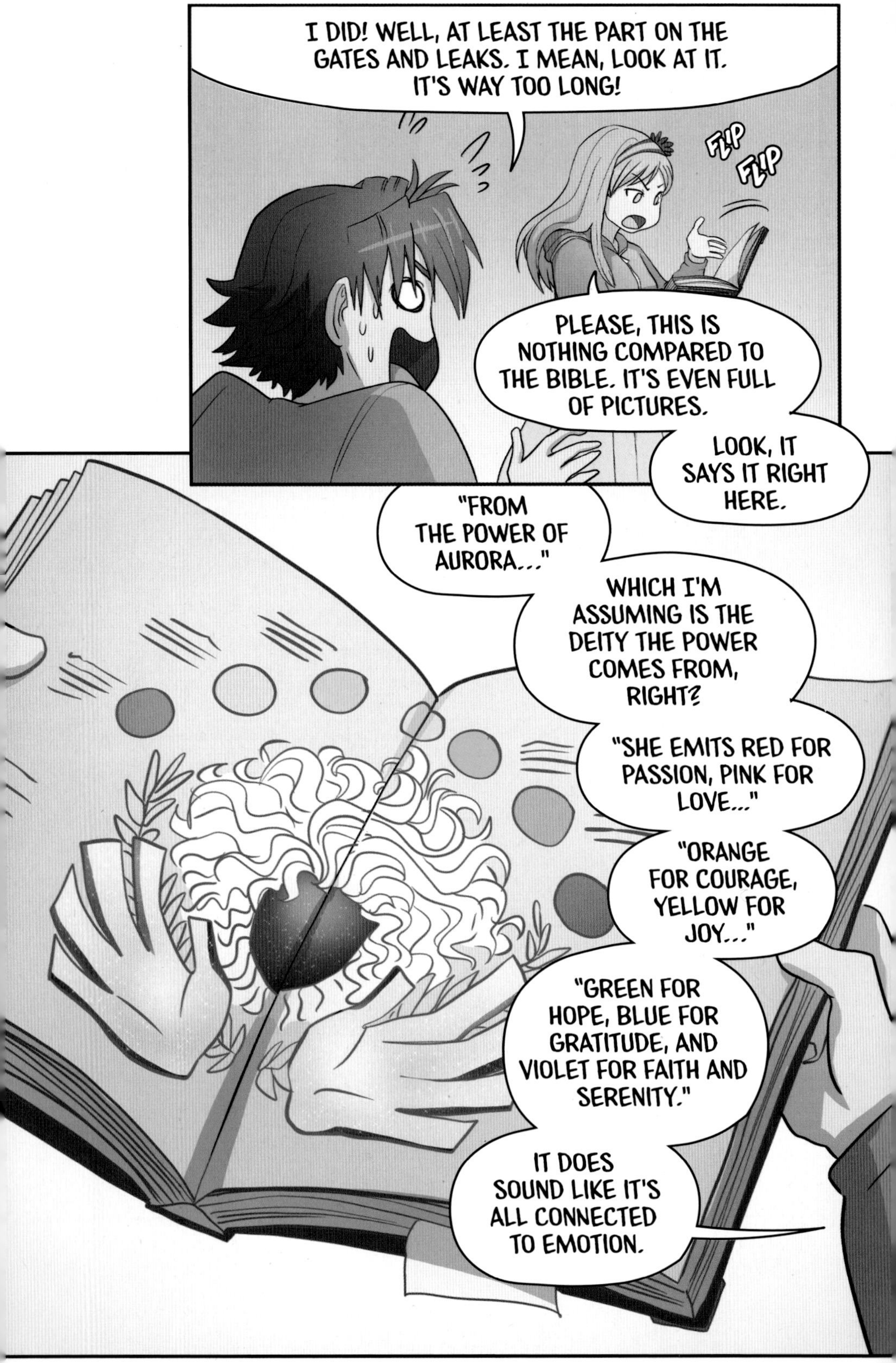
I DID! WELL, AT LEAST THE PART ON THE GATES AND LEAKS. I MEAN, LOOK AT IT. IT'S WAY TOO LONG!
FLIP FLIP
PLEASE, THIS IS NOTHING COMPARED TO THE BIBLE. IT'S EVEN FULL OF PICTURES.
LOOK, IT SAYS IT RIGHT HERE.
"FROM THE POWER OF AURORA..."
WHICH I'M ASSUMING IS THE DEITY THE POWER COMES FROM, RIGHT?
"SHE EMITS RED FOR PASSION, PINK FOR LOVE..."
"ORANGE FOR COURAGE, YELLOW FOR JOY..."
"GREEN FOR HOPE, BLUE FOR GRATITUDE, AND VIOLET FOR FAITH AND SERENITY."
IT DOES SOUND LIKE IT'S ALL CONNECTED TO EMOTION.

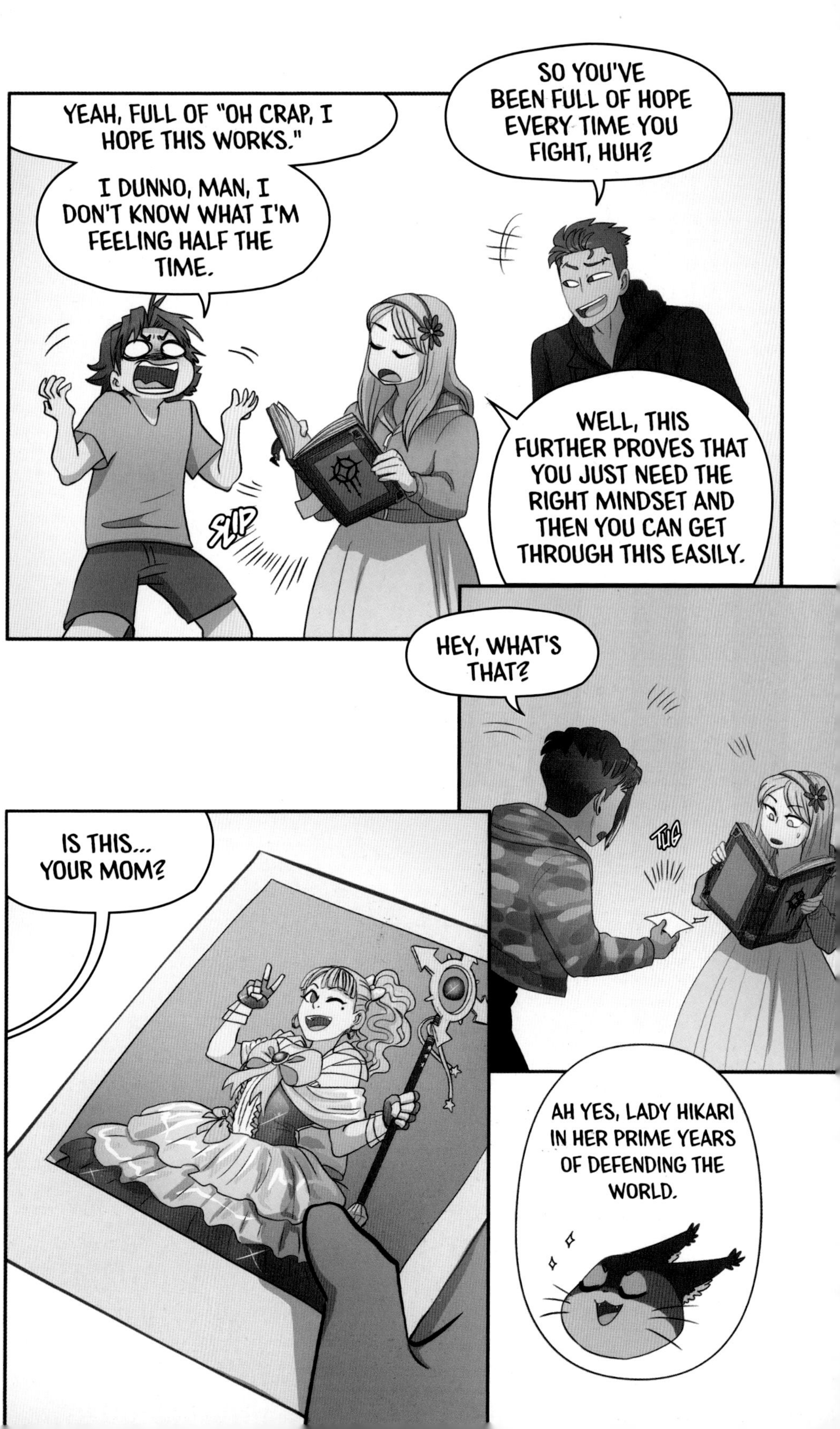
YEAH, FULL OF "OH CRAP, I HOPE THIS WORKS."
I DUNNO, MAN, I DON'T KNOW WHAT I'M FEELING HALF THE TIME.
SO YOU'VE BEEN FULL OF HOPE EVERY TIME YOU FIGHT, HUH?
SLIP
WELL, THIS FURTHER PROVES THAT YOU JUST NEED THE RIGHT MINDSET AND THEN YOU CAN GET THROUGH THIS EASILY.
HEY, WHAT'S THAT?
TUG
IS THIS... YOUR MOM?
AH YES, LADY HIKARI IN HER PRIME YEARS OF DEFENDING THE WORLD.

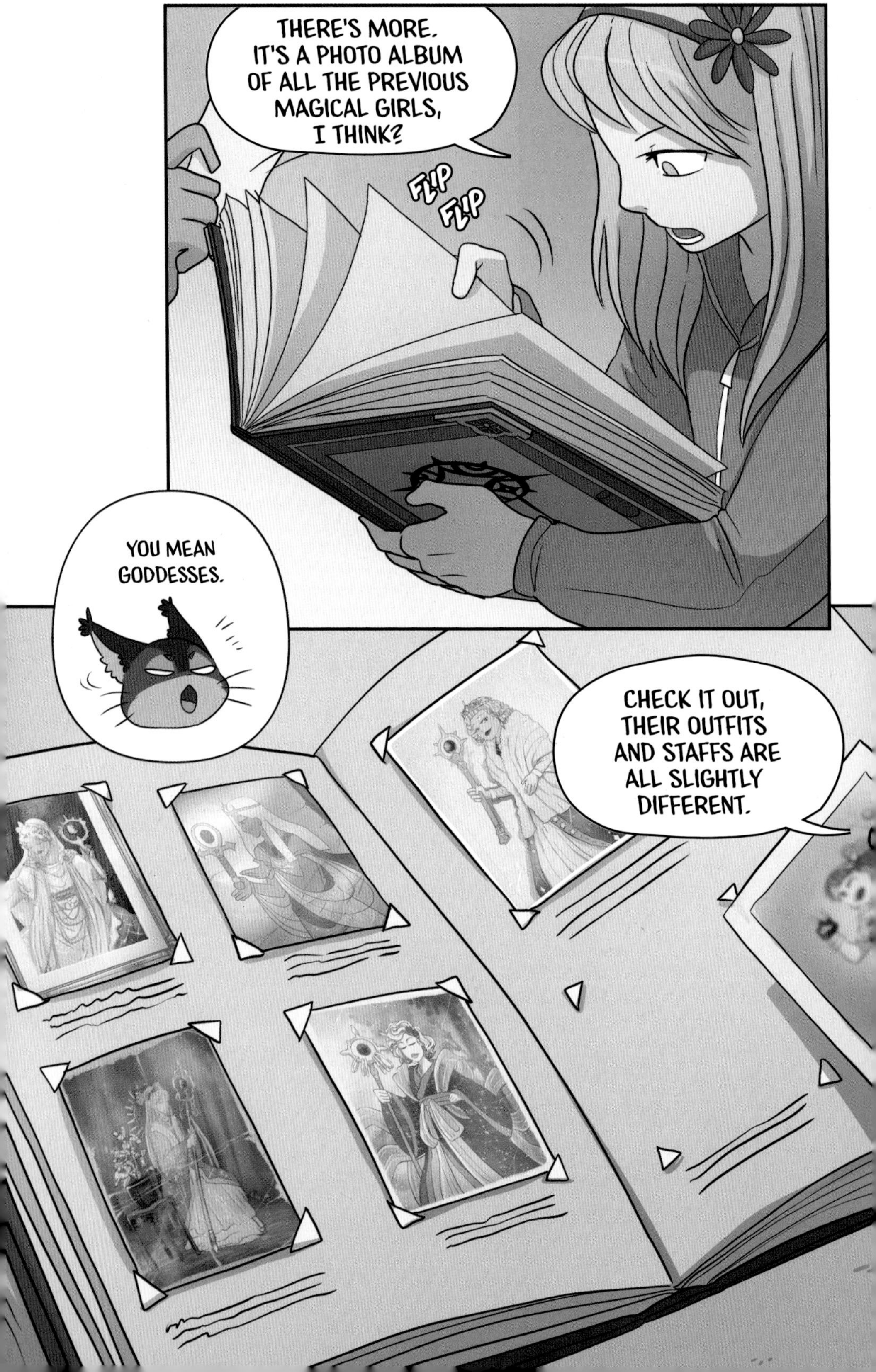
THERE'S MORE. IT'S A PHOTO ALBUM OF ALL THE PREVIOUS MAGICAL GIRLS, I THINK?
FLIP FLIP
YOU MEAN GODDESSES.
CHECK IT OUT, THEIR OUTFITS AND STAFFS ARE ALL SLIGHTLY DIFFERENT.

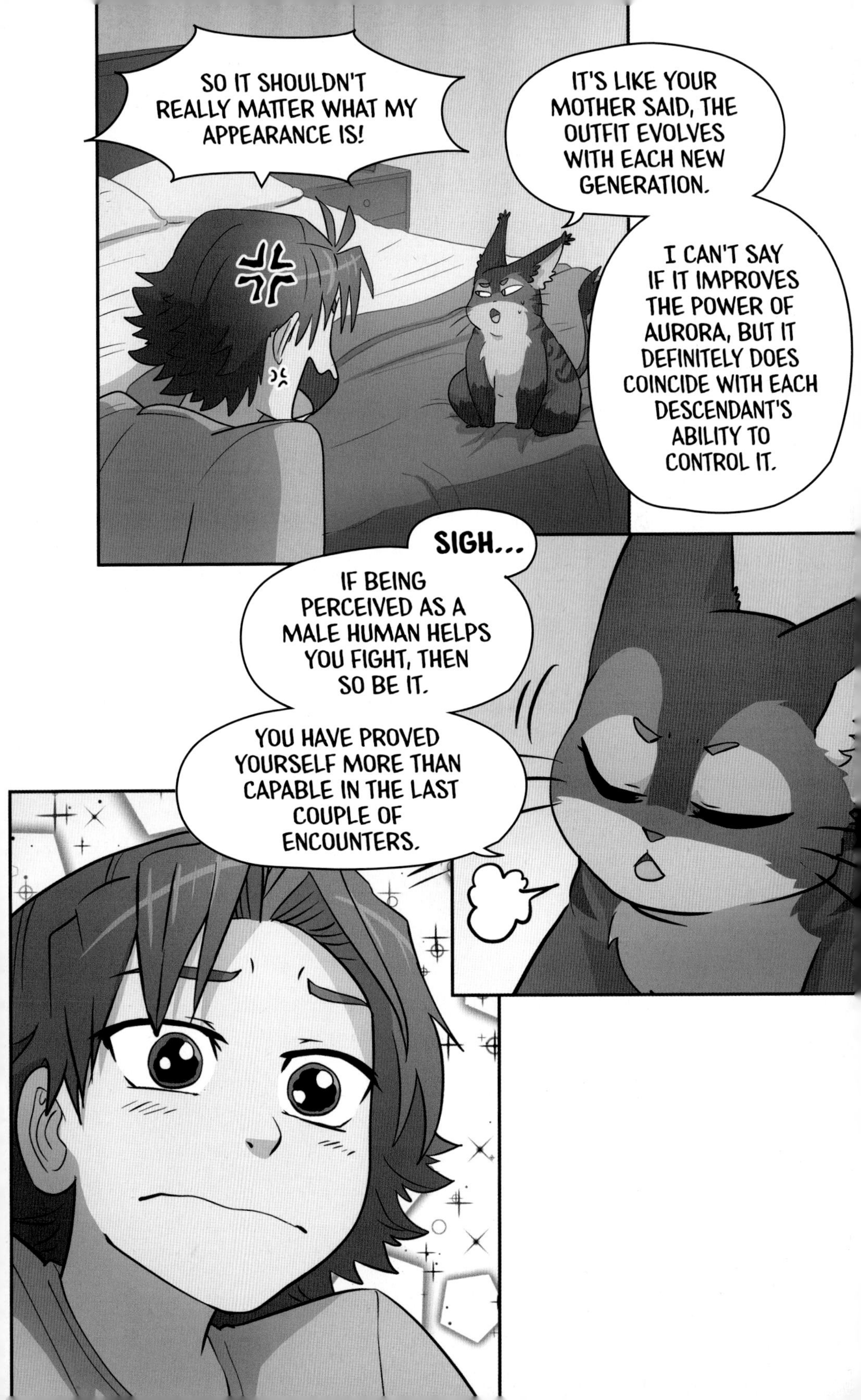
SO IT SHOULDN'T REALLY MATTER WHAT MY APPEARANCE IS!
IT'S LIKE YOUR MOTHER SAID, THE OUTFIT EVOLVES WITH EACH NEW GENERATION.
I CAN'T SAY IF IT IMPROVES THE POWER OF AURORA, BUT IT DEFINITELY DOES COINCIDE WITH EACH DESCENDANT'S ABILITY TO CONTROL IT.
SIGH...
IF BEING PERCEIVED AS A MALE HUMAN HELPS YOU FIGHT, THEN SO BE IT.
YOU HAVE PROVED YOURSELF MORE THAN CAPABLE IN THE LAST COUPLE OF ENCOUNTERS.

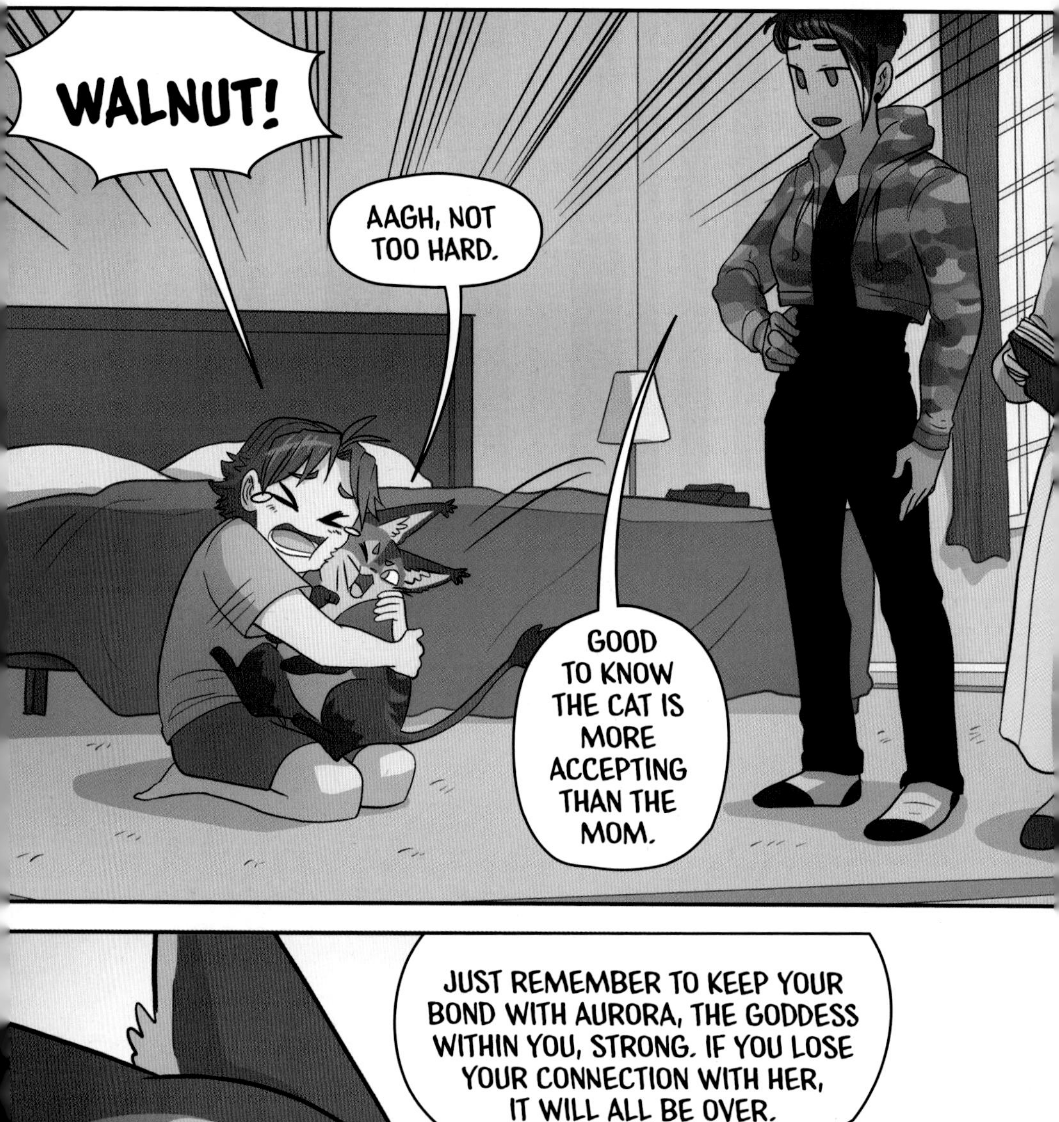
WALNUT!
AAGH, NOT TOO HARD.
GOOD TO KNOW THE CAT IS MORE ACCEPTING THAN THE MOM.

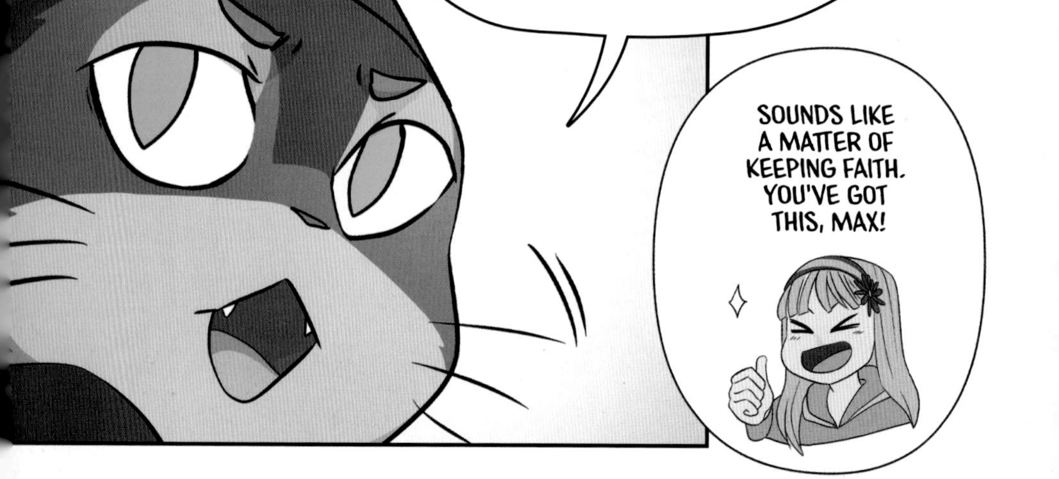
JUST REMEMBER TO KEEP YOUR BOND WITH AURORA, THE GODDESS WITHIN YOU, STRONG. IF YOU LOSE YOUR CONNECTION WITH HER, IT WILL ALL BE OVER.
SOUNDS LIKE A MATTER OF KEEPING FAITH. YOU'VE GOT THIS, MAX!

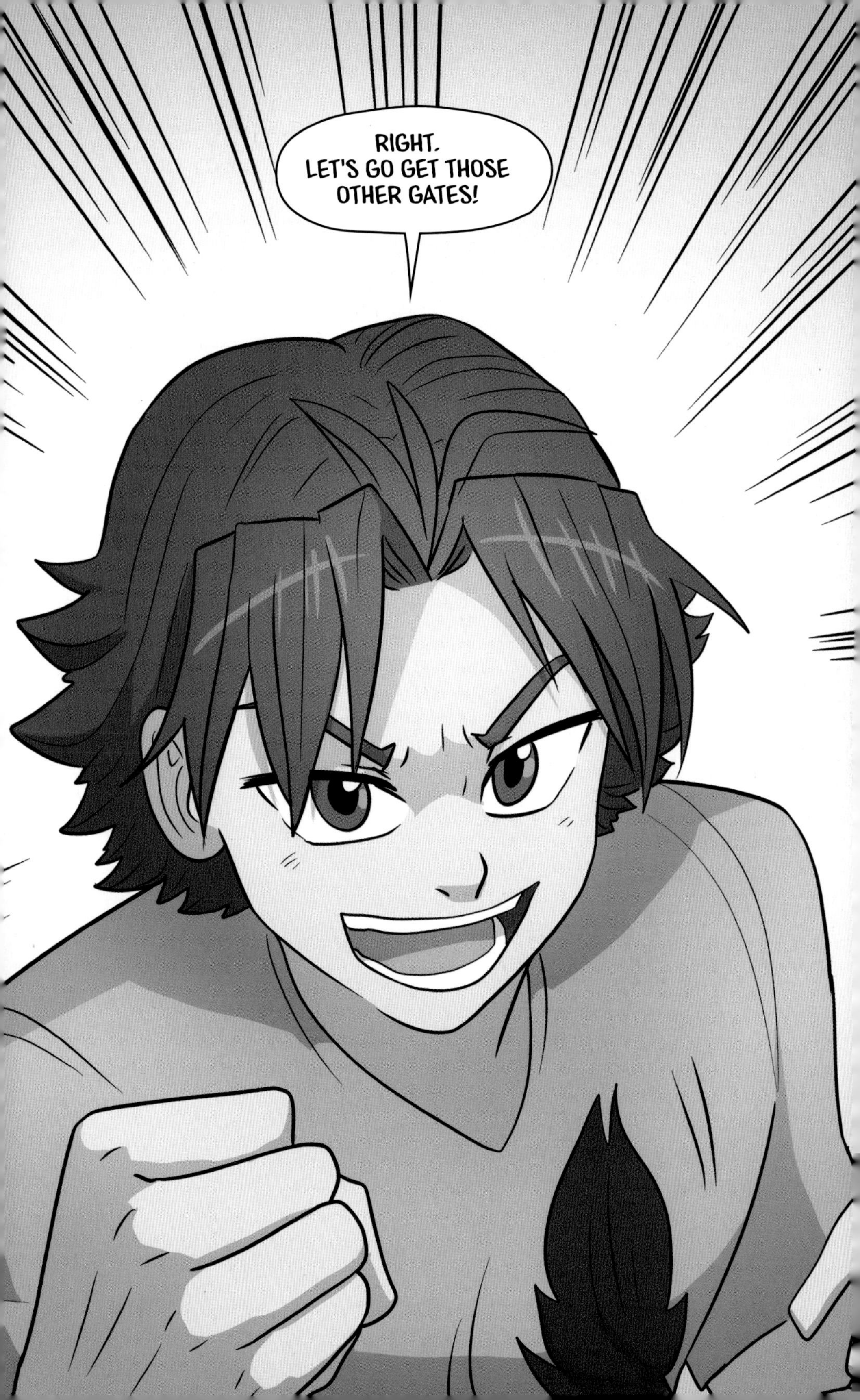
RIGHT.
LET'S GO GET THOSE
OTHER GATES!

EPISODE 20:
DETERMINATION

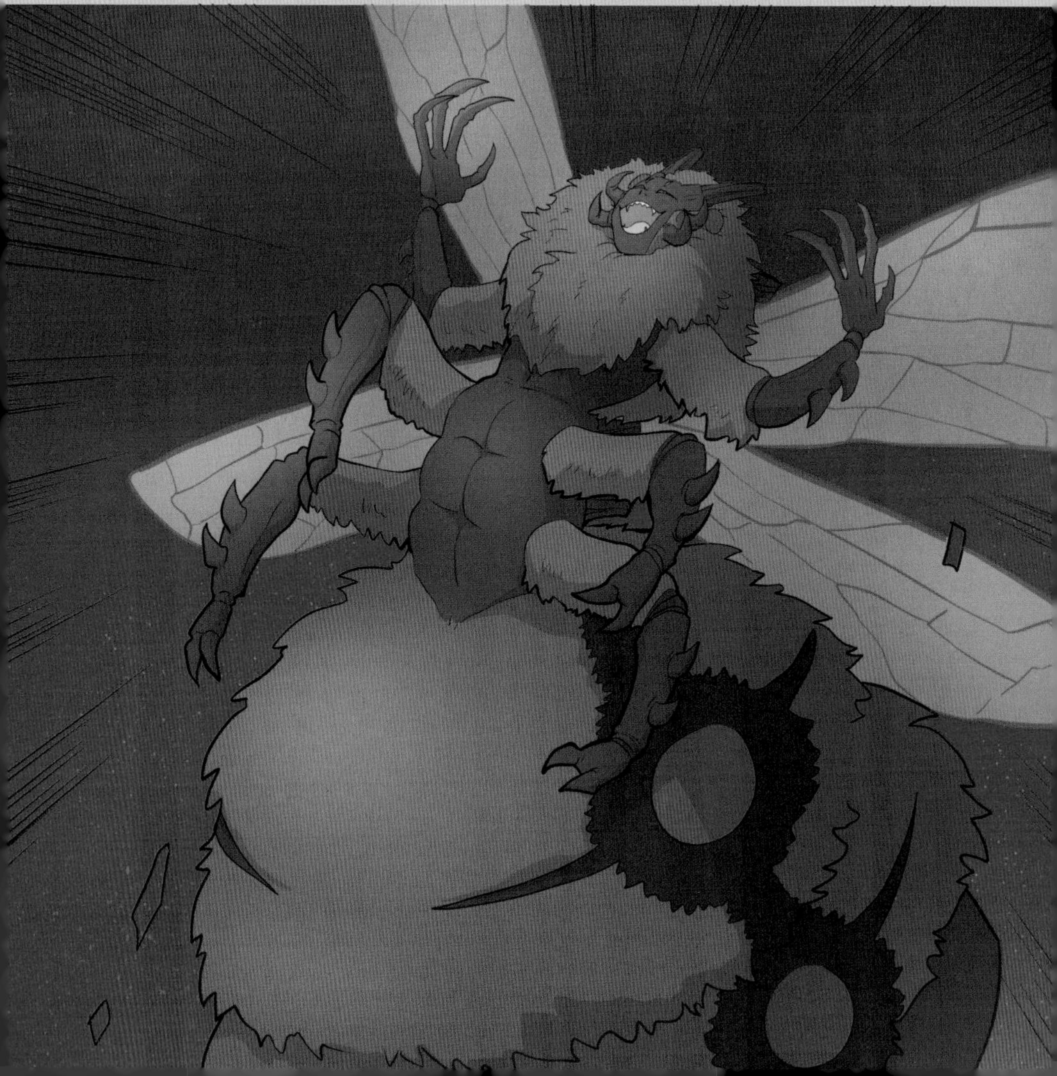

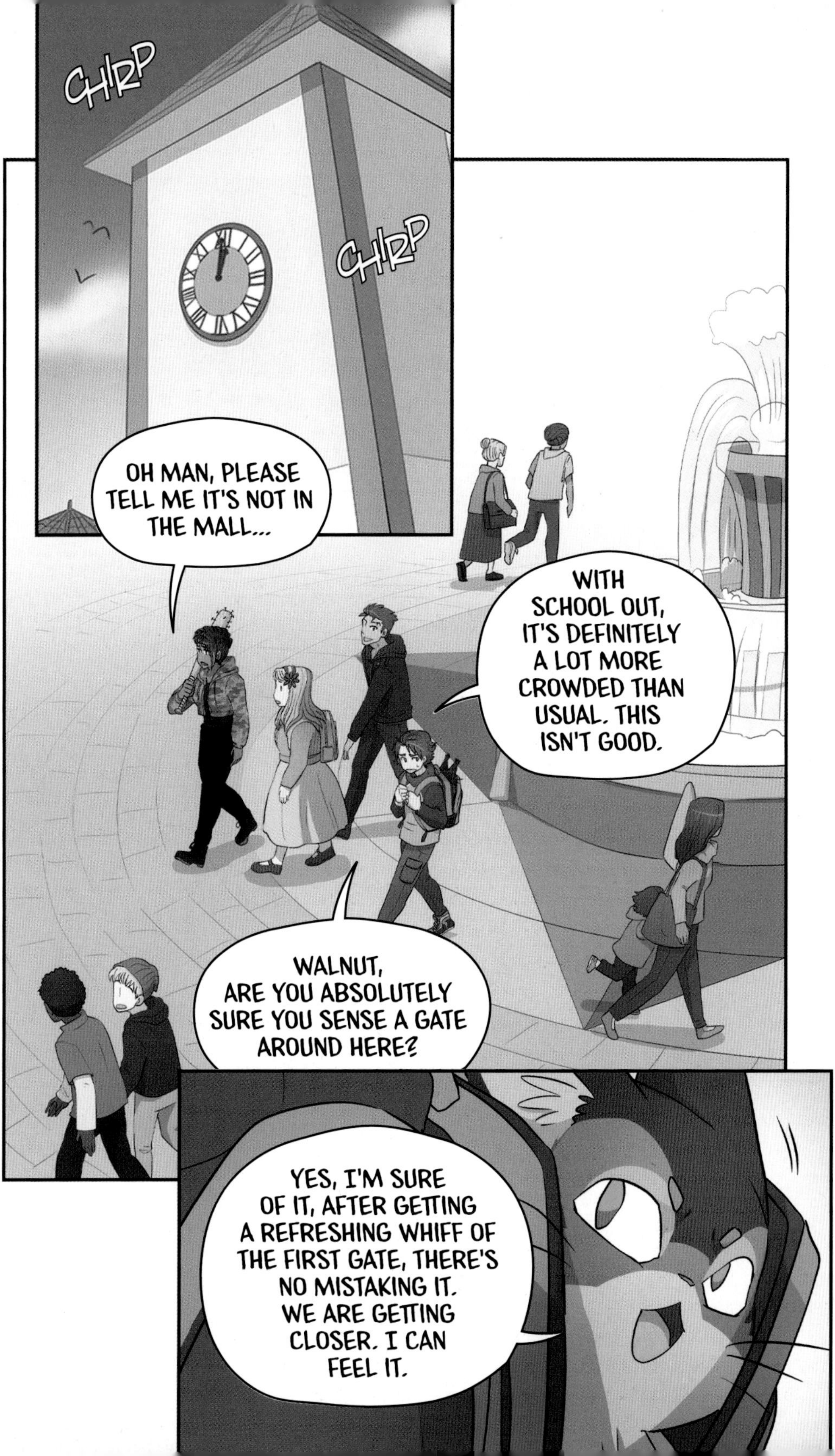
CHIRP
CHIRP
OH MAN, PLEASE TELL ME IT'S NOT IN THE MALL...
WITH SCHOOL OUT, IT'S DEFINITELY A LOT MORE CROWDED THAN USUAL. THIS ISN'T GOOD.
WALNUT, ARE YOU ABSOLUTELY SURE YOU SENSE A GATE AROUND HERE?
YES, I'M SURE OF IT, AFTER GETTING A REFRESHING WHIFF OF THE FIRST GATE, THERE'S NO MISTAKING IT. WE ARE GETTING CLOSER. I CAN FEEL IT.

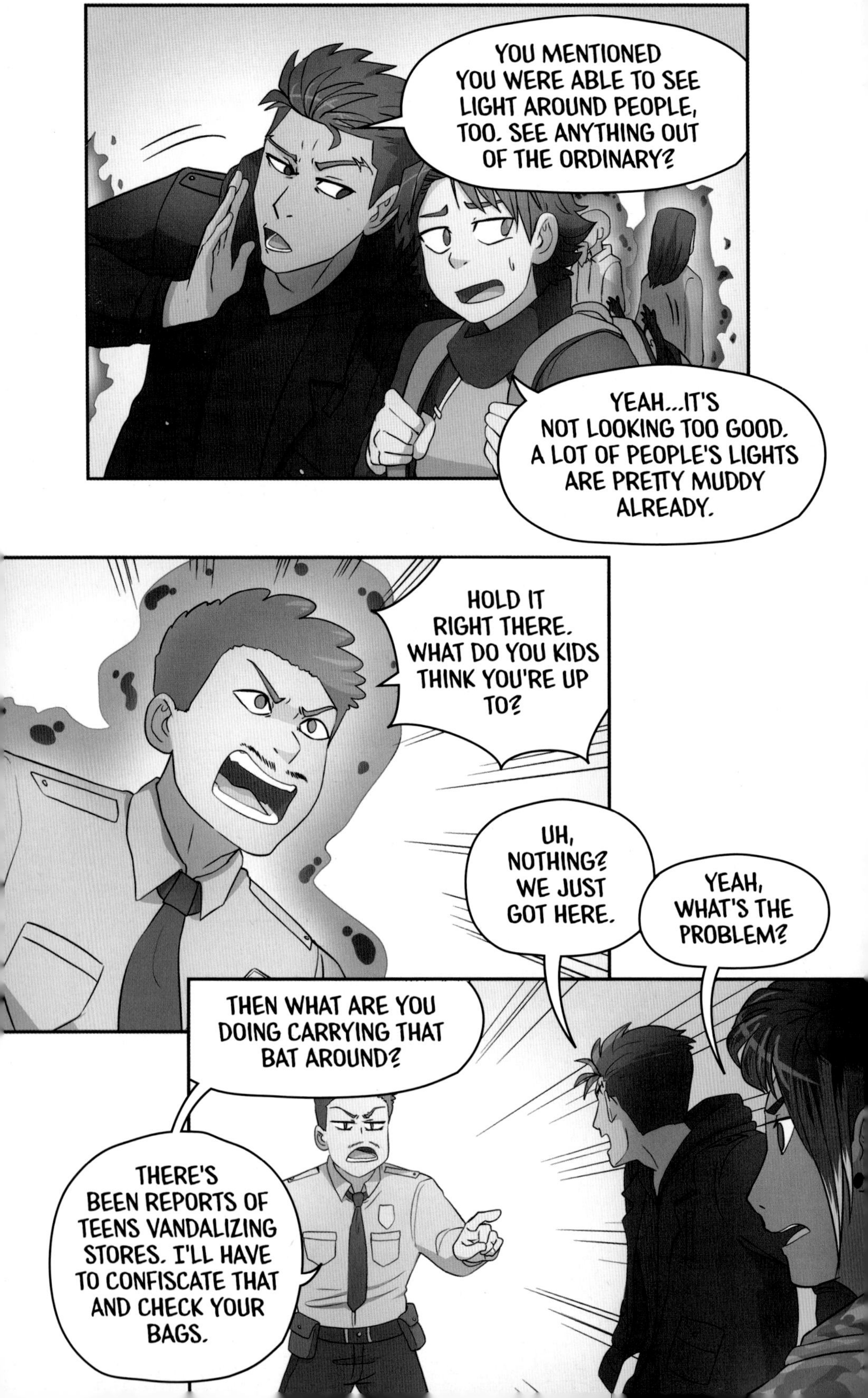
YOU MENTIONED YOU WERE ABLE TO SEE LIGHT AROUND PEOPLE, TOO. SEE ANYTHING OUT OF THE ORDINARY?
YEAH...IT'S NOT LOOKING TOO GOOD. A LOT OF PEOPLE'S LIGHTS ARE PRETTY MUDDY ALREADY.
HOLD IT RIGHT THERE. WHAT DO YOU KIDS THINK YOU'RE UP TO?
UH, NOTHING? WE JUST GOT HERE.
YEAH, WHAT'S THE PROBLEM?
THEN WHAT ARE YOU DOING CARRYING THAT BAT AROUND?
THERE'S BEEN REPORTS OF TEENS VANDALIZING STORES. I'LL HAVE TO CONFISCATE THAT AND CHECK YOUR BAGS.

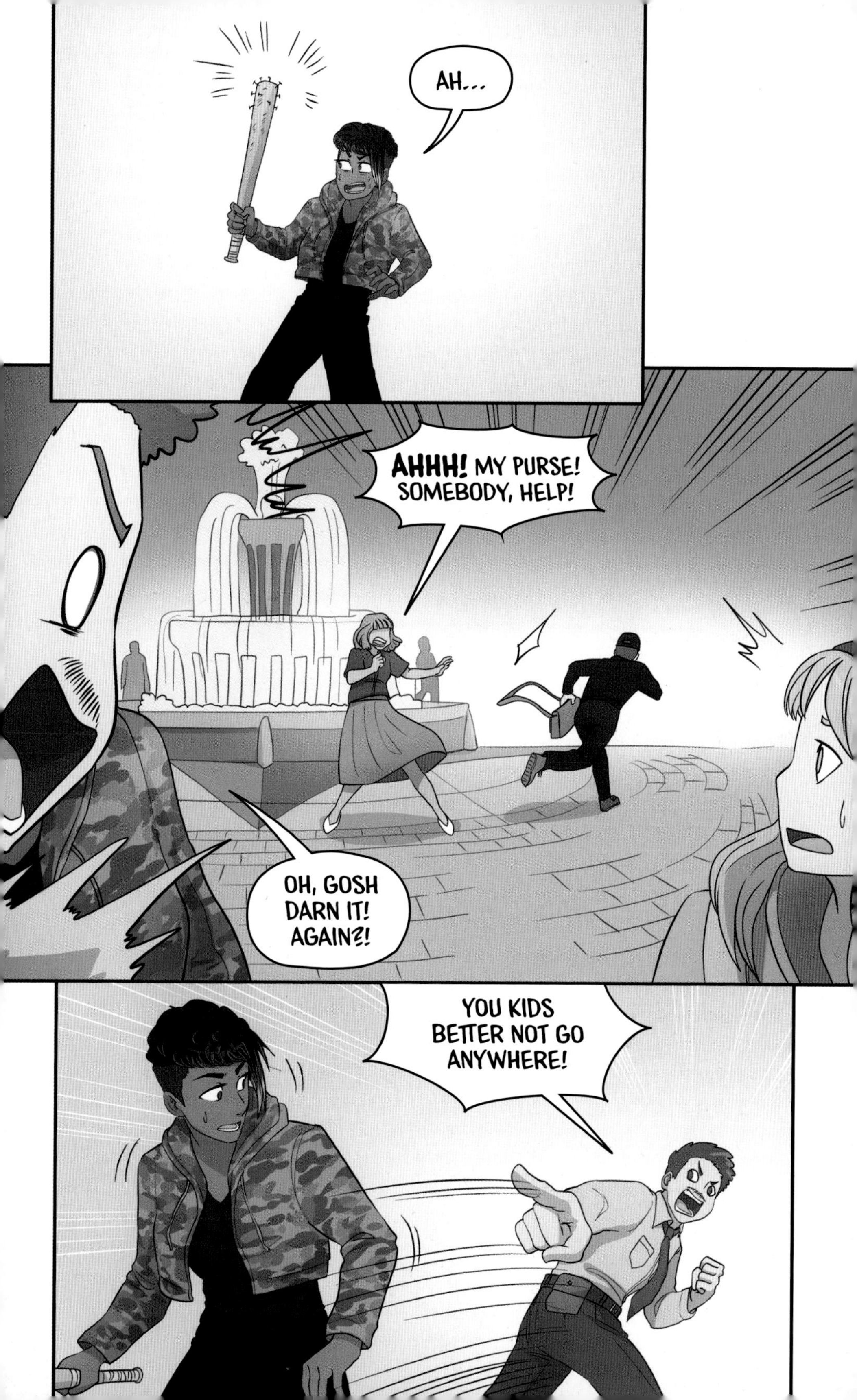
AH...
AHHH! MY PURSE! SOMEBODY, HELP!
OH, GOSH DARN IT! AGAIN?!
YOU KIDS BETTER NOT GO ANYWHERE!

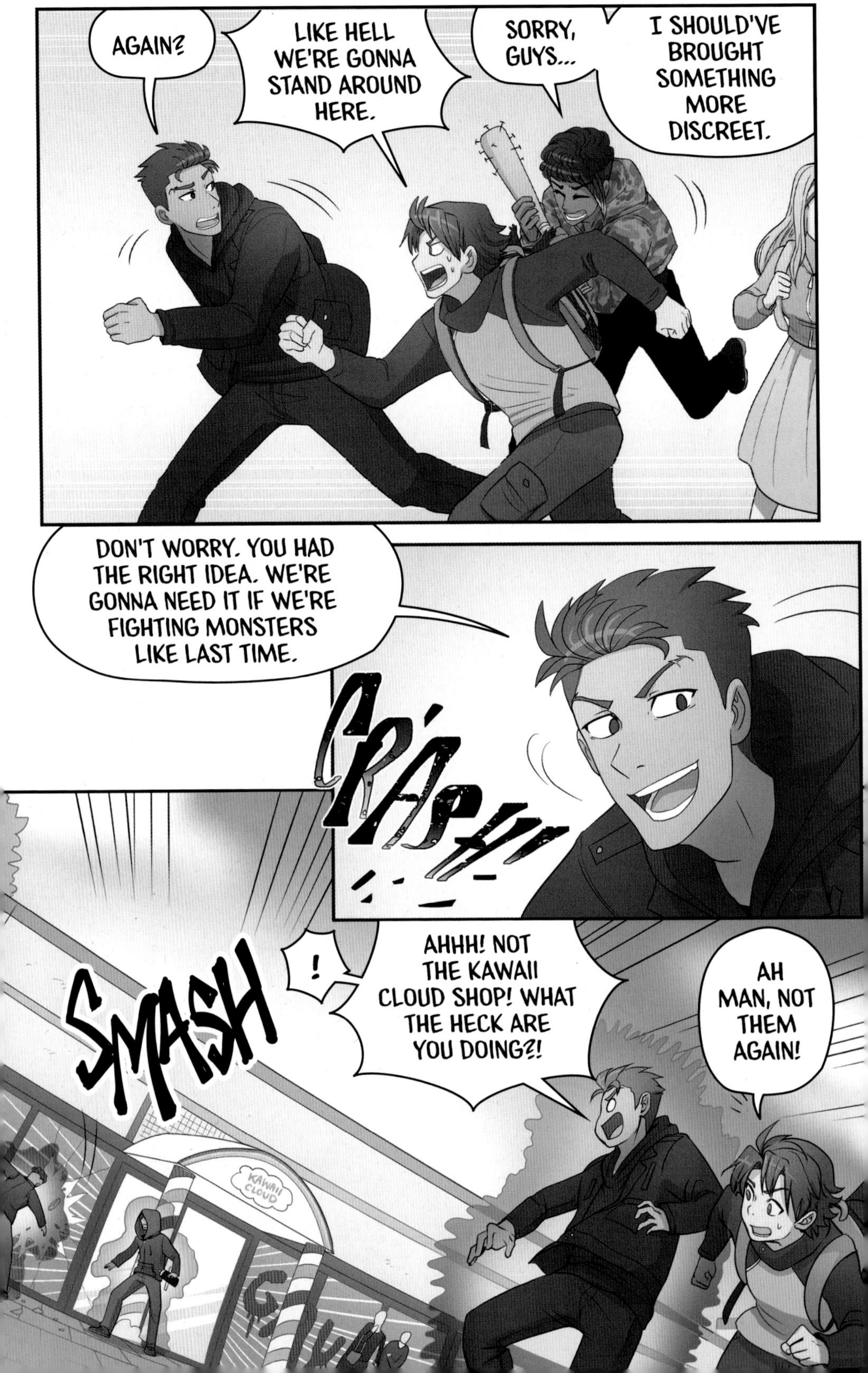
AGAIN?
LIKE HELL WE'RE GONNA STAND AROUND HERE.
SORRY, GUYS...
I SHOULD'VE BROUGHT SOMETHING MORE DISCREET.
DON'T WORRY. YOU HAD THE RIGHT IDEA. WE'RE GONNA NEED IT IF WE'RE FIGHTING MONSTERS LIKE LAST TIME.
CRASH!!
SMASH
!
AHHH! NOT THE KAWAII CLOUD SHOP! WHAT THE HECK ARE YOU DOING?!
AH MAN, NOT THEM AGAIN!
KAWAII CLOUD

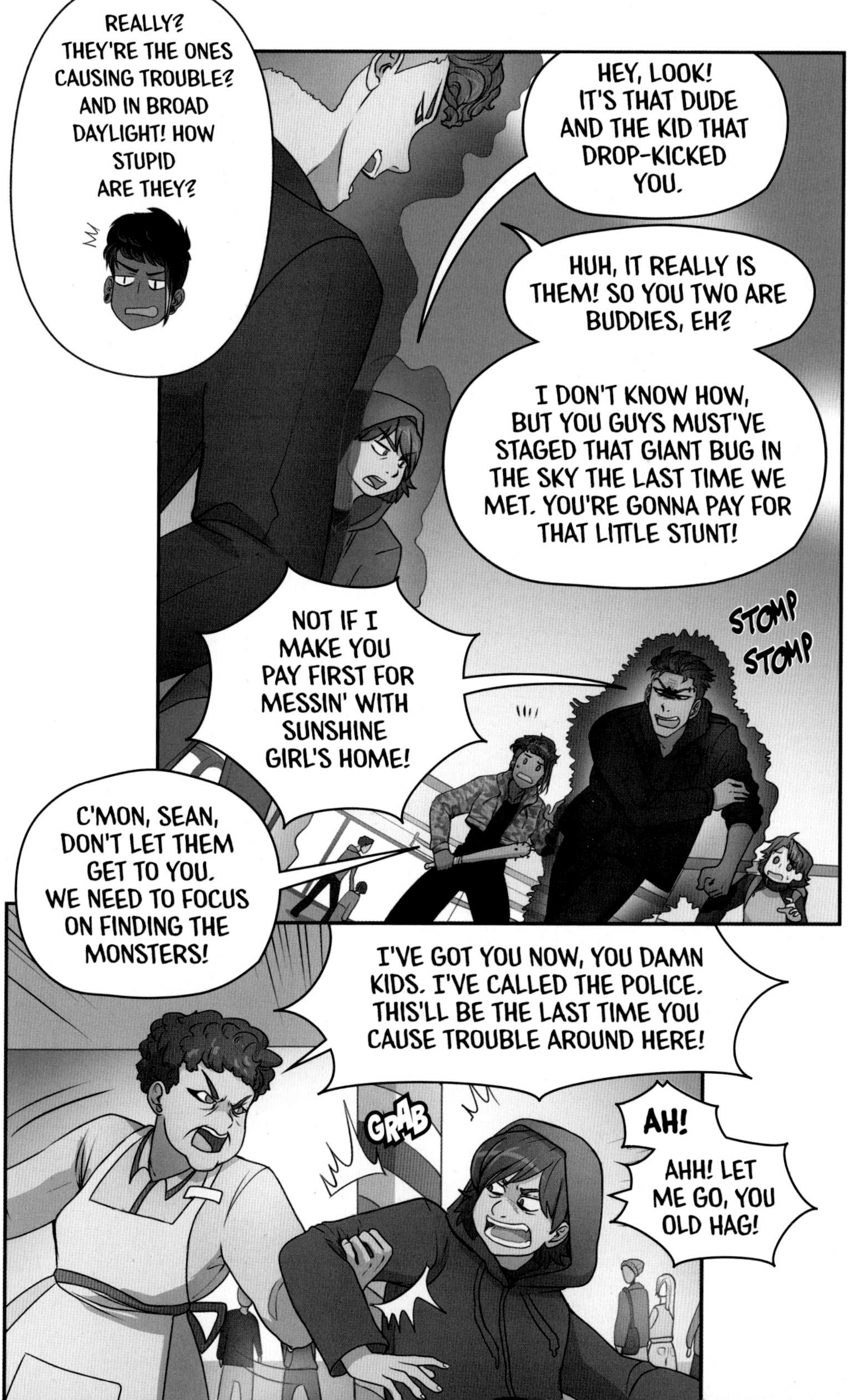
REALLY? THEY'RE THE ONES CAUSING TROUBLE? AND IN BROAD DAYLIGHT! HOW STUPID ARE THEY?
HEY, LOOK! IT'S THAT DUDE AND THE KID THAT DROP-KICKED YOU.
HUH, IT REALLY IS THEM! SO YOU TWO ARE BUDDIES, EH?
I DON'T KNOW HOW, BUT YOU GUYS MUST'VE STAGED THAT GIANT BUG IN THE SKY THE LAST TIME WE MET. YOU'RE GONNA PAY FOR THAT LITTLE STUNT!
NOT IF I MAKE YOU PAY FIRST FOR MESSIN' WITH SUNSHINE GIRL'S HOME!
STOMP
STOMP
C'MON, SEAN, DON'T LET THEM GET TO YOU. WE NEED TO FOCUS ON FINDING THE MONSTERS!
I'VE GOT YOU NOW, YOU DAMN KIDS. I'VE CALLED THE POLICE. THIS'LL BE THE LAST TIME YOU CAUSE TROUBLE AROUND HERE!
GRAB
AH!
AHH! LET ME GO, YOU OLD HAG!

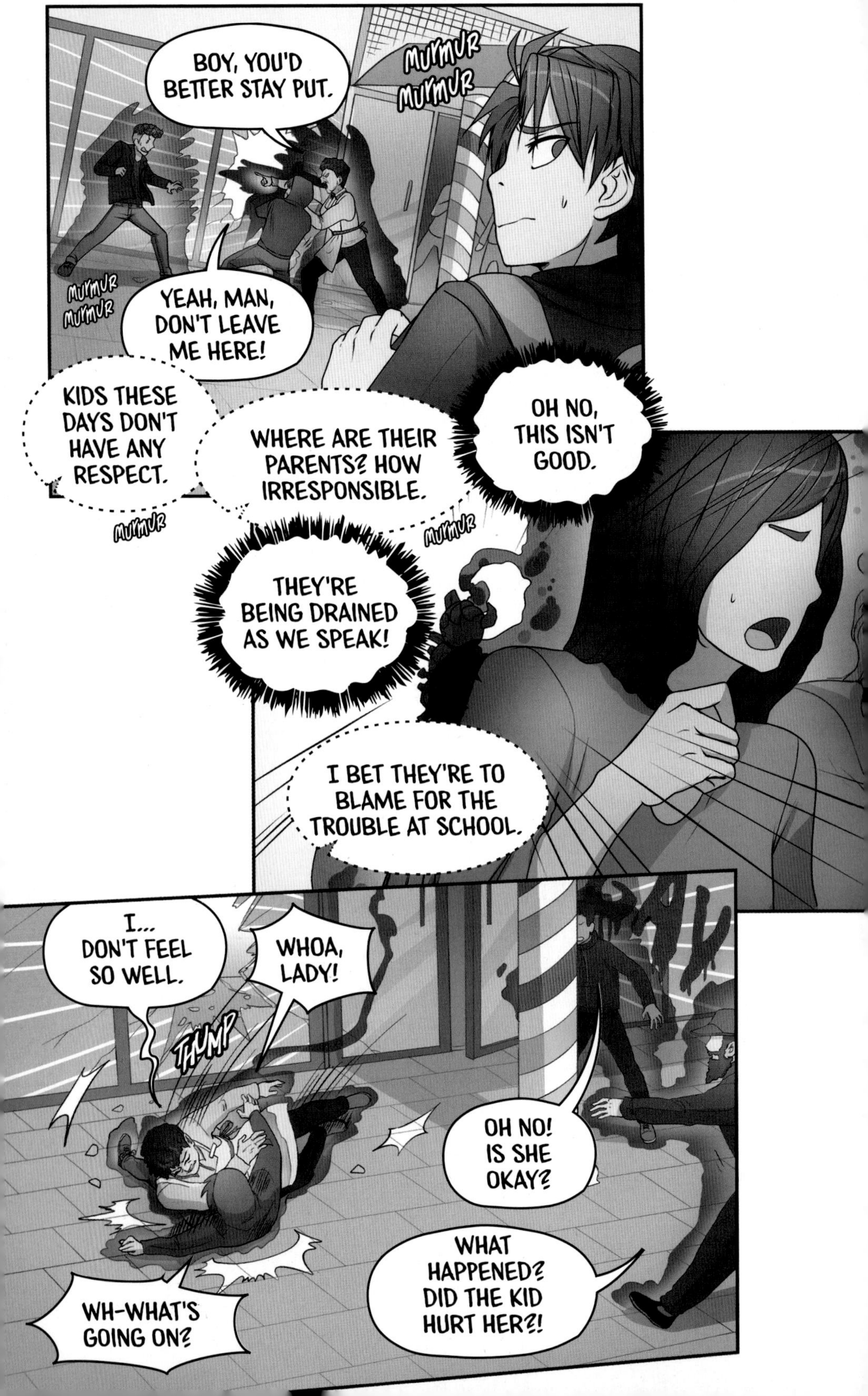
BOY, YOU'D BETTER STAY PUT.
MURMUR MURMUR
YEAH, MAN, DON'T LEAVE ME HERE!
MURMUR MURMUR
KIDS THESE DAYS DON'T HAVE ANY RESPECT.
WHERE ARE THEIR PARENTS? HOW IRRESPONSIBLE.
MURMUR
MURMUR
OH NO, THIS ISN'T GOOD.
THEY'RE BEING DRAINED AS WE SPEAK!
I BET THEY'RE TO BLAME FOR THE TROUBLE AT SCHOOL.
I... DON'T FEEL SO WELL.
WHOA, LADY!
THUMP
OH NO! IS SHE OKAY?
WHAT HAPPENED? DID THE KID HURT HER?!
WH-WHAT'S GOING ON?

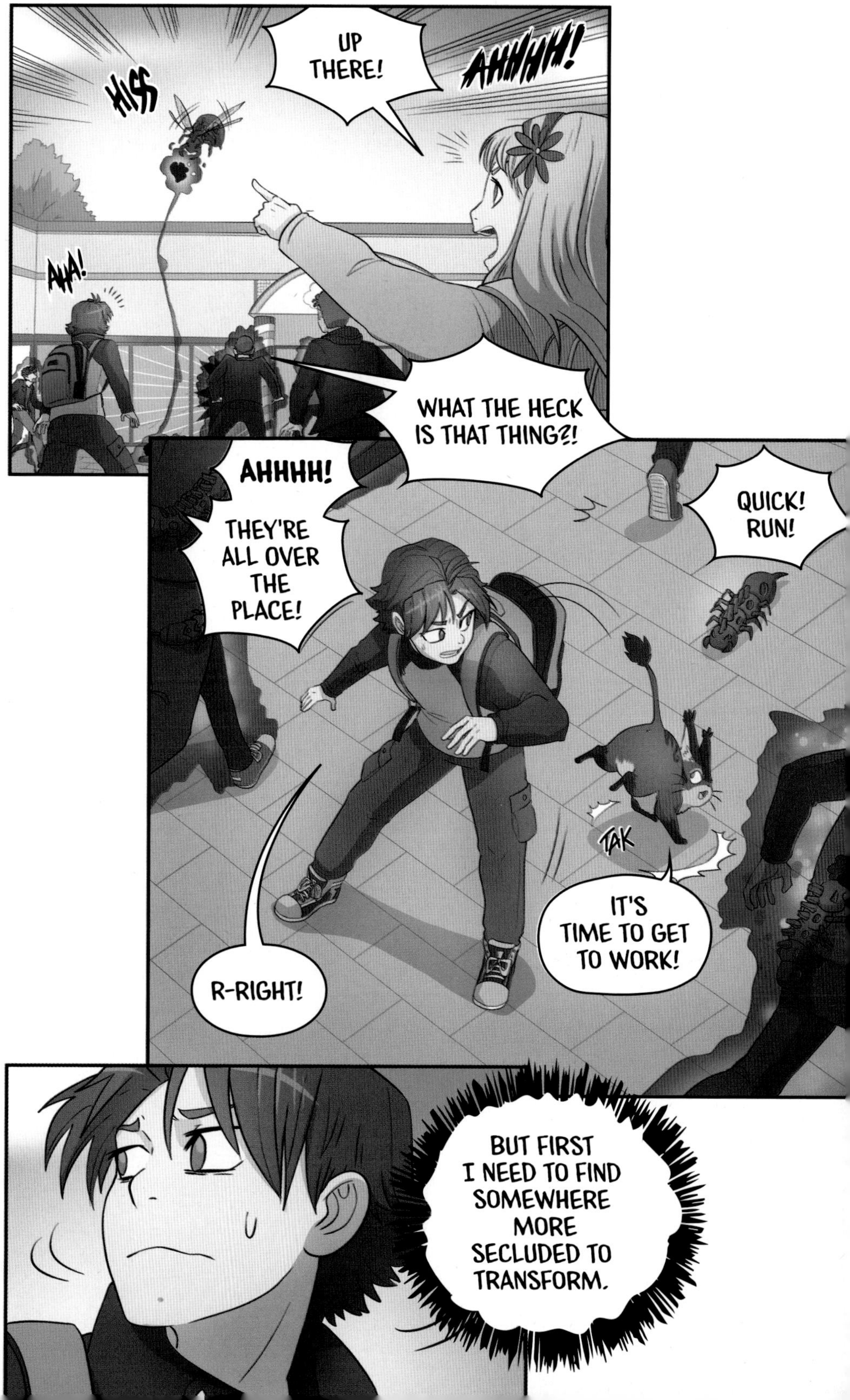
HISS
UP THERE!
AHHHH!
AHA!
WHAT THE HECK IS THAT THING?!
AHHHH!
THEY'RE ALL OVER THE PLACE!
QUICK! RUN!
TAK
IT'S TIME TO GET TO WORK!
R-RIGHT!
BUT FIRST I NEED TO FIND SOMEWHERE MORE SECLUDED TO TRANSFORM.

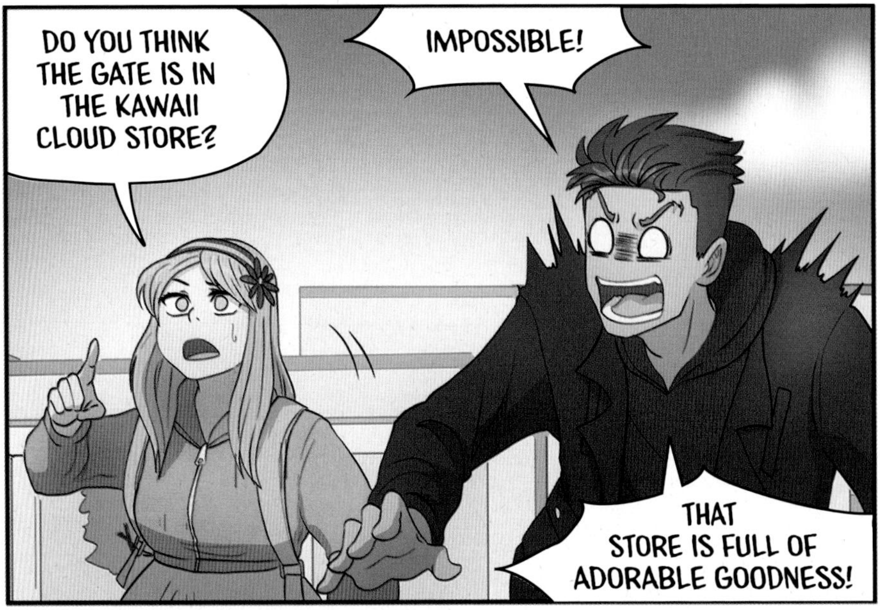
DO YOU THINK THE GATE IS IN THE KAWAII CLOUD STORE?
IMPOSSIBLE!
THAT STORE IS FULL OF ADORABLE GOODNESS!

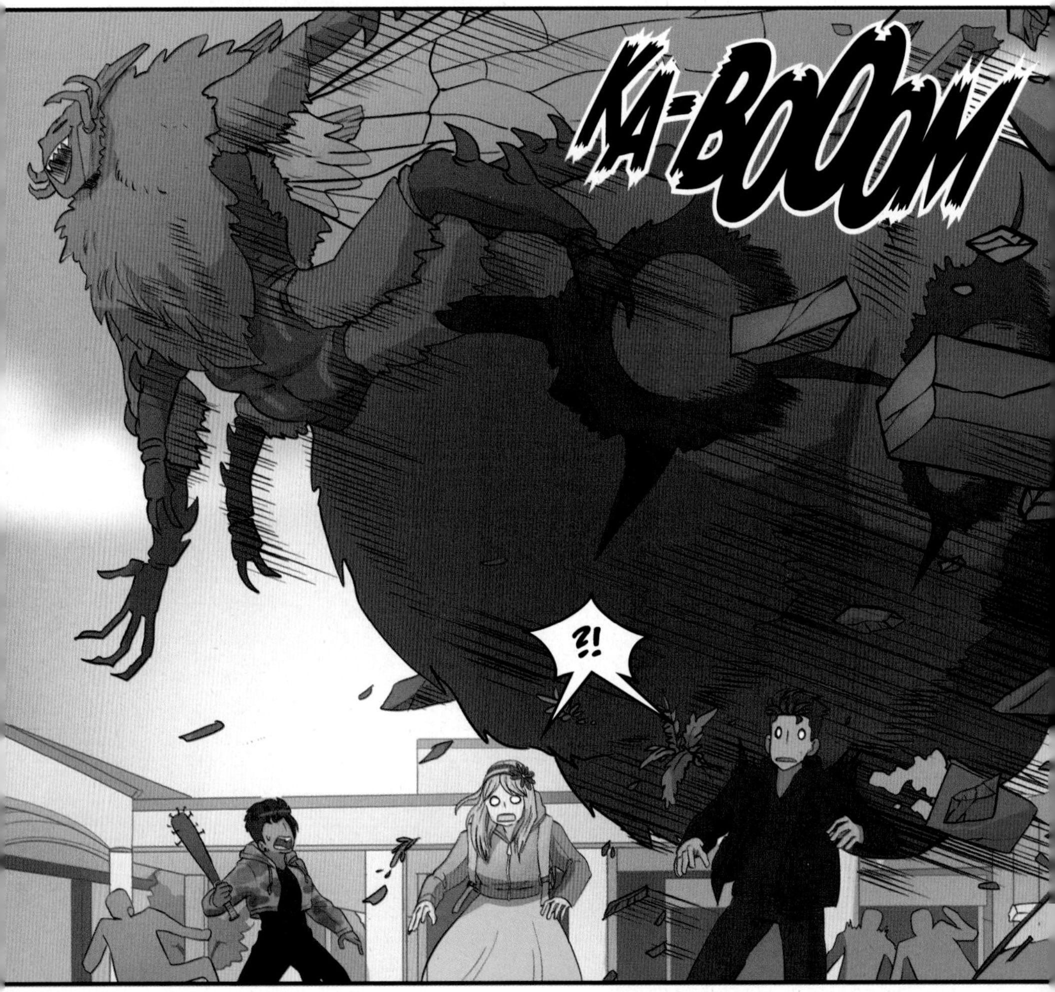
KA-BOOOM
?!

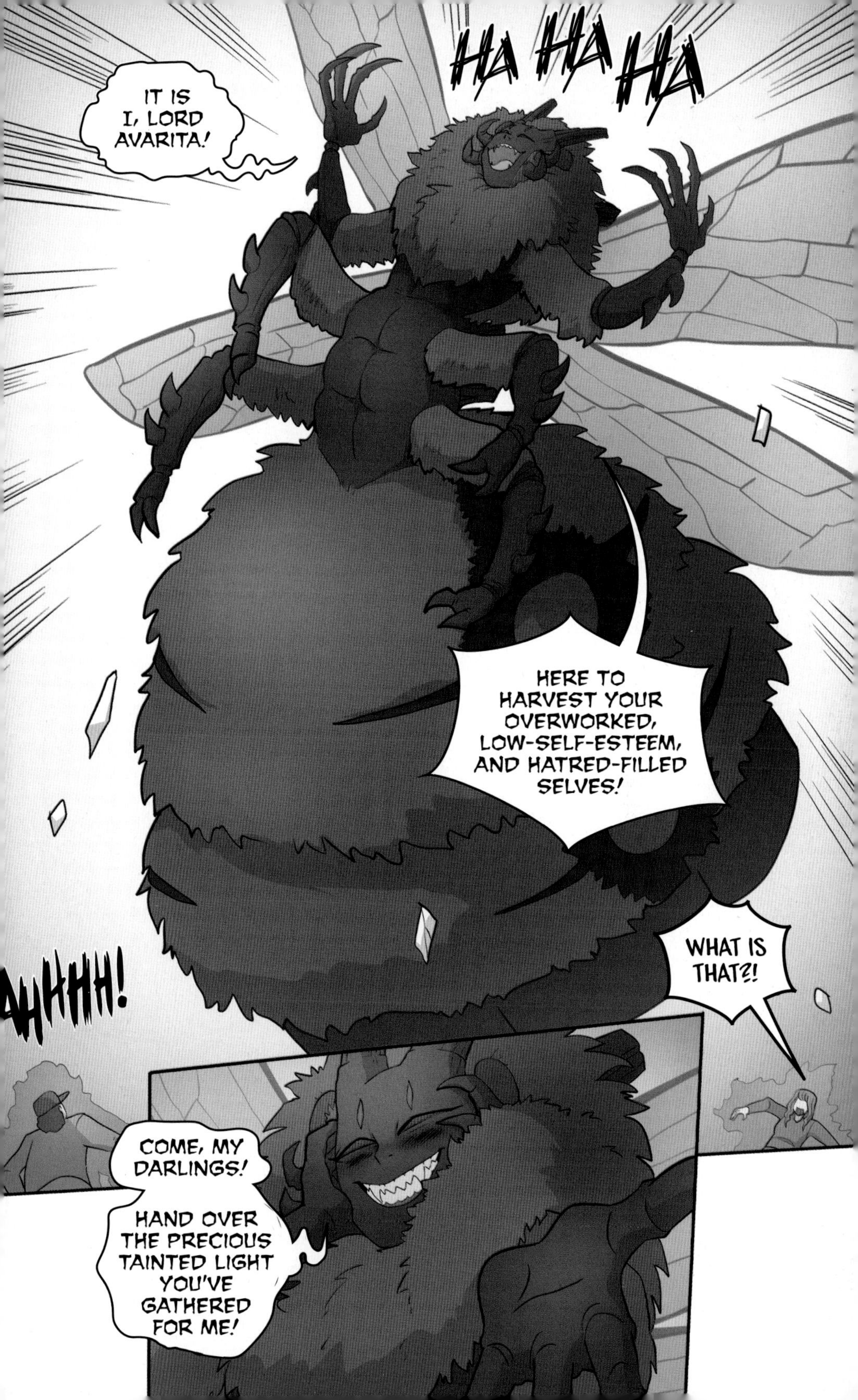
HA HA HA HA
IT IS I, LORD AVARITA!
HERE TO HARVEST YOUR OVERWORKED, LOW-SELF-ESTEEM, AND HATRED-FILLED SELVES!
AHHHH!
WHAT IS THAT?!
COME, MY DARLINGS!
HAND OVER THE PRECIOUS TAINTED LIGHT YOU'VE GATHERED FOR ME!

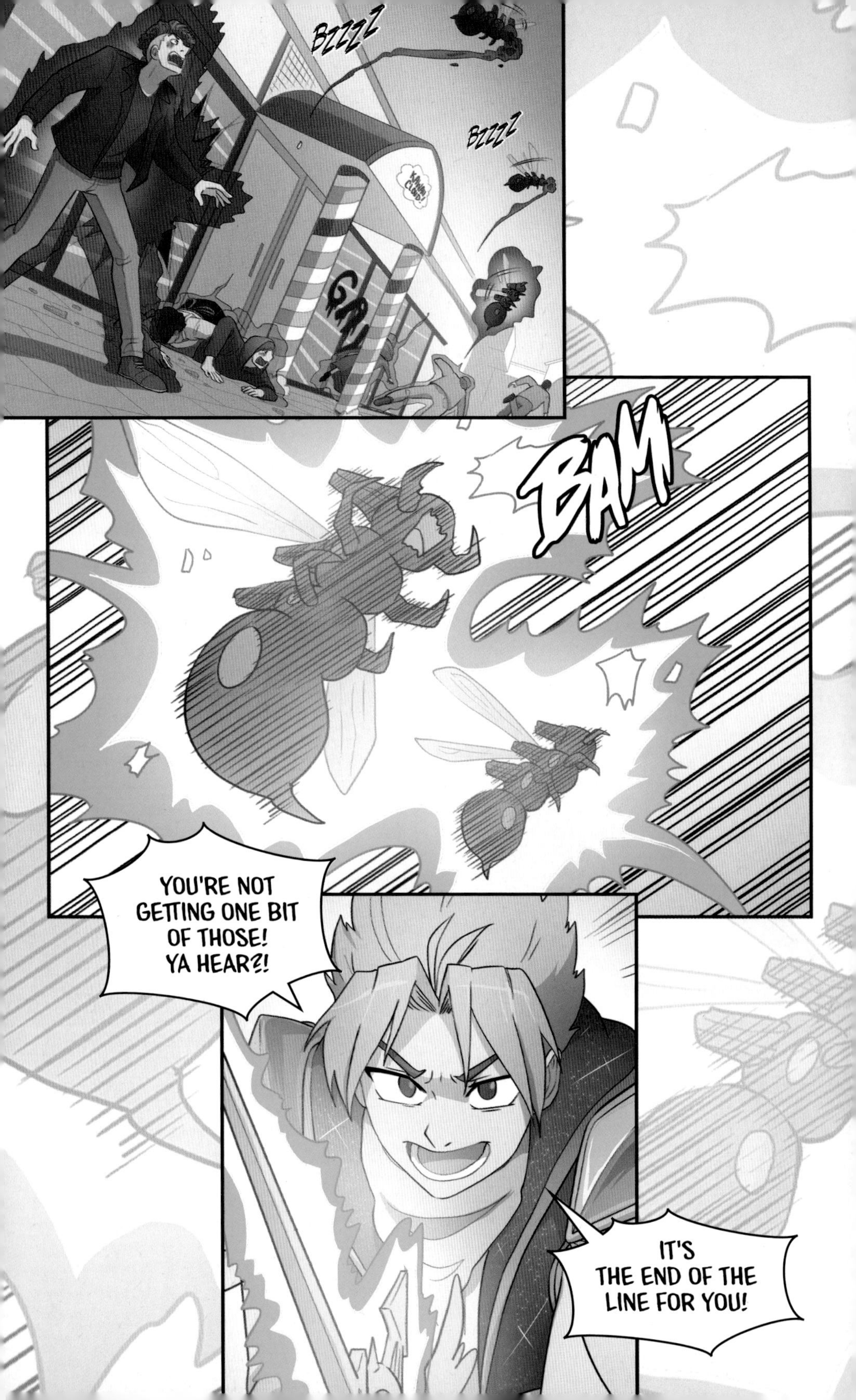
BZZZZ
BZZZZ
BAM
YOU'RE NOT GETTING ONE BIT OF THOSE! YA HEAR?!
IT'S THE END OF THE LINE FOR YOU!

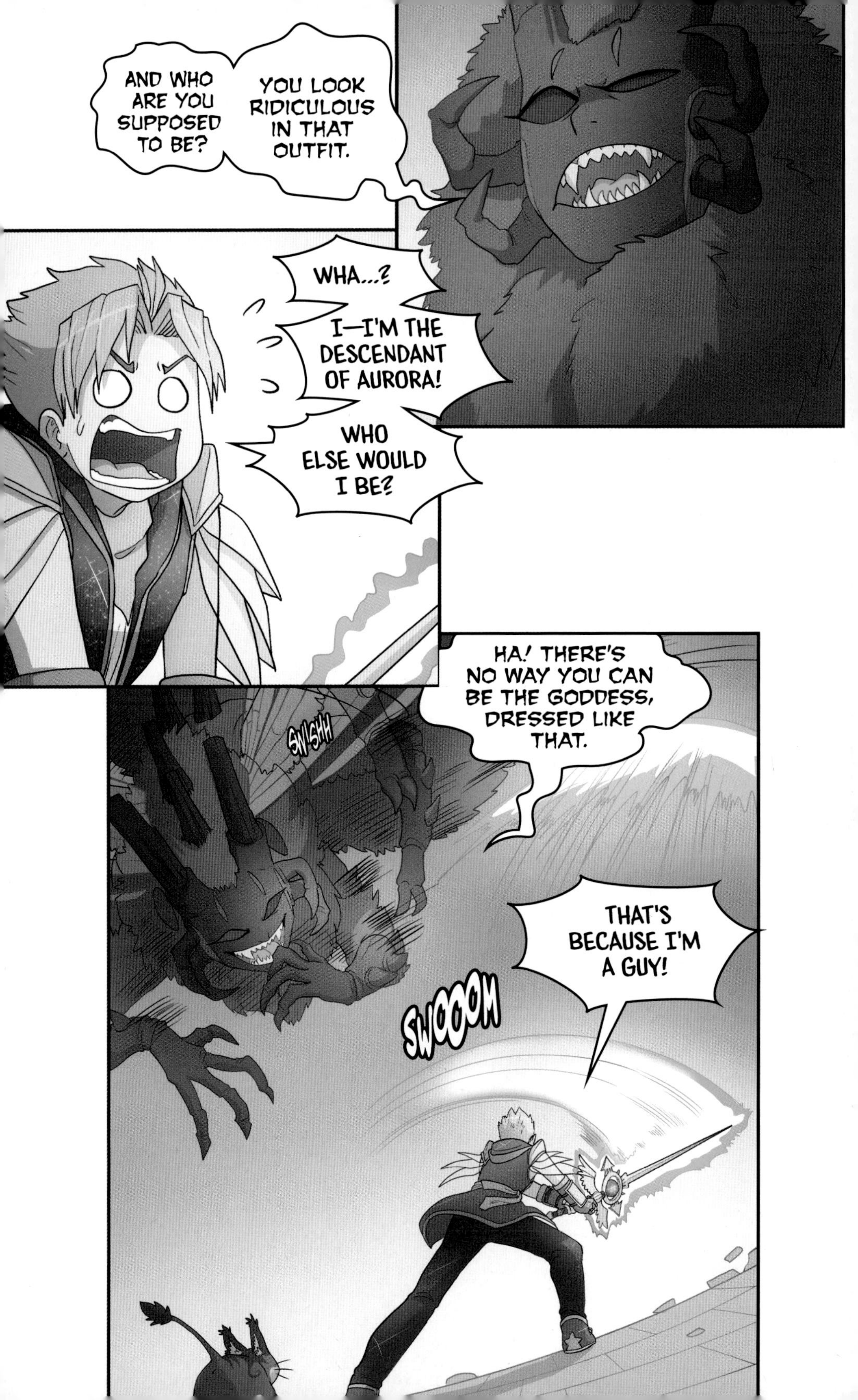
YOU LOOK RIDICULOUS IN THAT OUTFIT.
AND WHO ARE YOU SUPPOSED TO BE?
WHA...?
I—I'M THE DESCENDANT OF AURORA!
WHO ELSE WOULD I BE?
HA! THERE'S NO WAY YOU CAN BE THE GODDESS, DRESSED LIKE THAT.
SWISHH
THAT'S BECAUSE I'M A GUY!
SWOOOM

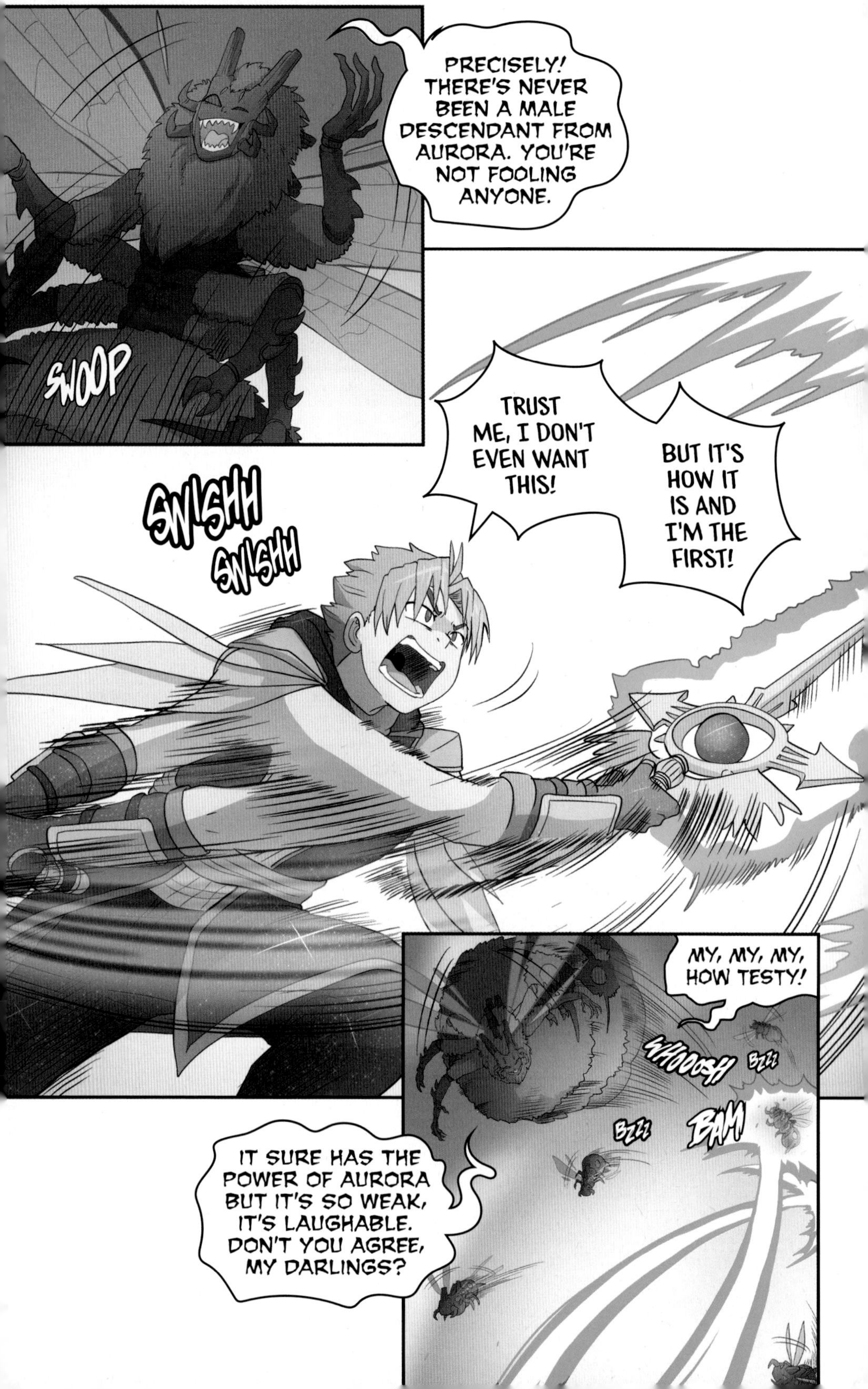
PRECISELY! THERE'S NEVER BEEN A MALE DESCENDANT FROM AURORA. YOU'RE NOT FOOLING ANYONE.
SWOOP
TRUST ME, I DON'T EVEN WANT THIS!
BUT IT'S HOW IT IS AND I'M THE FIRST!
SWISHH
SWISHH
MY, MY, MY, HOW TESTY!
WHOOOSH
BZZZ
BZZZ
BAM
IT SURE HAS THE POWER OF AURORA BUT IT'S SO WEAK, IT'S LAUGHABLE. DON'T YOU AGREE, MY DARLINGS?

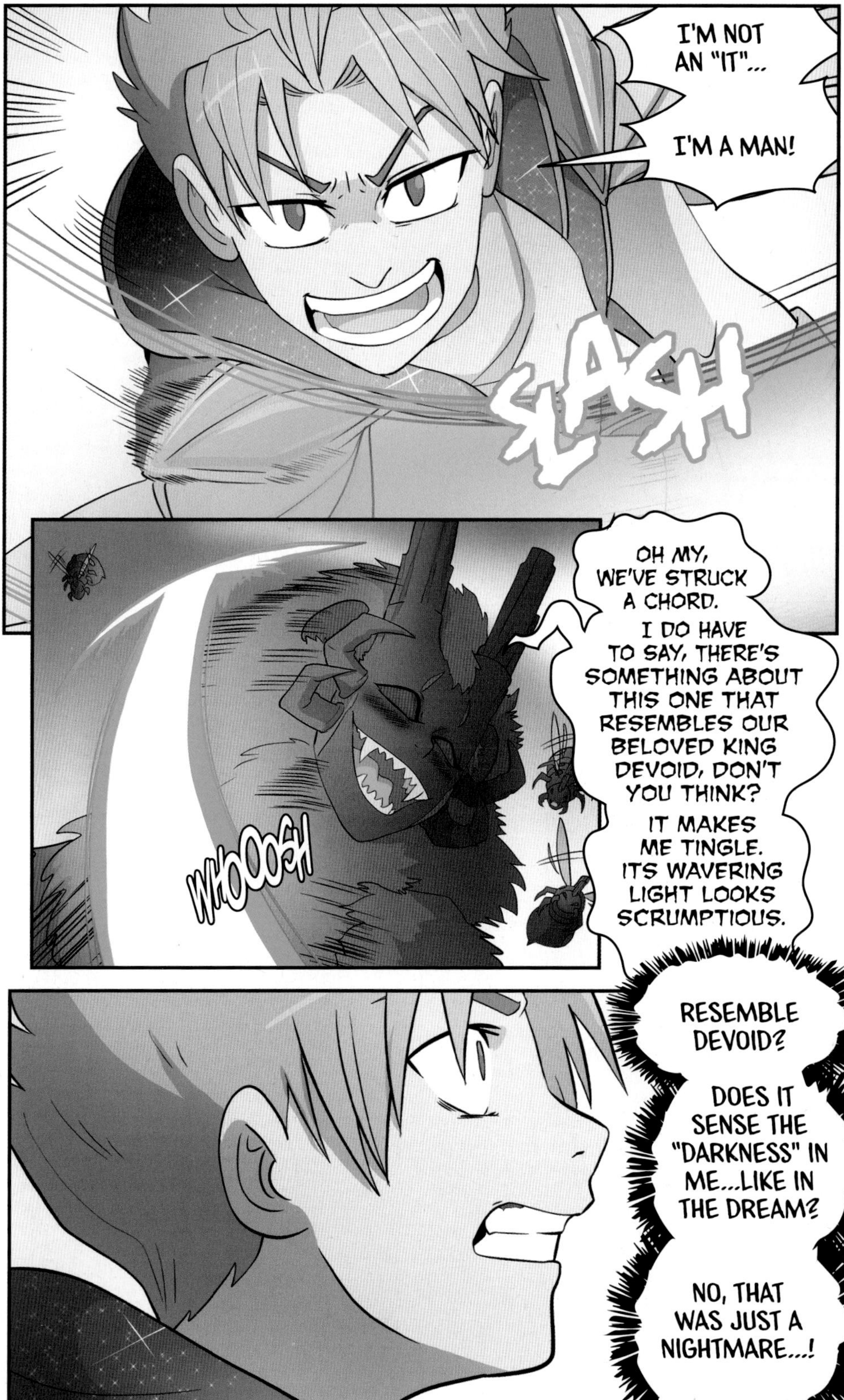
I'M NOT AN "IT"...
I'M A MAN!
SLASH
OH MY, WE'VE STRUCK A CHORD.
I DO HAVE TO SAY, THERE'S SOMETHING ABOUT THIS ONE THAT RESEMBLES OUR BELOVED KING DEVOID, DON'T YOU THINK?
IT MAKES ME TINGLE. ITS WAVERING LIGHT LOOKS SCRUMPTIOUS.
WHOOOSH
RESEMBLE DEVOID?
DOES IT SENSE THE "DARKNESS" IN ME...LIKE IN THE DREAM?
NO, THAT WAS JUST A NIGHTMARE...!

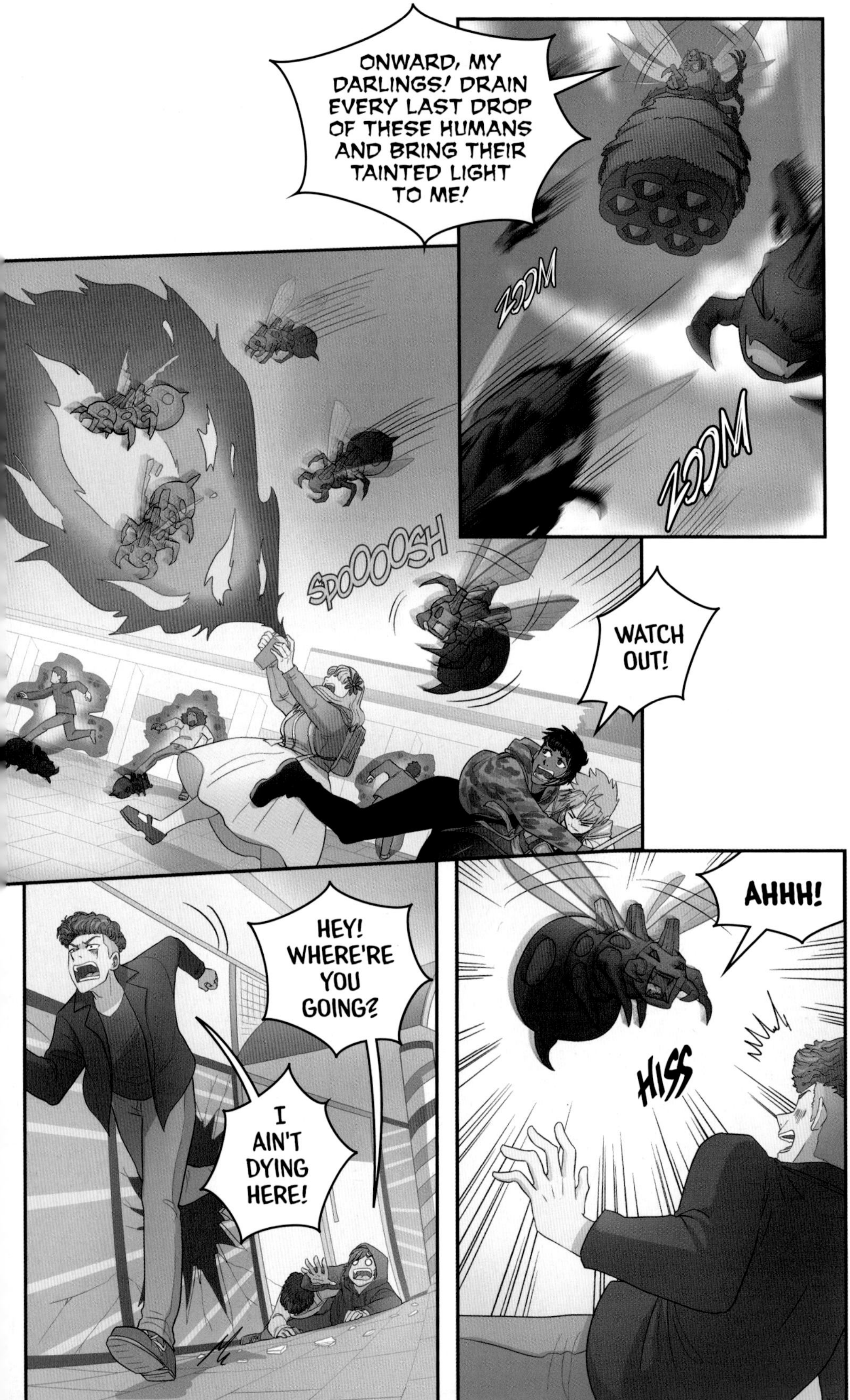
ONWARD, MY DARLINGS! DRAIN EVERY LAST DROP OF THESE HUMANS AND BRING THEIR TAINTED LIGHT TO ME!
ZOOM
ZOOM
SPOOOOSH
WATCH OUT!
HEY! WHERE'RE YOU GOING?
I AIN'T DYING HERE!
AHHH!
HISS

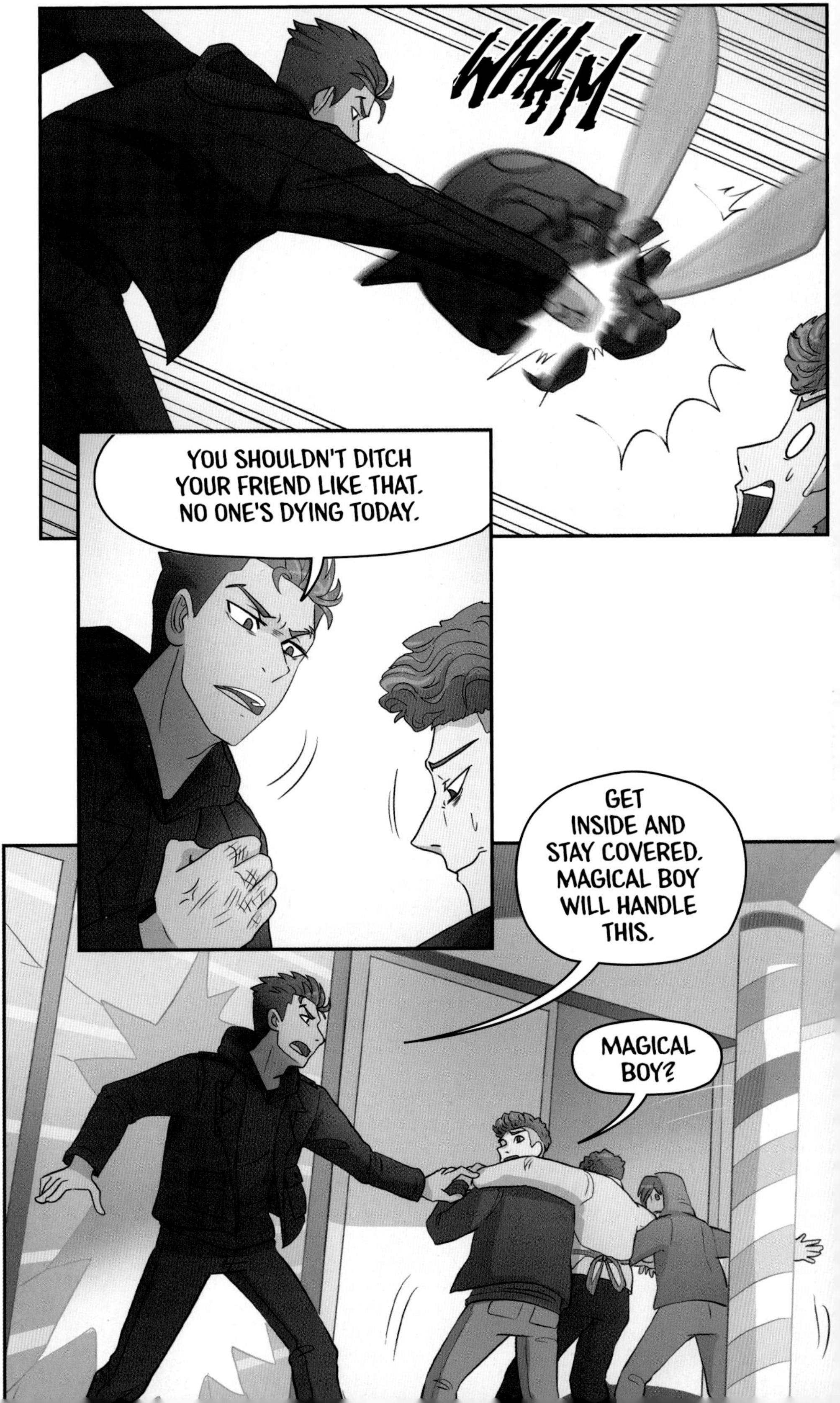
WHAM
YOU SHOULDN'T DITCH YOUR FRIEND LIKE THAT. NO ONE'S DYING TODAY.
GET INSIDE AND STAY COVERED. MAGICAL BOY WILL HANDLE THIS.
MAGICAL BOY?

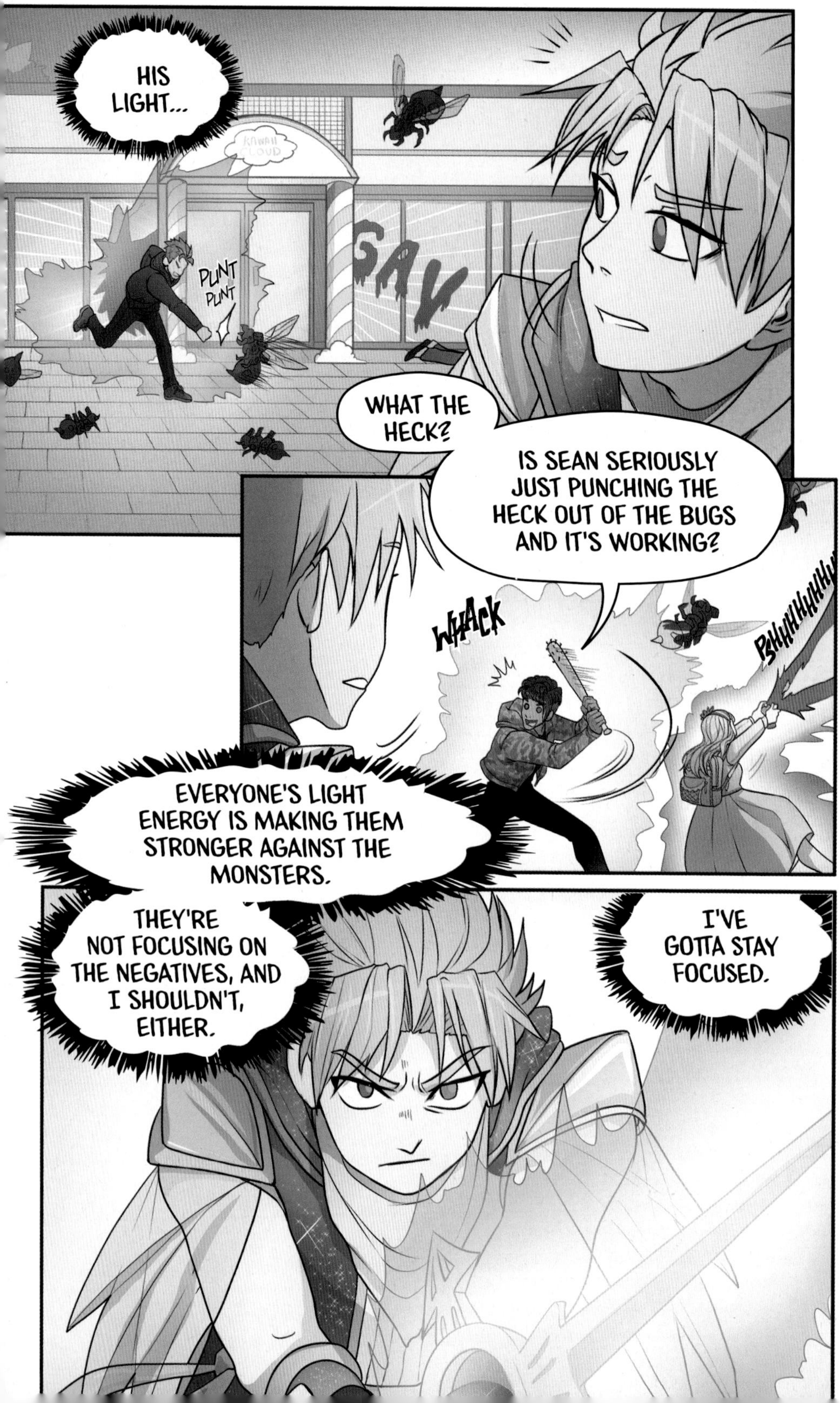
HIS LIGHT...
KAWAII CLOUD
PUNT PUNT
SAV
WHAT THE HECK?
IS SEAN SERIOUSLY JUST PUNCHING THE HECK OUT OF THE BUGS AND IT'S WORKING?
WHACK
BSHHHHHHH
EVERYONE'S LIGHT ENERGY IS MAKING THEM STRONGER AGAINST THE MONSTERS.
THEY'RE NOT FOCUSING ON THE NEGATIVES, AND I SHOULDN'T, EITHER.
I'VE GOTTA STAY FOCUSED.

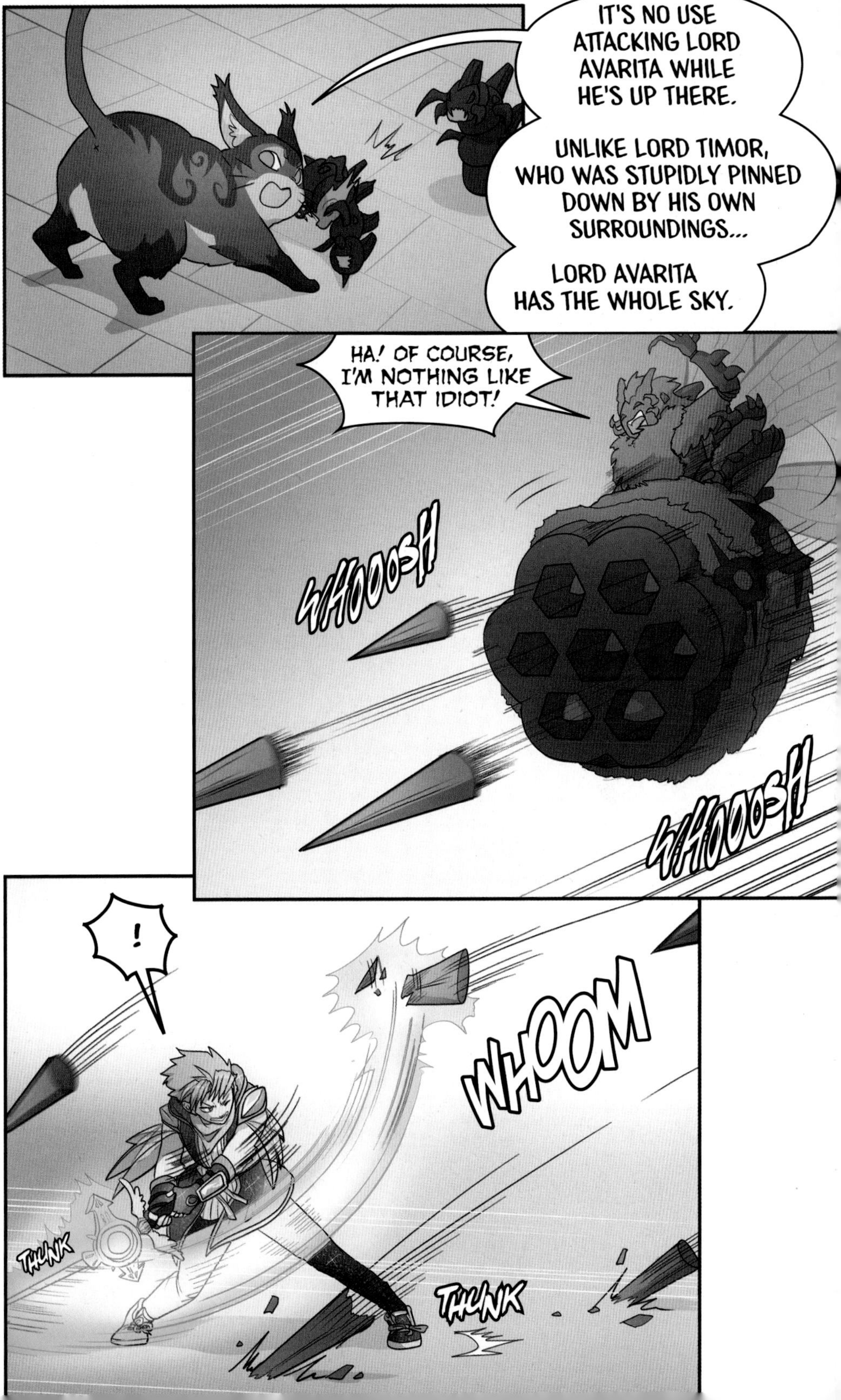
IT'S NO USE ATTACKING LORD AVARITA WHILE HE'S UP THERE.
UNLIKE LORD TIMOR, WHO WAS STUPIDLY PINNED DOWN BY HIS OWN SURROUNDINGS...
LORD AVARITA HAS THE WHOLE SKY.
HA! OF COURSE, I'M NOTHING LIKE THAT IDIOT!
WHOOOSH
WHOOOSH
!
WHOOM
THUNK
THUNK

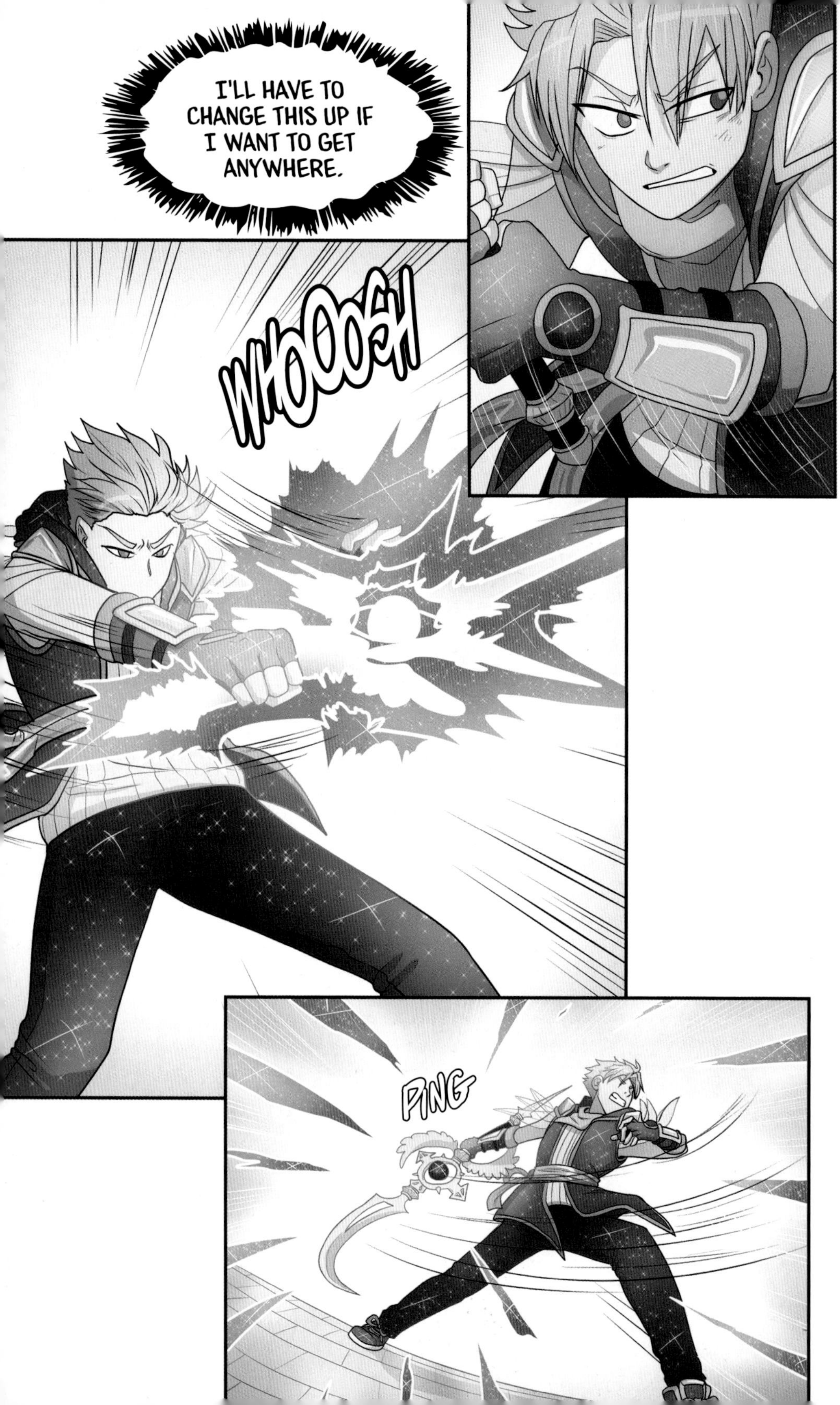
I'LL HAVE TO CHANGE THIS UP IF I WANT TO GET ANYWHERE.
WHOOOSH
PING

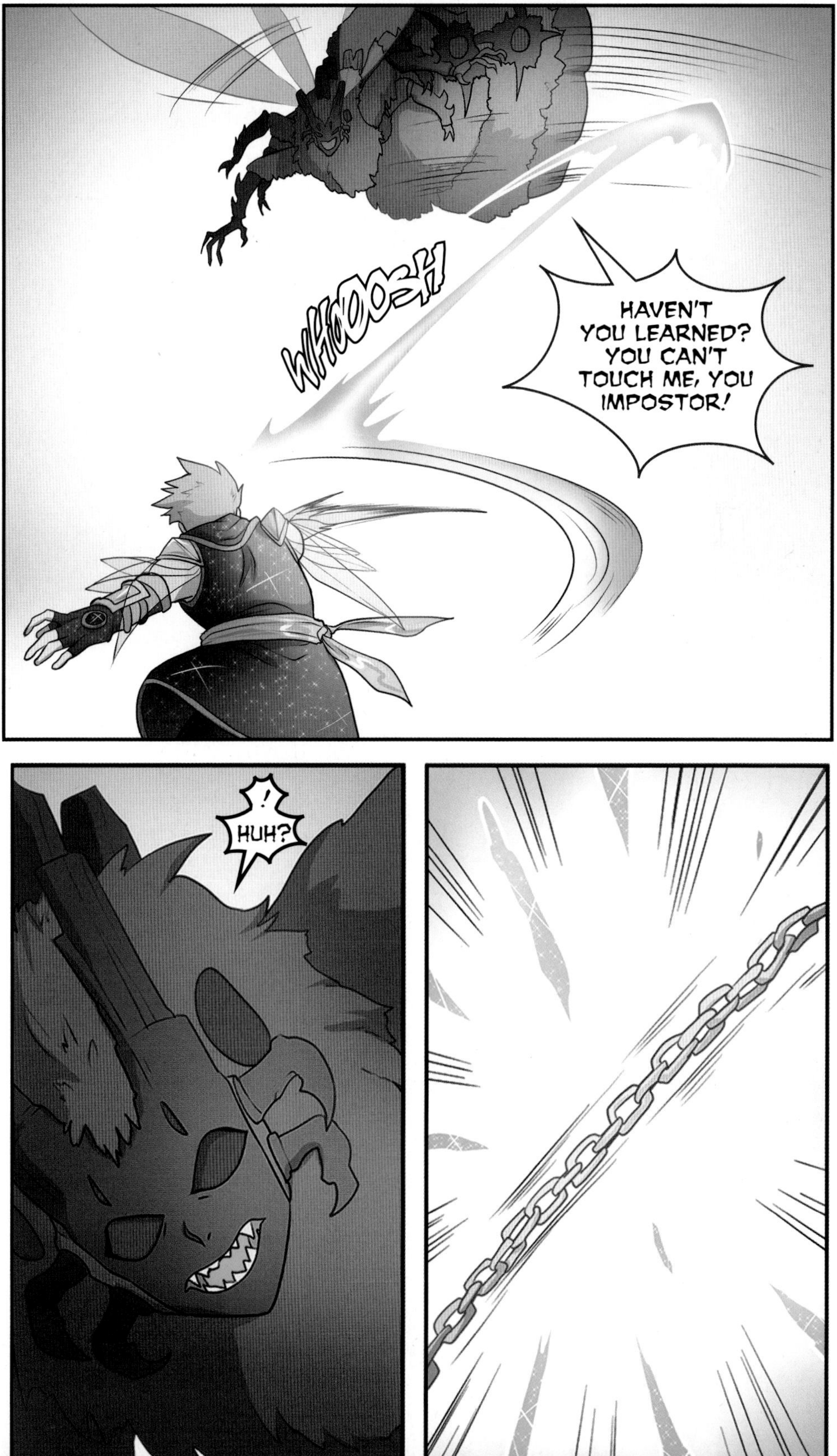
WHOOOSH
HAVEN'T YOU LEARNED? YOU CAN'T TOUCH ME, YOU IMPOSTOR!
!
HUH?

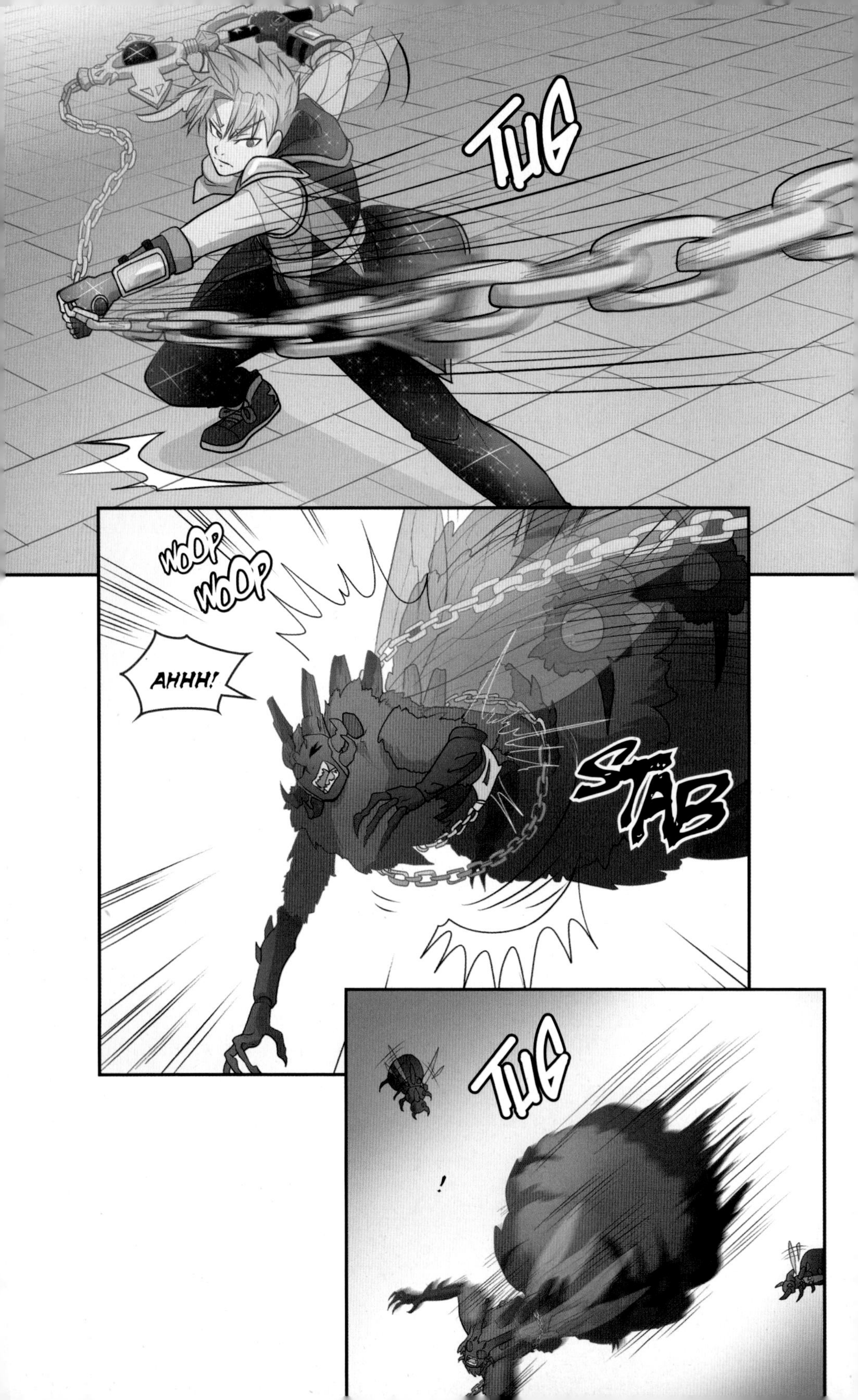
TUG
WOOP WOOP
AHHH!
STAB
TUG
!

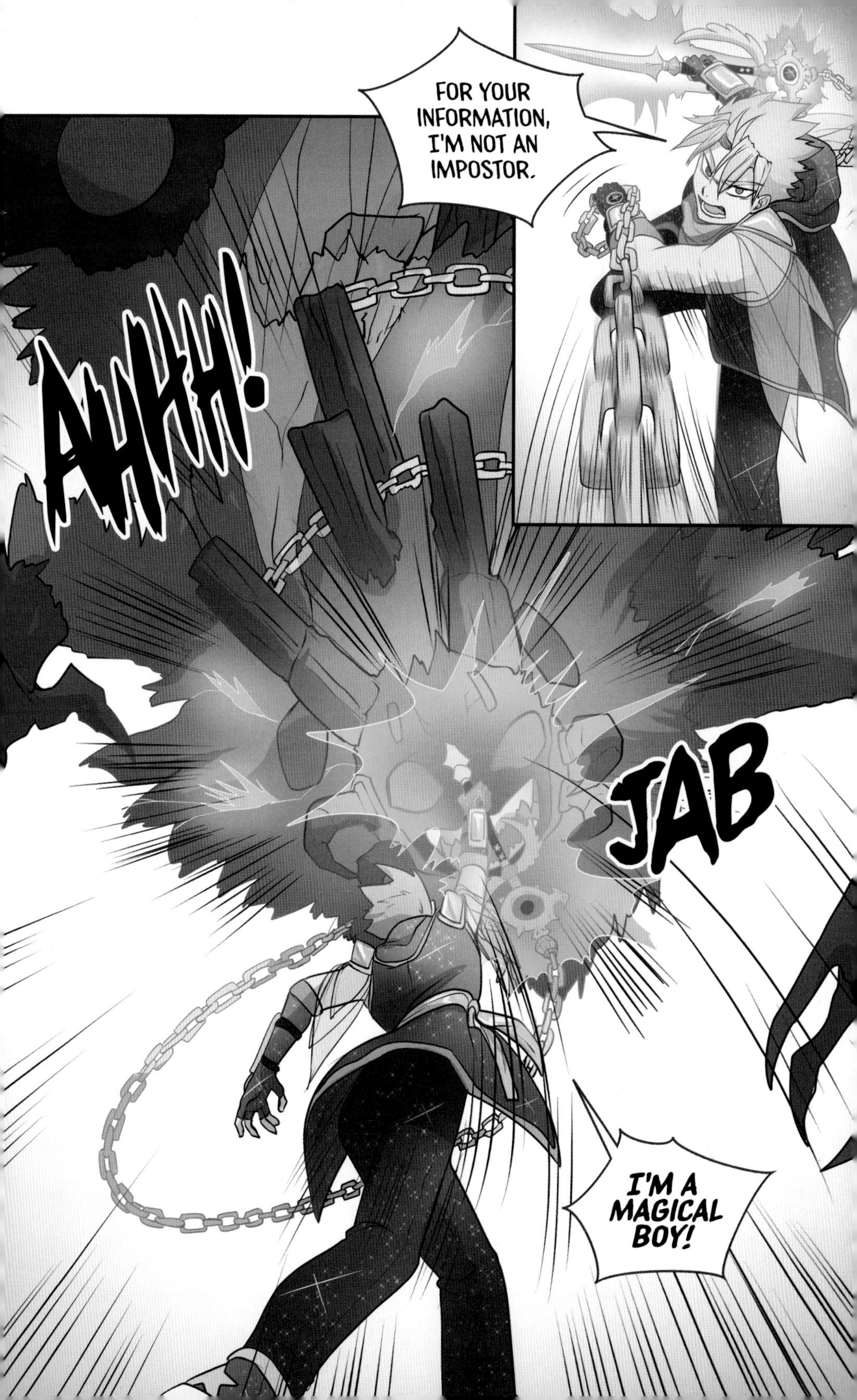
FOR YOUR INFORMATION, I'M NOT AN IMPOSTOR.
AHHH!
JAB
I'M A MAGICAL BOY!

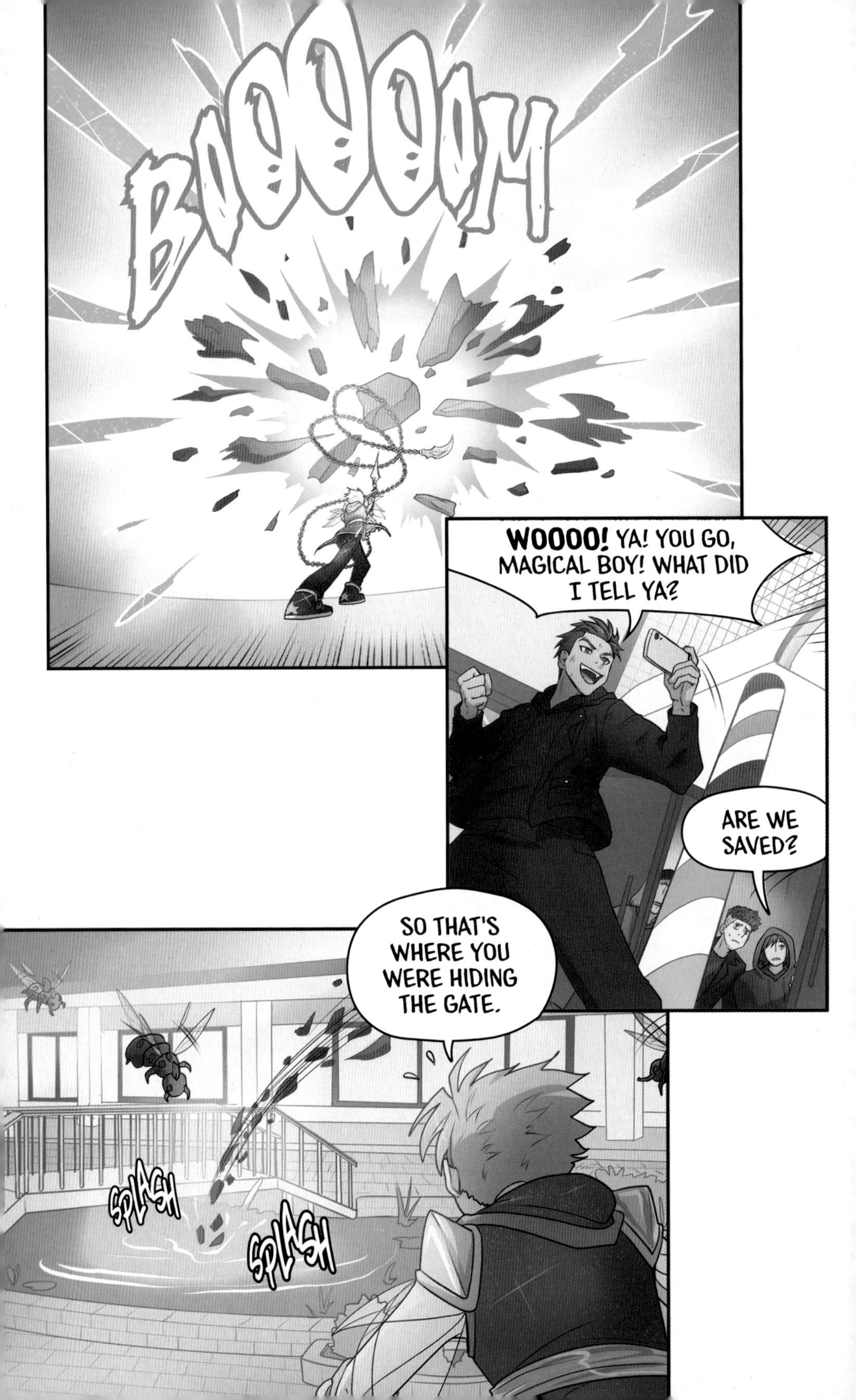
BOOOOOM
WOOOO! YA! YOU GO, MAGICAL BOY! WHAT DID I TELL YA?
ARE WE SAVED?
SO THAT'S WHERE YOU WERE HIDING THE GATE.
SPLASH
SPLASH

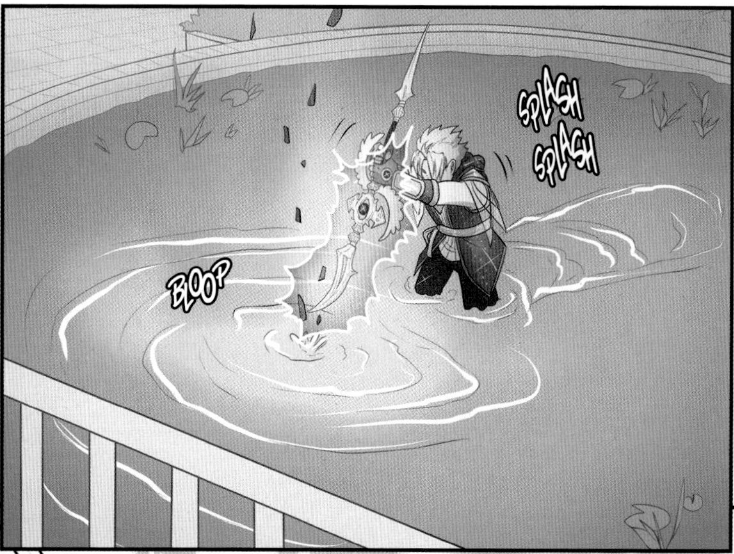
SPLASH
SPLASH
BLOOP

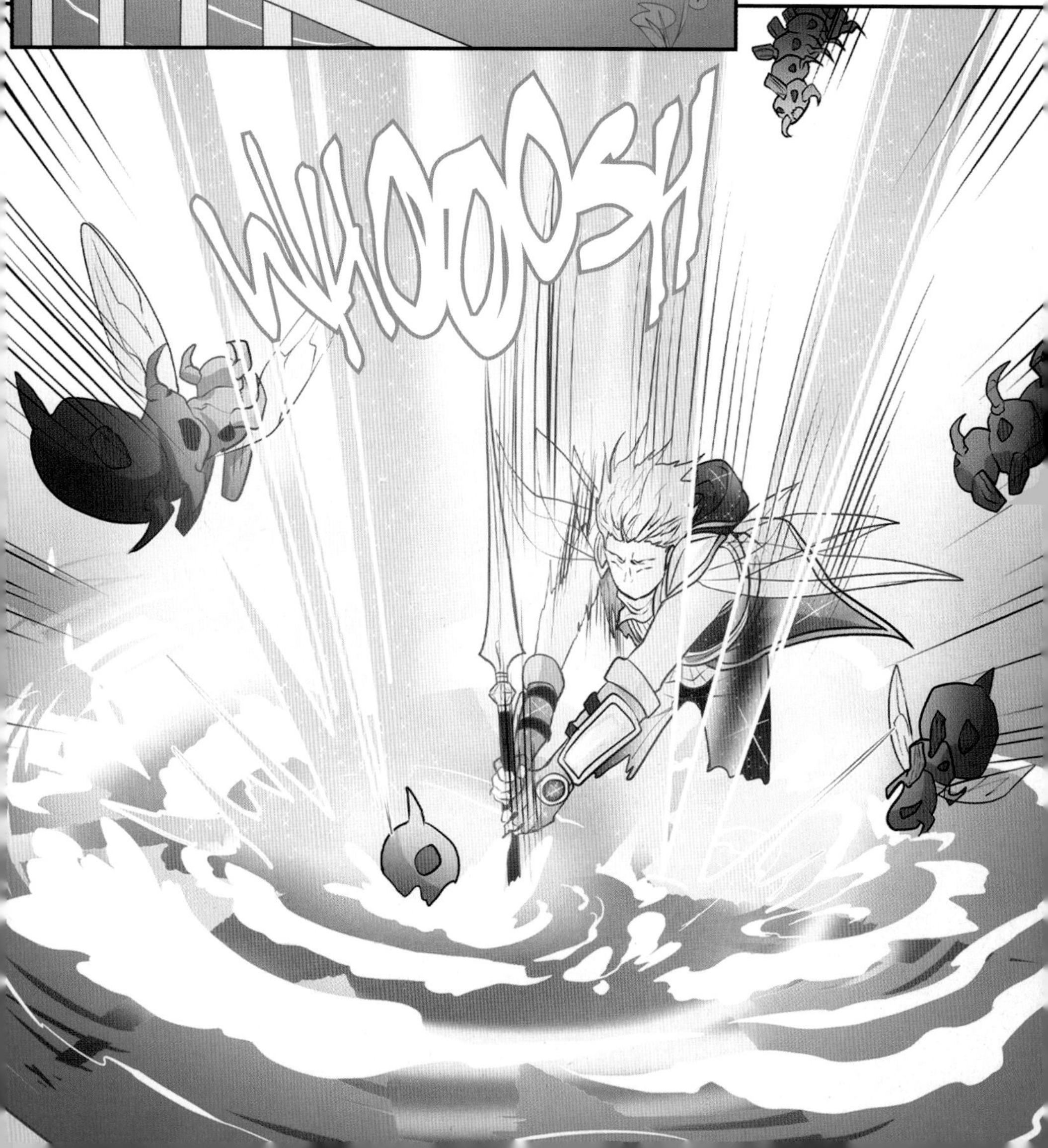
WHOOOSH

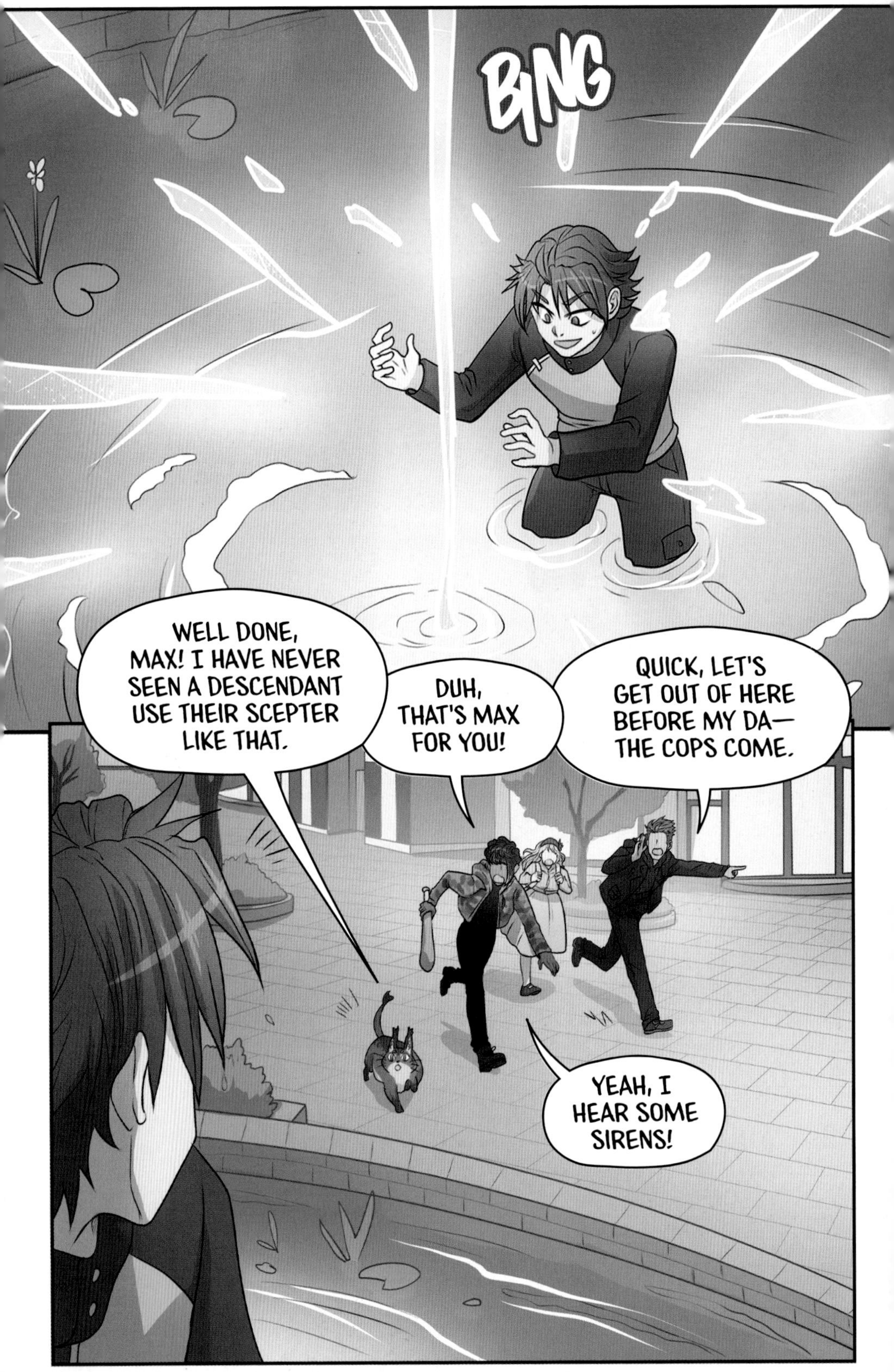
BING
WELL DONE, MAX! I HAVE NEVER SEEN A DESCENDANT USE THEIR SCEPTER LIKE THAT.
DUH, THAT'S MAX FOR YOU!
QUICK, LET'S GET OUT OF HERE BEFORE MY DA— THE COPS COME.
YEAH, I HEAR SOME SIRENS!

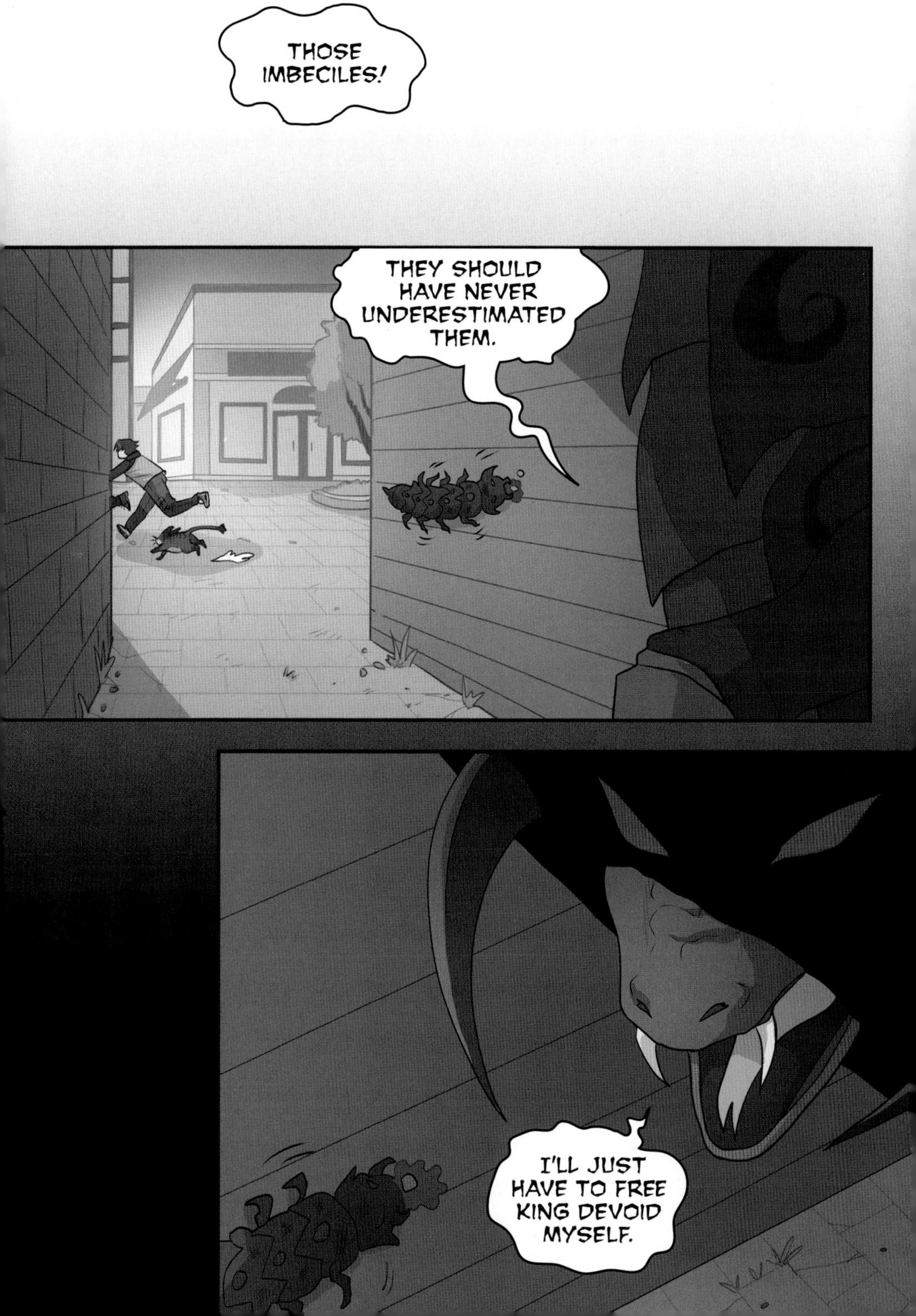
THOSE IMBECILES!
THEY SHOULD HAVE NEVER UNDERESTIMATED THEM.
I'LL JUST HAVE TO FREE KING DEVOID MYSELF.

EPISODE 21:
OUTED

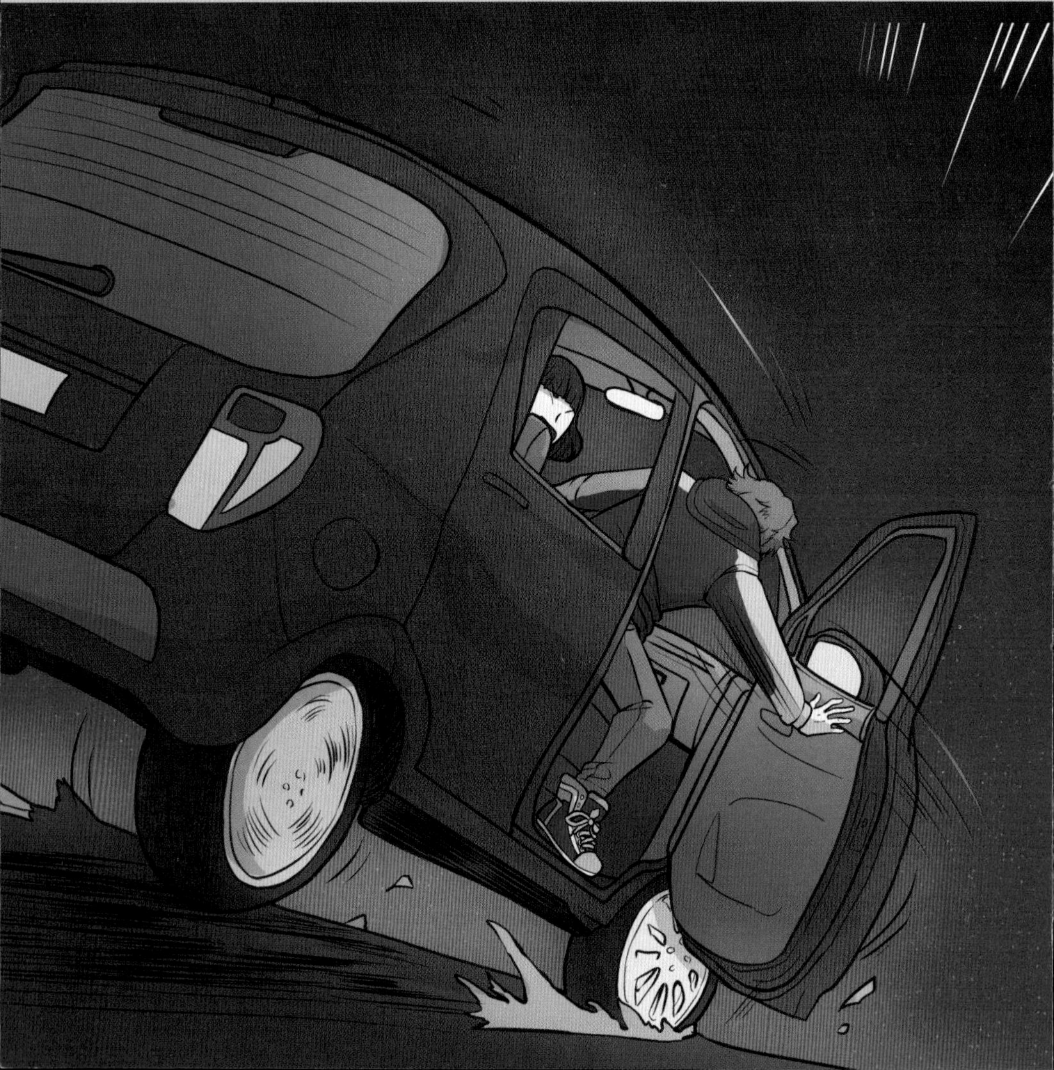

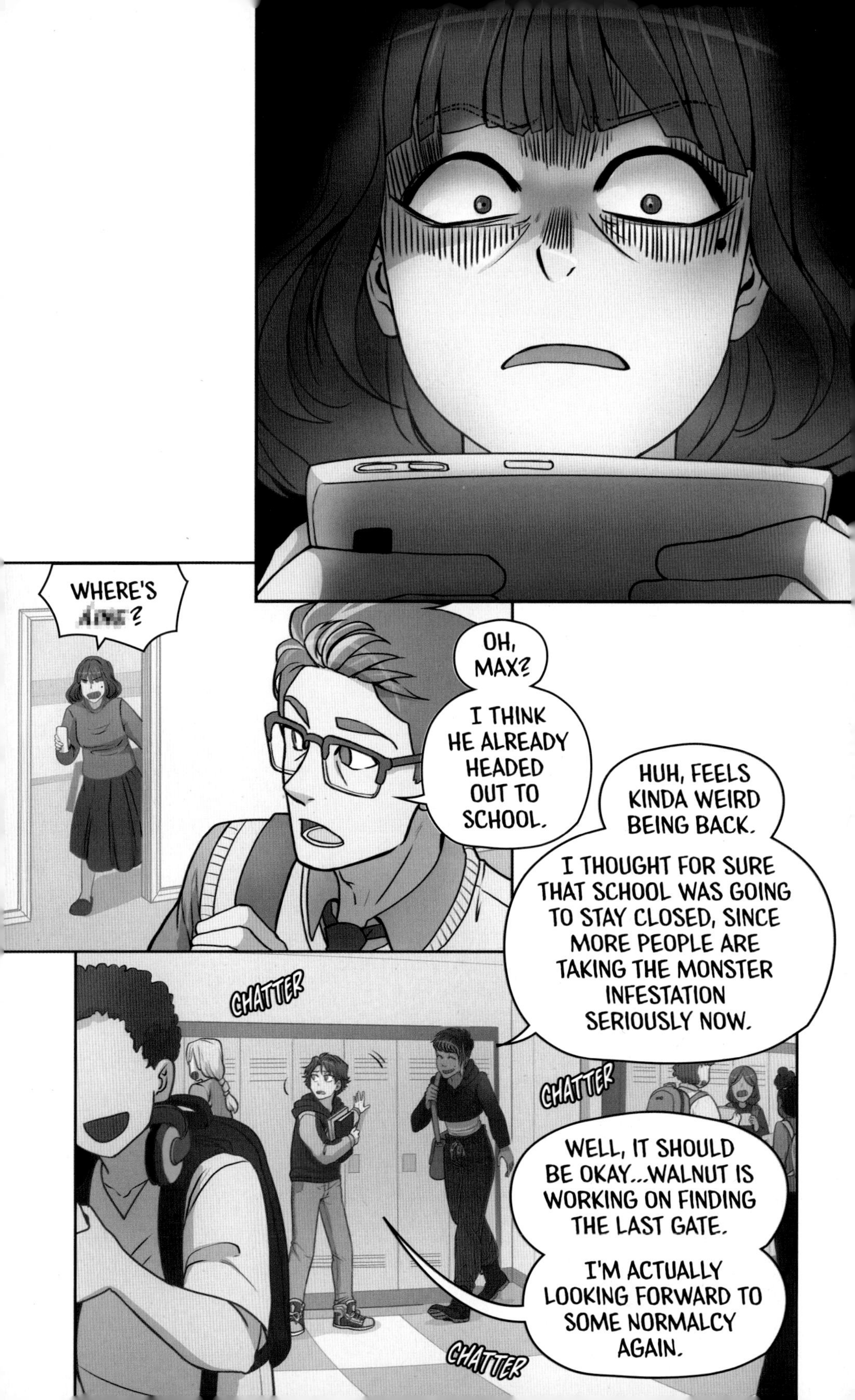
WHERE'S ?
OH, MAX?
I THINK HE ALREADY HEADED OUT TO SCHOOL.
HUH, FEELS KINDA WEIRD BEING BACK.
I THOUGHT FOR SURE THAT SCHOOL WAS GOING TO STAY CLOSED, SINCE MORE PEOPLE ARE TAKING THE MONSTER INFESTATION SERIOUSLY NOW.
CHATTER
CHATTER
WELL, IT SHOULD BE OKAY...WALNUT IS WORKING ON FINDING THE LAST GATE.
I'M ACTUALLY LOOKING FORWARD TO SOME NORMALCY AGAIN.
CHATTER

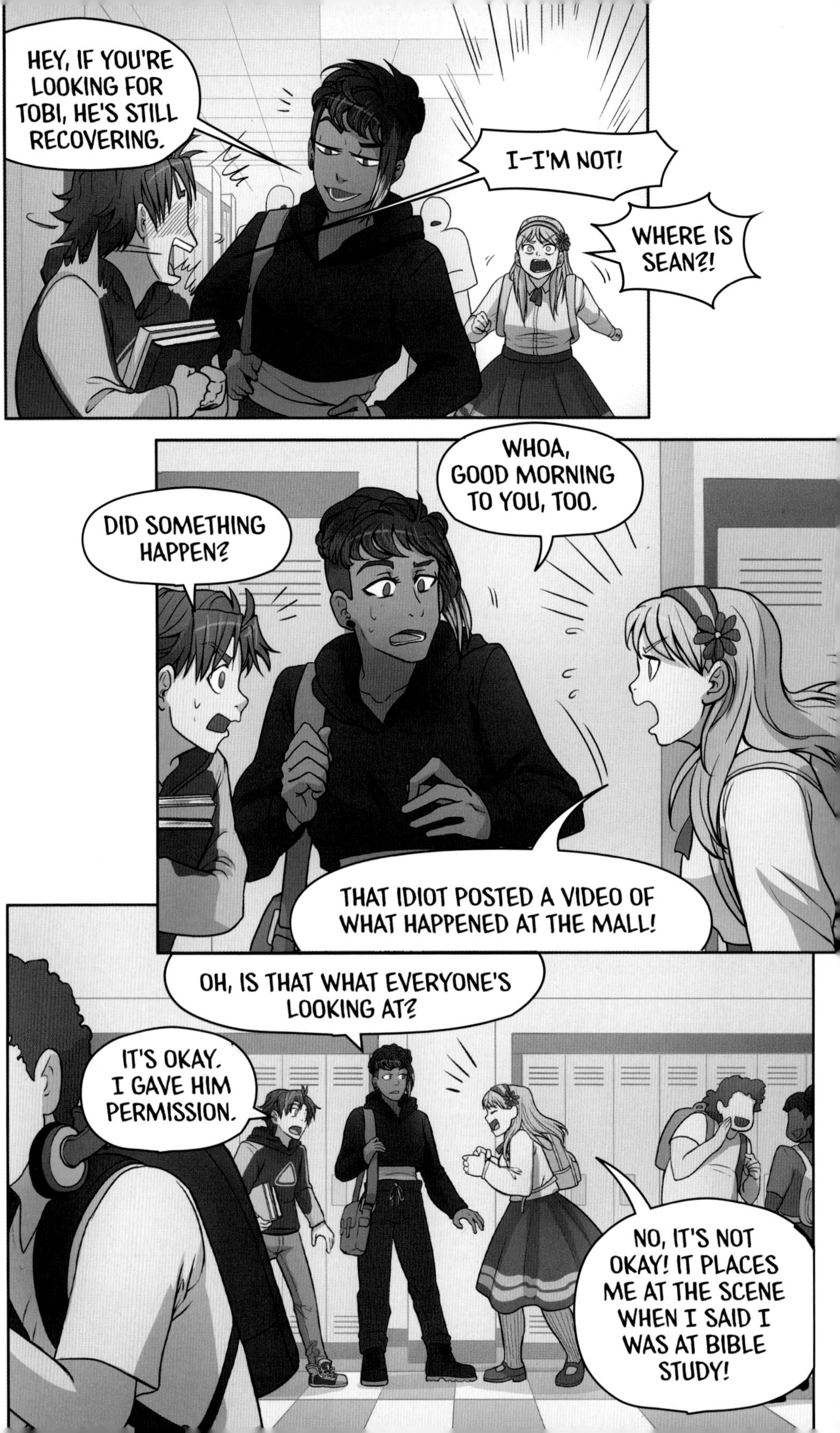
HEY, IF YOU'RE LOOKING FOR TOBI, HE'S STILL RECOVERING.
I-I'M NOT!
WHERE IS SEAN?!
WHOA, GOOD MORNING TO YOU, TOO.
DID SOMETHING HAPPEN?
THAT IDIOT POSTED A VIDEO OF WHAT HAPPENED AT THE MALL!
OH, IS THAT WHAT EVERYONE'S LOOKING AT?
IT'S OKAY. I GAVE HIM PERMISSION.
NO, IT'S NOT OKAY! IT PLACES ME AT THE SCENE WHEN I SAID I WAS AT BIBLE STUDY!

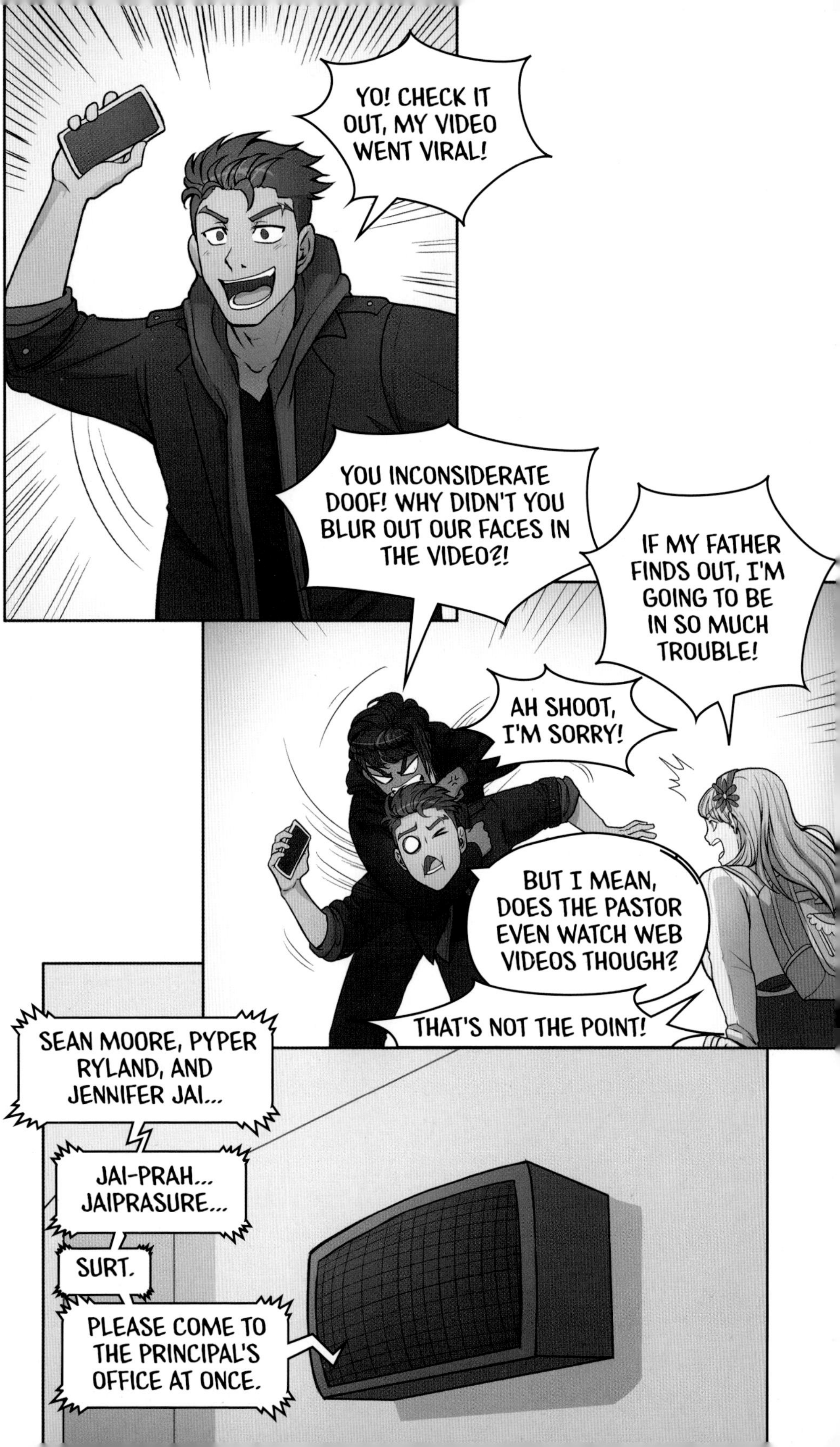
YO! CHECK IT OUT, MY VIDEO WENT VIRAL!
YOU INCONSIDERATE DOOF! WHY DIDN'T YOU BLUR OUT OUR FACES IN THE VIDEO?!
IF MY FATHER FINDS OUT, I'M GOING TO BE IN SO MUCH TROUBLE!
AH SHOOT, I'M SORRY!
BUT I MEAN, DOES THE PASTOR EVEN WATCH WEB VIDEOS THOUGH?
THAT'S NOT THE POINT!
SEAN MOORE, PYPER RYLAND, AND JENNIFER JAI...
JAI-PRAH... JAIPRASURE...
SURT.
PLEASE COME TO THE PRINCIPAL'S OFFICE AT ONCE.

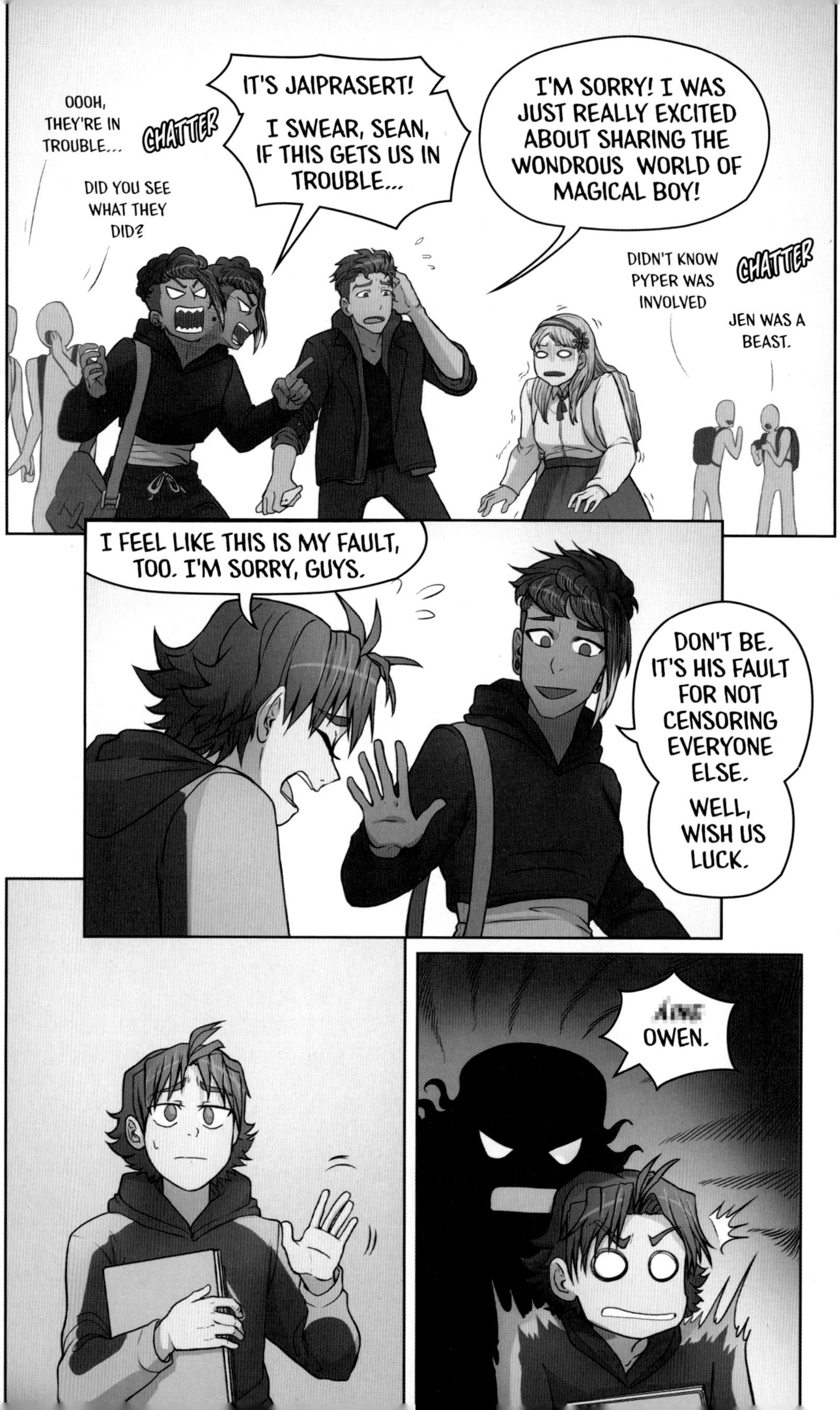
OOOH, THEY'RE IN TROUBLE...
CHATTER
DID YOU SEE WHAT THEY DID?
IT'S JAIPRASERT!
I SWEAR, SEAN, IF THIS GETS US IN TROUBLE...
I'M SORRY! I WAS JUST REALLY EXCITED ABOUT SHARING THE WONDROUS WORLD OF MAGICAL BOY!
DIDN'T KNOW PYPER WAS INVOLVED
CHATTER
JEN WAS A BEAST.
I FEEL LIKE THIS IS MY FAULT, TOO. I'M SORRY, GUYS.
DON'T BE. IT'S HIS FAULT FOR NOT CENSORING EVERYONE ELSE.
WELL, WISH US LUCK.
OWEN.

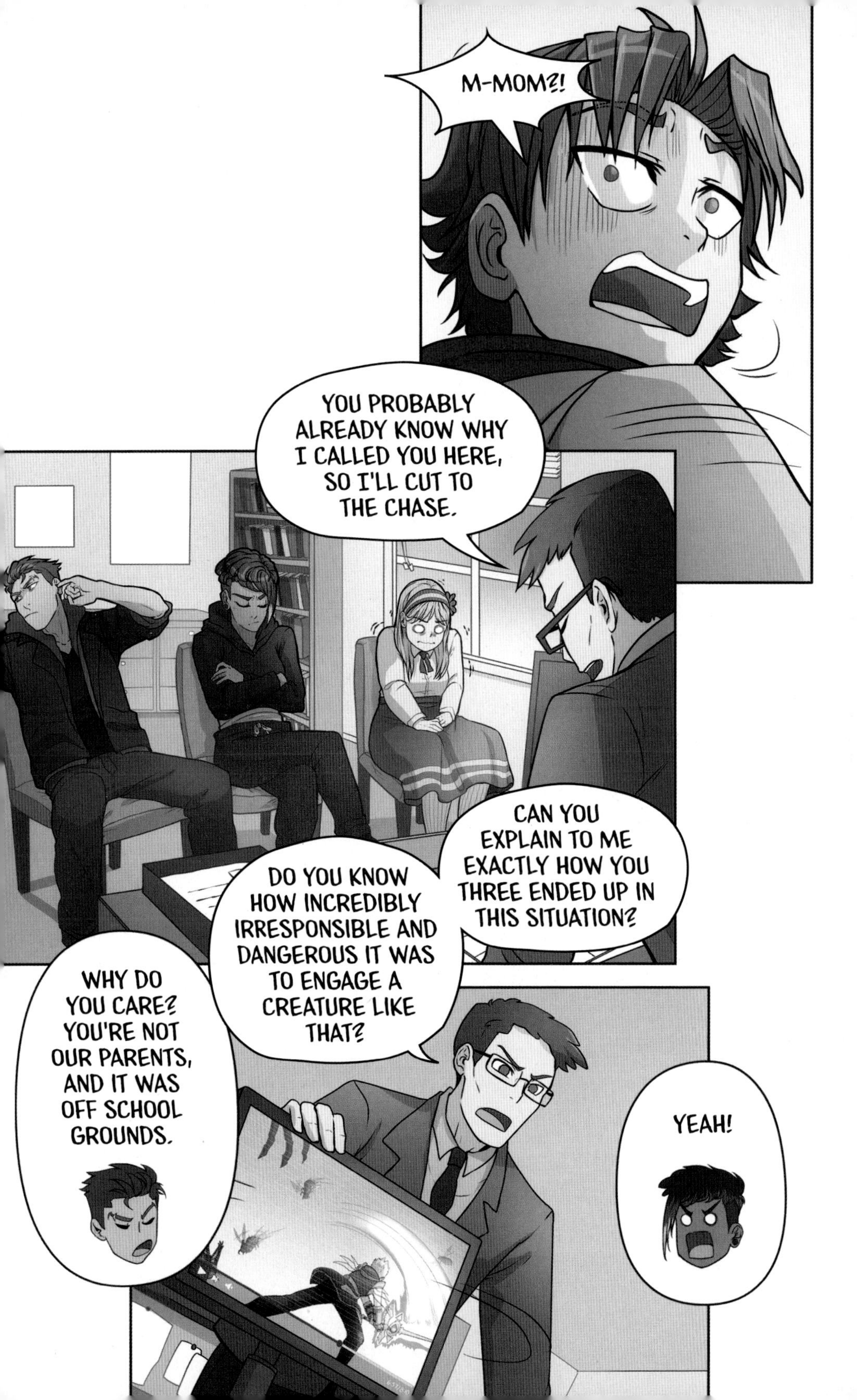
M-MOM?!
YOU PROBABLY ALREADY KNOW WHY I CALLED YOU HERE, SO I'LL CUT TO THE CHASE.
CAN YOU EXPLAIN TO ME EXACTLY HOW YOU THREE ENDED UP IN THIS SITUATION?
DO YOU KNOW HOW INCREDIBLY IRRESPONSIBLE AND DANGEROUS IT WAS TO ENGAGE A CREATURE LIKE THAT?
WHY DO YOU CARE? YOU'RE NOT OUR PARENTS, AND IT WAS OFF SCHOOL GROUNDS.
YEAH!

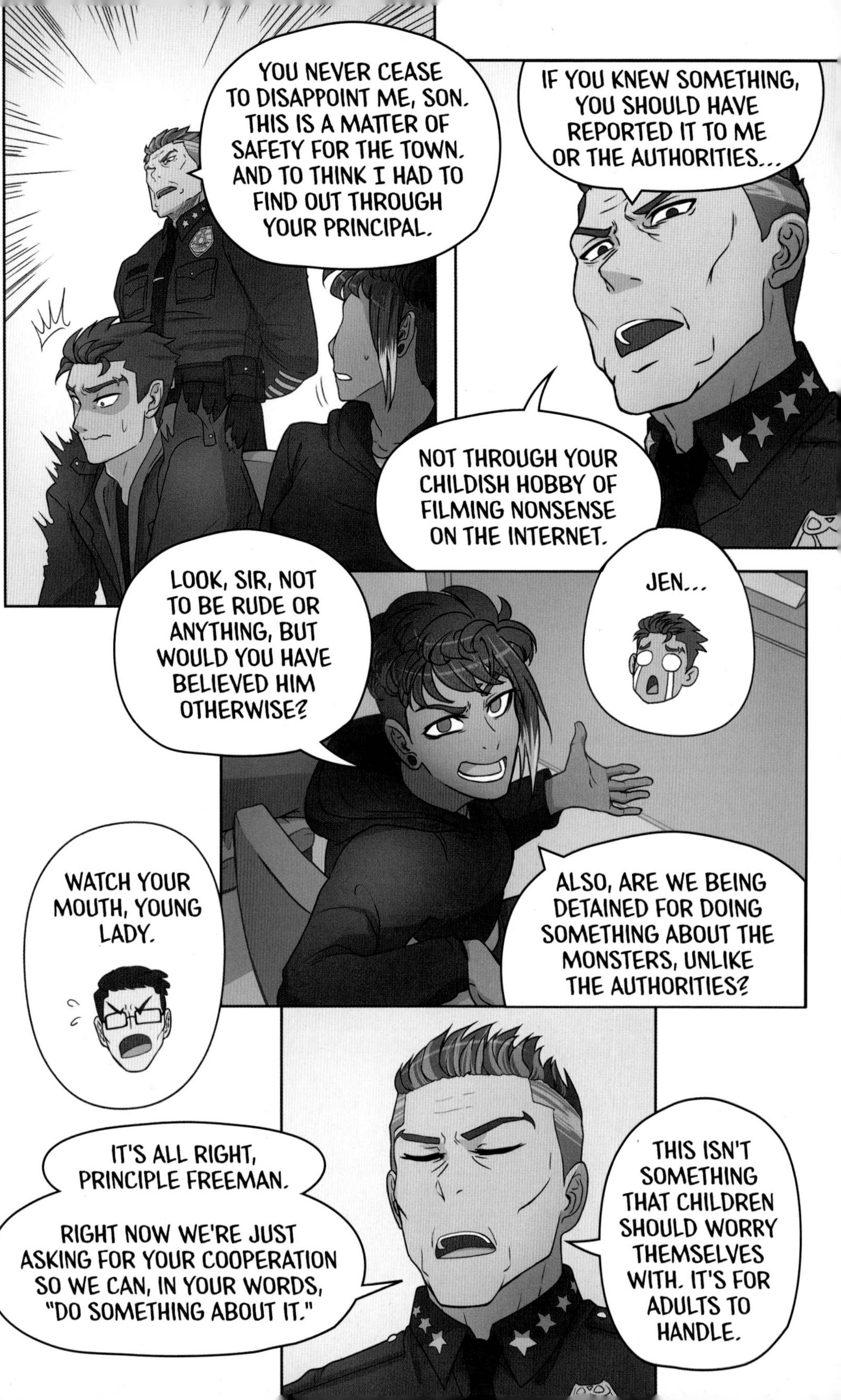
YOU NEVER CEASE TO DISAPPOINT ME, SON. THIS IS A MATTER OF SAFETY FOR THE TOWN. AND TO THINK I HAD TO FIND OUT THROUGH YOUR PRINCIPAL.
IF YOU KNEW SOMETHING, YOU SHOULD HAVE REPORTED IT TO ME OR THE AUTHORITIES...
NOT THROUGH YOUR CHILDISH HOBBY OF FILMING NONSENSE ON THE INTERNET.
LOOK, SIR, NOT TO BE RUDE OR ANYTHING, BUT WOULD YOU HAVE BELIEVED HIM OTHERWISE?
JEN...
ALSO, ARE WE BEING DETAINED FOR DOING SOMETHING ABOUT THE MONSTERS, UNLIKE THE AUTHORITIES?
WATCH YOUR MOUTH, YOUNG LADY.
IT'S ALL RIGHT, PRINCIPLE FREEMAN.
RIGHT NOW WE'RE JUST ASKING FOR YOUR COOPERATION SO WE CAN, IN YOUR WORDS, "DO SOMETHING ABOUT IT."
THIS ISN'T SOMETHING THAT CHILDREN SHOULD WORRY THEMSELVES WITH. IT'S FOR ADULTS TO HANDLE.

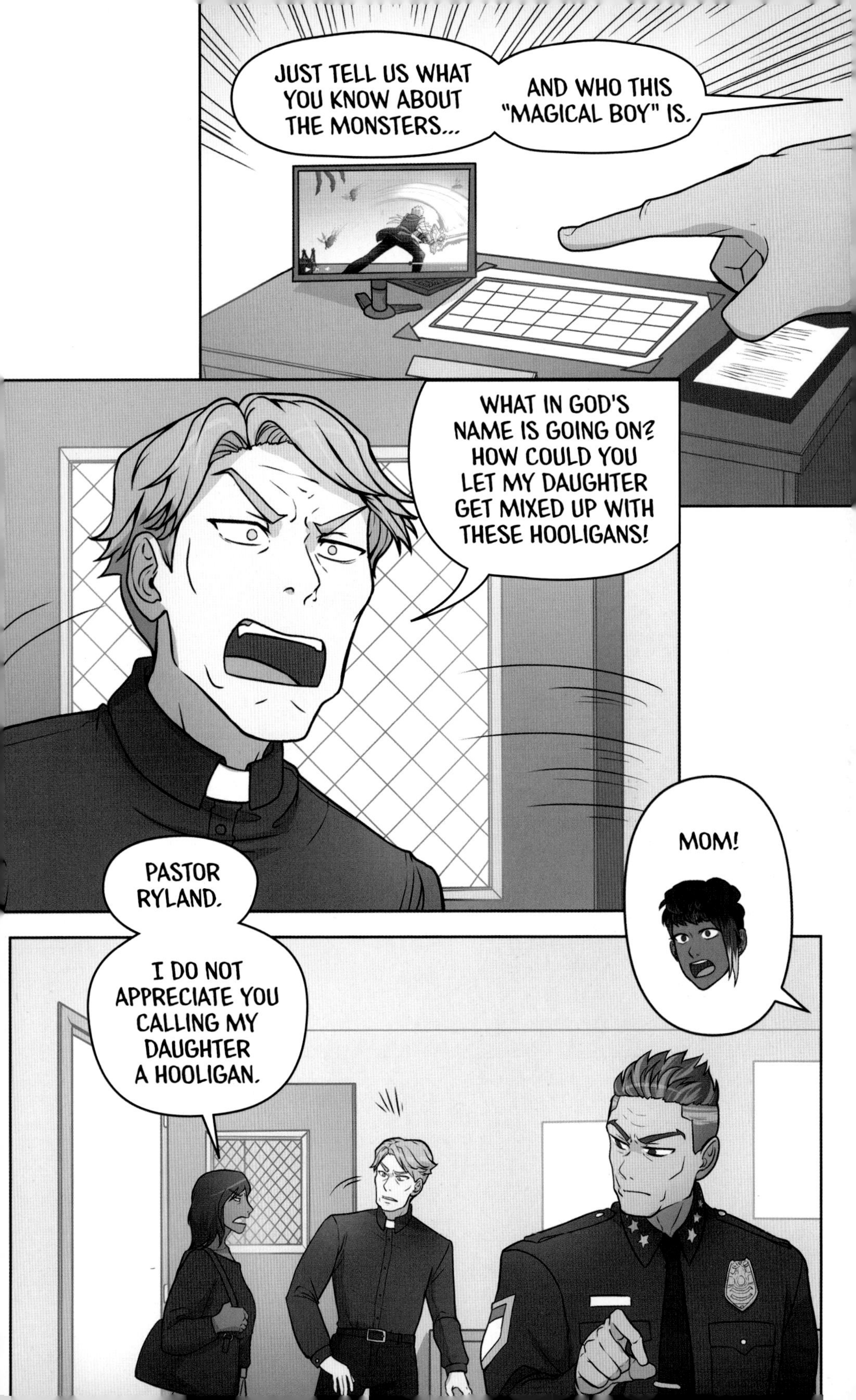
JUST TELL US WHAT YOU KNOW ABOUT THE MONSTERS...
AND WHO THIS "MAGICAL BOY" IS.
WHAT IN GOD'S NAME IS GOING ON? HOW COULD YOU LET MY DAUGHTER GET MIXED UP WITH THESE HOOLIGANS!
MOM!
PASTOR RYLAND.
I DO NOT APPRECIATE YOU CALLING MY DAUGHTER A HOOLIGAN.

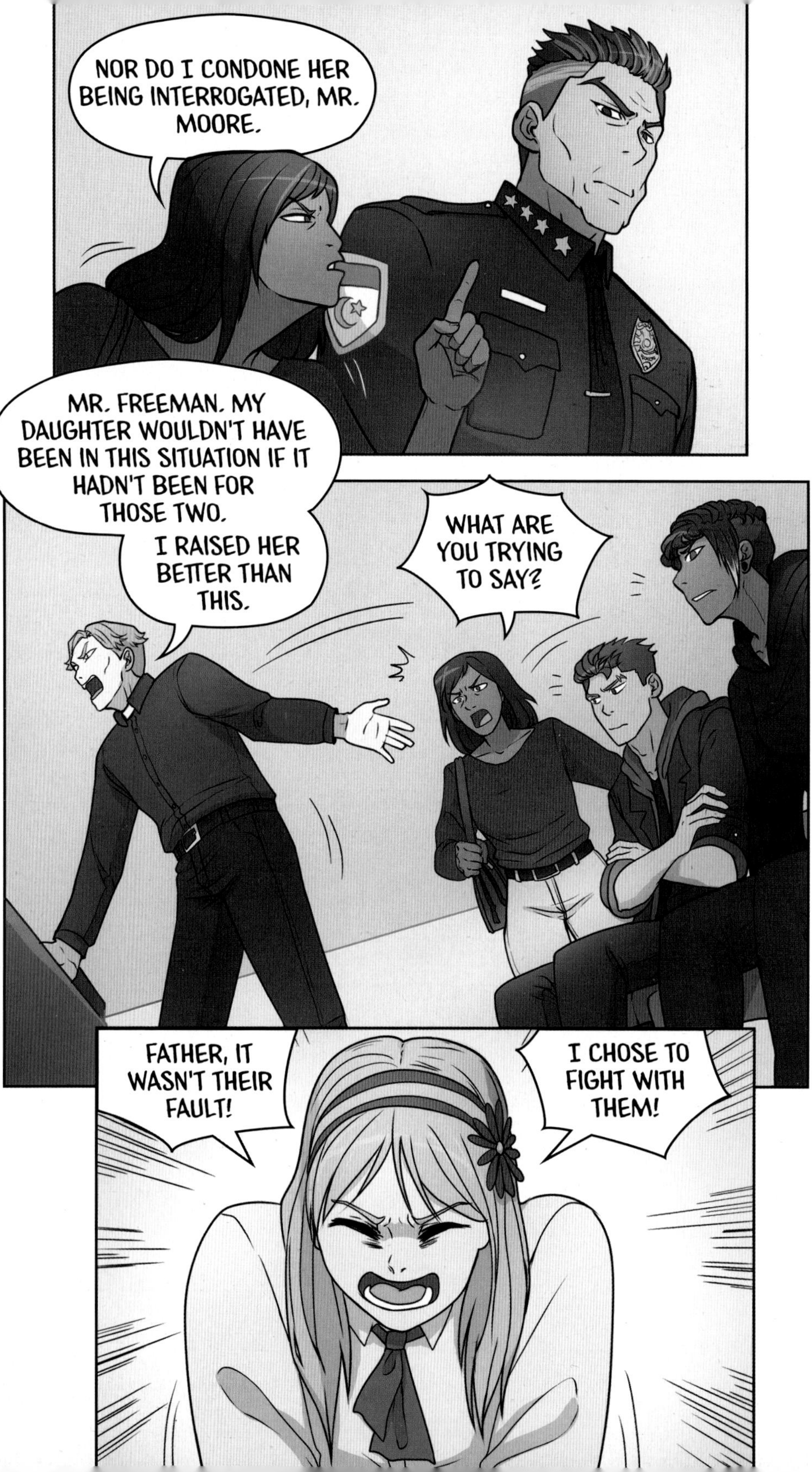
NOR DO I CONDONE HER BEING INTERROGATED, MR. MOORE.
MR. FREEMAN. MY DAUGHTER WOULDN'T HAVE BEEN IN THIS SITUATION IF IT HADN'T BEEN FOR THOSE TWO.
I RAISED HER BETTER THAN THIS.
WHAT ARE YOU TRYING TO SAY?
FATHER, IT WASN'T THEIR FAULT!
I CHOSE TO FIGHT WITH THEM!

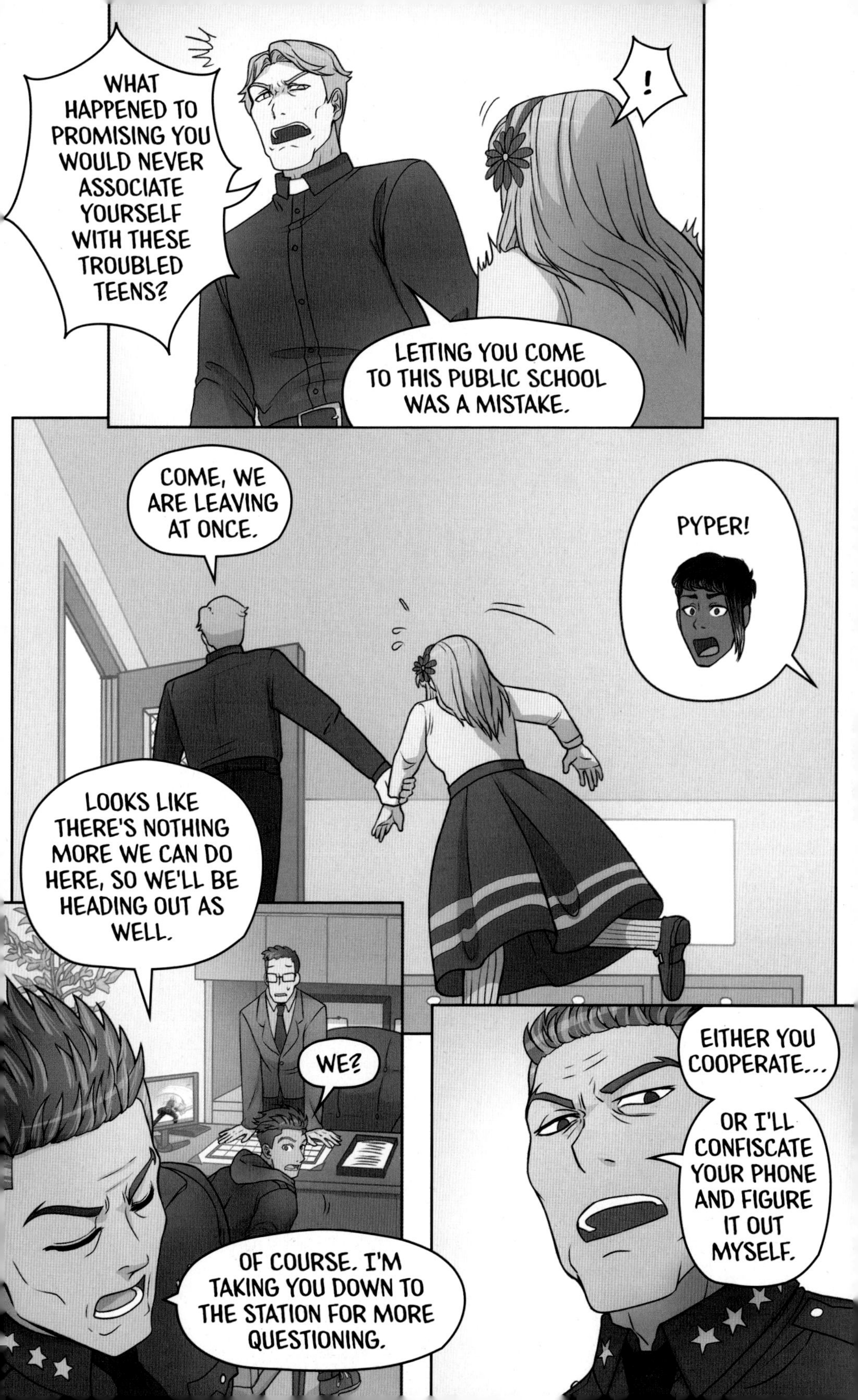
WHAT HAPPENED TO PROMISING YOU WOULD NEVER ASSOCIATE YOURSELF WITH THESE TROUBLED TEENS?
!
LETTING YOU COME TO THIS PUBLIC SCHOOL WAS A MISTAKE.
COME, WE ARE LEAVING AT ONCE.
PYPER!
LOOKS LIKE THERE'S NOTHING MORE WE CAN DO HERE, SO WE'LL BE HEADING OUT AS WELL.
WE?
OF COURSE. I'M TAKING YOU DOWN TO THE STATION FOR MORE QUESTIONING.
EITHER YOU COOPERATE...
OR I'LL CONFISCATE YOUR PHONE AND FIGURE IT OUT MYSELF.

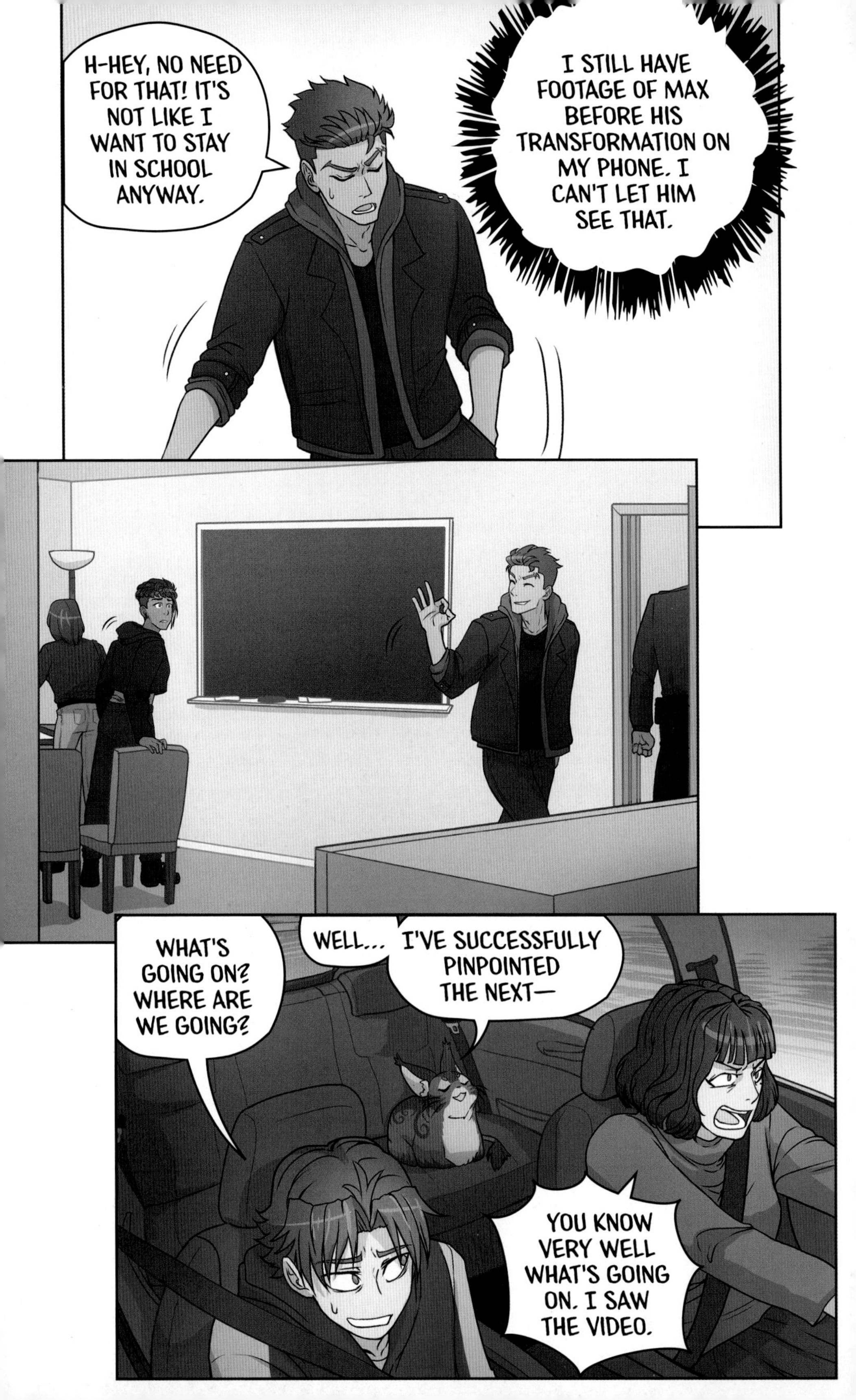
H-HEY, NO NEED FOR THAT! IT'S NOT LIKE I WANT TO STAY IN SCHOOL ANYWAY.
I STILL HAVE FOOTAGE OF MAX BEFORE HIS TRANSFORMATION ON MY PHONE. I CAN'T LET HIM SEE THAT.
WHAT'S GOING ON? WHERE ARE WE GOING?
WELL...
I'VE SUCCESSFULLY PINPOINTED THE NEXT—
YOU KNOW VERY WELL WHAT'S GOING ON. I SAW THE VIDEO.

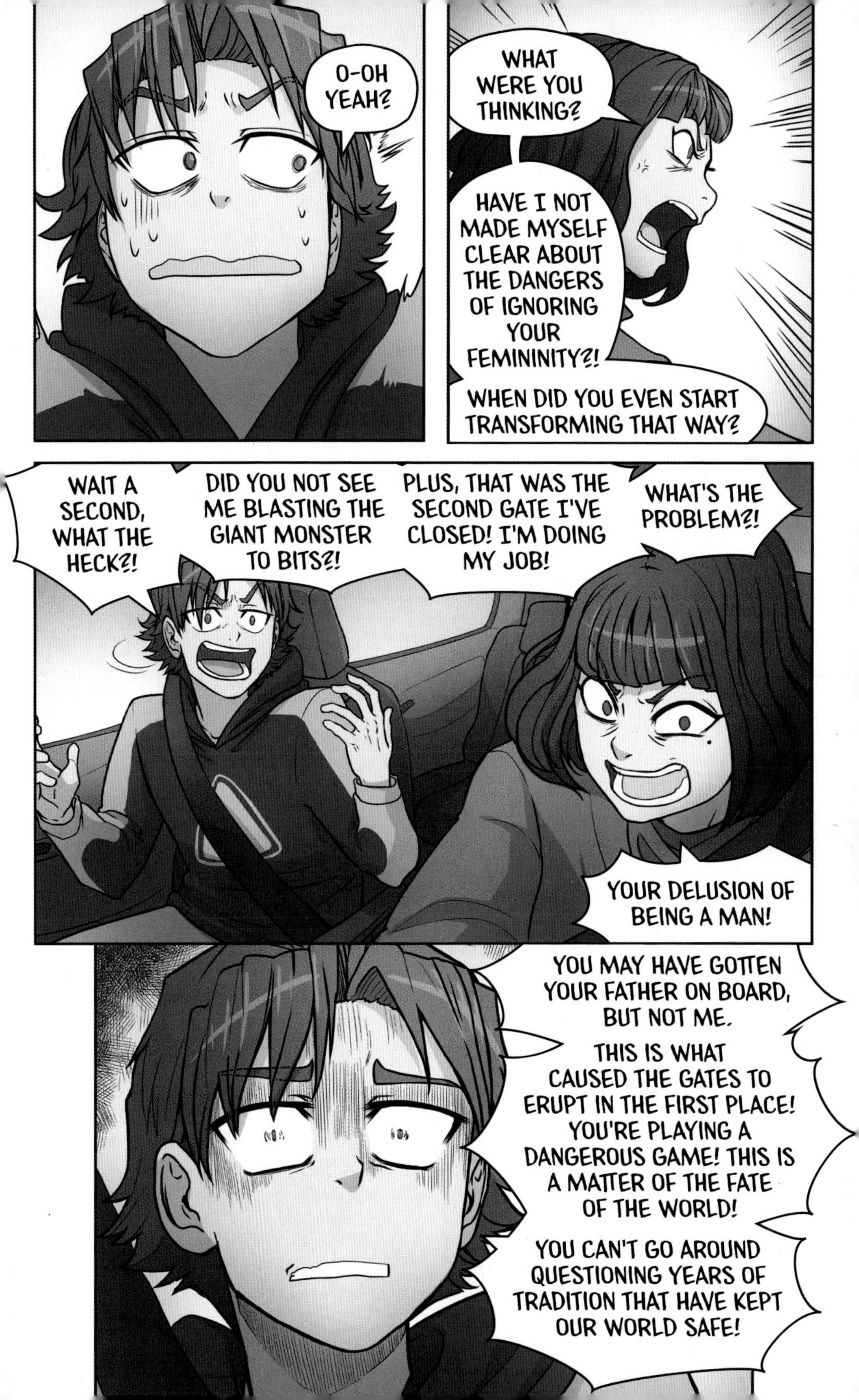

O-OH YEAH?
WHAT WERE YOU THINKING?
HAVE I NOT MADE MYSELF CLEAR ABOUT THE DANGERS OF IGNORING YOUR FEMININITY?!
WHEN DID YOU EVEN START TRANSFORMING THAT WAY?
WAIT A SECOND, WHAT THE HECK?!
DID YOU NOT SEE ME BLASTING THE GIANT MONSTER TO BITS?!
PLUS, THAT WAS THE SECOND GATE I'VE CLOSED! I'M DOING MY JOB!
WHAT'S THE PROBLEM?!
YOUR DELUSION OF BEING A MAN!
YOU MAY HAVE GOTTEN YOUR FATHER ON BOARD, BUT NOT ME.
THIS IS WHAT CAUSED THE GATES TO ERUPT IN THE FIRST PLACE! YOU'RE PLAYING A DANGEROUS GAME! THIS IS A MATTER OF THE FATE OF THE WORLD!
YOU CAN'T GO AROUND QUESTIONING YEARS OF TRADITION THAT HAVE KEPT OUR WORLD SAFE!

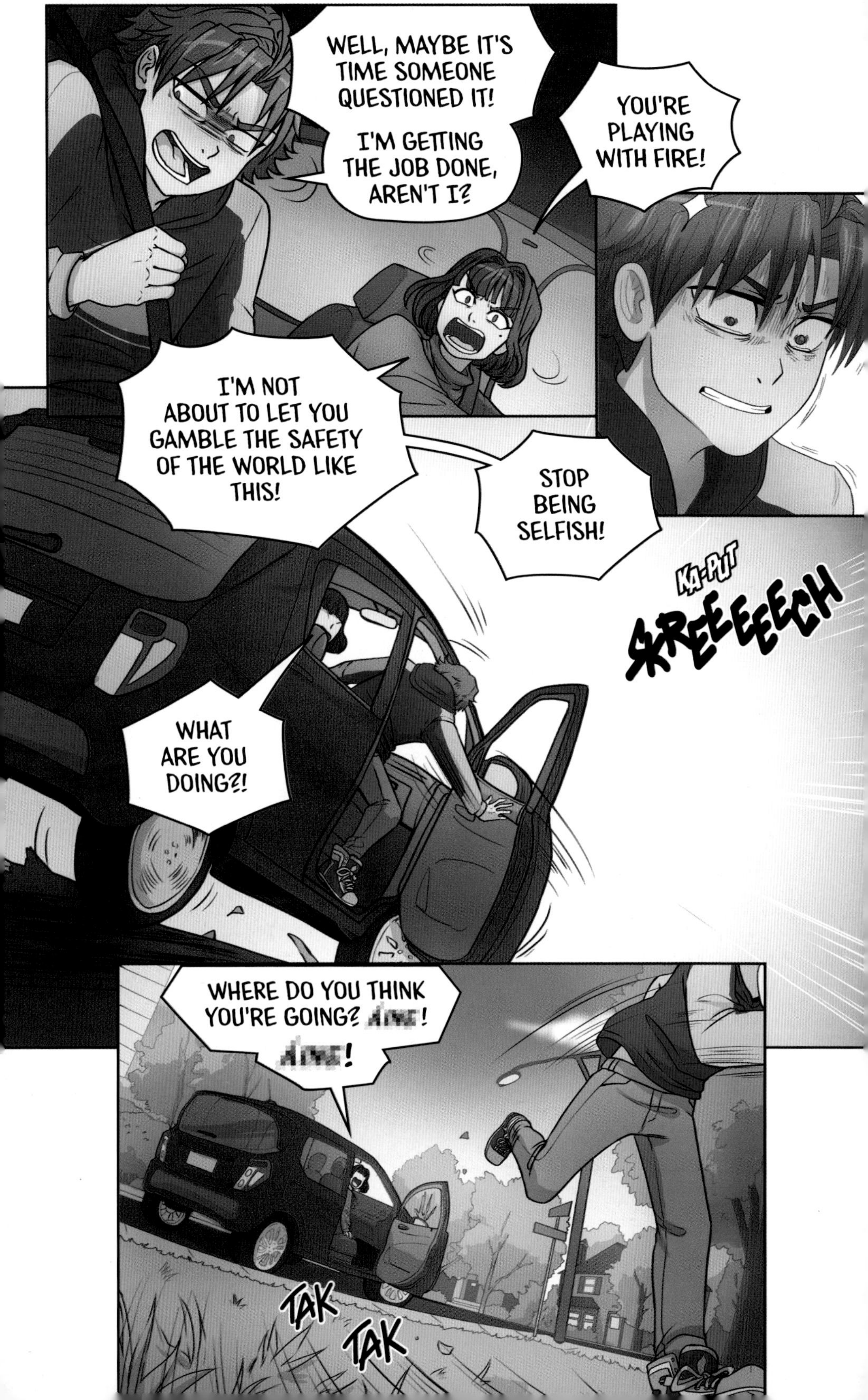
WELL, MAYBE IT'S TIME SOMEONE QUESTIONED IT!
I'M GETTING THE JOB DONE, AREN'T I?
YOU'RE PLAYING WITH FIRE!
I'M NOT ABOUT TO LET YOU GAMBLE THE SAFETY OF THE WORLD LIKE THIS!
STOP BEING SELFISH!
KA-PUT
SKREEEEECH
WHAT ARE YOU DOING?!
WHERE DO YOU THINK YOU'RE GOING? [redacted]!
[redacted]!
TAK
TAK

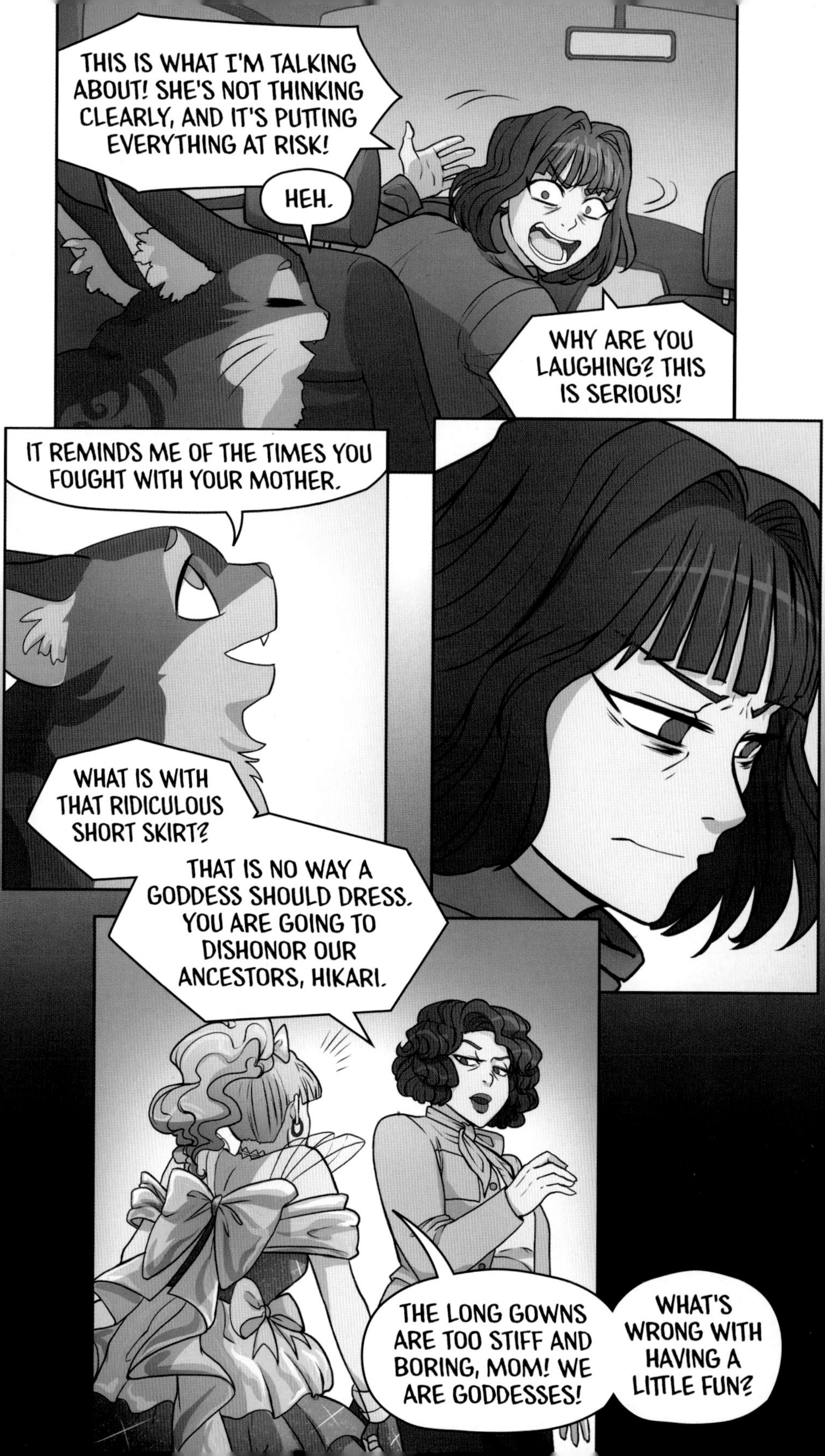
THIS IS WHAT I'M TALKING ABOUT! SHE'S NOT THINKING CLEARLY, AND IT'S PUTTING EVERYTHING AT RISK!
HEH.
WHY ARE YOU LAUGHING? THIS IS SERIOUS!
IT REMINDS ME OF THE TIMES YOU FOUGHT WITH YOUR MOTHER.
WHAT IS WITH THAT RIDICULOUS SHORT SKIRT?
THAT IS NO WAY A GODDESS SHOULD DRESS. YOU ARE GOING TO DISHONOR OUR ANCESTORS, HIKARI.
THE LONG GOWNS ARE TOO STIFF AND BORING, MOM! WE ARE GODDESSES!
WHAT'S WRONG WITH HAVING A LITTLE FUN?

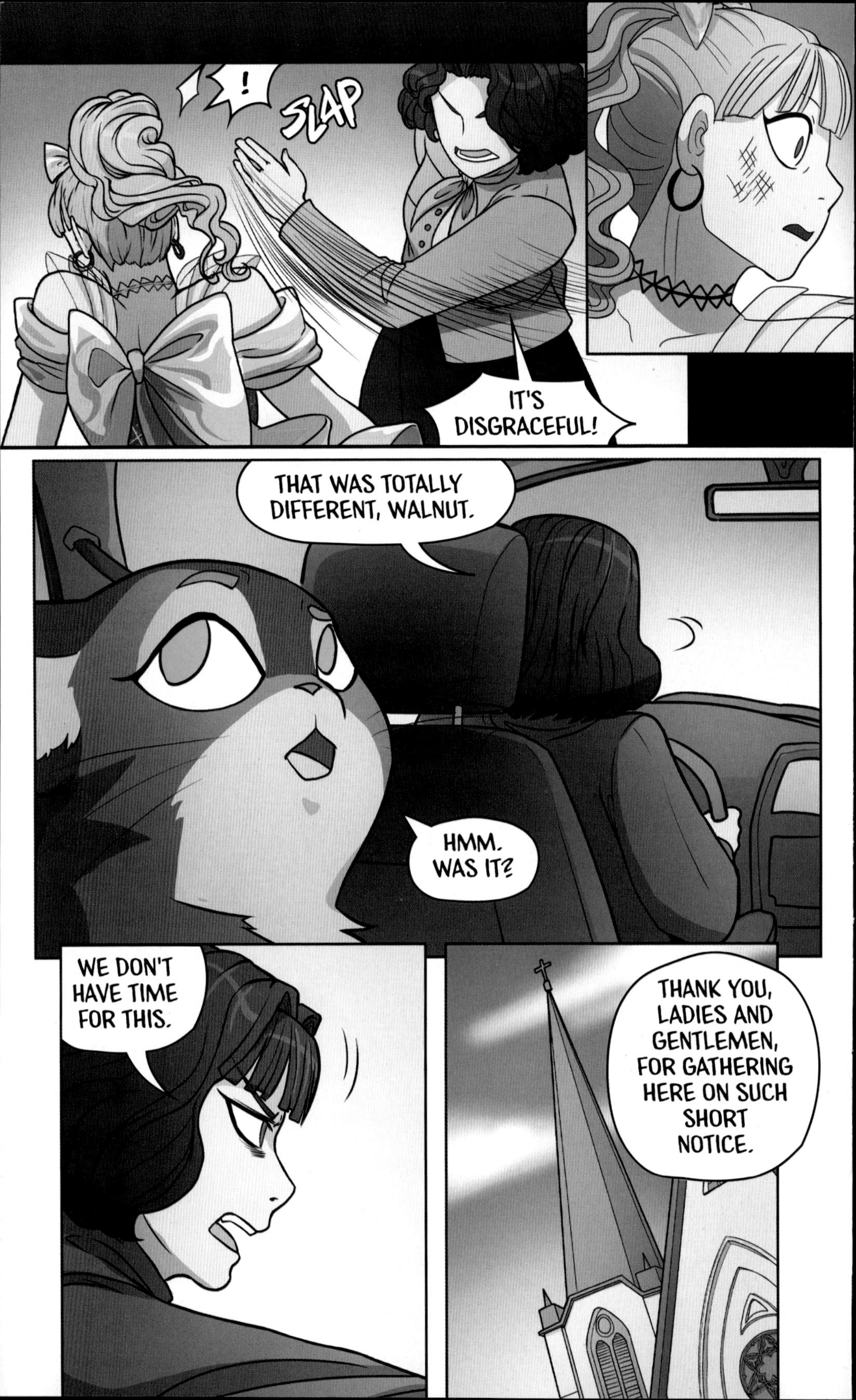
!
SLAP
IT'S DISGRACEFUL!
THAT WAS TOTALLY DIFFERENT, WALNUT.
HMM. WAS IT?
WE DON'T HAVE TIME FOR THIS.
THANK YOU, LADIES AND GENTLEMEN, FOR GATHERING HERE ON SUCH SHORT NOTICE.

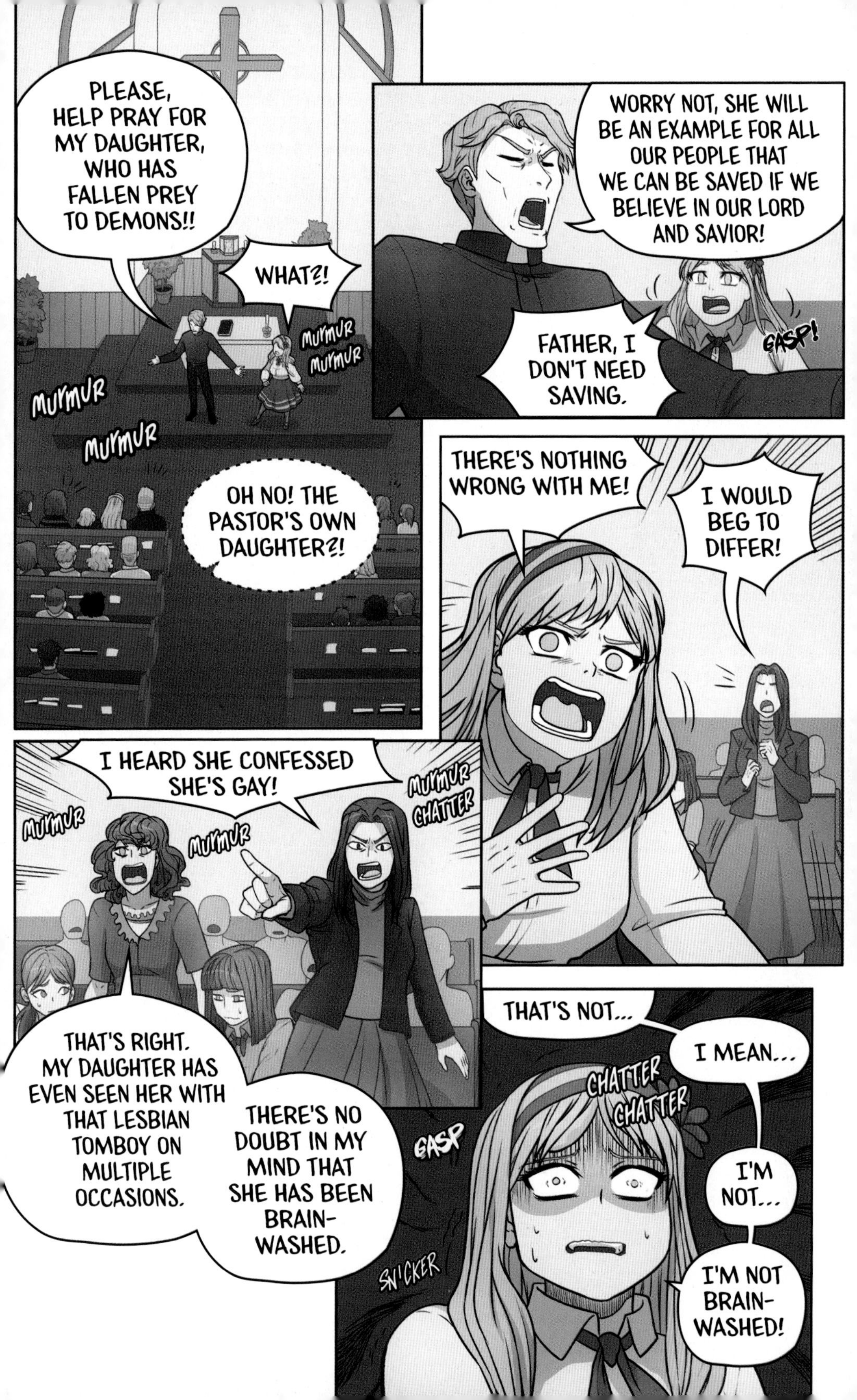
PLEASE, HELP PRAY FOR MY DAUGHTER, WHO HAS FALLEN PREY TO DEMONS!!
WHAT?!
MURMUR MURMUR
MURMUR
MURMUR
WORRY NOT, SHE WILL BE AN EXAMPLE FOR ALL OUR PEOPLE THAT WE CAN BE SAVED IF WE BELIEVE IN OUR LORD AND SAVIOR!
GASP!
FATHER, I DON'T NEED SAVING.
OH NO! THE PASTOR'S OWN DAUGHTER?!
THERE'S NOTHING WRONG WITH ME!
I WOULD BEG TO DIFFER!
I HEARD SHE CONFESSED SHE'S GAY!
MURMUR
MURMUR
MURMUR CHATTER
THAT'S RIGHT. MY DAUGHTER HAS EVEN SEEN HER WITH THAT LESBIAN TOMBOY ON MULTIPLE OCCASIONS.
THERE'S NO DOUBT IN MY MIND THAT SHE HAS BEEN BRAIN-WASHED.
THAT'S NOT...
I MEAN...
CHATTER CHATTER
GASP
I'M NOT...
SNICKER
I'M NOT BRAIN-WASHED!

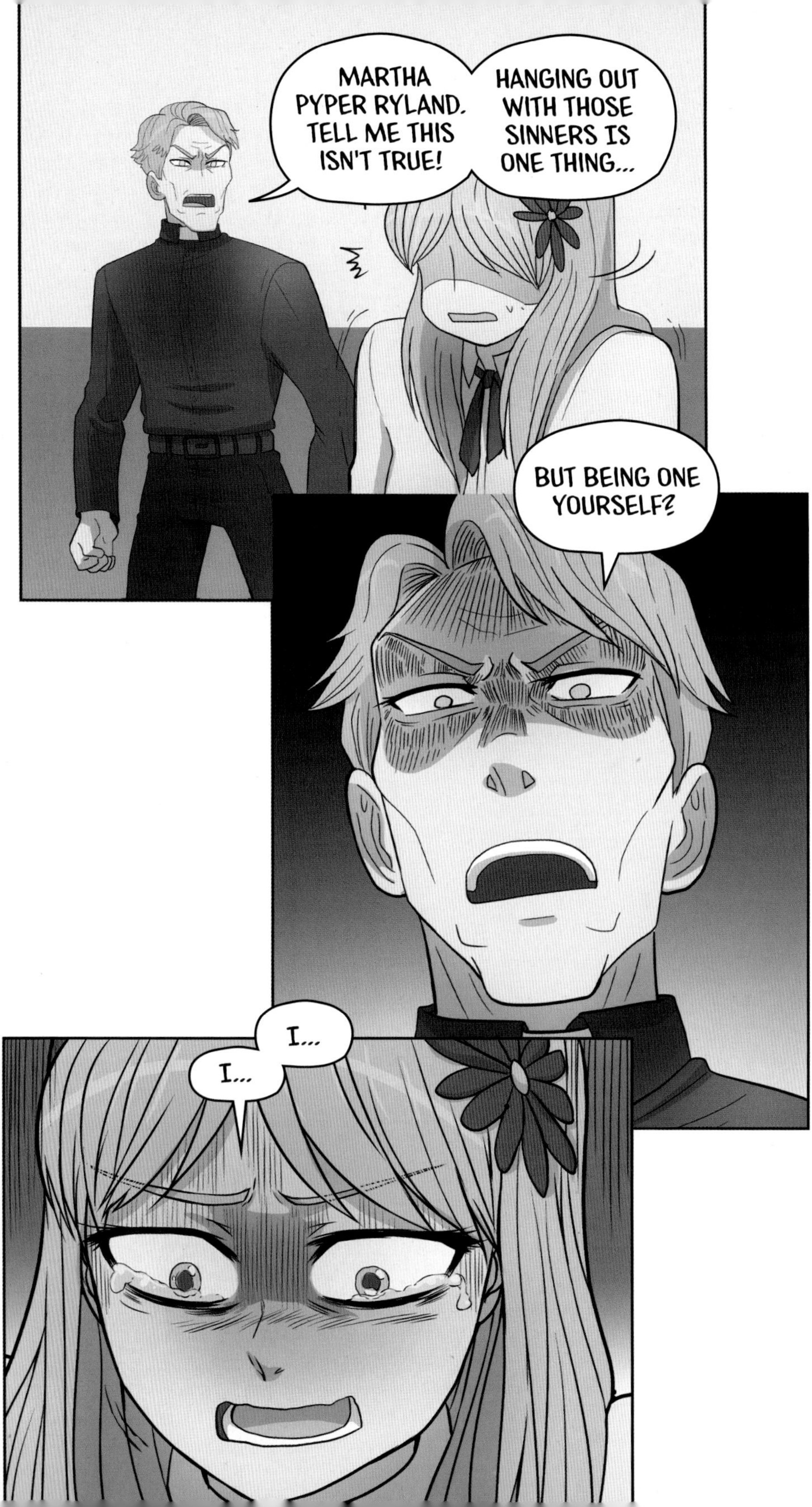
MARTHA PYPER RYLAND. TELL ME THIS ISN'T TRUE!
HANGING OUT WITH THOSE SINNERS IS ONE THING...
BUT BEING ONE YOURSELF?
I...
I...

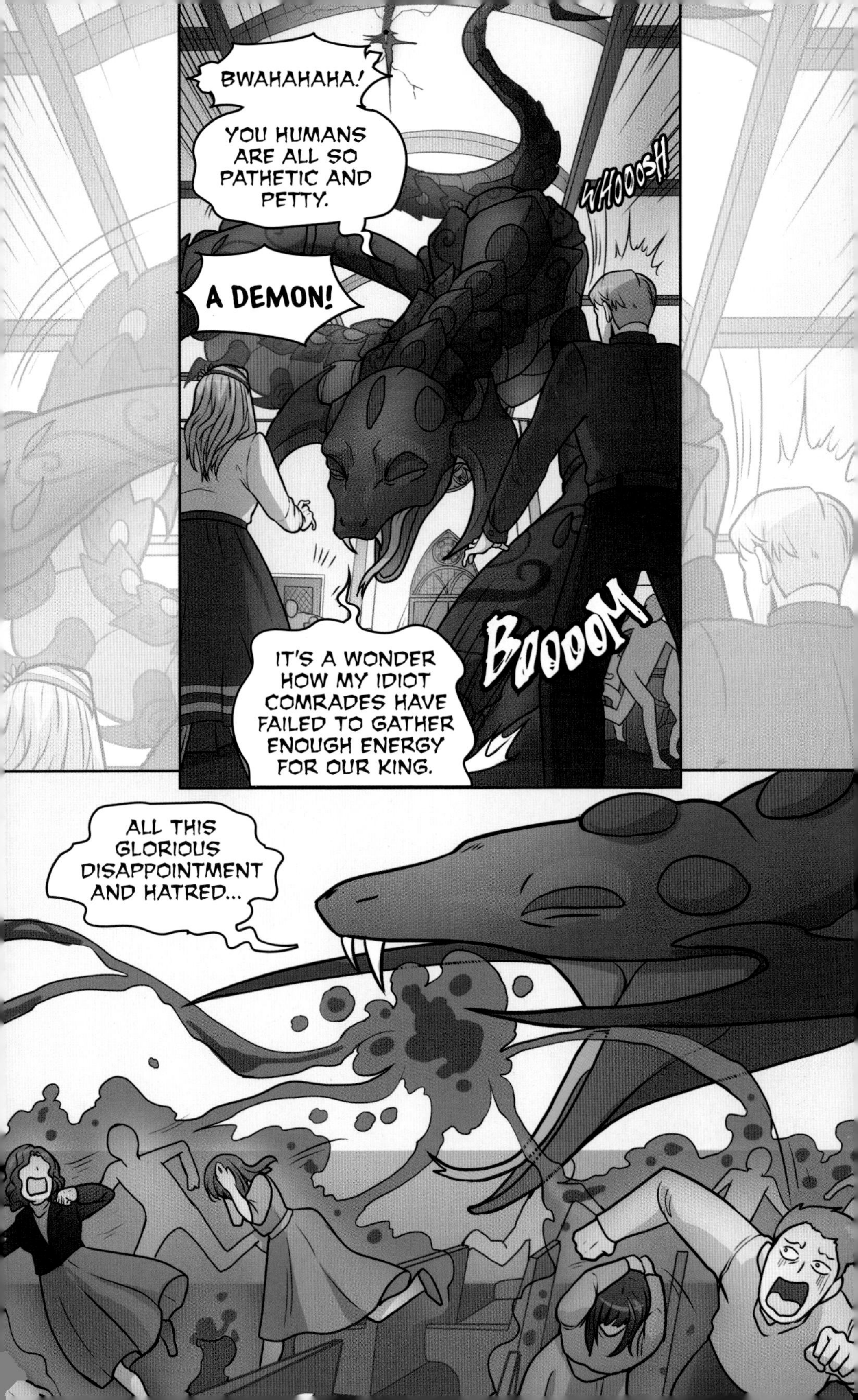
BWAHAHAHA!
YOU HUMANS ARE ALL SO PATHETIC AND PETTY.
WHOOOSH
A DEMON!
BOOOOM
IT'S A WONDER HOW MY IDIOT COMRADES HAVE FAILED TO GATHER ENOUGH ENERGY FOR OUR KING.
ALL THIS GLORIOUS DISAPPOINTMENT AND HATRED...

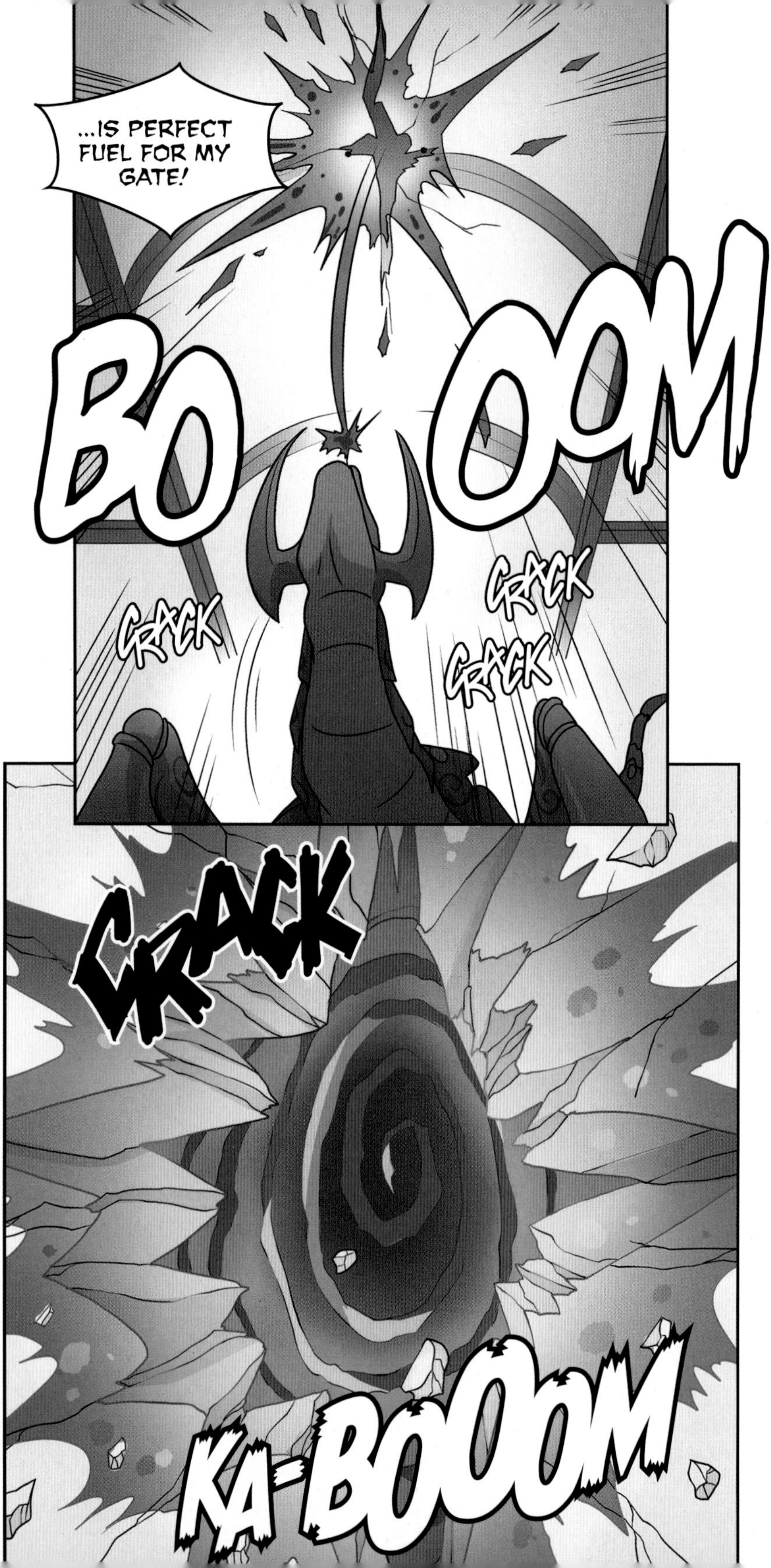
...IS PERFECT FUEL FOR MY GATE!
BOOOOM
CRACK
CRACK
CRACK
CRACK
KA-BOOOOM

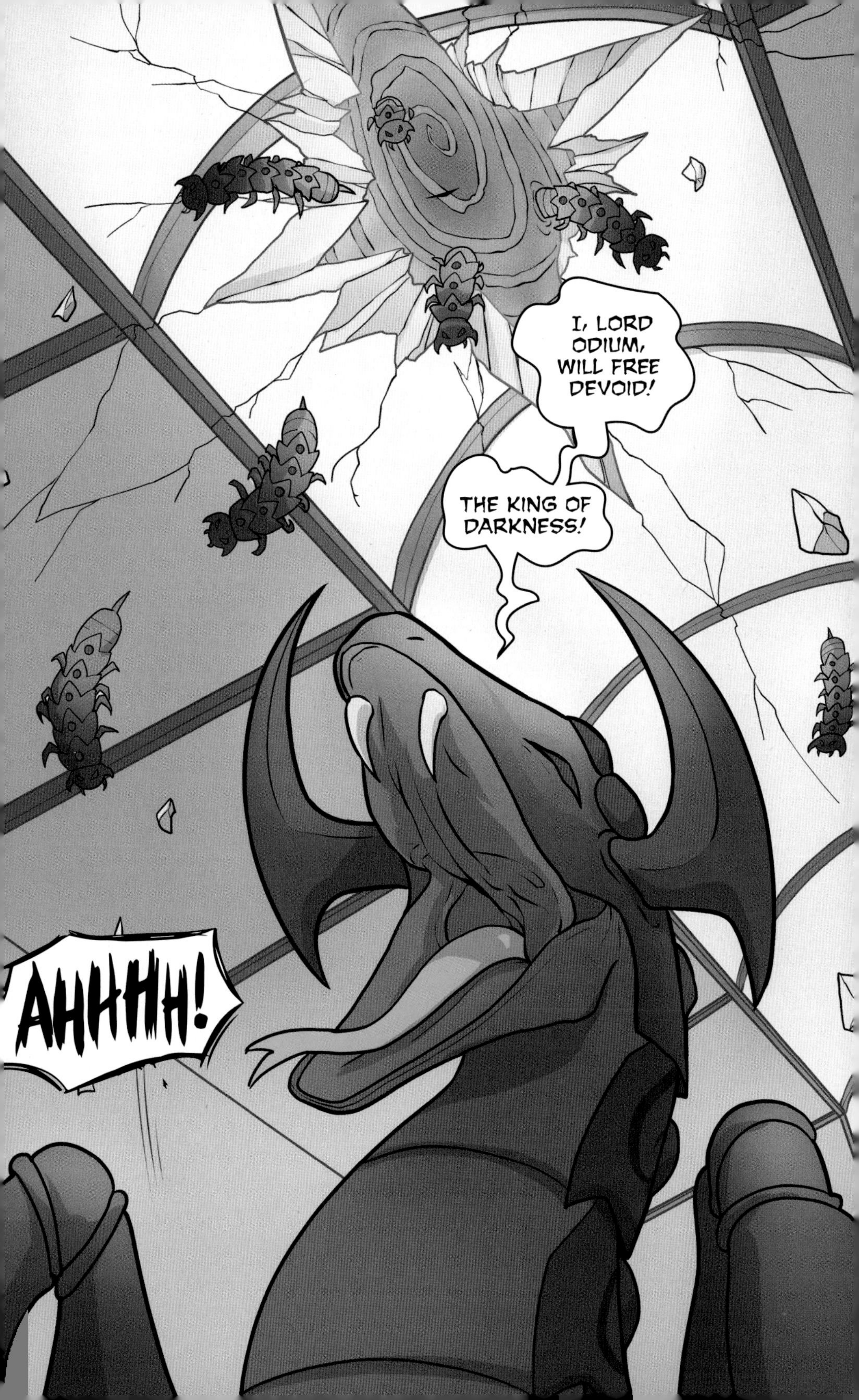
I, LORD ODIUM, WILL FREE DEVOID!
THE KING OF DARKNESS!
AHHHH!

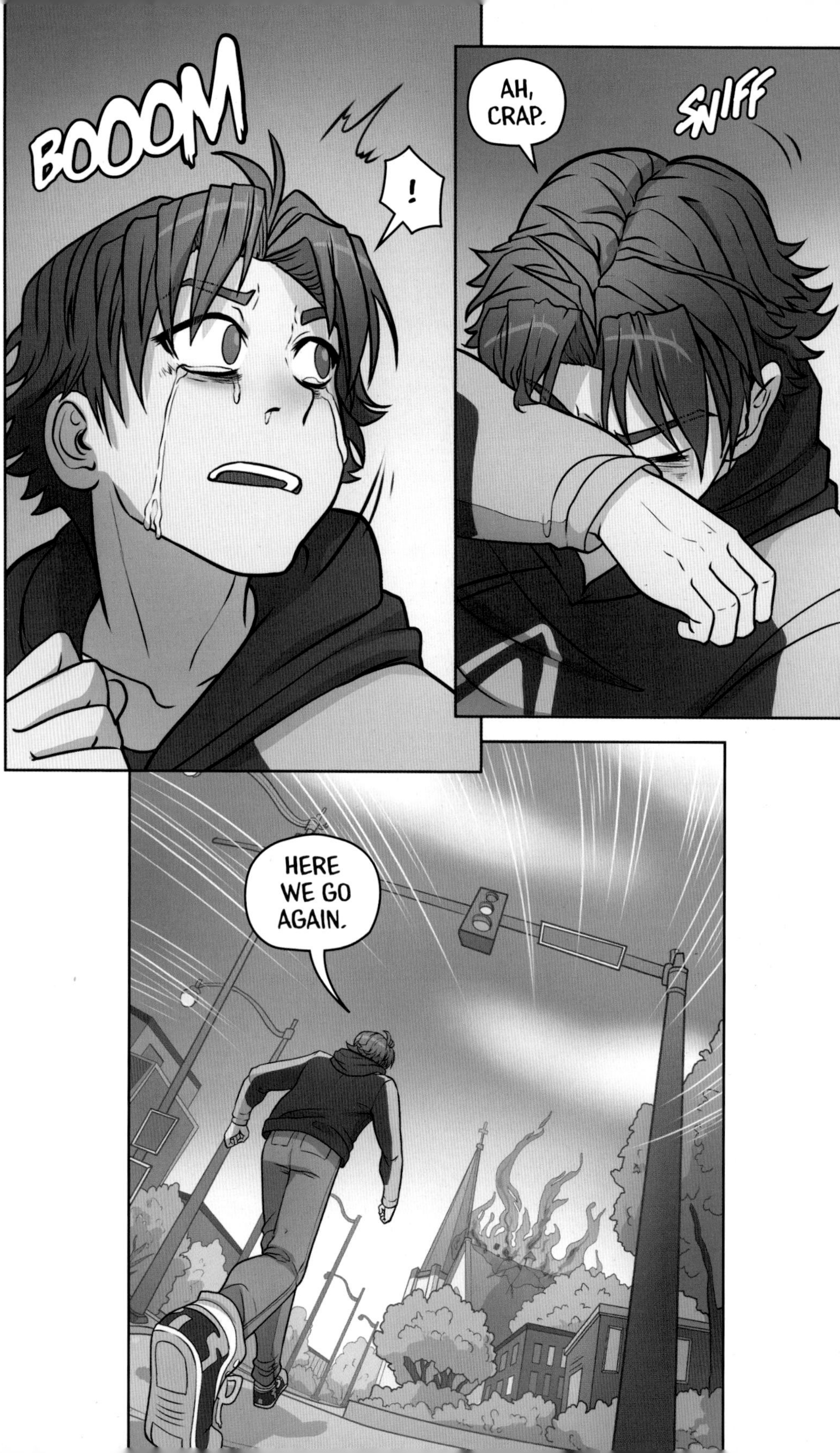
BOOOM
!
AH, CRAP.
SNIFF
HERE WE GO AGAIN.

EPISODE 22:
PAST & PRESENT

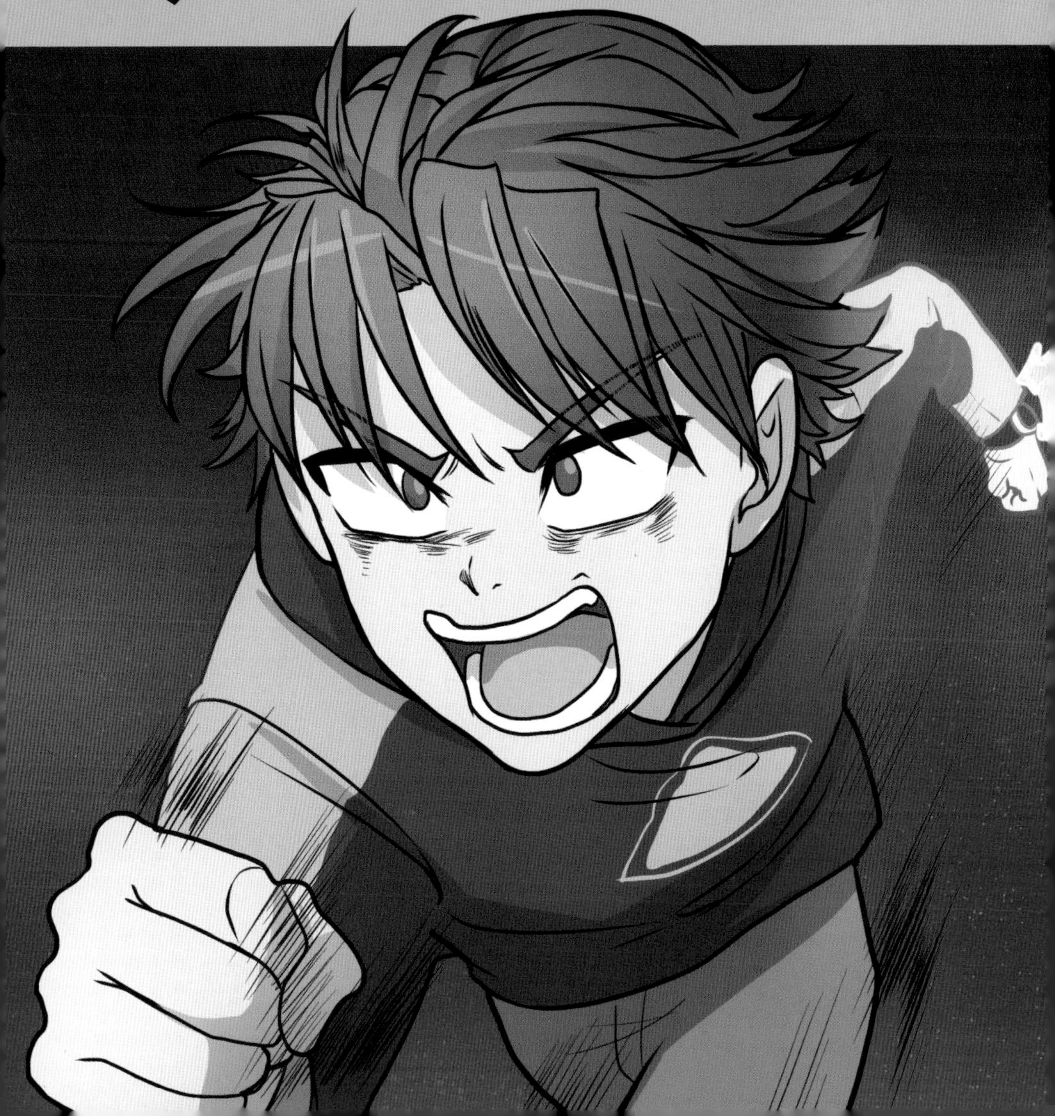

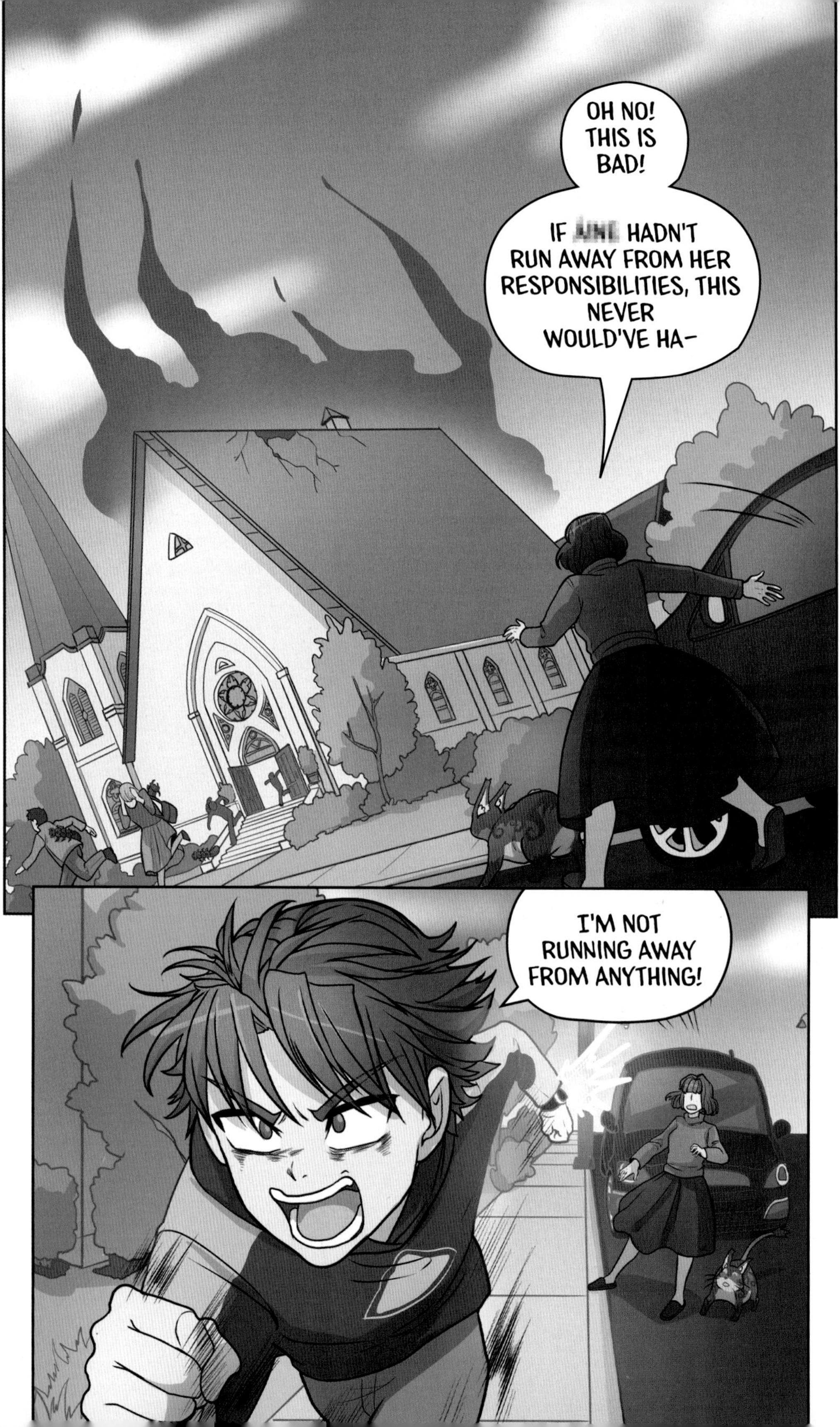
OH NO! THIS IS BAD!
IF [redacted] HADN'T RUN AWAY FROM HER RESPONSIBILITIES, THIS NEVER WOULD'VE HA-
I'M NOT RUNNING AWAY FROM ANYTHING!

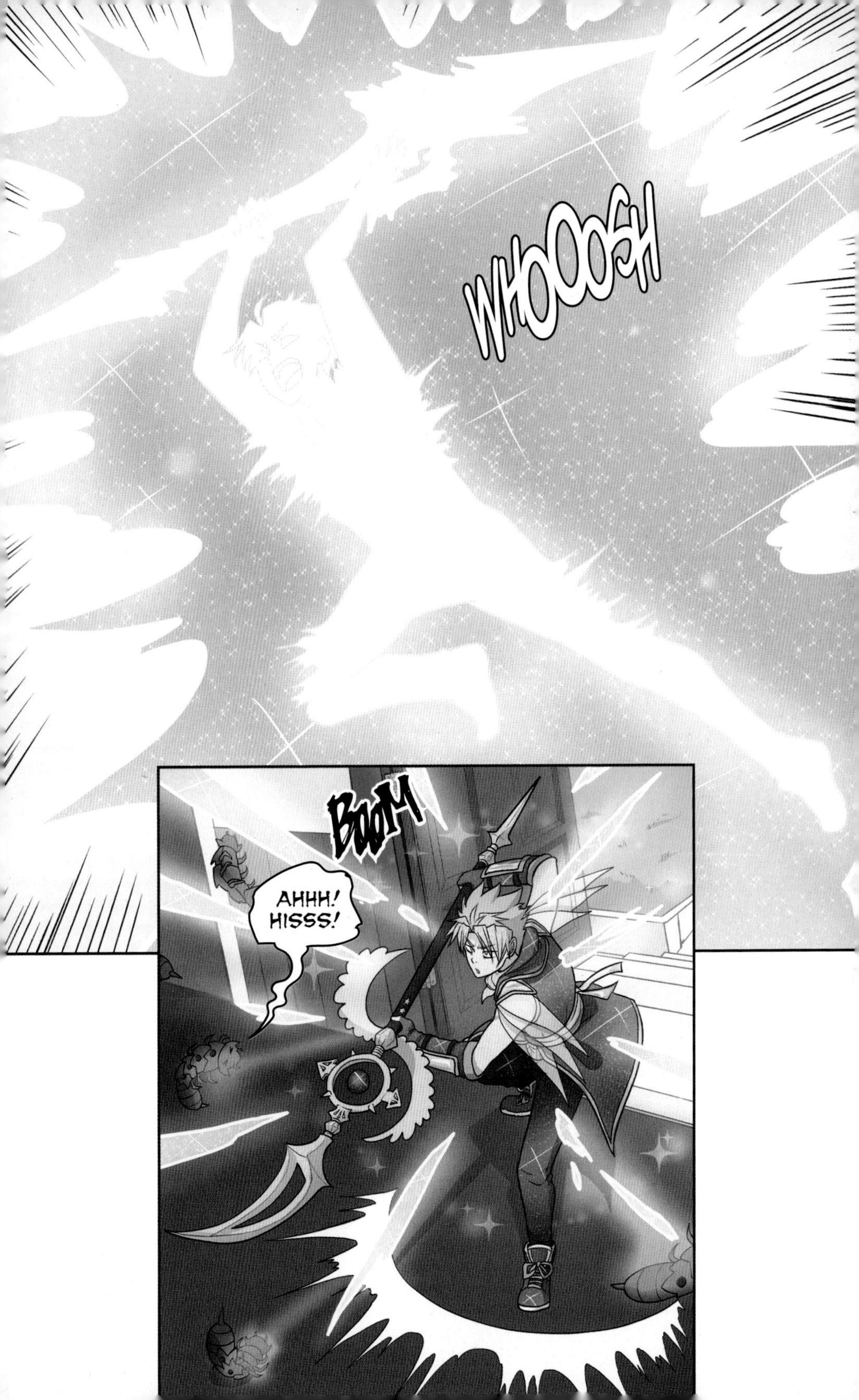
WHOOOSH
BOOM
AHHH! HISSS!

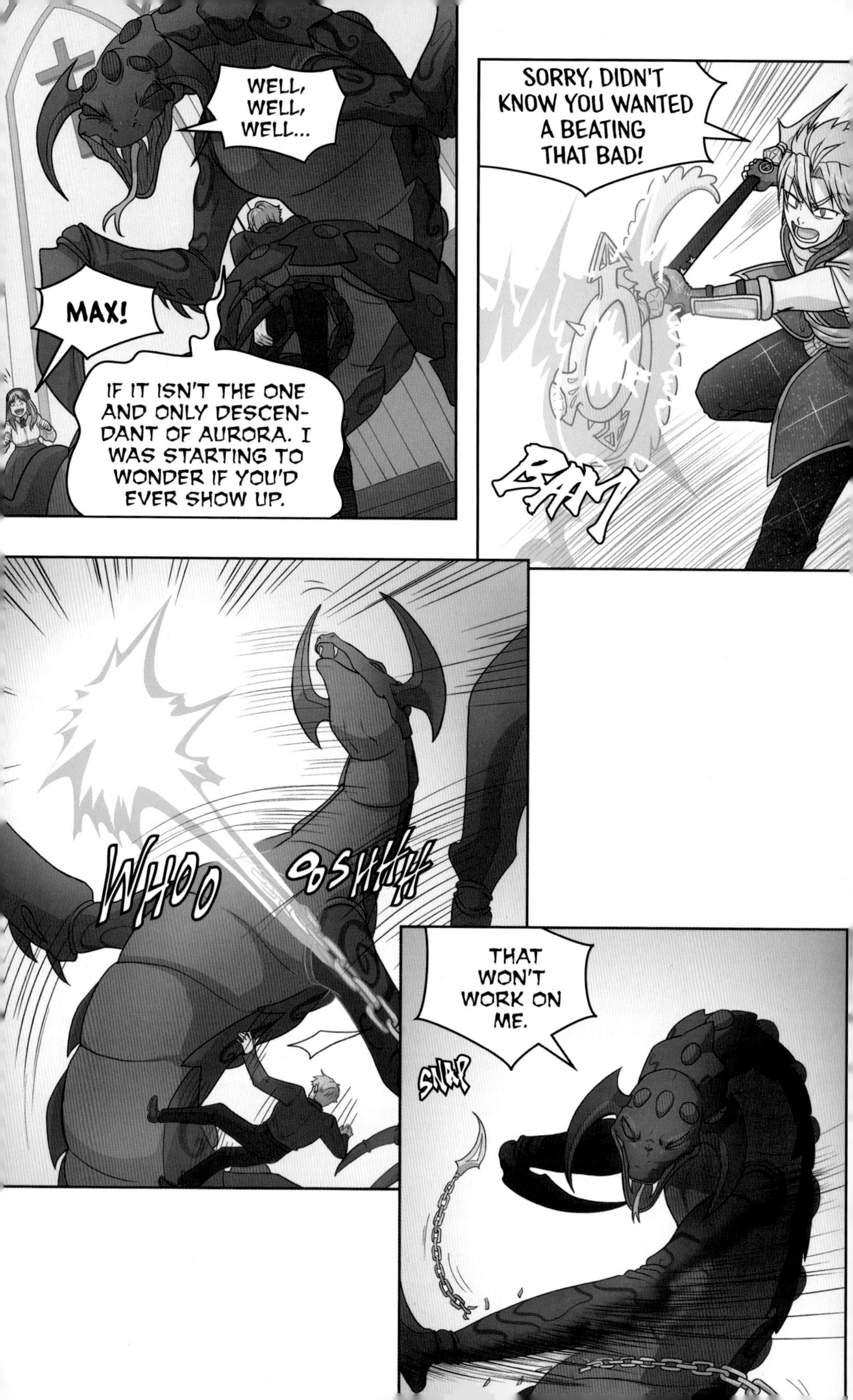

WELL, WELL, WELL...
MAX!
IF IT ISN'T THE ONE AND ONLY DESCENDANT OF AURORA. I WAS STARTING TO WONDER IF YOU'D EVER SHOW UP.
SORRY, DIDN'T KNOW YOU WANTED A BEATING THAT BAD!
BAM
WHOOOSHHH
THAT WON'T WORK ON ME.
SNAP

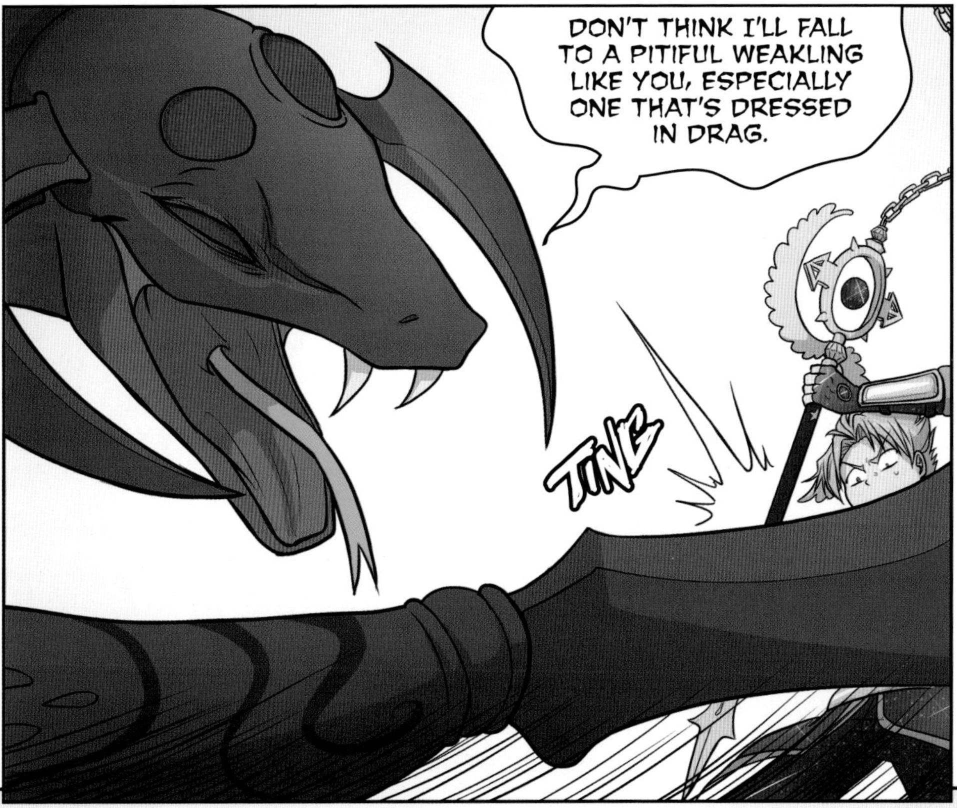
DON'T THINK I'LL FALL TO A PITIFUL WEAKLING LIKE YOU, ESPECIALLY ONE THAT'S DRESSED IN DRAG.
TING
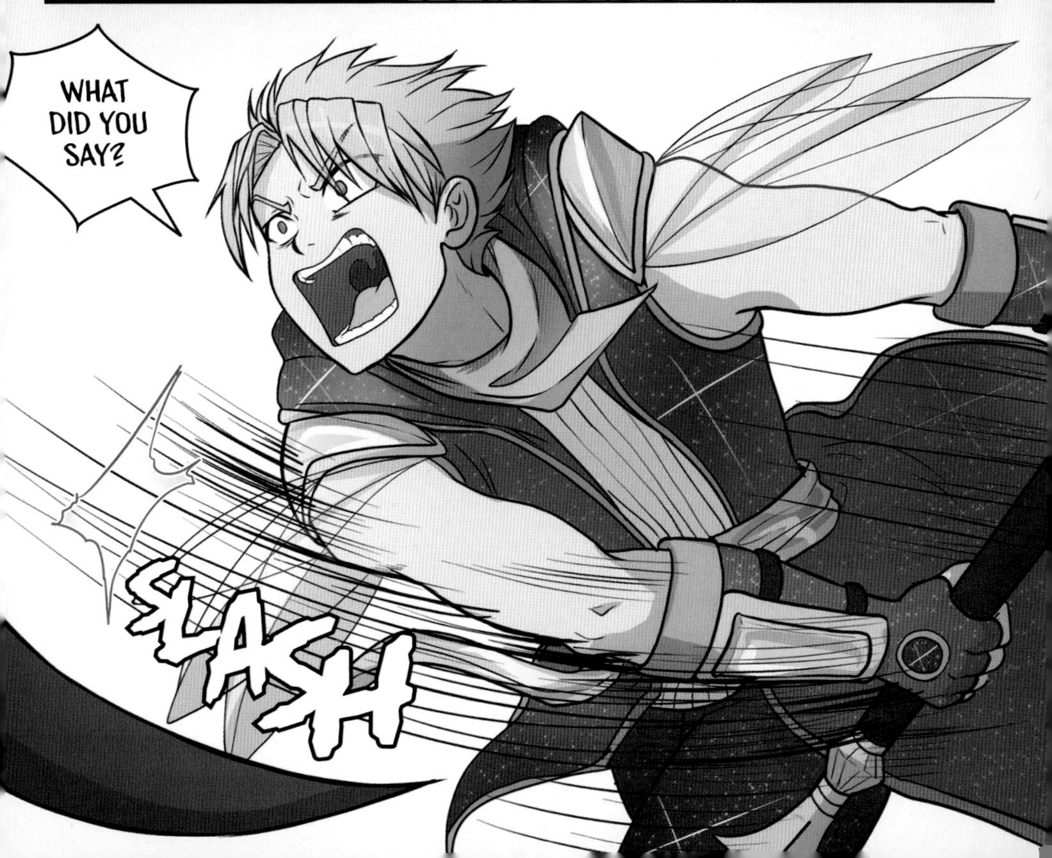
WHAT DID YOU SAY?
SLASH

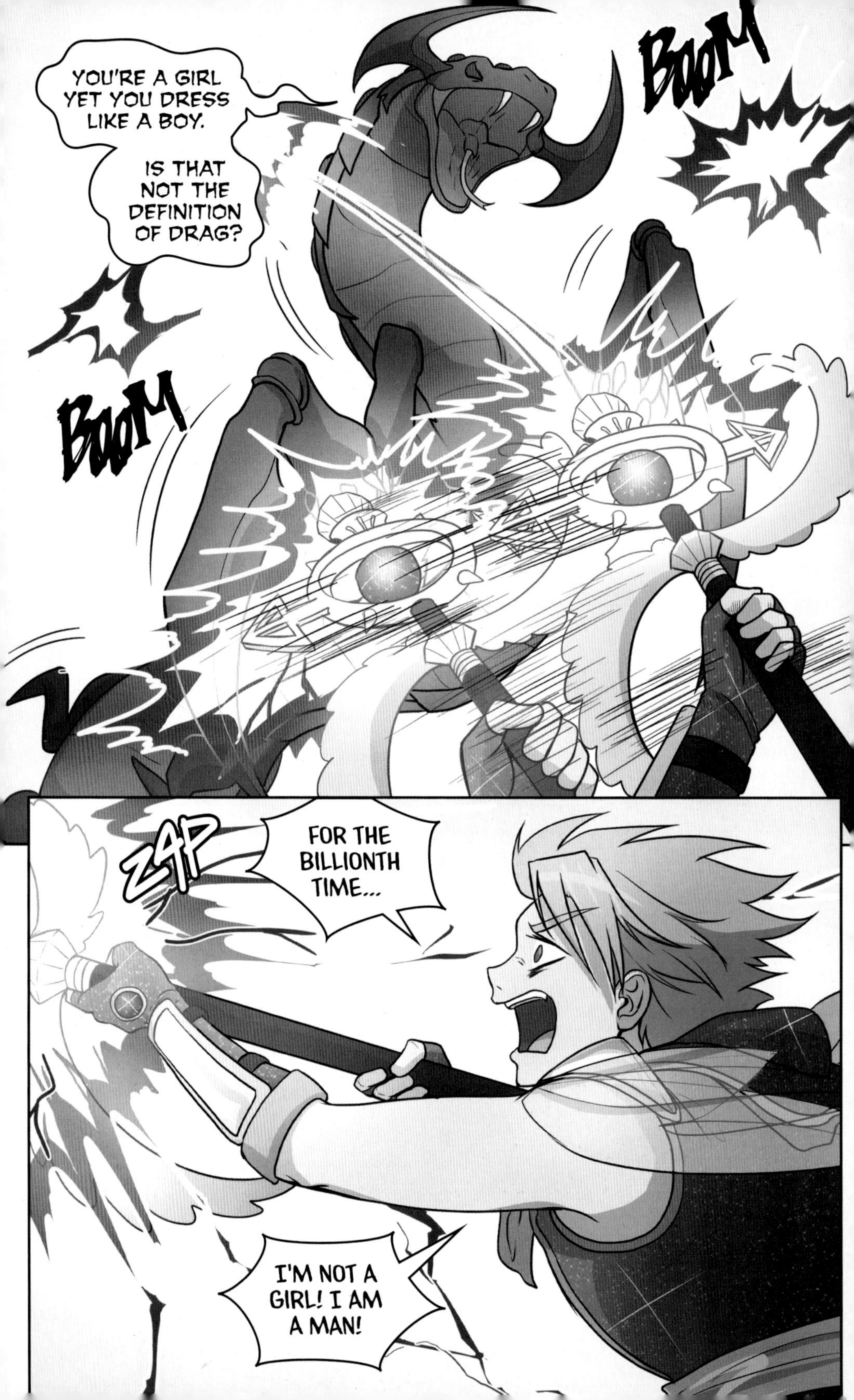

YOU'RE A GIRL YET YOU DRESS LIKE A BOY.
IS THAT NOT THE DEFINITION OF DRAG?
BOOM
BOOM
ZAP
FOR THE BILLIONTH TIME...
I'M NOT A GIRL! I AM A MAN!

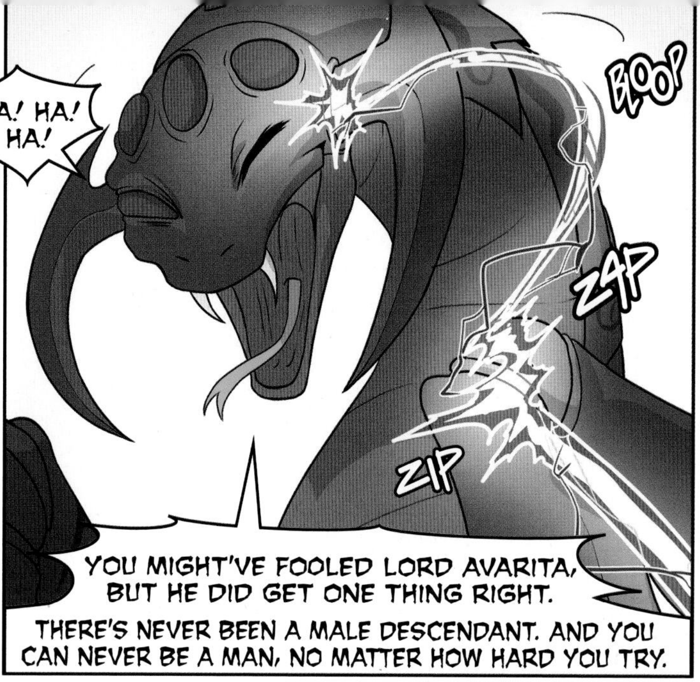
HA! HA! HA!
BLOOP
ZAP
ZIP
YOU MIGHT'VE FOOLED LORD AVARITA, BUT HE DID GET ONE THING RIGHT.
THERE'S NEVER BEEN A MALE DESCENDANT. AND YOU CAN NEVER BE A MAN, NO MATTER HOW HARD YOU TRY.

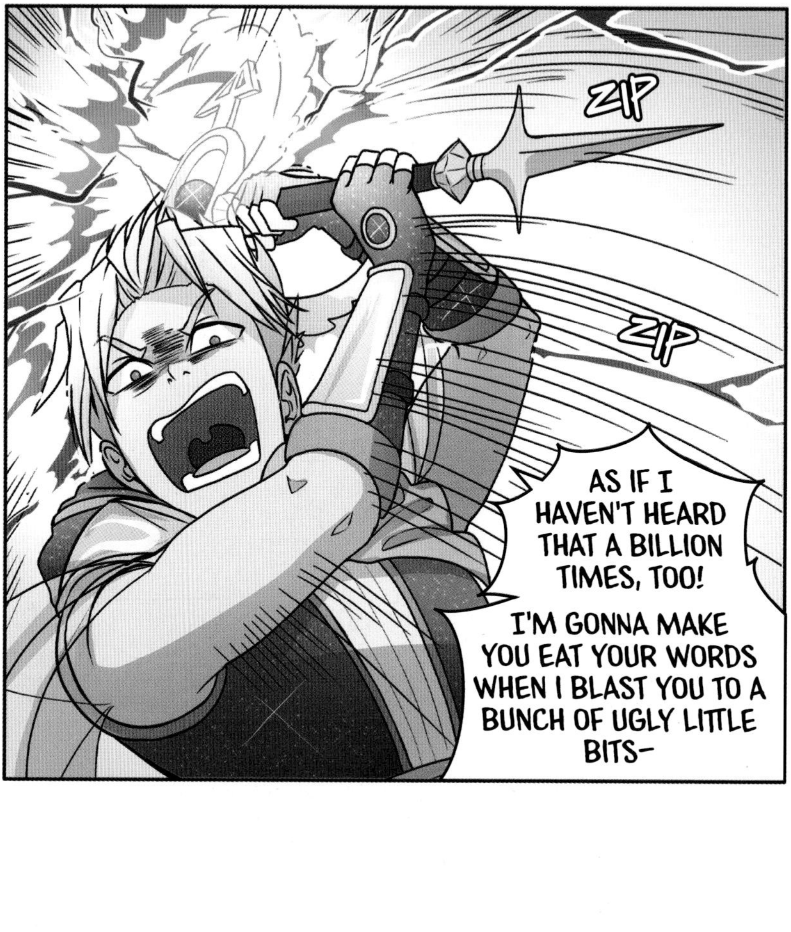
ZIP
ZIP
AS IF I HAVEN'T HEARD THAT A BILLION TIMES, TOO!
I'M GONNA MAKE YOU EAT YOUR WORDS WHEN I BLAST YOU TO A BUNCH OF UGLY LITTLE BITS-

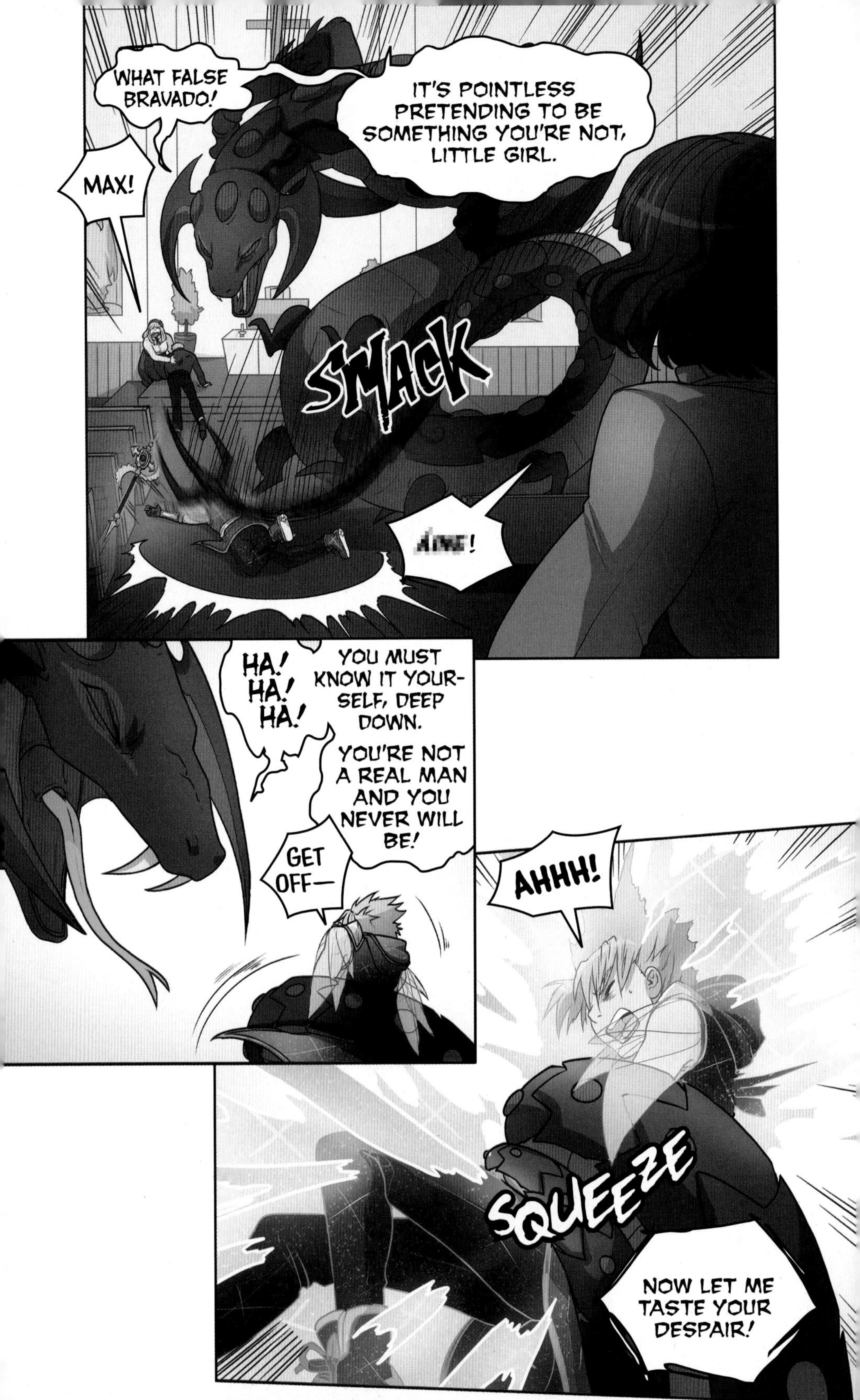
WHAT FALSE BRAVADO!
IT'S POINTLESS PRETENDING TO BE SOMETHING YOU'RE NOT, LITTLE GIRL.
MAX!
SMACK
[redacted]!
HA! HA! HA!
YOU MUST KNOW IT YOUR-SELF, DEEP DOWN.
YOU'RE NOT A REAL MAN AND YOU NEVER WILL BE!
GET OFF—
AHHH!
SQUEEZE
NOW LET ME TASTE YOUR DESPAIR!

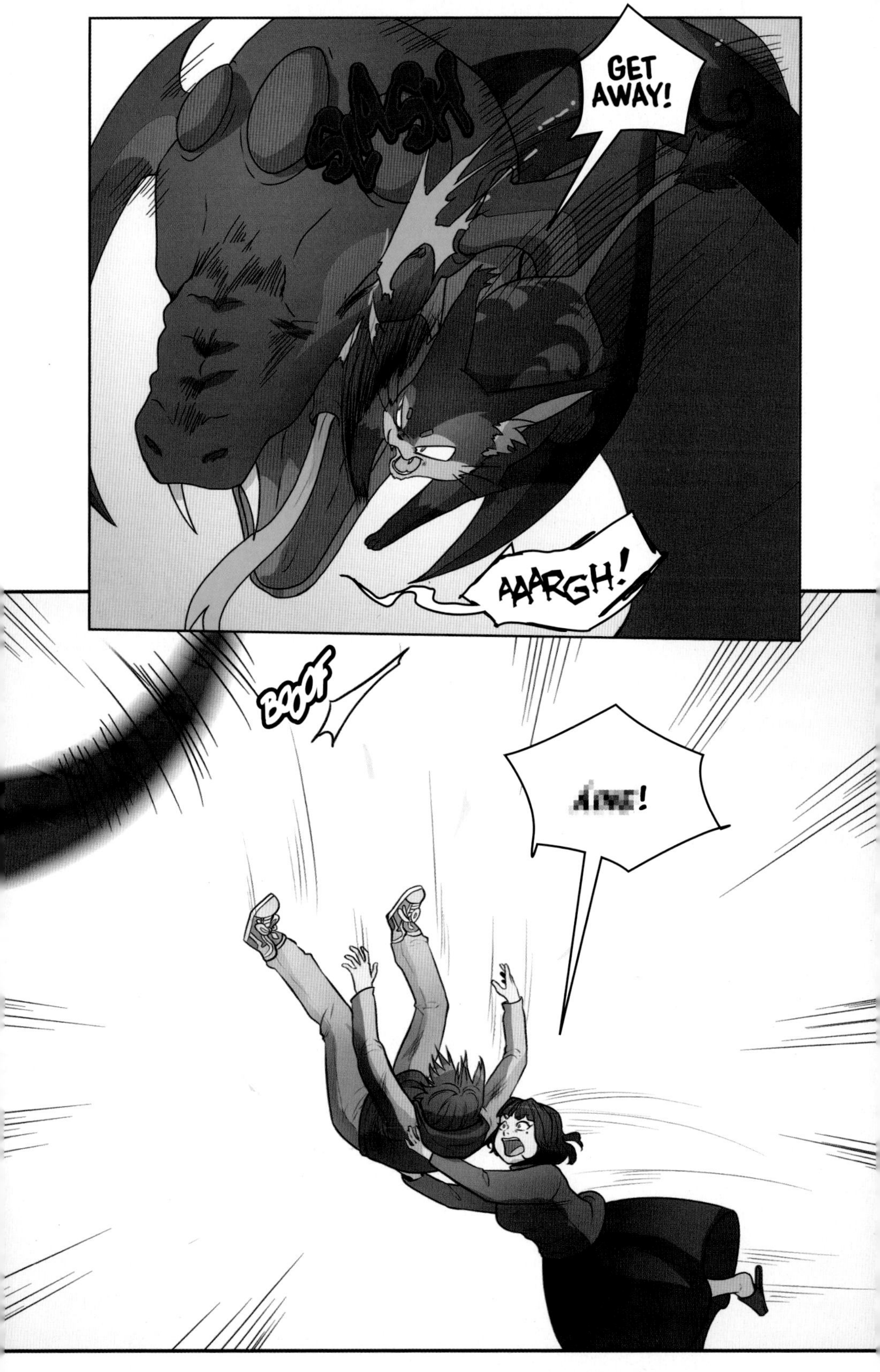
SLASH
GET AWAY!
AAARGH!
BOOF
[redacted]!

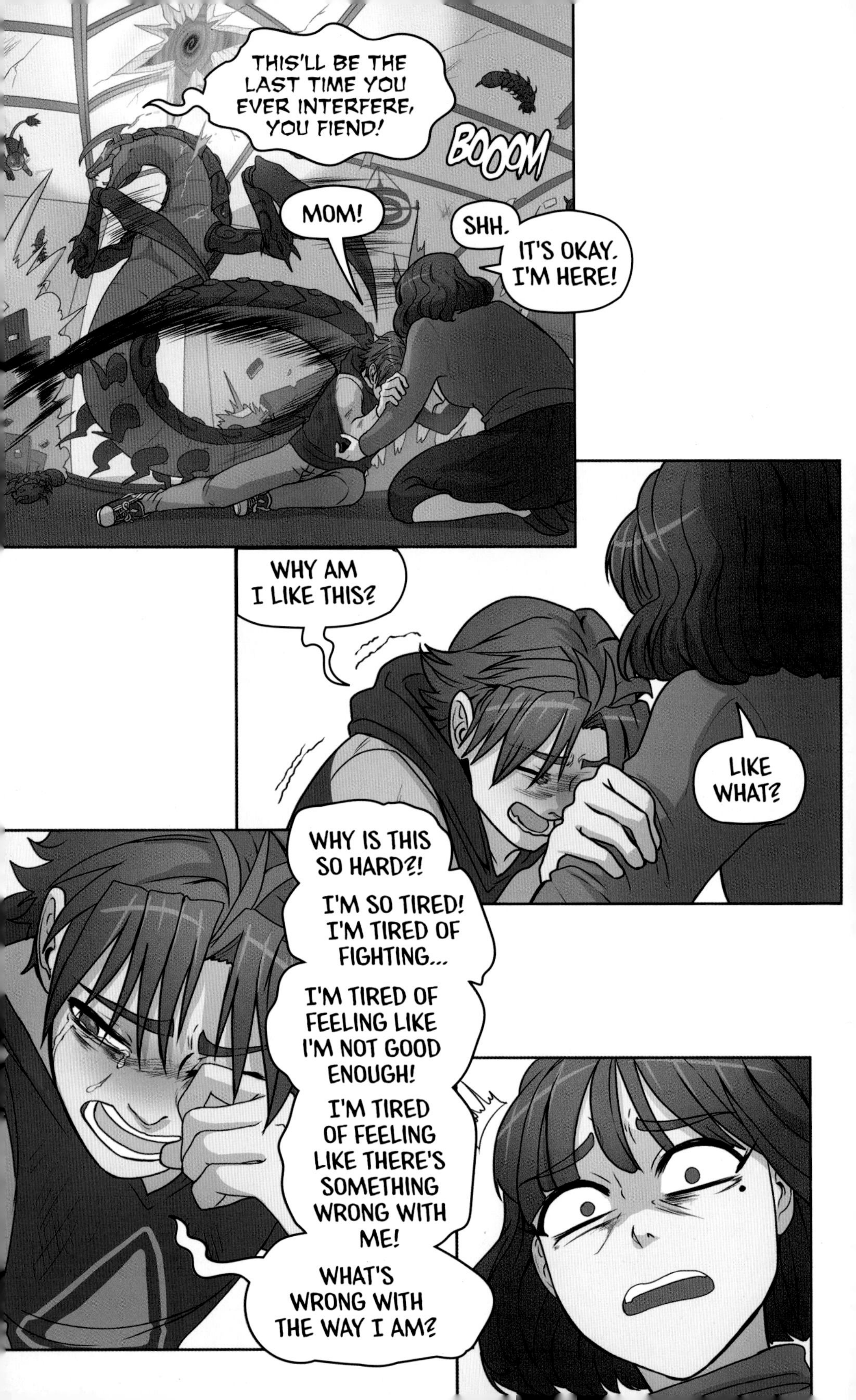

THIS'LL BE THE LAST TIME YOU EVER INTERFERE, YOU FIEND!
BOOOM
MOM!
SHH.
IT'S OKAY. I'M HERE!
WHY AM I LIKE THIS?
LIKE WHAT?
WHY IS THIS SO HARD?!
I'M SO TIRED! I'M TIRED OF FIGHTING...
I'M TIRED OF FEELING LIKE I'M NOT GOOD ENOUGH!
I'M TIRED OF FEELING LIKE THERE'S SOMETHING WRONG WITH ME!
WHAT'S WRONG WITH THE WAY I AM?

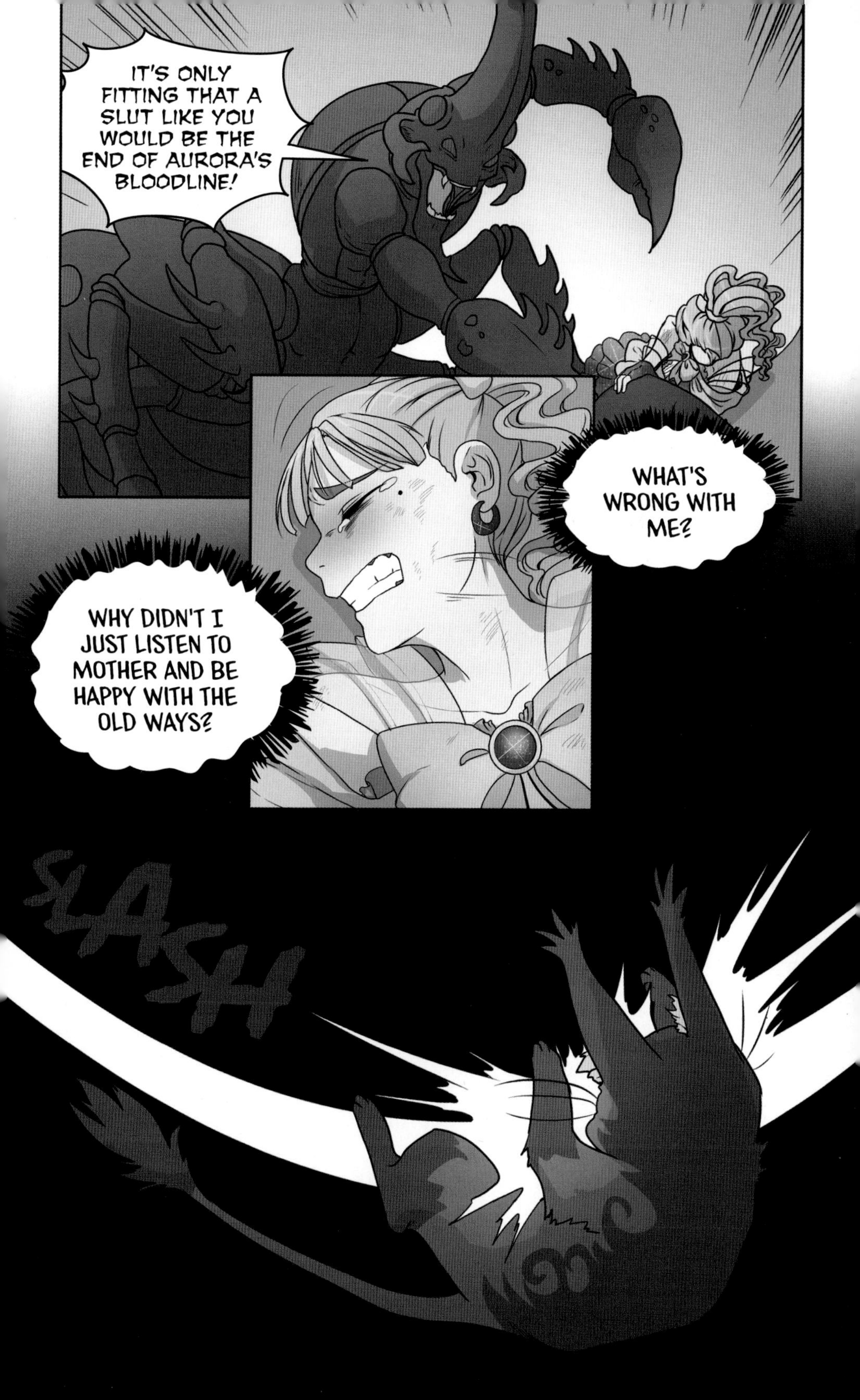
IT'S ONLY FITTING THAT A SLUT LIKE YOU WOULD BE THE END OF AURORA'S BLOODLINE!
WHAT'S WRONG WITH ME?
WHY DIDN'T I JUST LISTEN TO MOTHER AND BE HAPPY WITH THE OLD WAYS?
SLASH

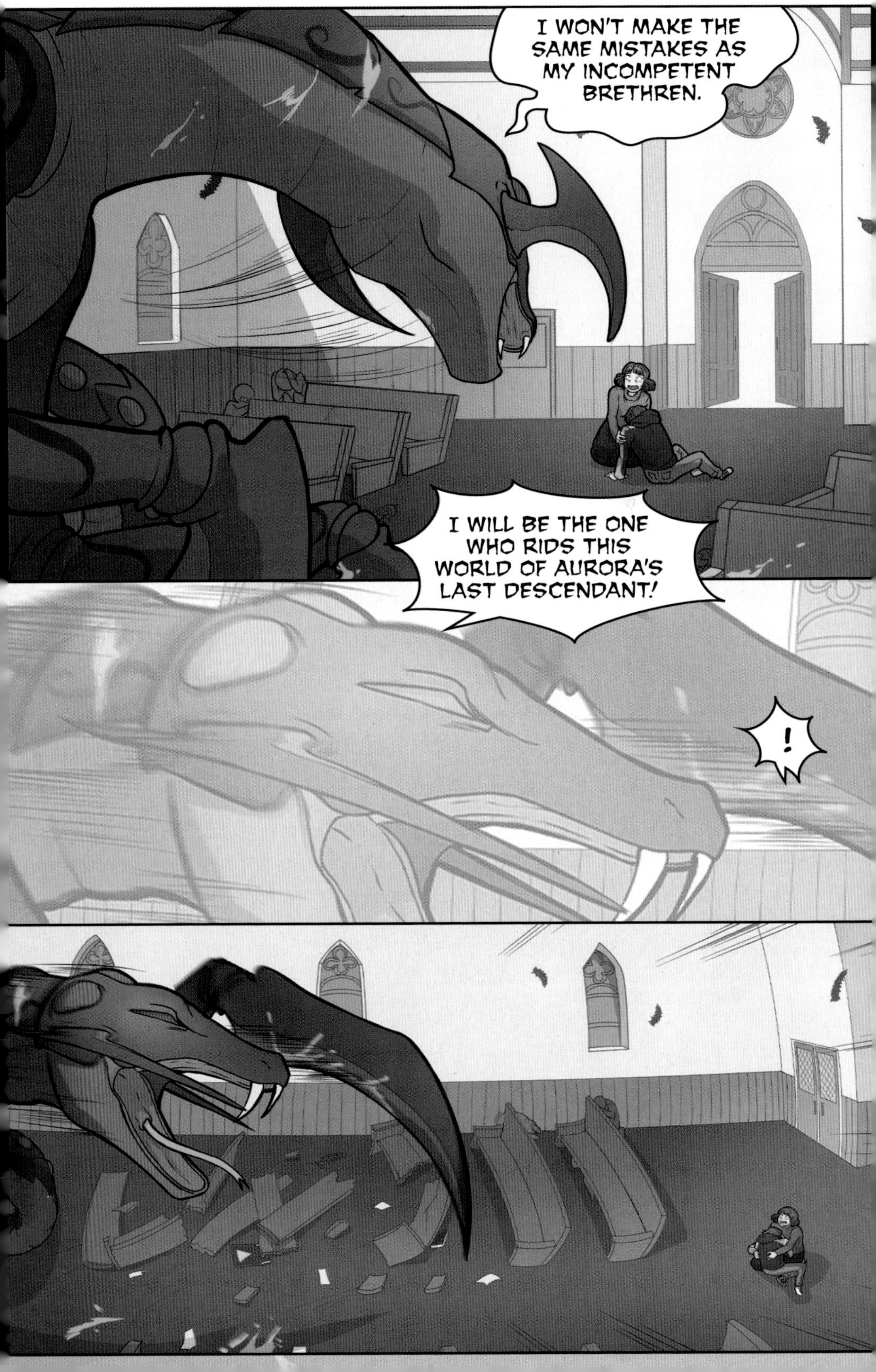
I WON'T MAKE THE SAME MISTAKES AS MY INCOMPETENT BRETHREN.
I WILL BE THE ONE WHO RIDS THIS WORLD OF AURORA'S LAST DESCENDANT!
!

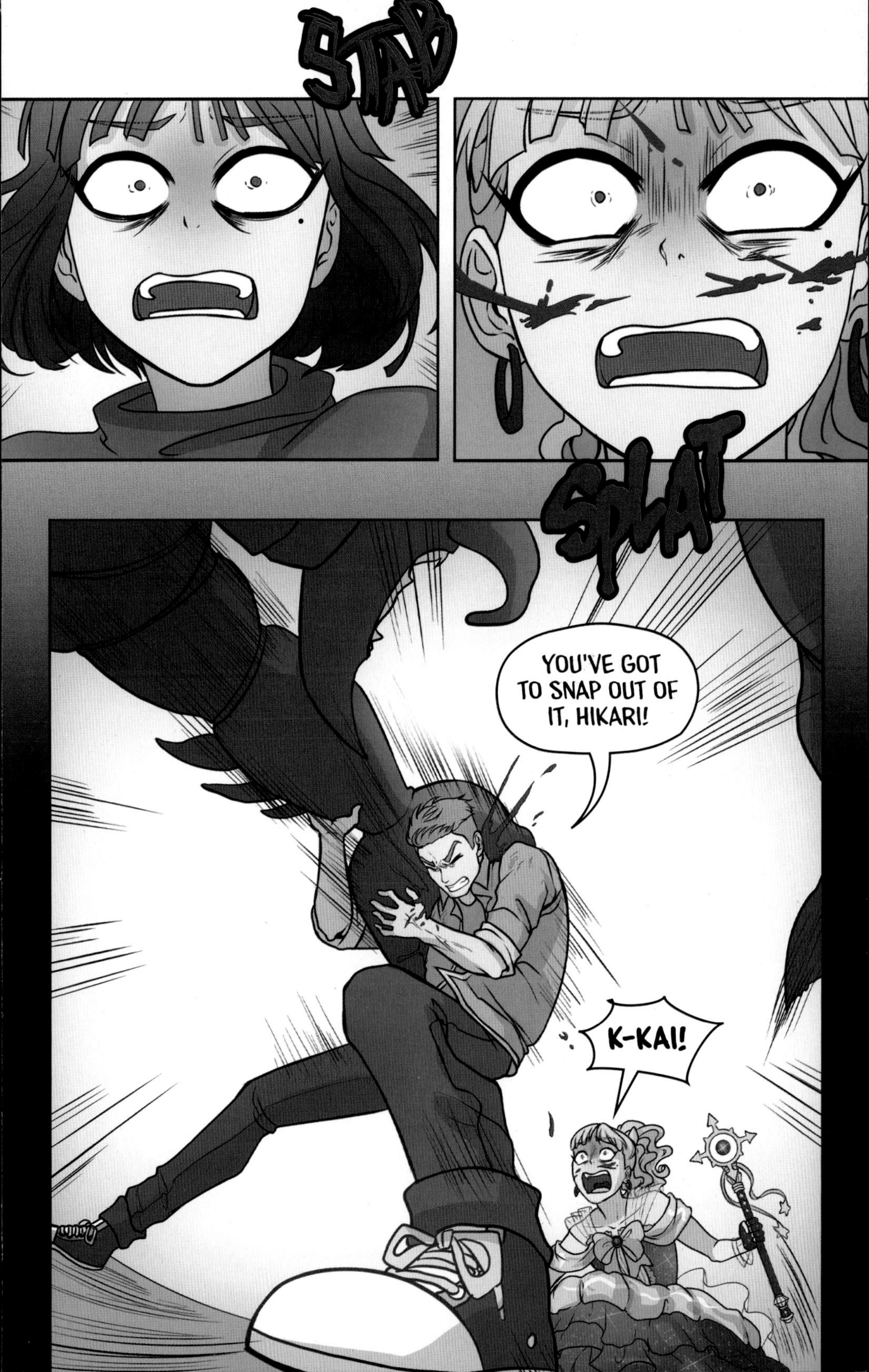
STAB
SPLAT
YOU'VE GOT TO SNAP OUT OF IT, HIKARI!
K-KAI!

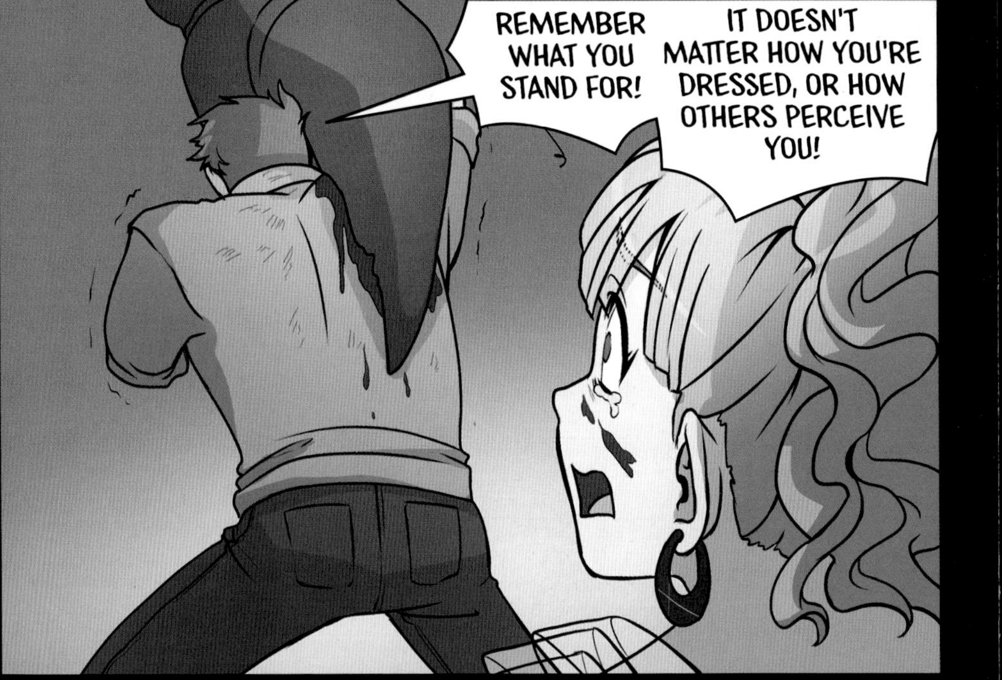
REMEMBER WHAT YOU STAND FOR!
IT DOESN'T MATTER HOW YOU'RE DRESSED, OR HOW OTHERS PERCEIVE YOU!

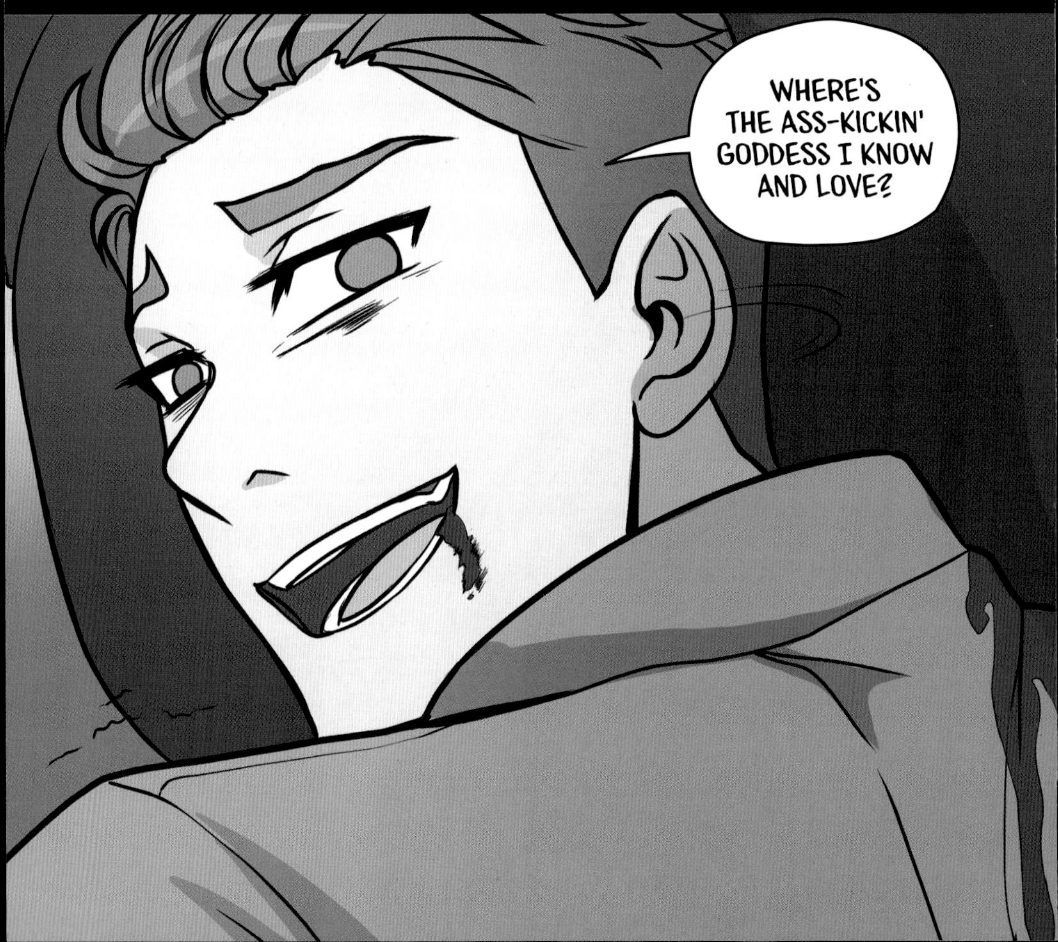
WHERE'S THE ASS-KICKIN' GODDESS I KNOW AND LOVE?

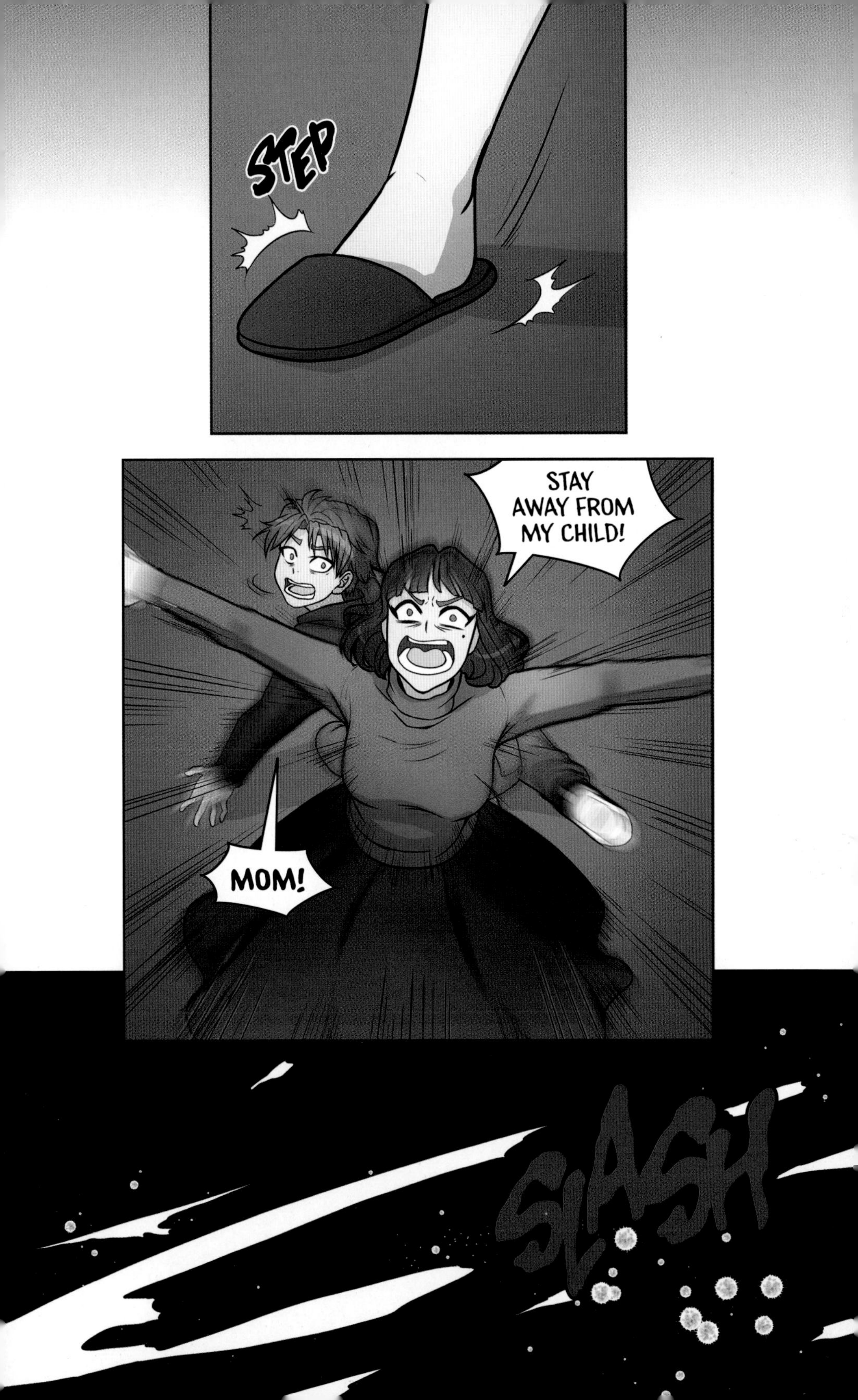
STEP
STAY AWAY FROM MY CHILD!
MOM!
SLASH

EPISODE 23:
THE WRATH OF DEVOID

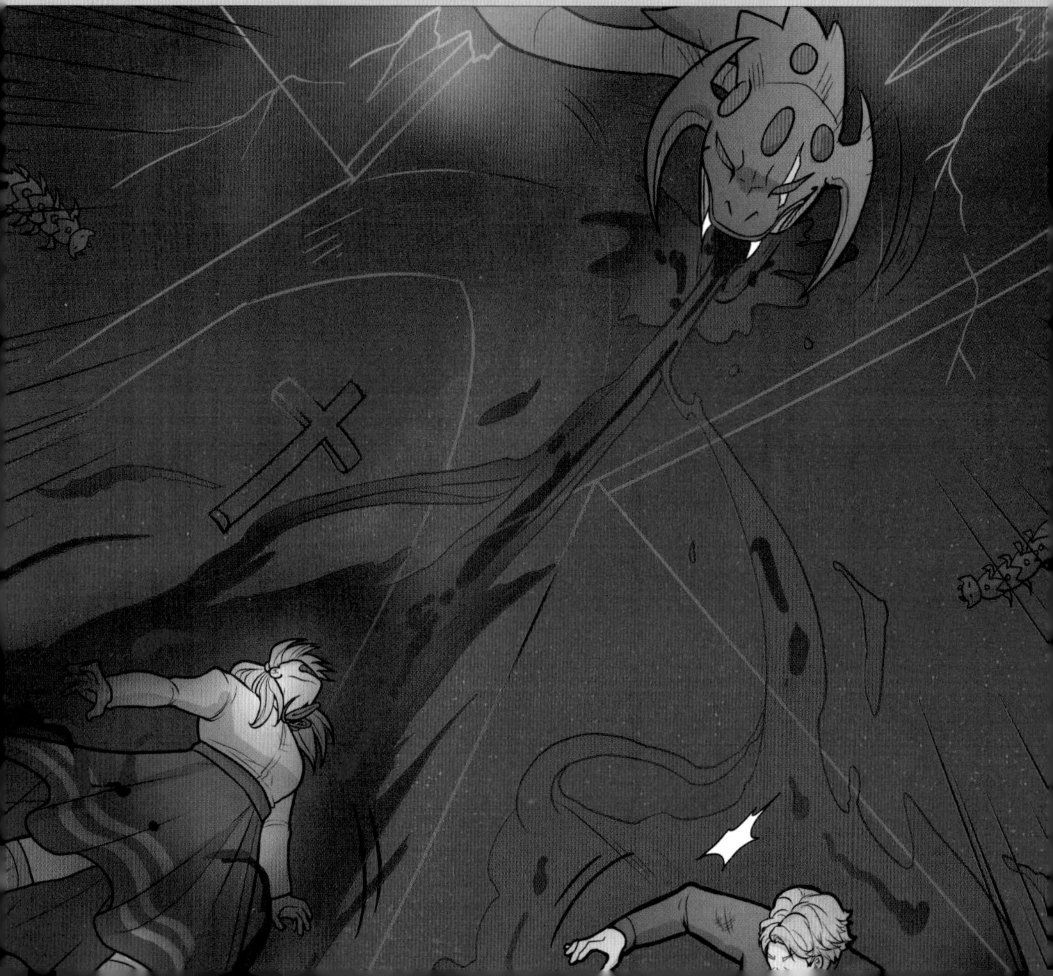

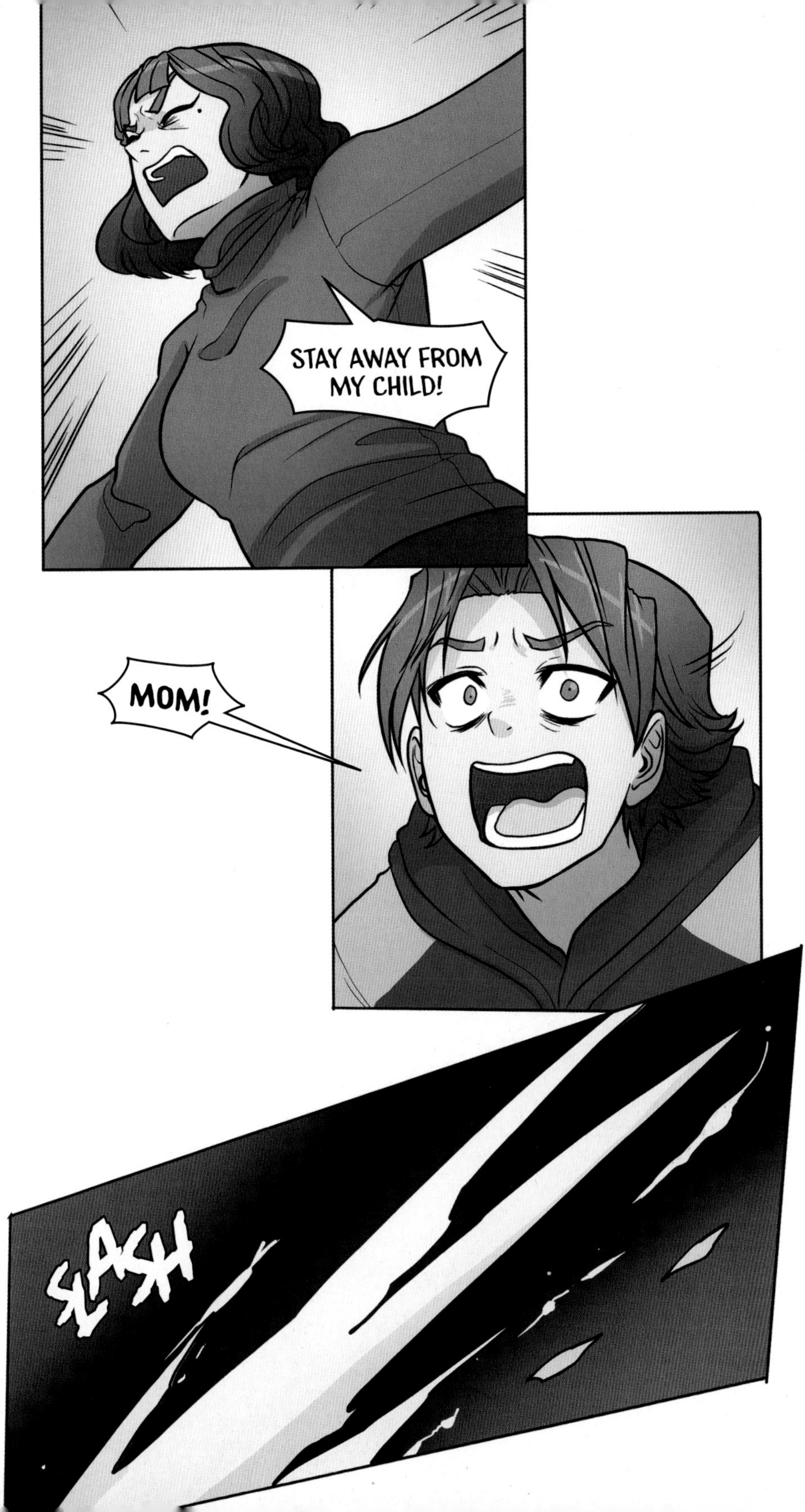
STAY AWAY FROM MY CHILD!
MOM!
SLASH

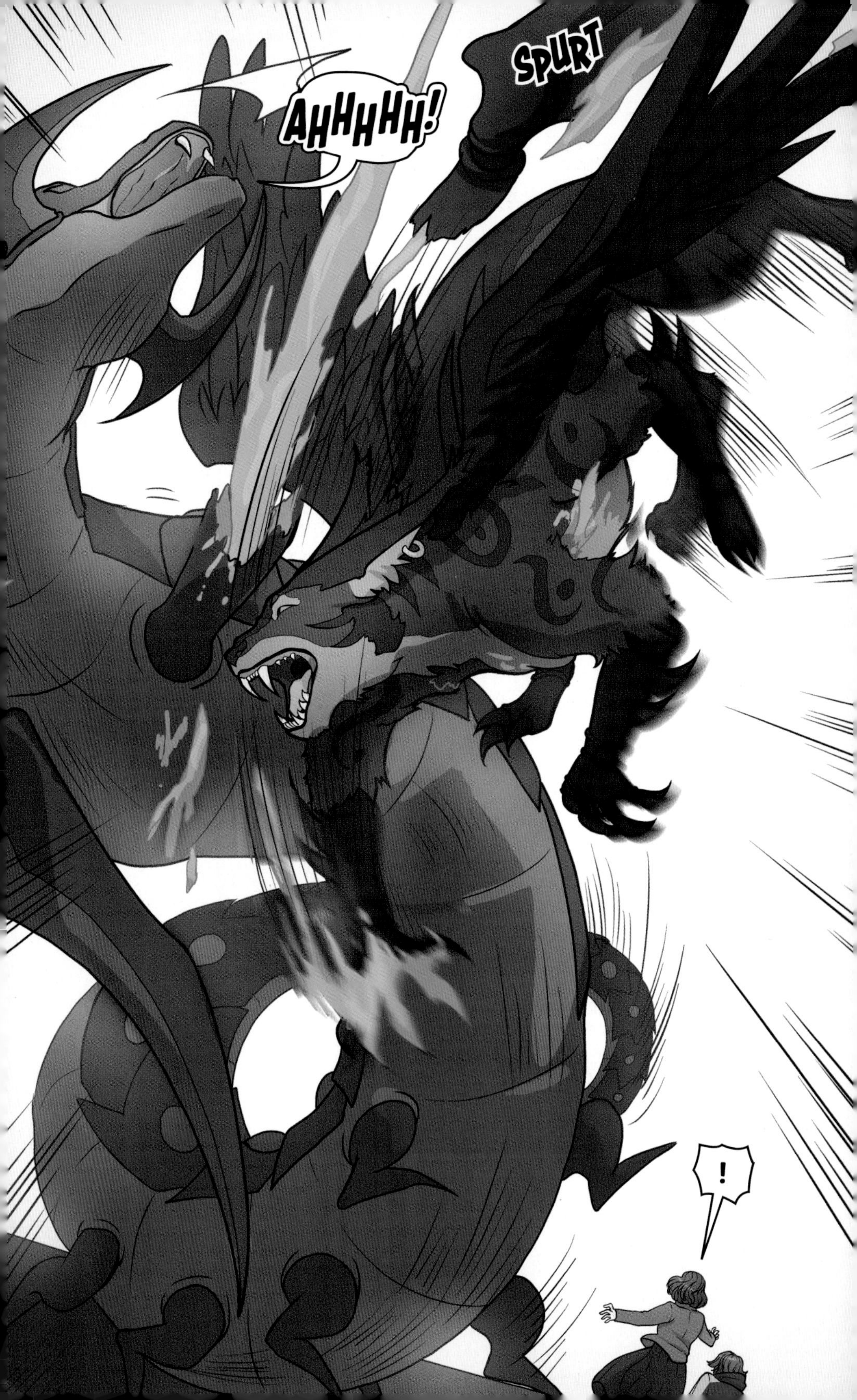
AHHHHH!
SPURT
!

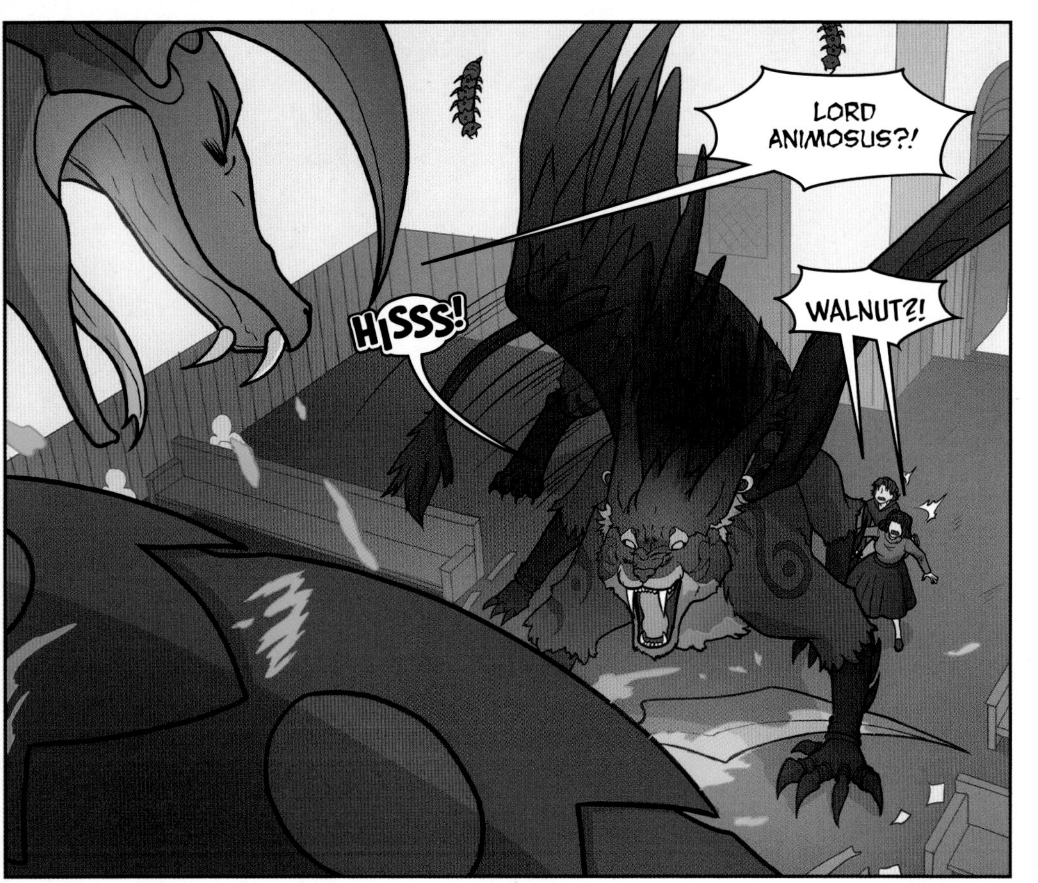
LORD ANIMOSUS?!
HISSS!
WALNUT?!

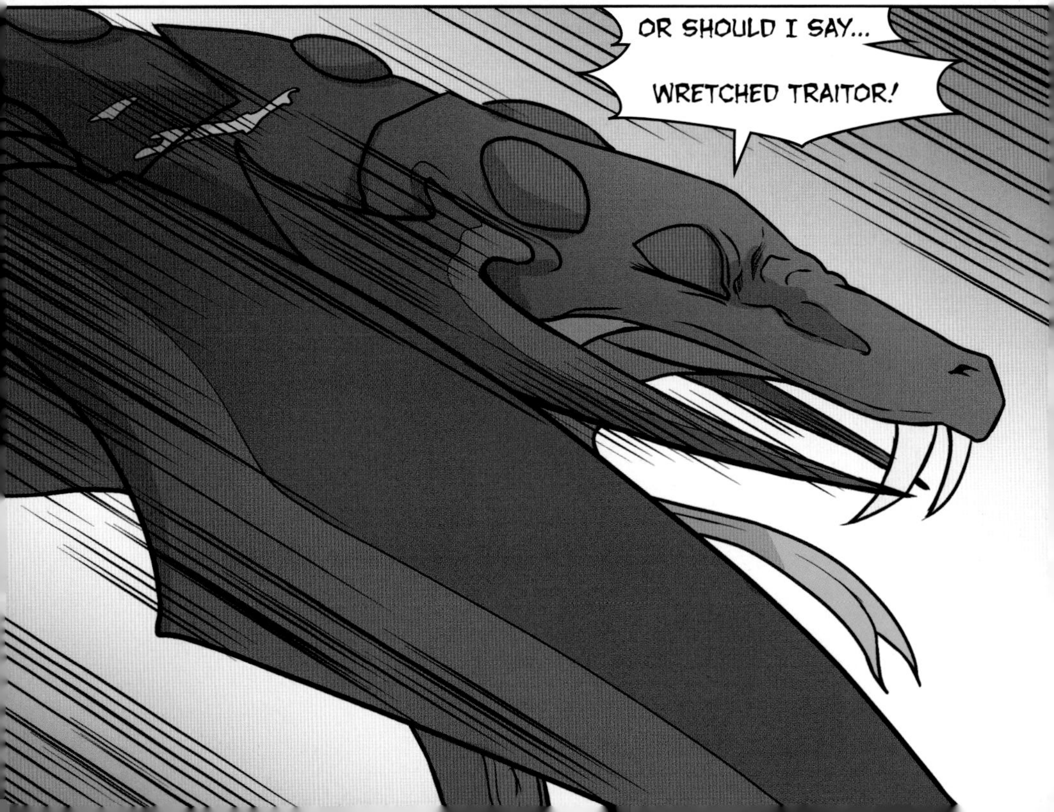
OR SHOULD I SAY...
WRETCHED TRAITOR!

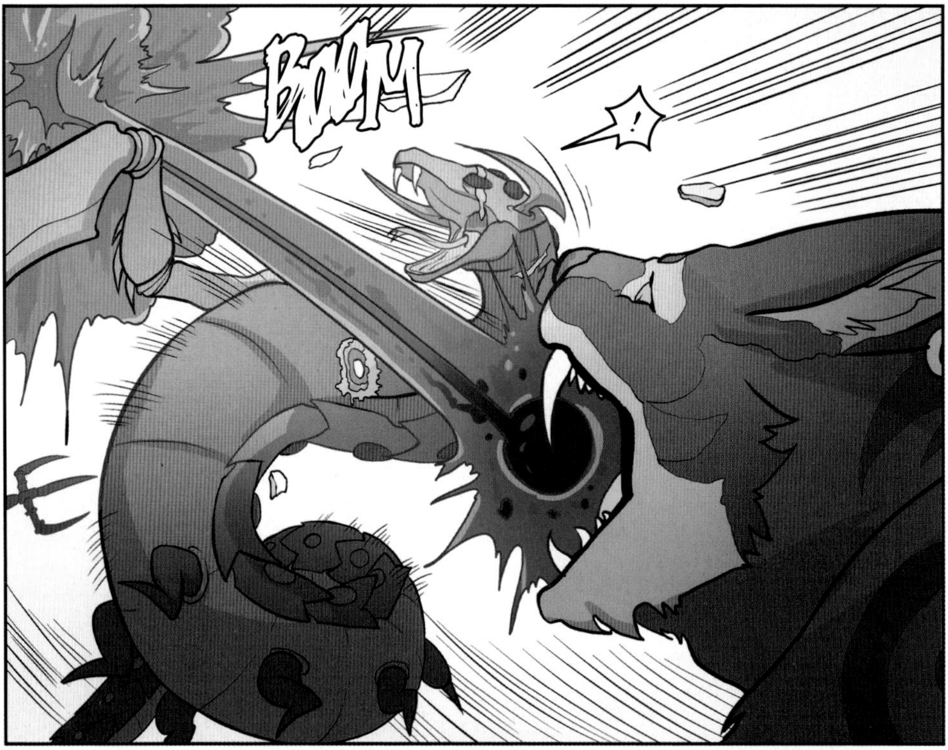
BOOM
!

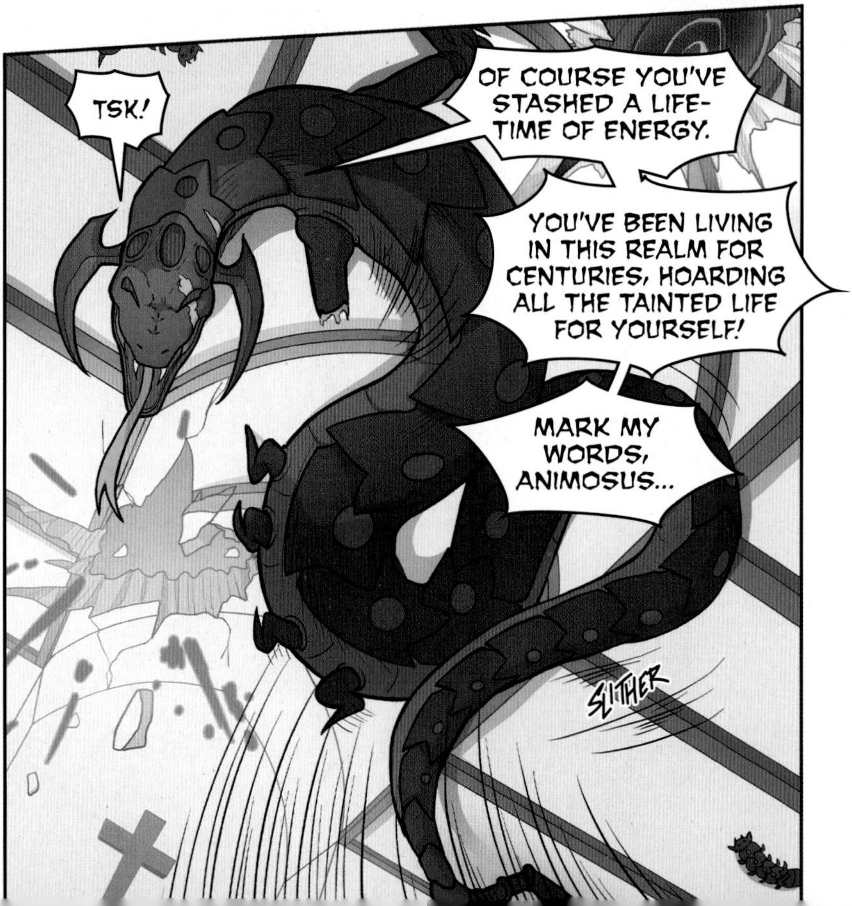
TSK!
OF COURSE YOU'VE STASHED A LIFE-TIME OF ENERGY.
YOU'VE BEEN LIVING IN THIS REALM FOR CENTURIES, HOARDING ALL THE TAINTED LIFE FOR YOURSELF!
MARK MY WORDS, ANIMOSUS...
SLITHER

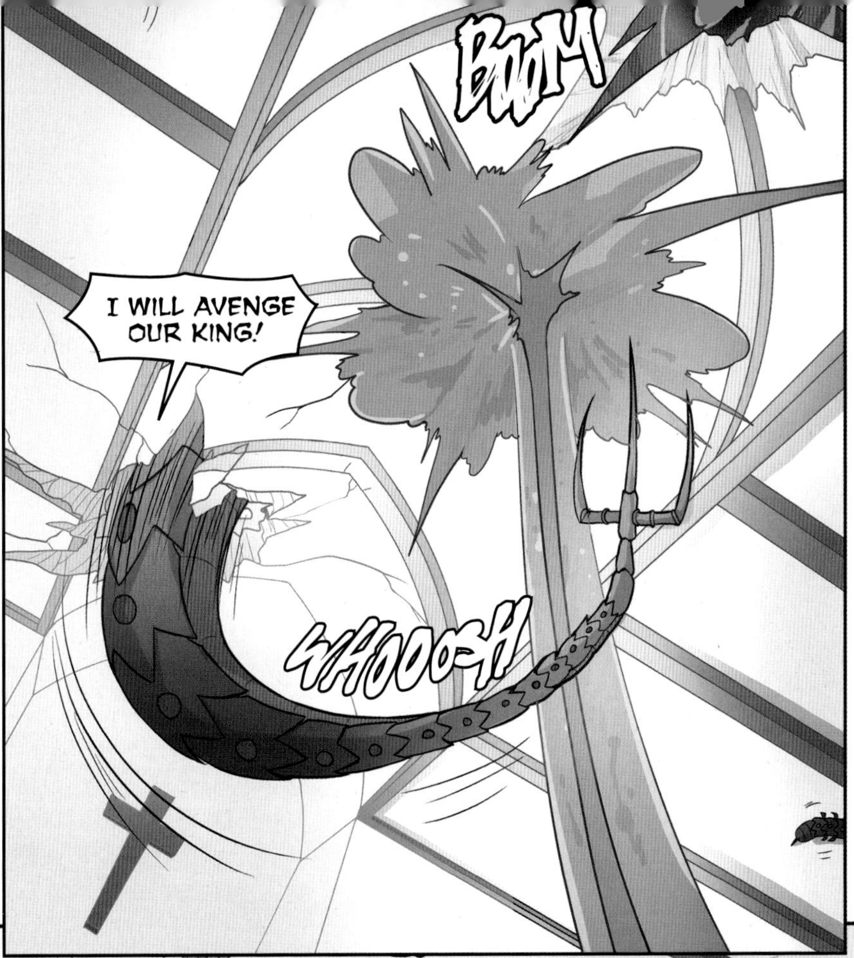
BOOM
I WILL AVENGE OUR KING!
WHOOOSH

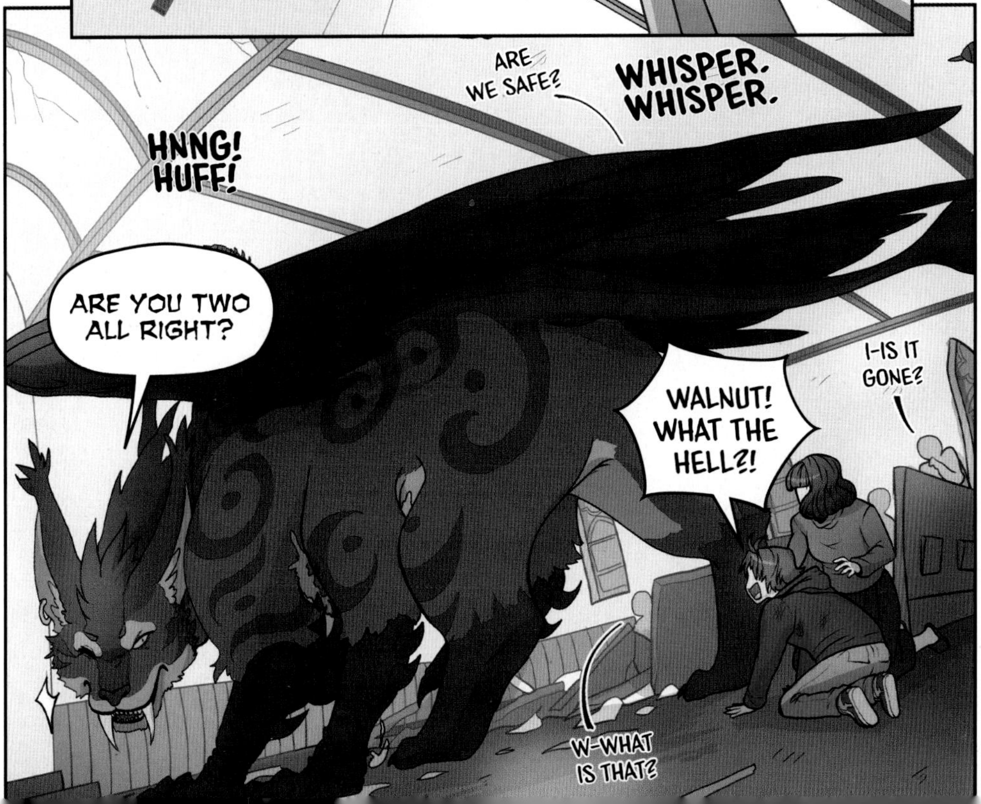
ARE WE SAFE?
WHISPER. WHISPER.
HNNG! HUFF!
ARE YOU TWO ALL RIGHT?
WALNUT! WHAT THE HELL?!
I-IS IT GONE?
W-WHAT IS THAT?

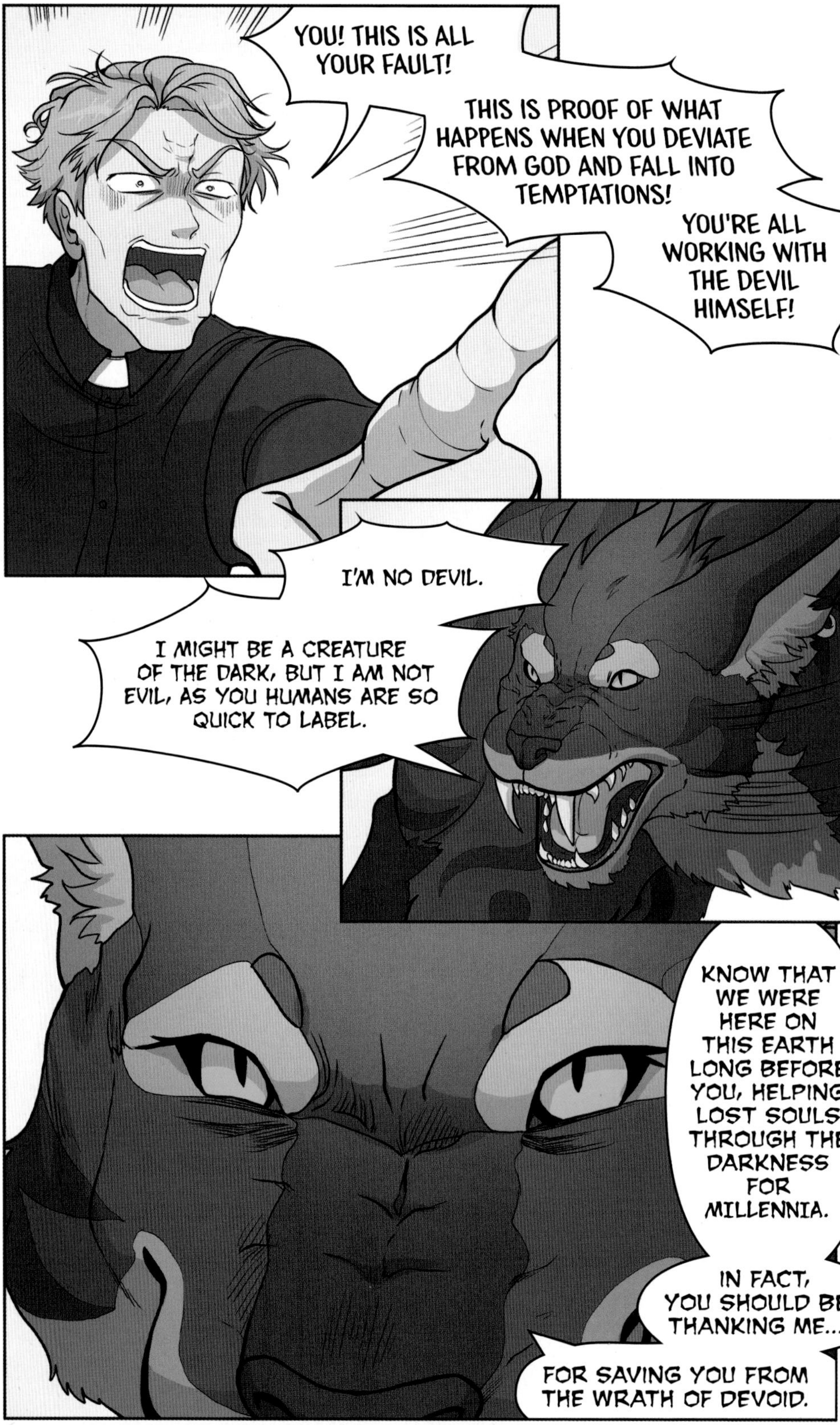
YOU! THIS IS ALL YOUR FAULT!
THIS IS PROOF OF WHAT HAPPENS WHEN YOU DEVIATE FROM GOD AND FALL INTO TEMPTATIONS!
YOU'RE ALL WORKING WITH THE DEVIL HIMSELF!
I'M NO DEVIL.
I MIGHT BE A CREATURE OF THE DARK, BUT I AM NOT EVIL, AS YOU HUMANS ARE SO QUICK TO LABEL.
KNOW THAT WE WERE HERE ON THIS EARTH LONG BEFORE YOU, HELPING LOST SOULS THROUGH THE DARKNESS FOR MILLENNIA.
IN FACT, YOU SHOULD BE THANKING ME...
FOR SAVING YOU FROM THE WRATH OF DEVOID.

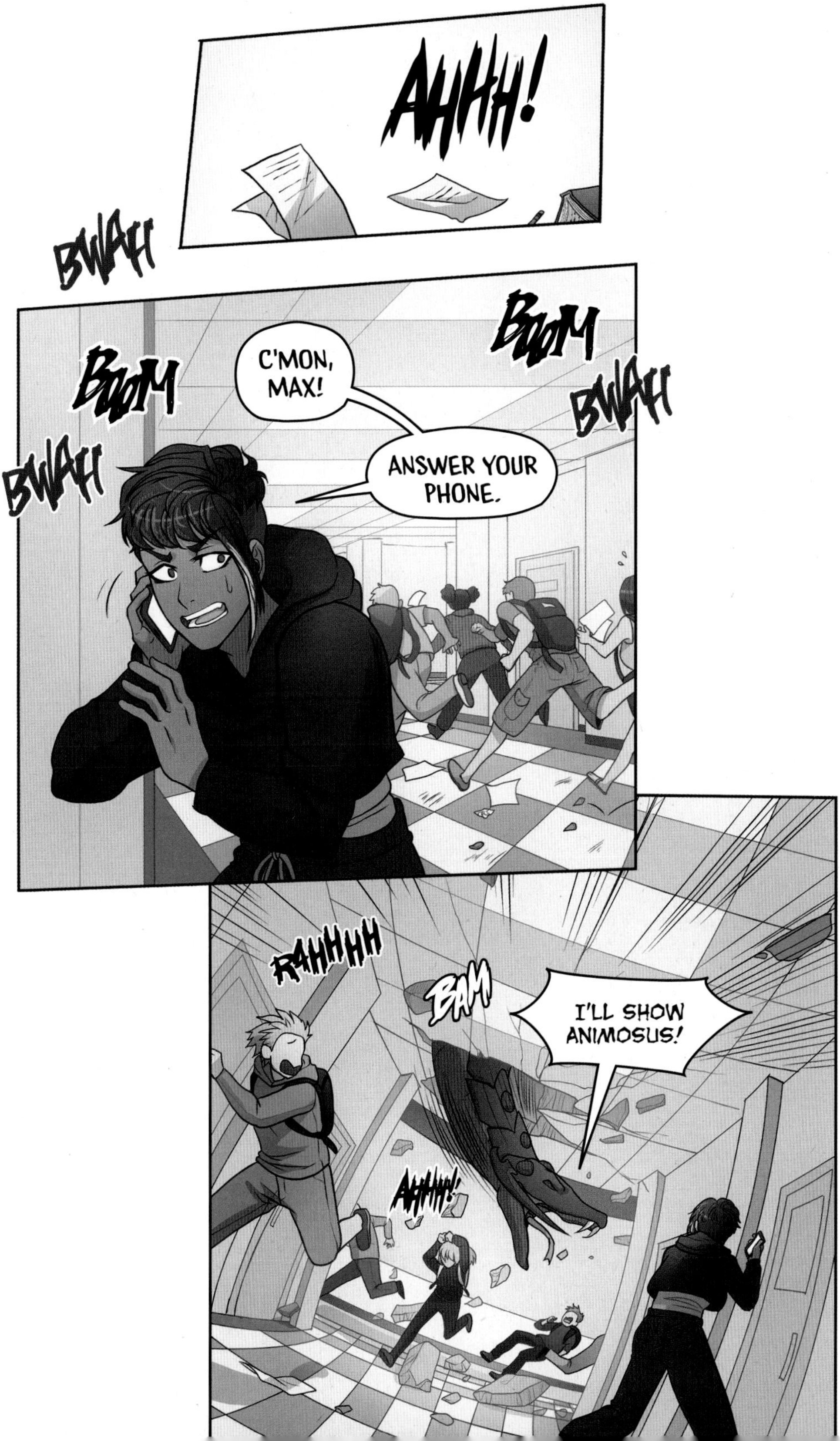
AHHH!
BWAH
BOOM
BWAH
C'MON, MAX!
ANSWER YOUR PHONE.
BOOM
BWAH
RAHHHH
BAM
I'LL SHOW ANIMOSUS!
AHHH!

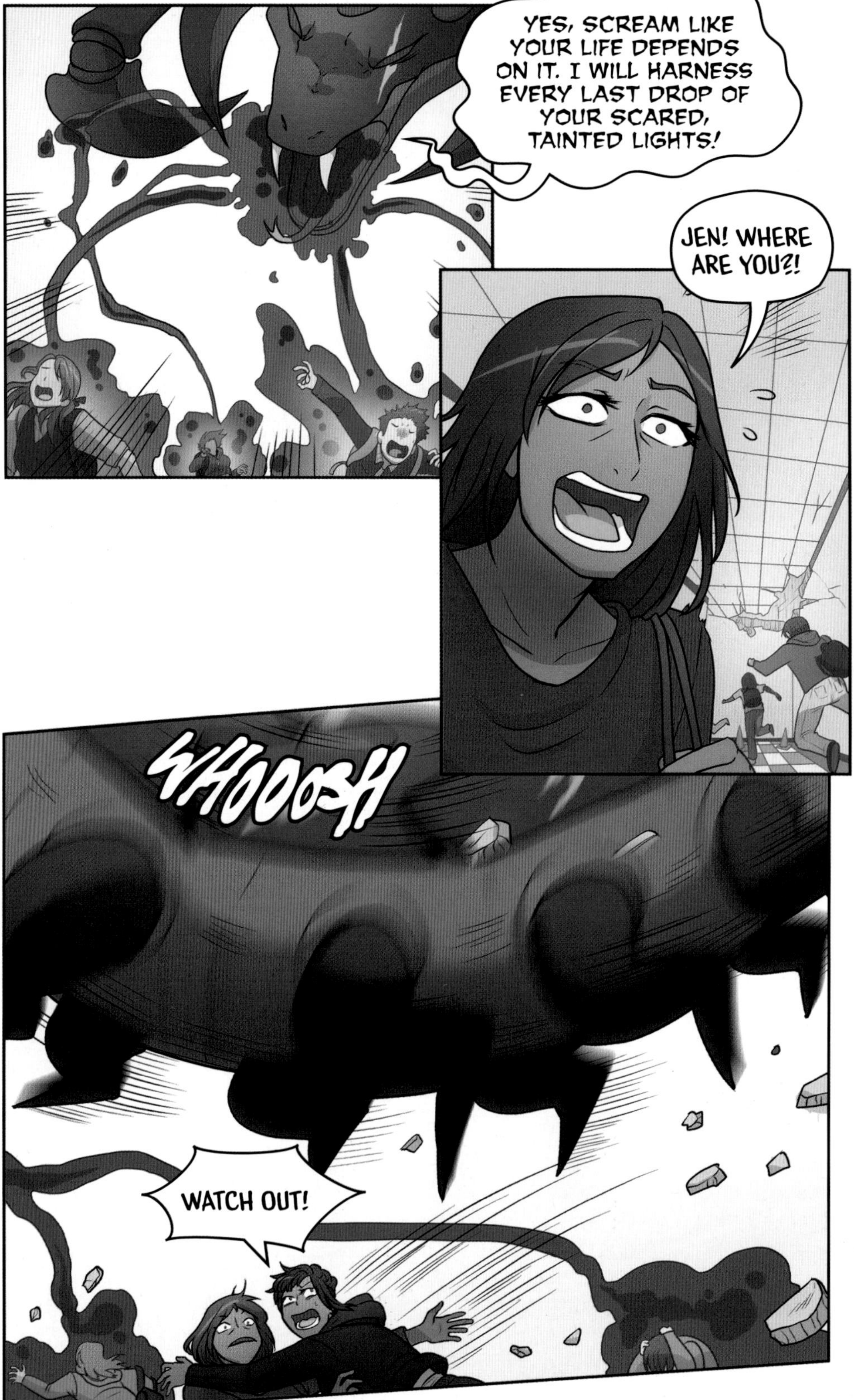
YES, SCREAM LIKE YOUR LIFE DEPENDS ON IT. I WILL HARNESS EVERY LAST DROP OF YOUR SCARED, TAINTED LIGHTS!
JEN! WHERE ARE YOU?!
WHOOOSH
WATCH OUT!

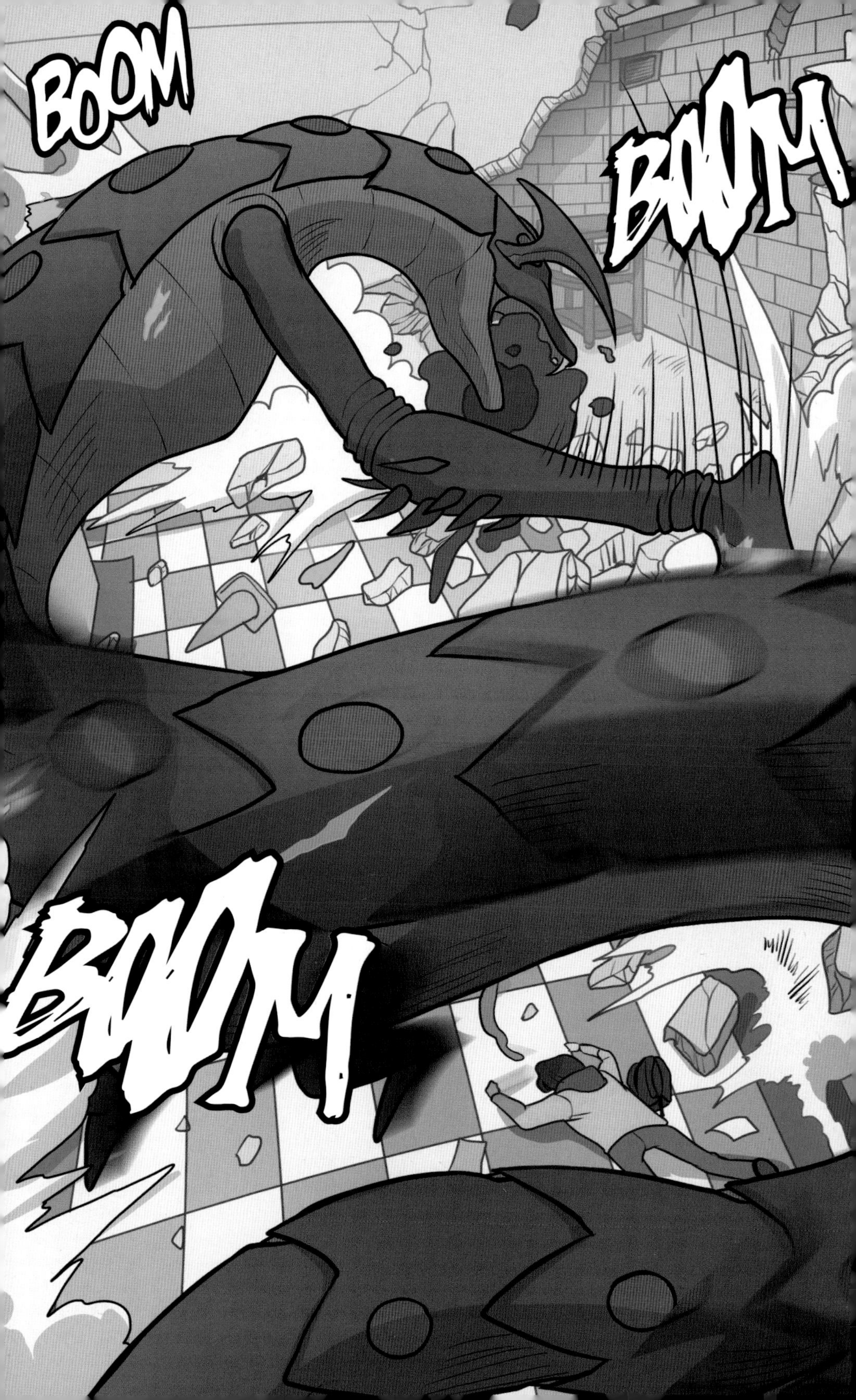
BOOM
BOOM
BOOM

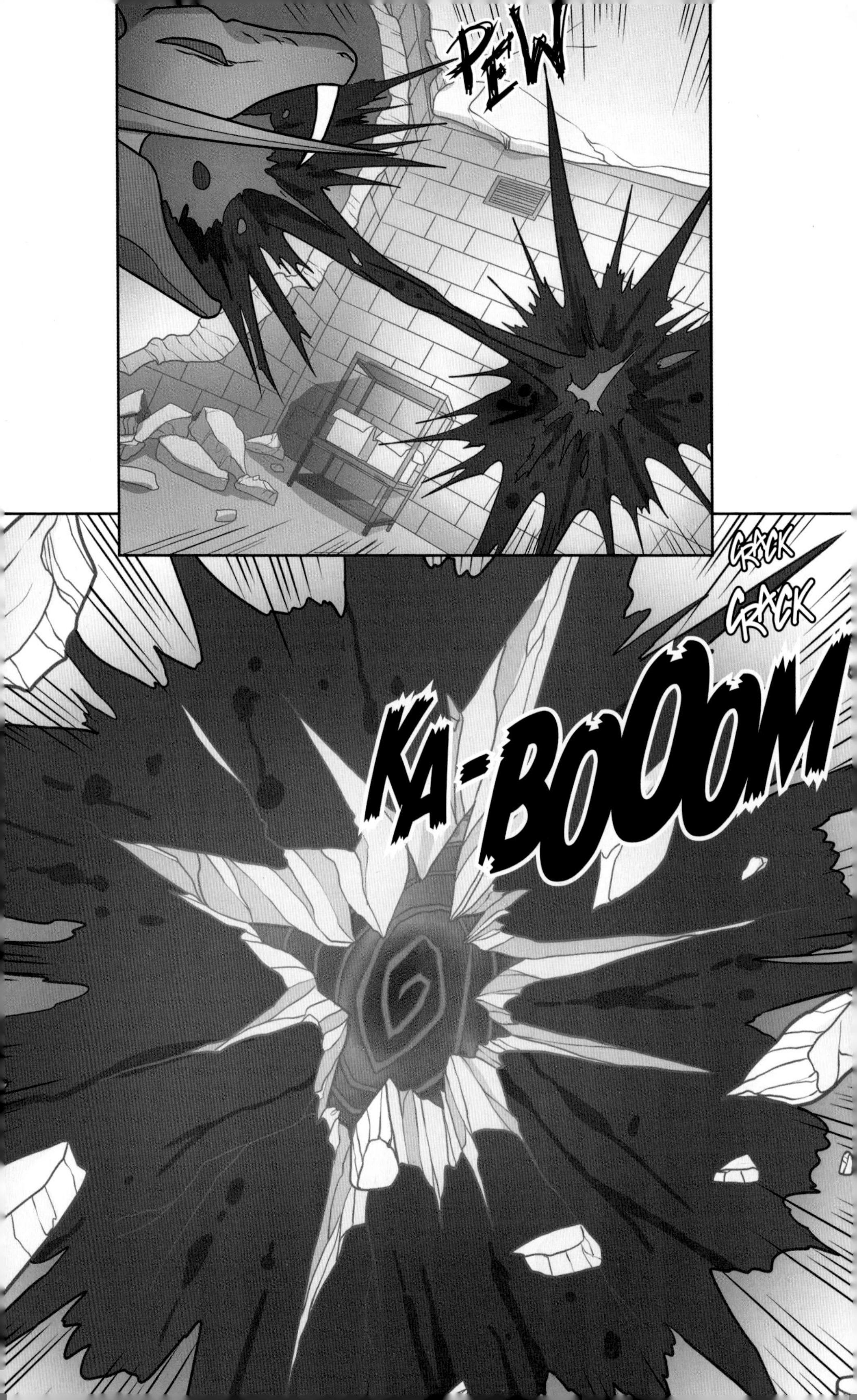
PEW
CRACK
CRACK
KA-BOOOOM

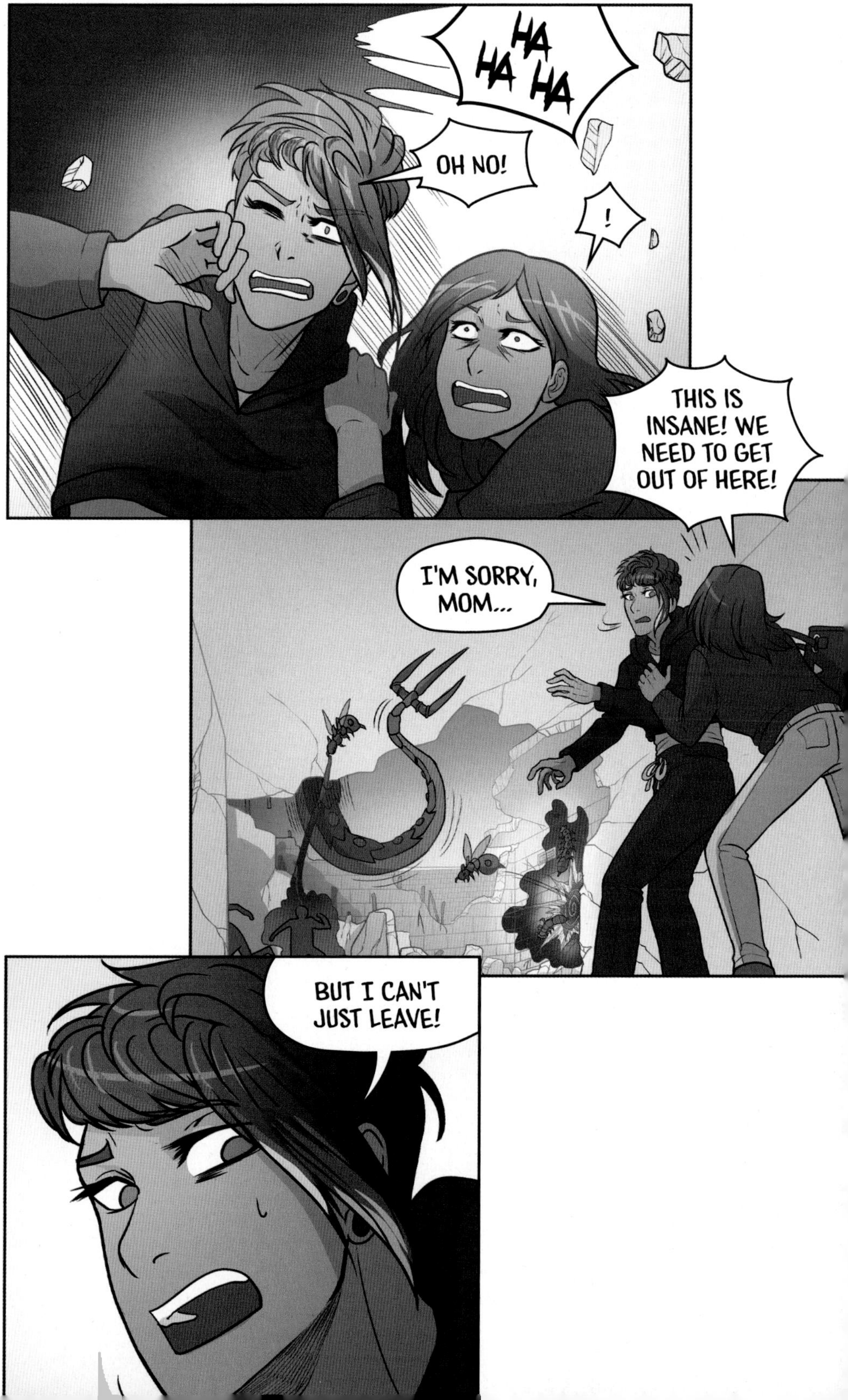
HA HA HA
OH NO!
!
THIS IS INSANE! WE NEED TO GET OUT OF HERE!
I'M SORRY, MOM...
BUT I CAN'T JUST LEAVE!

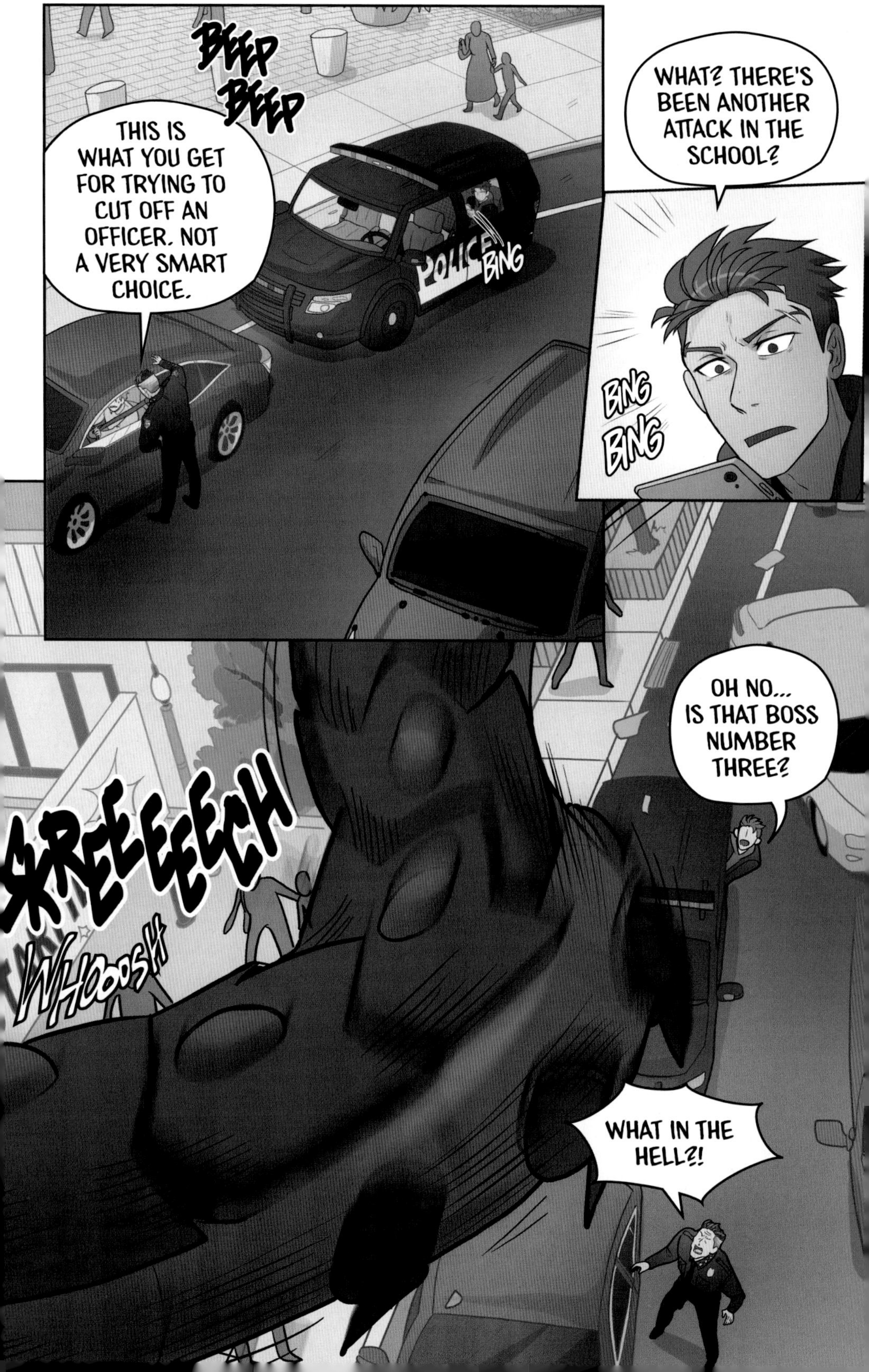
BEEP
BEEP
THIS IS WHAT YOU GET FOR TRYING TO CUT OFF AN OFFICER. NOT A VERY SMART CHOICE.
POLICE
BING
WHAT? THERE'S BEEN ANOTHER ATTACK IN THE SCHOOL?
BING
BING
SKREEEEECH
WHOOOSH
OH NO... IS THAT BOSS NUMBER THREE?
WHAT IN THE HELL?!

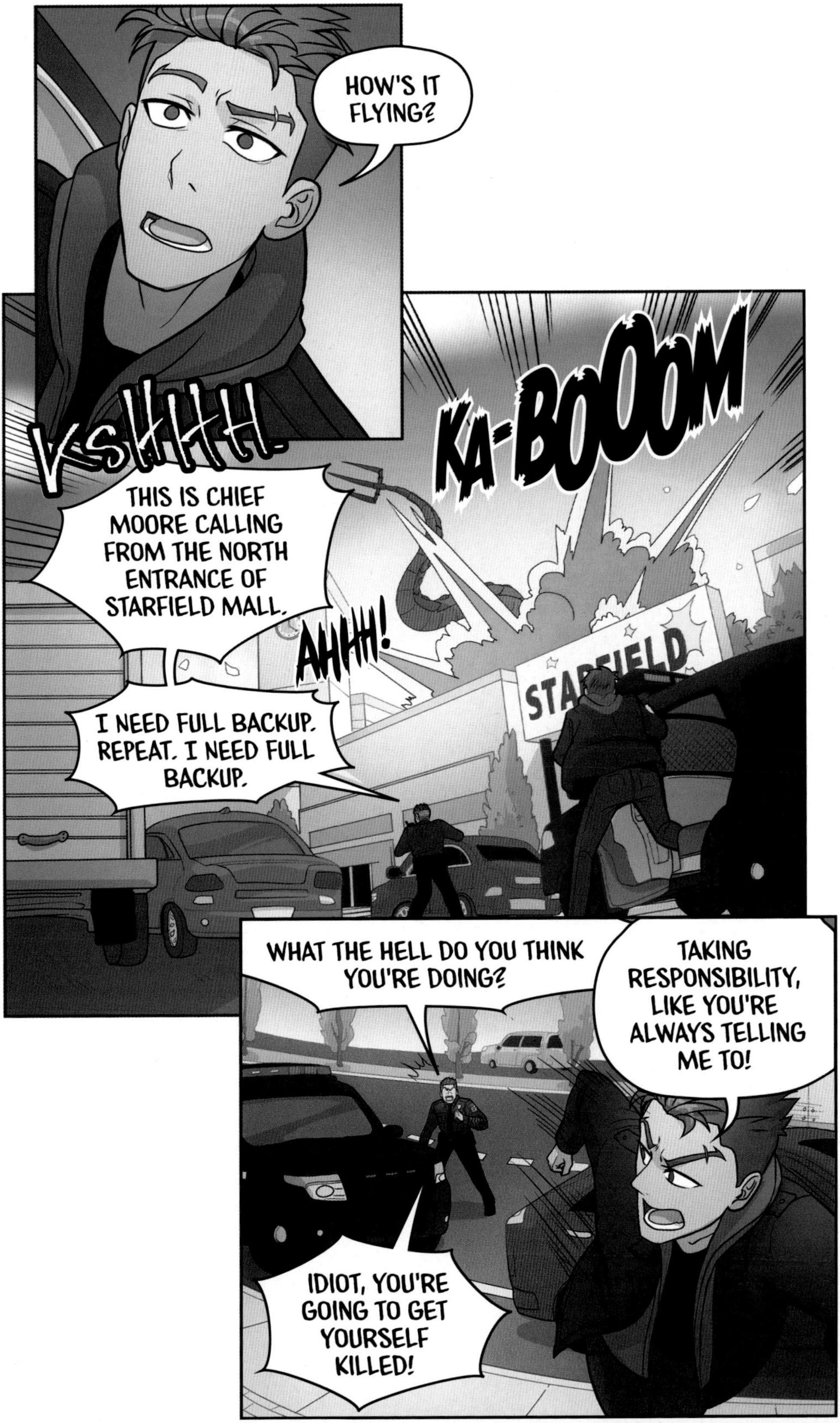

HOW'S IT FLYING?
KSHHH.
THIS IS CHIEF MOORE CALLING FROM THE NORTH ENTRANCE OF STARFIELD MALL.
KA-BOOOOM
AHHH!
STARFIELD
I NEED FULL BACKUP. REPEAT. I NEED FULL BACKUP.
WHAT THE HELL DO YOU THINK YOU'RE DOING?
TAKING RESPONSIBILITY, LIKE YOU'RE ALWAYS TELLING ME TO!
IDIOT, YOU'RE GOING TO GET YOURSELF KILLED!

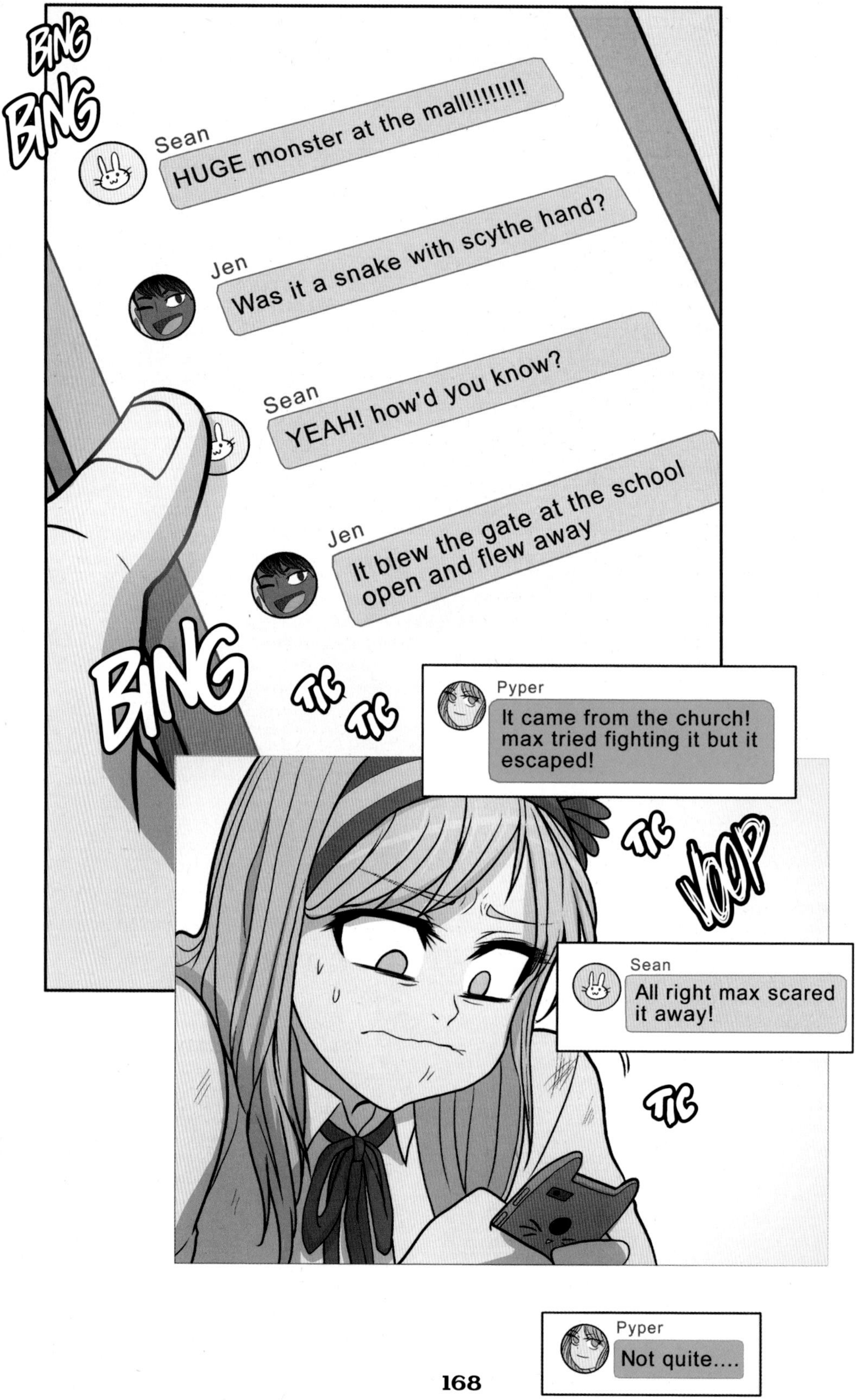
BING
BING
Sean
HUGE monster at the mall!!!!!!!!
Jen
Was it a snake with scythe hand?
Sean
YEAH! how'd you know?
Jen
It blew the gate at the school open and flew away
BING
TIC
TIC
Pyper
It came from the church! max tried fighting it but it escaped!
TIC
VOOP
Sean
All right max scared it away!
TIC
Pyper
Not quite....

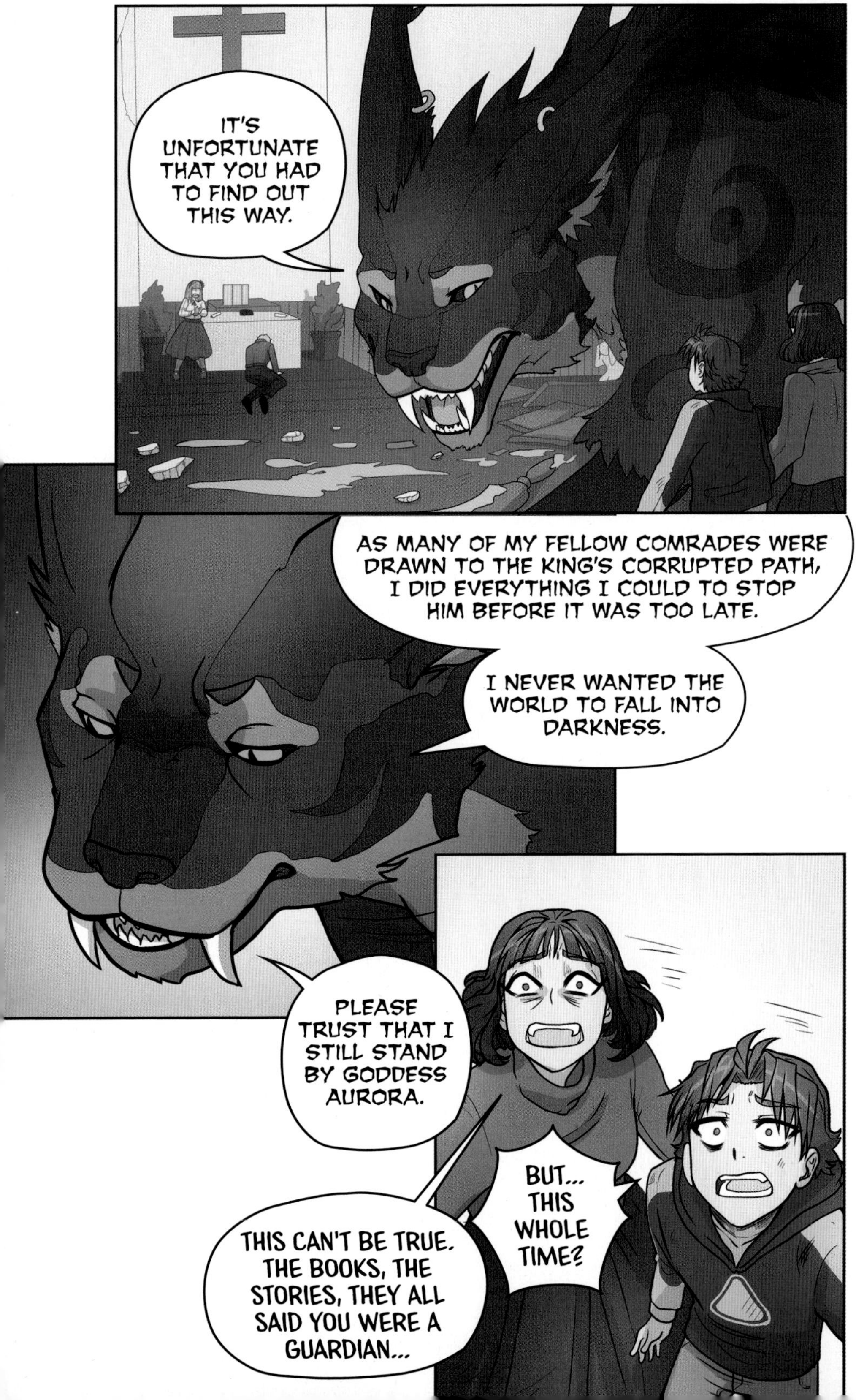
IT'S UNFORTUNATE THAT YOU HAD TO FIND OUT THIS WAY.
AS MANY OF MY FELLOW COMRADES WERE DRAWN TO THE KING'S CORRUPTED PATH, I DID EVERYTHING I COULD TO STOP HIM BEFORE IT WAS TOO LATE.
I NEVER WANTED THE WORLD TO FALL INTO DARKNESS.
PLEASE TRUST THAT I STILL STAND BY GODDESS AURORA.
THIS CAN'T BE TRUE. THE BOOKS, THE STORIES, THEY ALL SAID YOU WERE A GUARDIAN...
BUT... THIS WHOLE TIME?

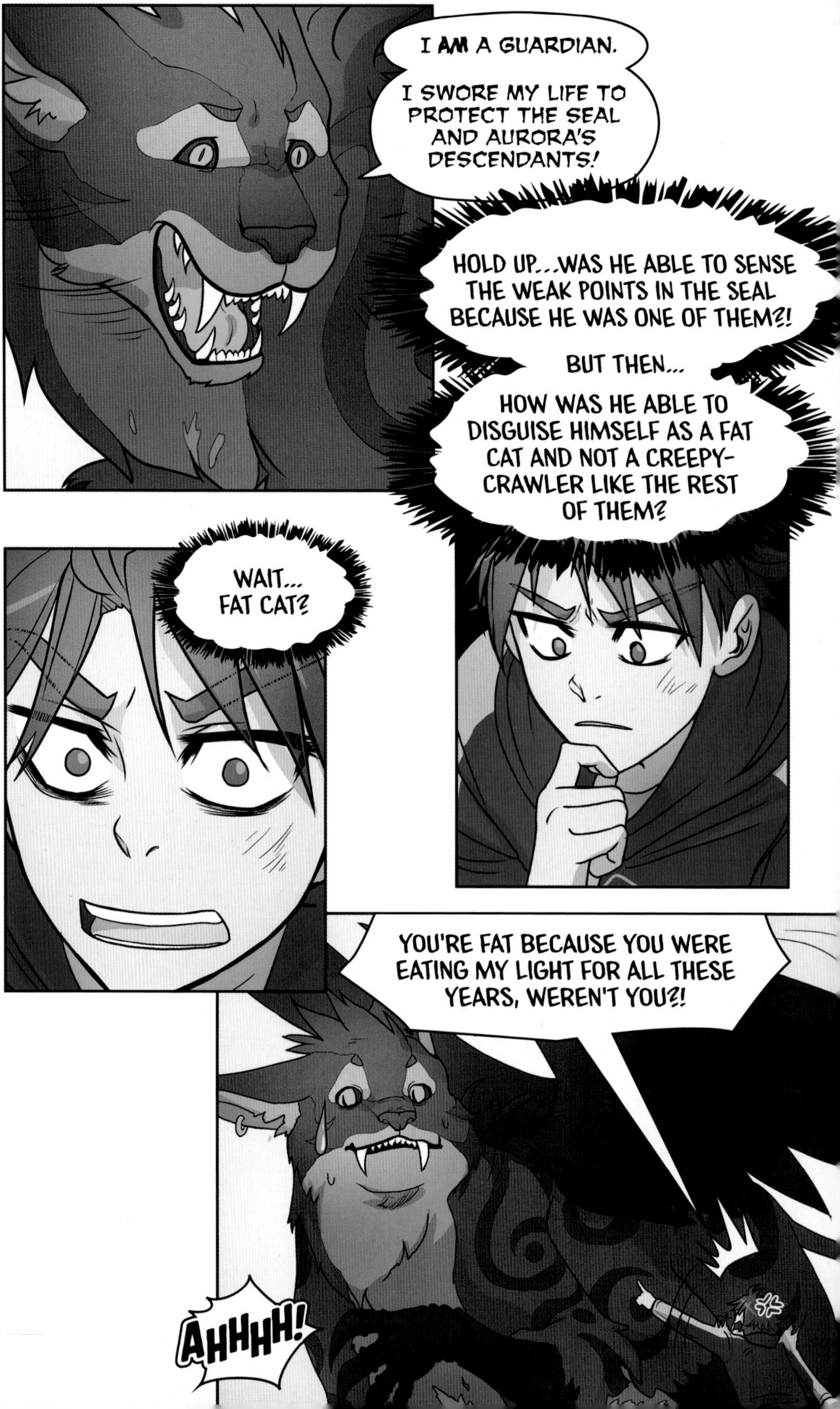
I AM A GUARDIAN.
I SWORE MY LIFE TO PROTECT THE SEAL AND AURORA'S DESCENDANTS!
HOLD UP...WAS HE ABLE TO SENSE THE WEAK POINTS IN THE SEAL BECAUSE HE WAS ONE OF THEM?!
BUT THEN...
HOW WAS HE ABLE TO DISGUISE HIMSELF AS A FAT CAT AND NOT A CREEPY-CRAWLER LIKE THE REST OF THEM?
WAIT... FAT CAT?
YOU'RE FAT BECAUSE YOU WERE EATING MY LIGHT FOR ALL THESE YEARS, WEREN'T YOU?!
AHHHH!

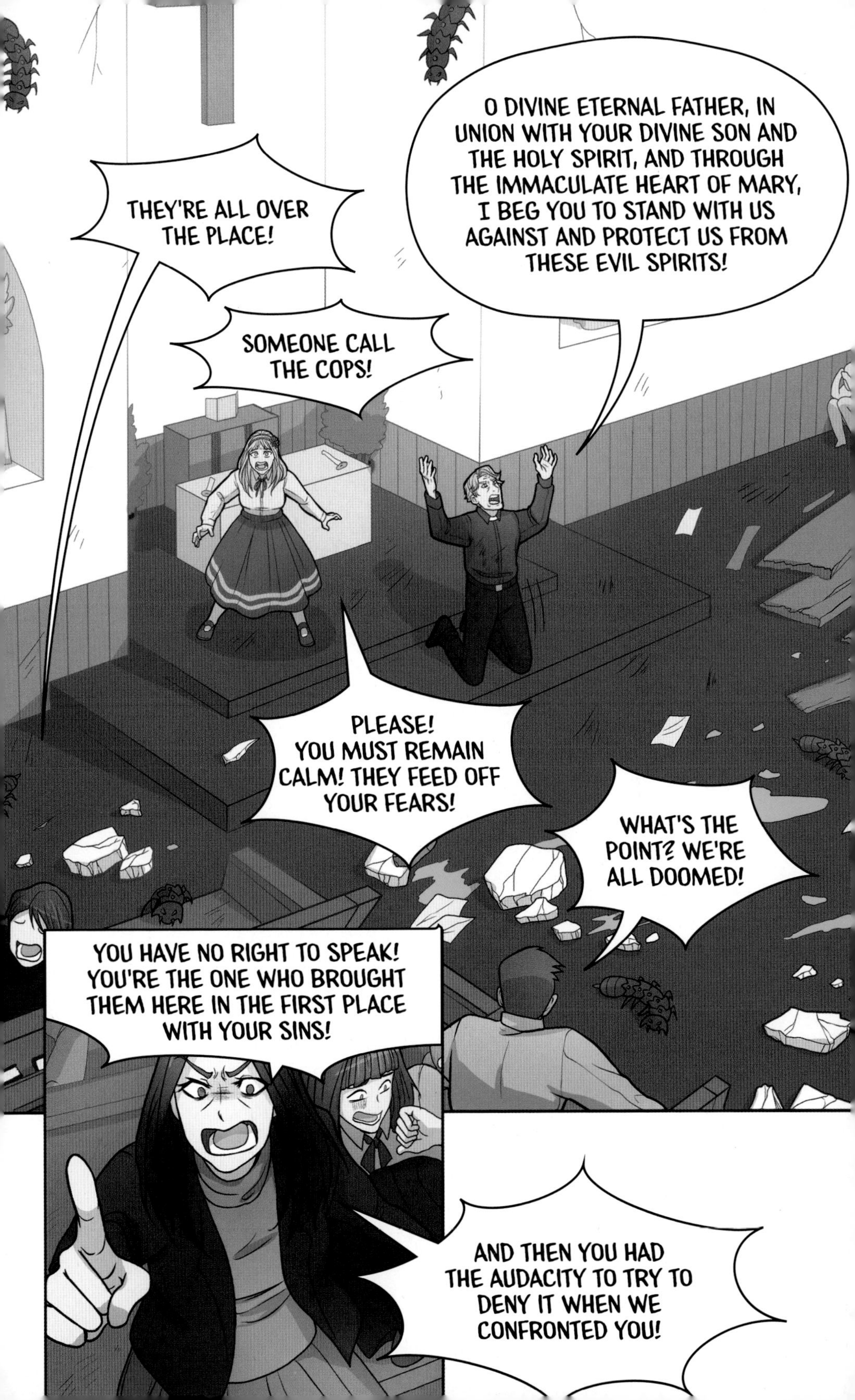
THEY'RE ALL OVER THE PLACE!
O DIVINE ETERNAL FATHER, IN UNION WITH YOUR DIVINE SON AND THE HOLY SPIRIT, AND THROUGH THE IMMACULATE HEART OF MARY, I BEG YOU TO STAND WITH US AGAINST AND PROTECT US FROM THESE EVIL SPIRITS!
SOMEONE CALL THE COPS!
PLEASE! YOU MUST REMAIN CALM! THEY FEED OFF YOUR FEARS!
WHAT'S THE POINT? WE'RE ALL DOOMED!
YOU HAVE NO RIGHT TO SPEAK! YOU'RE THE ONE WHO BROUGHT THEM HERE IN THE FIRST PLACE WITH YOUR SINS!
AND THEN YOU HAD THE AUDACITY TO TRY TO DENY IT WHEN WE CONFRONTED YOU!

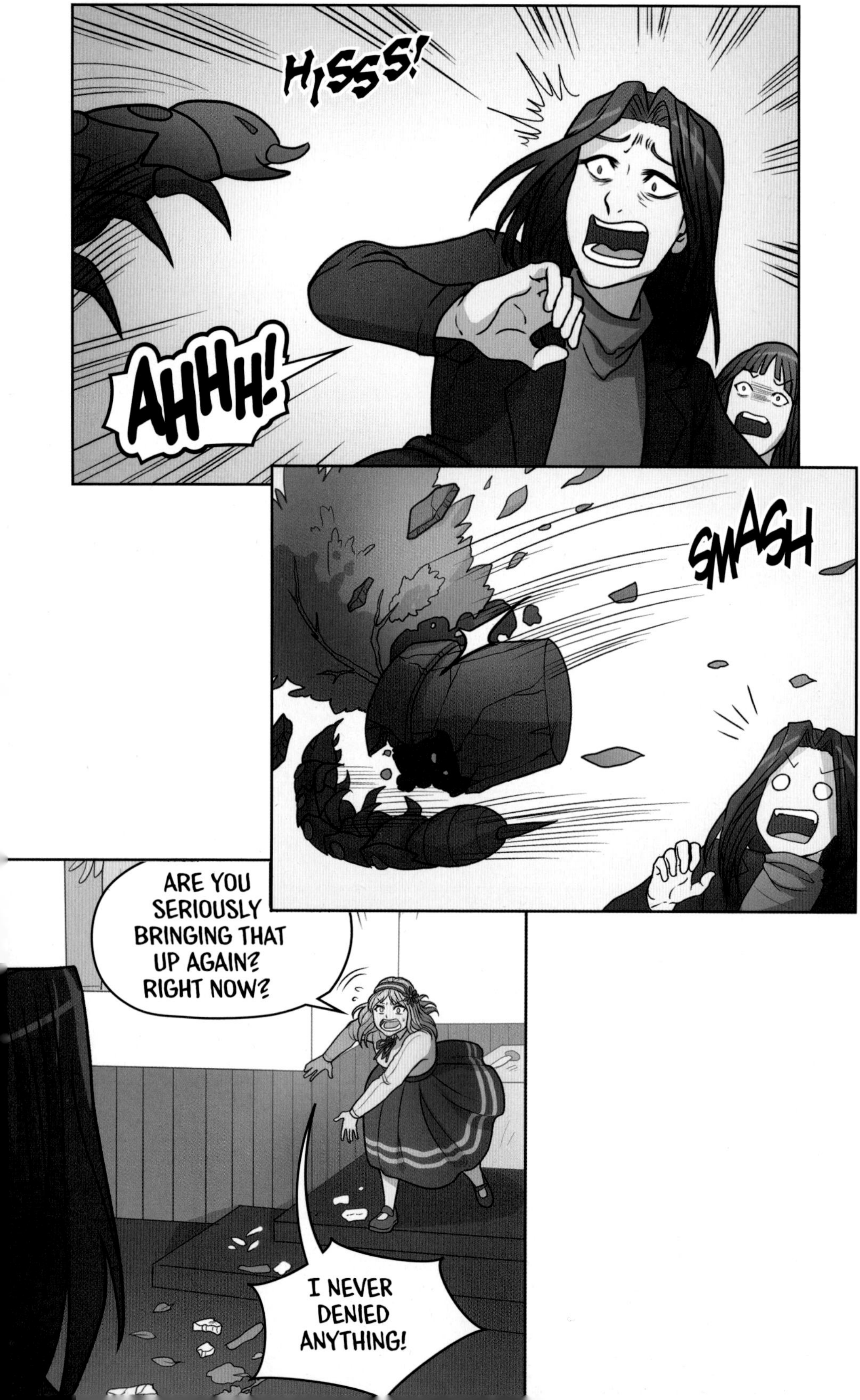
HISSS!
AHHH!
SMASH
ARE YOU SERIOUSLY BRINGING THAT UP AGAIN? RIGHT NOW?
I NEVER DENIED ANYTHING!

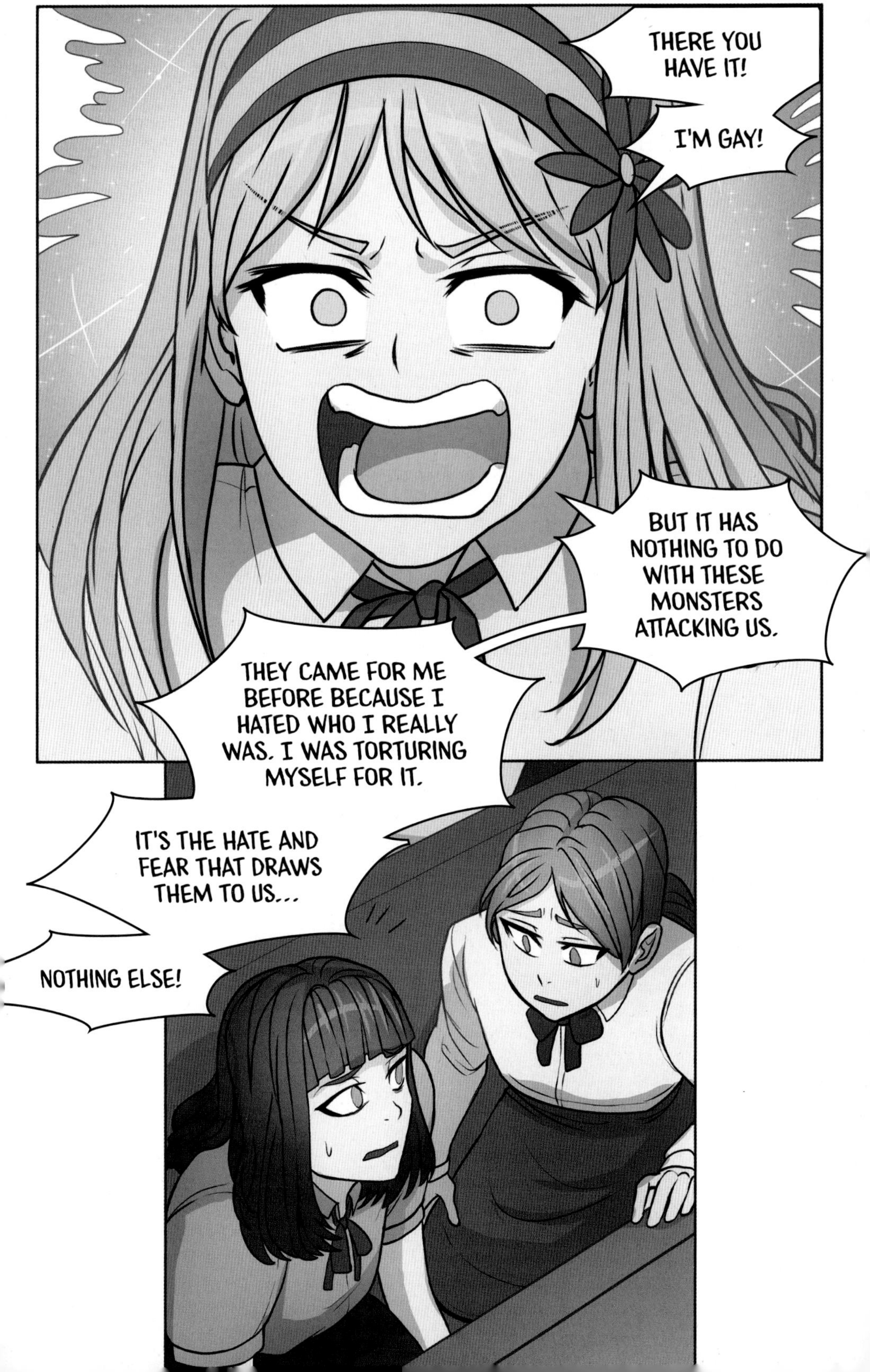
THERE YOU HAVE IT!
I'M GAY!
BUT IT HAS NOTHING TO DO WITH THESE MONSTERS ATTACKING US.
THEY CAME FOR ME BEFORE BECAUSE I HATED WHO I REALLY WAS. I WAS TORTURING MYSELF FOR IT.
IT'S THE HATE AND FEAR THAT DRAWS THEM TO US...
NOTHING ELSE!

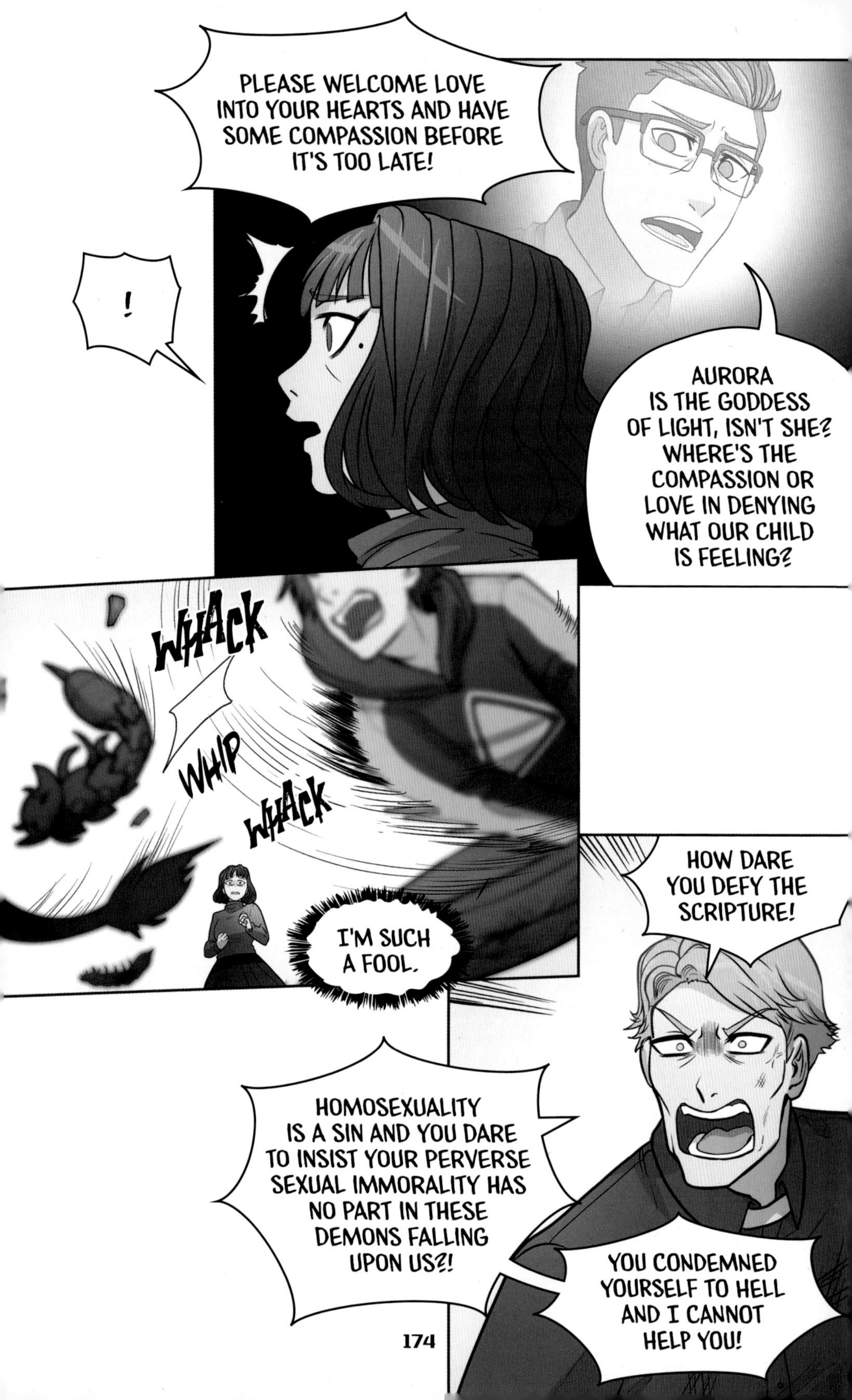
PLEASE WELCOME LOVE INTO YOUR HEARTS AND HAVE SOME COMPASSION BEFORE IT'S TOO LATE!
!
AURORA IS THE GODDESS OF LIGHT, ISN'T SHE? WHERE'S THE COMPASSION OR LOVE IN DENYING WHAT OUR CHILD IS FEELING?
WHACK
WHIP
WHACK
I'M SUCH A FOOL.
HOW DARE YOU DEFY THE SCRIPTURE!
HOMOSEXUALITY IS A SIN AND YOU DARE TO INSIST YOUR PERVERSE SEXUAL IMMORALITY HAS NO PART IN THESE DEMONS FALLING UPON US?!
YOU CONDEMNED YOURSELF TO HELL AND I CANNOT HELP YOU!

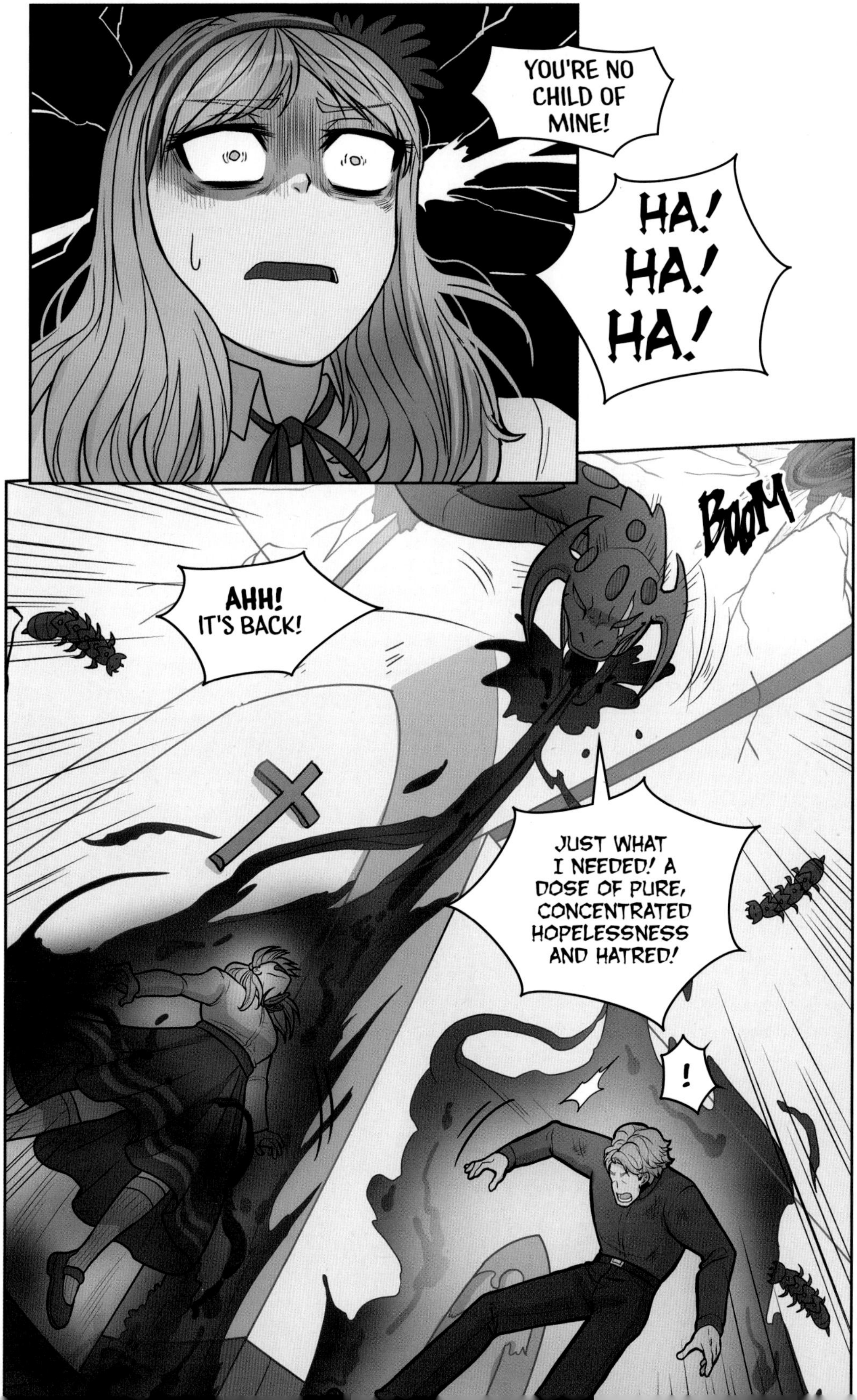
YOU'RE NO CHILD OF MINE!
HA! HA! HA!
BOOM
AHH! IT'S BACK!
JUST WHAT I NEEDED! A DOSE OF PURE, CONCENTRATED HOPELESSNESS AND HATRED!
!

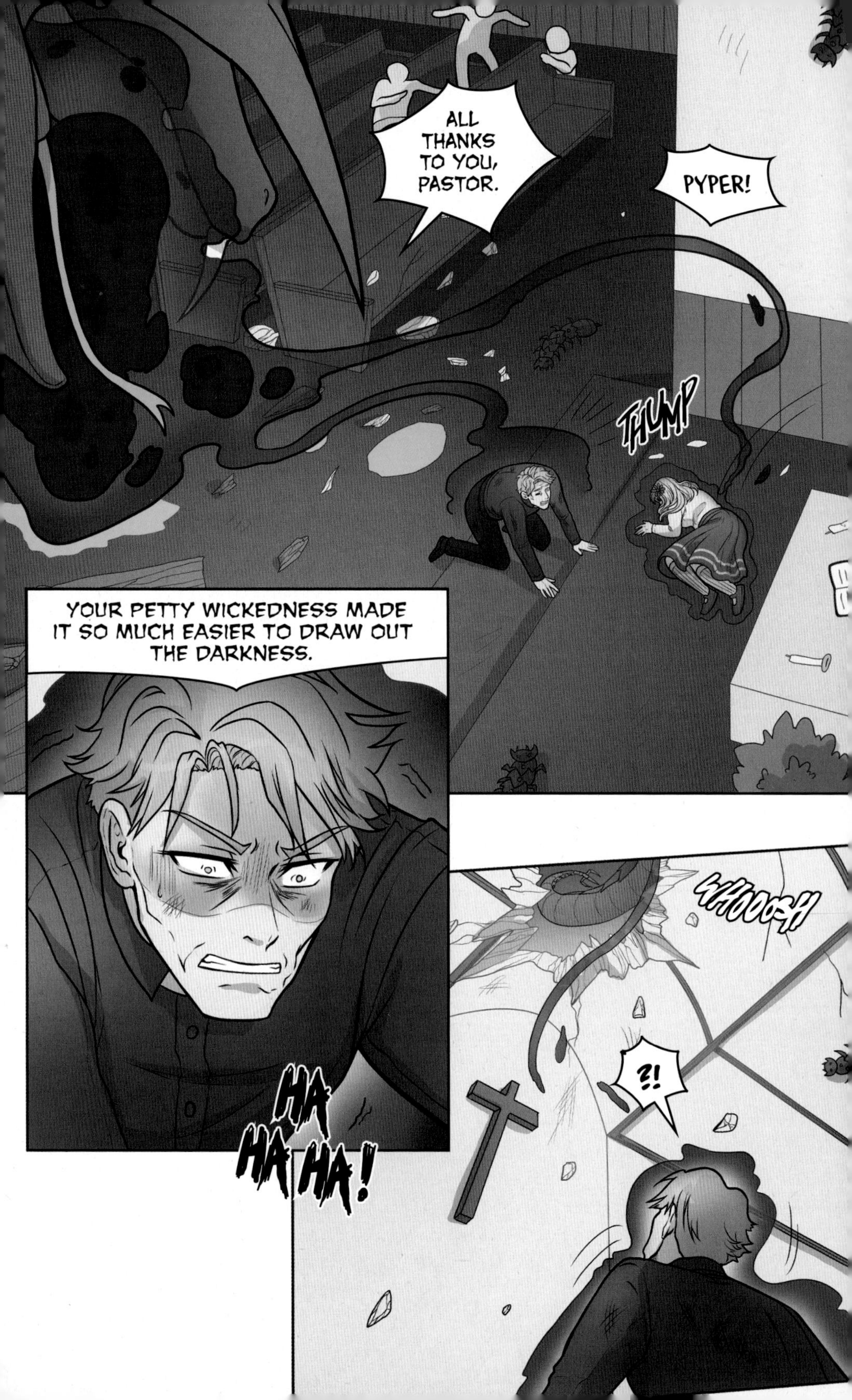
ALL THANKS TO YOU, PASTOR.
PYPER!
THUMP
YOUR PETTY WICKEDNESS MADE IT SO MUCH EASIER TO DRAW OUT THE DARKNESS.
HA HA HA HA!
WHOOOSH
?!

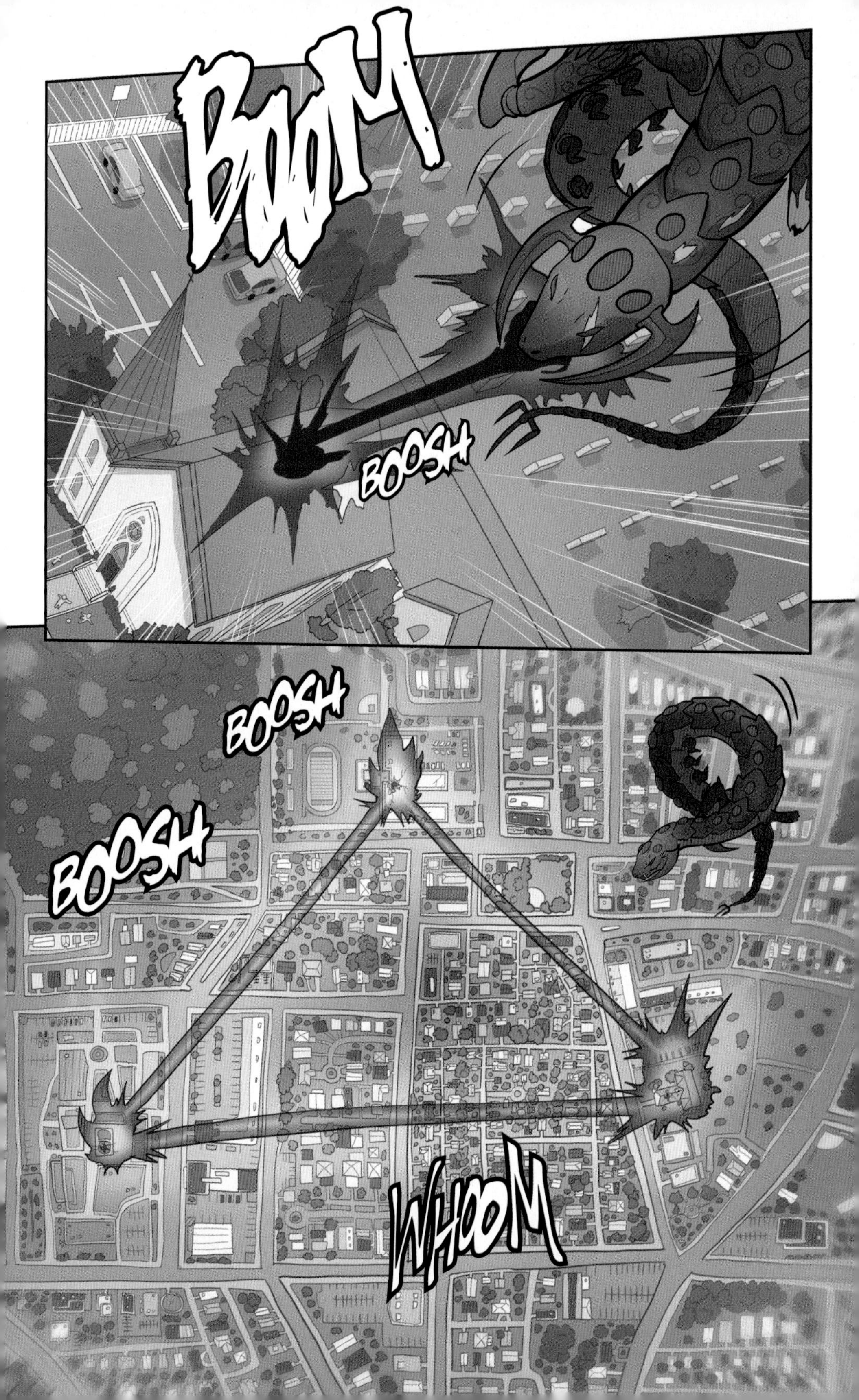
BOOM
BOOSH
BOOSH
BOOSH
WHOOM

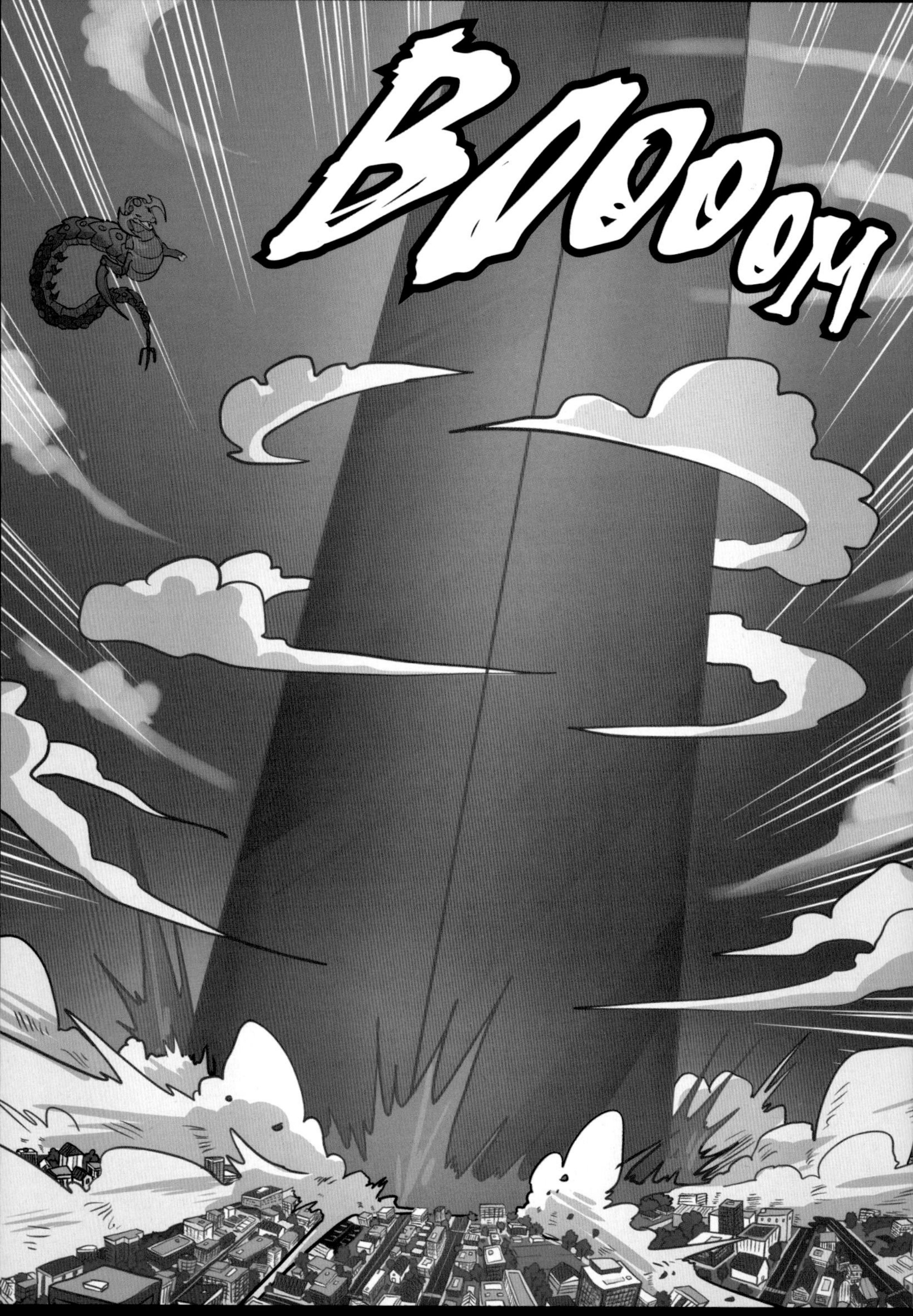
BLOOOOM

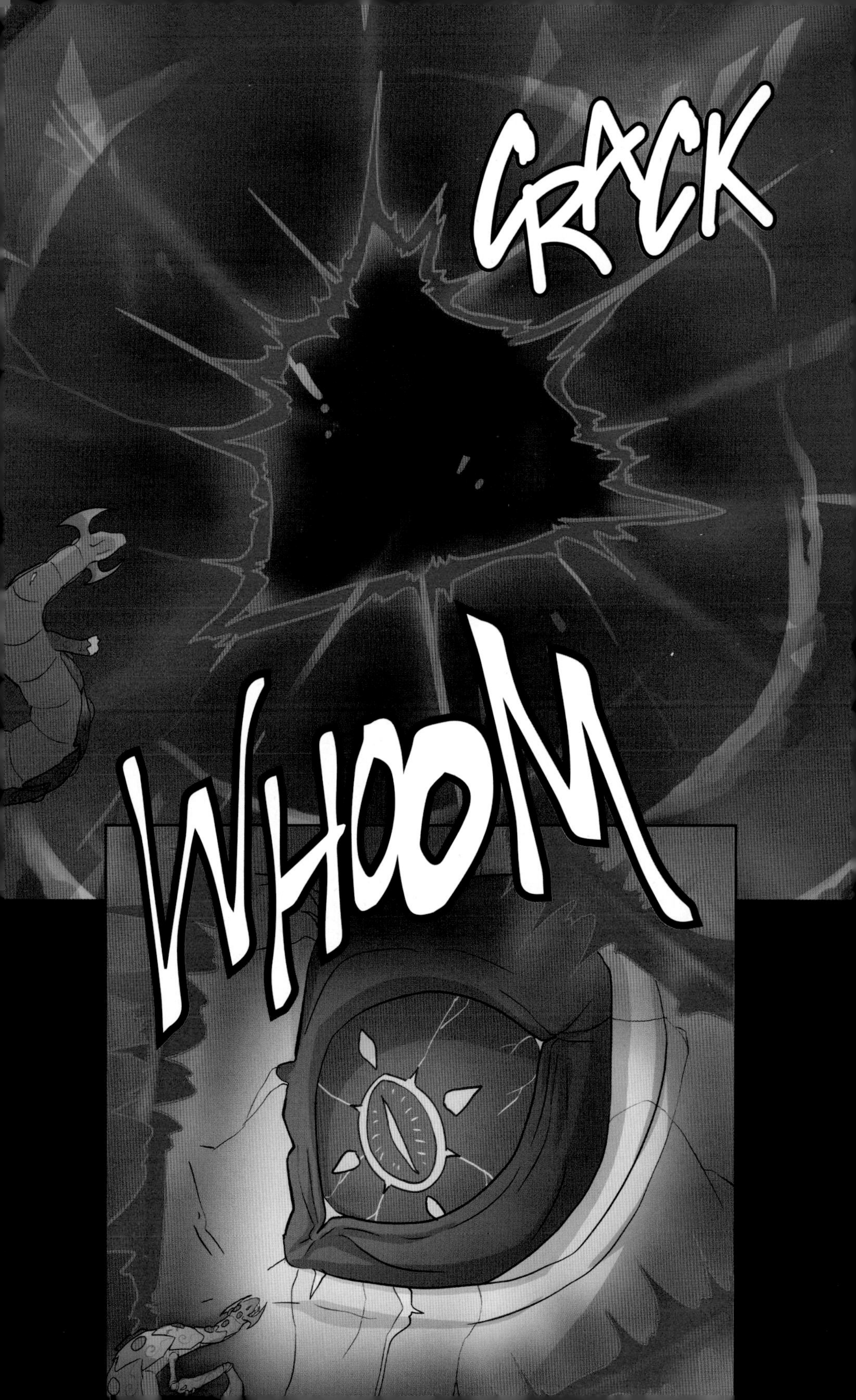
CRACK
WHOOM

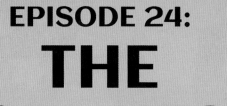

EPISODE 24:

THE DARKNESS FALLS (PT. 1)

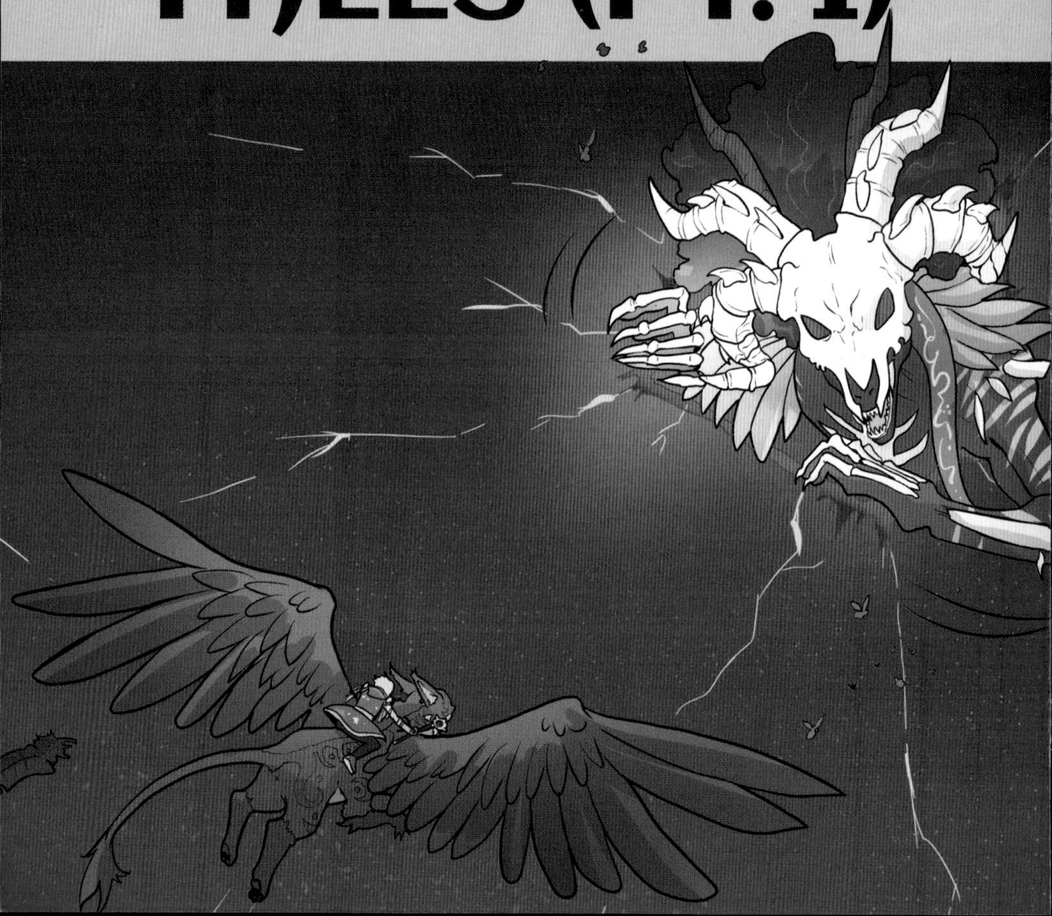

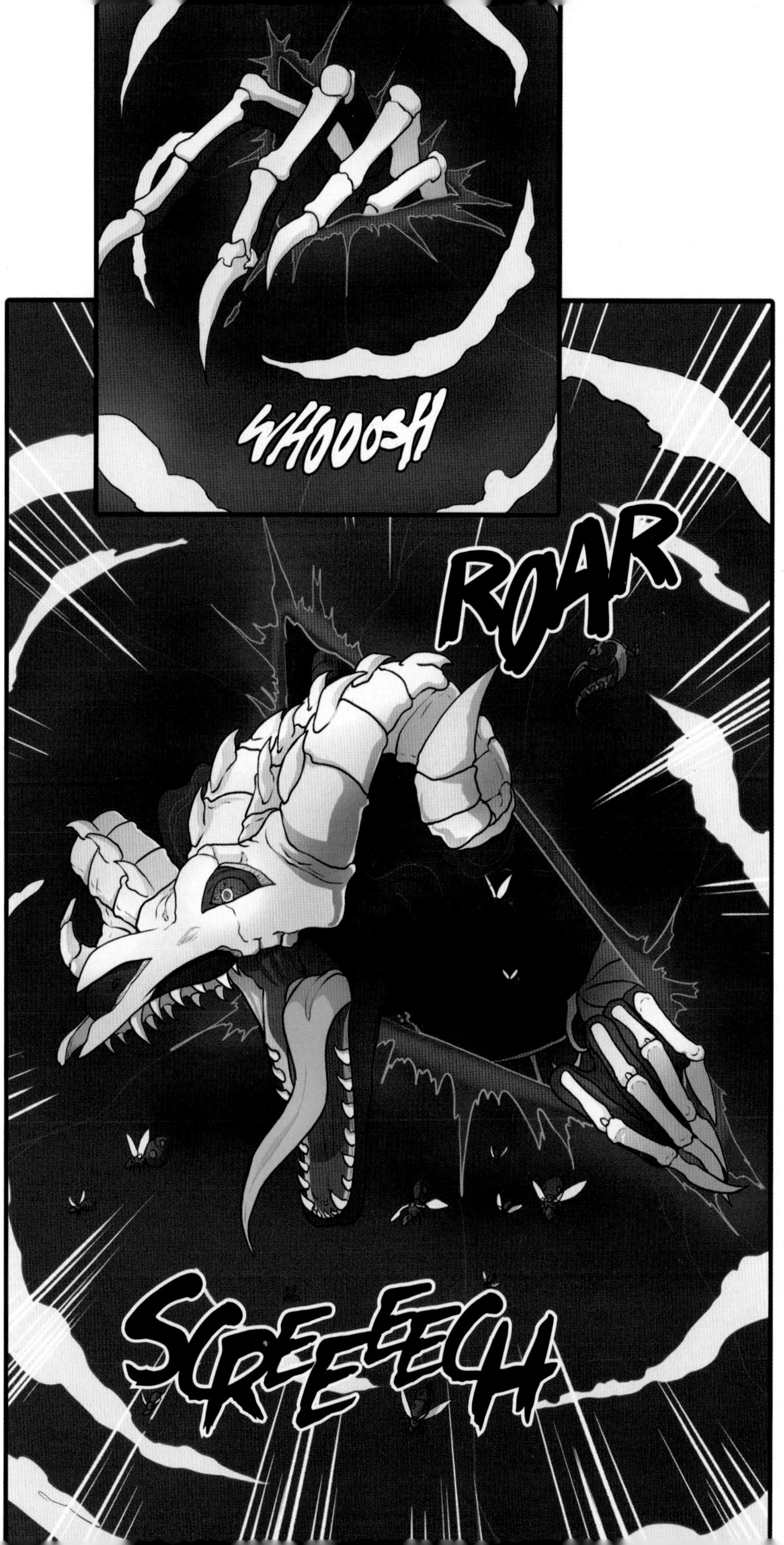
WHOOOSH
ROAR
SCREEEECH

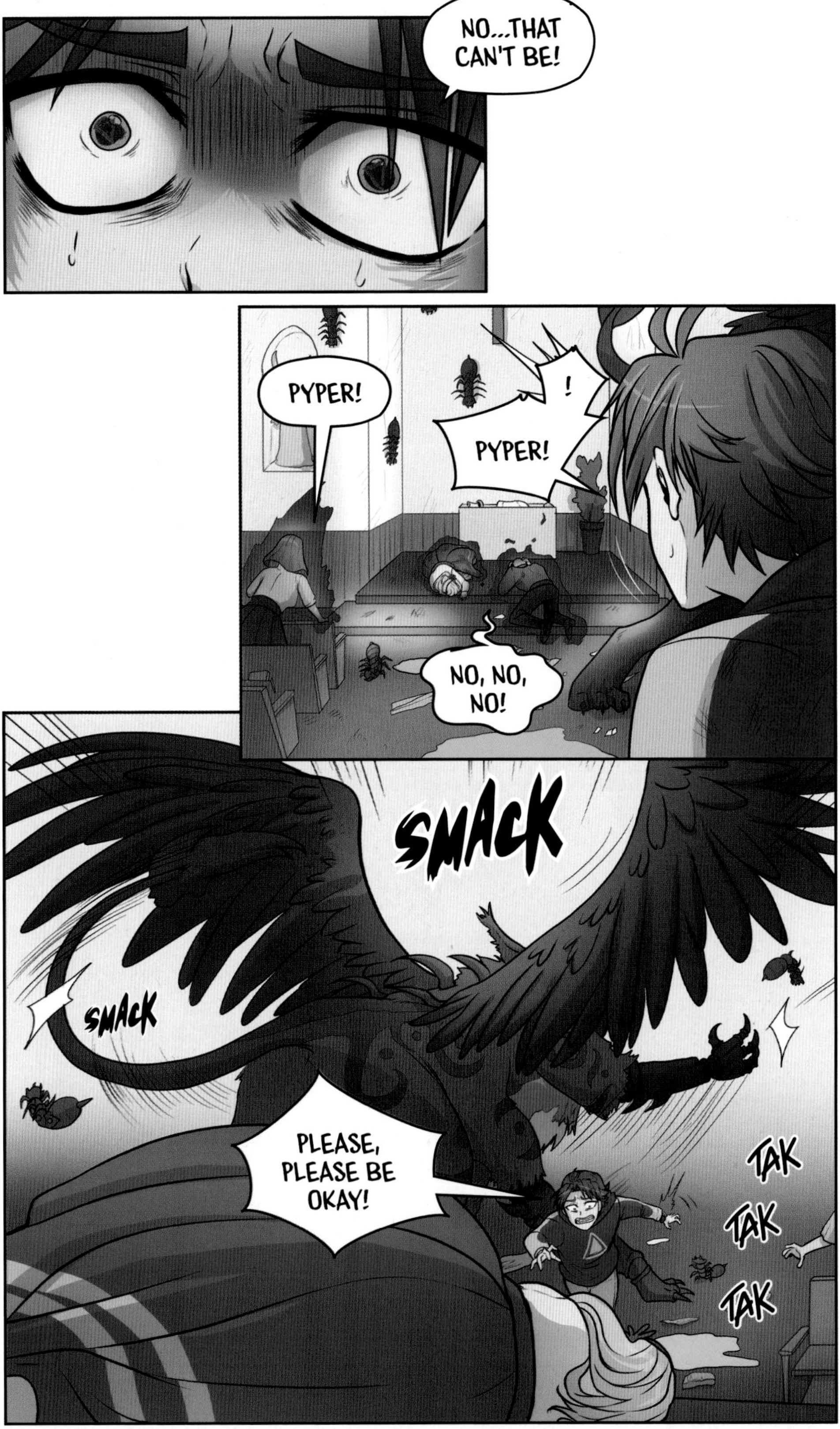
NO...THAT CAN'T BE!
PYPER!
!
PYPER!
NO, NO, NO!
SMACK
SMACK
PLEASE, PLEASE BE OKAY!
TAK
TAK
TAK

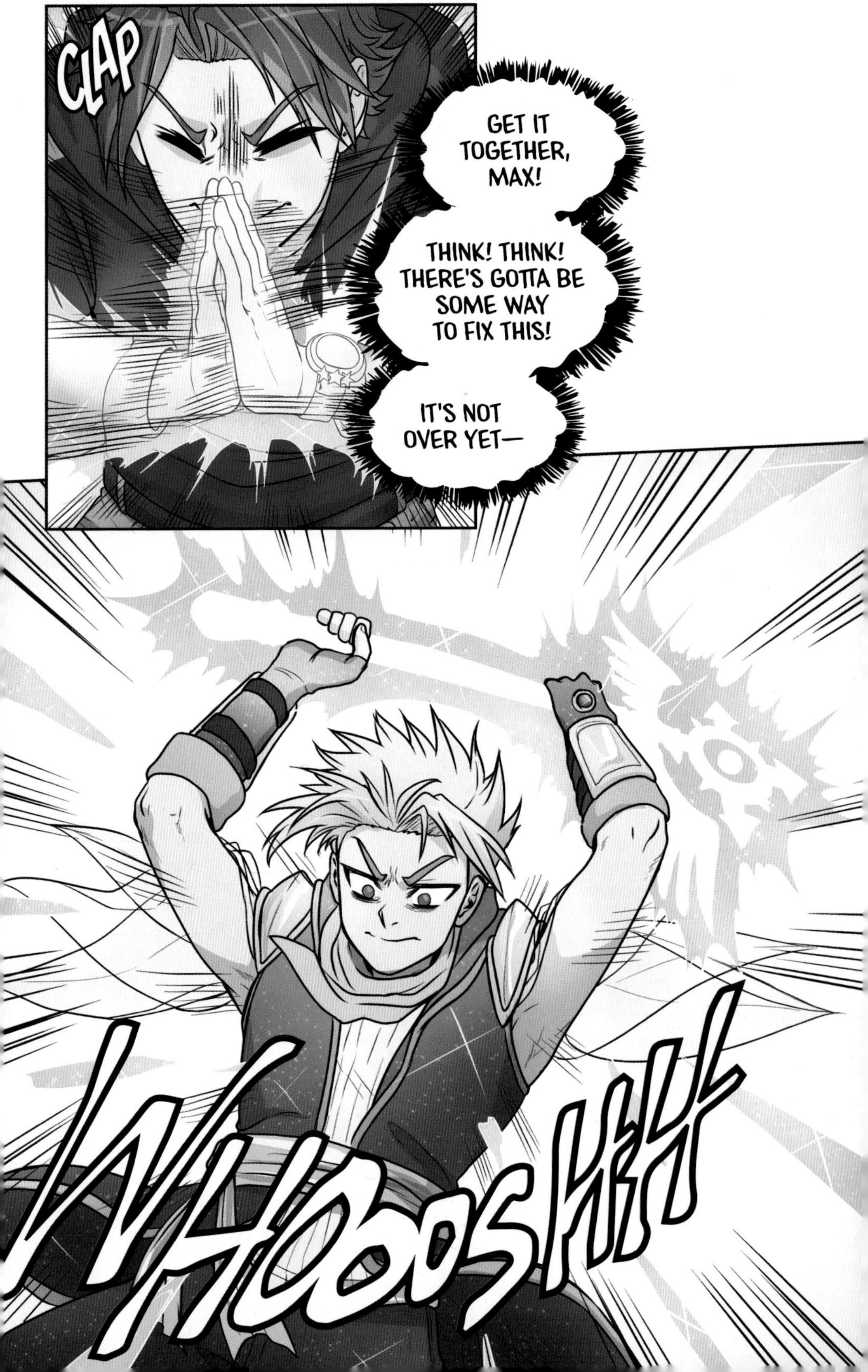
CLAP
GET IT TOGETHER, MAX!
THINK! THINK! THERE'S GOTTA BE SOME WAY TO FIX THIS!
IT'S NOT OVER YET—
WHOOSHHH

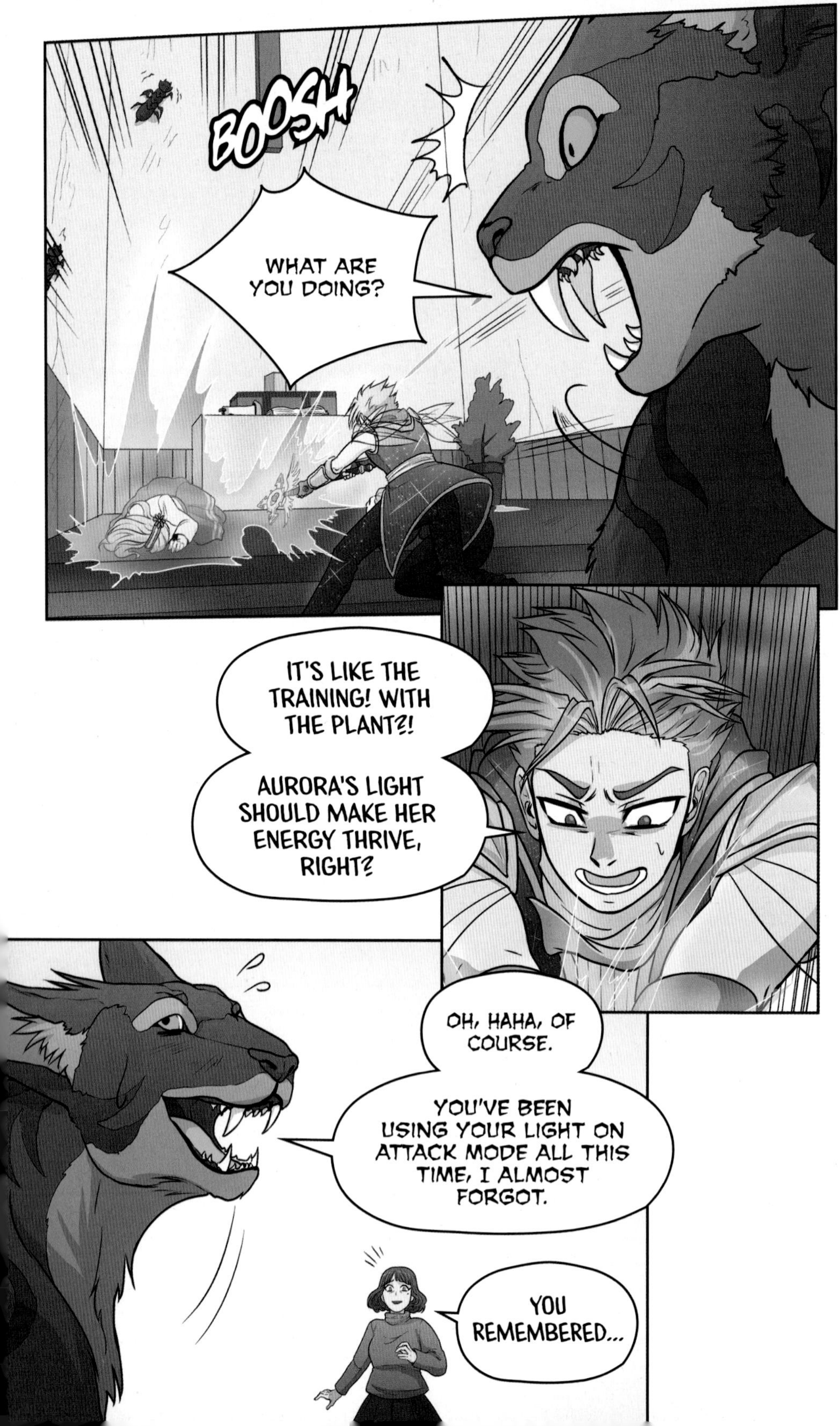
BOOSH
WHAT ARE YOU DOING?
IT'S LIKE THE TRAINING! WITH THE PLANT?!
AURORA'S LIGHT SHOULD MAKE HER ENERGY THRIVE, RIGHT?
OH, HAHA, OF COURSE.
YOU'VE BEEN USING YOUR LIGHT ON ATTACK MODE ALL THIS TIME, I ALMOST FORGOT.
YOU REMEMBERED...

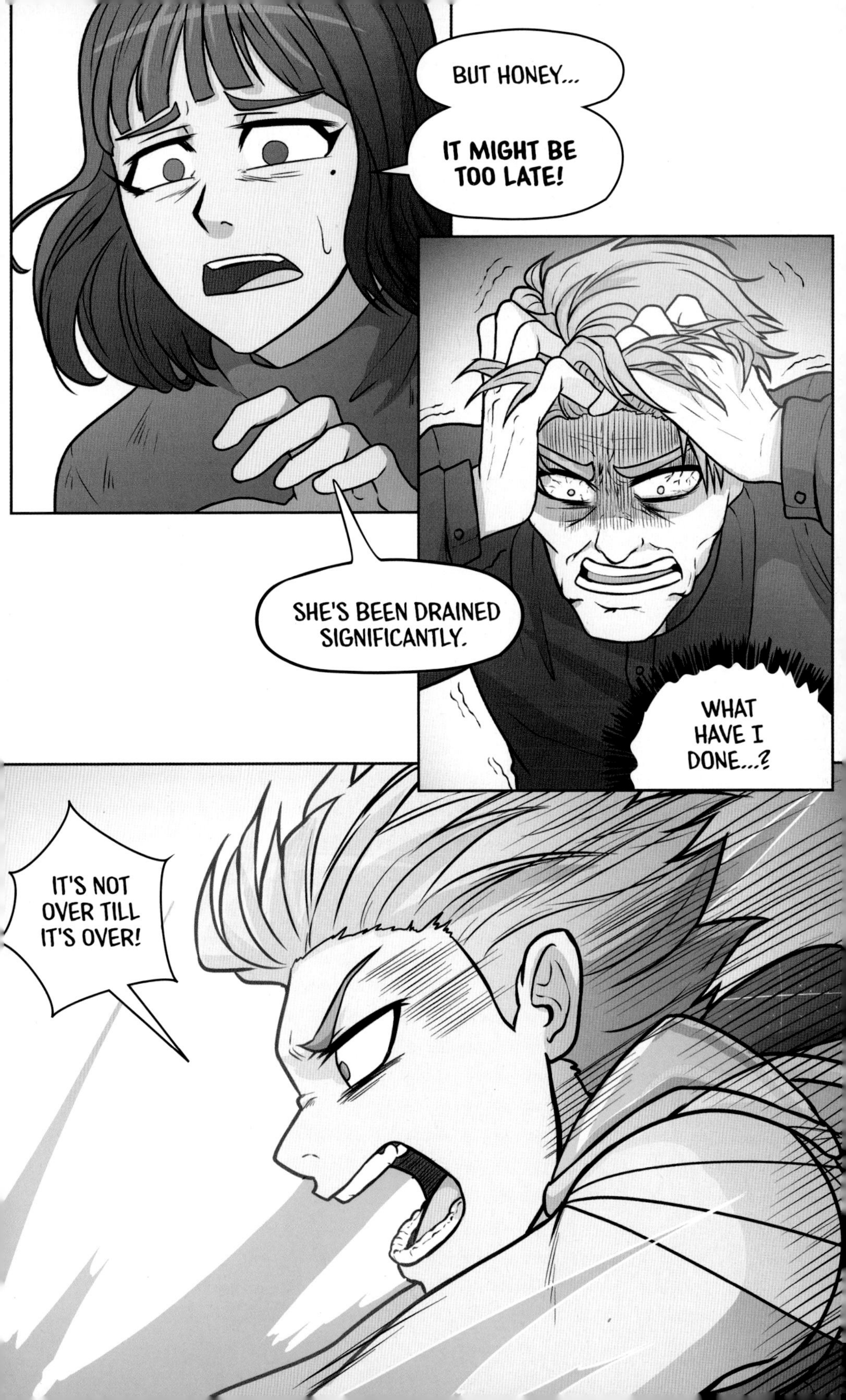
BUT HONEY...
IT MIGHT BE TOO LATE!
SHE'S BEEN DRAINED SIGNIFICANTLY.
WHAT HAVE I DONE...?
IT'S NOT OVER TILL IT'S OVER!

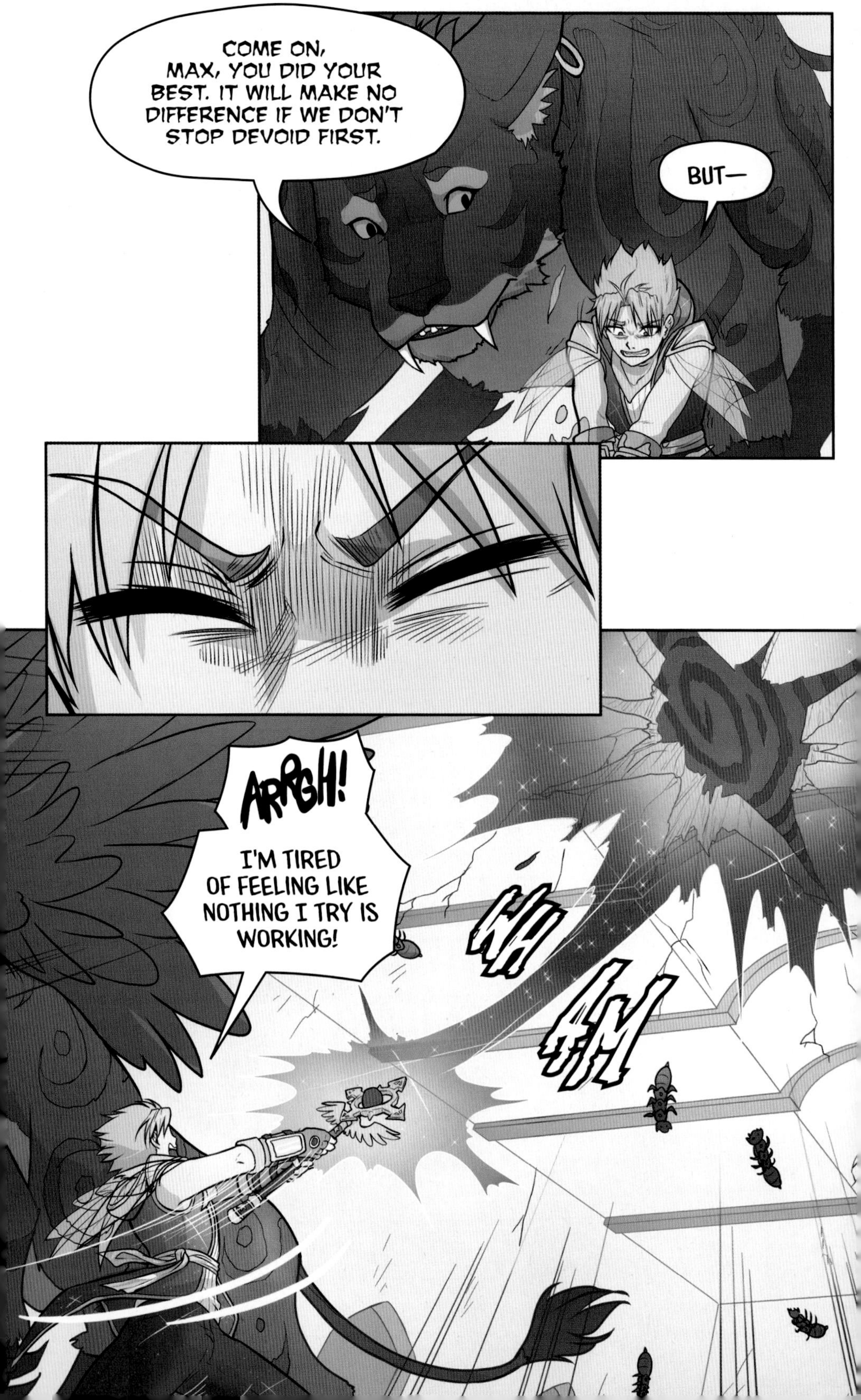
COME ON, MAX, YOU DID YOUR BEST. IT WILL MAKE NO DIFFERENCE IF WE DON'T STOP DEVOID FIRST.
BUT—
ARRGH!
I'M TIRED OF FEELING LIKE NOTHING I TRY IS WORKING!
WHHAM

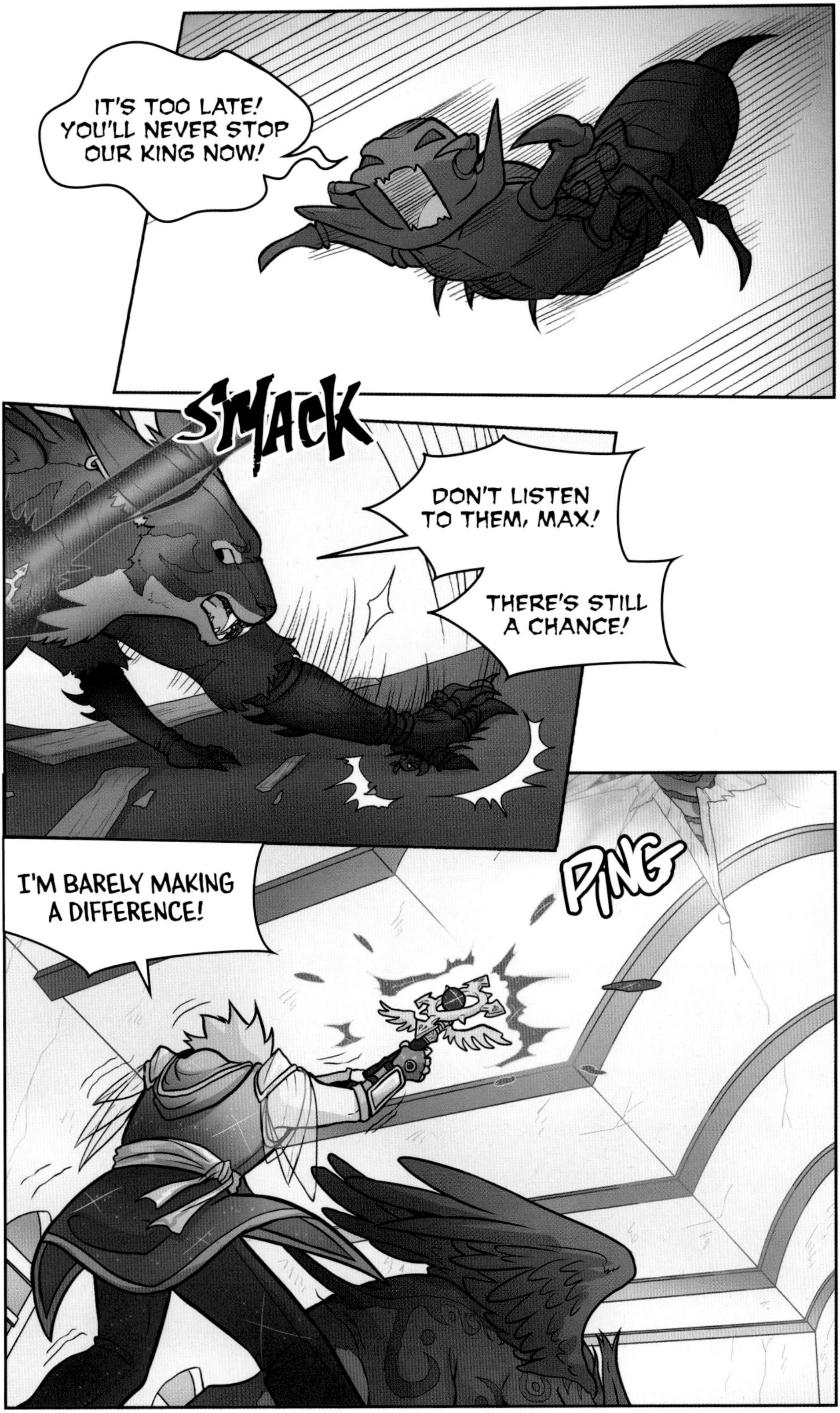
IT'S TOO LATE! YOU'LL NEVER STOP OUR KING NOW!
SMACK
DON'T LISTEN TO THEM, MAX!
THERE'S STILL A CHANCE!
I'M BARELY MAKING A DIFFERENCE!
PING

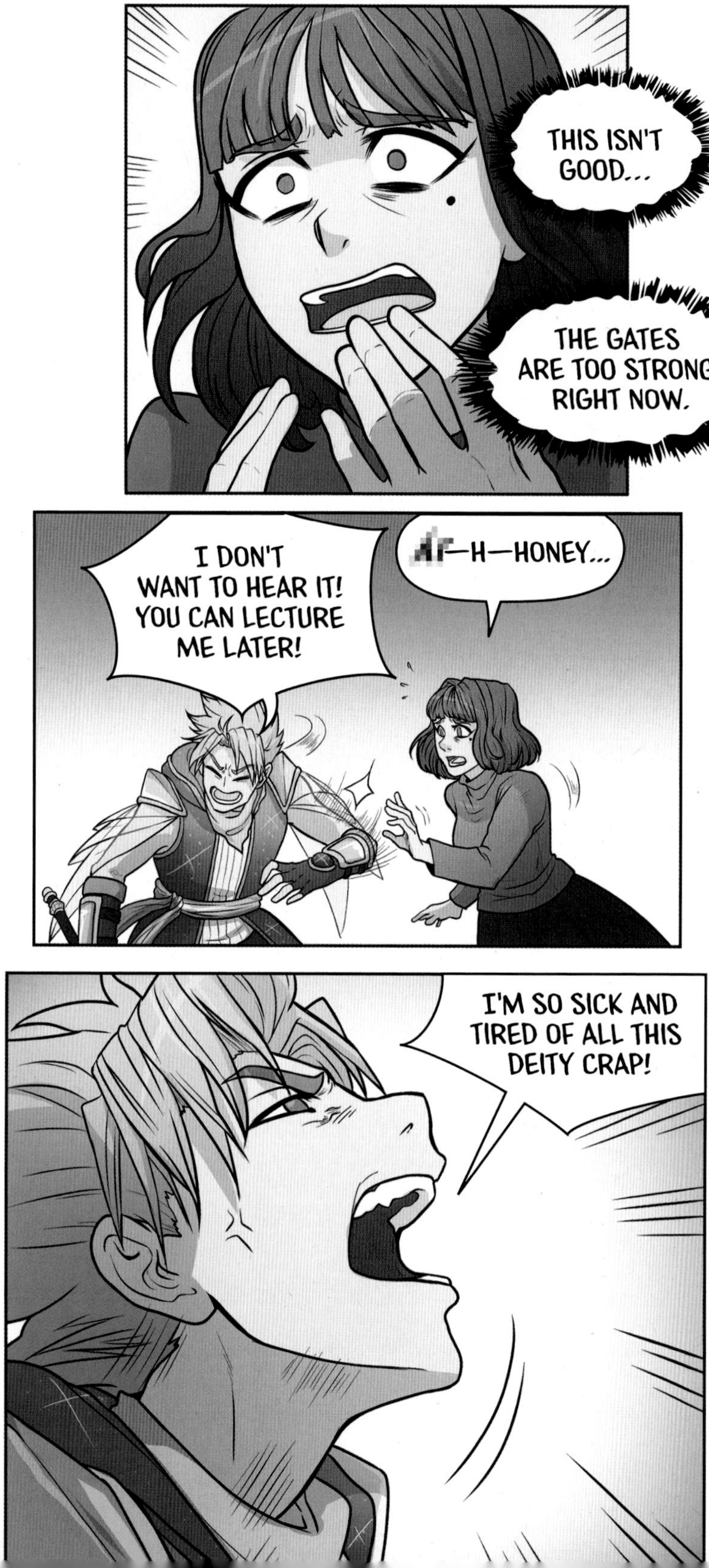
THIS ISN'T GOOD...
THE GATES ARE TOO STRONG RIGHT NOW.
I DON'T WANT TO HEAR IT! YOU CAN LECTURE ME LATER!
—H—HONEY...
I'M SO SICK AND TIRED OF ALL THIS DEITY CRAP!

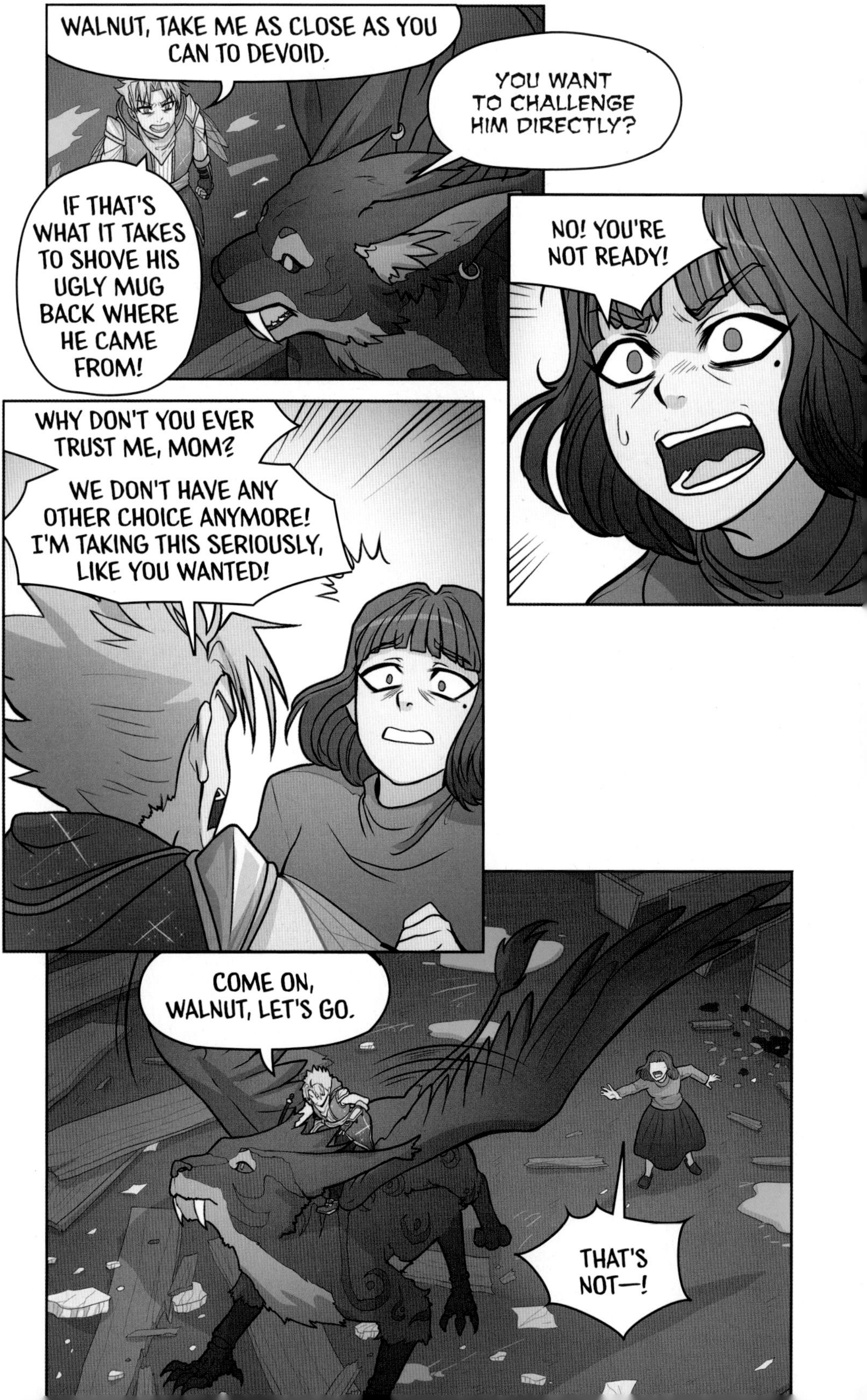
WALNUT, TAKE ME AS CLOSE AS YOU CAN TO DEVOID.
YOU WANT TO CHALLENGE HIM DIRECTLY?
IF THAT'S WHAT IT TAKES TO SHOVE HIS UGLY MUG BACK WHERE HE CAME FROM!
NO! YOU'RE NOT READY!
WHY DON'T YOU EVER TRUST ME, MOM?
WE DON'T HAVE ANY OTHER CHOICE ANYMORE! I'M TAKING THIS SERIOUSLY, LIKE YOU WANTED!
COME ON, WALNUT, LET'S GO.
THAT'S NOT—!

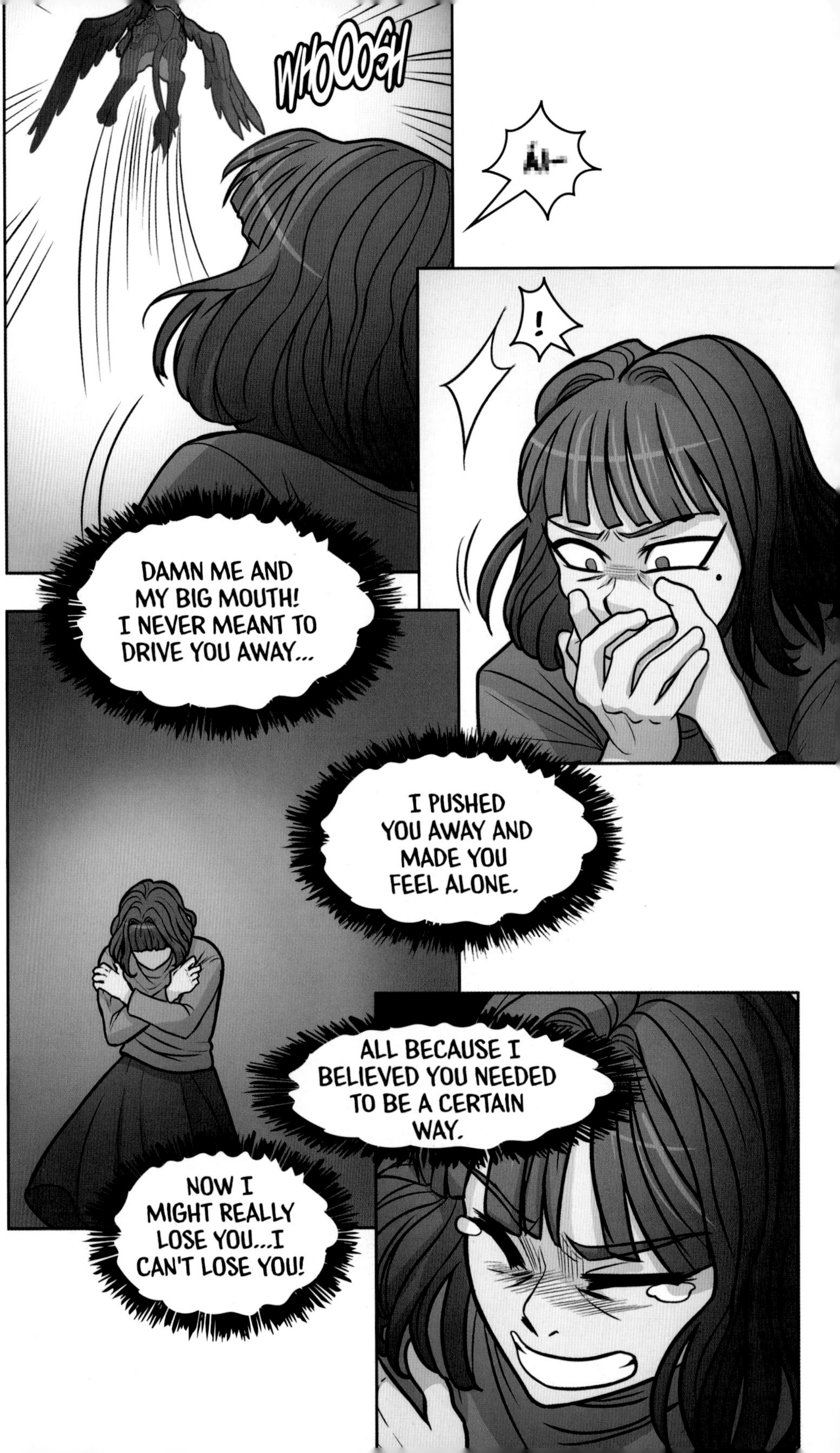
WHOOOSH
!
DAMN ME AND MY BIG MOUTH! I NEVER MEANT TO DRIVE YOU AWAY...
I PUSHED YOU AWAY AND MADE YOU FEEL ALONE.
ALL BECAUSE I BELIEVED YOU NEEDED TO BE A CERTAIN WAY.
NOW I MIGHT REALLY LOSE YOU...I CAN'T LOSE YOU!

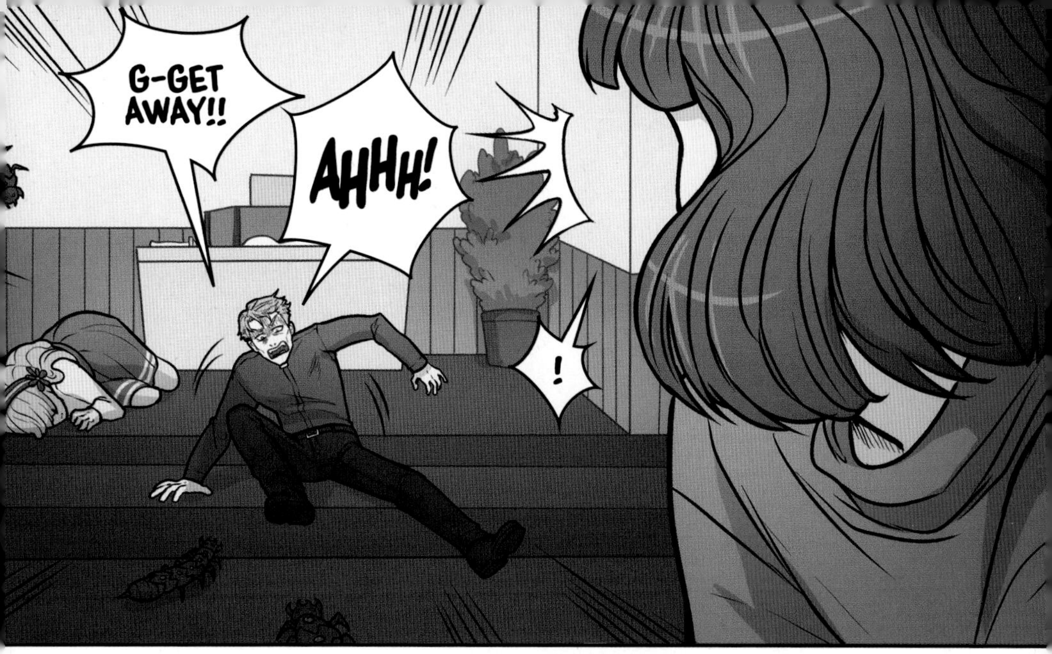
G-GET AWAY!!
AHHH!
!

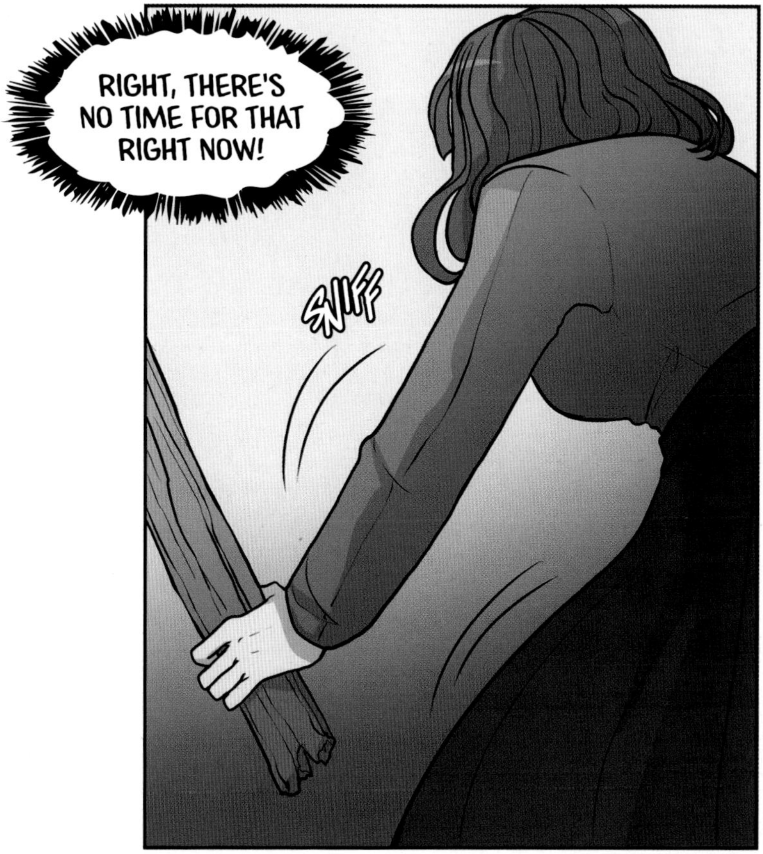
RIGHT, THERE'S NO TIME FOR THAT RIGHT NOW!
SNIFF

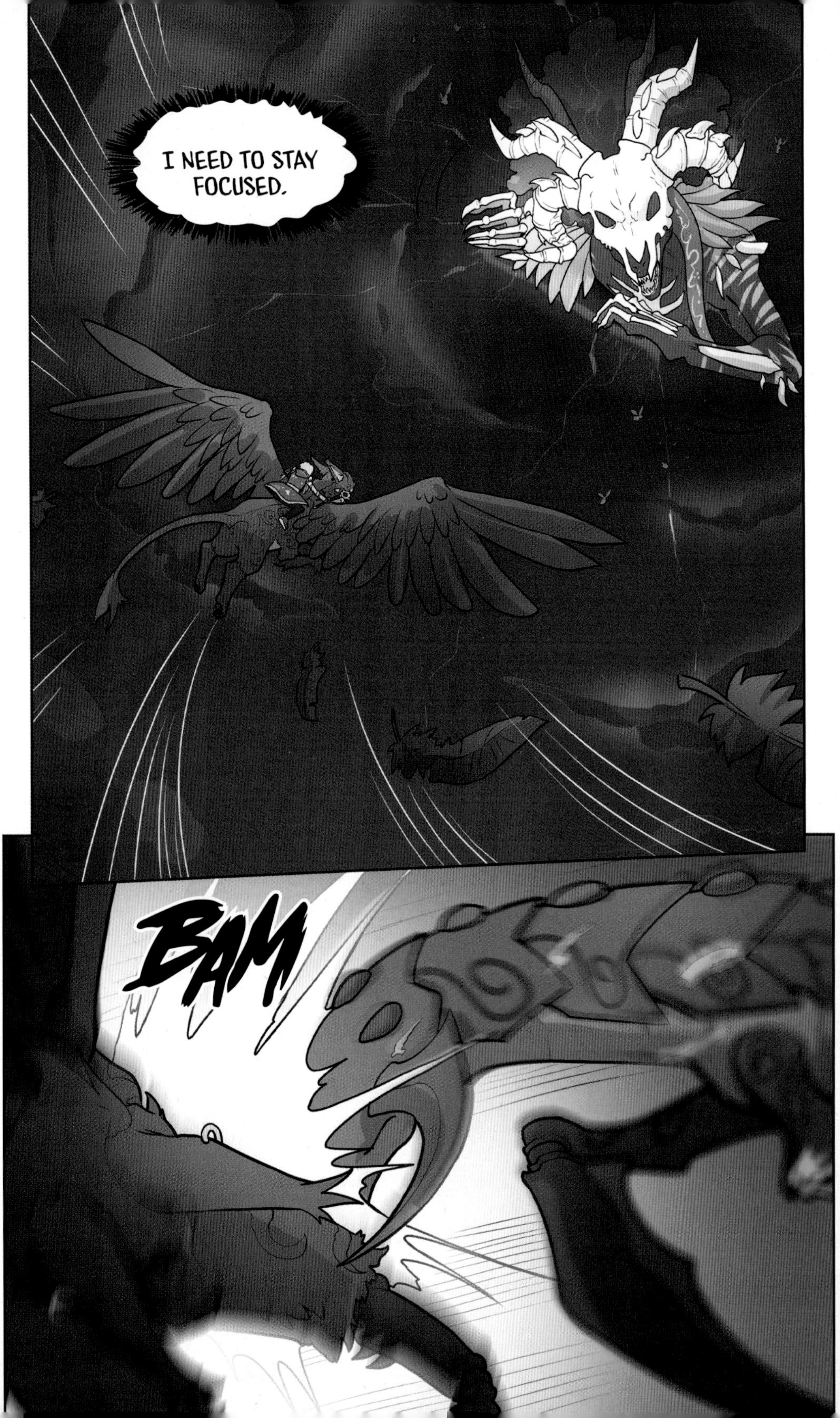
I NEED TO STAY FOCUSED.
BAM

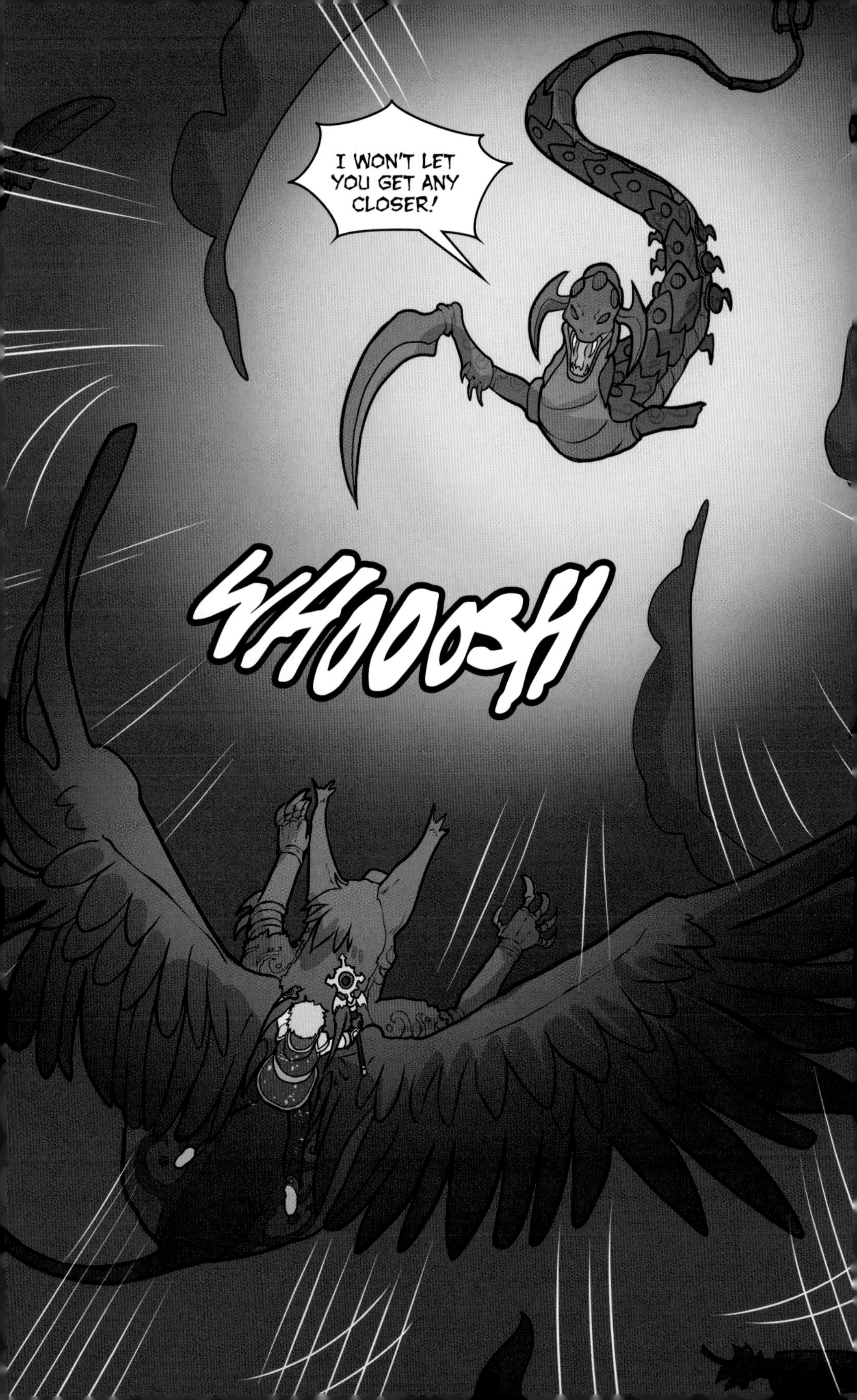
I WON'T LET YOU GET ANY CLOSER!
WHOOOSH

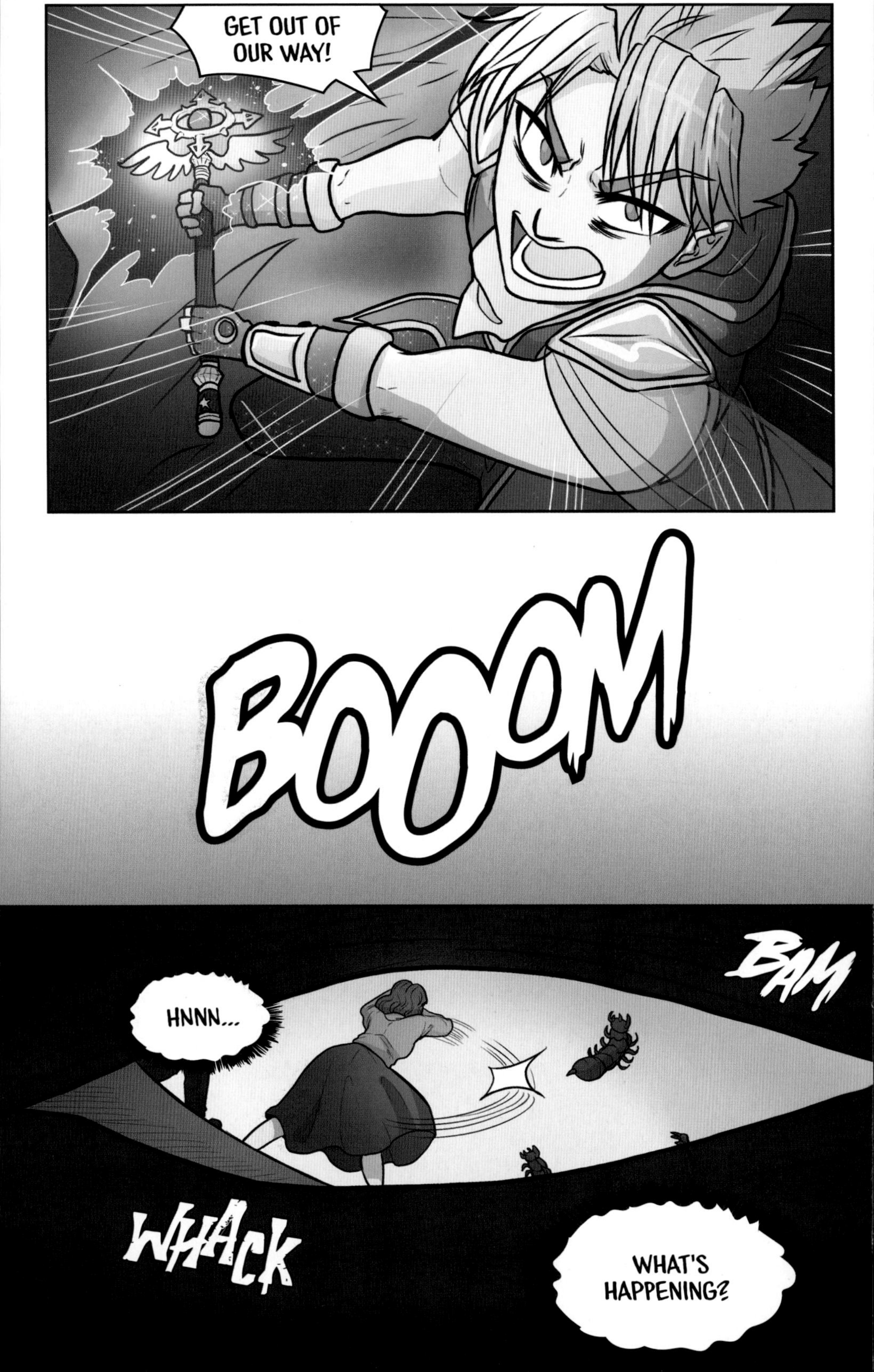
GET OUT OF OUR WAY!
BOOOM
BAM
HNNN...
WHACK
WHAT'S HAPPENING?

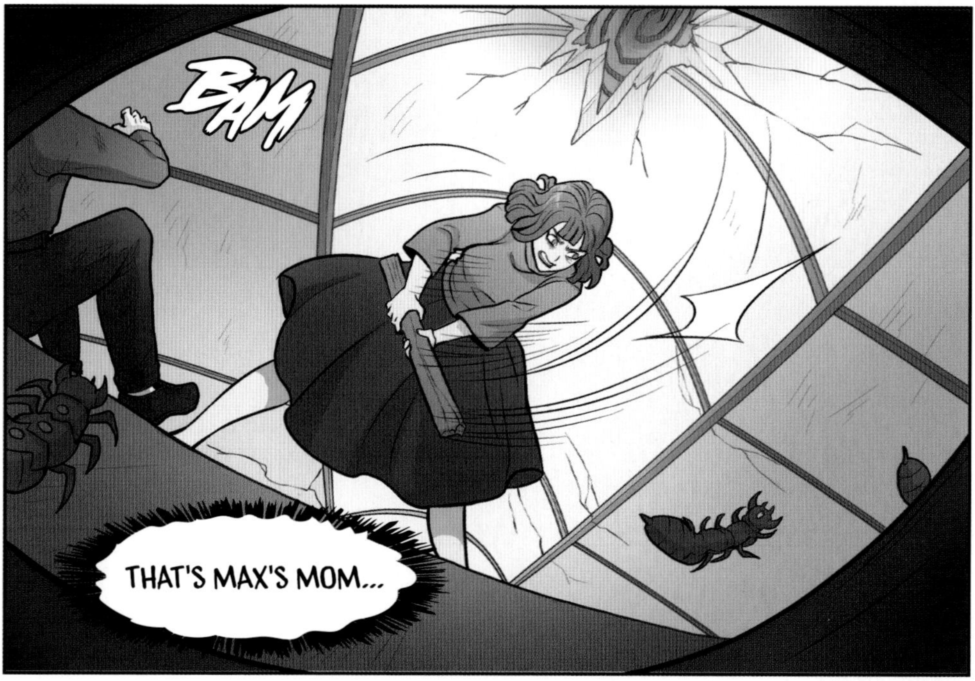
BAM
THAT'S MAX'S MOM...

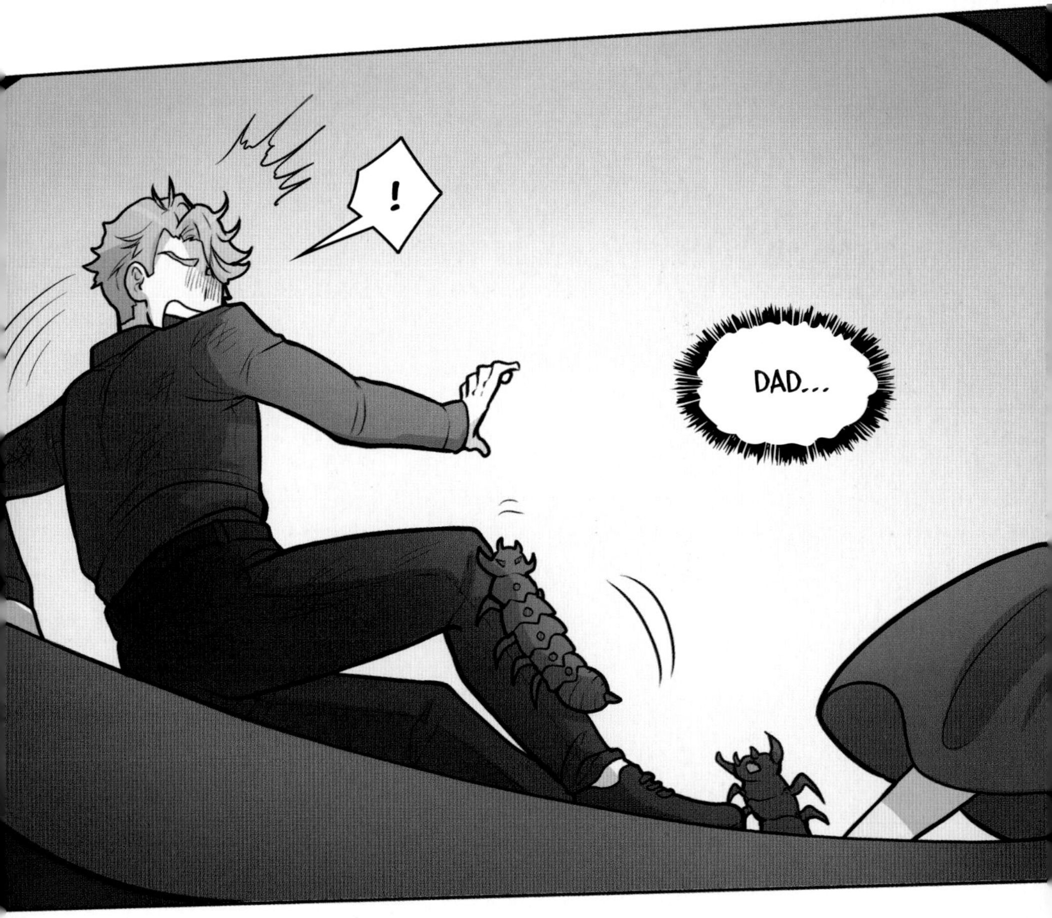
!
DAD...

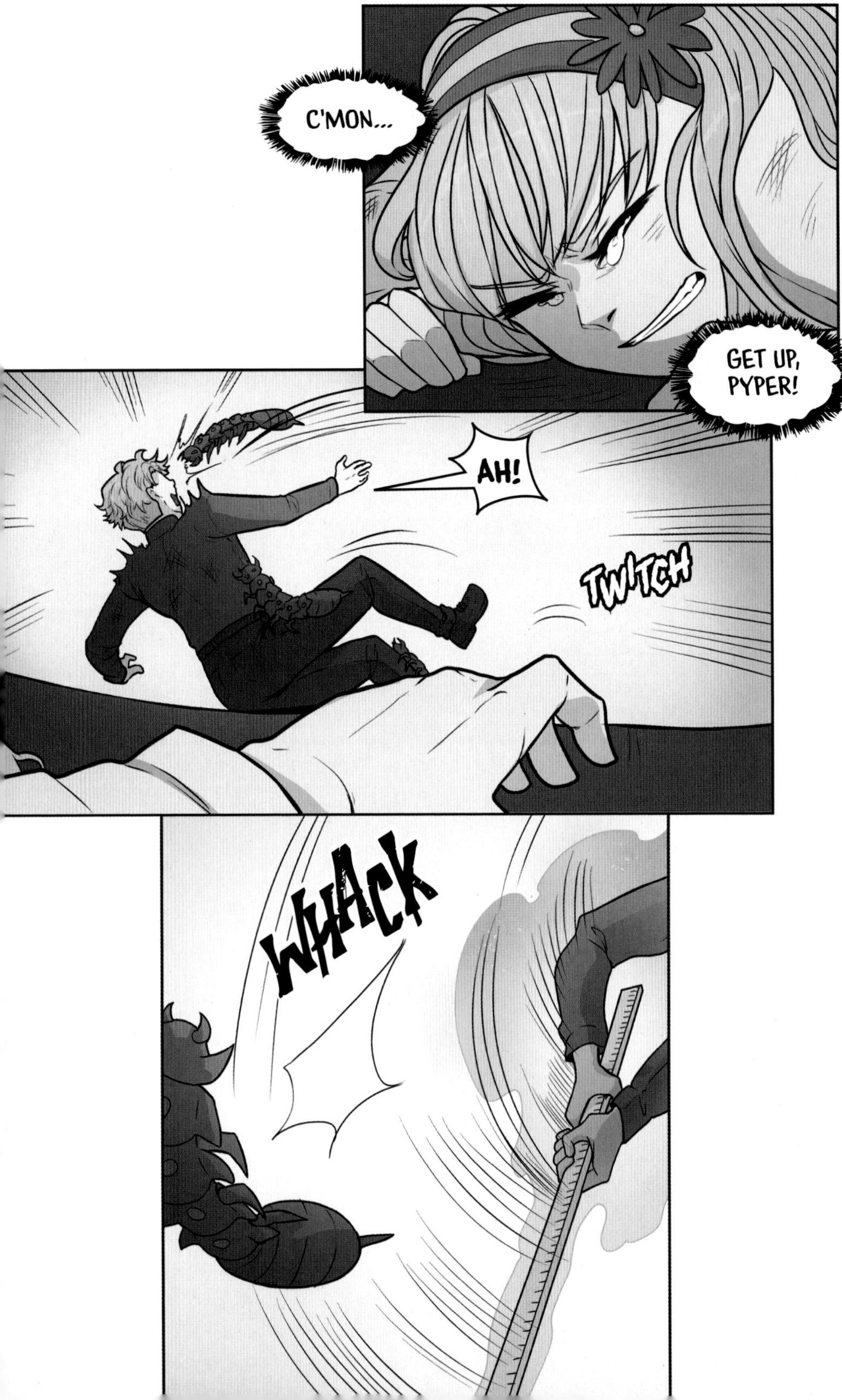
C'MON...
GET UP, PYPER!
AH!
TWITCH
WHACK

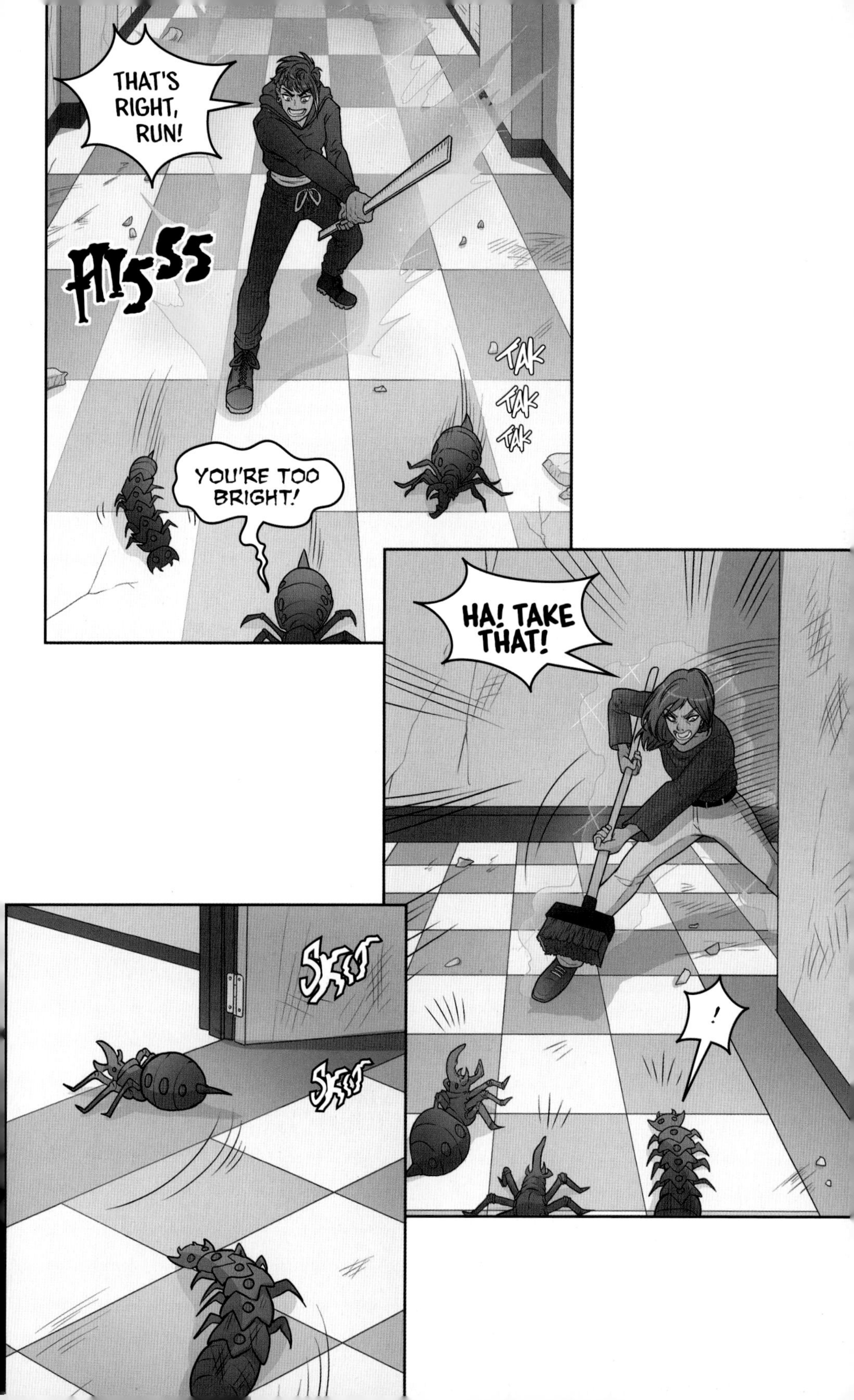
THAT'S RIGHT, RUN!
HISSS
TAK
TAK
TAK
YOU'RE TOO BRIGHT!
HA! TAKE THAT!
!
SKIT
SKIT

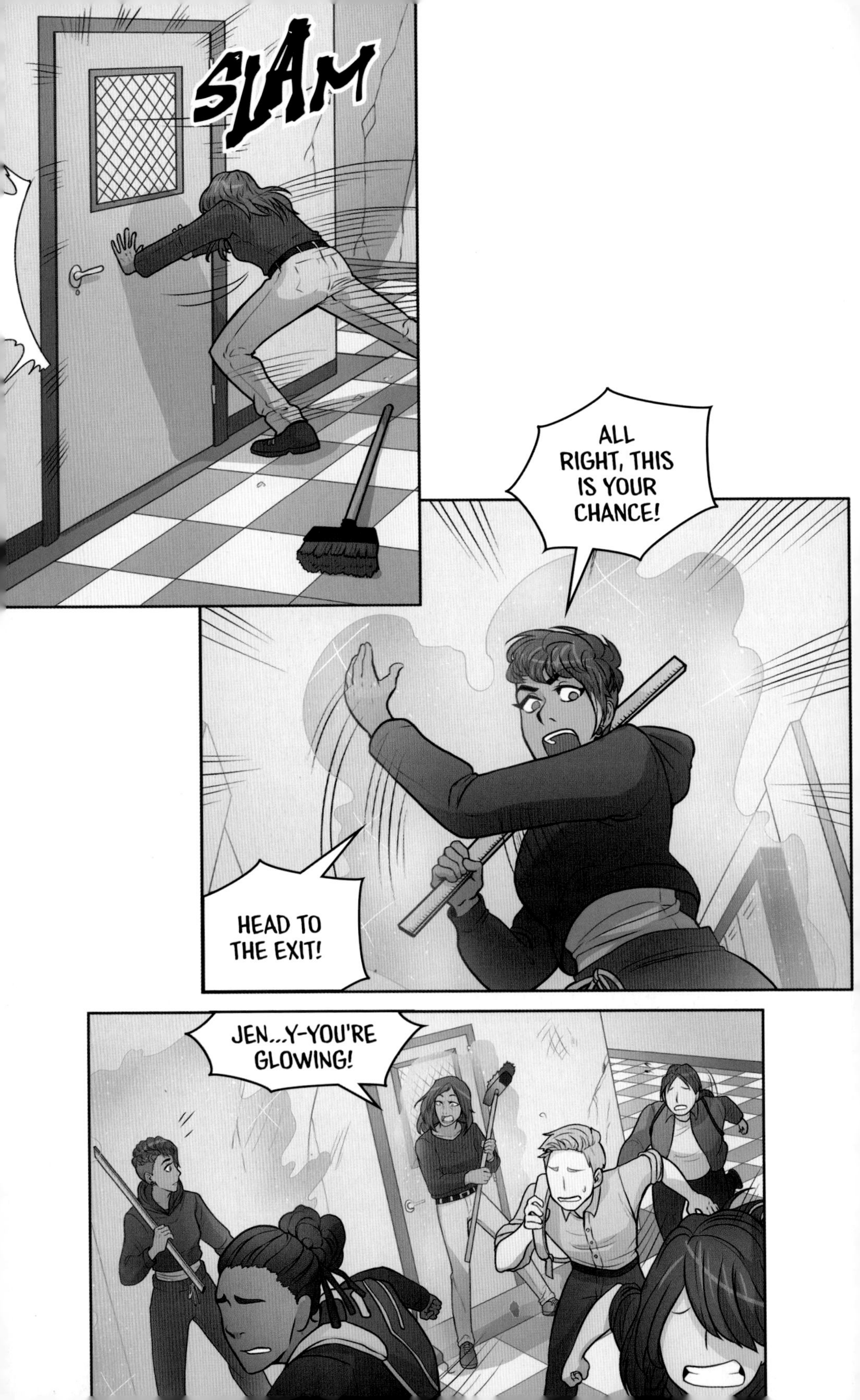
SLAM
ALL RIGHT, THIS IS YOUR CHANCE!
HEAD TO THE EXIT!
JEN...Y-YOU'RE GLOWING!

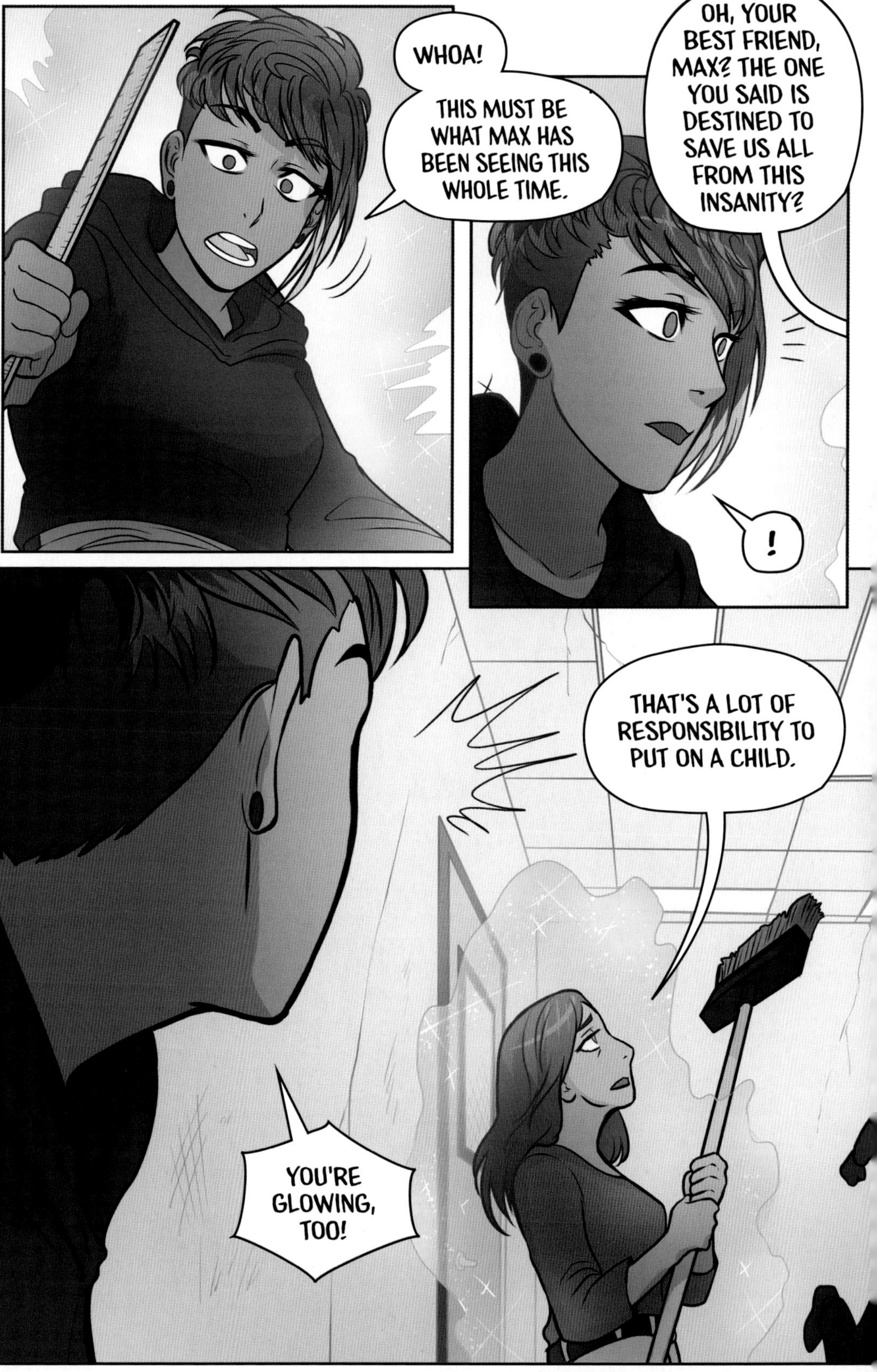
WHOA!
THIS MUST BE WHAT MAX HAS BEEN SEEING THIS WHOLE TIME.
OH, YOUR BEST FRIEND, MAX? THE ONE YOU SAID IS DESTINED TO SAVE US ALL FROM THIS INSANITY?
!
THAT'S A LOT OF RESPONSIBILITY TO PUT ON A CHILD.
YOU'RE GLOWING, TOO!

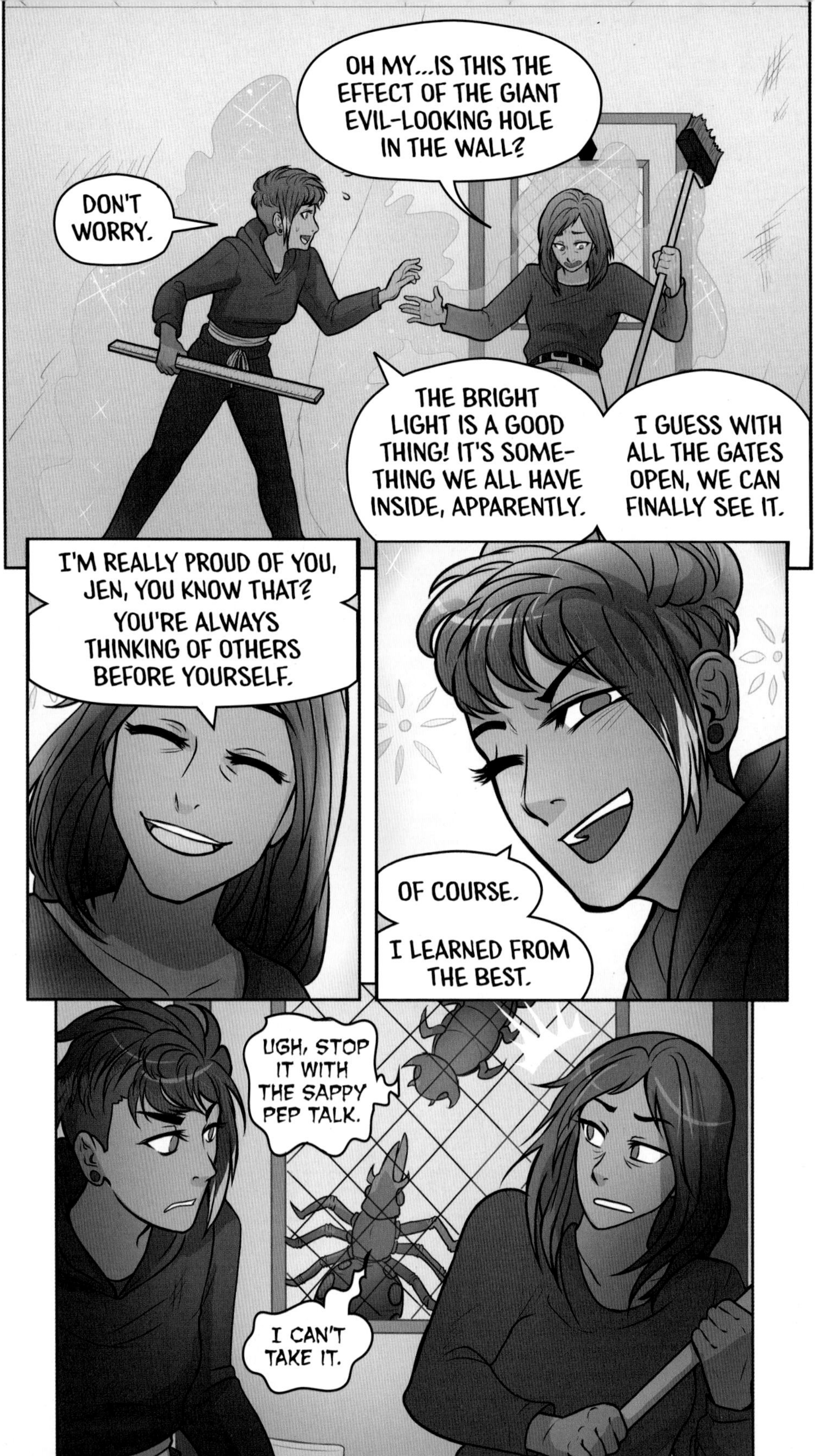
OH MY...IS THIS THE EFFECT OF THE GIANT EVIL-LOOKING HOLE IN THE WALL?
DON'T WORRY.
THE BRIGHT LIGHT IS A GOOD THING! IT'S SOME-THING WE ALL HAVE INSIDE, APPARENTLY.
I GUESS WITH ALL THE GATES OPEN, WE CAN FINALLY SEE IT.
I'M REALLY PROUD OF YOU, JEN, YOU KNOW THAT?
YOU'RE ALWAYS THINKING OF OTHERS BEFORE YOURSELF.
OF COURSE.
I LEARNED FROM THE BEST.
UGH, STOP IT WITH THE SAPPY PEP TALK.
I CAN'T TAKE IT.

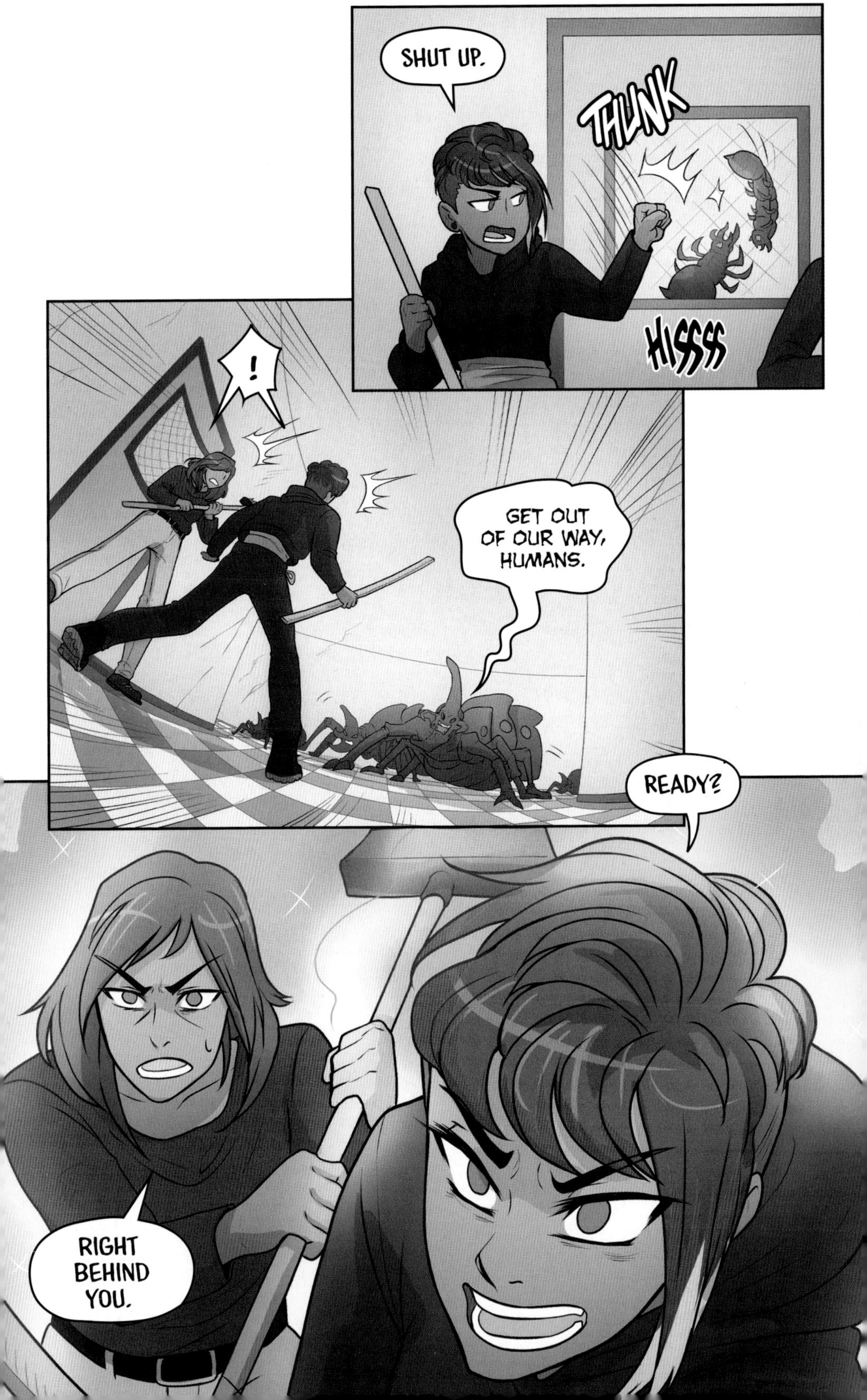
SHUT UP.
THUNK
HISSSS
!
GET OUT OF OUR WAY, HUMANS.
READY?
RIGHT BEHIND YOU.

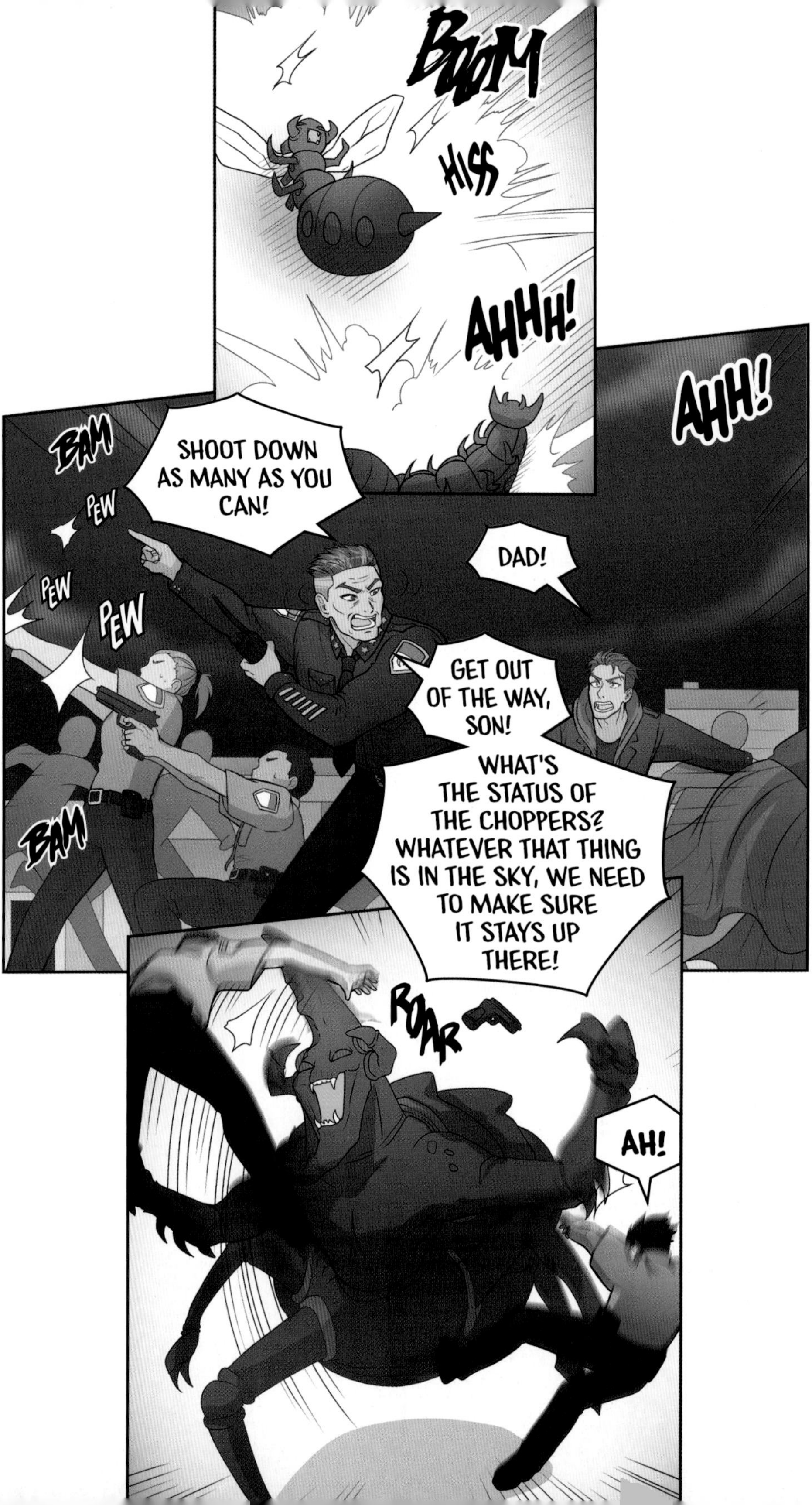
BOOM
HISS
AHHH!
AHH!
BAM
SHOOT DOWN AS MANY AS YOU CAN!
PEW
PEW
PEW
DAD!
GET OUT OF THE WAY, SON!
WHAT'S THE STATUS OF THE CHOPPERS? WHATEVER THAT THING IS IN THE SKY, WE NEED TO MAKE SURE IT STAYS UP THERE!
BAM
ROAR
AH!

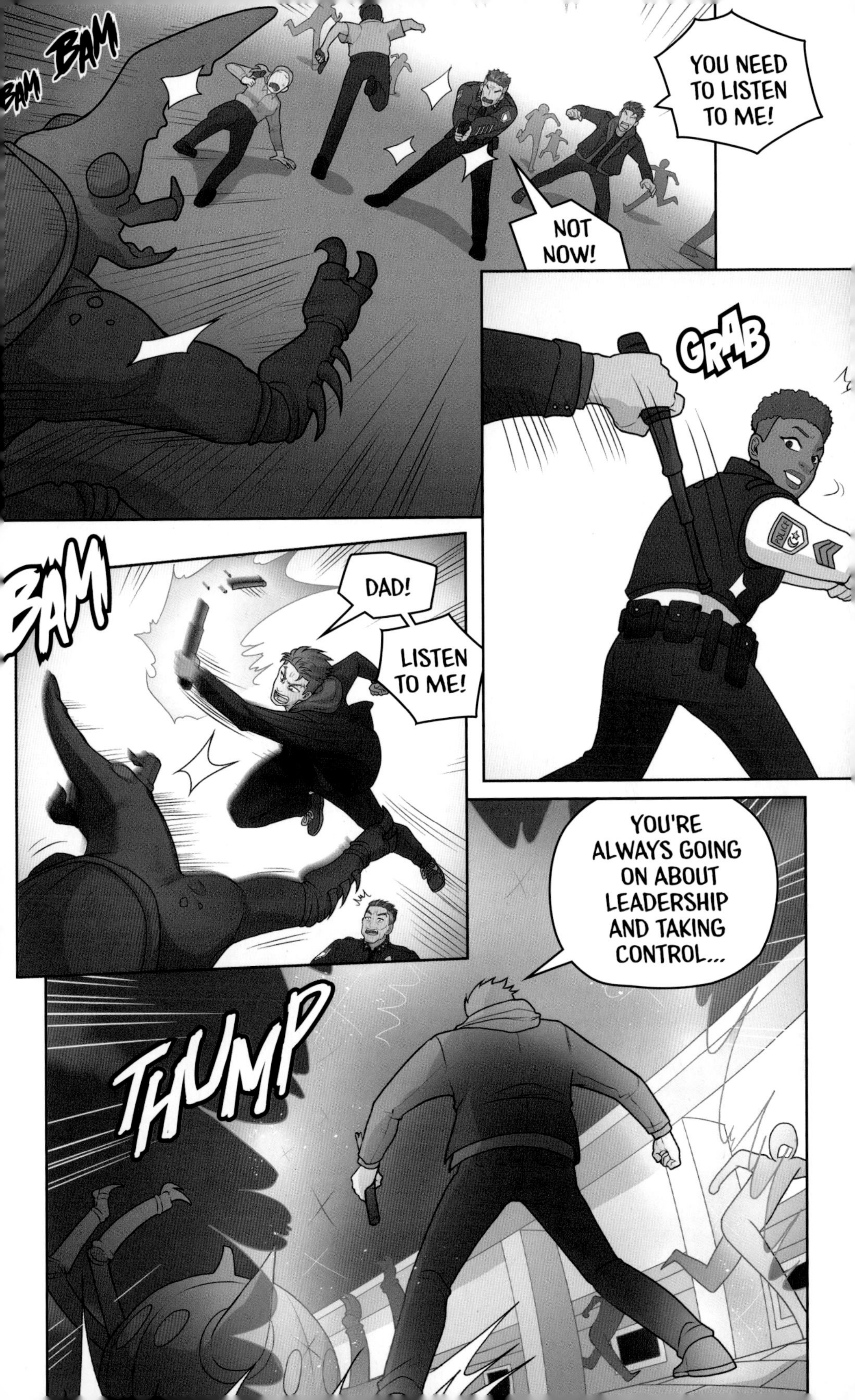
BAM BAM
BAM
YOU NEED TO LISTEN TO ME!
NOT NOW!
GRAB
BAM
DAD!
LISTEN TO ME!
THUMP
YOU'RE ALWAYS GOING ON ABOUT LEADERSHIP AND TAKING CONTROL...

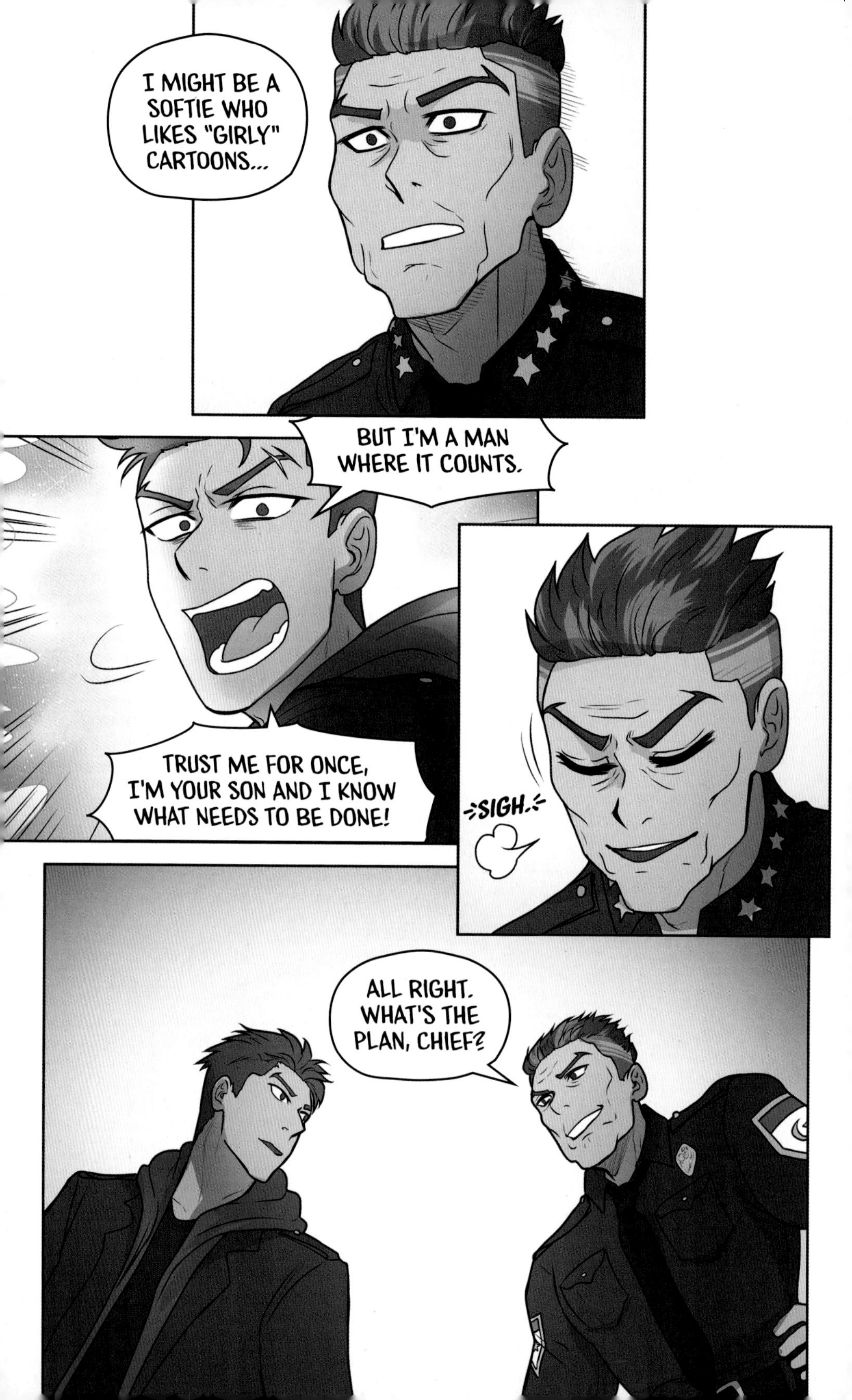
I MIGHT BE A SOFTIE WHO LIKES "GIRLY" CARTOONS...
BUT I'M A MAN WHERE IT COUNTS.
TRUST ME FOR ONCE, I'M YOUR SON AND I KNOW WHAT NEEDS TO BE DONE!
SIGH.
ALL RIGHT. WHAT'S THE PLAN, CHIEF?

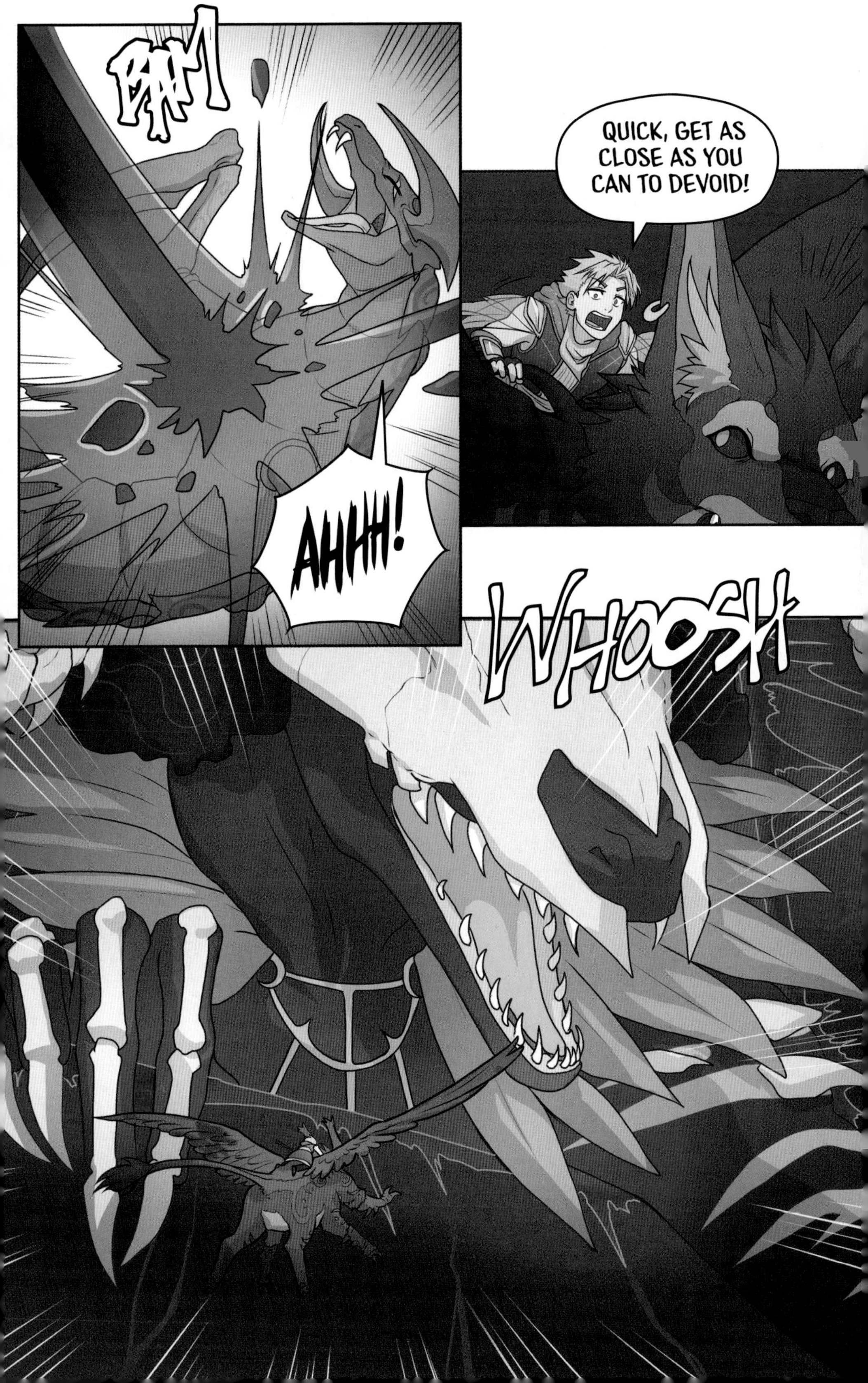
BAM
AHHH!
QUICK, GET AS CLOSE AS YOU CAN TO DEVOID!
WHOOSH

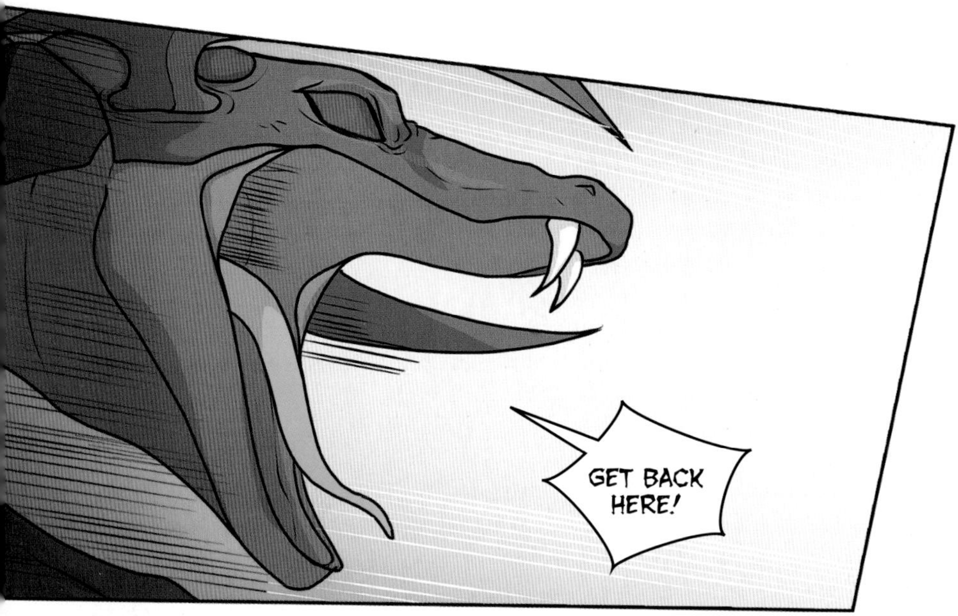
GET BACK
HERE!

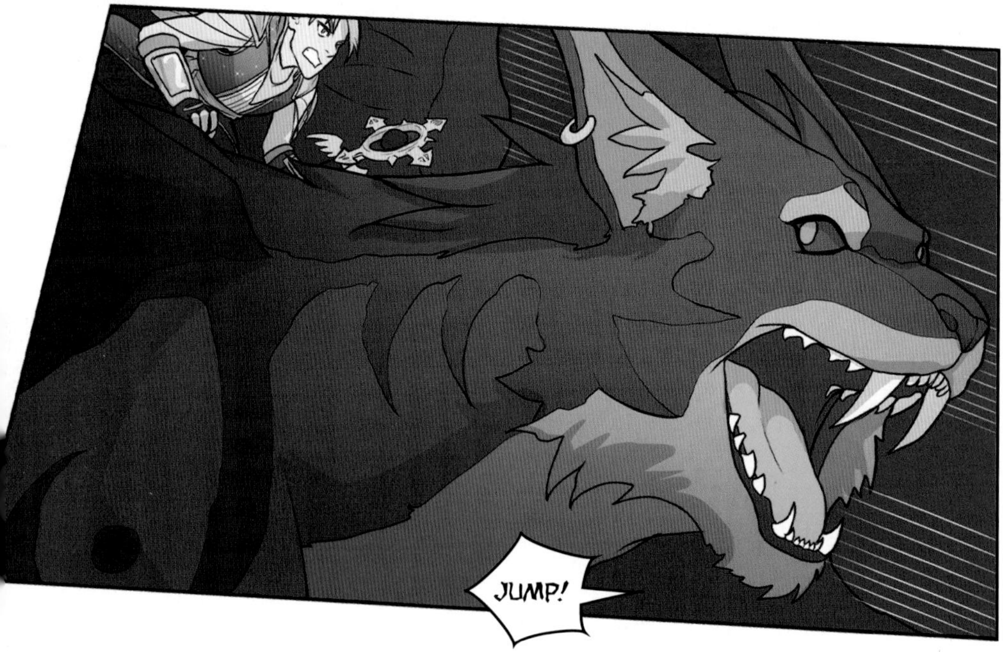
JUMP!

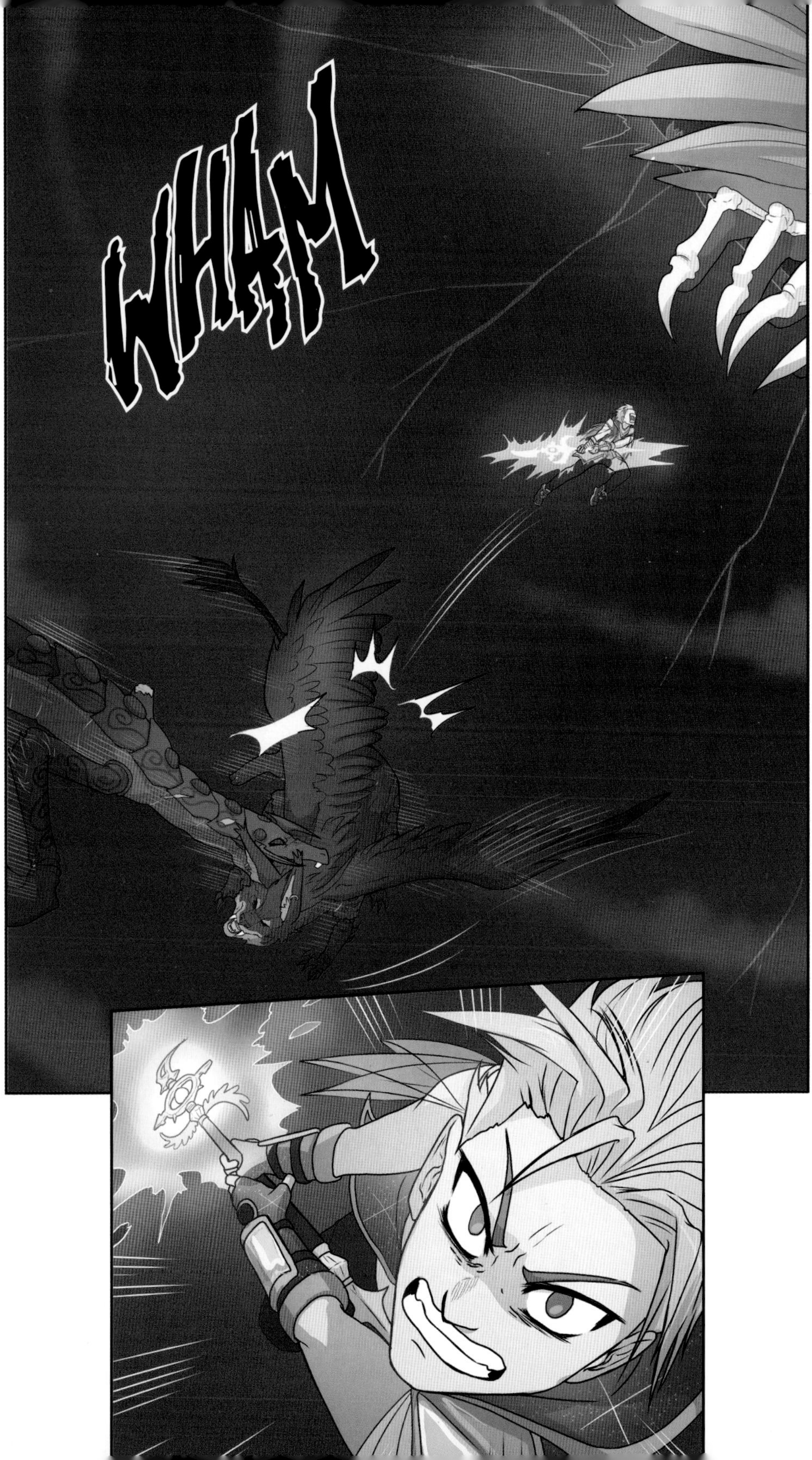
WHAM

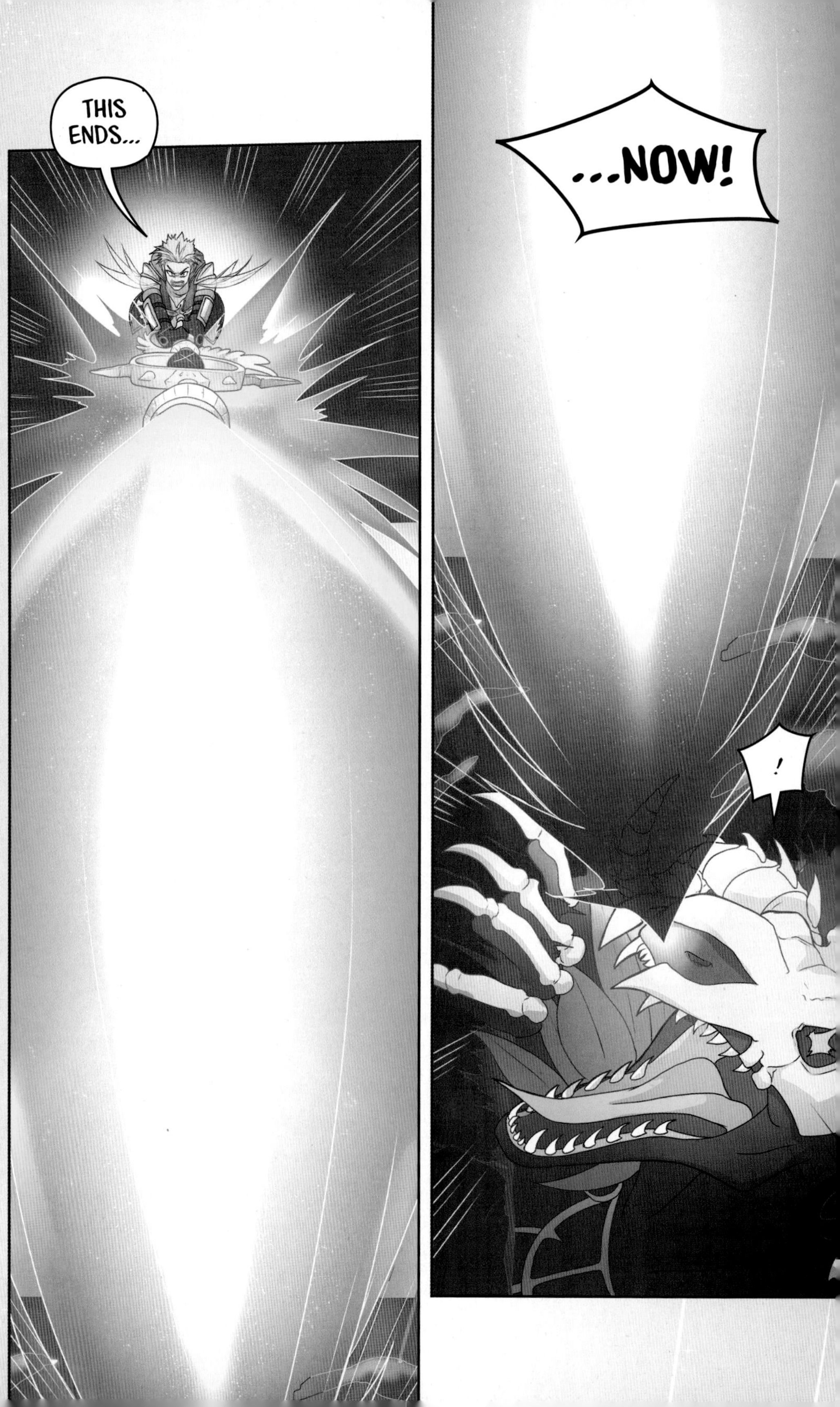
THIS ENDS...
...NOW!
!

EPISODE 25:
THE DARKNESS FALLS (PT. 2)

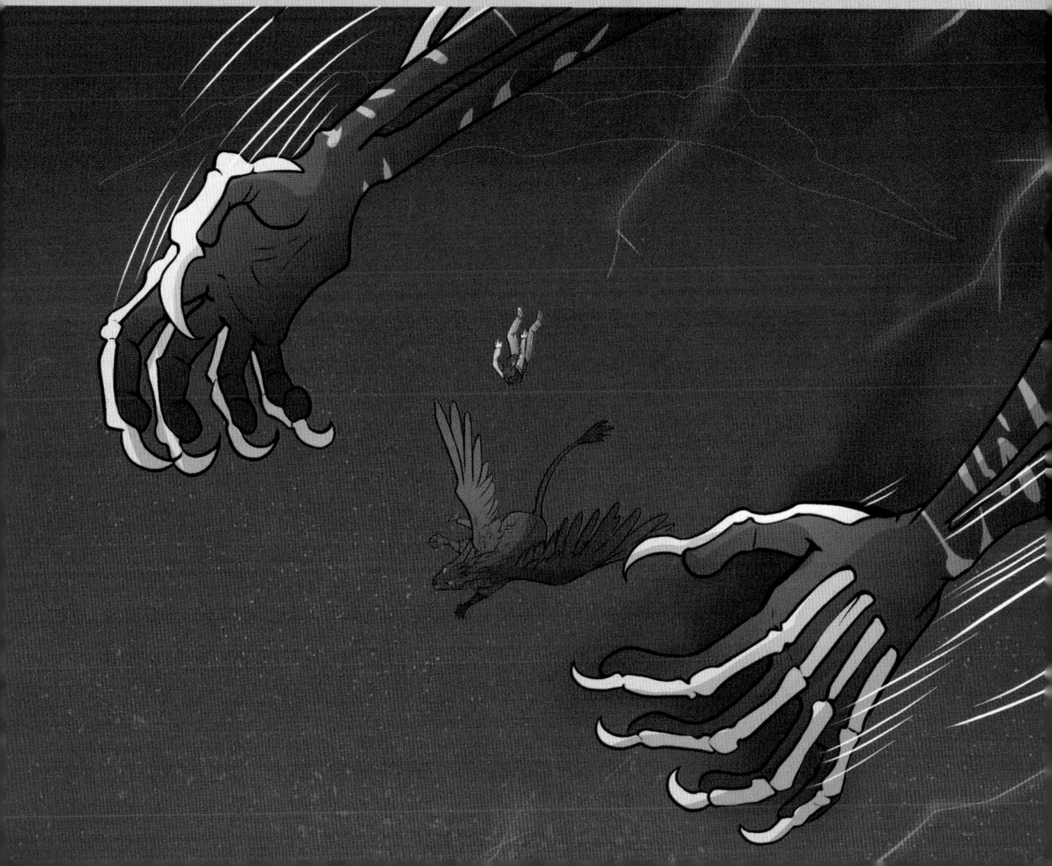

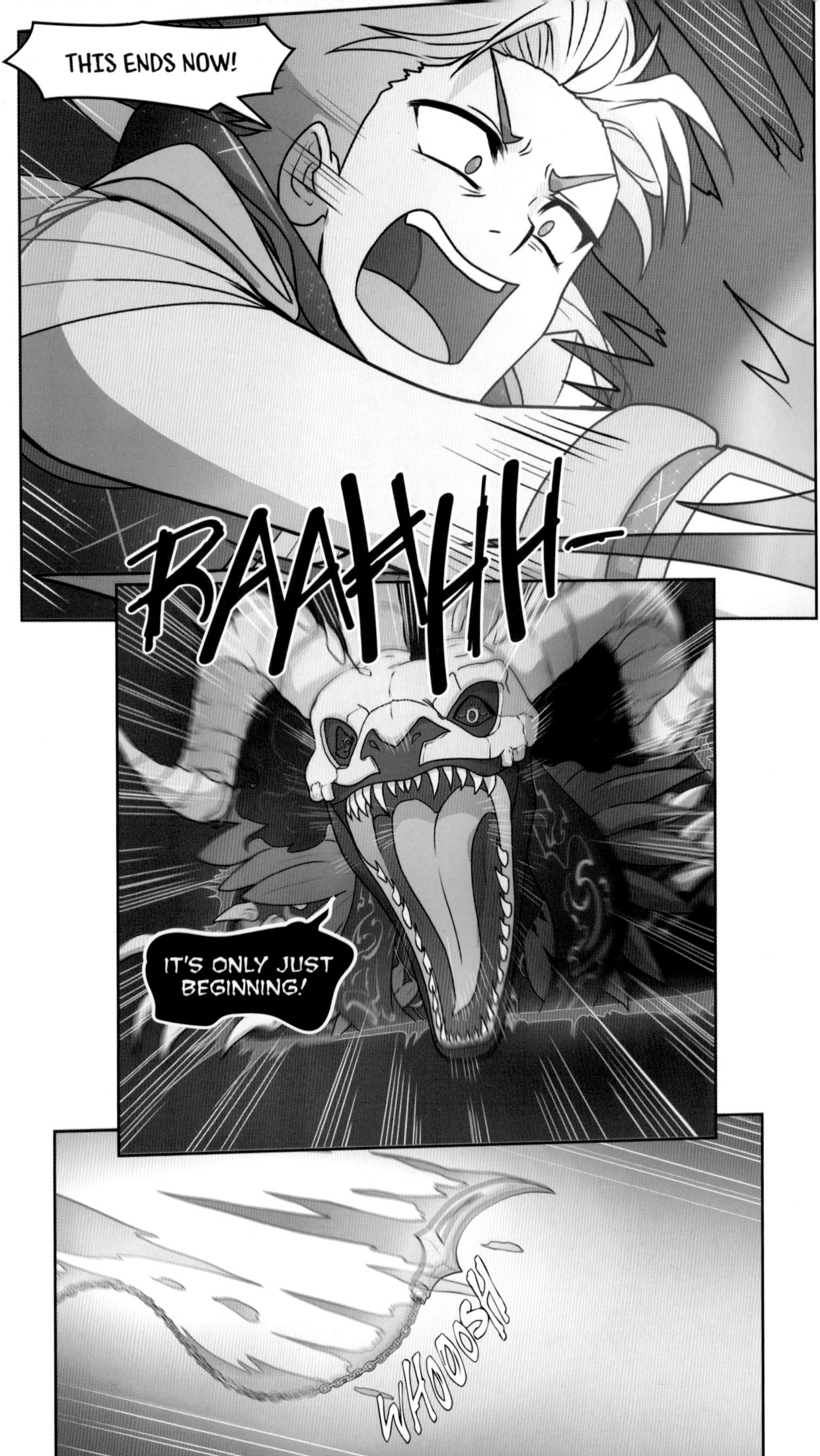
THIS ENDS NOW!
RAAHHH-
IT'S ONLY JUST BEGINNING!
WHOOOSH

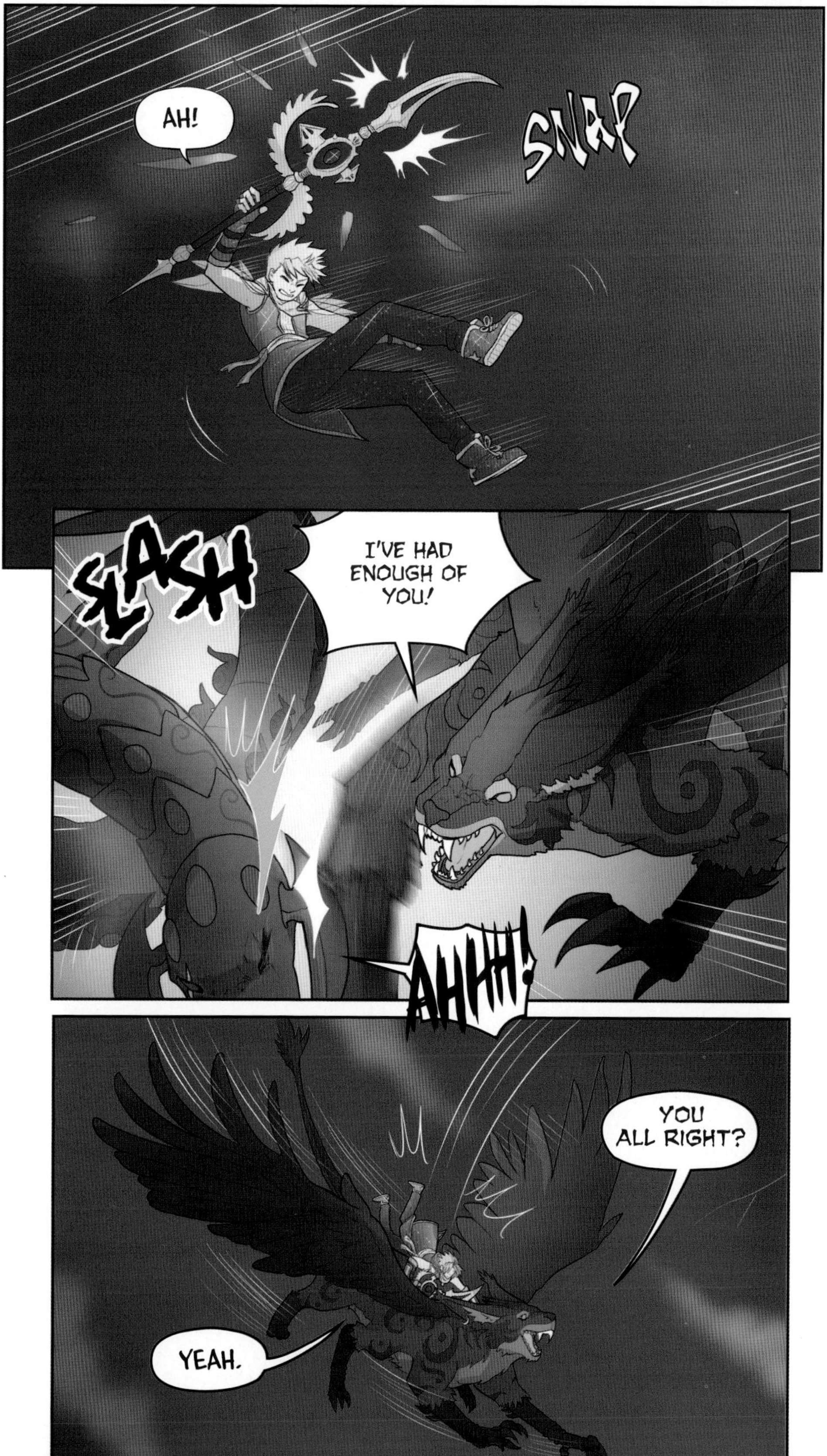
AH!
SNAP
SLASH
I'VE HAD ENOUGH OF YOU!
AHHH!
YOU ALL RIGHT?
YEAH.

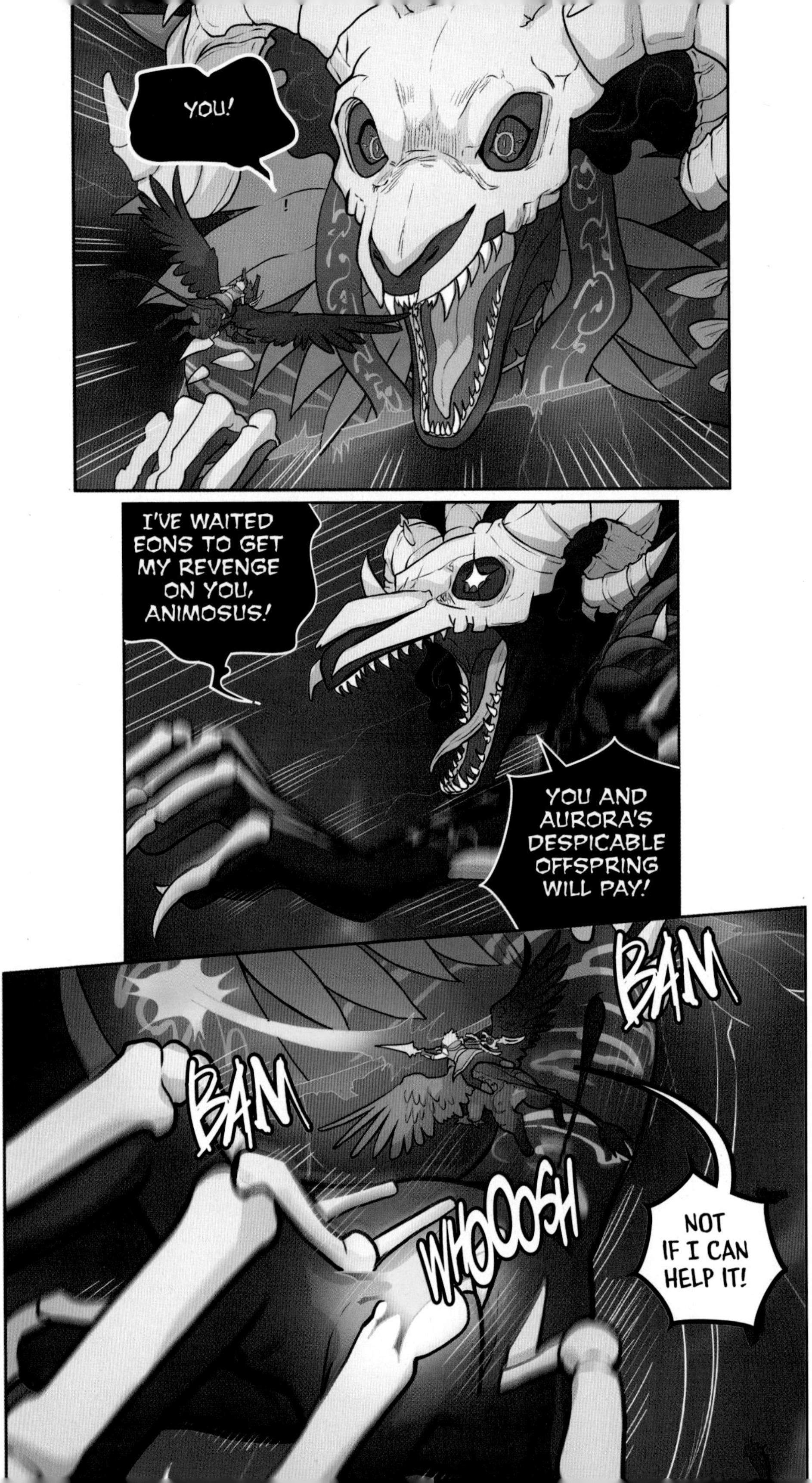
YOU!
I'VE WAITED EONS TO GET MY REVENGE ON YOU, ANIMOSUS!
YOU AND AURORA'S DESPICABLE OFFSPRING WILL PAY!
BAM
BAM
WHOOOSH
NOT IF I CAN HELP IT!

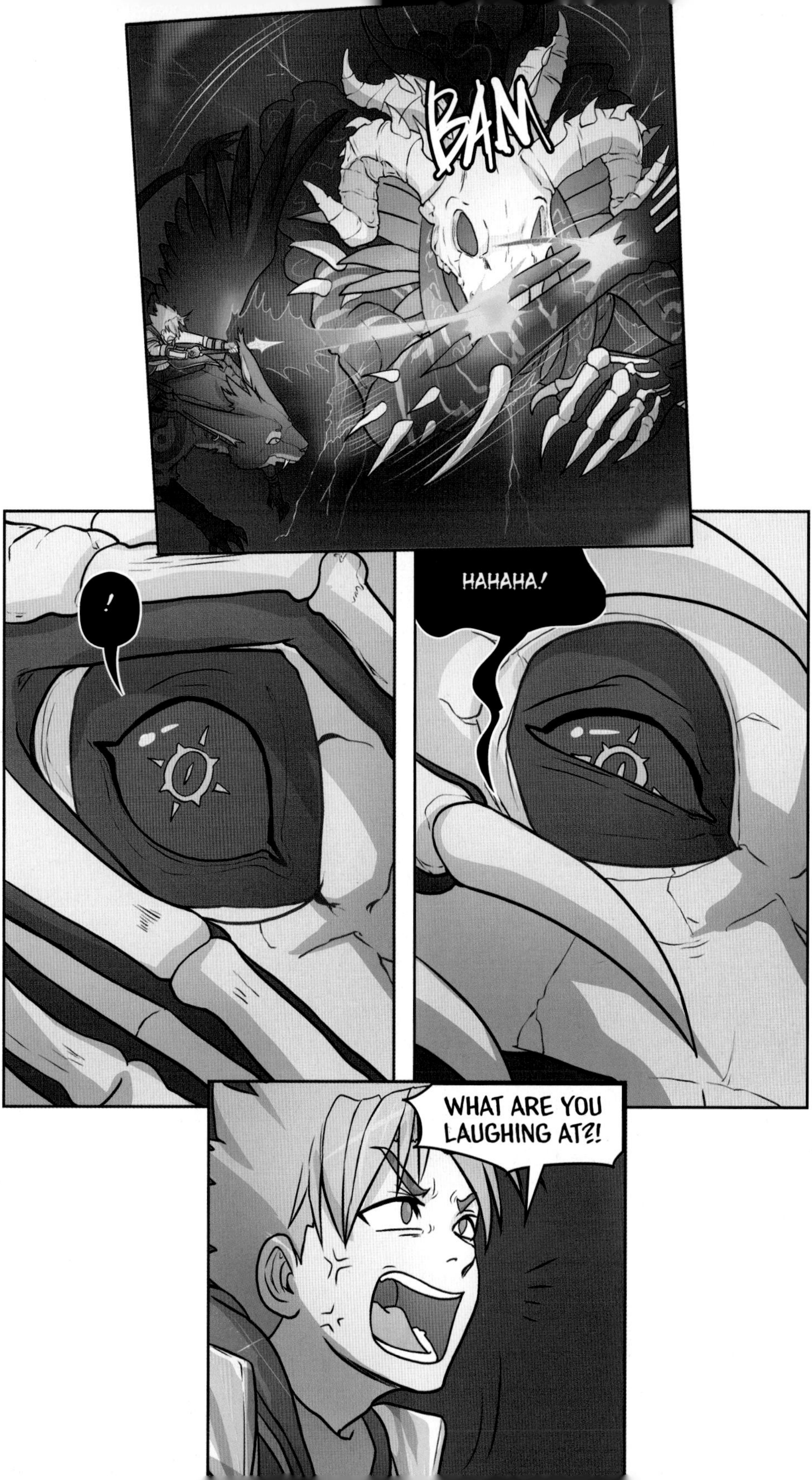
BAM
!
HAHAHA!
WHAT ARE YOU LAUGHING AT?!

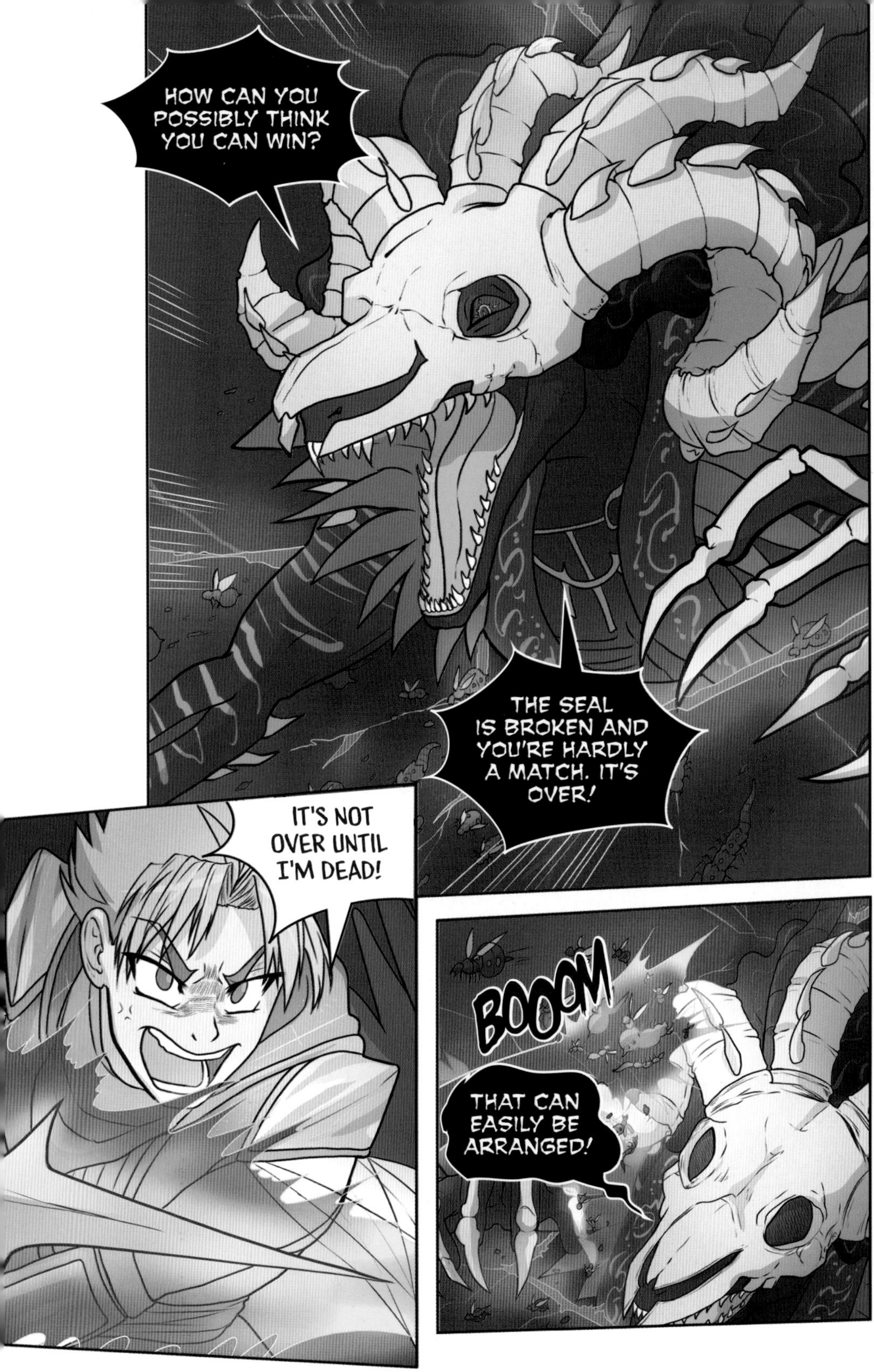
HOW CAN YOU POSSIBLY THINK YOU CAN WIN?
THE SEAL IS BROKEN AND YOU'RE HARDLY A MATCH. IT'S OVER!
IT'S NOT OVER UNTIL I'M DEAD!
BOOOM
THAT CAN EASILY BE ARRANGED!

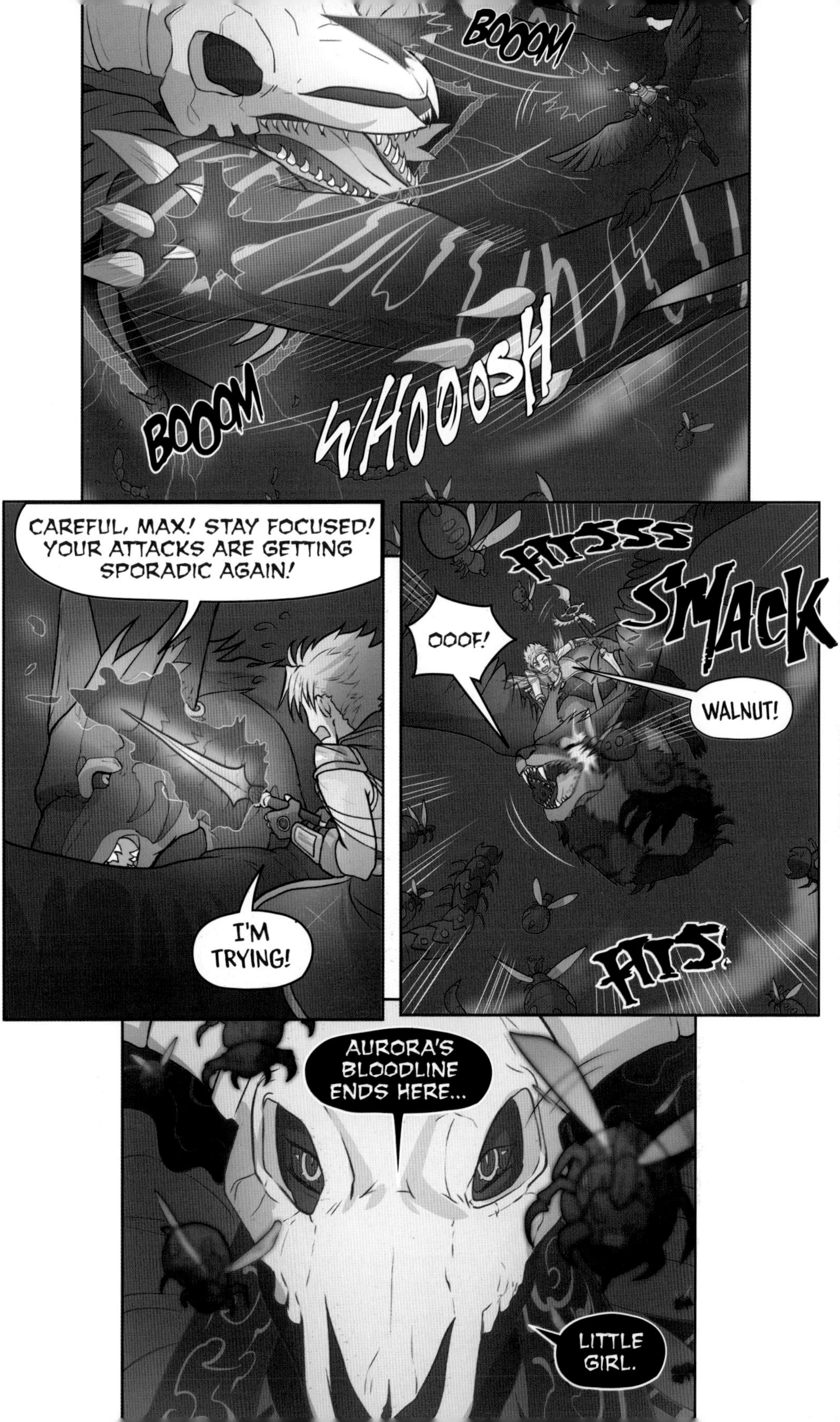
BOOOM
BOOOM
WHOOOSH
CAREFUL, MAX! STAY FOCUSED! YOUR ATTACKS ARE GETTING SPORADIC AGAIN!
I'M TRYING!
FTTSSS
SMACK
OOOF!
WALNUT!
FTTS!
AURORA'S BLOODLINE ENDS HERE...
LITTLE GIRL.

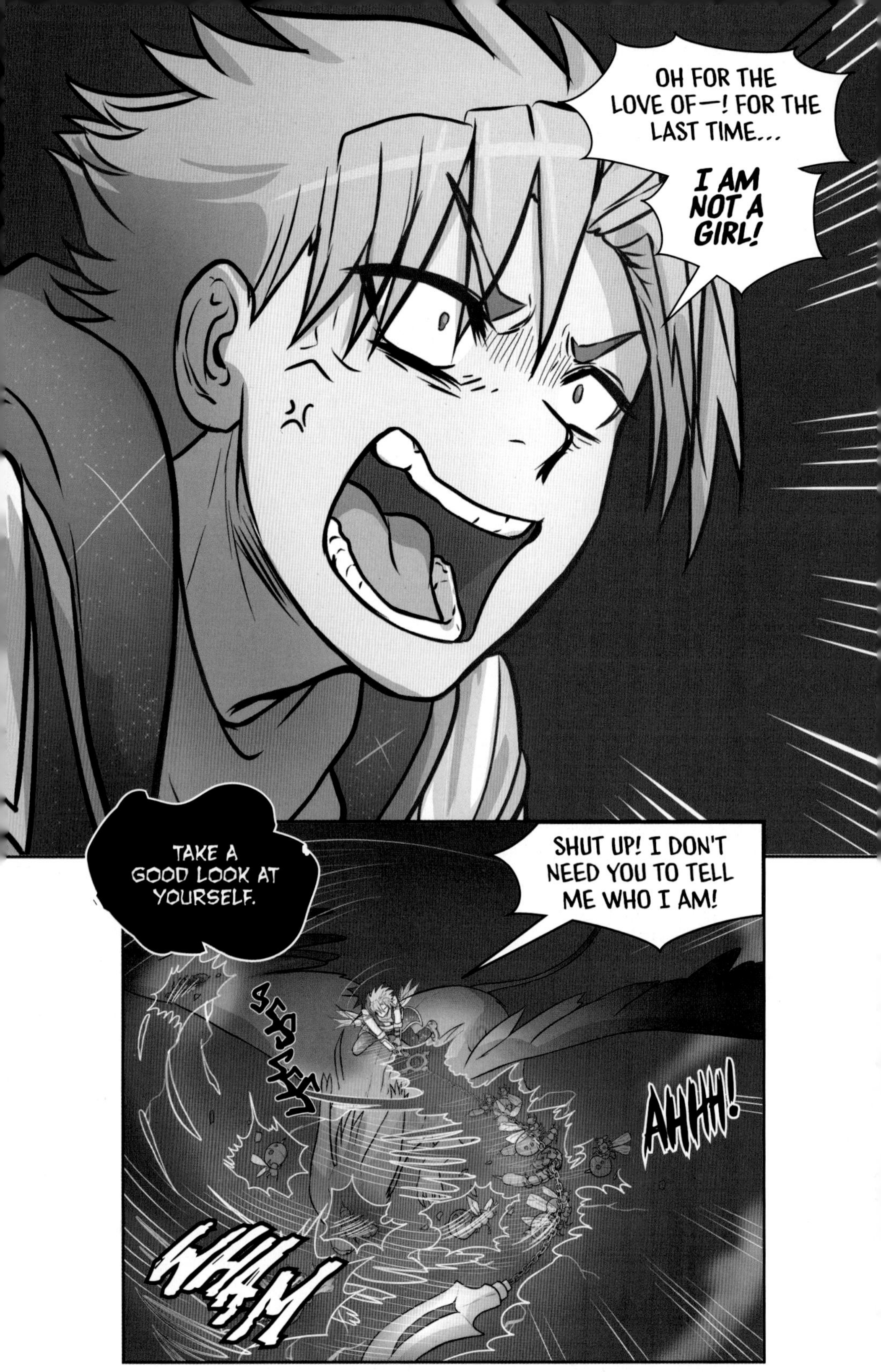
OH FOR THE LOVE OF—! FOR THE LAST TIME...
I AM NOT A GIRL!
TAKE A GOOD LOOK AT YOURSELF.
SHUT UP! I DON'T NEED YOU TO TELL ME WHO I AM!
SSSCCCH
AHHH!
WHAM

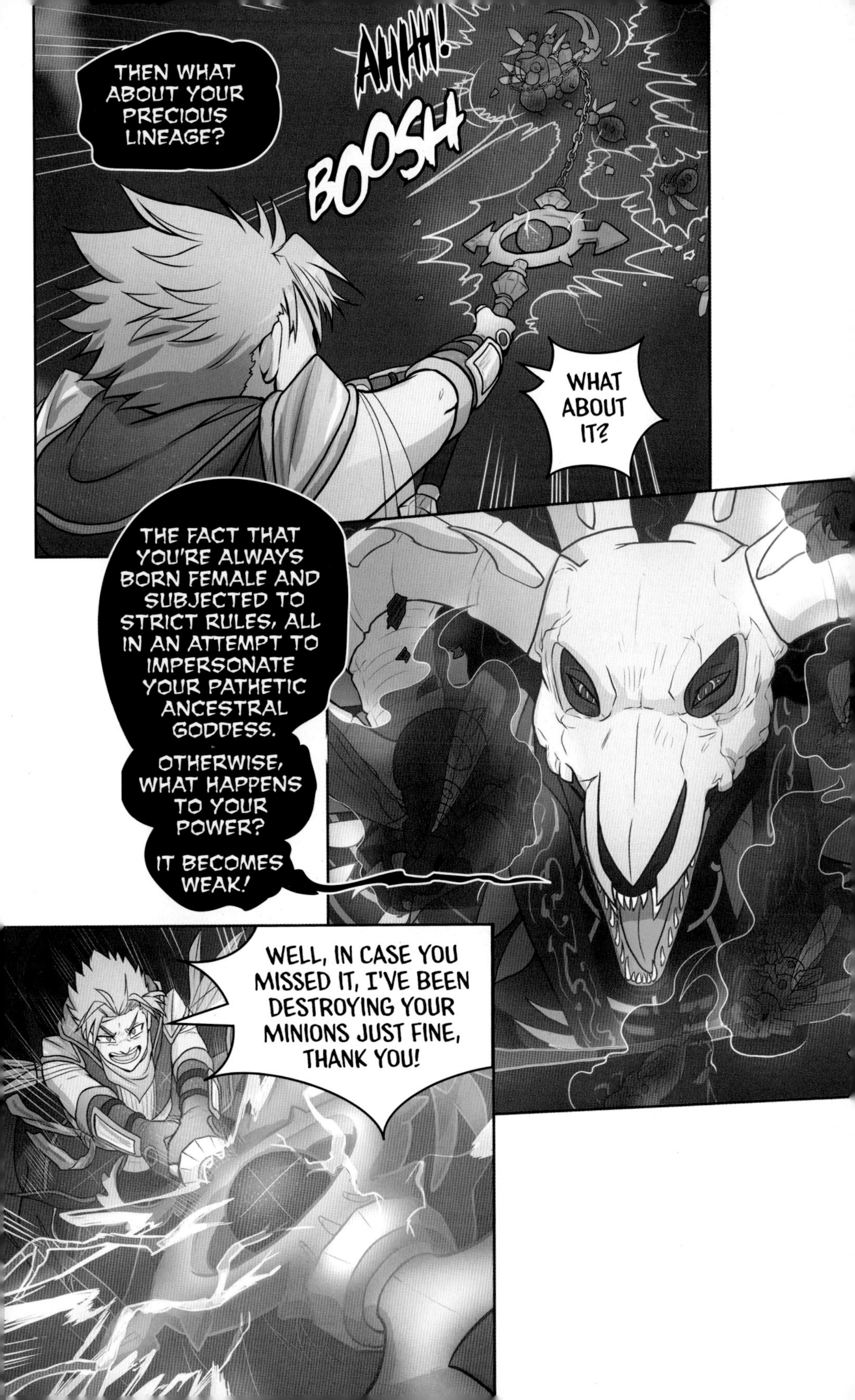
THEN WHAT ABOUT YOUR PRECIOUS LINEAGE?
AHHH!
BOOSH
WHAT ABOUT IT?
THE FACT THAT YOU'RE ALWAYS BORN FEMALE AND SUBJECTED TO STRICT RULES, ALL IN AN ATTEMPT TO IMPERSONATE YOUR PATHETIC ANCESTRAL GODDESS.
OTHERWISE, WHAT HAPPENS TO YOUR POWER?
IT BECOMES WEAK!
WELL, IN CASE YOU MISSED IT, I'VE BEEN DESTROYING YOUR MINIONS JUST FINE, THANK YOU!

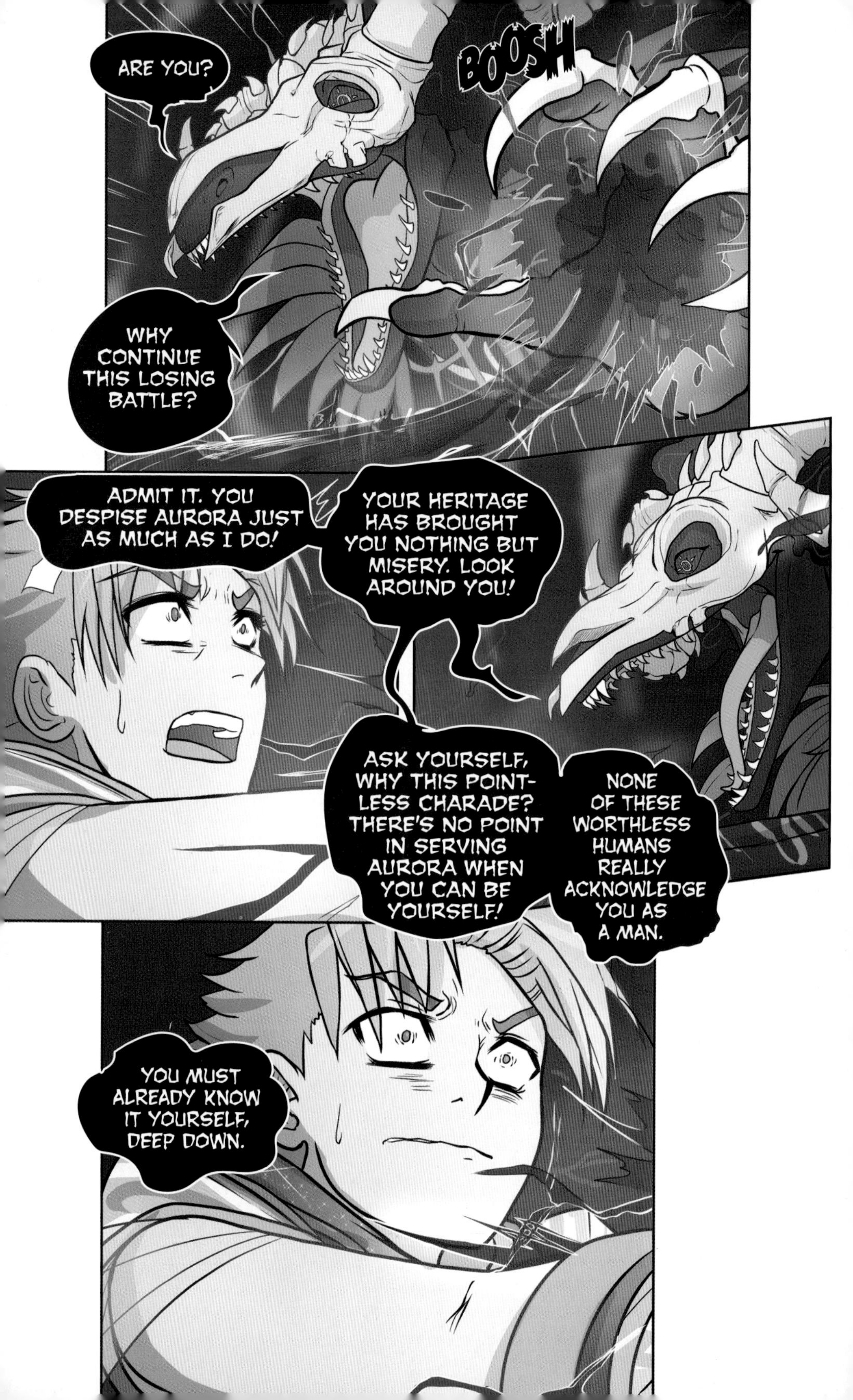
ARE YOU?
BOOSH
WHY CONTINUE THIS LOSING BATTLE?
ADMIT IT. YOU DESPISE AURORA JUST AS MUCH AS I DO!
YOUR HERITAGE HAS BROUGHT YOU NOTHING BUT MISERY. LOOK AROUND YOU!
ASK YOURSELF, WHY THIS POINT-LESS CHARADE? THERE'S NO POINT IN SERVING AURORA WHEN YOU CAN BE YOURSELF!
NONE OF THESE WORTHLESS HUMANS REALLY ACKNOWLEDGE YOU AS A MAN.
YOU MUST ALREADY KNOW IT YOURSELF, DEEP DOWN.

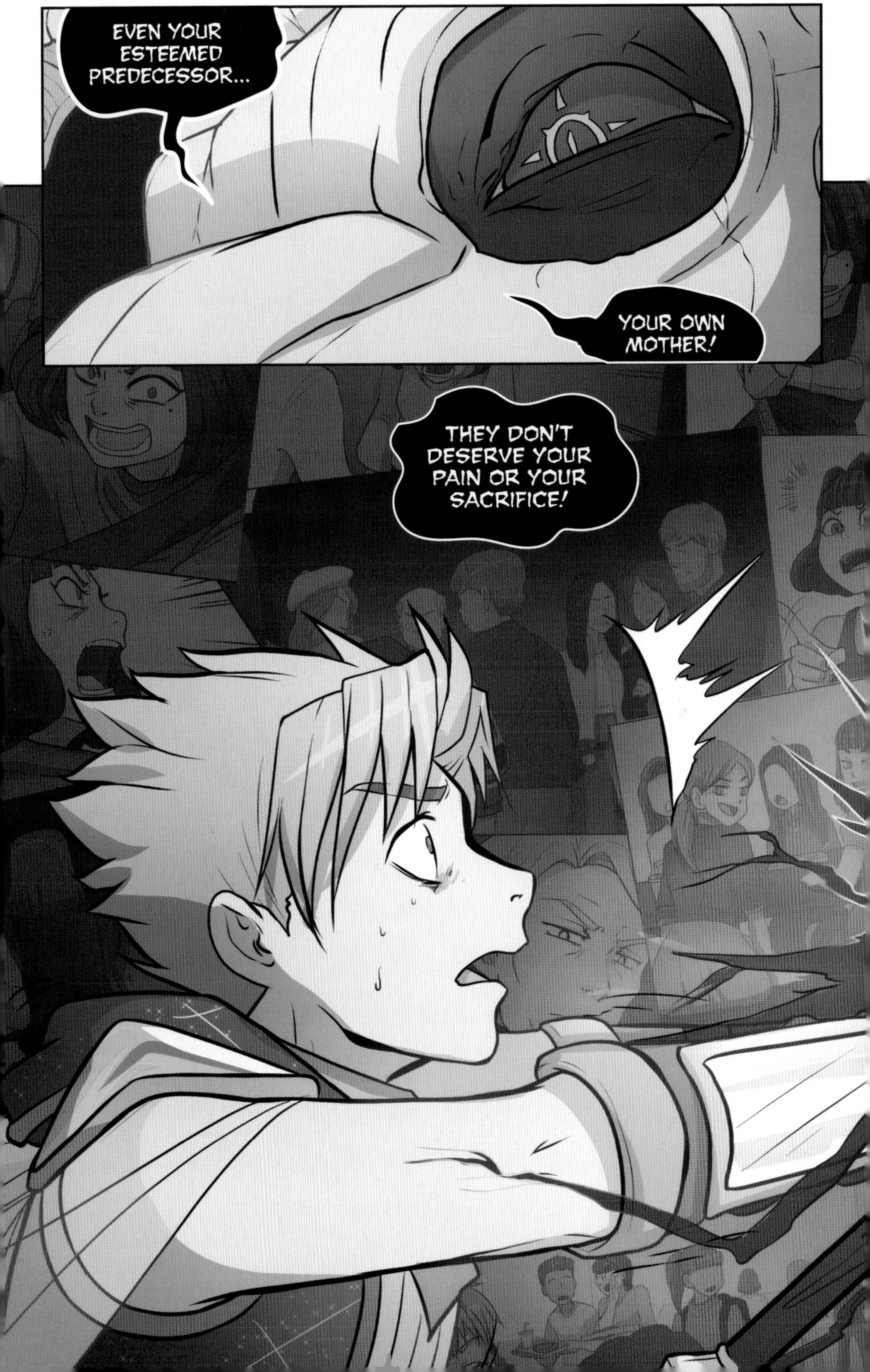
EVEN YOUR ESTEEMED PREDECESSOR...
YOUR OWN MOTHER!
THEY DON'T DESERVE YOUR PAIN OR YOUR SACRIFICE!

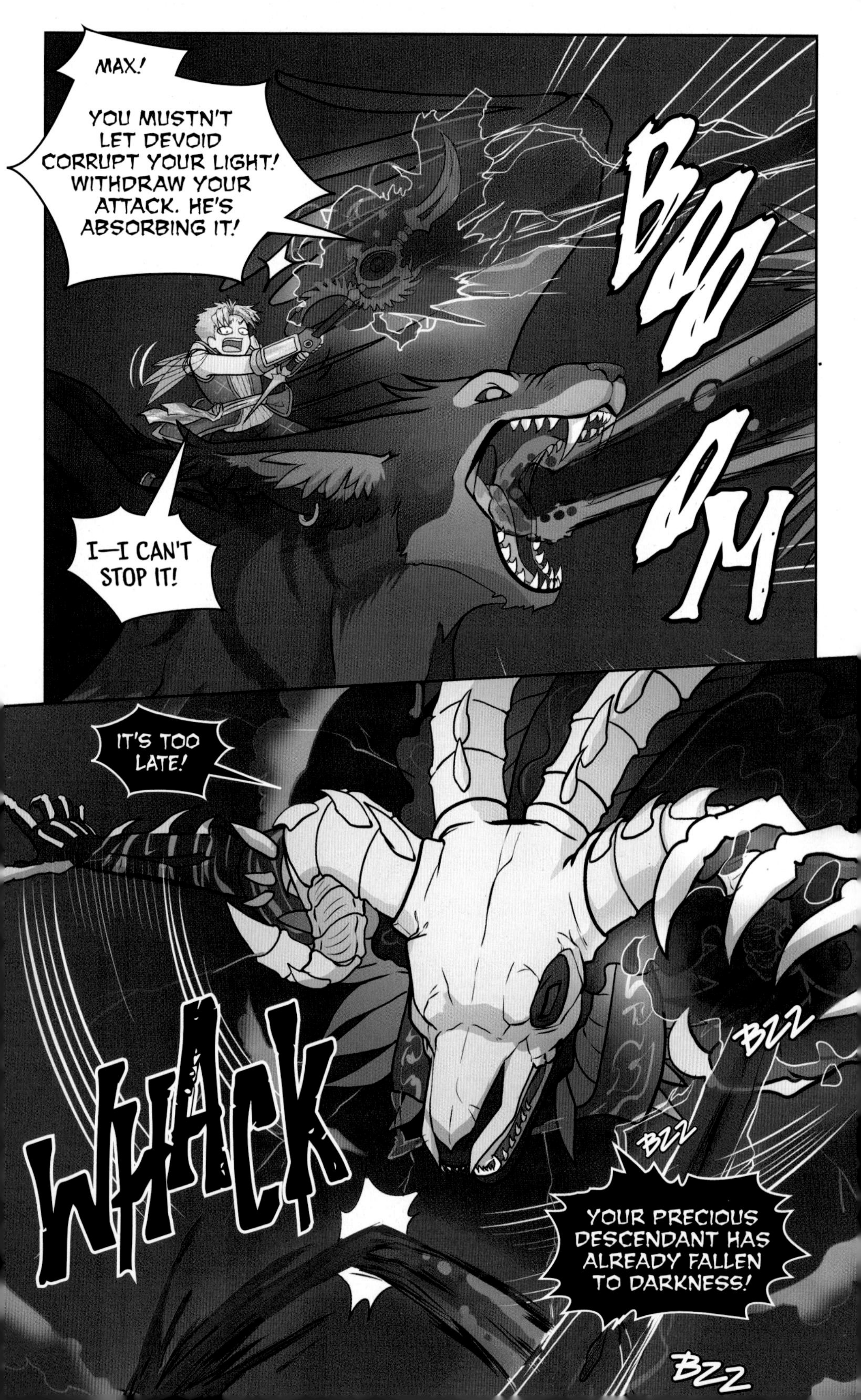
MAX!
YOU MUSTN'T LET DEVOID CORRUPT YOUR LIGHT! WITHDRAW YOUR ATTACK. HE'S ABSORBING IT!
BOOOM
I—I CAN'T STOP IT!
IT'S TOO LATE!
WHACK
BZZ
BZZ
YOUR PRECIOUS DESCENDANT HAS ALREADY FALLEN TO DARKNESS!
BZZ

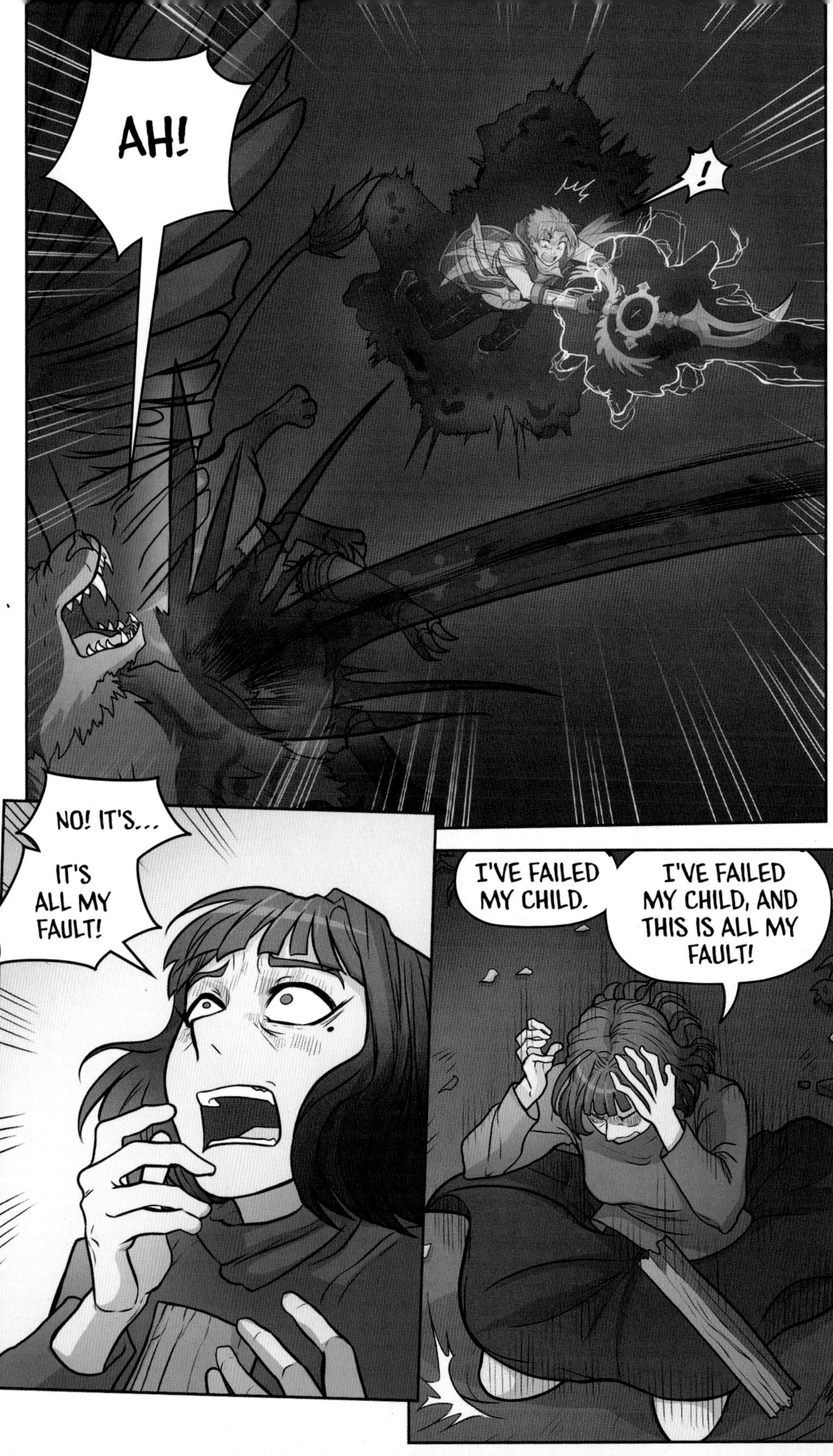
AH!
!
NO! IT'S...
IT'S ALL MY FAULT!
I'VE FAILED MY CHILD.
I'VE FAILED MY CHILD, AND THIS IS ALL MY FAULT!

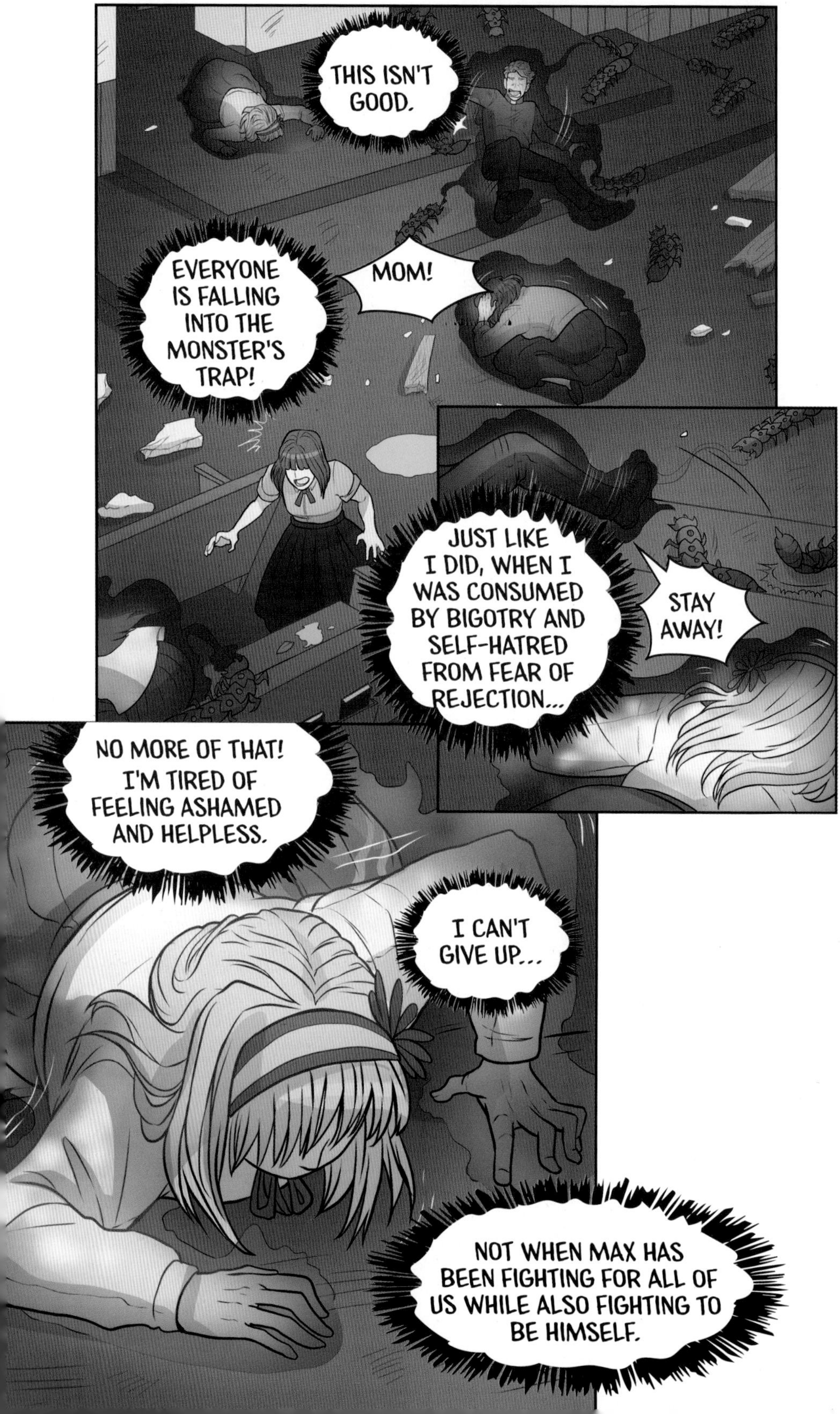
THIS ISN'T GOOD.
EVERYONE IS FALLING INTO THE MONSTER'S TRAP!
MOM!
JUST LIKE I DID, WHEN I WAS CONSUMED BY BIGOTRY AND SELF-HATRED FROM FEAR OF REJECTION...
STAY AWAY!
NO MORE OF THAT! I'M TIRED OF FEELING ASHAMED AND HELPLESS.
I CAN'T GIVE UP...
NOT WHEN MAX HAS BEEN FIGHTING FOR ALL OF US WHILE ALSO FIGHTING TO BE HIMSELF.

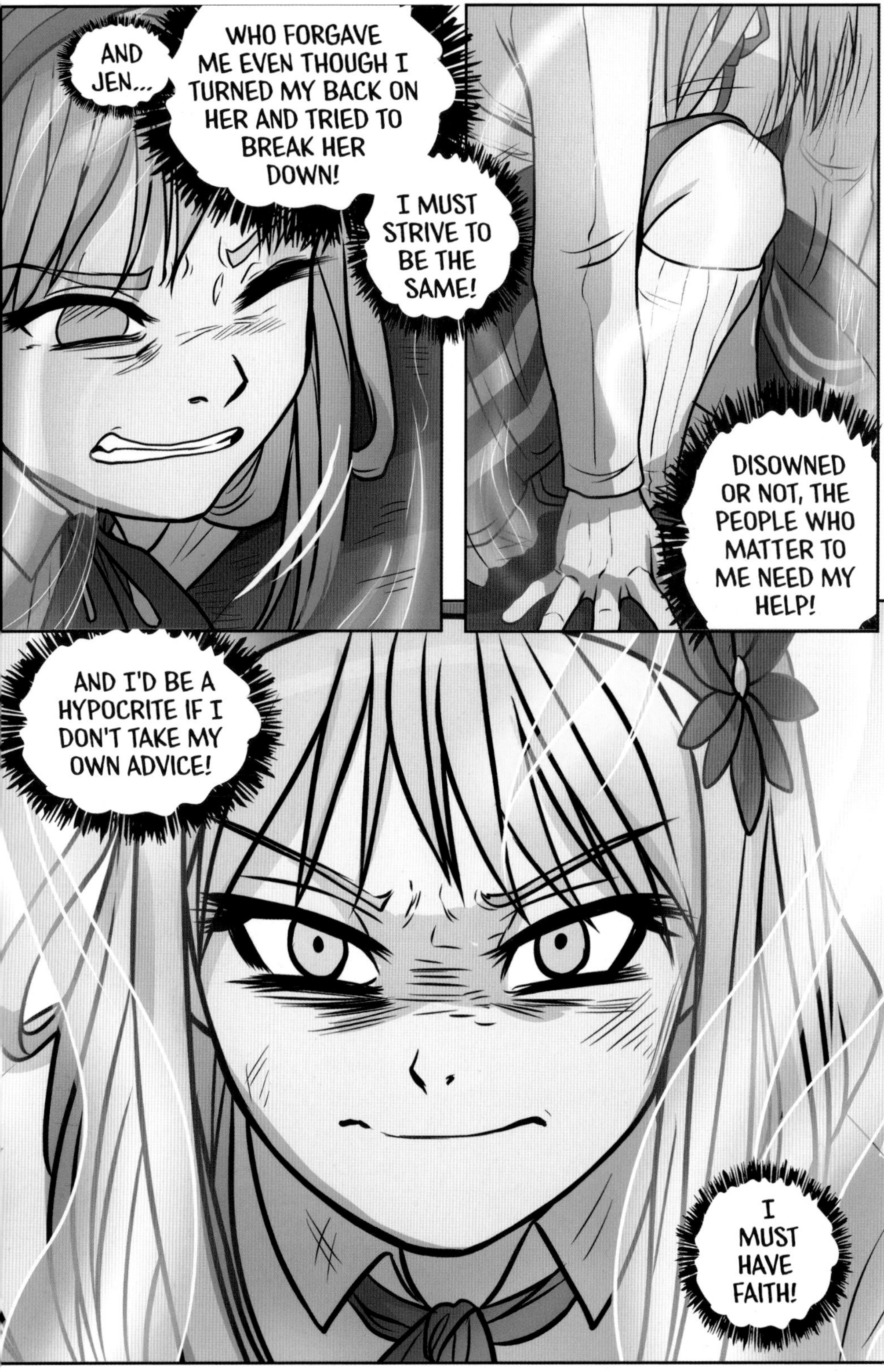
AND JEN...
WHO FORGAVE ME EVEN THOUGH I TURNED MY BACK ON HER AND TRIED TO BREAK HER DOWN!
I MUST STRIVE TO BE THE SAME!
DISOWNED OR NOT, THE PEOPLE WHO MATTER TO ME NEED MY HELP!
AND I'D BE A HYPOCRITE IF I DON'T TAKE MY OWN ADVICE!
I MUST HAVE FAITH!

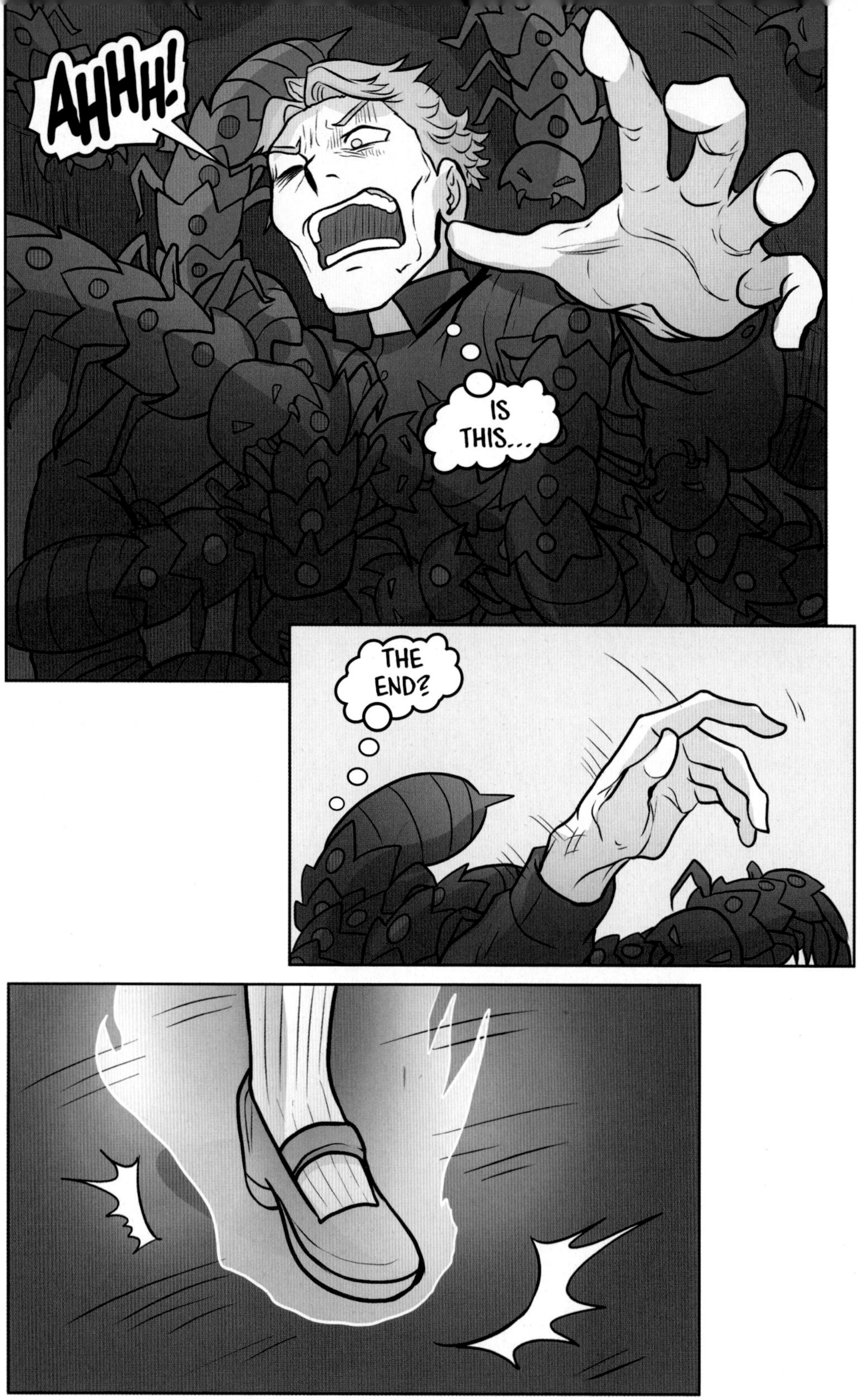
AHHH!
IS THIS...
THE END?

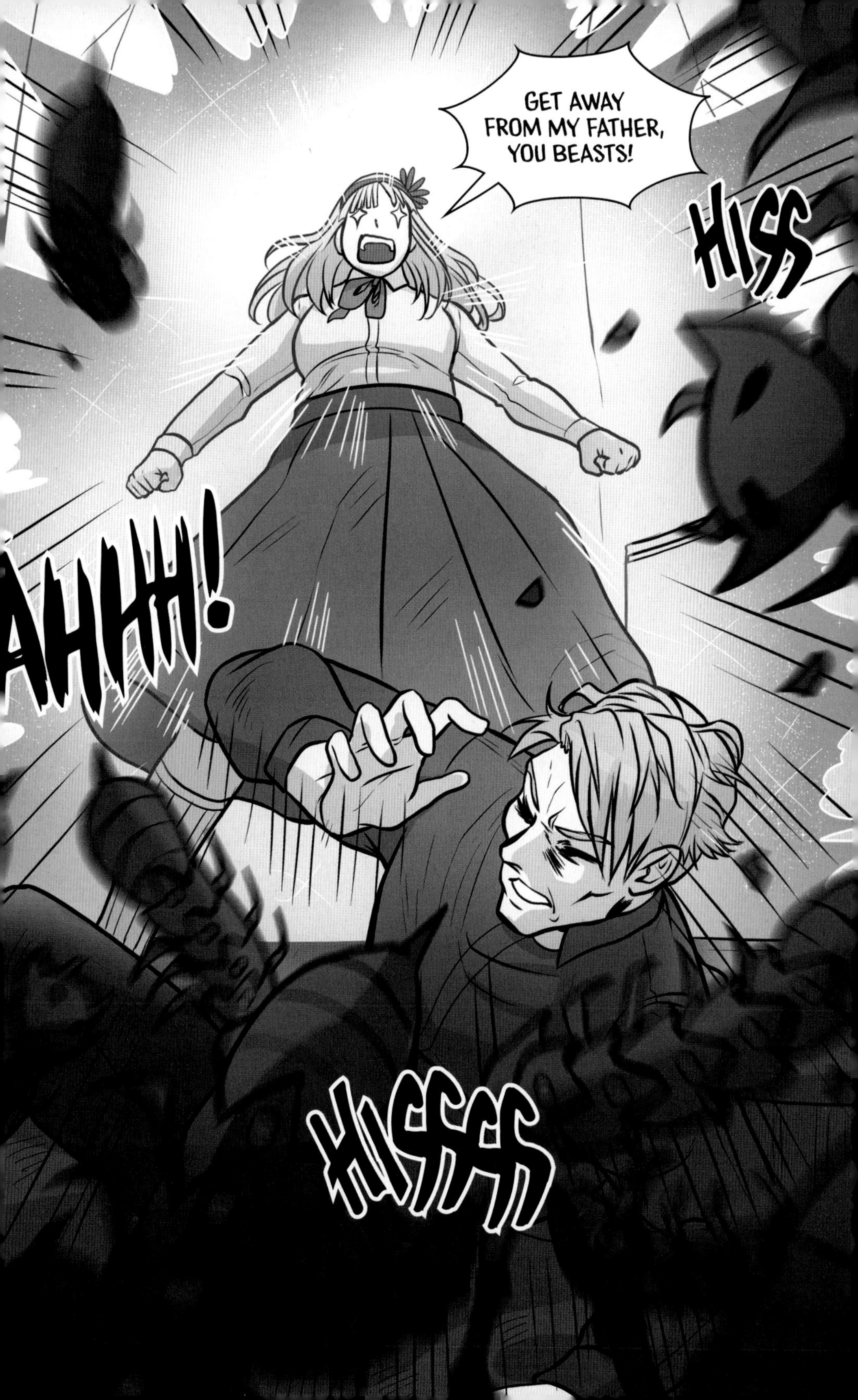
GET AWAY FROM MY FATHER, YOU BEASTS!
HISS
AHHH!
HISSSS

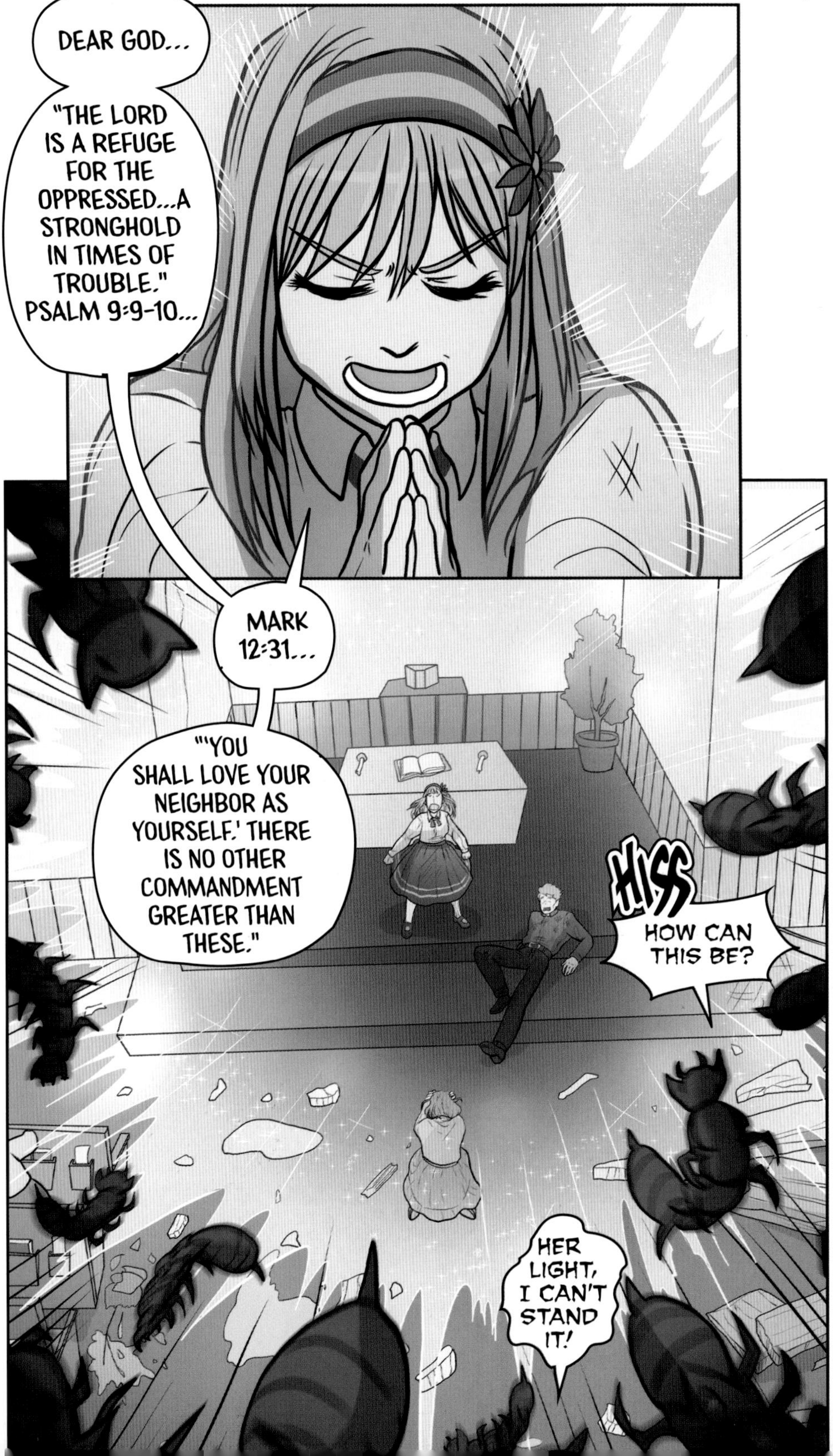

DEAR GOD...
"THE LORD IS A REFUGE FOR THE OPPRESSED...A STRONGHOLD IN TIMES OF TROUBLE." PSALM 9:9-10...
MARK 12:31...
"'YOU SHALL LOVE YOUR NEIGHBOR AS YOURSELF.' THERE IS NO OTHER COMMANDMENT GREATER THAN THESE."
HISS
HOW CAN THIS BE?
HER LIGHT, I CAN'T STAND IT!

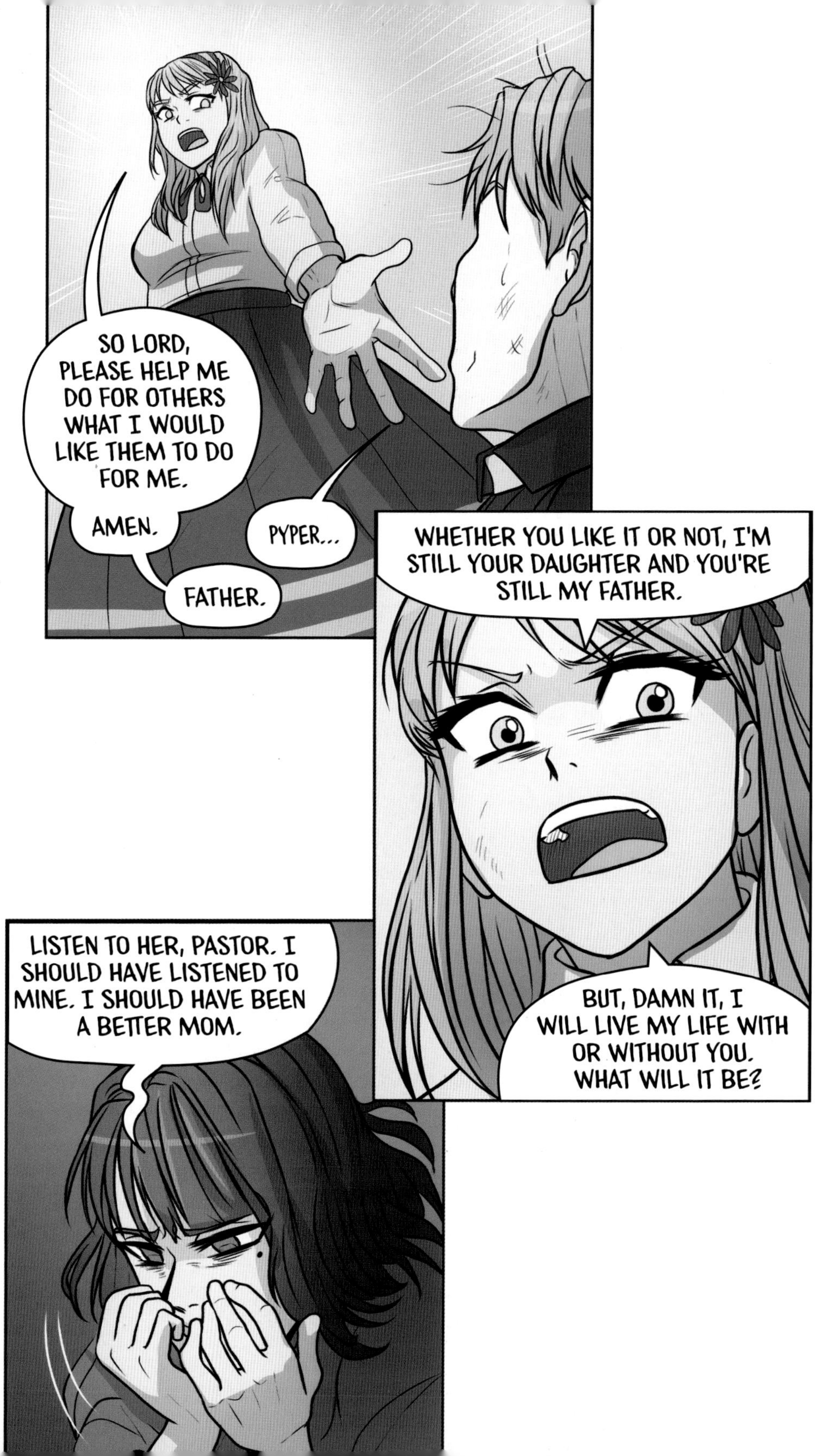
SO LORD, PLEASE HELP ME DO FOR OTHERS WHAT I WOULD LIKE THEM TO DO FOR ME.
AMEN.
FATHER.
PYPER...
WHETHER YOU LIKE IT OR NOT, I'M STILL YOUR DAUGHTER AND YOU'RE STILL MY FATHER.
BUT, DAMN IT, I WILL LIVE MY LIFE WITH OR WITHOUT YOU. WHAT WILL IT BE?
LISTEN TO HER, PASTOR. I SHOULD HAVE LISTENED TO MINE. I SHOULD HAVE BEEN A BETTER MOM.

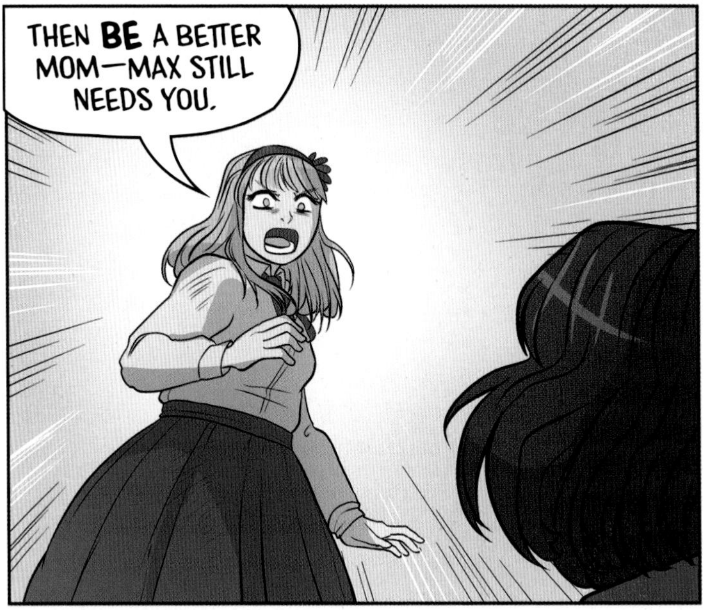
THEN **BE** A BETTER MOM—MAX STILL NEEDS YOU.

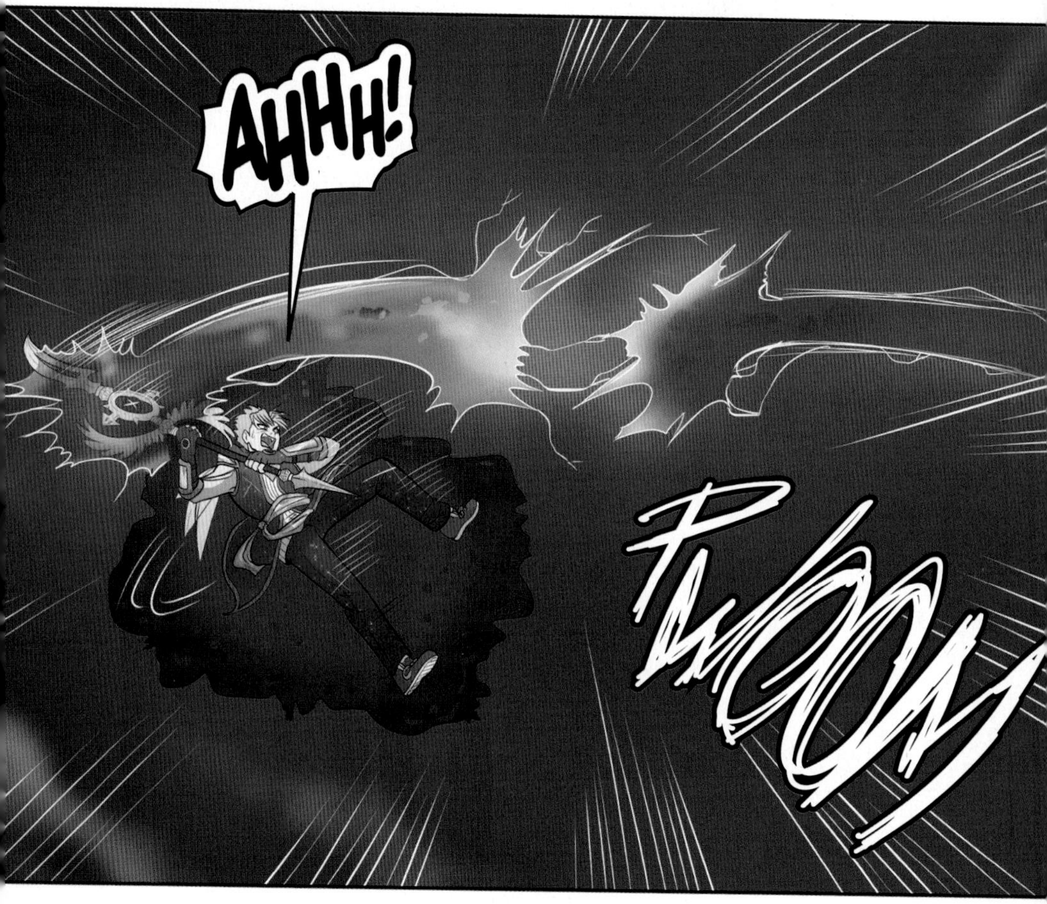
AHHH!
PWOOM

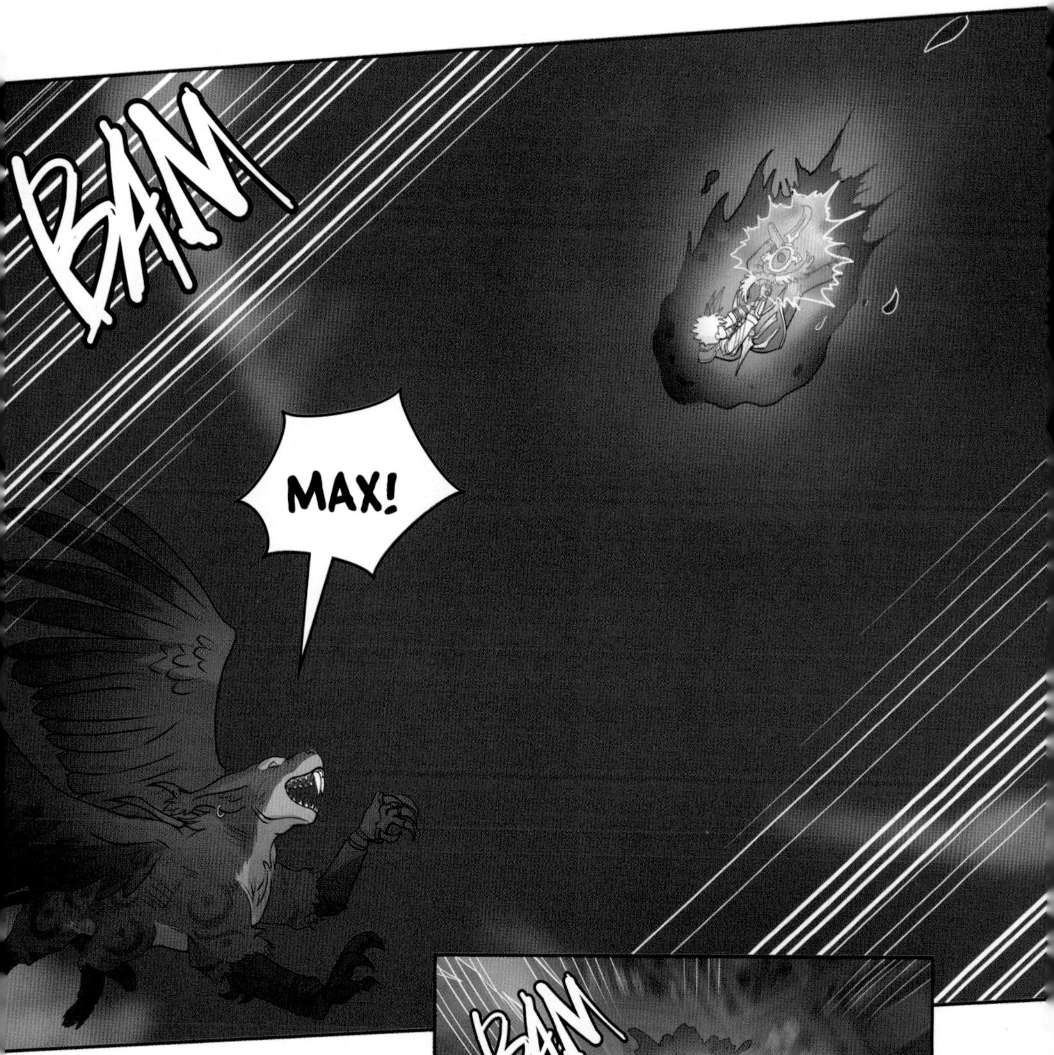
BAM
MAX!

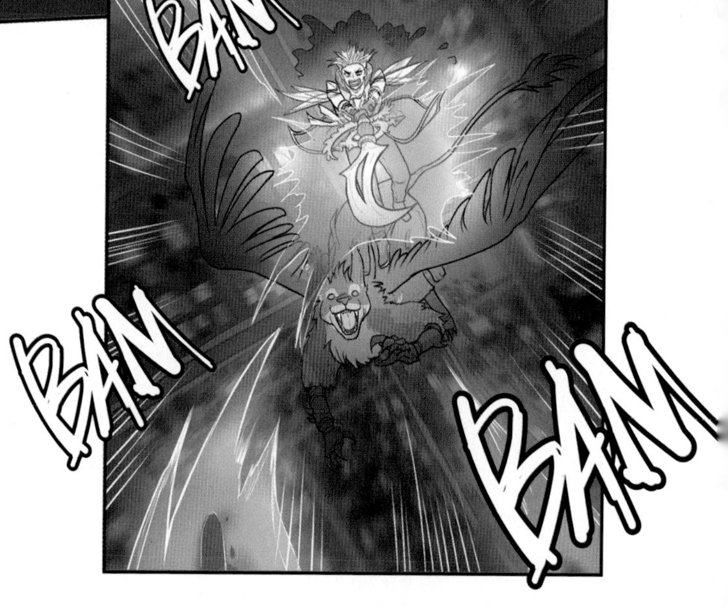
BAM
BAM
BAM

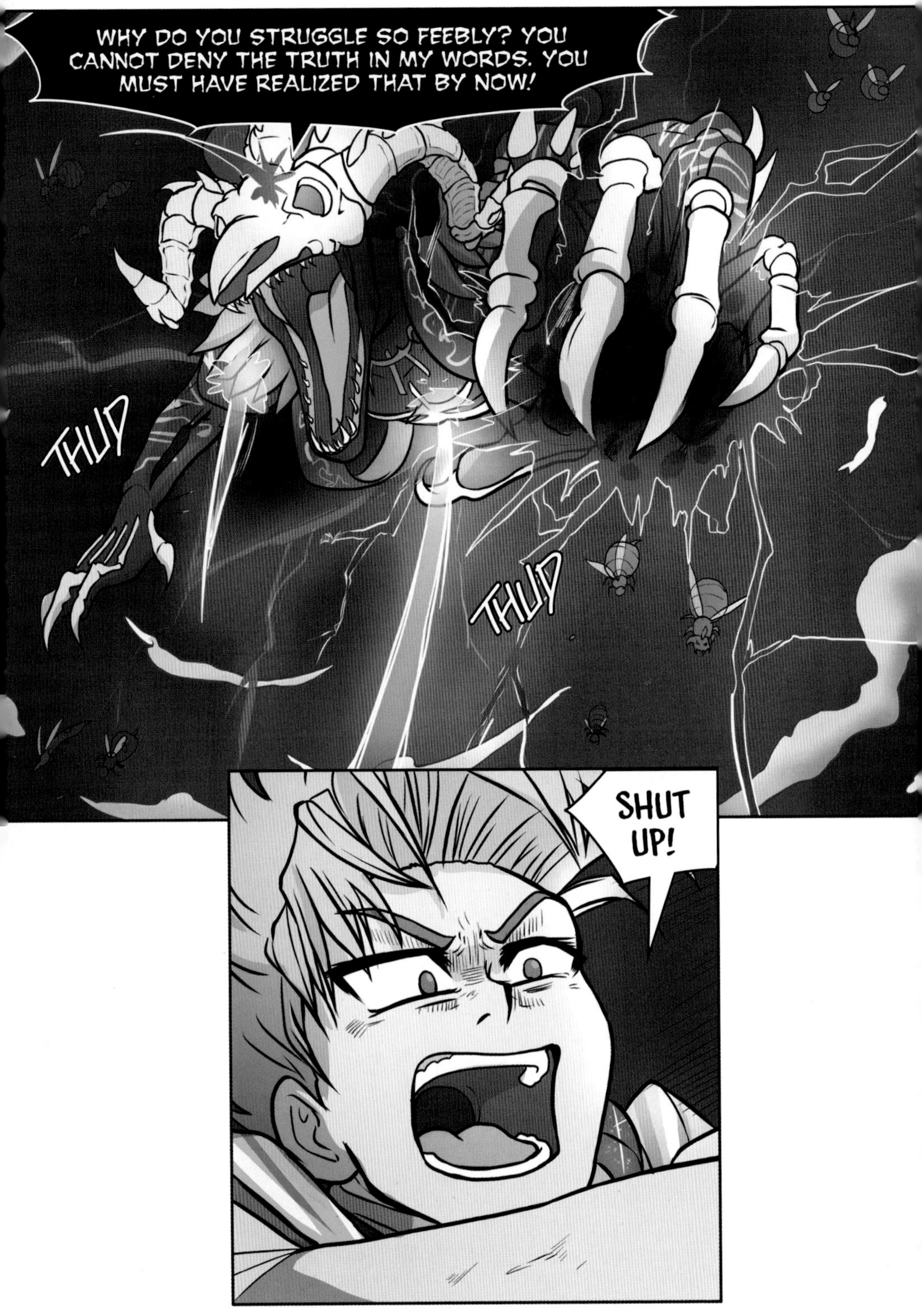
WHY DO YOU STRUGGLE SO FEEBLY? YOU CANNOT DENY THE TRUTH IN MY WORDS. YOU MUST HAVE REALIZED THAT BY NOW!
THUD
THUD
SHUT UP!

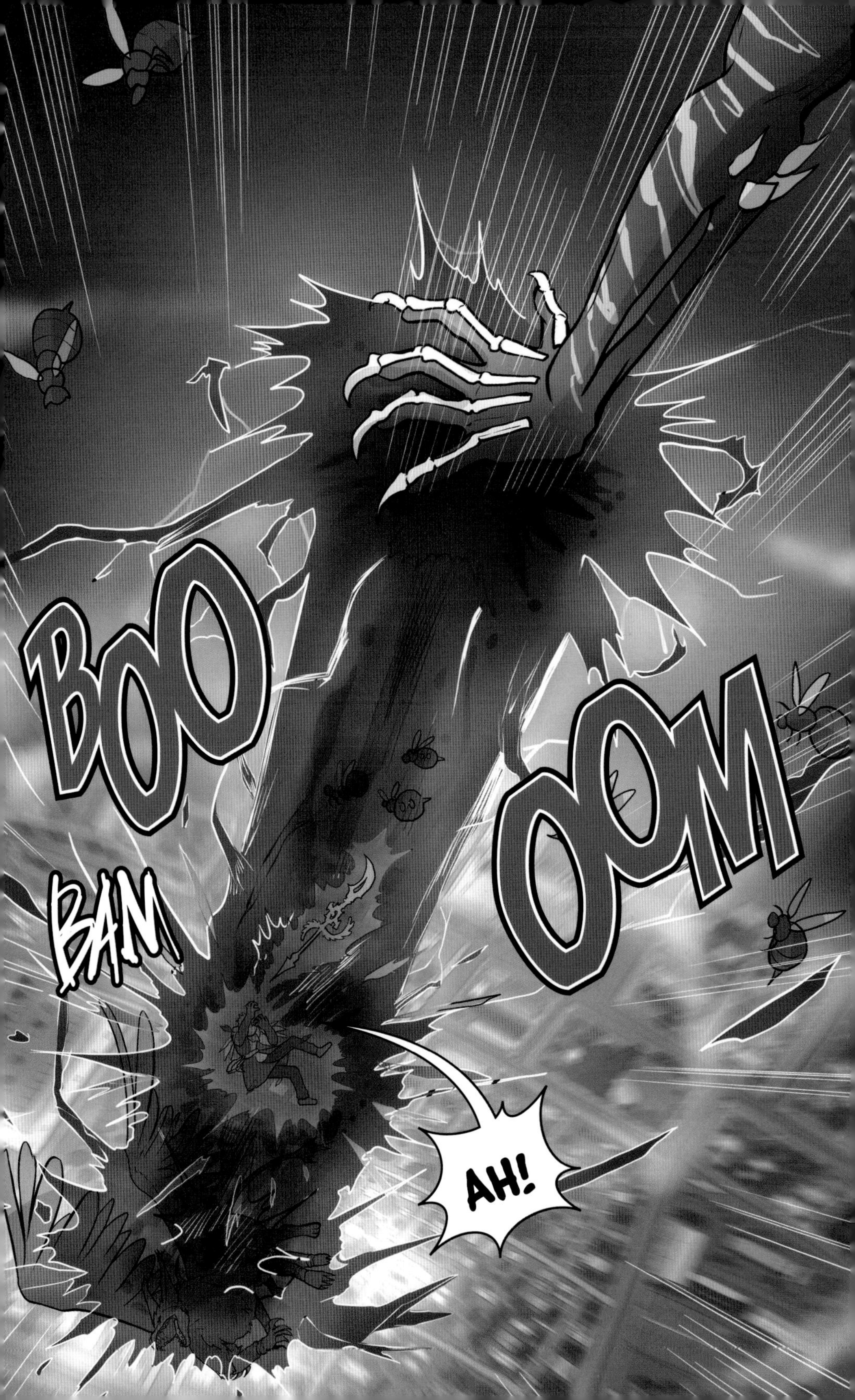
BOOOOM
BAM
AH!

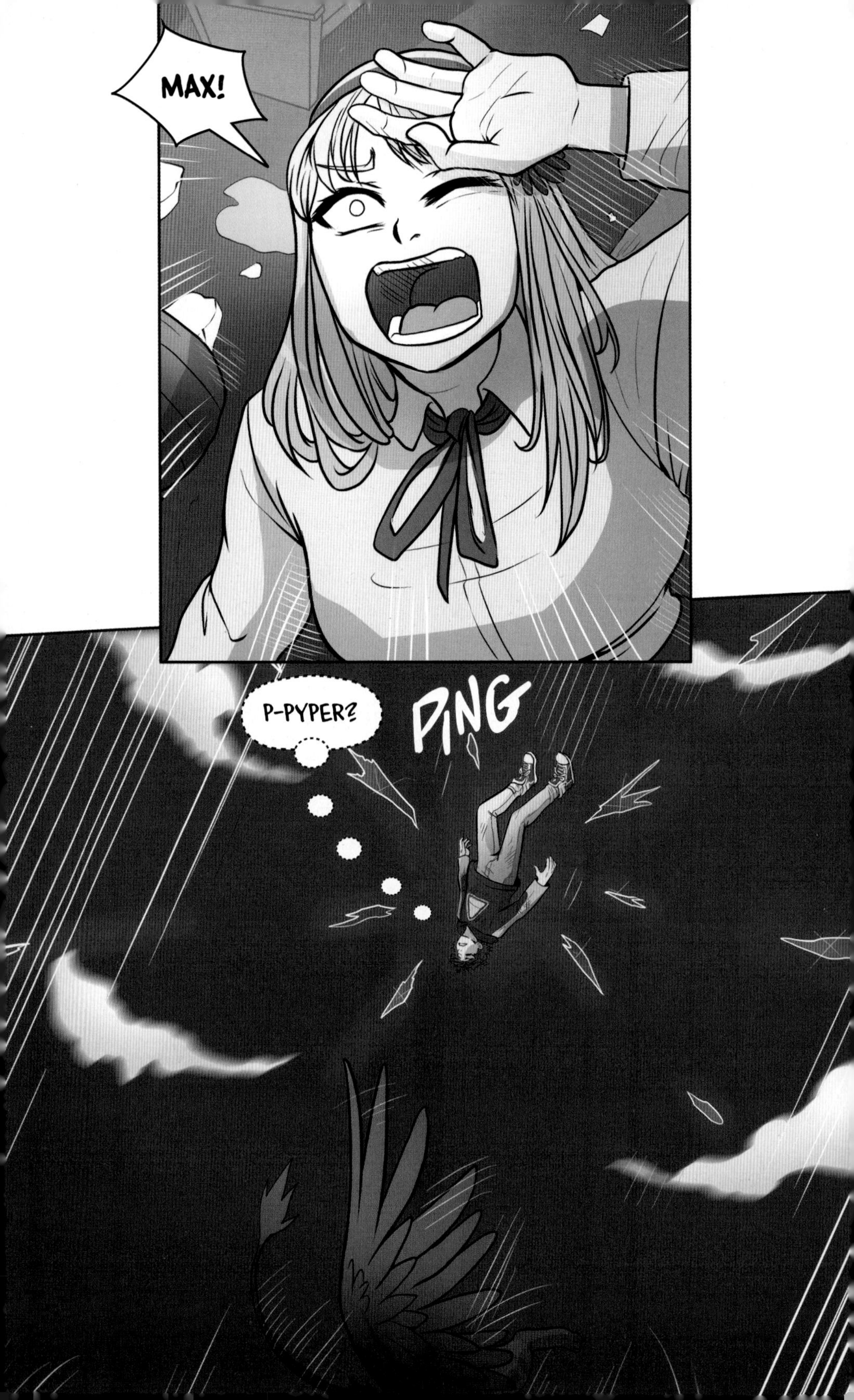
MAX!
P-PYPER?
PING

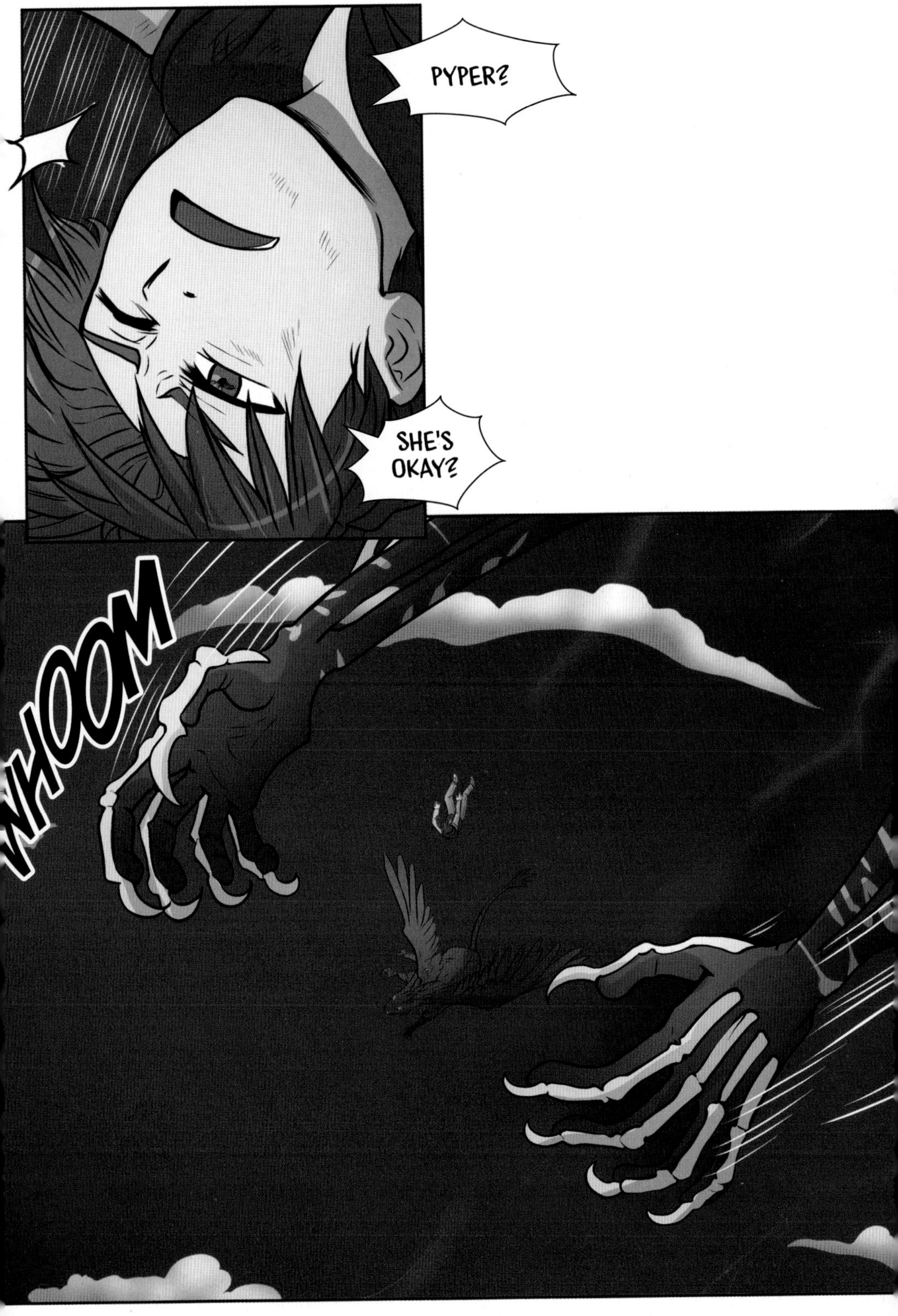
PYPER?
SHE'S OKAY?
WHOOM

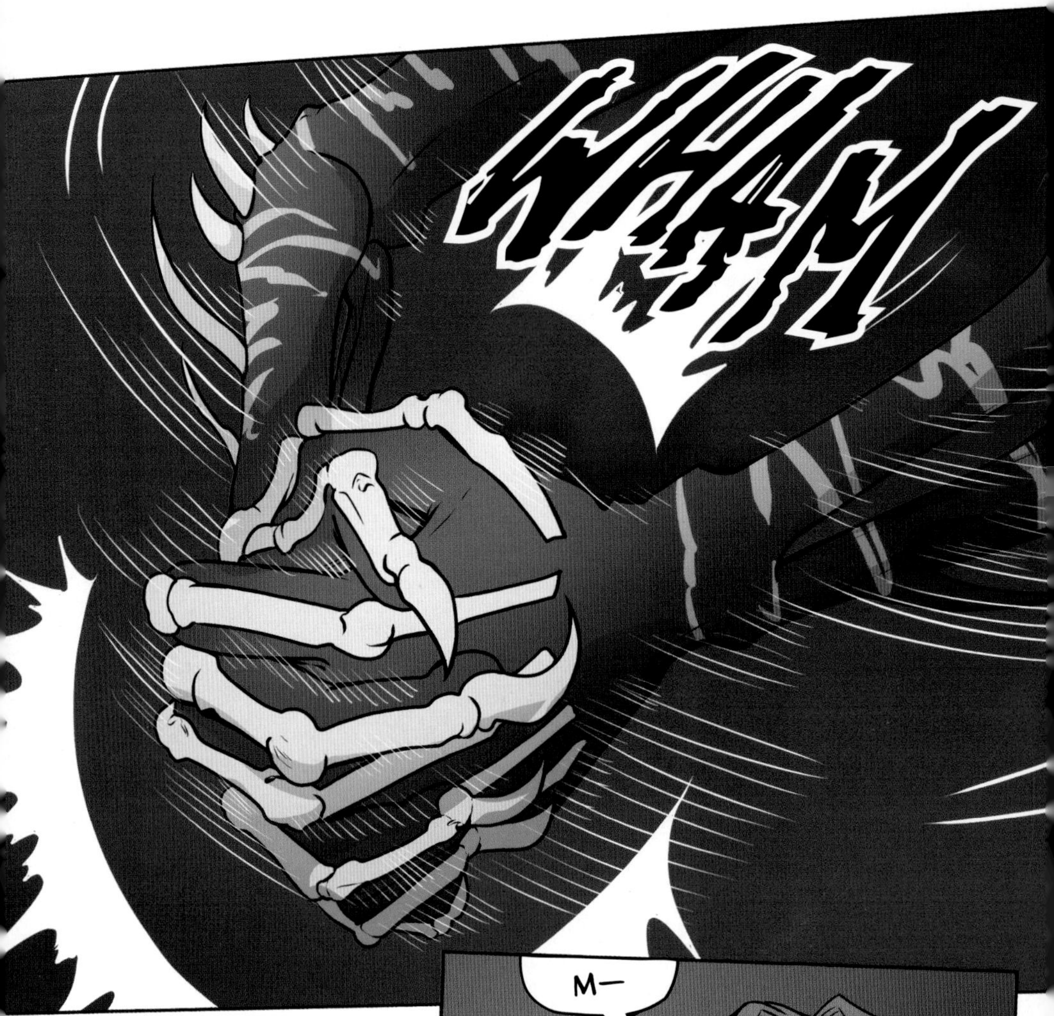
WHAM

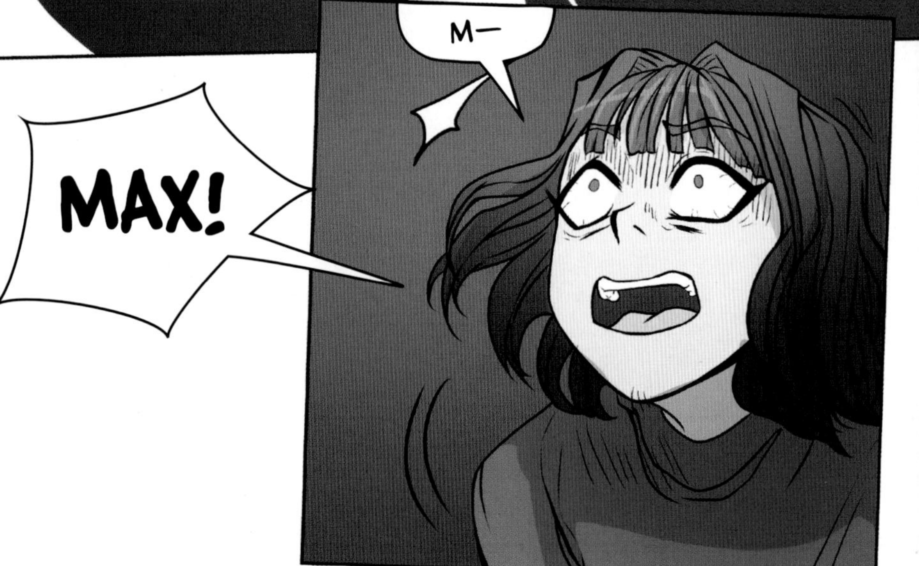
M—
MAX!

EPISODE 26:

THE GODDESS WITHIN (PT. 1)

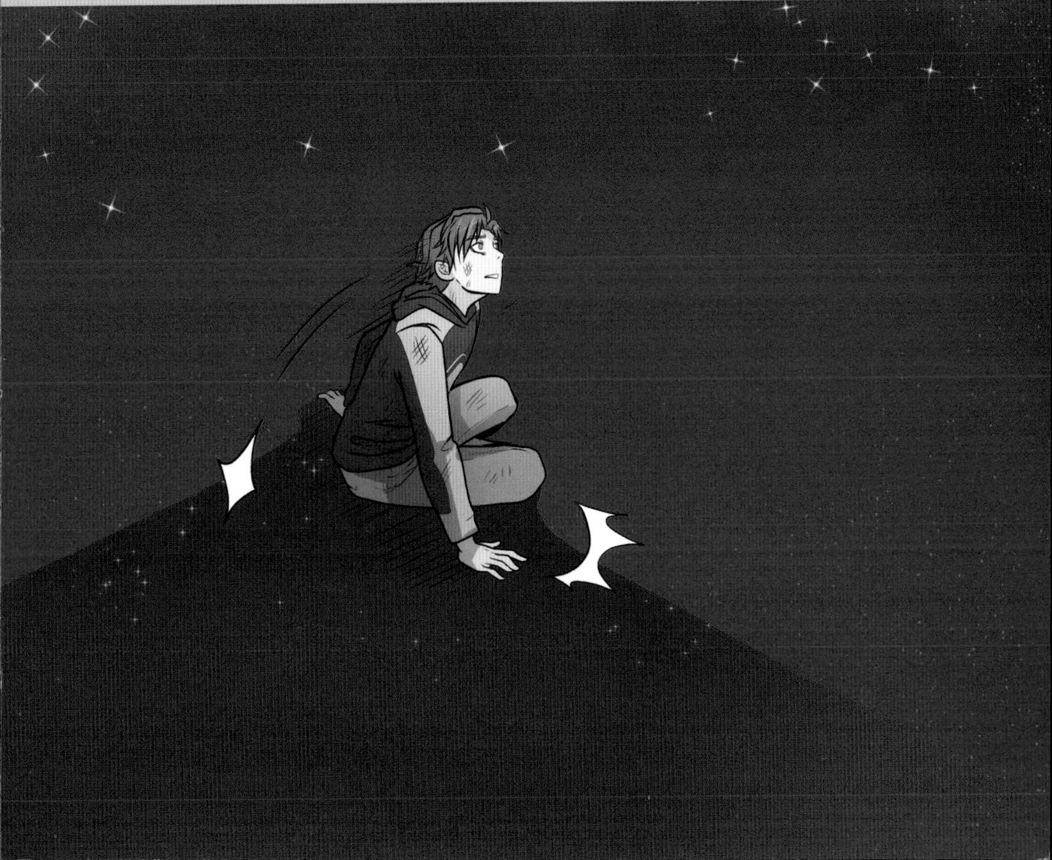

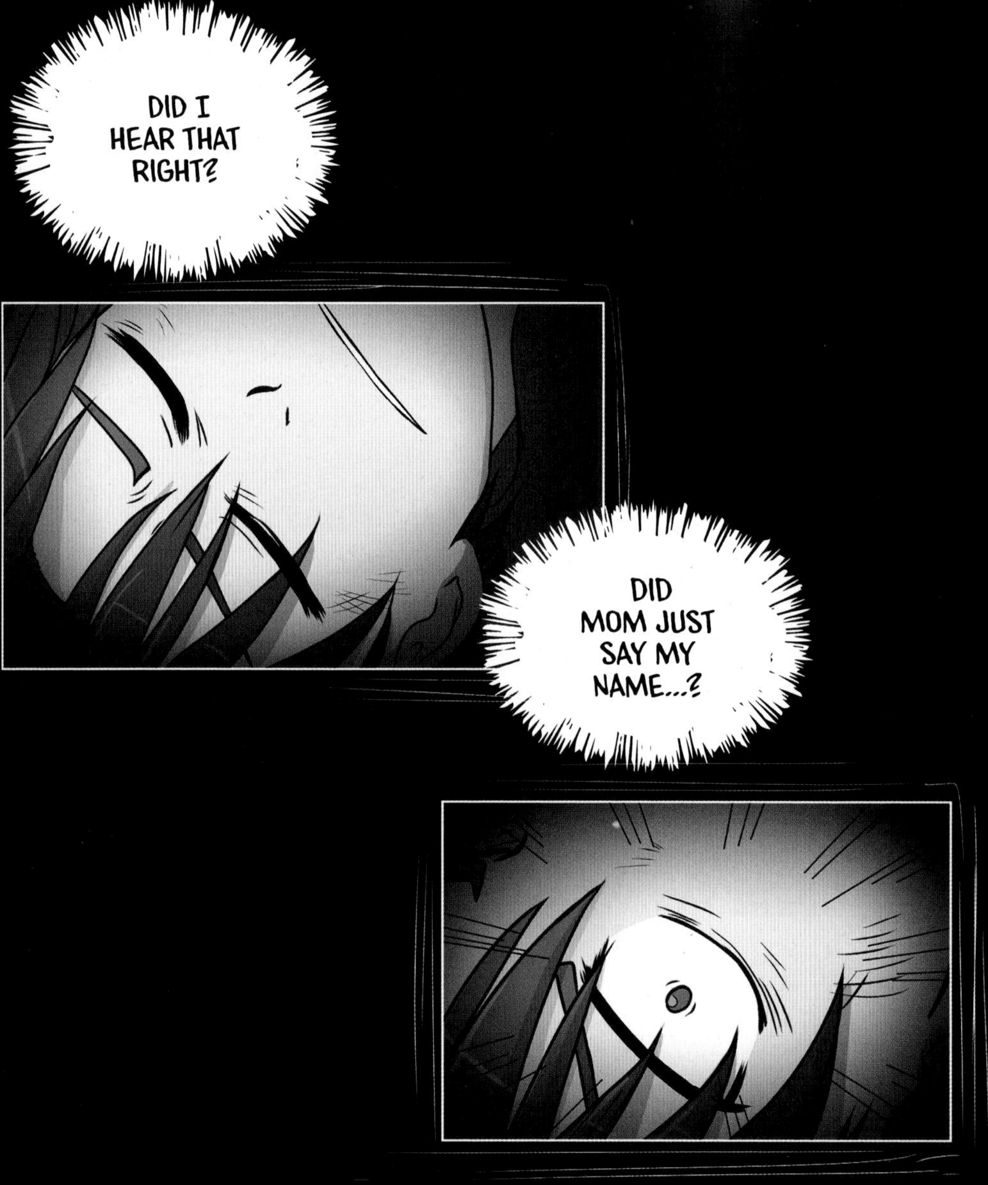
DID I HEAR THAT RIGHT?
DID MOM JUST SAY MY NAME...?

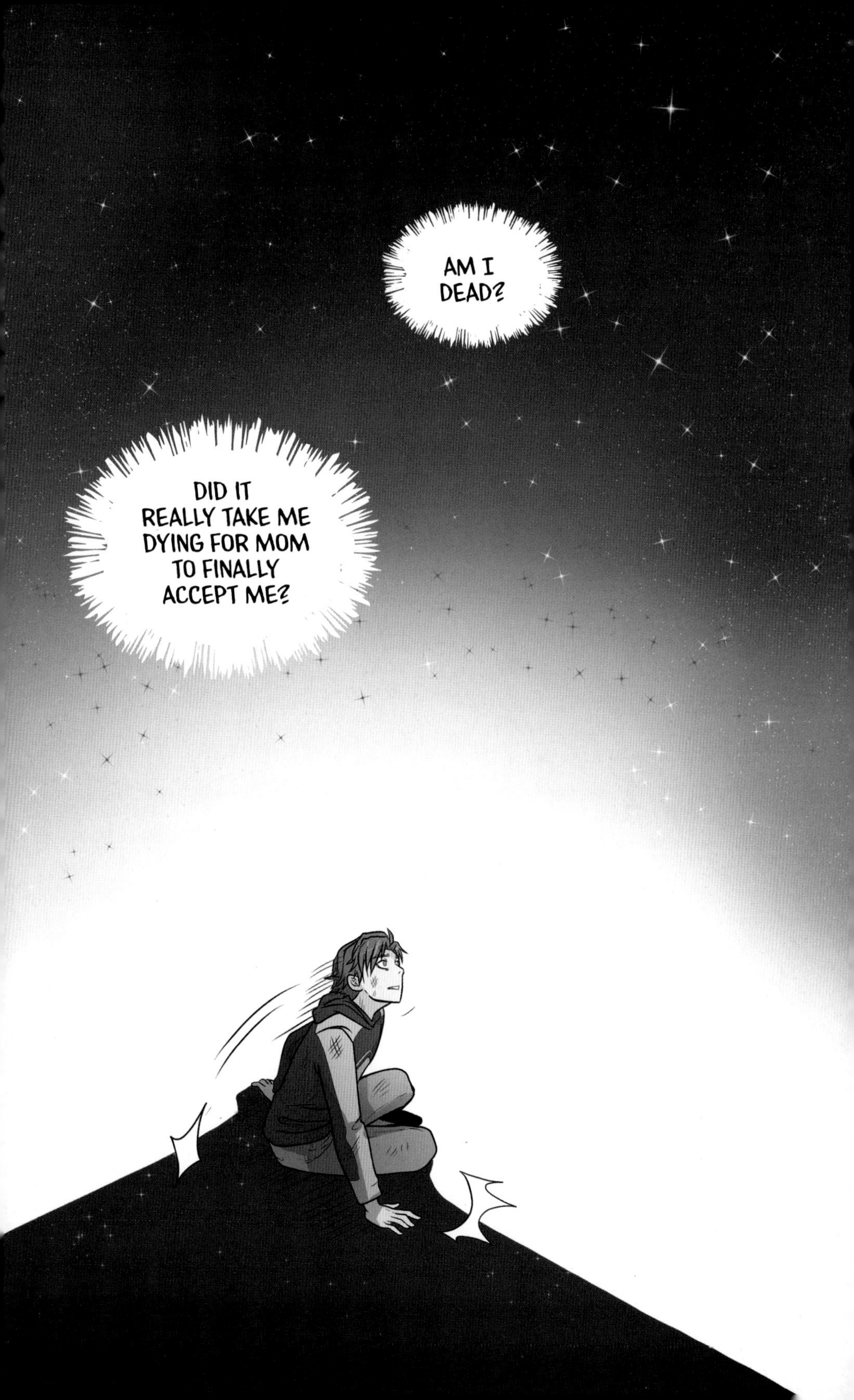
AM I DEAD?
DID IT REALLY TAKE ME DYING FOR MOM TO FINALLY ACCEPT ME?

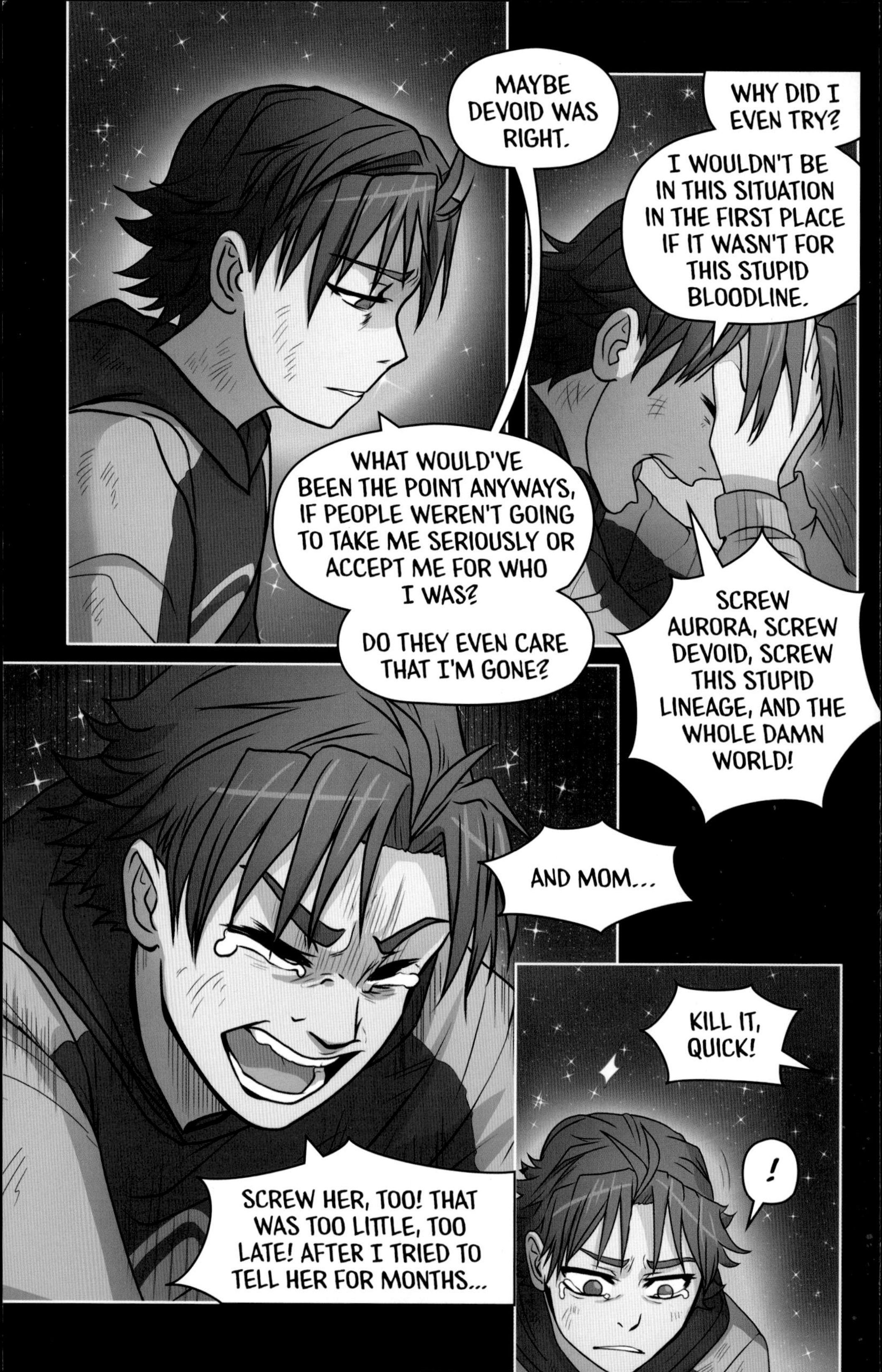
MAYBE DEVOID WAS RIGHT.
WHY DID I EVEN TRY?
I WOULDN'T BE IN THIS SITUATION IN THE FIRST PLACE IF IT WASN'T FOR THIS STUPID BLOODLINE.
WHAT WOULD'VE BEEN THE POINT ANYWAYS, IF PEOPLE WEREN'T GOING TO TAKE ME SERIOUSLY OR ACCEPT ME FOR WHO I WAS?
DO THEY EVEN CARE THAT I'M GONE?
SCREW AURORA, SCREW DEVOID, SCREW THIS STUPID LINEAGE, AND THE WHOLE DAMN WORLD!
AND MOM...
SCREW HER, TOO! THAT WAS TOO LITTLE, TOO LATE! AFTER I TRIED TO TELL HER FOR MONTHS...
KILL IT, QUICK!
!

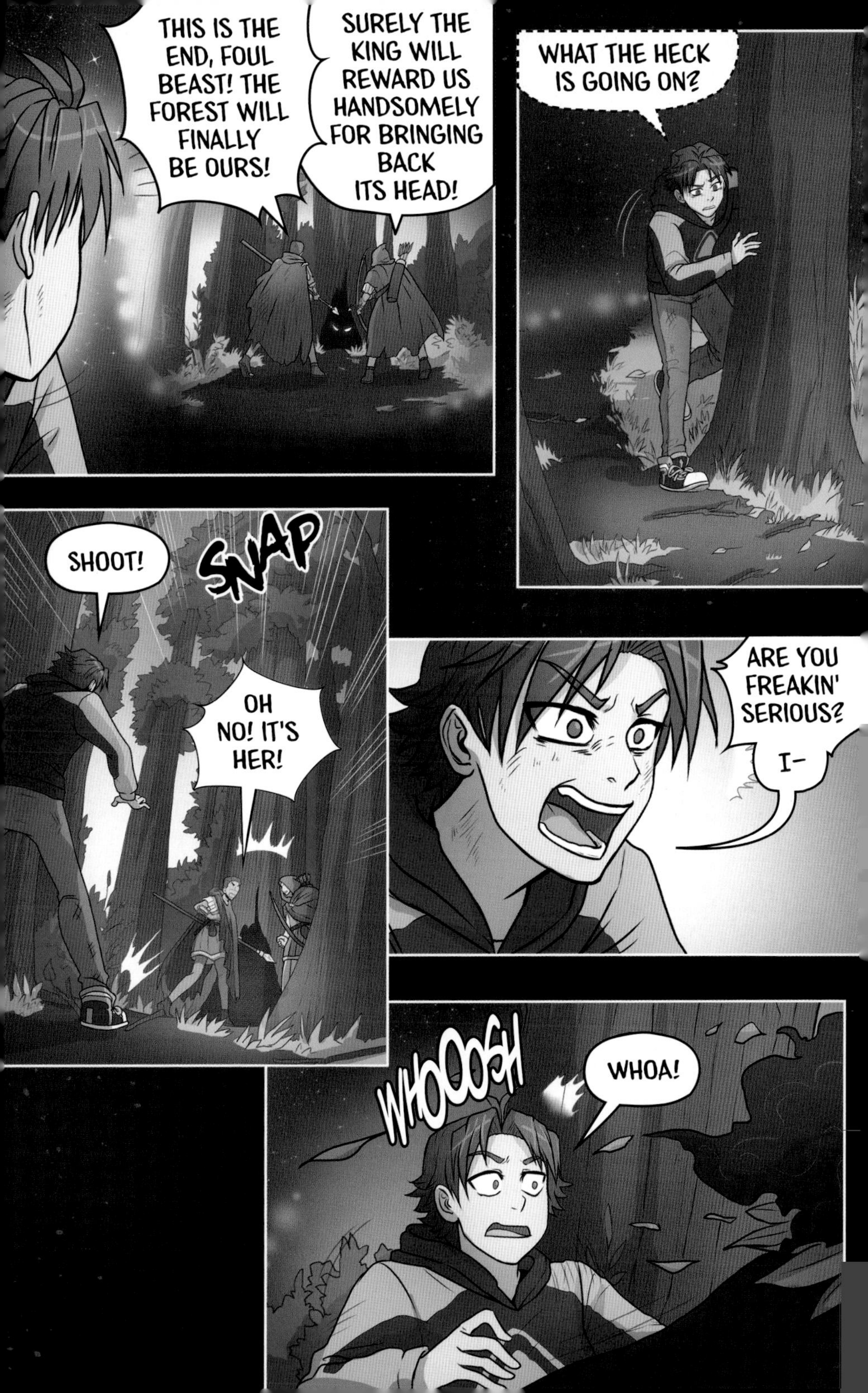

THIS IS THE END, FOUL BEAST! THE FOREST WILL FINALLY BE OURS!
SURELY THE KING WILL REWARD US HANDSOMELY FOR BRINGING BACK ITS HEAD!
WHAT THE HECK IS GOING ON?
SHOOT!
SNAP
OH NO! IT'S HER!
ARE YOU FREAKIN' SERIOUS?
I-
WHOOOSH
WHOA!

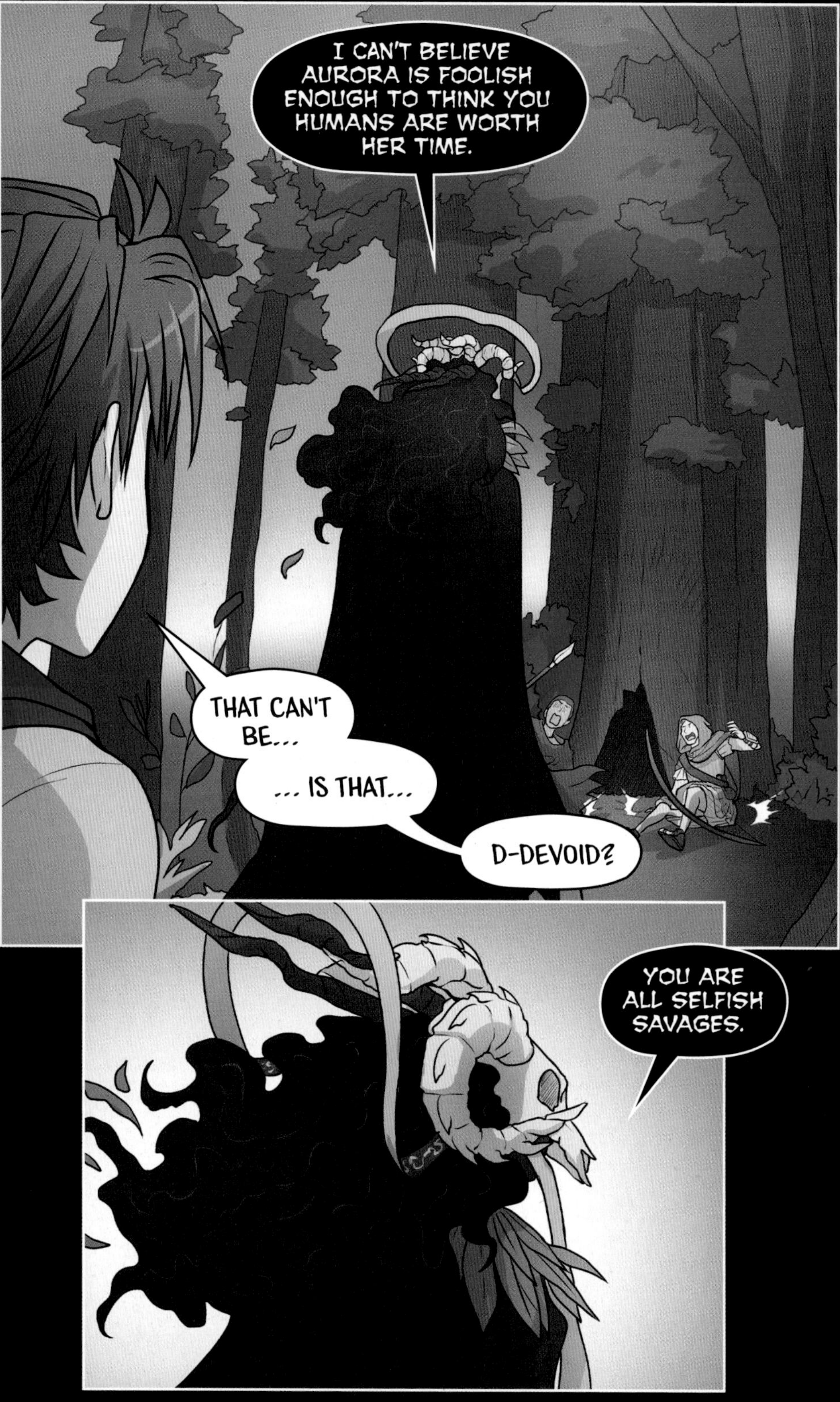
I CAN'T BELIEVE AURORA IS FOOLISH ENOUGH TO THINK YOU HUMANS ARE WORTH HER TIME.
THAT CAN'T BE...
... IS THAT...
D-DEVOID?
YOU ARE ALL SELFISH SAVAGES.

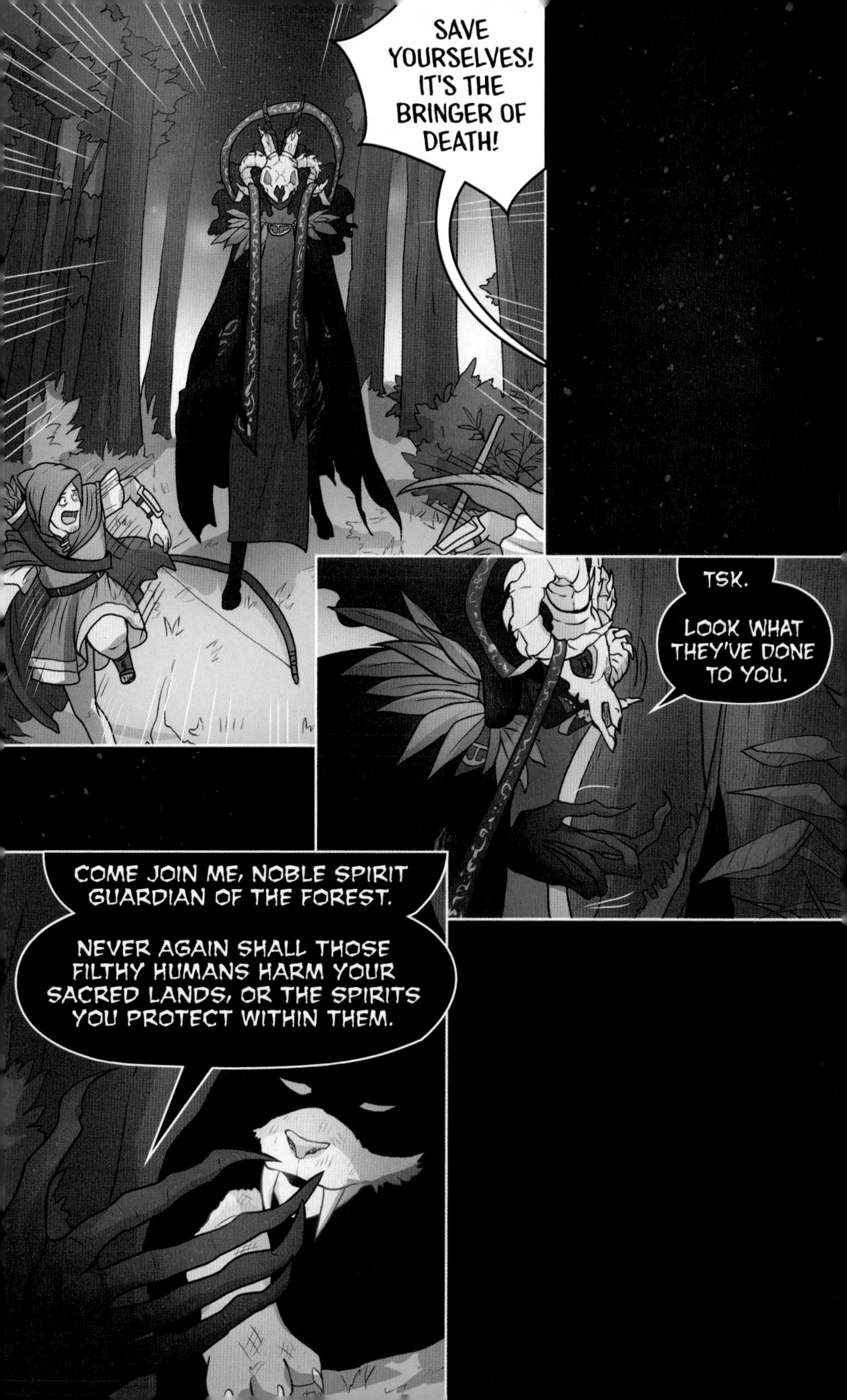
SAVE YOURSELVES! IT'S THE BRINGER OF DEATH!
TSK.
LOOK WHAT THEY'VE DONE TO YOU.
COME JOIN ME, NOBLE SPIRIT GUARDIAN OF THE FOREST.
NEVER AGAIN SHALL THOSE FILTHY HUMANS HARM YOUR SACRED LANDS, OR THE SPIRITS YOU PROTECT WITHIN THEM.

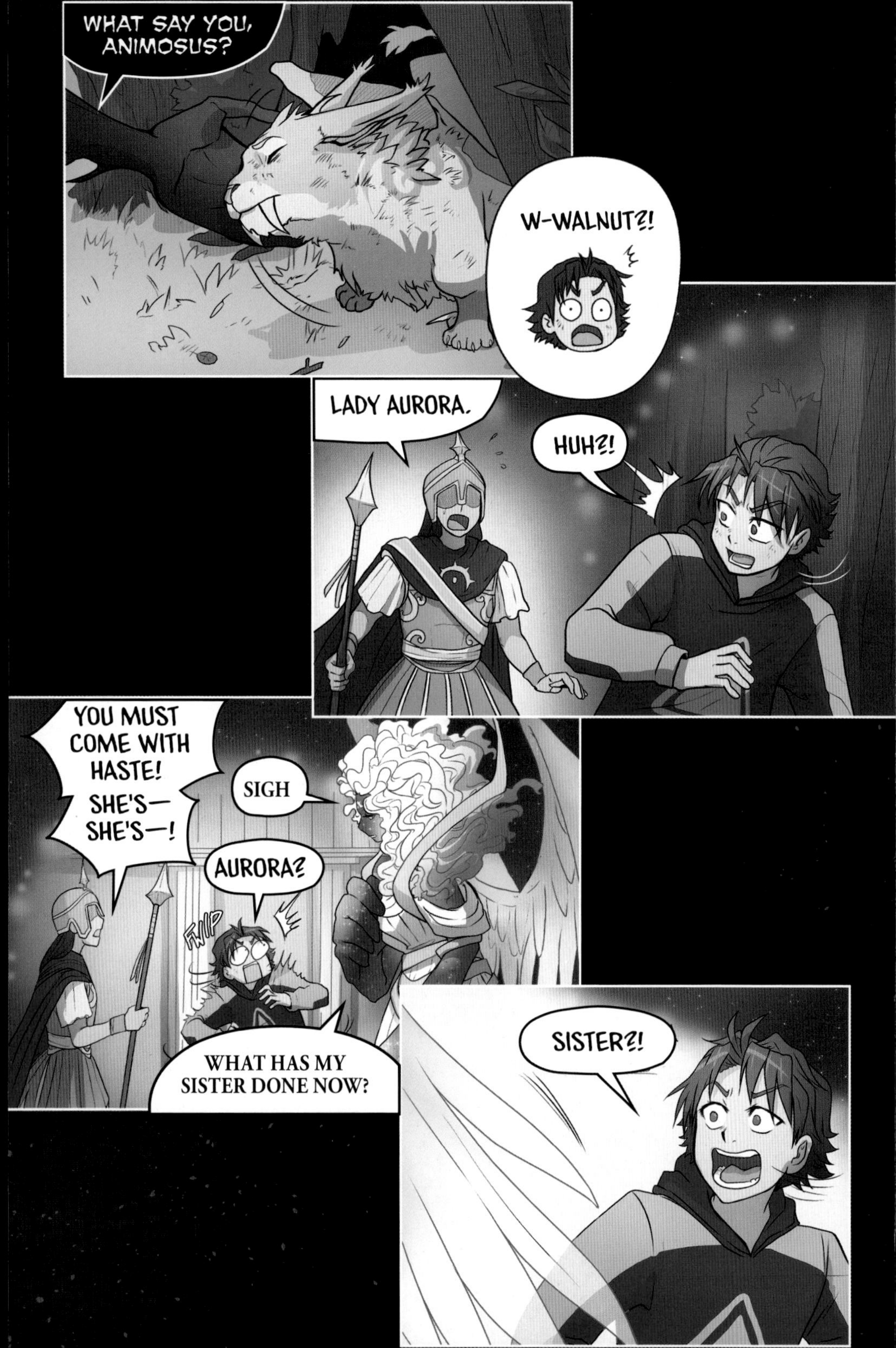
WHAT SAY YOU, ANIMOSUS?
W-WALNUT?!
LADY AURORA.
HUH?!
YOU MUST COME WITH HASTE! SHE'S— SHE'S—!
SIGH
AURORA?
FWIP
WHAT HAS MY SISTER DONE NOW?
SISTER?!

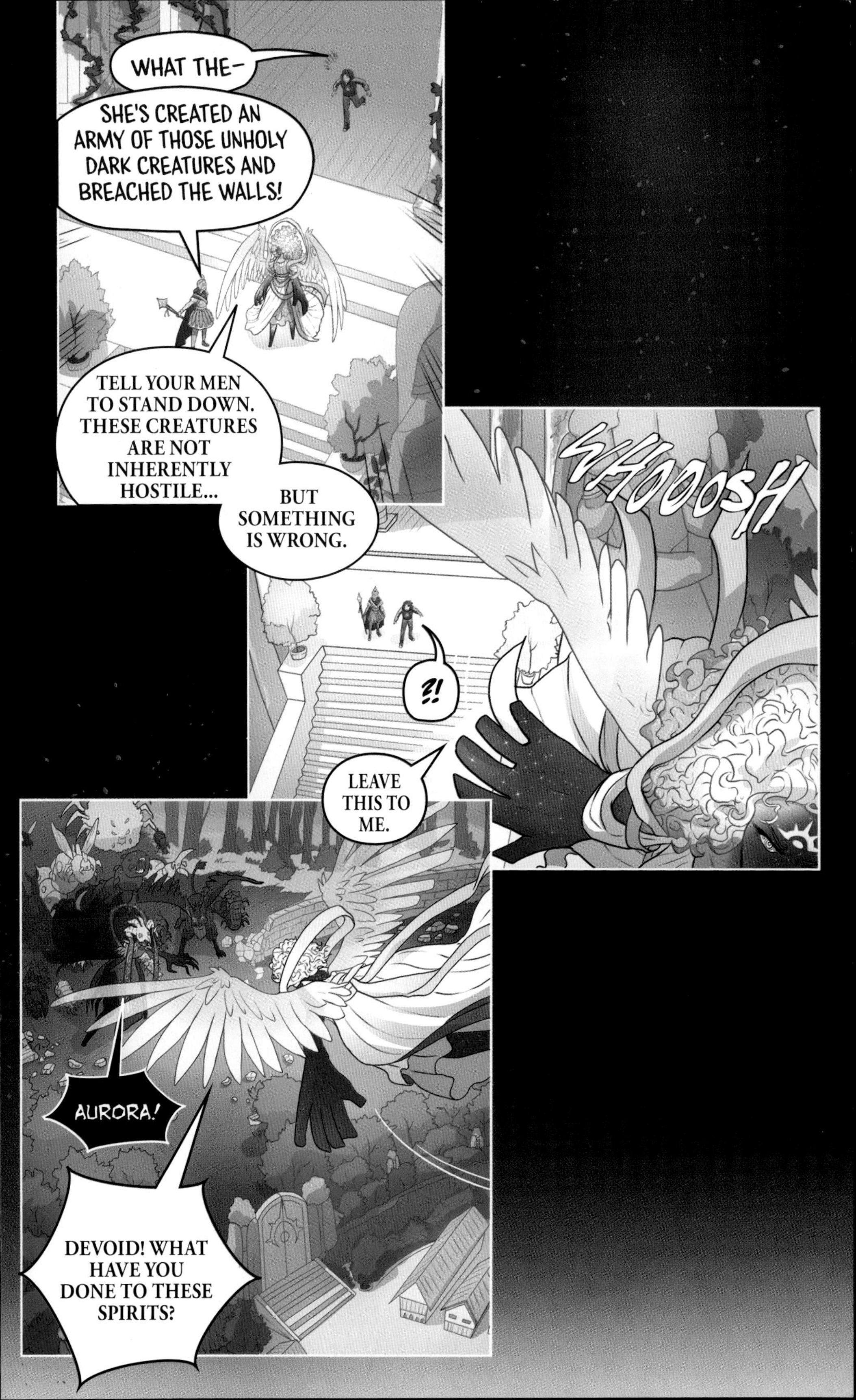
WHAT THE–
SHE'S CREATED AN ARMY OF THOSE UNHOLY DARK CREATURES AND BREACHED THE WALLS!
TELL YOUR MEN TO STAND DOWN. THESE CREATURES ARE NOT INHERENTLY HOSTILE...
BUT SOMETHING IS WRONG.
WHOOOSH
?!
LEAVE THIS TO ME.
AURORA!
DEVOID! WHAT HAVE YOU DONE TO THESE SPIRITS?

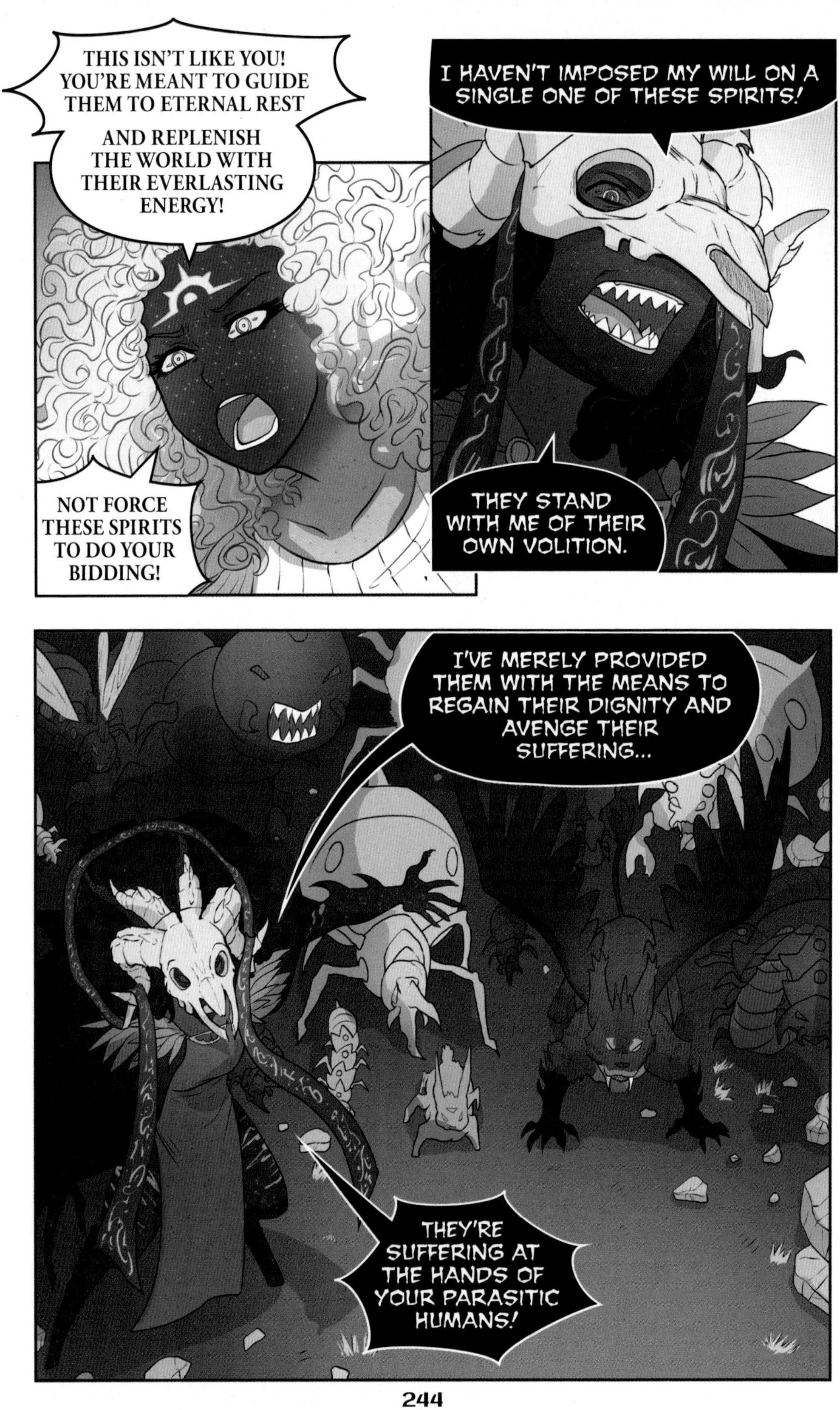
THIS ISN'T LIKE YOU! YOU'RE MEANT TO GUIDE THEM TO ETERNAL REST
AND REPLENISH THE WORLD WITH THEIR EVERLASTING ENERGY!
NOT FORCE THESE SPIRITS TO DO YOUR BIDDING!
I HAVEN'T IMPOSED MY WILL ON A SINGLE ONE OF THESE SPIRITS!
THEY STAND WITH ME OF THEIR OWN VOLITION.
I'VE MERELY PROVIDED THEM WITH THE MEANS TO REGAIN THEIR DIGNITY AND AVENGE THEIR SUFFERING...
THEY'RE SUFFERING AT THE HANDS OF YOUR PARASITIC HUMANS!

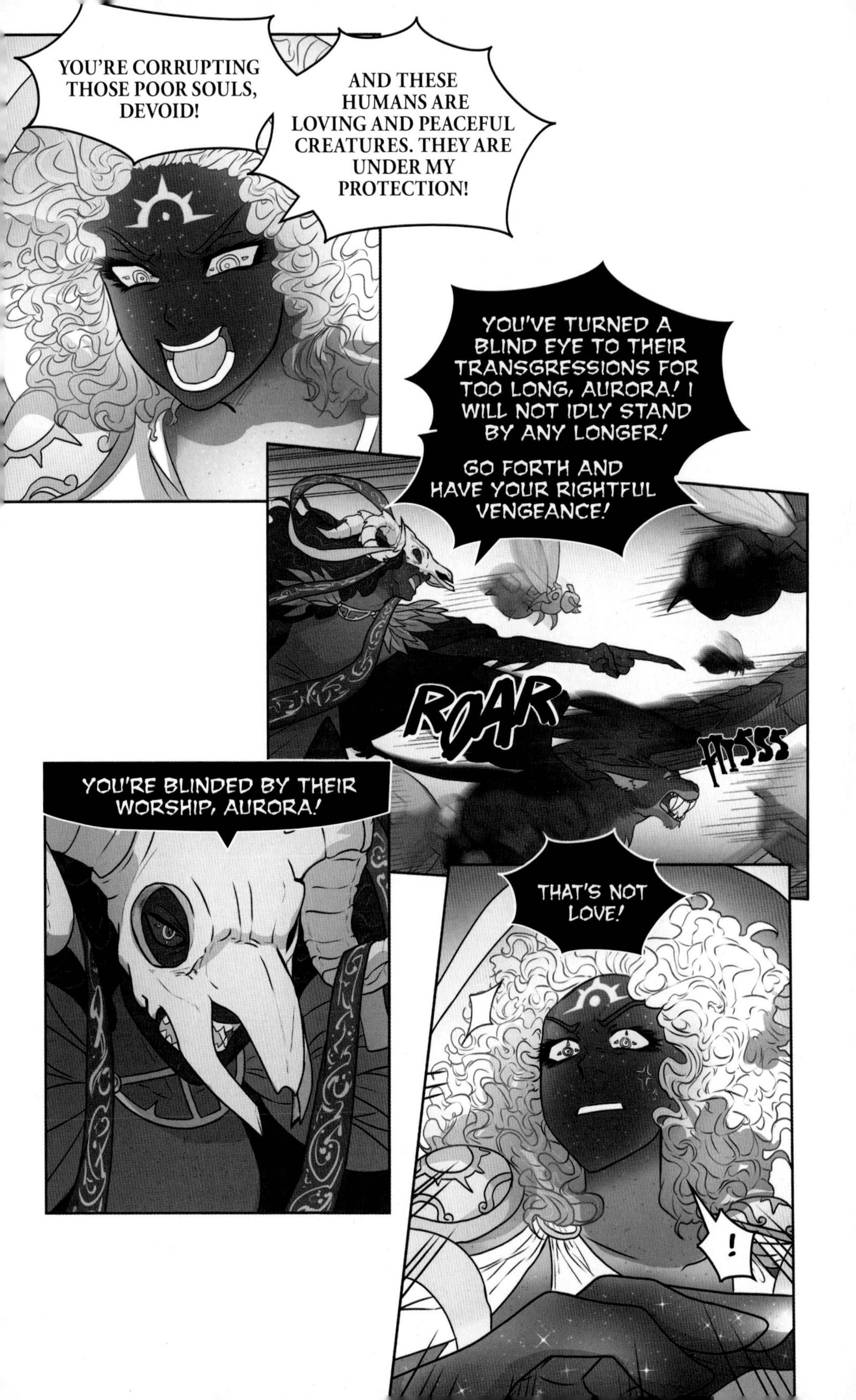
YOU'RE CORRUPTING THOSE POOR SOULS, DEVOID!
AND THESE HUMANS ARE LOVING AND PEACEFUL CREATURES. THEY ARE UNDER MY PROTECTION!
YOU'VE TURNED A BLIND EYE TO THEIR TRANSGRESSIONS FOR TOO LONG, AURORA! I WILL NOT IDLY STAND BY ANY LONGER!
GO FORTH AND HAVE YOUR RIGHTFUL VENGEANCE!
ROAR
HISSSS
YOU'RE BLINDED BY THEIR WORSHIP, AURORA!
THAT'S NOT LOVE!
!

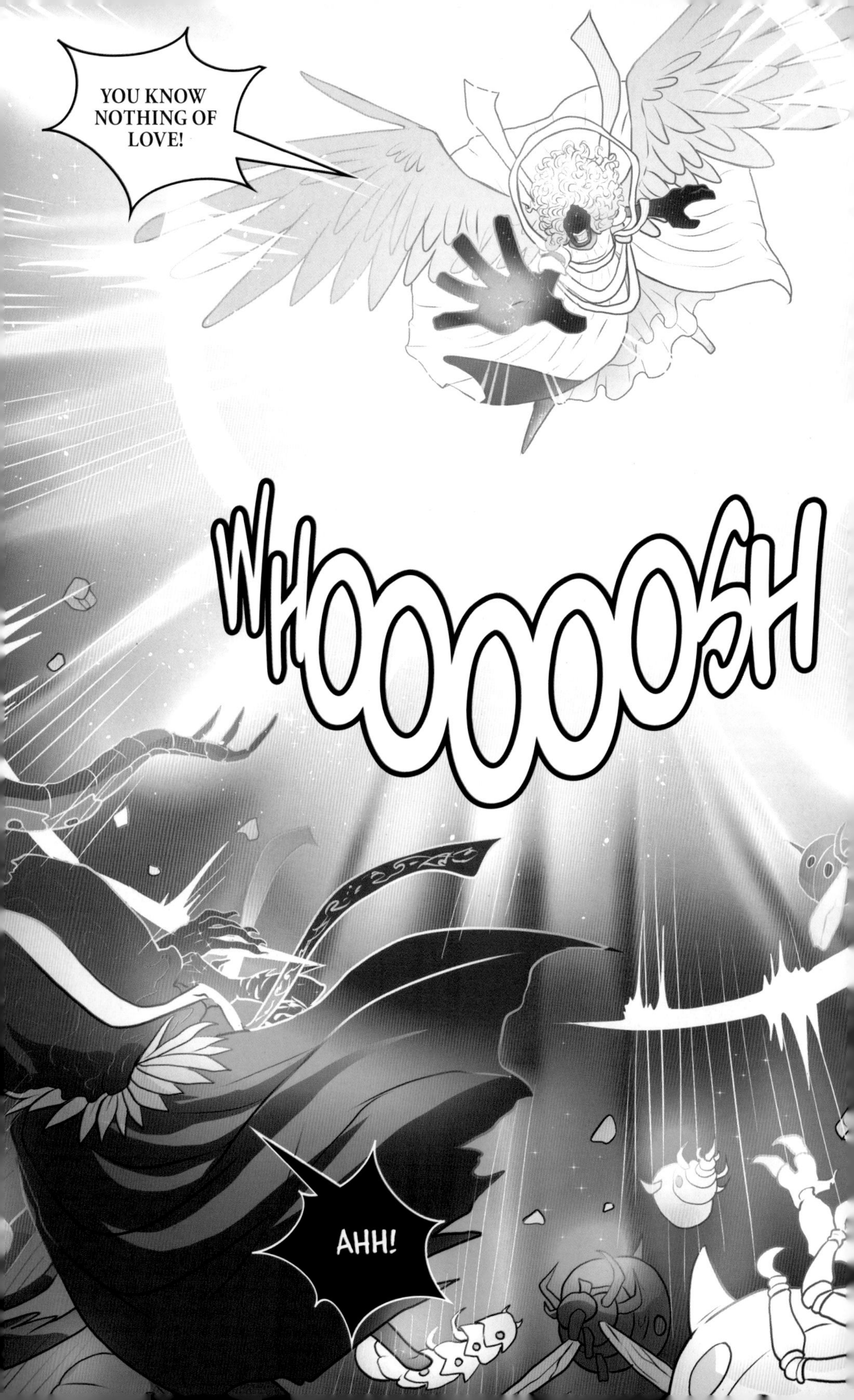
YOU KNOW NOTHING OF LOVE!
WHOOOOOSH
AHH!

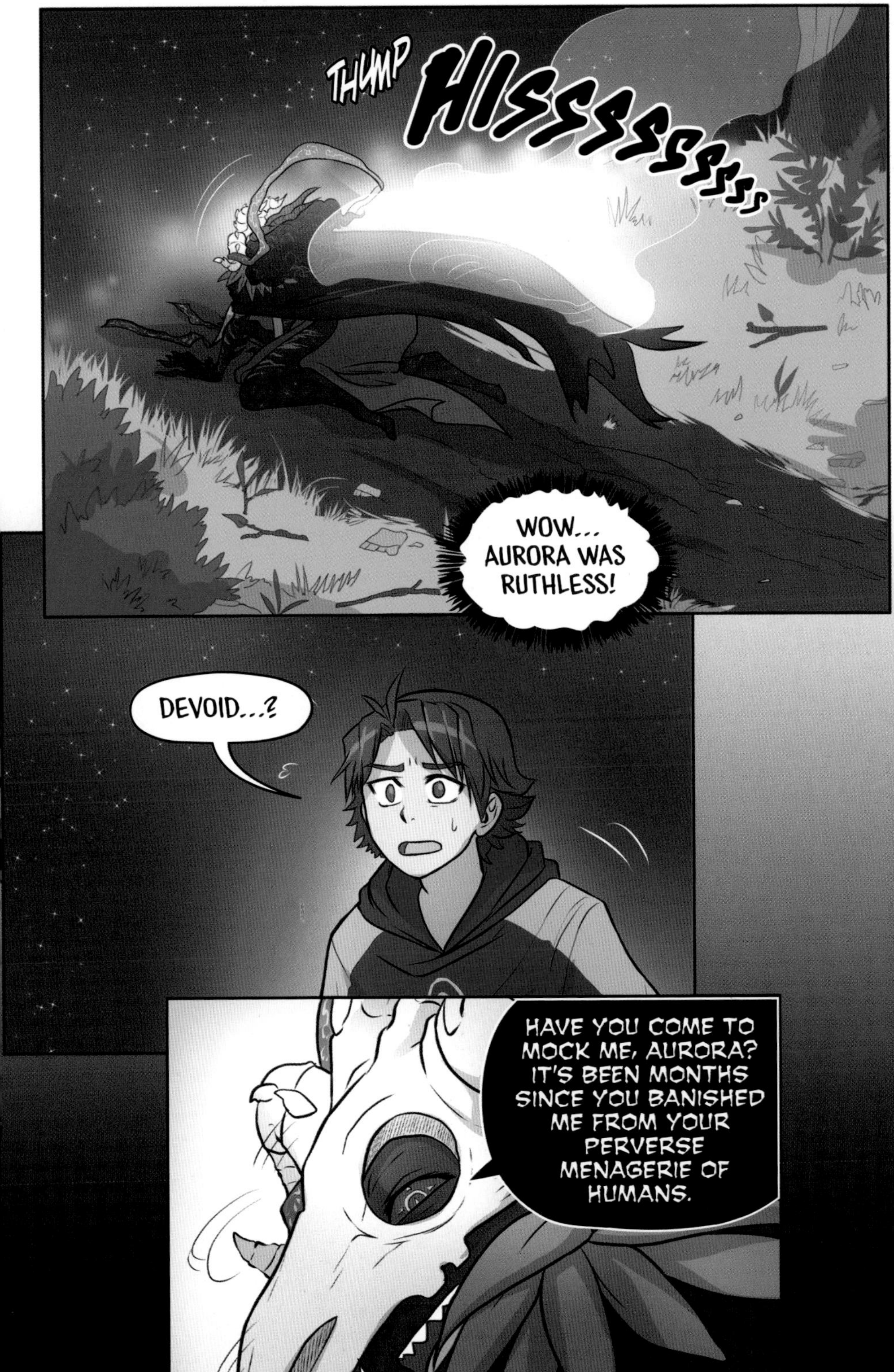
THUMP
HISSSSSSSSS
WOW... AURORA WAS RUTHLESS!
DEVOID...?
HAVE YOU COME TO MOCK ME, AURORA? IT'S BEEN MONTHS SINCE YOU BANISHED ME FROM YOUR PERVERSE MENAGERIE OF HUMANS.

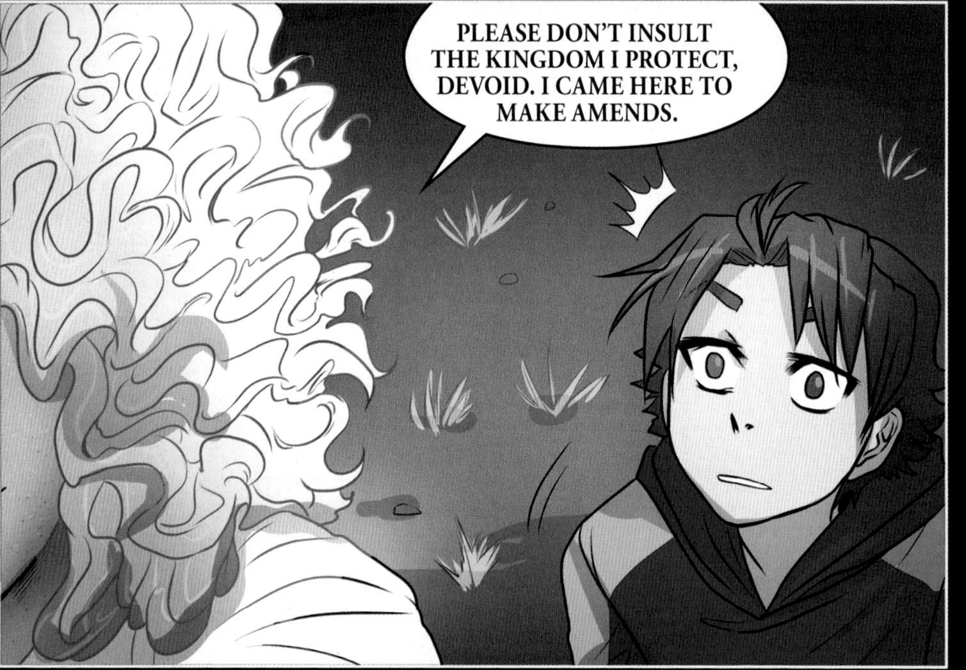
PLEASE DON'T INSULT THE KINGDOM I PROTECT, DEVOID. I CAME HERE TO MAKE AMENDS.

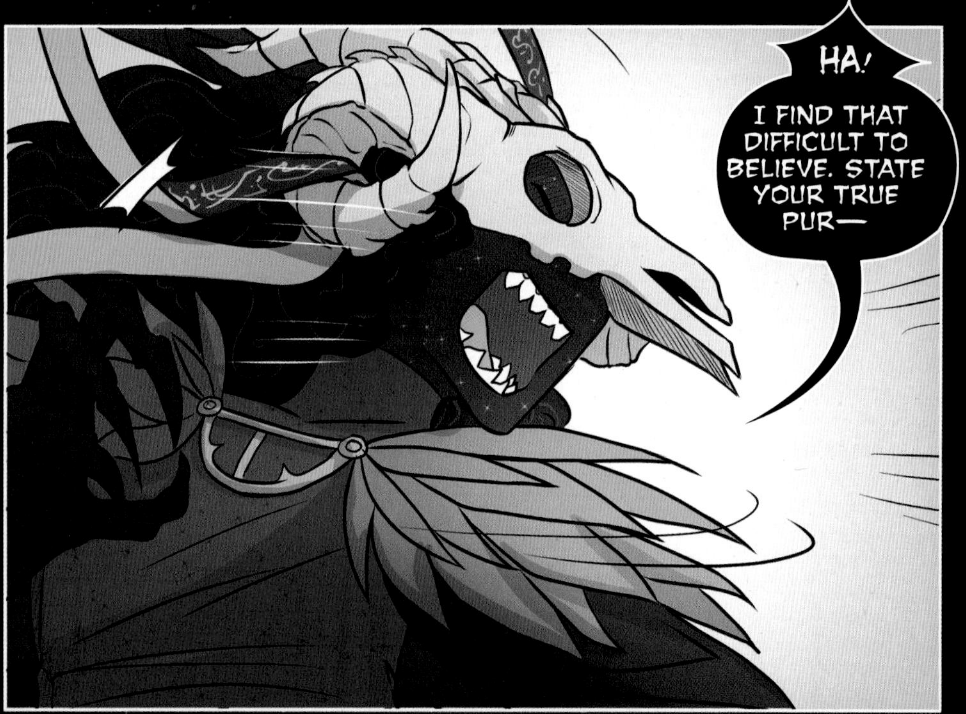
HA!
I FIND THAT DIFFICULT TO BELIEVE. STATE YOUR TRUE PUR—

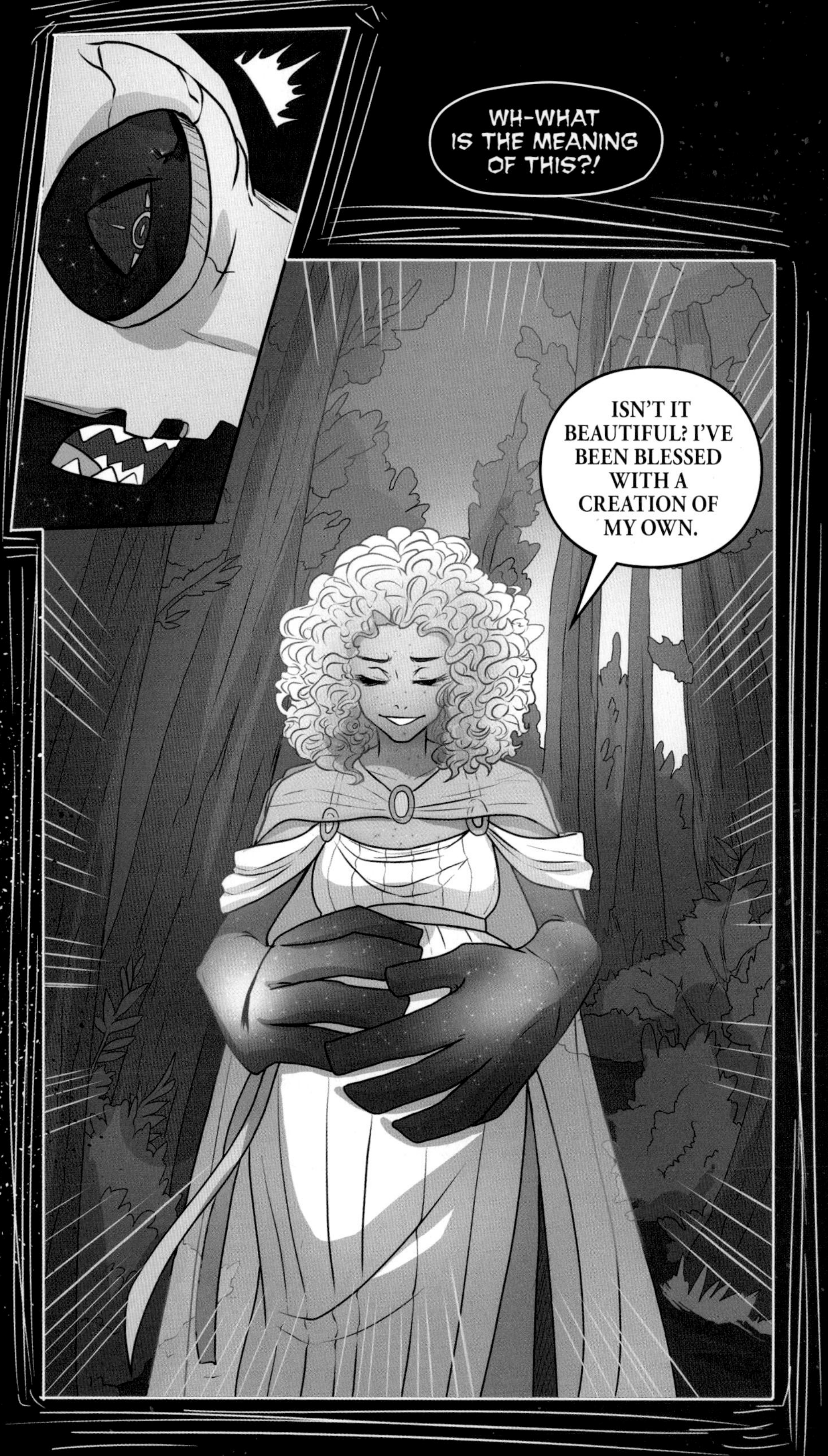
WH-WHAT IS THE MEANING OF THIS?!
ISN'T IT BEAUTIFUL? I'VE BEEN BLESSED WITH A CREATION OF MY OWN.

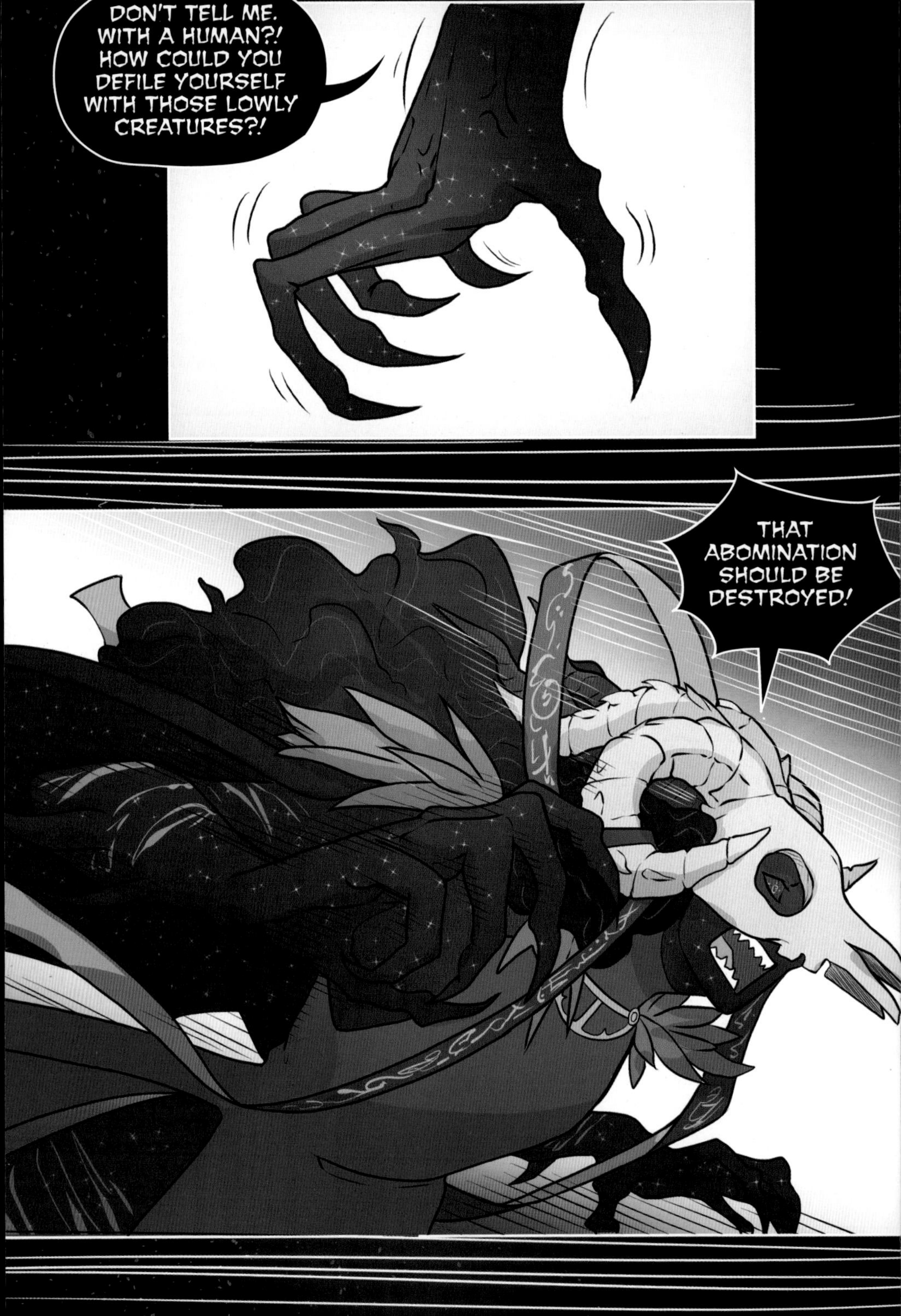
DON'T TELL ME. WITH A HUMAN?! HOW COULD YOU DEFILE YOURSELF WITH THOSE LOWLY CREATURES?!
THAT ABOMINATION SHOULD BE DESTROYED!

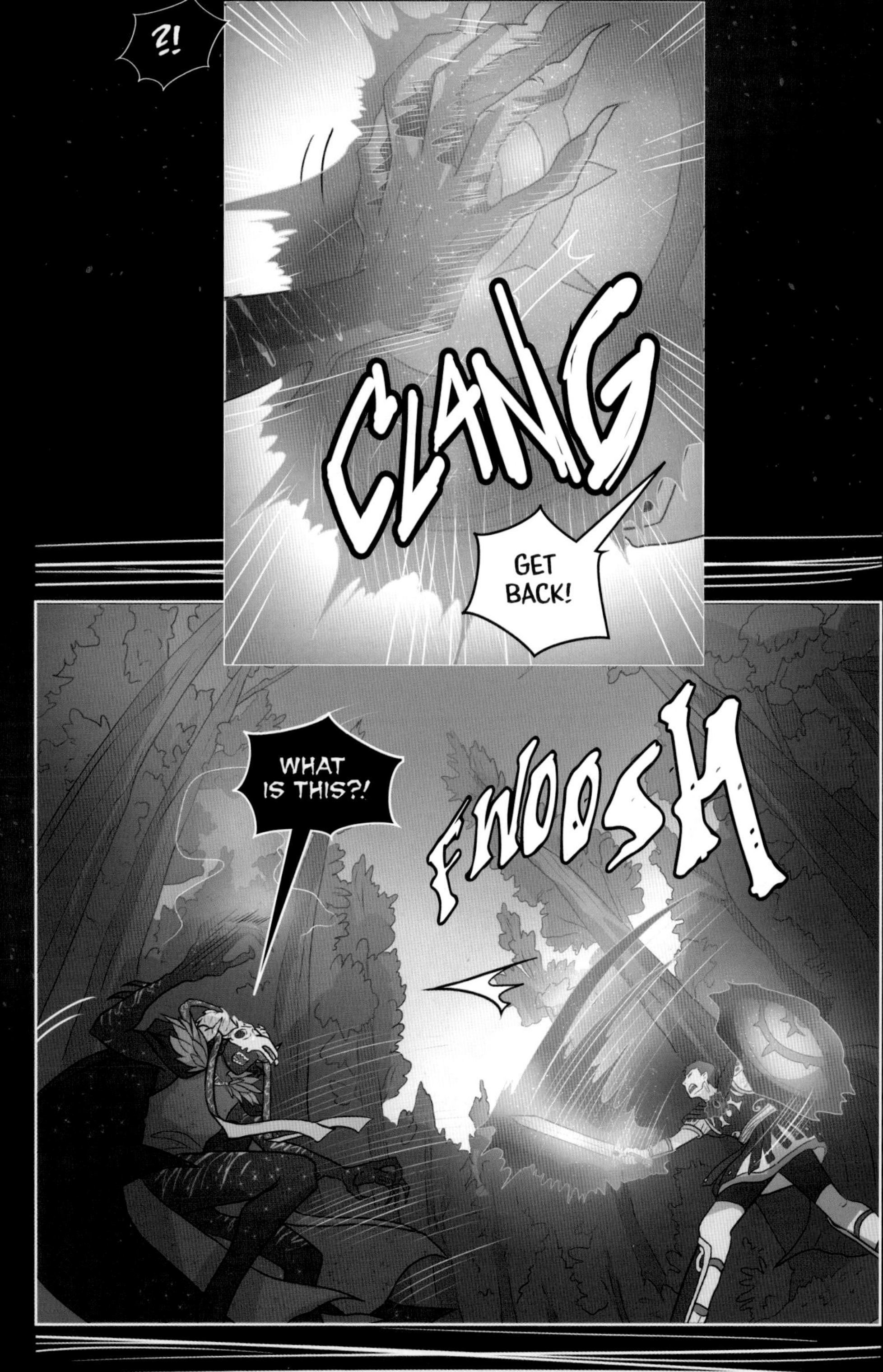
?!
CLANG
GET BACK!
WHAT IS THIS?!
FWOOSH

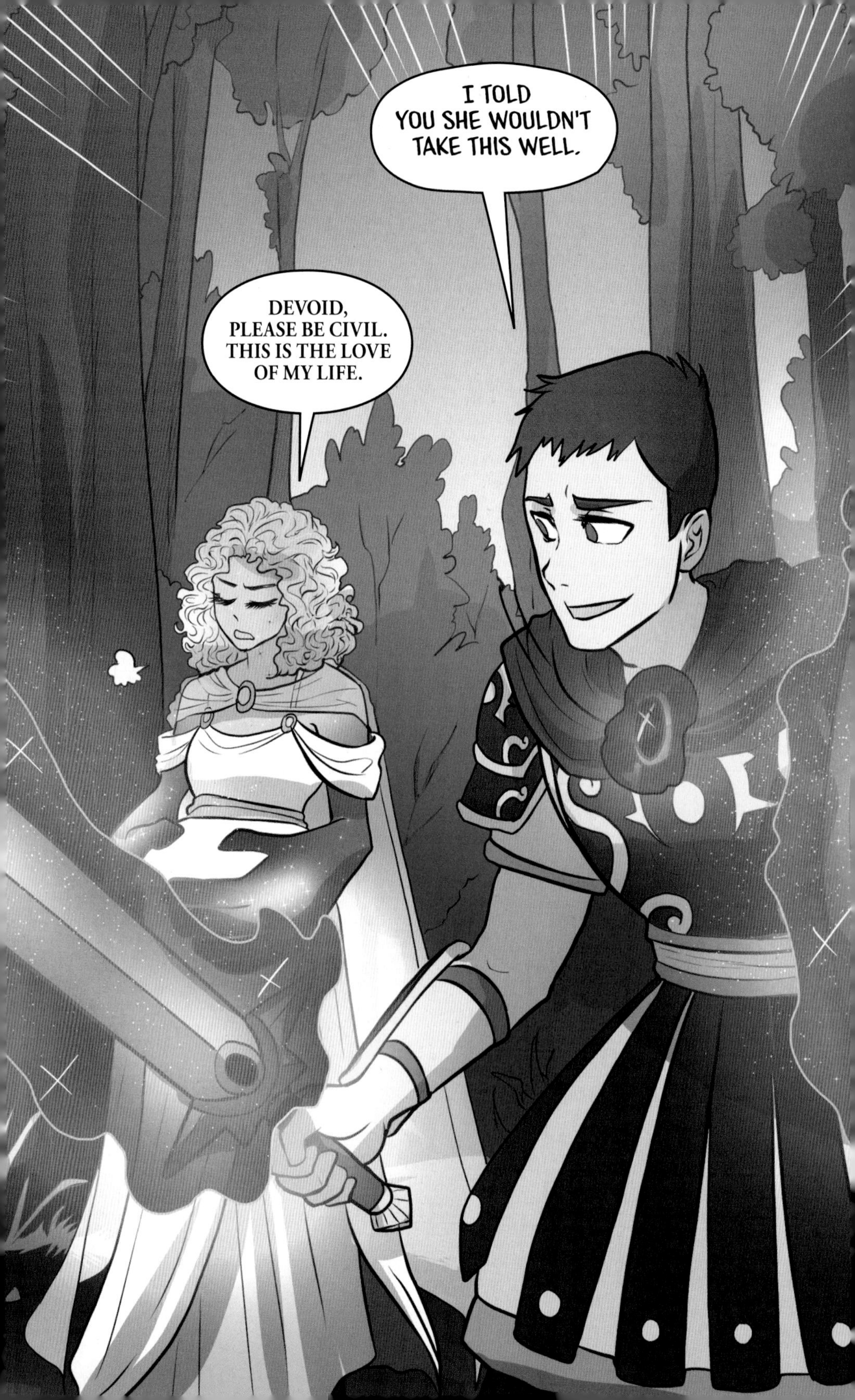
DEVOID, PLEASE BE CIVIL. THIS IS THE LOVE OF MY LIFE.
I TOLD YOU SHE WOULDN'T TAKE THIS WELL.

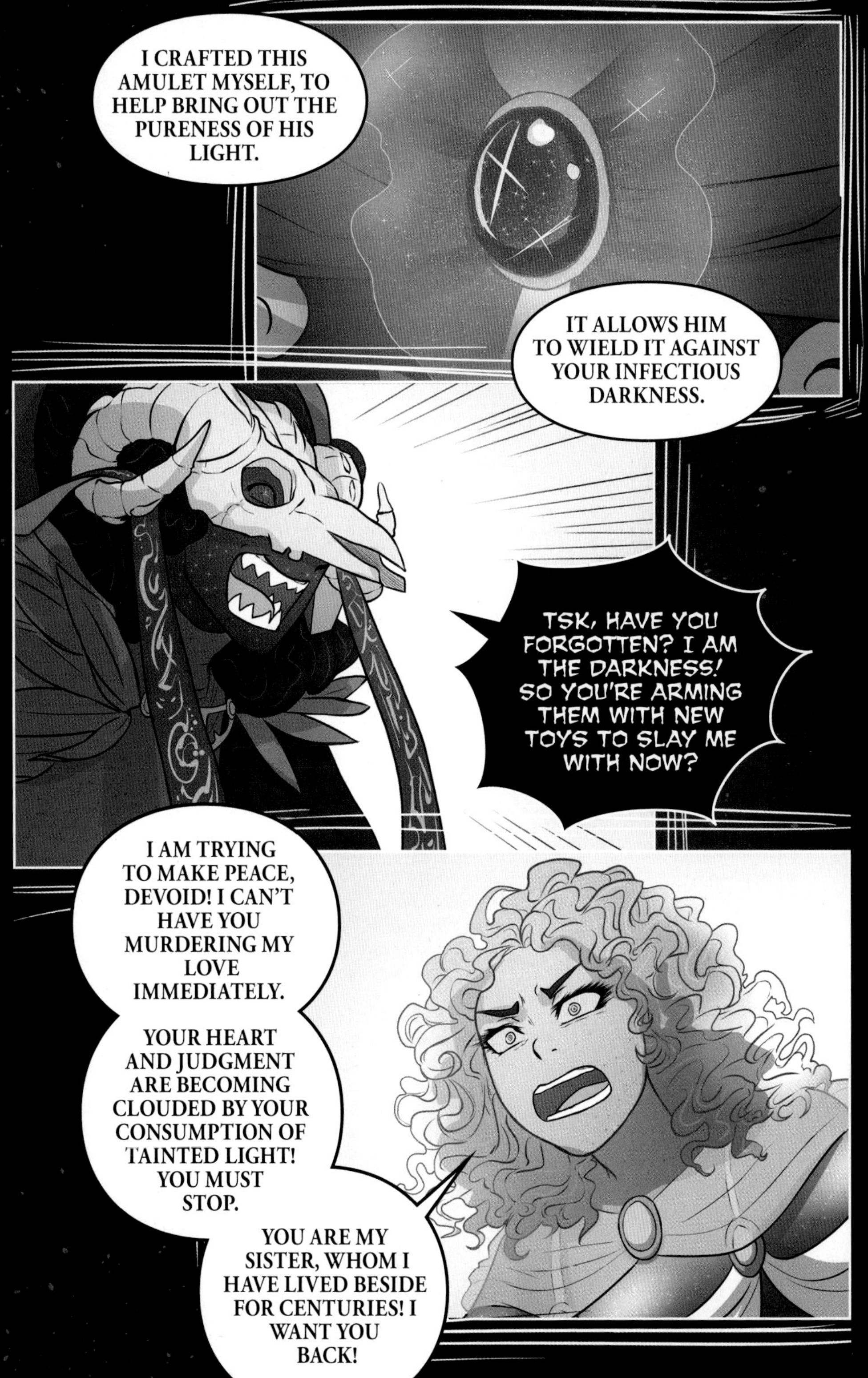
I CRAFTED THIS AMULET MYSELF, TO HELP BRING OUT THE PURENESS OF HIS LIGHT.
IT ALLOWS HIM TO WIELD IT AGAINST YOUR INFECTIOUS DARKNESS.
TSK, HAVE YOU FORGOTTEN? I AM THE DARKNESS! SO YOU'RE ARMING THEM WITH NEW TOYS TO SLAY ME WITH NOW?
I AM TRYING TO MAKE PEACE, DEVOID! I CAN'T HAVE YOU MURDERING MY LOVE IMMEDIATELY.
YOUR HEART AND JUDGMENT ARE BECOMING CLOUDED BY YOUR CONSUMPTION OF TAINTED LIGHT! YOU MUST STOP.
YOU ARE MY SISTER, WHOM I HAVE LIVED BESIDE FOR CENTURIES! I WANT YOU BACK!

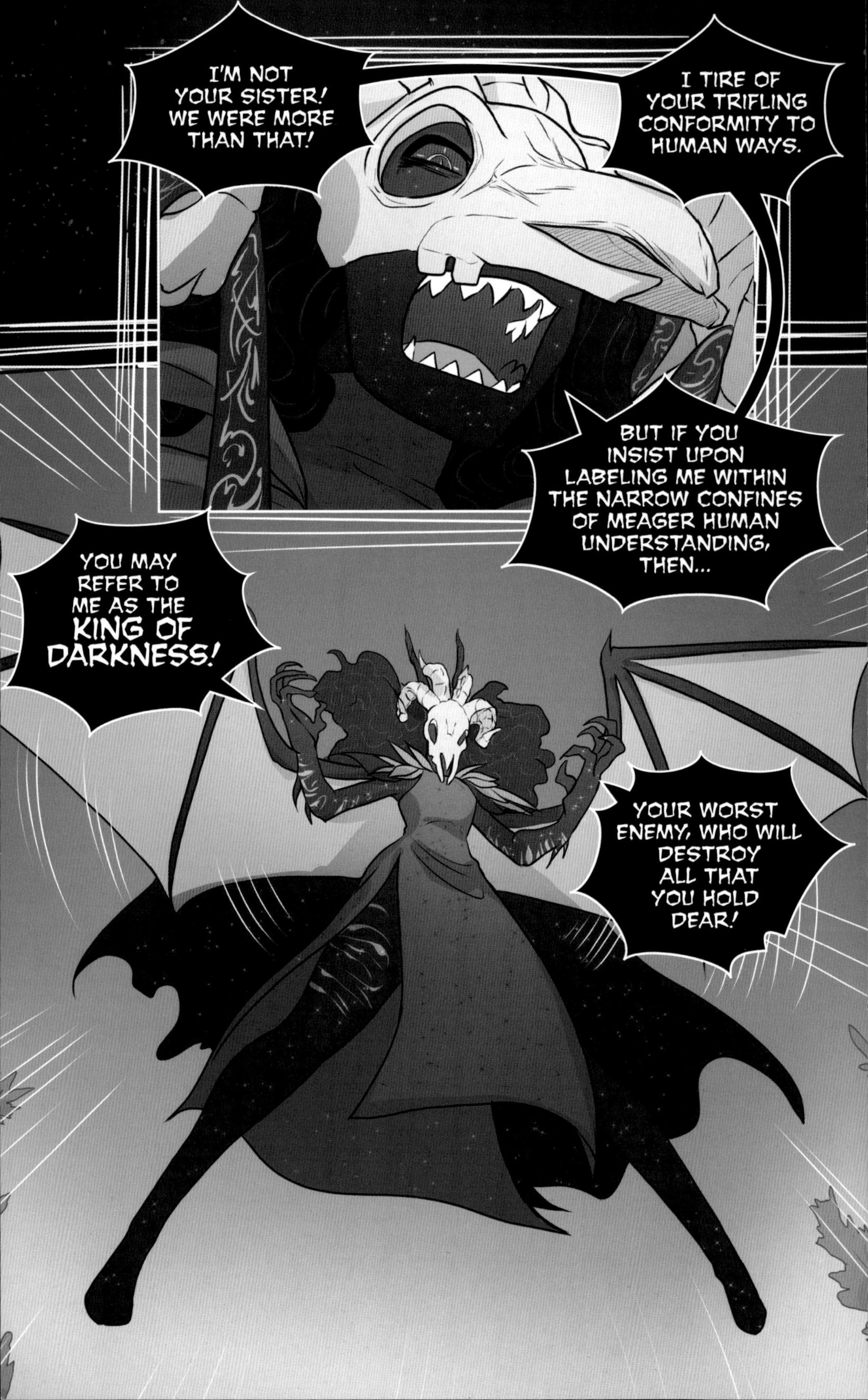
I'M NOT YOUR SISTER! WE WERE MORE THAN THAT!
I TIRE OF YOUR TRIFLING CONFORMITY TO HUMAN WAYS.
BUT IF YOU INSIST UPON LABELING ME WITHIN THE NARROW CONFINES OF MEAGER HUMAN UNDERSTANDING, THEN...
YOU MAY REFER TO ME AS THE KING OF DARKNESS!
YOUR WORST ENEMY, WHO WILL DESTROY ALL THAT YOU HOLD DEAR!

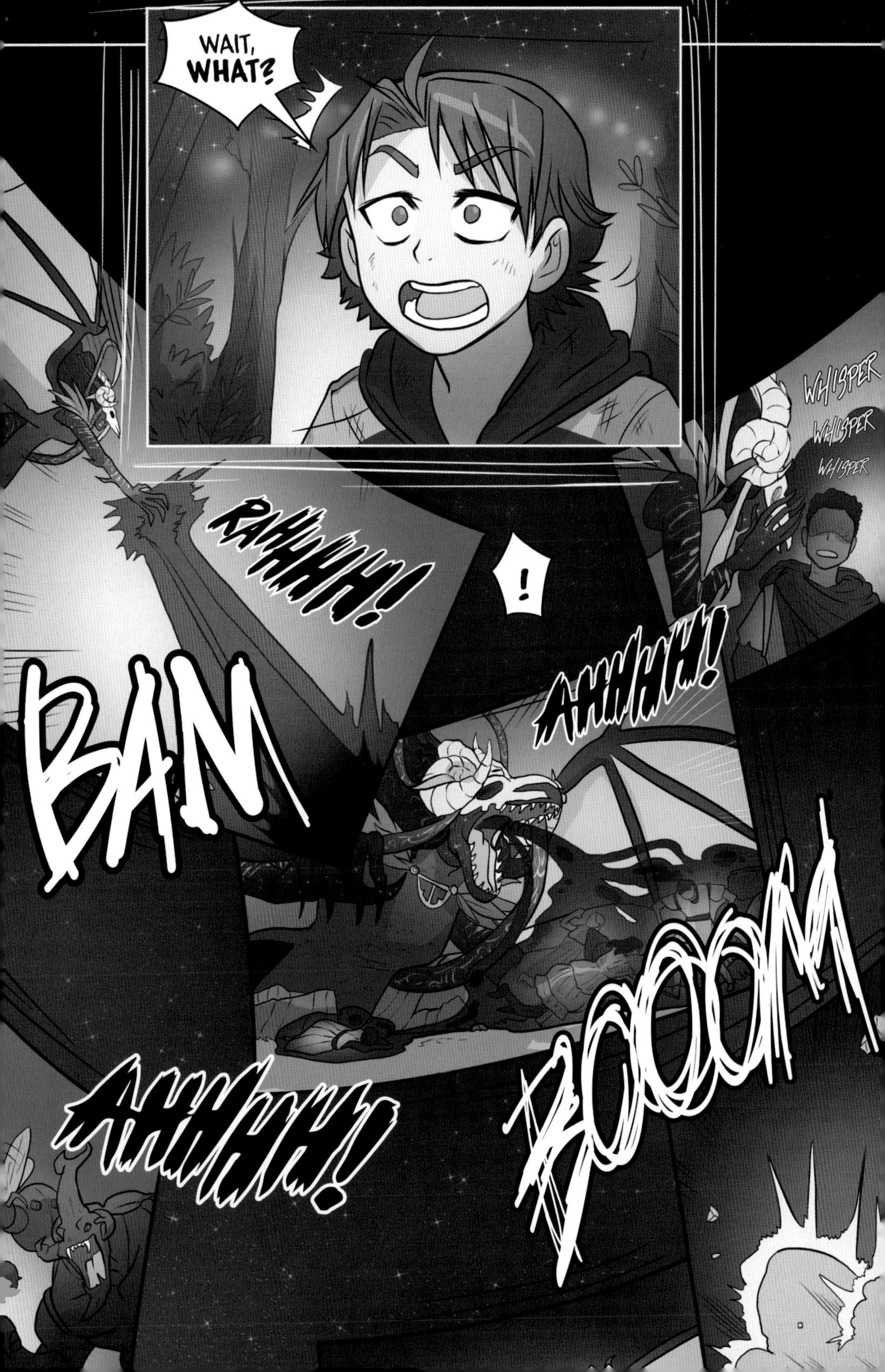
WAIT, WHAT?
WHISPER
WHISPER
WHISPER
RAHHHH!
!
BAM
AHHHH!
AHHHHH!
ZOOOOM

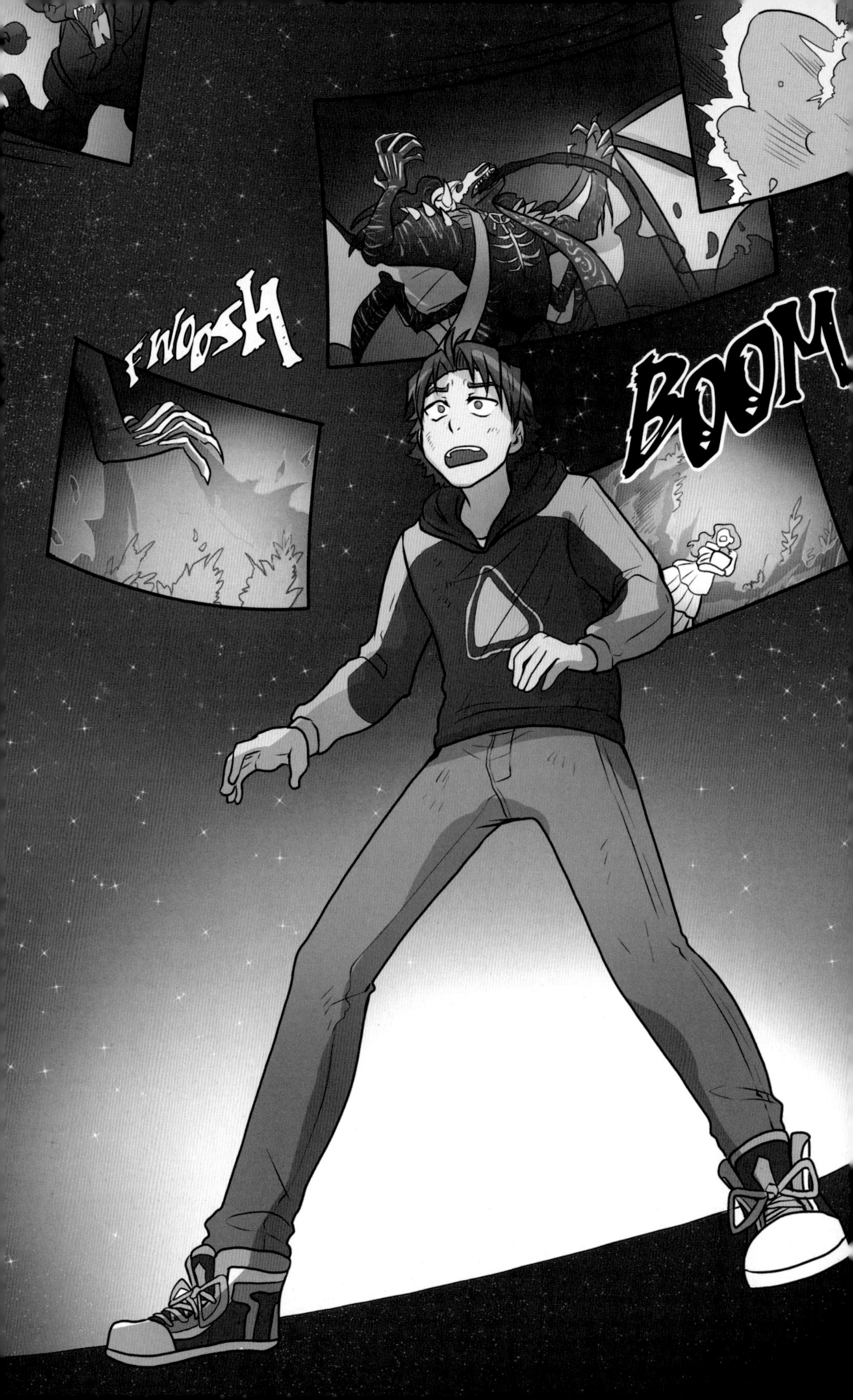
FWOOSH
BOOM

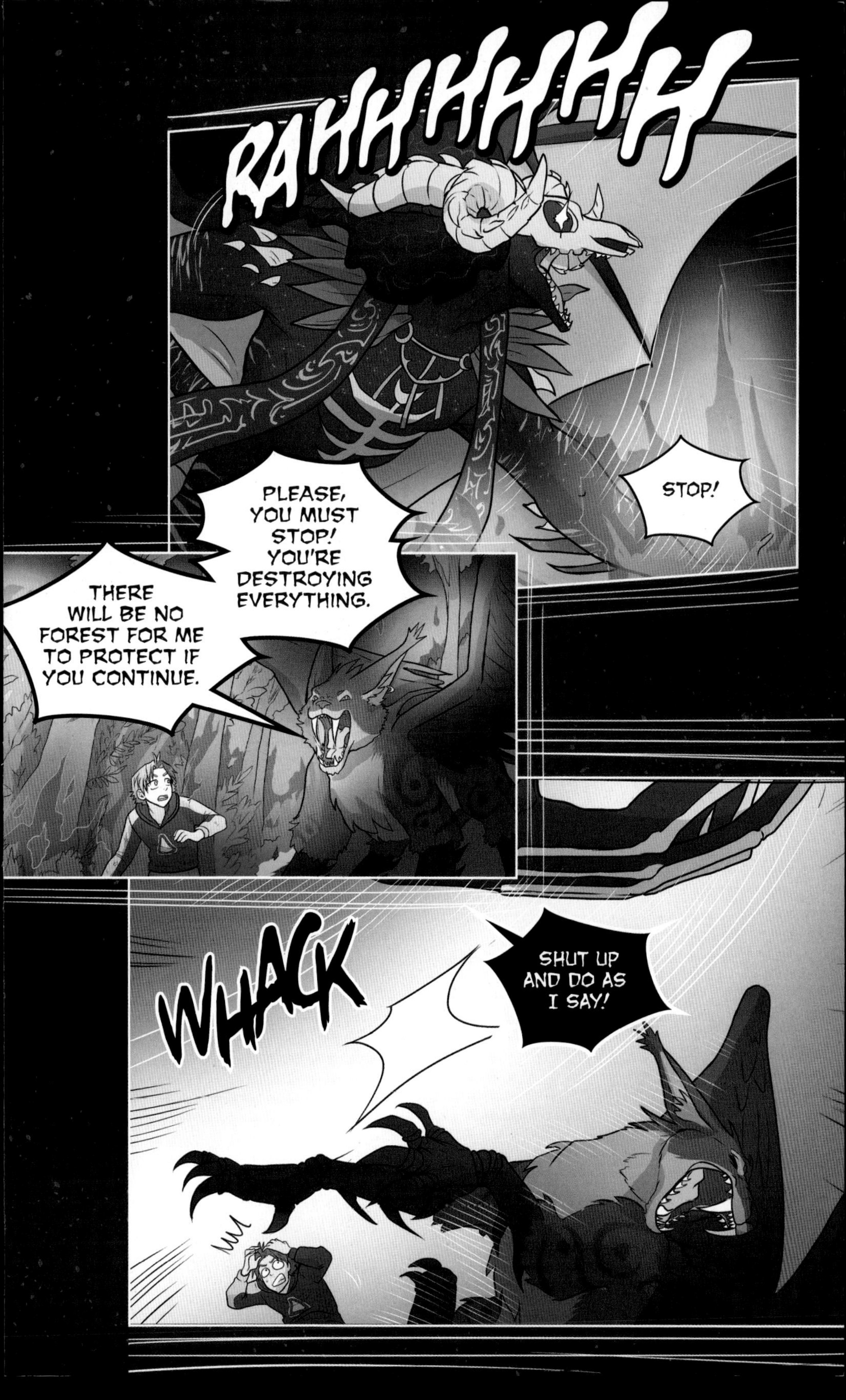
RAHHHHHHH
STOP!
PLEASE, YOU MUST STOP! YOU'RE DESTROYING EVERYTHING.
THERE WILL BE NO FOREST FOR ME TO PROTECT IF YOU CONTINUE.
WHACK
SHUT UP AND DO AS I SAY!

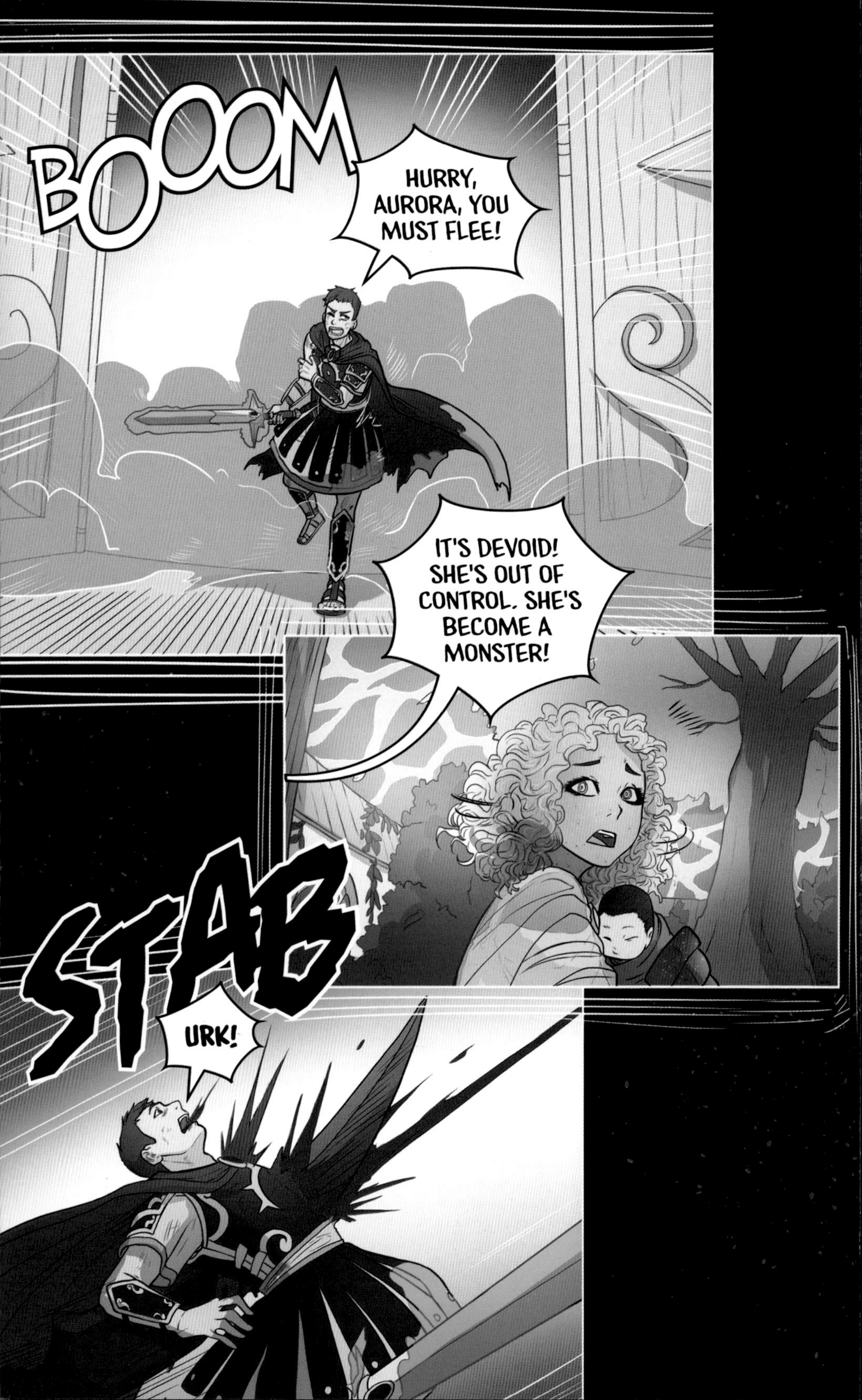
BOOOM
HURRY, AURORA, YOU MUST FLEE!
IT'S DEVOID! SHE'S OUT OF CONTROL. SHE'S BECOME A MONSTER!
STAB
URK!

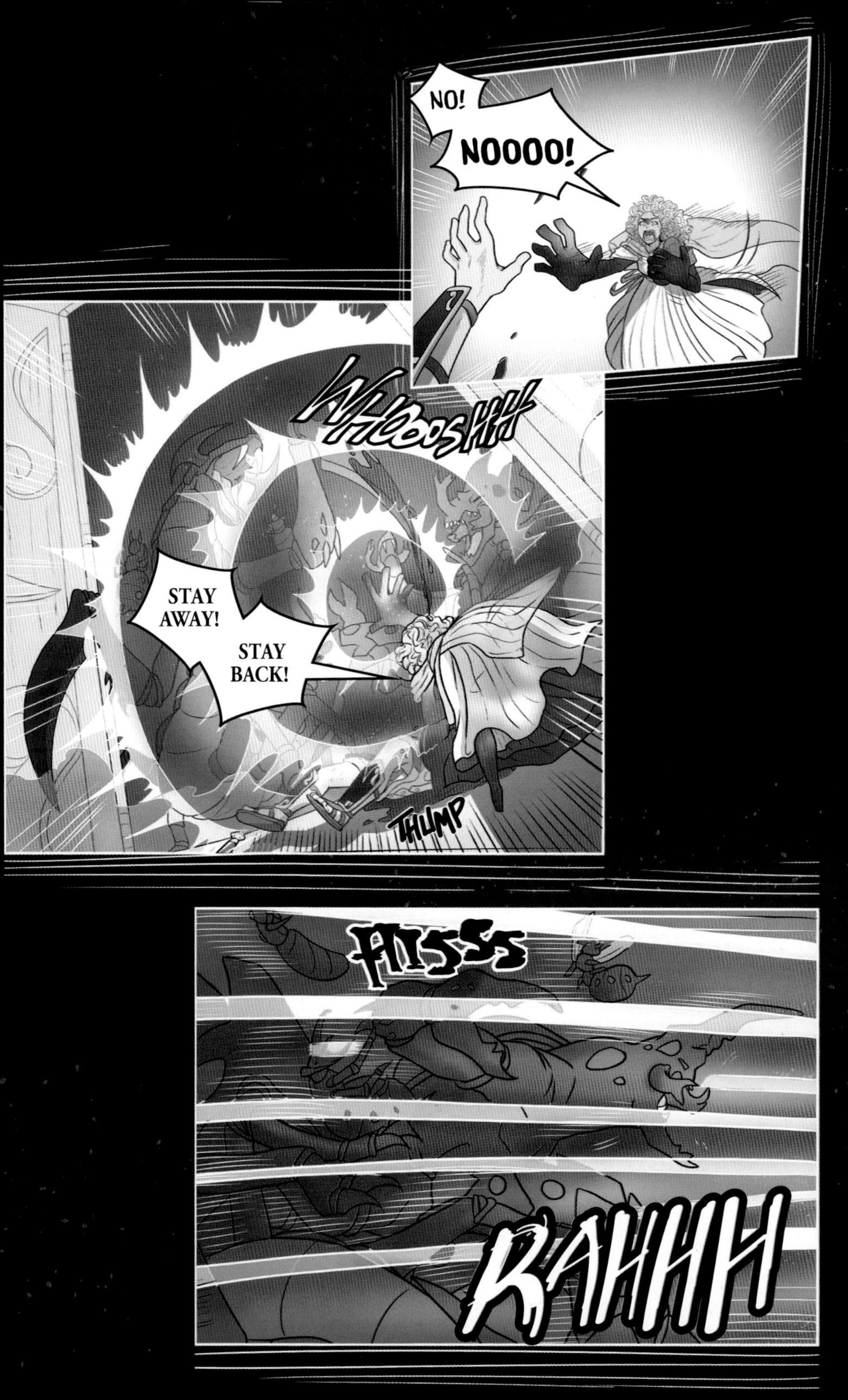
NO!
NOOOO!
WHOOOSHHH
STAY AWAY!
STAY BACK!
THUMP
HISSS
RAHHH

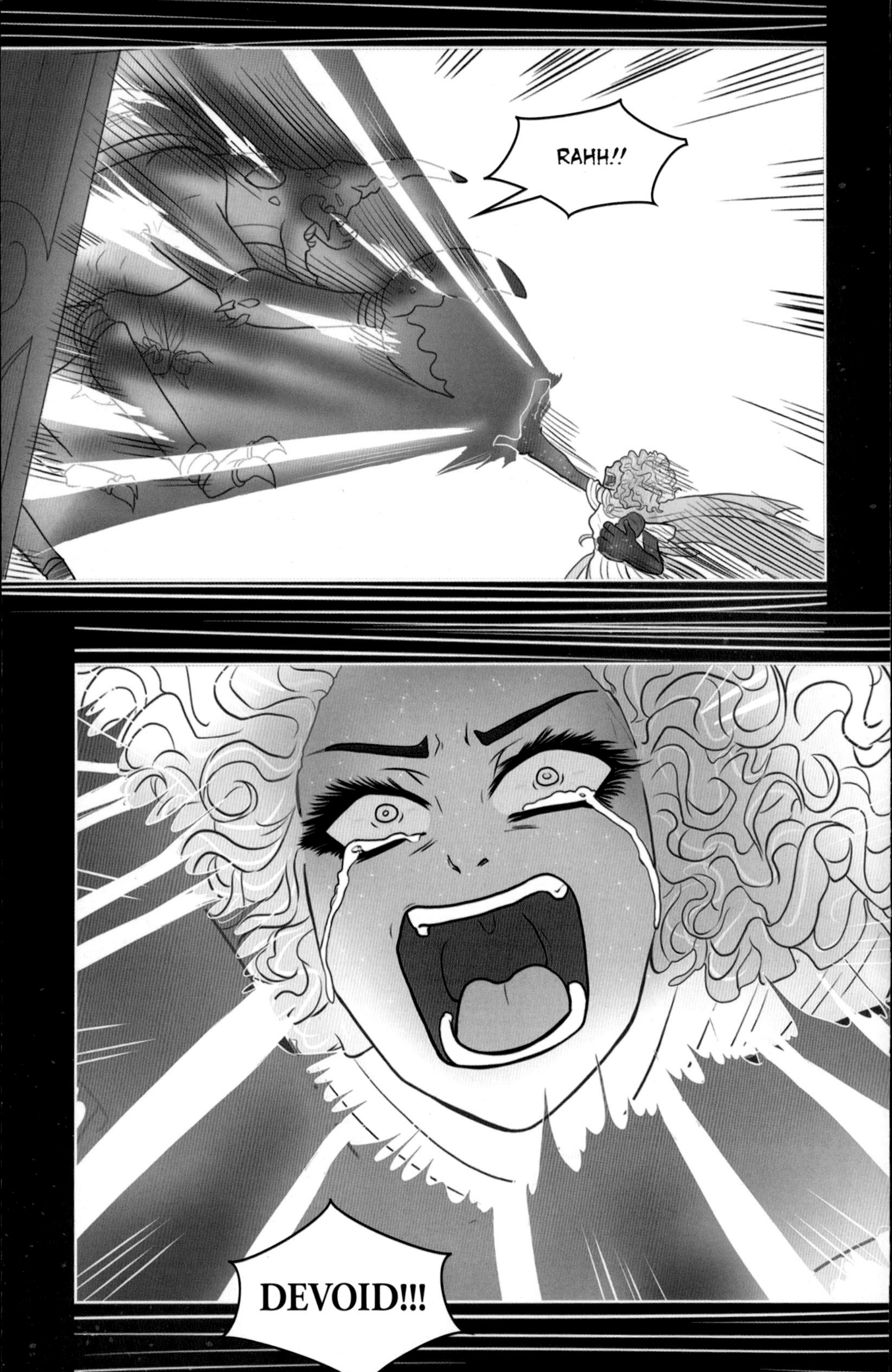
RAHH!!
DEVOID!!!

EPISODE 27:
THE GODDESS WITHIN (PT. 2)

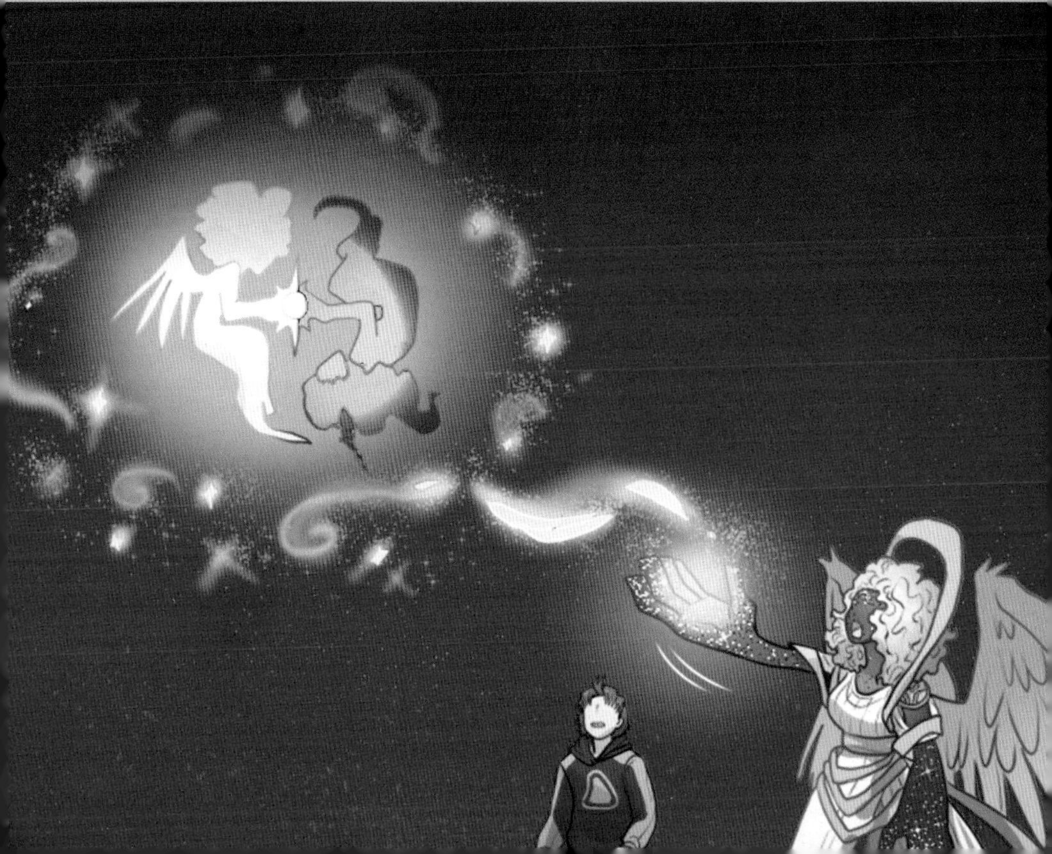

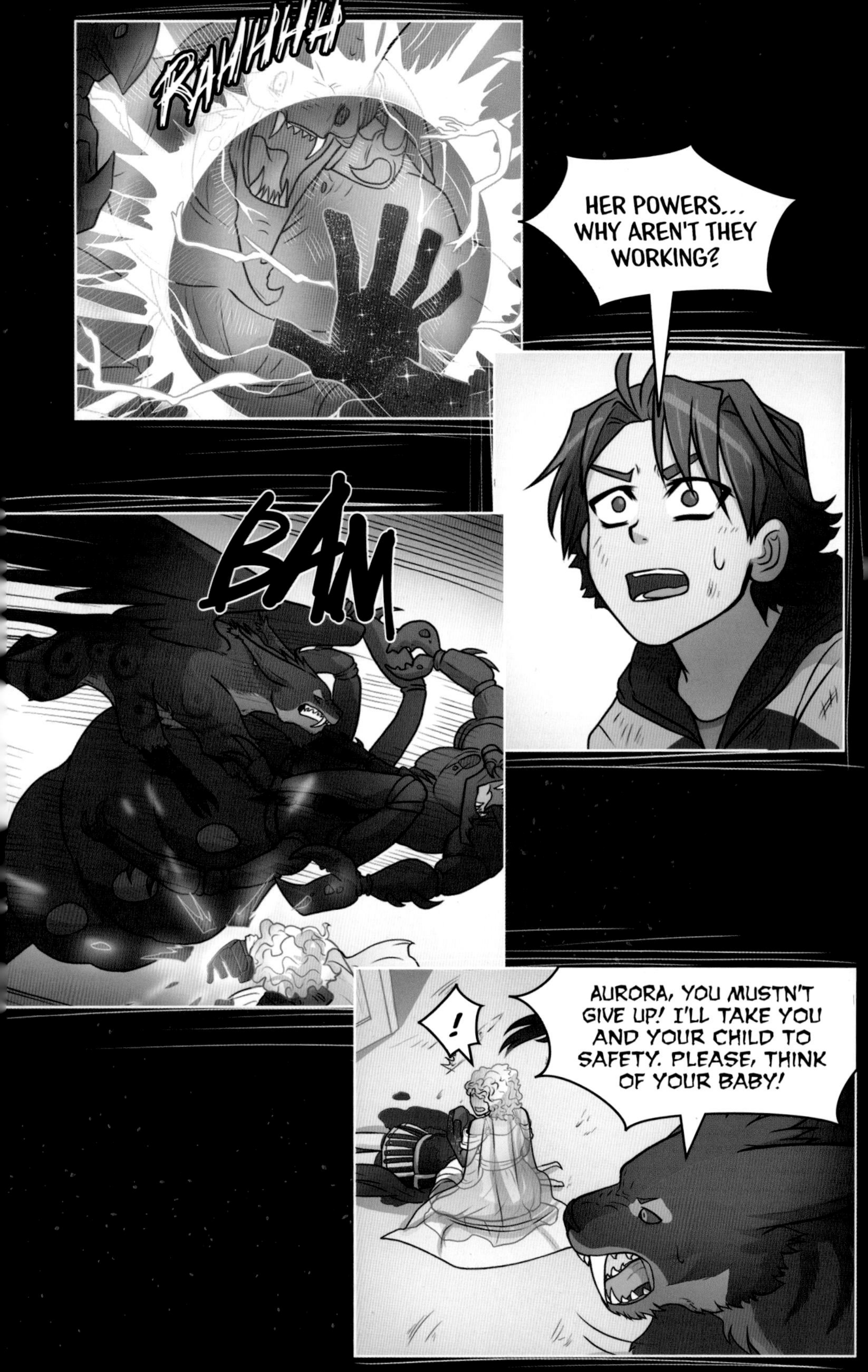
RAHHHH
HER POWERS... WHY AREN'T THEY WORKING?
BAM
!
AURORA, YOU MUSTN'T GIVE UP! I'LL TAKE YOU AND YOUR CHILD TO SAFETY. PLEASE, THINK OF YOUR BABY!

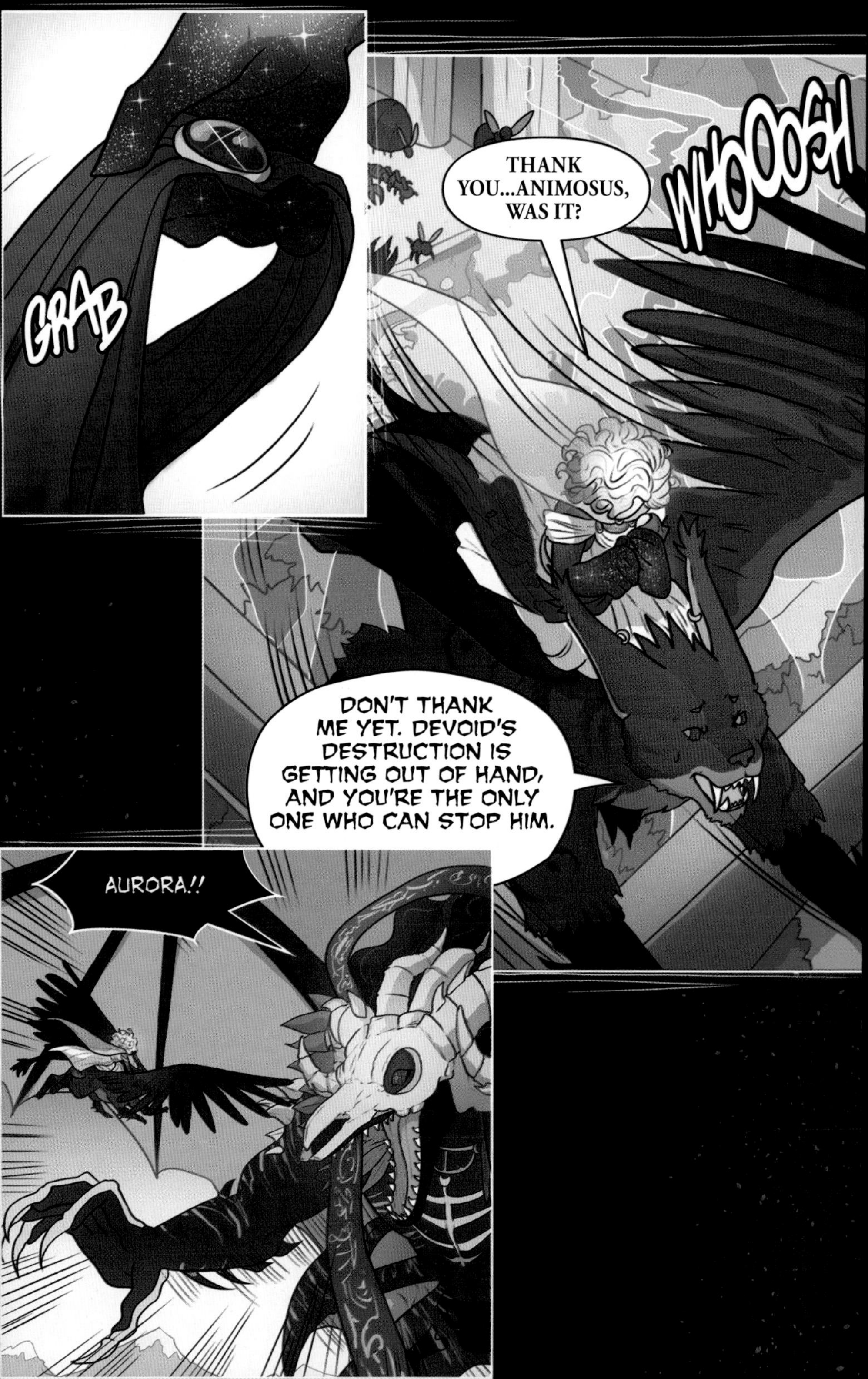
GRAB
THANK YOU...ANIMOSUS, WAS IT?
WHOOOSH
DON'T THANK ME YET. DEVOID'S DESTRUCTION IS GETTING OUT OF HAND, AND YOU'RE THE ONLY ONE WHO CAN STOP HIM.
AURORA!!

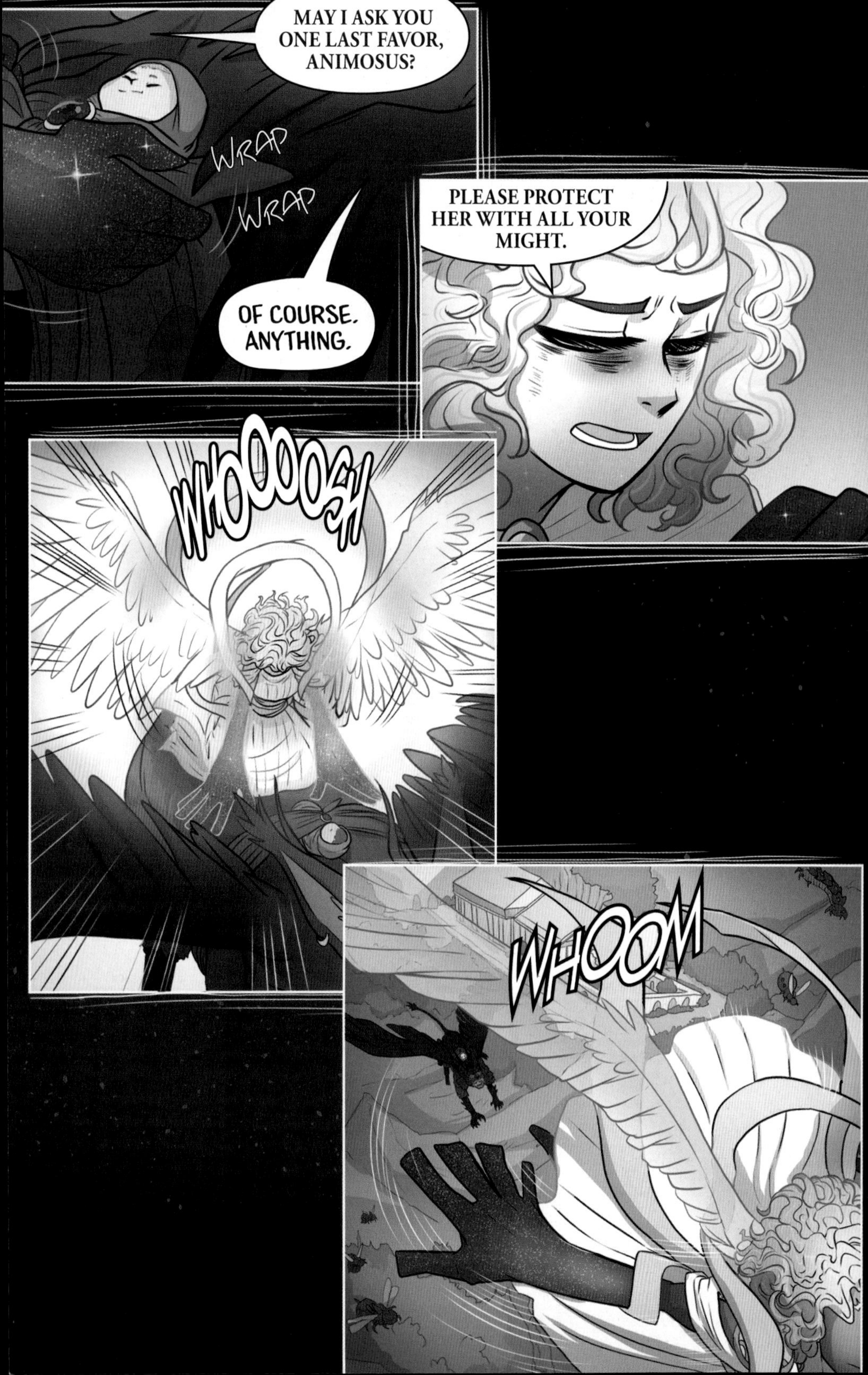
MAY I ASK YOU ONE LAST FAVOR, ANIMOSUS?
WRAP
WRAP
OF COURSE. ANYTHING.
PLEASE PROTECT HER WITH ALL YOUR MIGHT.
WHOOOOSH
WHOOM

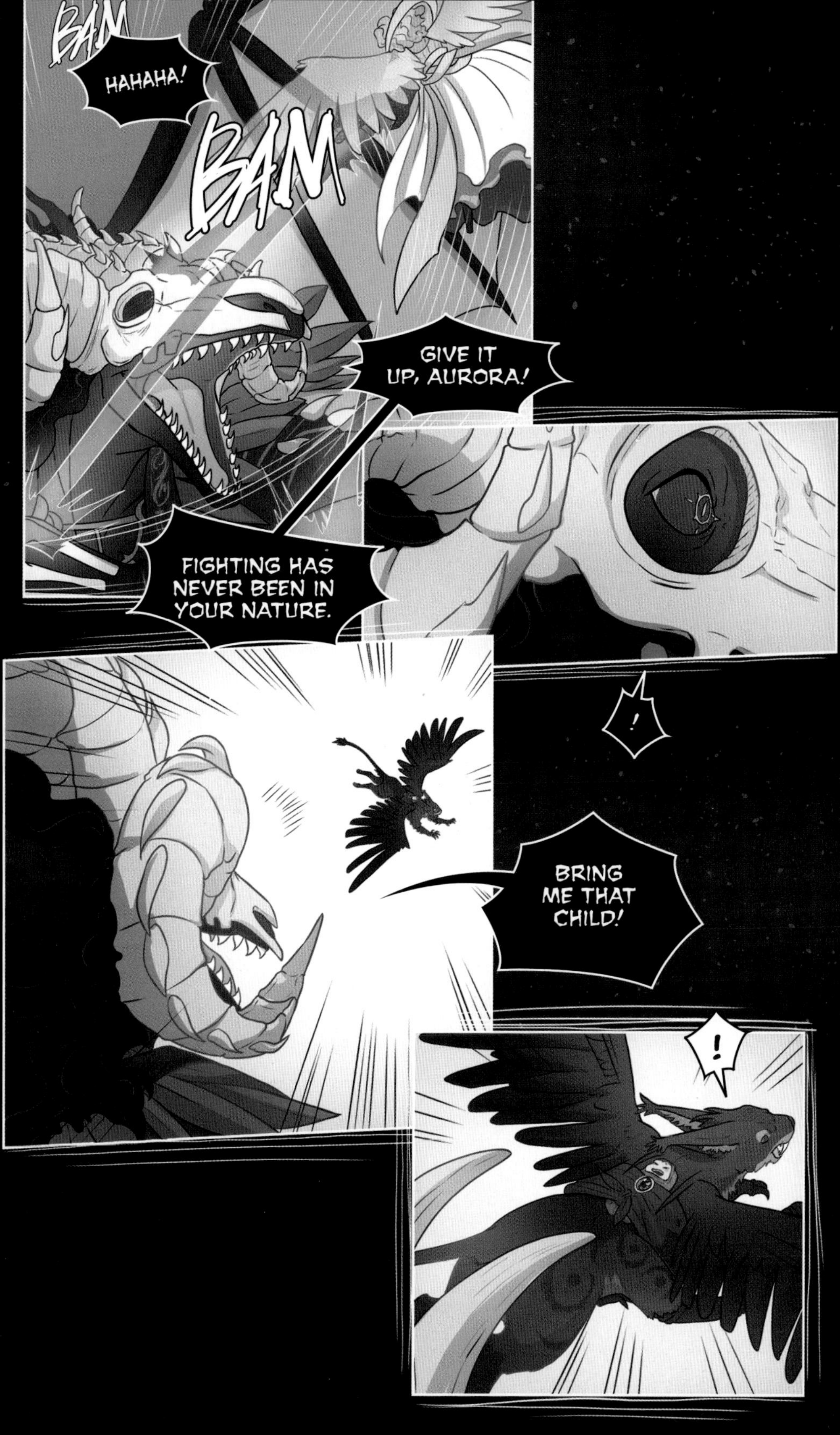
BAM
HAHAHA!
BAM
GIVE IT UP, AURORA!
FIGHTING HAS NEVER BEEN IN YOUR NATURE.
!
BRING ME THAT CHILD!
!

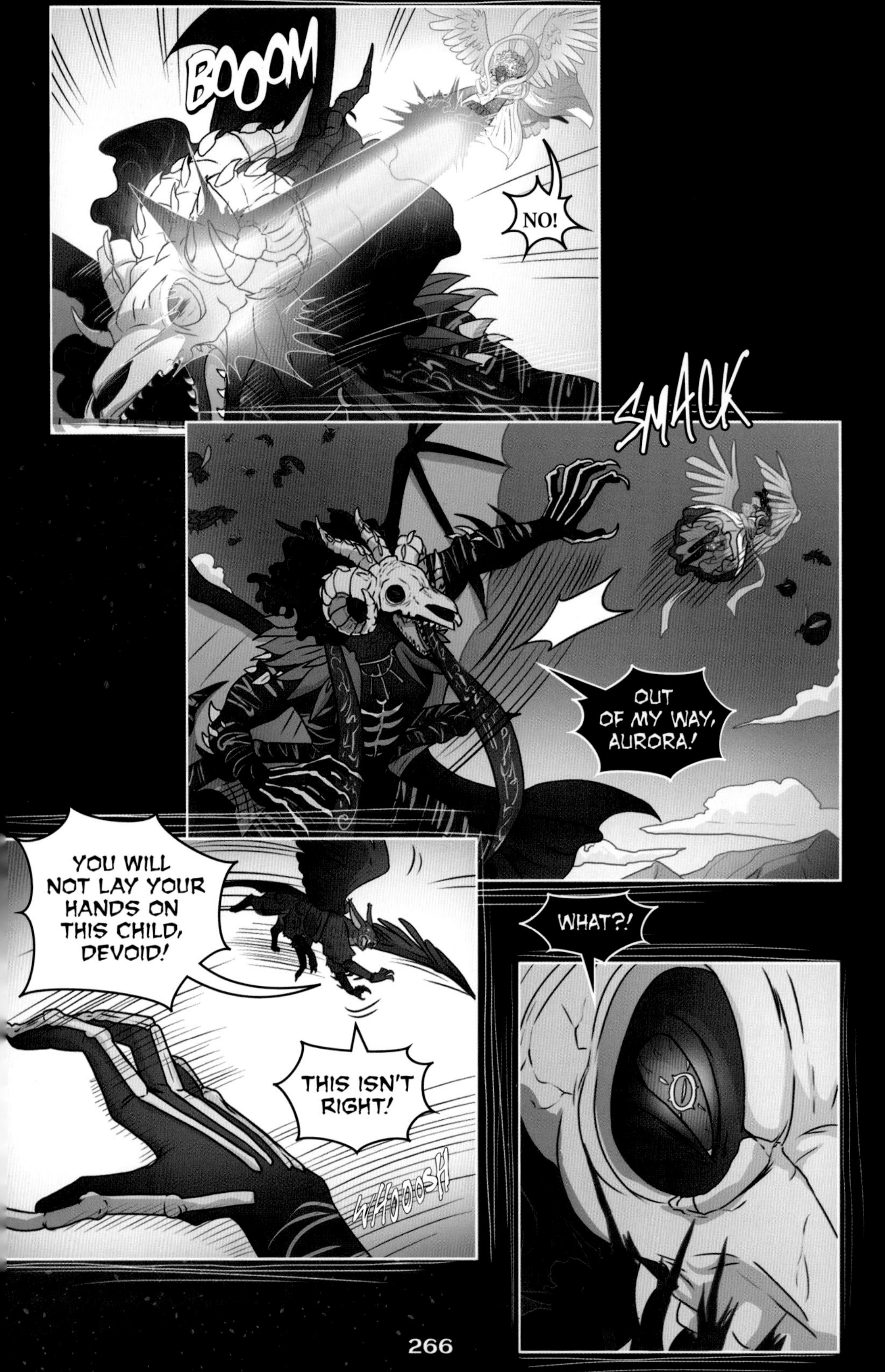
BOOOM
NO!
SMACK
OUT OF MY WAY, AURORA!
YOU WILL NOT LAY YOUR HANDS ON THIS CHILD, DEVOID!
THIS ISN'T RIGHT!
WHOOOSH
WHAT?!

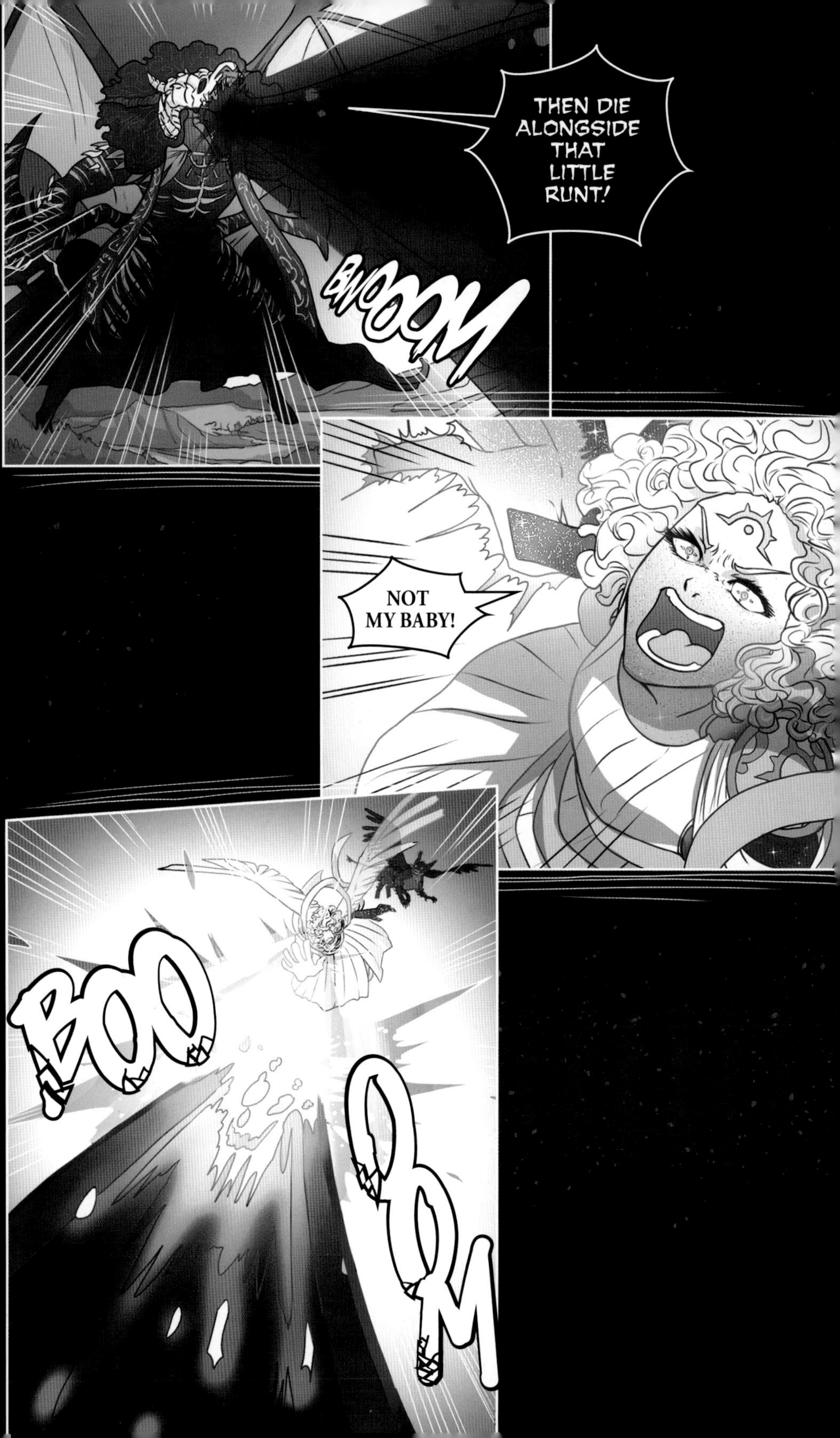
THEN DIE ALONGSIDE THAT LITTLE RUNT!
BWOOOM
NOT MY BABY!
BOOOOM

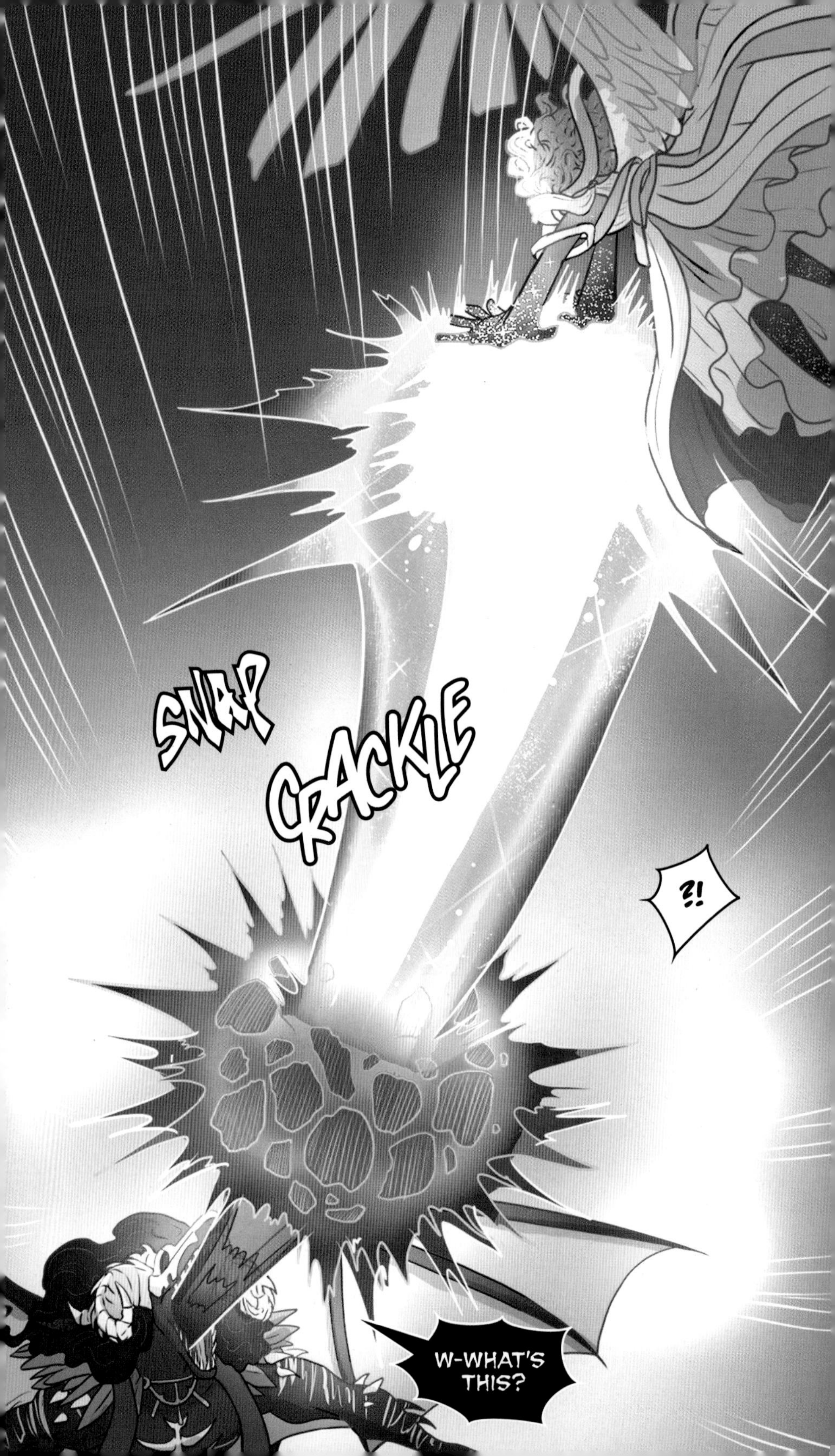
SNAP
CRACKLE
?!
W-WHAT'S THIS?

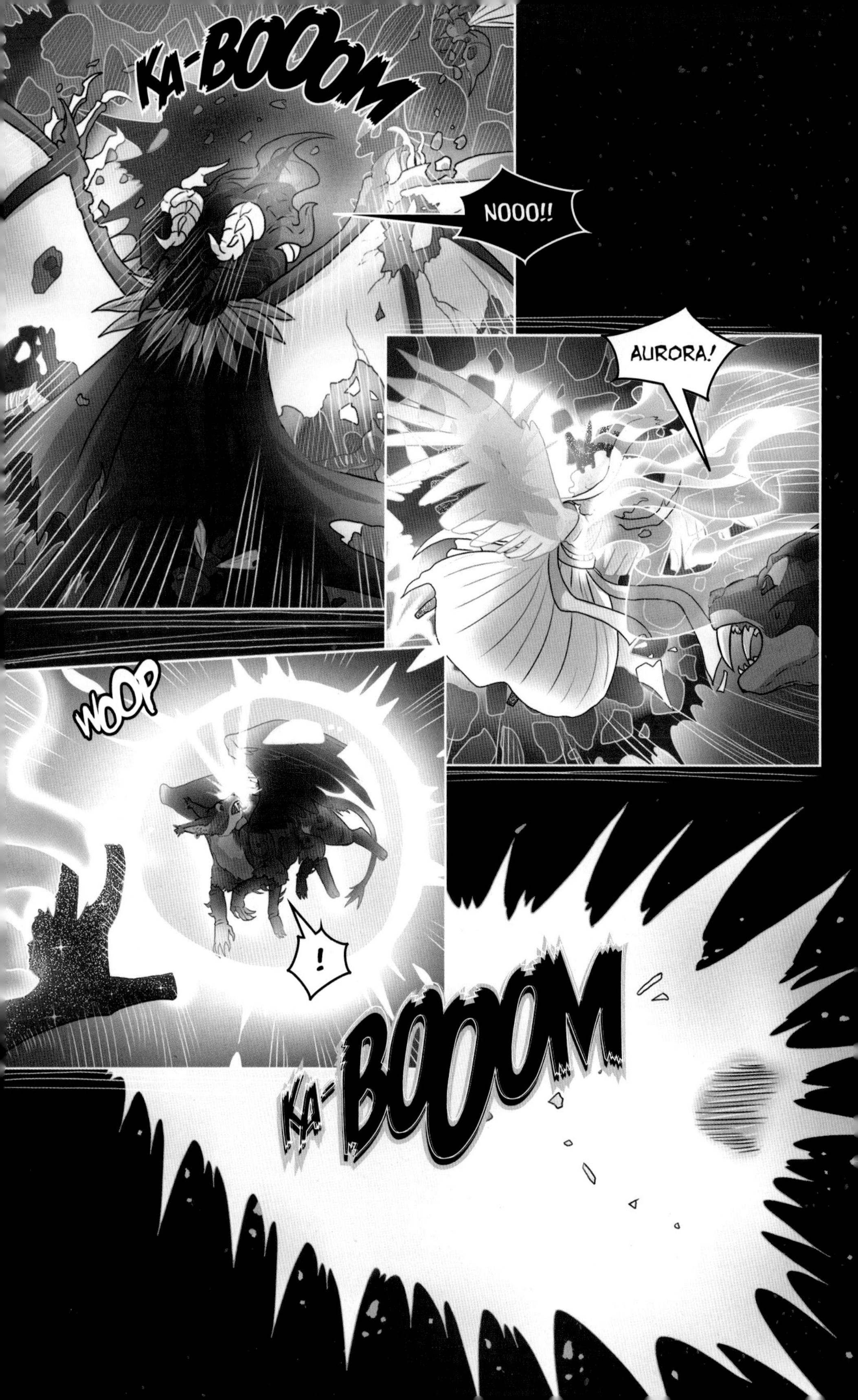
KA-BOOOM
NOOO!!
AURORA!
WOOP
!
KA-BOOOM

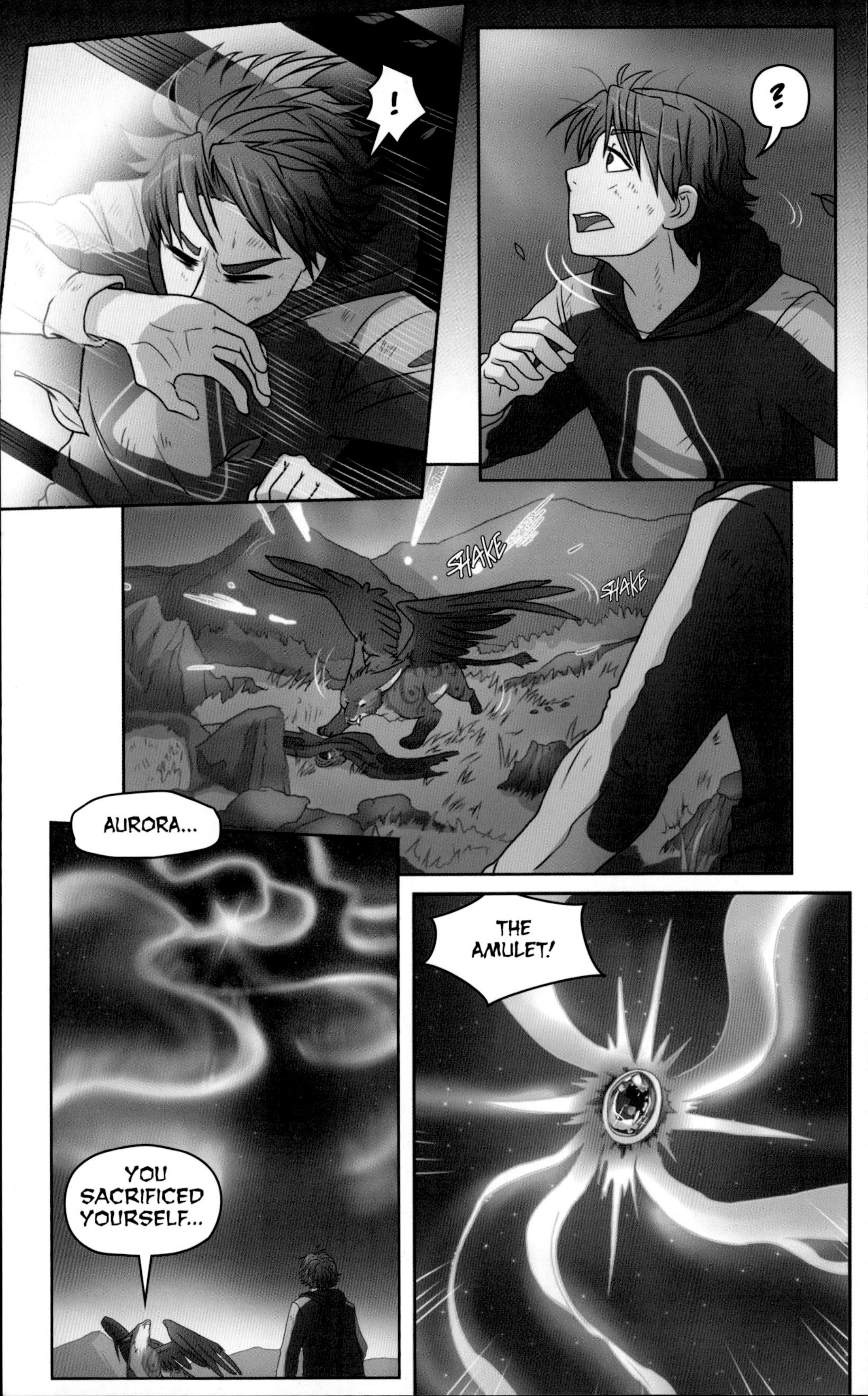
!
?
SHAKE
SHAKE
AURORA...
YOU SACRIFICED YOURSELF...
THE AMULET!

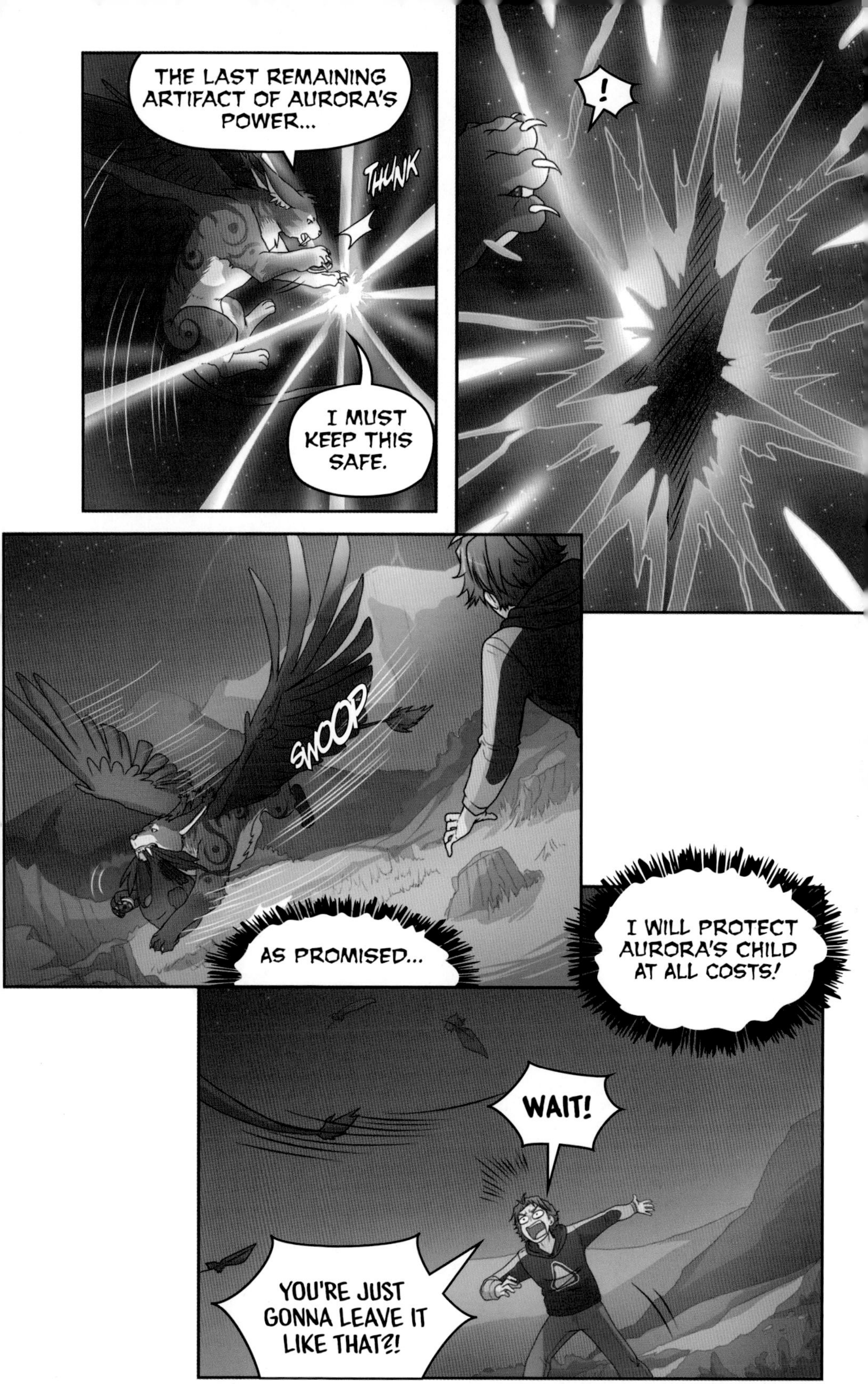
THE LAST REMAINING ARTIFACT OF AURORA'S POWER...
THUNK
I MUST KEEP THIS SAFE.
!
SWOOP
AS PROMISED...
I WILL PROTECT AURORA'S CHILD AT ALL COSTS!
WAIT!
YOU'RE JUST GONNA LEAVE IT LIKE THAT?!

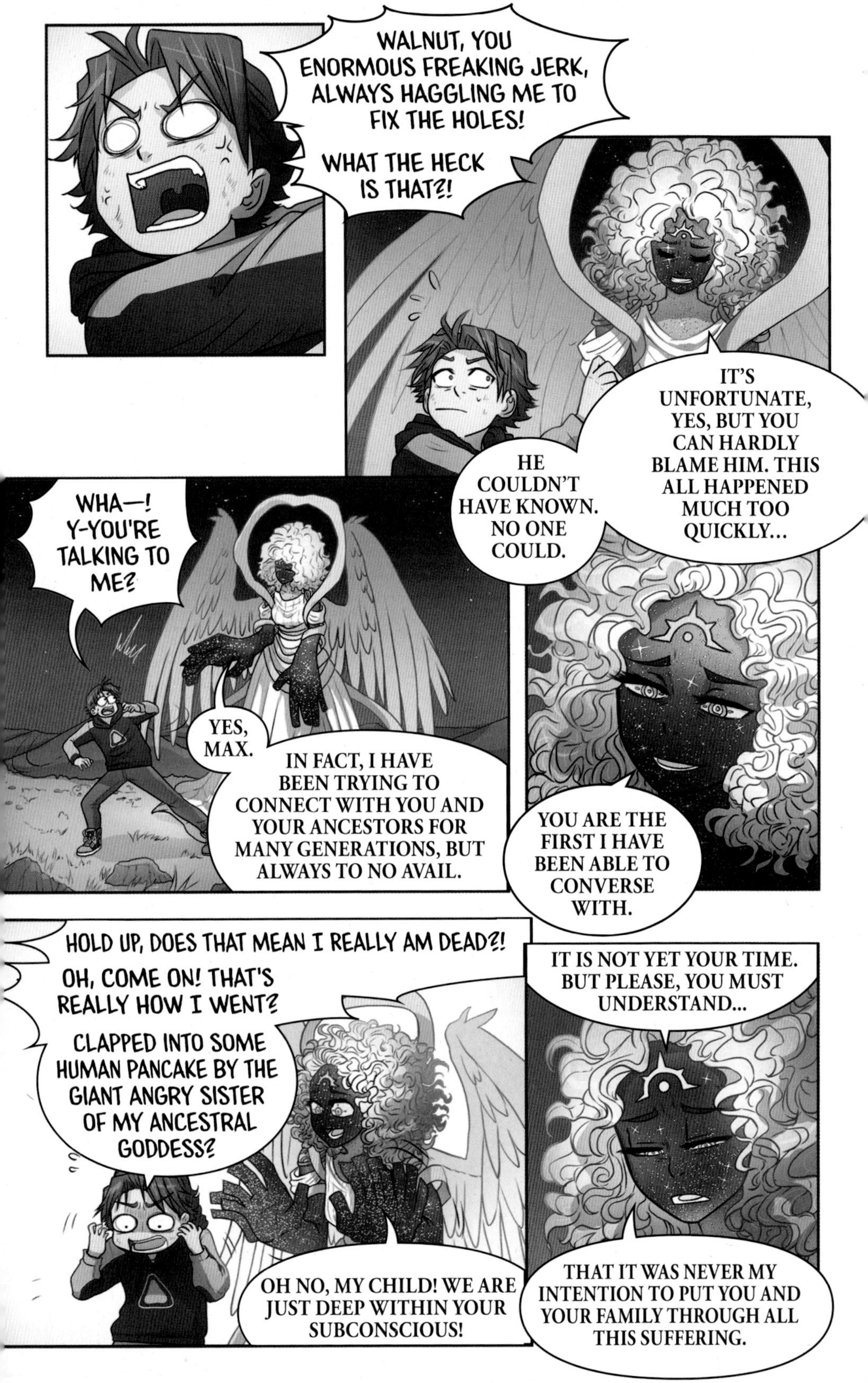
WALNUT, YOU ENORMOUS FREAKING JERK, ALWAYS HAGGLING ME TO FIX THE HOLES!
WHAT THE HECK IS THAT?!
IT'S UNFORTUNATE, YES, BUT YOU CAN HARDLY BLAME HIM. THIS ALL HAPPENED MUCH TOO QUICKLY...
HE COULDN'T HAVE KNOWN. NO ONE COULD.
WHA—! Y-YOU'RE TALKING TO ME?
YES, MAX.
IN FACT, I HAVE BEEN TRYING TO CONNECT WITH YOU AND YOUR ANCESTORS FOR MANY GENERATIONS, BUT ALWAYS TO NO AVAIL.
YOU ARE THE FIRST I HAVE BEEN ABLE TO CONVERSE WITH.
HOLD UP, DOES THAT MEAN I REALLY AM DEAD?!
OH, COME ON! THAT'S REALLY HOW I WENT?
CLAPPED INTO SOME HUMAN PANCAKE BY THE GIANT ANGRY SISTER OF MY ANCESTRAL GODDESS?
OH NO, MY CHILD! WE ARE JUST DEEP WITHIN YOUR SUBCONSCIOUS!
IT IS NOT YET YOUR TIME. BUT PLEASE, YOU MUST UNDERSTAND...
THAT IT WAS NEVER MY INTENTION TO PUT YOU AND YOUR FAMILY THROUGH ALL THIS SUFFERING.

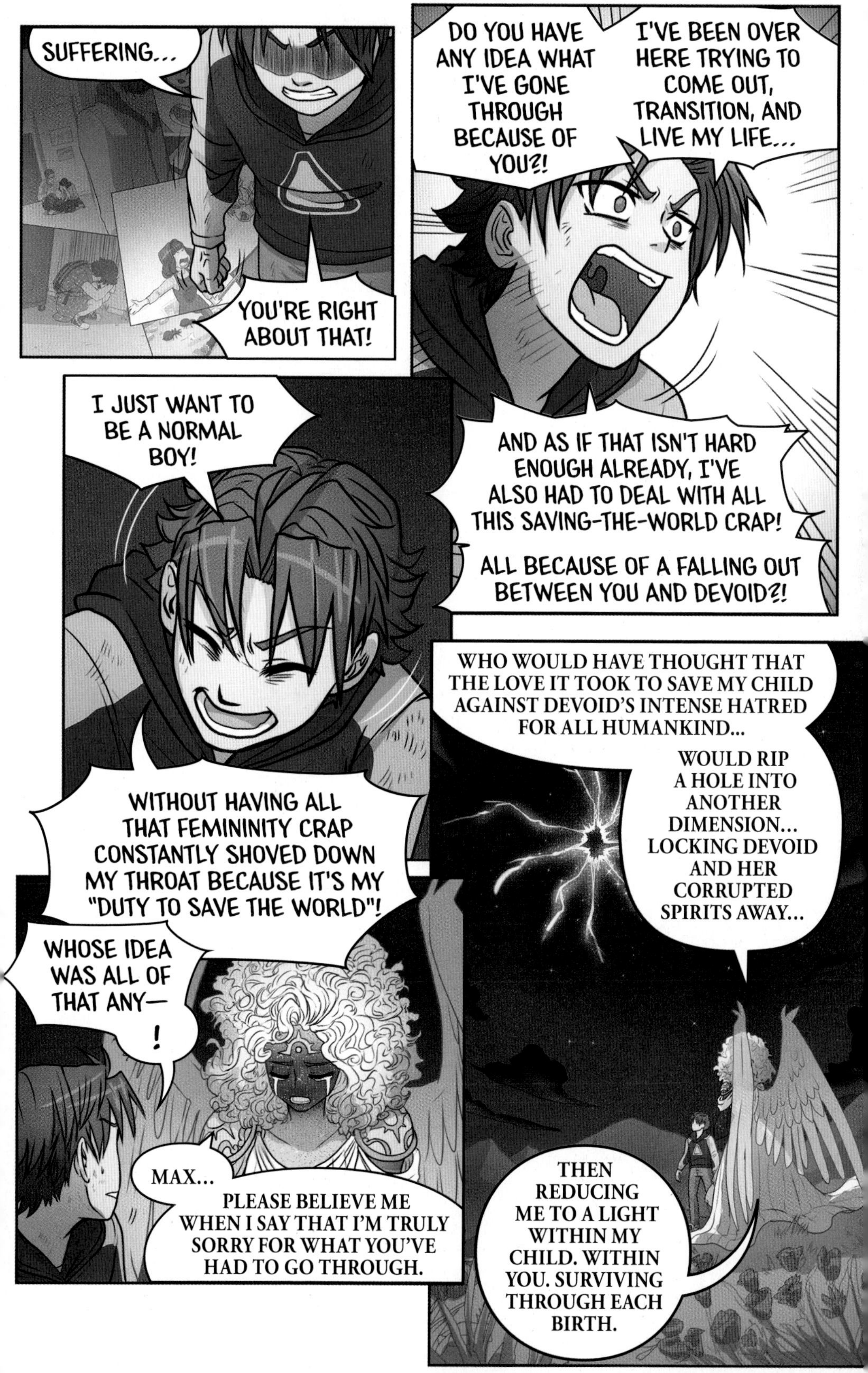
SUFFERING...
YOU'RE RIGHT ABOUT THAT!
DO YOU HAVE ANY IDEA WHAT I'VE GONE THROUGH BECAUSE OF YOU?!
I'VE BEEN OVER HERE TRYING TO COME OUT, TRANSITION, AND LIVE MY LIFE...
AND AS IF THAT ISN'T HARD ENOUGH ALREADY, I'VE ALSO HAD TO DEAL WITH ALL THIS SAVING-THE-WORLD CRAP!
ALL BECAUSE OF A FALLING OUT BETWEEN YOU AND DEVOID?!
I JUST WANT TO BE A NORMAL BOY!
WITHOUT HAVING ALL THAT FEMININITY CRAP CONSTANTLY SHOVED DOWN MY THROAT BECAUSE IT'S MY "DUTY TO SAVE THE WORLD"!
WHOSE IDEA WAS ALL OF THAT ANY—
!
MAX...
PLEASE BELIEVE ME WHEN I SAY THAT I'M TRULY SORRY FOR WHAT YOU'VE HAD TO GO THROUGH.
WHO WOULD HAVE THOUGHT THAT THE LOVE IT TOOK TO SAVE MY CHILD AGAINST DEVOID'S INTENSE HATRED FOR ALL HUMANKIND...
WOULD RIP A HOLE INTO ANOTHER DIMENSION... LOCKING DEVOID AND HER CORRUPTED SPIRITS AWAY...
THEN REDUCING ME TO A LIGHT WITHIN MY CHILD. WITHIN YOU. SURVIVING THROUGH EACH BIRTH.

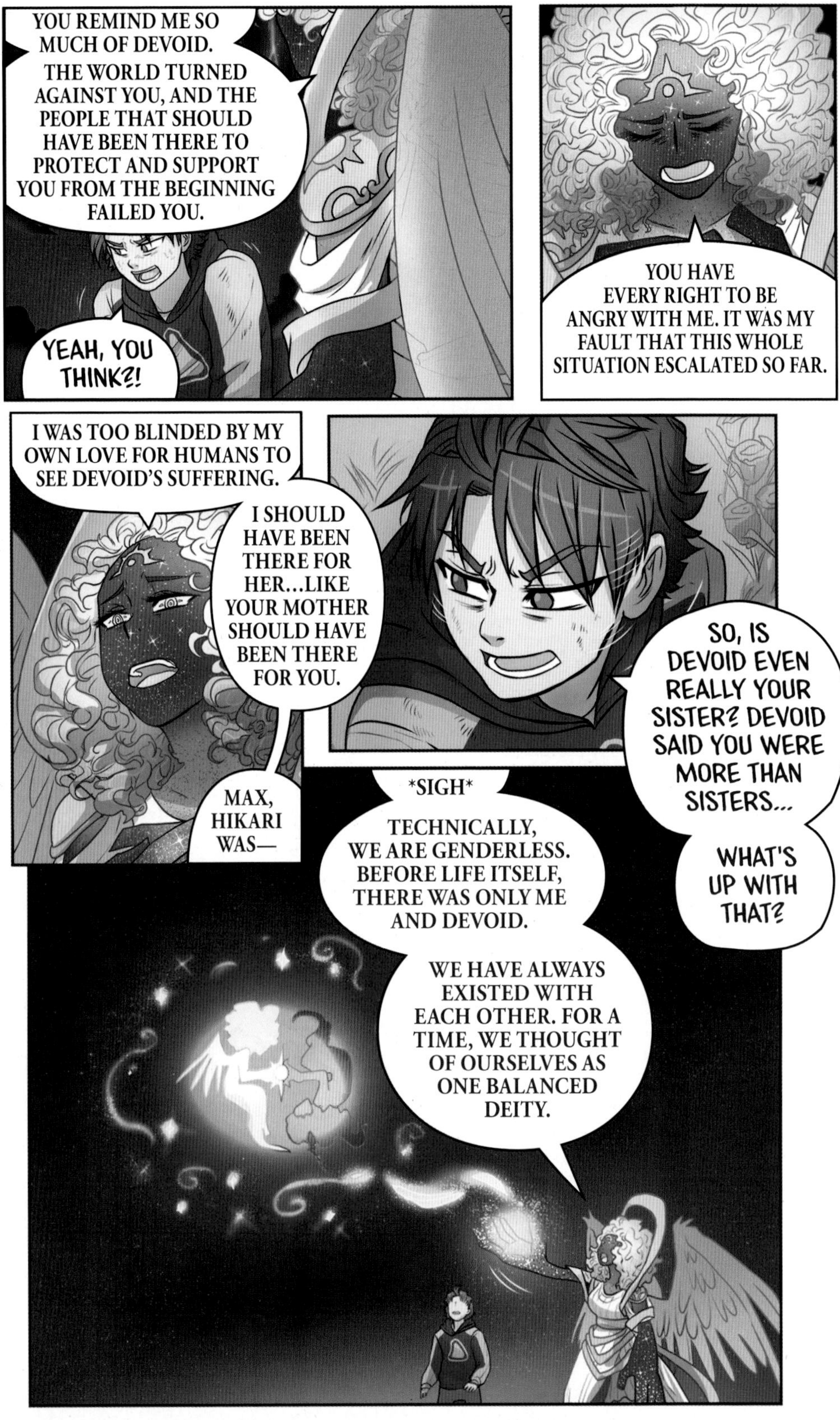
YOU REMIND ME SO MUCH OF DEVOID.
THE WORLD TURNED AGAINST YOU, AND THE PEOPLE THAT SHOULD HAVE BEEN THERE TO PROTECT AND SUPPORT YOU FROM THE BEGINNING FAILED YOU.
YEAH, YOU THINK?!
YOU HAVE EVERY RIGHT TO BE ANGRY WITH ME. IT WAS MY FAULT THAT THIS WHOLE SITUATION ESCALATED SO FAR.
I WAS TOO BLINDED BY MY OWN LOVE FOR HUMANS TO SEE DEVOID'S SUFFERING.
I SHOULD HAVE BEEN THERE FOR HER...LIKE YOUR MOTHER SHOULD HAVE BEEN THERE FOR YOU.
MAX, HIKARI WAS—
SO, IS DEVOID EVEN REALLY YOUR SISTER? DEVOID SAID YOU WERE MORE THAN SISTERS...
WHAT'S UP WITH THAT?
SIGH
TECHNICALLY, WE ARE GENDERLESS. BEFORE LIFE ITSELF, THERE WAS ONLY ME AND DEVOID.
WE HAVE ALWAYS EXISTED WITH EACH OTHER. FOR A TIME, WE THOUGHT OF OURSELVES AS ONE BALANCED DEITY.

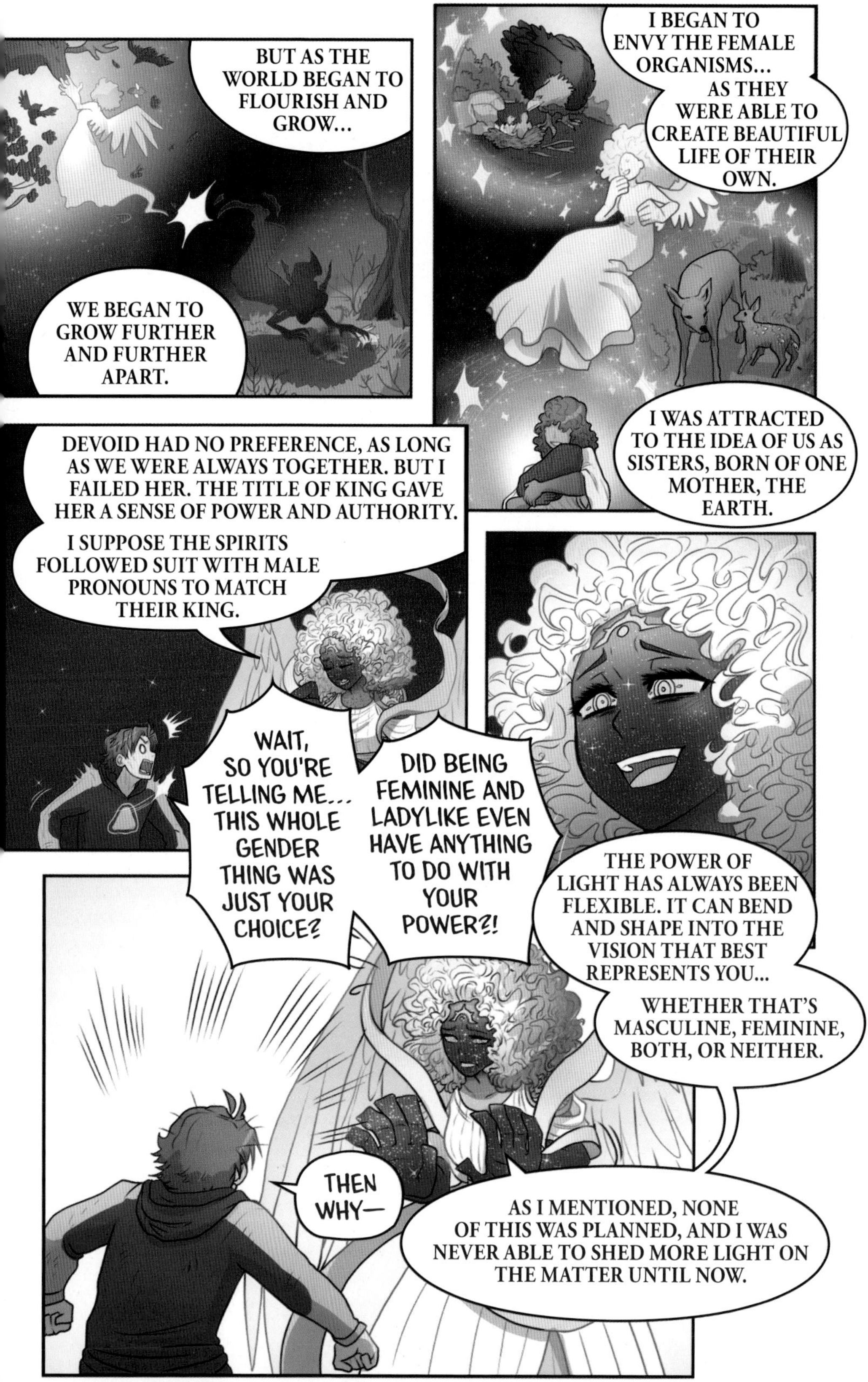
BUT AS THE WORLD BEGAN TO FLOURISH AND GROW...
WE BEGAN TO GROW FURTHER AND FURTHER APART.
I BEGAN TO ENVY THE FEMALE ORGANISMS... AS THEY WERE ABLE TO CREATE BEAUTIFUL LIFE OF THEIR OWN.
I WAS ATTRACTED TO THE IDEA OF US AS SISTERS, BORN OF ONE MOTHER, THE EARTH.
DEVOID HAD NO PREFERENCE, AS LONG AS WE WERE ALWAYS TOGETHER. BUT I FAILED HER. THE TITLE OF KING GAVE HER A SENSE OF POWER AND AUTHORITY.
I SUPPOSE THE SPIRITS FOLLOWED SUIT WITH MALE PRONOUNS TO MATCH THEIR KING.
WAIT, SO YOU'RE TELLING ME... THIS WHOLE GENDER THING WAS JUST YOUR CHOICE?
DID BEING FEMININE AND LADYLIKE EVEN HAVE ANYTHING TO DO WITH YOUR POWER?!
THE POWER OF LIGHT HAS ALWAYS BEEN FLEXIBLE. IT CAN BEND AND SHAPE INTO THE VISION THAT BEST REPRESENTS YOU...
WHETHER THAT'S MASCULINE, FEMININE, BOTH, OR NEITHER.
THEN WHY—
AS I MENTIONED, NONE OF THIS WAS PLANNED, AND I WAS NEVER ABLE TO SHED MORE LIGHT ON THE MATTER UNTIL NOW.

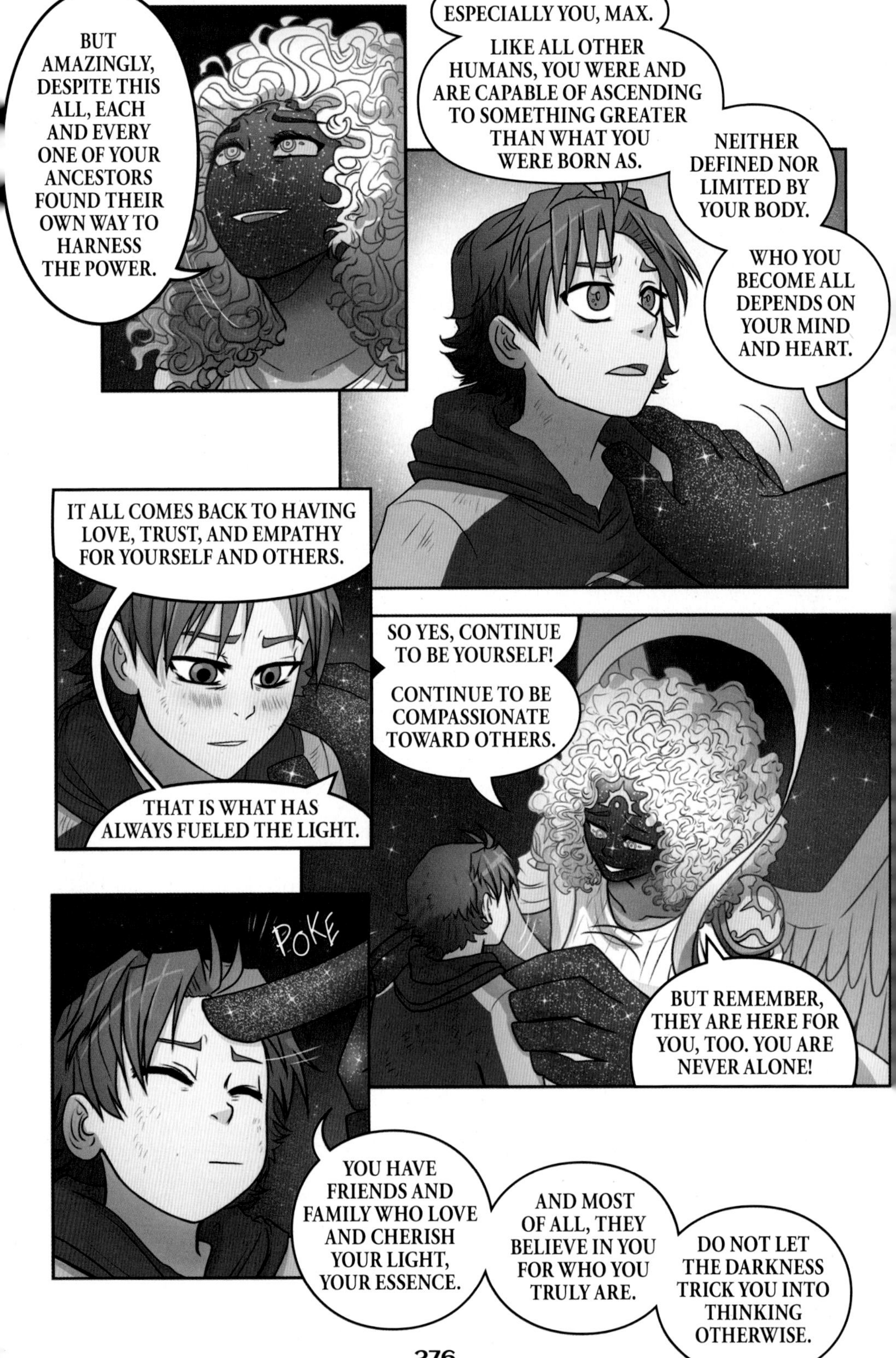
BUT AMAZINGLY, DESPITE THIS ALL, EACH AND EVERY ONE OF YOUR ANCESTORS FOUND THEIR OWN WAY TO HARNESS THE POWER.
ESPECIALLY YOU, MAX.
LIKE ALL OTHER HUMANS, YOU WERE AND ARE CAPABLE OF ASCENDING TO SOMETHING GREATER THAN WHAT YOU WERE BORN AS.
NEITHER DEFINED NOR LIMITED BY YOUR BODY.
WHO YOU BECOME ALL DEPENDS ON YOUR MIND AND HEART.
IT ALL COMES BACK TO HAVING LOVE, TRUST, AND EMPATHY FOR YOURSELF AND OTHERS.
THAT IS WHAT HAS ALWAYS FUELED THE LIGHT.
SO YES, CONTINUE TO BE YOURSELF!
CONTINUE TO BE COMPASSIONATE TOWARD OTHERS.
BUT REMEMBER, THEY ARE HERE FOR YOU, TOO. YOU ARE NEVER ALONE!
POKE
YOU HAVE FRIENDS AND FAMILY WHO LOVE AND CHERISH YOUR LIGHT, YOUR ESSENCE.
AND MOST OF ALL, THEY BELIEVE IN YOU FOR WHO YOU TRULY ARE.
DO NOT LET THE DARKNESS TRICK YOU INTO THINKING OTHERWISE.

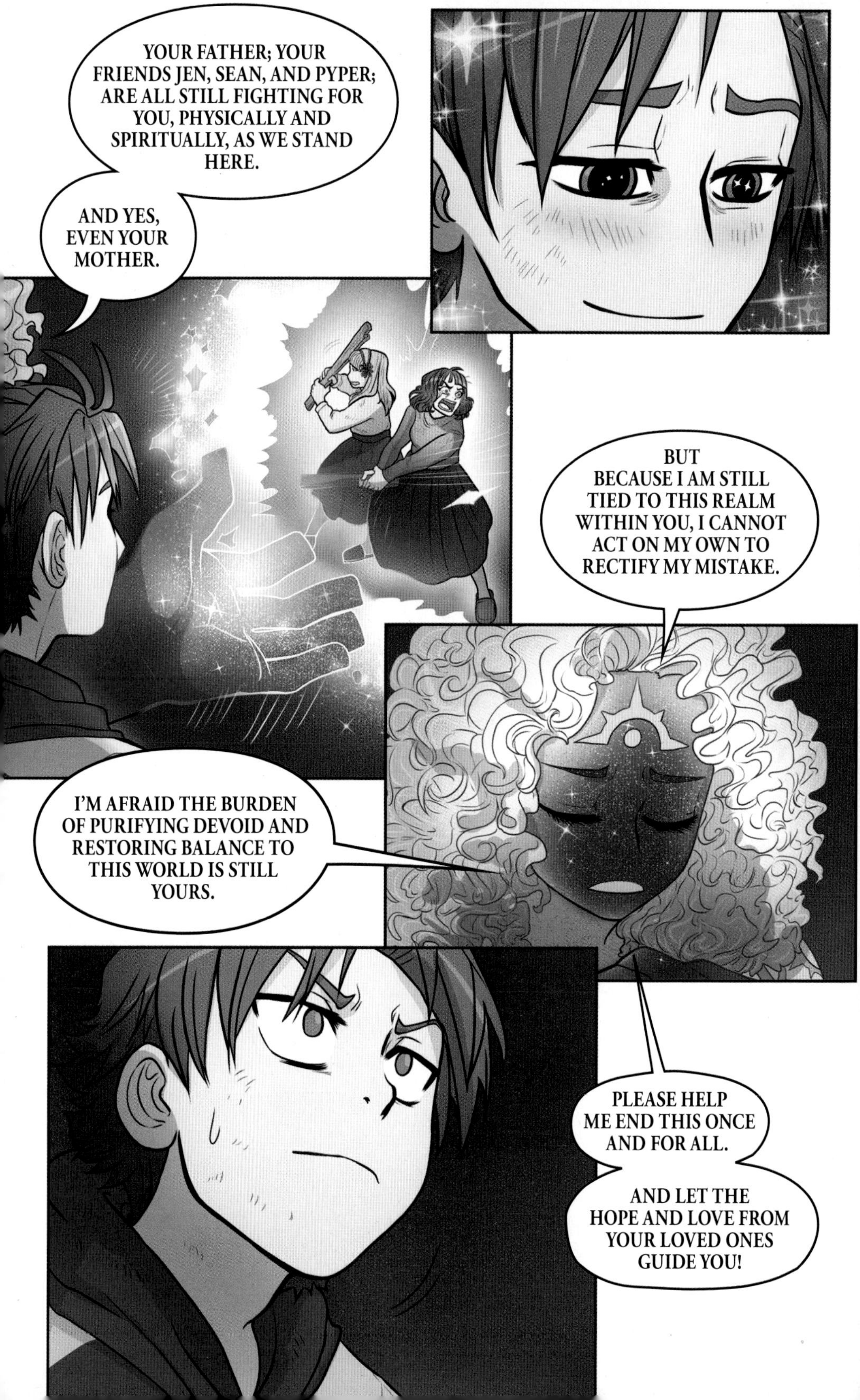
YOUR FATHER; YOUR FRIENDS JEN, SEAN, AND PYPER; ARE ALL STILL FIGHTING FOR YOU, PHYSICALLY AND SPIRITUALLY, AS WE STAND HERE.
AND YES, EVEN YOUR MOTHER.
BUT BECAUSE I AM STILL TIED TO THIS REALM WITHIN YOU, I CANNOT ACT ON MY OWN TO RECTIFY MY MISTAKE.
I'M AFRAID THE BURDEN OF PURIFYING DEVOID AND RESTORING BALANCE TO THIS WORLD IS STILL YOURS.
PLEASE HELP ME END THIS ONCE AND FOR ALL.
AND LET THE HOPE AND LOVE FROM YOUR LOVED ONES GUIDE YOU!

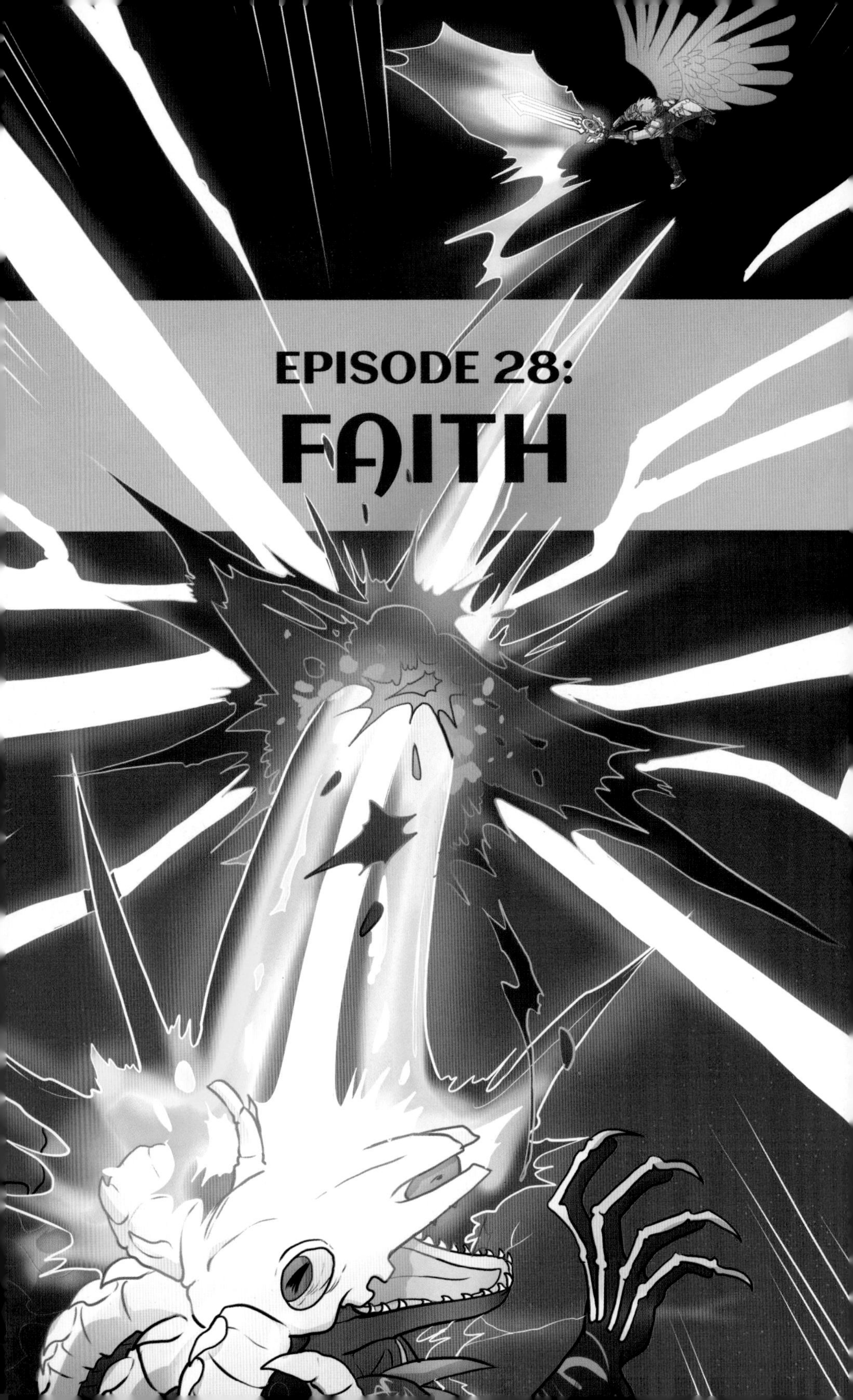
EPISODE 28:
FAITH

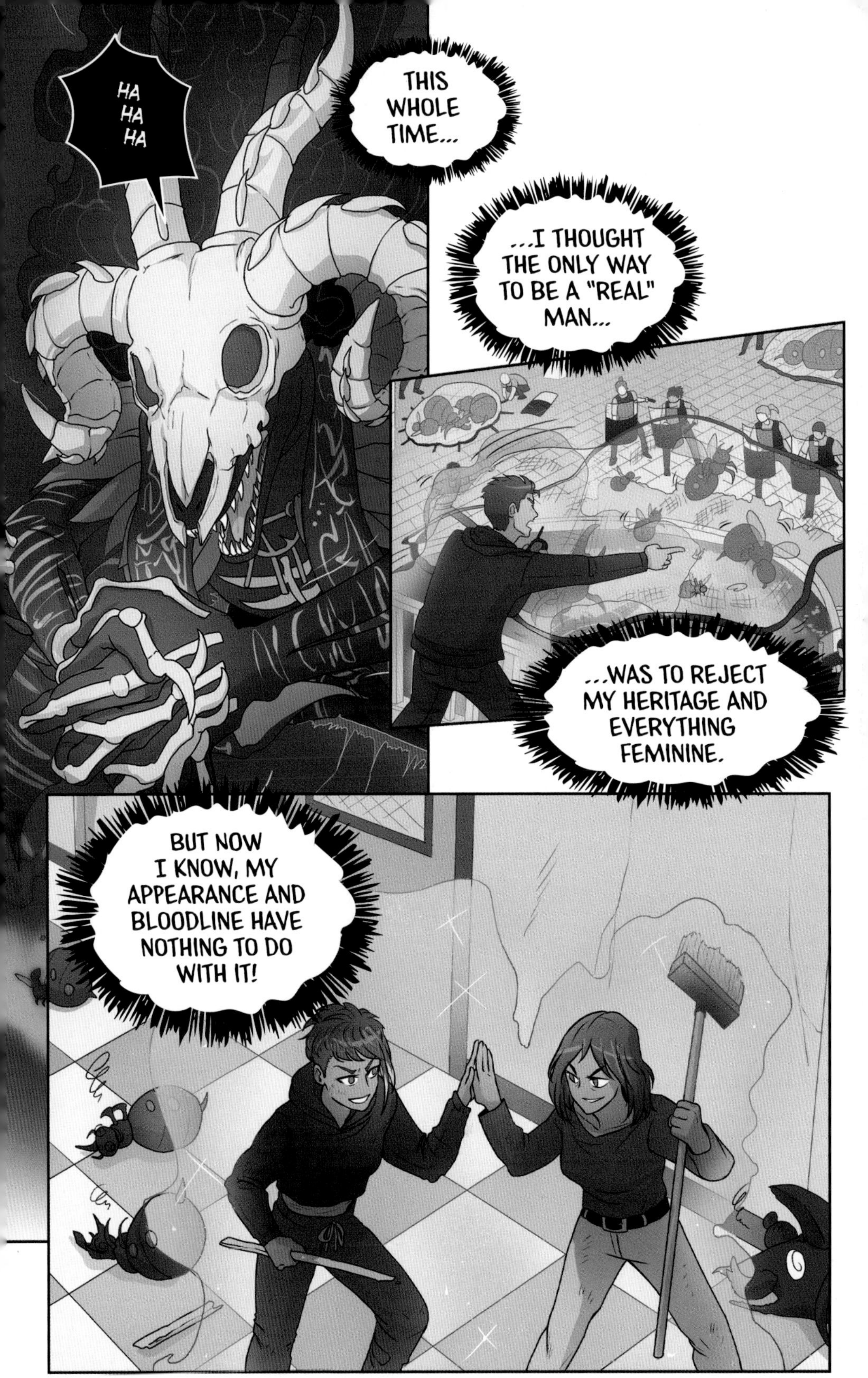
HA HA HA
THIS WHOLE TIME...
...I THOUGHT THE ONLY WAY TO BE A "REAL" MAN...
...WAS TO REJECT MY HERITAGE AND EVERYTHING FEMININE.
BUT NOW I KNOW, MY APPEARANCE AND BLOODLINE HAVE NOTHING TO DO WITH IT!

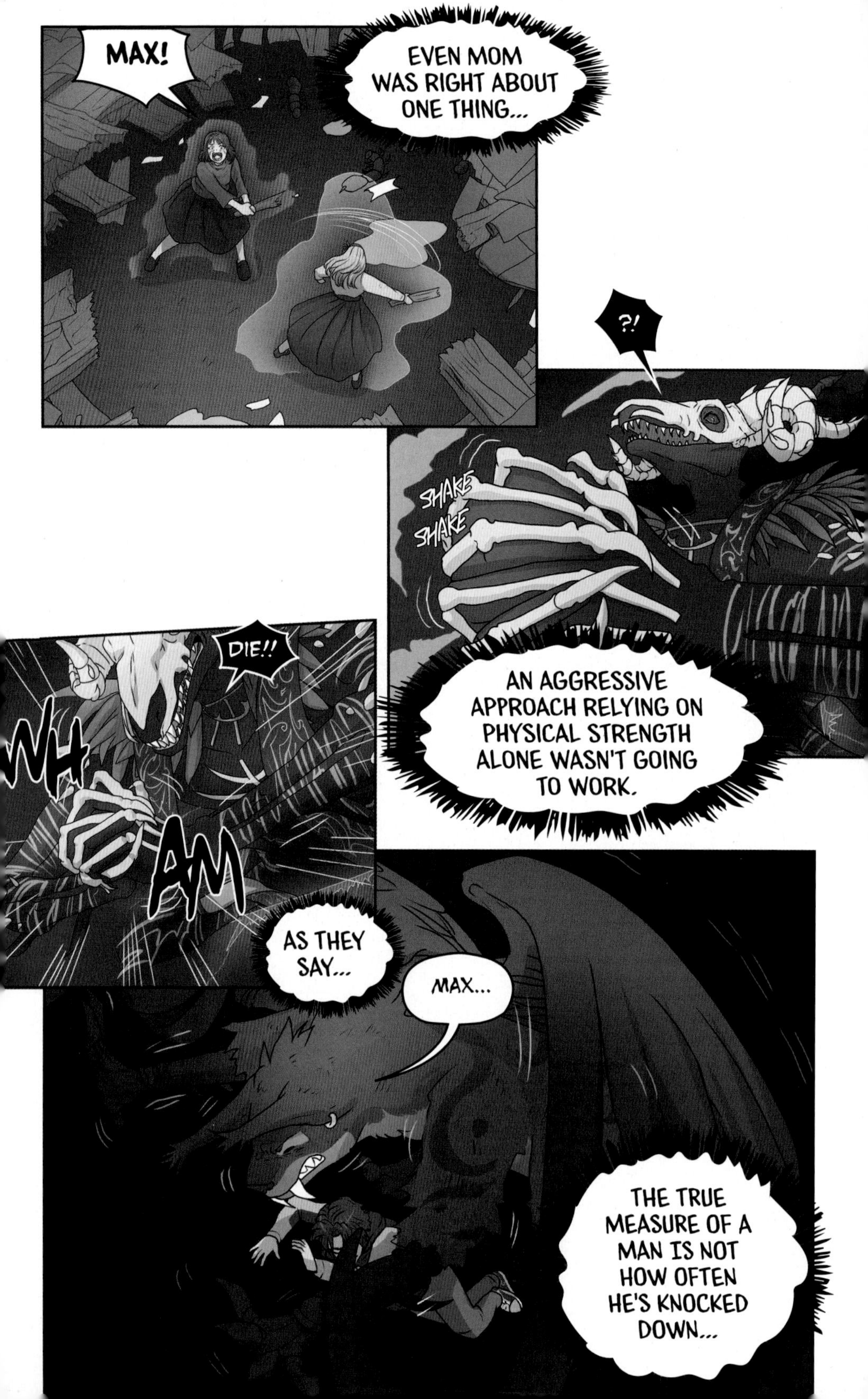
MAX!
EVEN MOM WAS RIGHT ABOUT ONE THING...
?!
SHAKE
SHAKE
AN AGGRESSIVE APPROACH RELYING ON PHYSICAL STRENGTH ALONE WASN'T GOING TO WORK.
DIE!!
WH
AM
AS THEY SAY...
MAX...
THE TRUE MEASURE OF A MAN IS NOT HOW OFTEN HE'S KNOCKED DOWN...

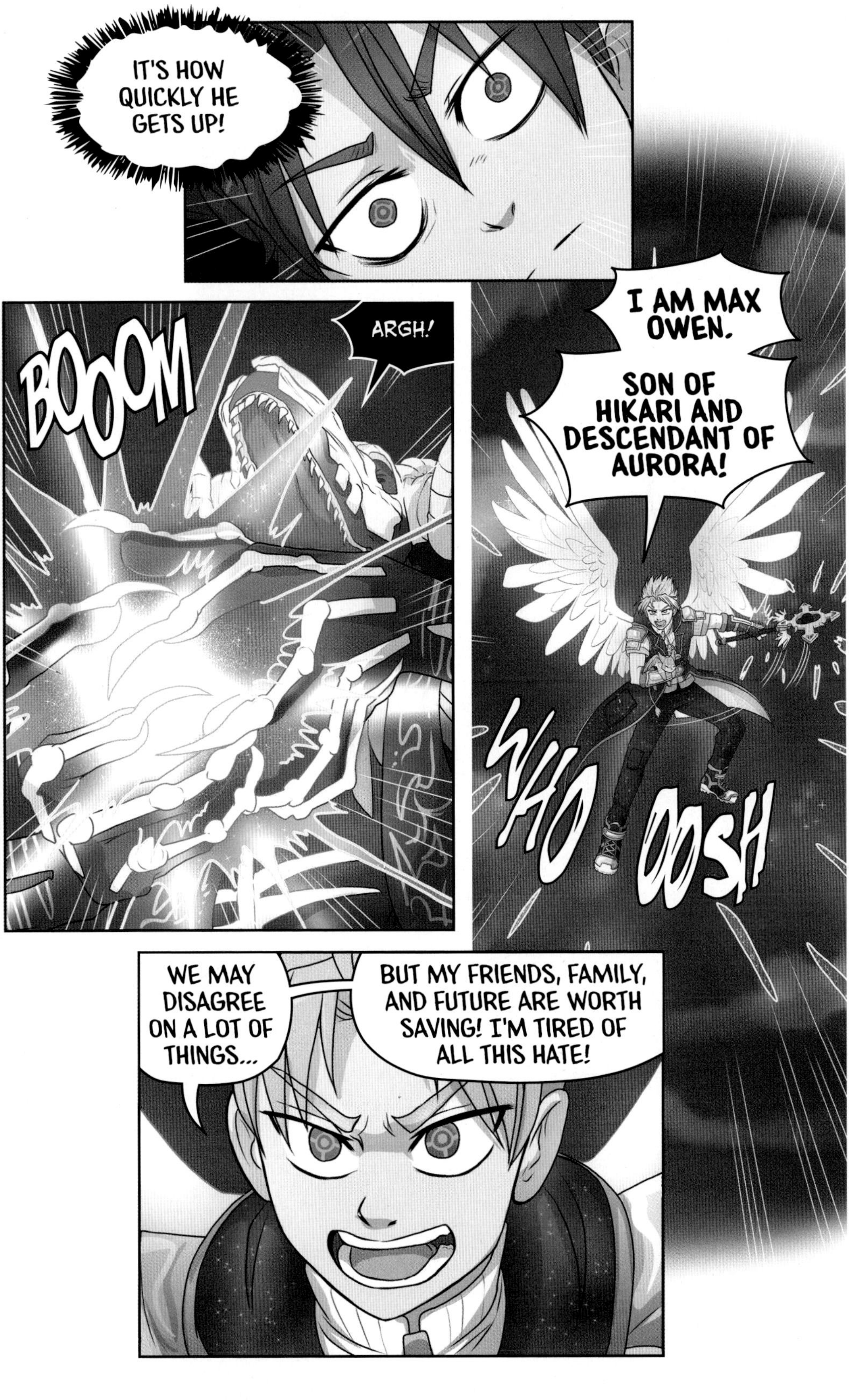
IT'S HOW QUICKLY HE GETS UP!
BOOOM
ARGH!
I AM MAX OWEN.
SON OF HIKARI AND DESCENDANT OF AURORA!
WHOOOSH
WE MAY DISAGREE ON A LOT OF THINGS...
BUT MY FRIENDS, FAMILY, AND FUTURE ARE WORTH SAVING! I'M TIRED OF ALL THIS HATE!

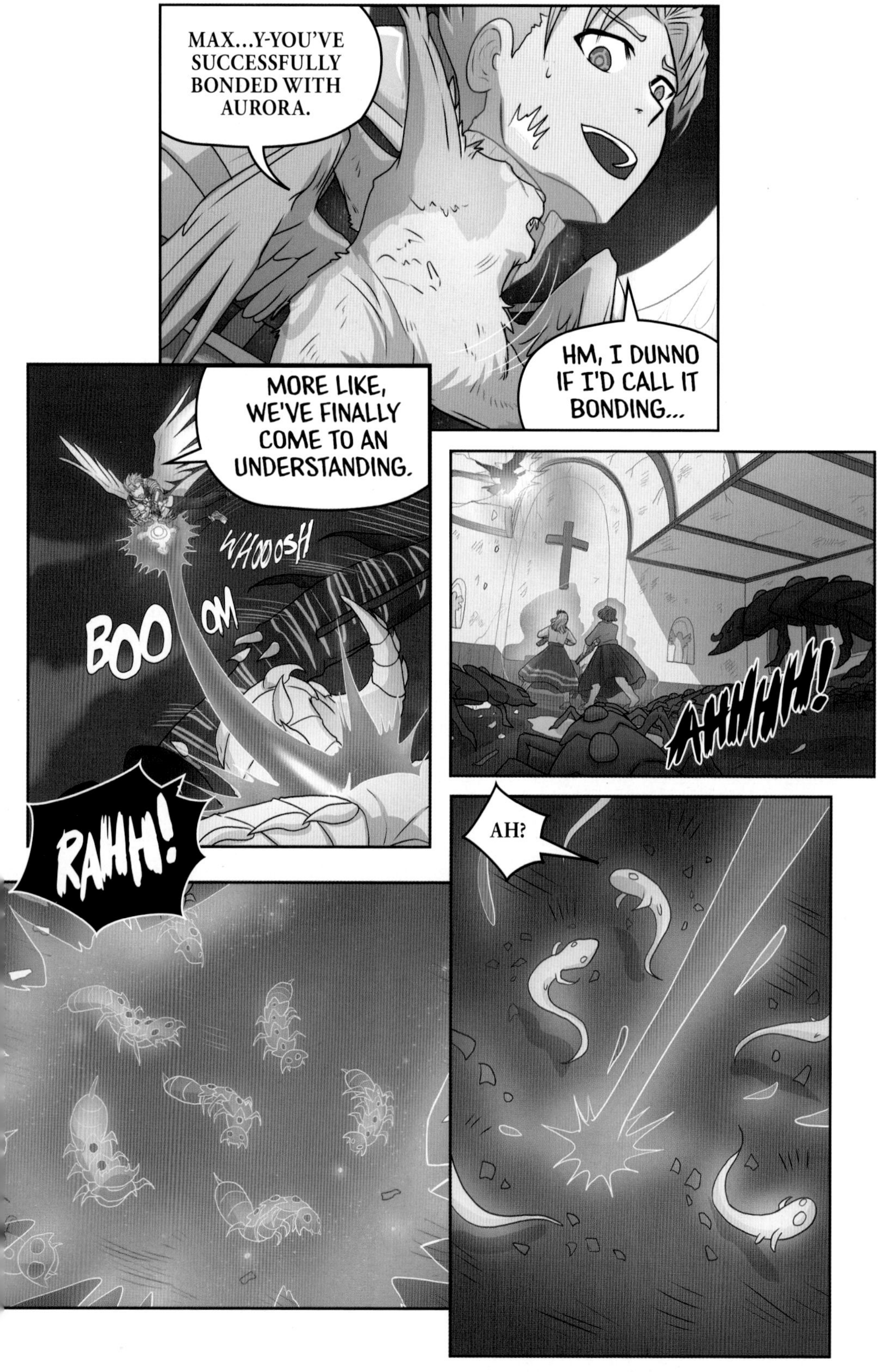
MAX...Y-YOU'VE SUCCESSFULLY BONDED WITH AURORA.
HM, I DUNNO IF I'D CALL IT BONDING...
MORE LIKE, WE'VE FINALLY COME TO AN UNDERSTANDING.
WHOOOSH
BOOOM
AHHHHH!
RAHH!
AH?

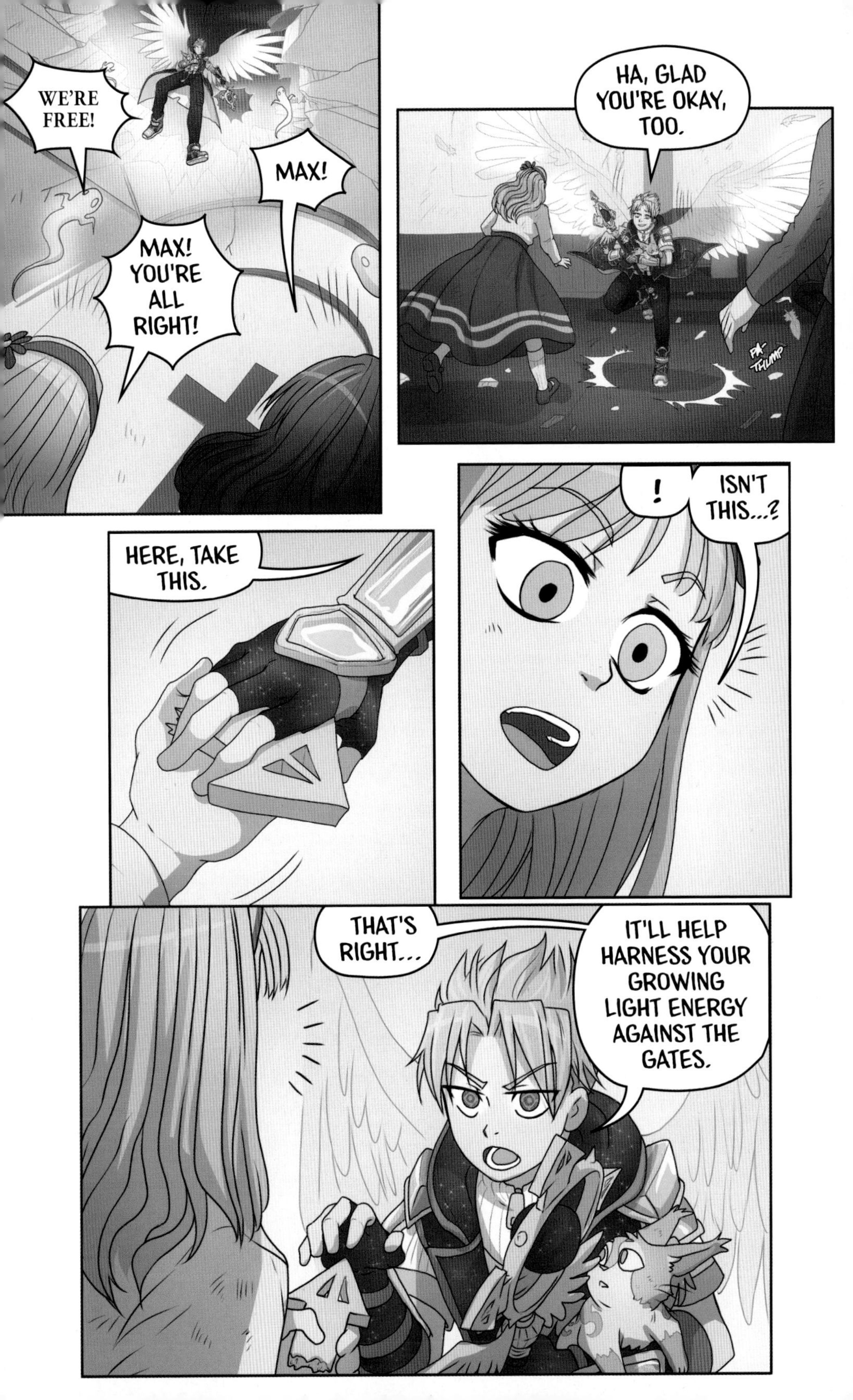
WE'RE FREE!
MAX!
MAX! YOU'RE ALL RIGHT!
HA, GLAD YOU'RE OKAY, TOO.
PA-THUMP
HERE, TAKE THIS.
!
ISN'T THIS...?
THAT'S RIGHT...
IT'LL HELP HARNESS YOUR GROWING LIGHT ENERGY AGAINST THE GATES.

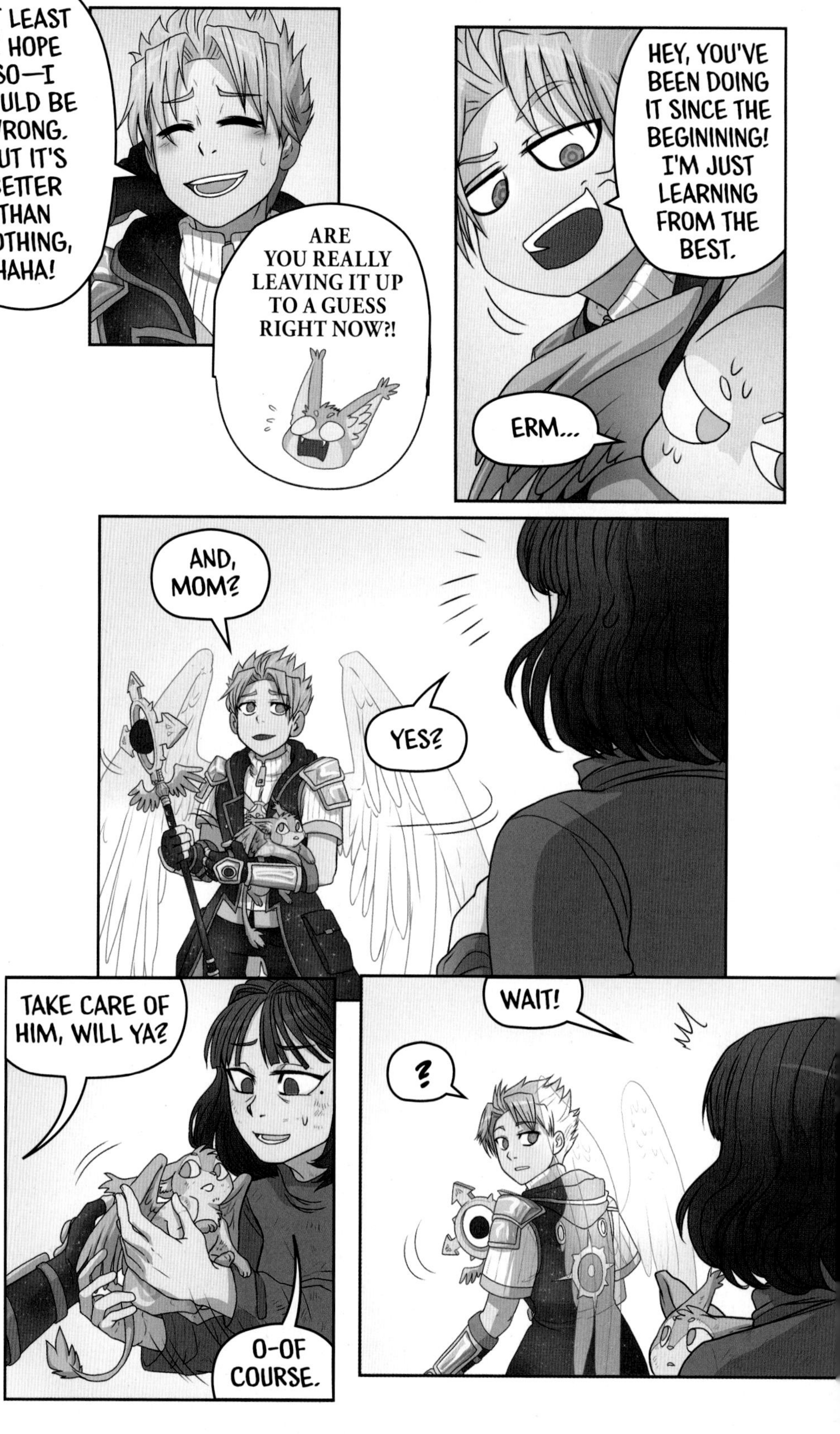
AT LEAST I HOPE SO—I COULD BE WRONG. BUT IT'S BETTER THAN NOTHING, HAHA!
ARE YOU REALLY LEAVING IT UP TO A GUESS RIGHT NOW?!
HEY, YOU'VE BEEN DOING IT SINCE THE BEGININING! I'M JUST LEARNING FROM THE BEST.
ERM...
AND, MOM?
YES?
TAKE CARE OF HIM, WILL YA?
O-OF COURSE.
WAIT!
?

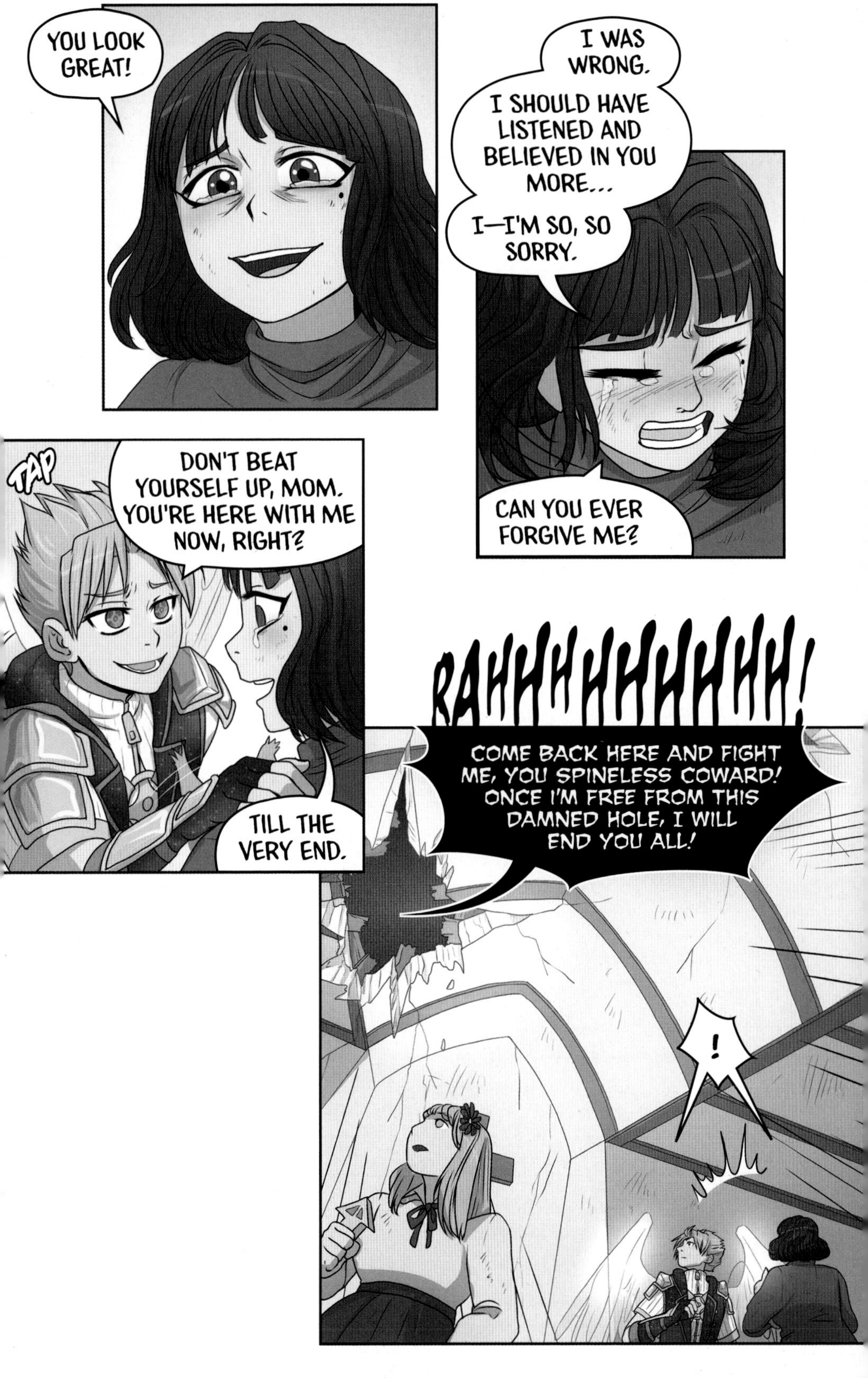
YOU LOOK GREAT!
I WAS WRONG.
I SHOULD HAVE LISTENED AND BELIEVED IN YOU MORE...
I—I'M SO, SO SORRY.
CAN YOU EVER FORGIVE ME?
TAP
DON'T BEAT YOURSELF UP, MOM. YOU'RE HERE WITH ME NOW, RIGHT?
TILL THE VERY END.
RAHHHHHHHHHH!
COME BACK HERE AND FIGHT ME, YOU SPINELESS COWARD! ONCE I'M FREE FROM THIS DAMNED HOLE, I WILL END YOU ALL!
!

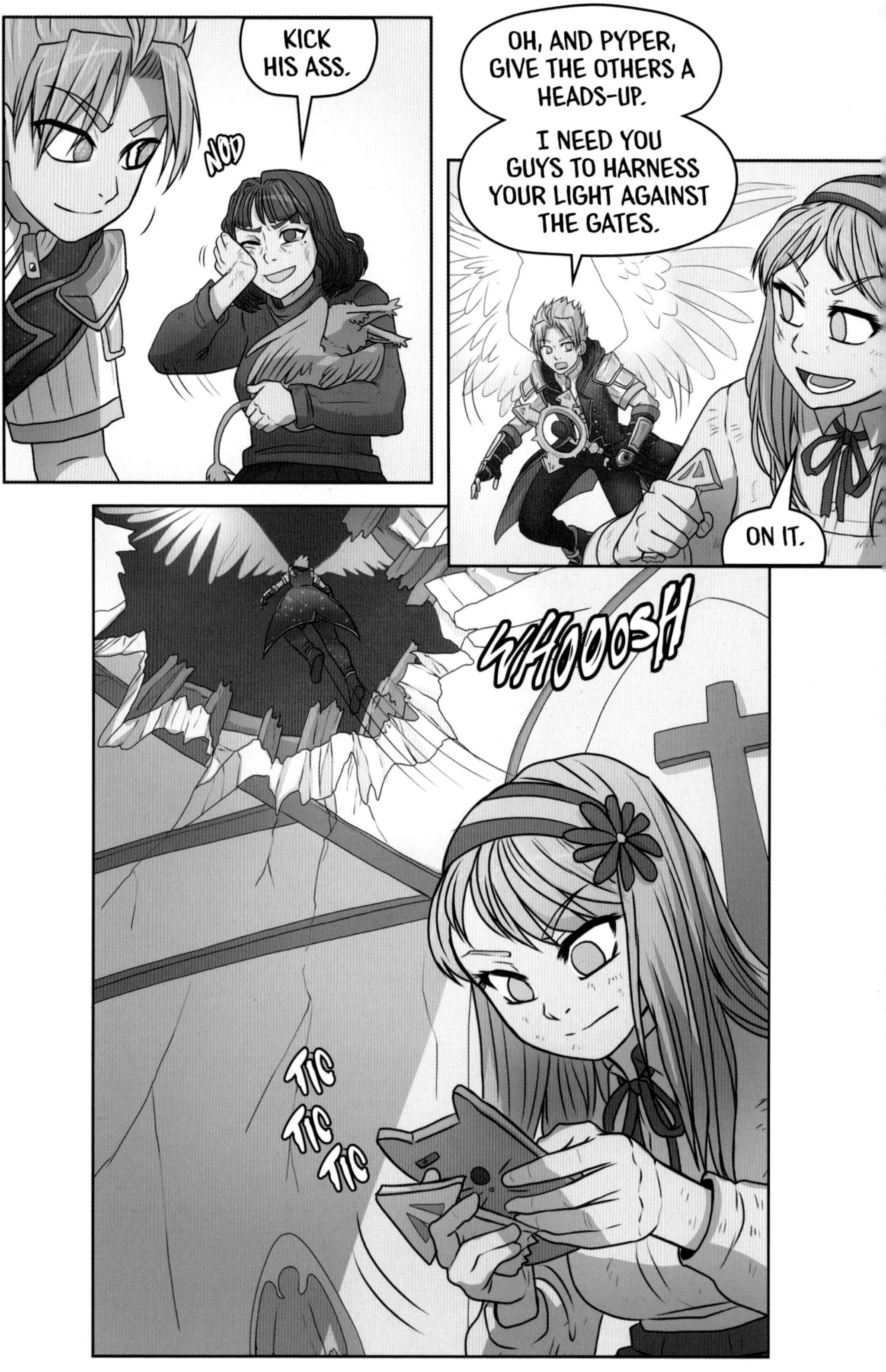
KICK HIS ASS.
NOD
OH, AND PYPER, GIVE THE OTHERS A HEADS-UP.
I NEED YOU GUYS TO HARNESS YOUR LIGHT AGAINST THE GATES.
ON IT.
WHOOOOSH
TIC
TIC
TIC

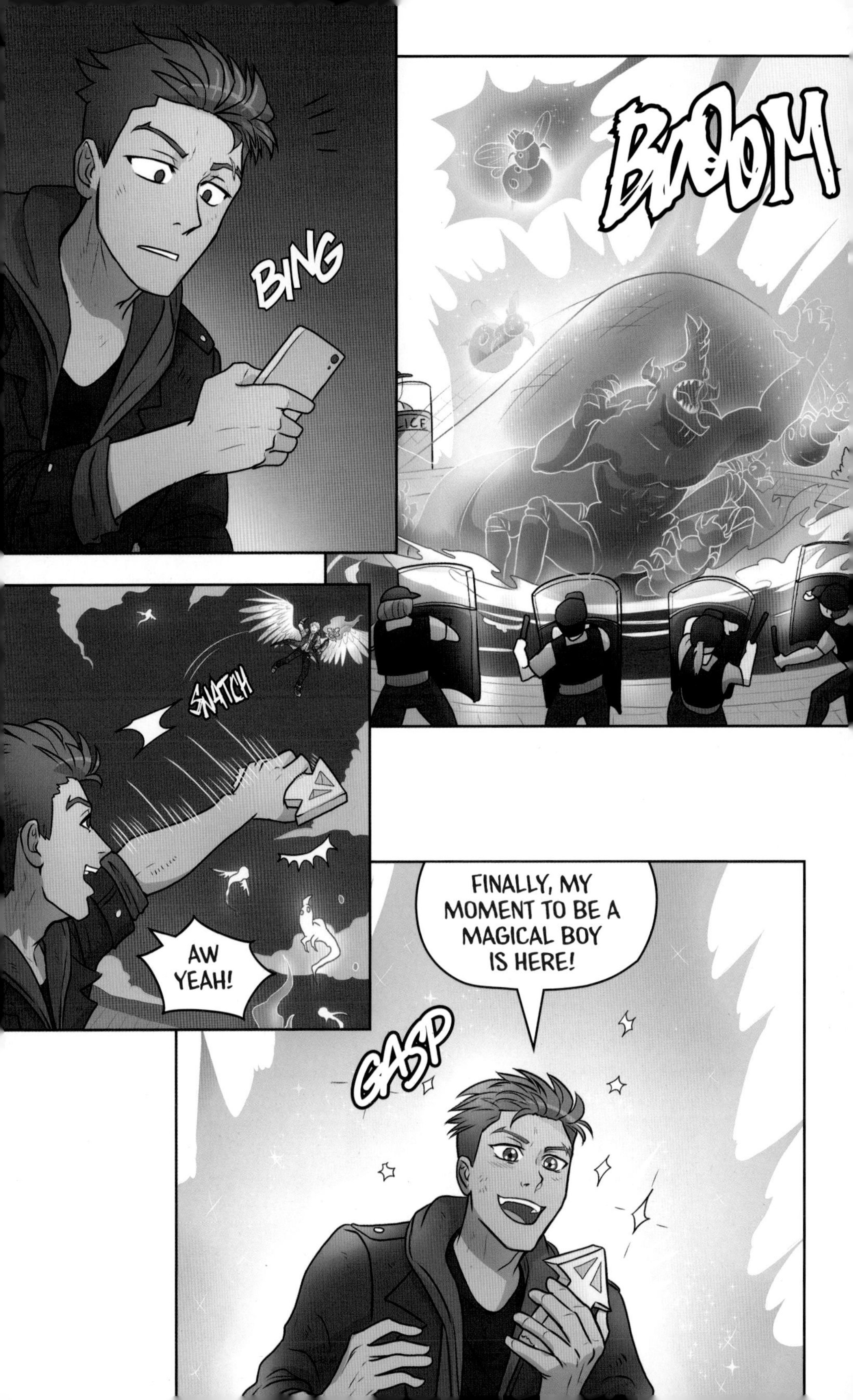
BING
BOOM
SNATCH
AW YEAH!
GASP
FINALLY, MY MOMENT TO BE A MAGICAL BOY IS HERE!

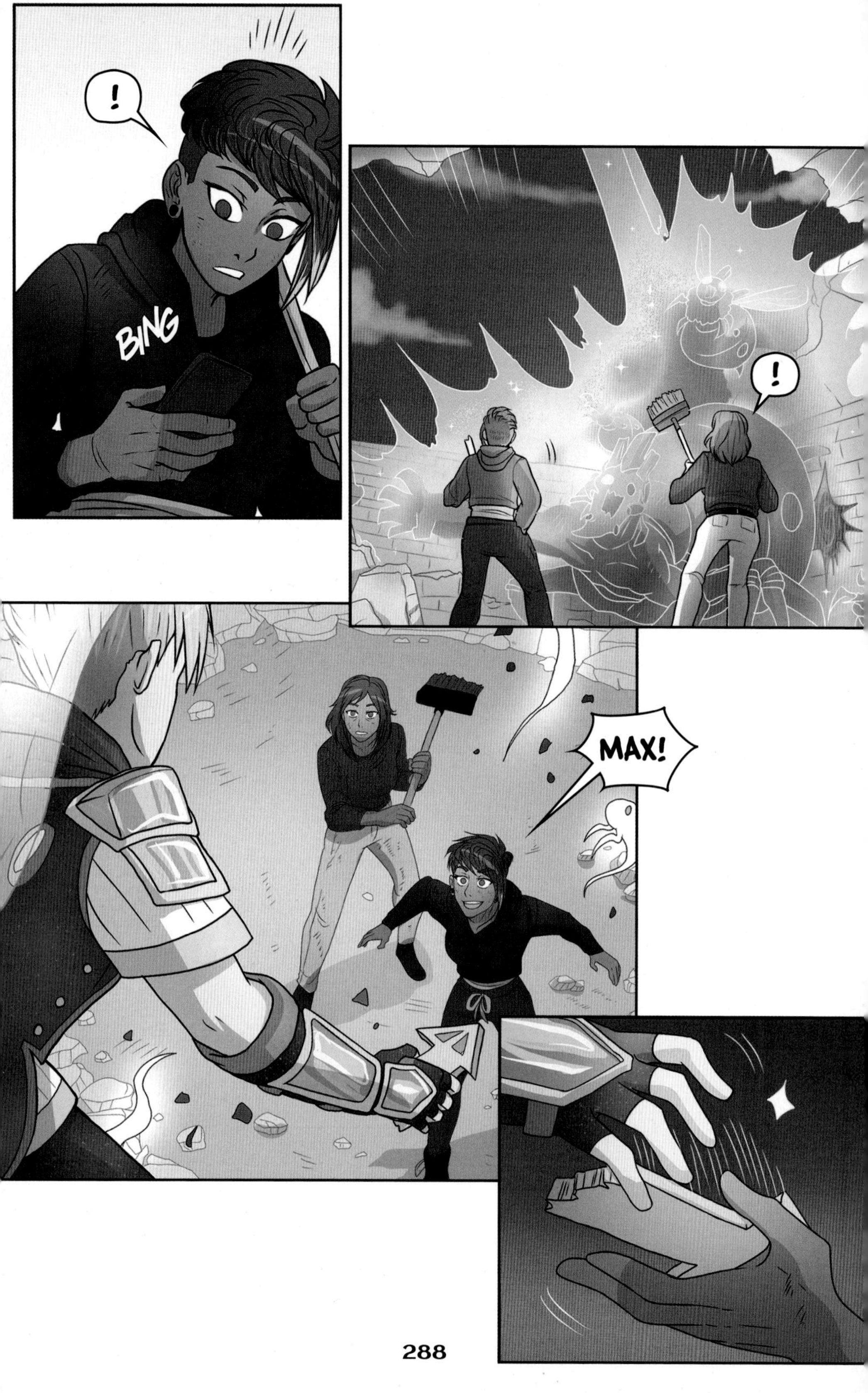
!
BING
!
MAX!

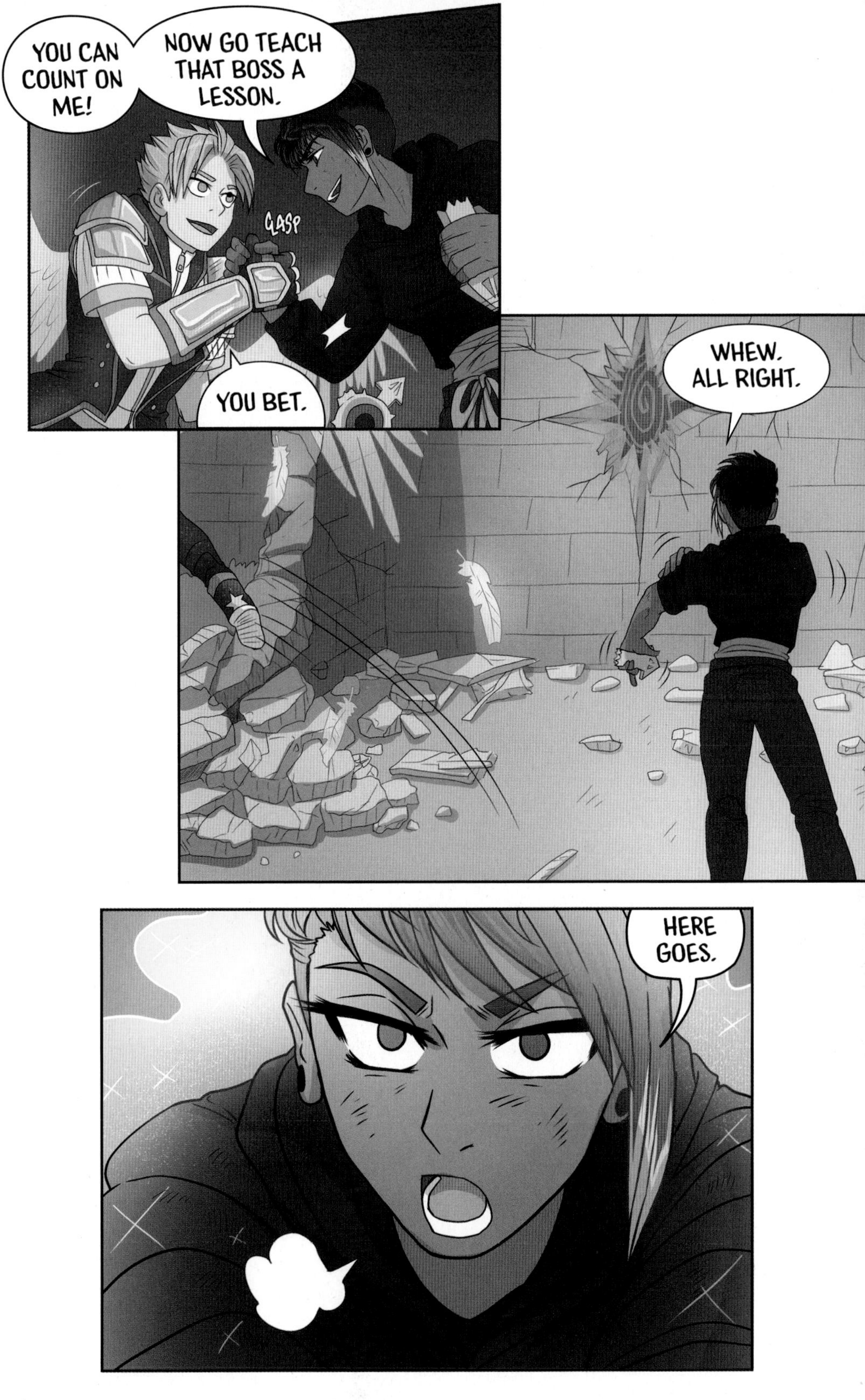
YOU CAN COUNT ON ME!
NOW GO TEACH THAT BOSS A LESSON.
CLASP
YOU BET.
WHEW. ALL RIGHT.
HERE GOES.

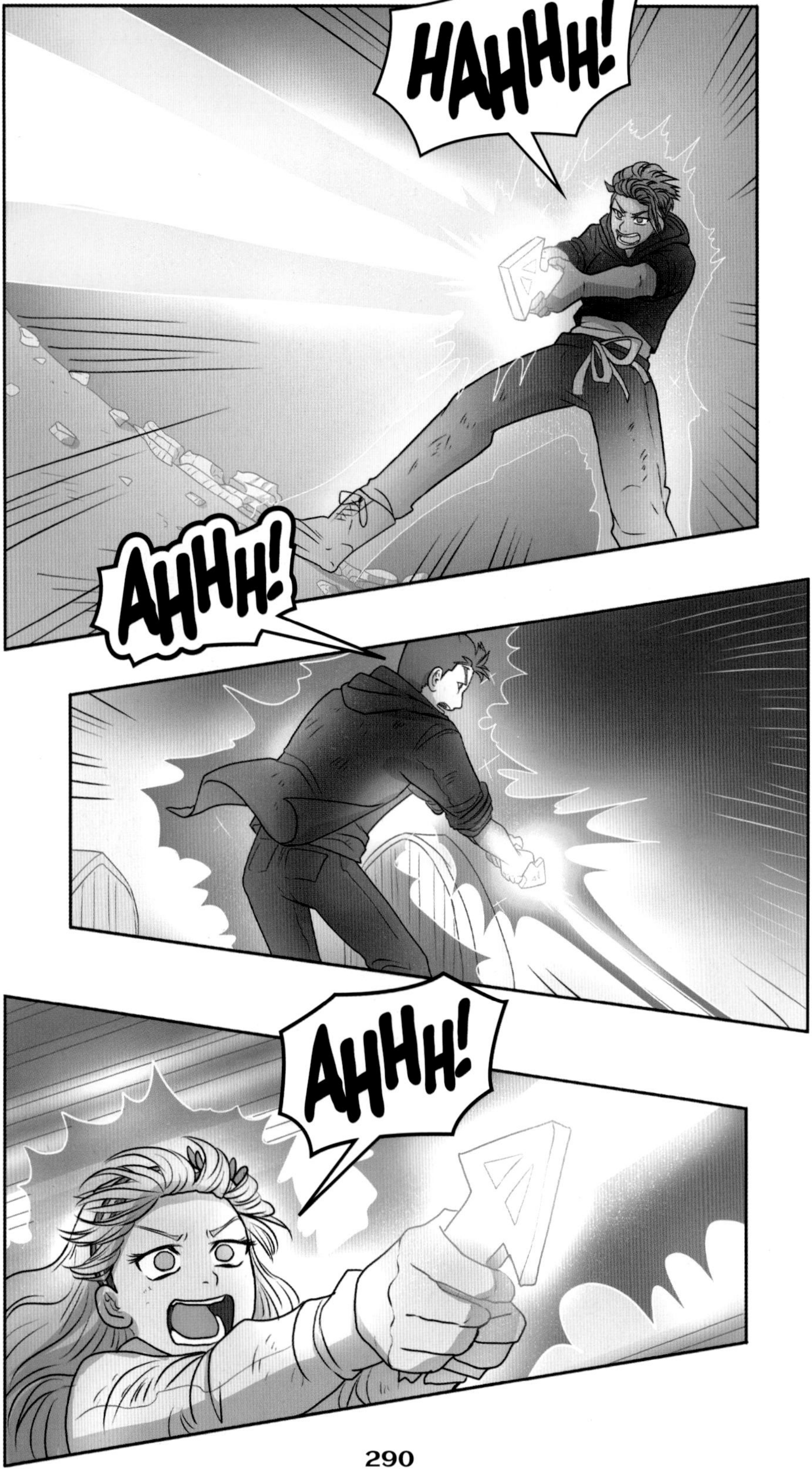
HAHHH!
AHHH!
AHHH!

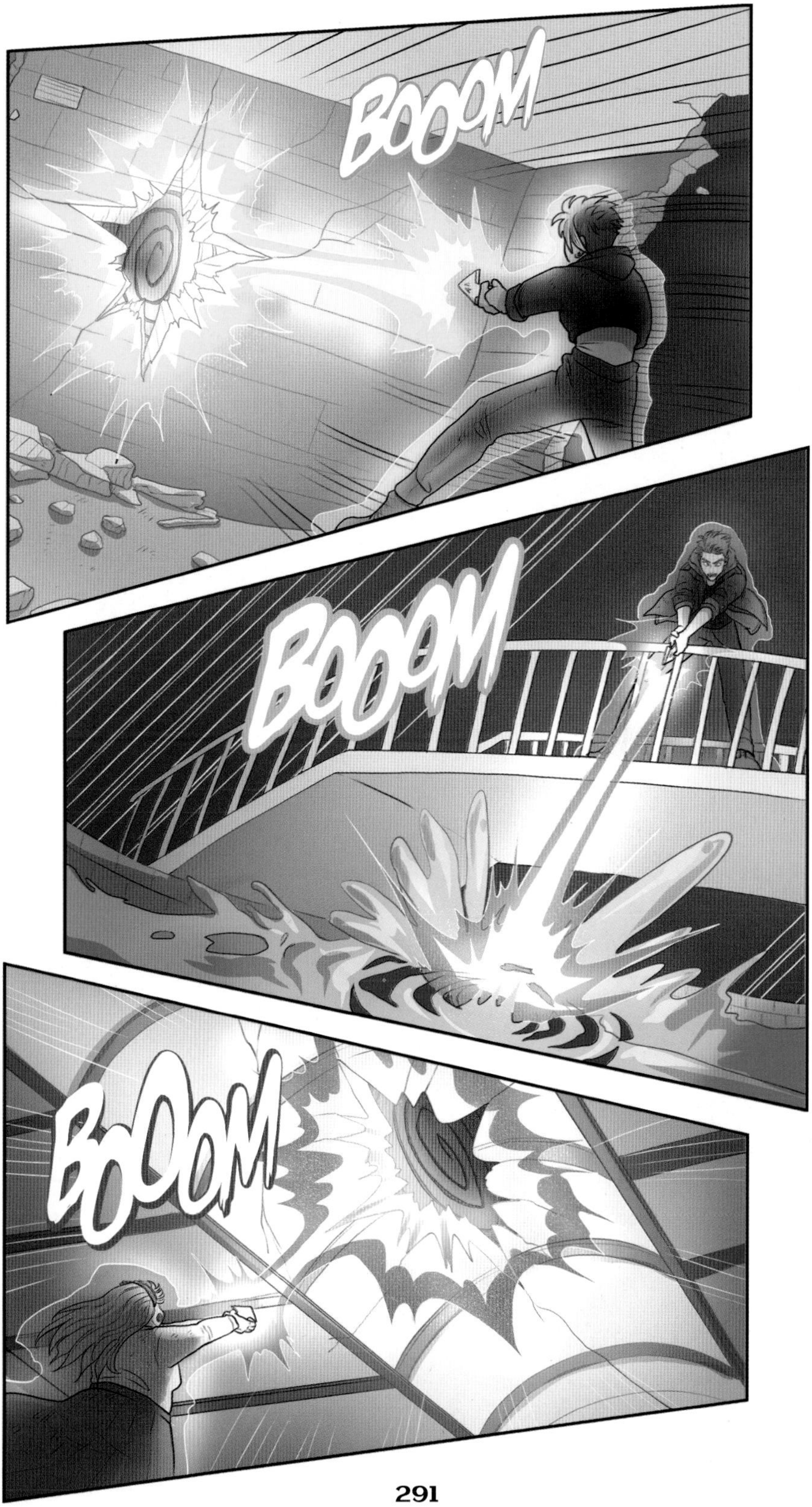
BOOOM
BOOOM
BOOOM

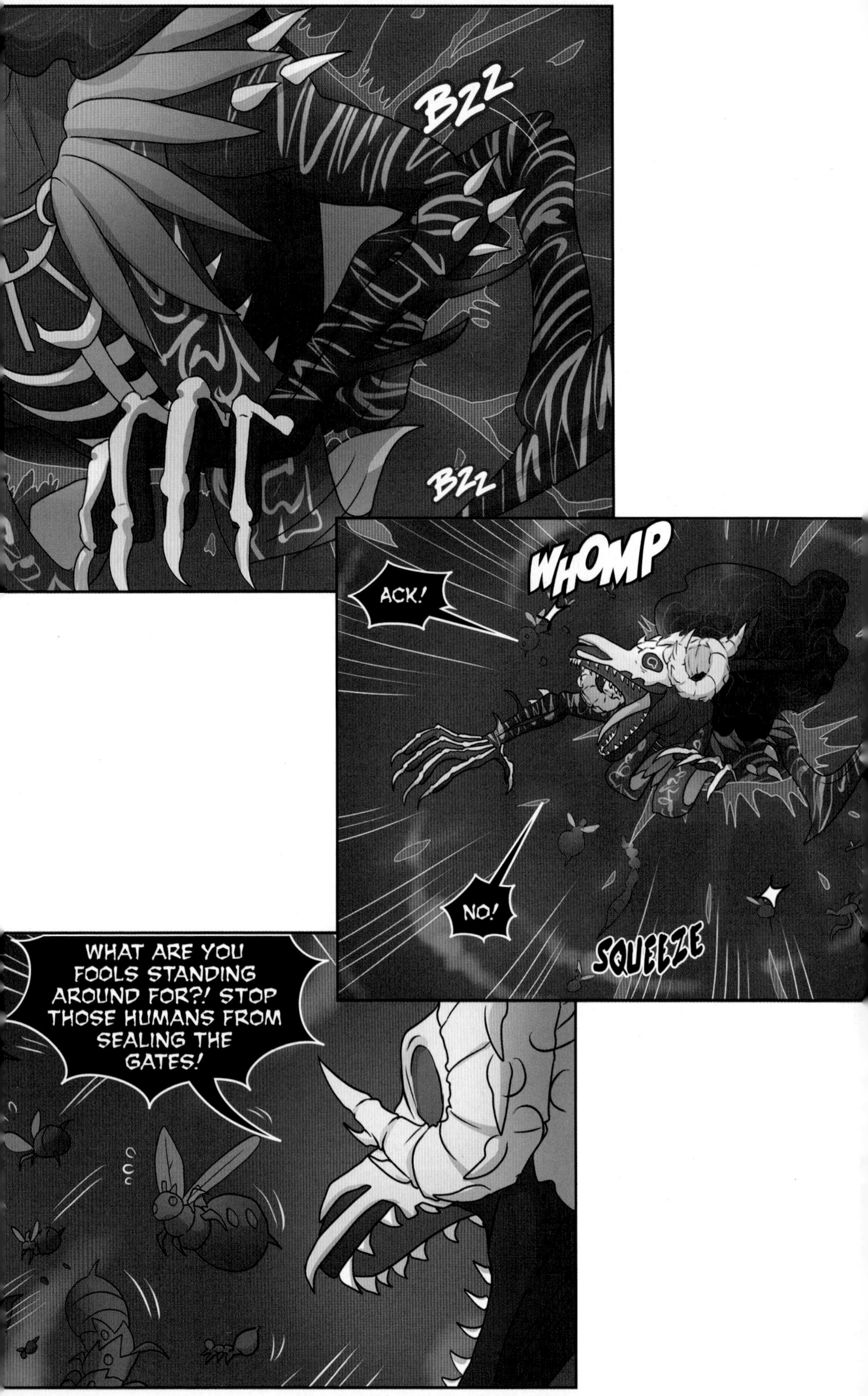
BZZ
BZZ
WHOMP
ACK!
NO!
SQUEEZE
WHAT ARE YOU FOOLS STANDING AROUND FOR?! STOP THOSE HUMANS FROM SEALING THE GATES!

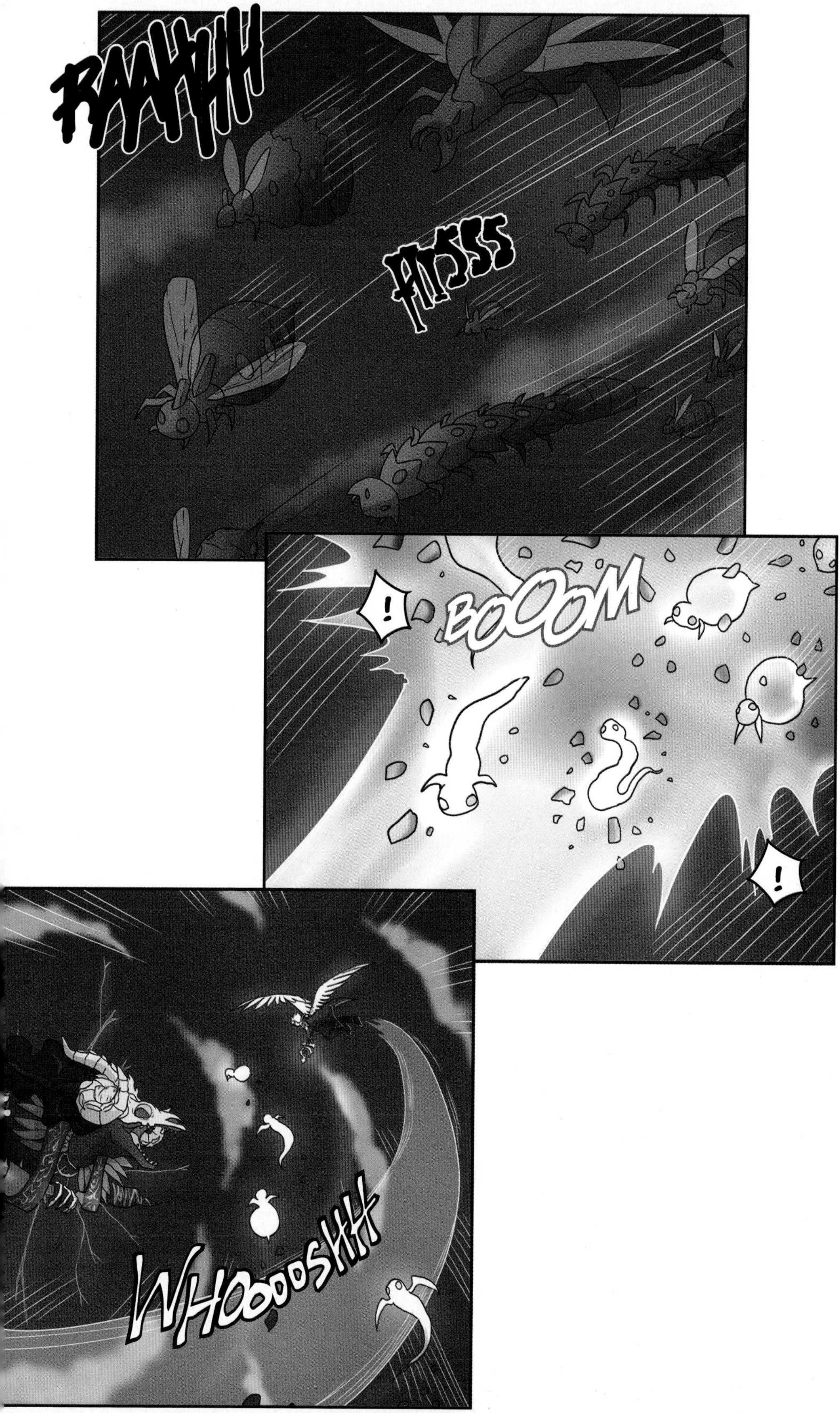
RAAHHH
HISSS
BOOOOM
!
!
WHOooosHH

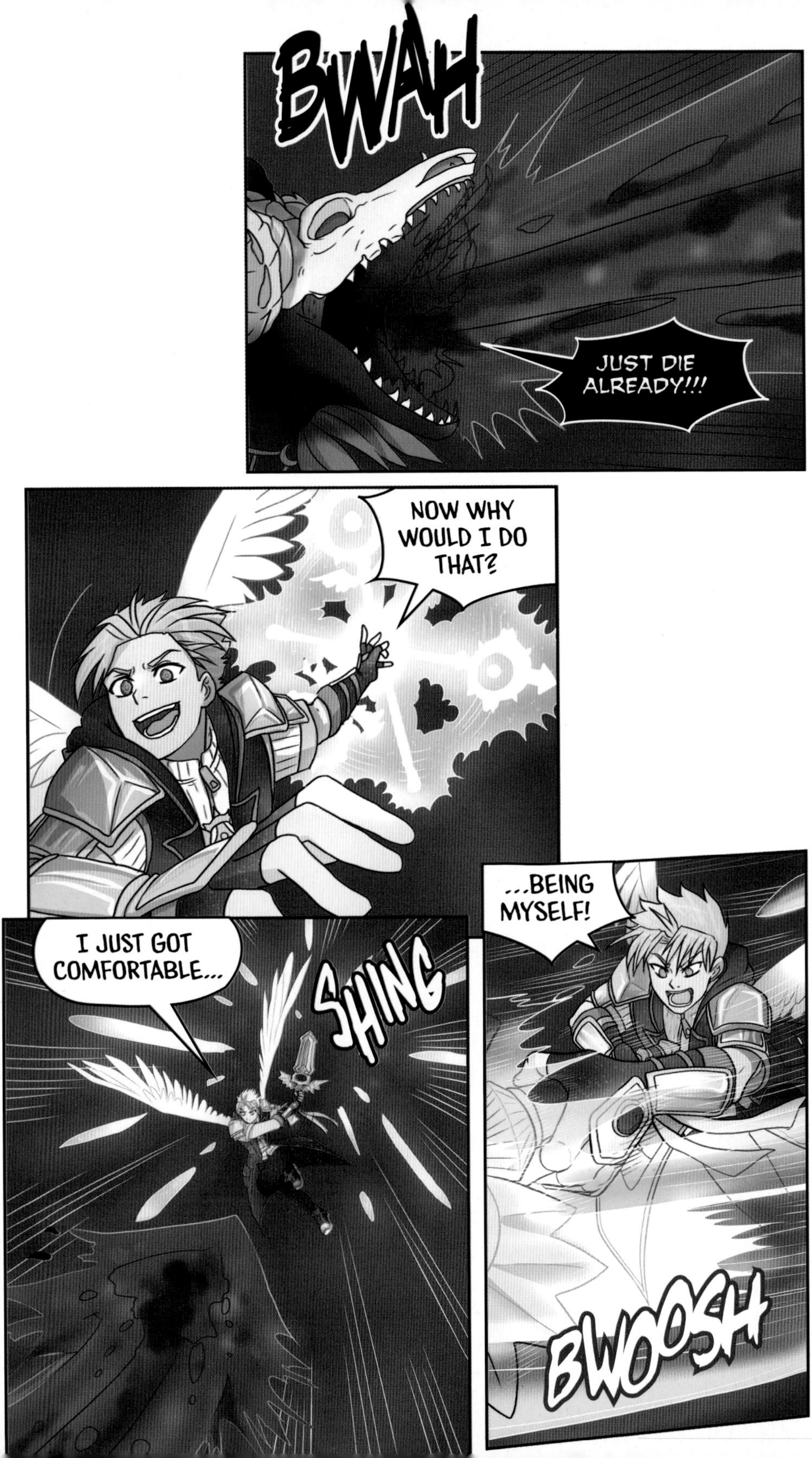
BWAH
JUST DIE ALREADY!!!
NOW WHY WOULD I DO THAT?
I JUST GOT COMFORTABLE...
SHING
...BEING MYSELF!
BWOOSH

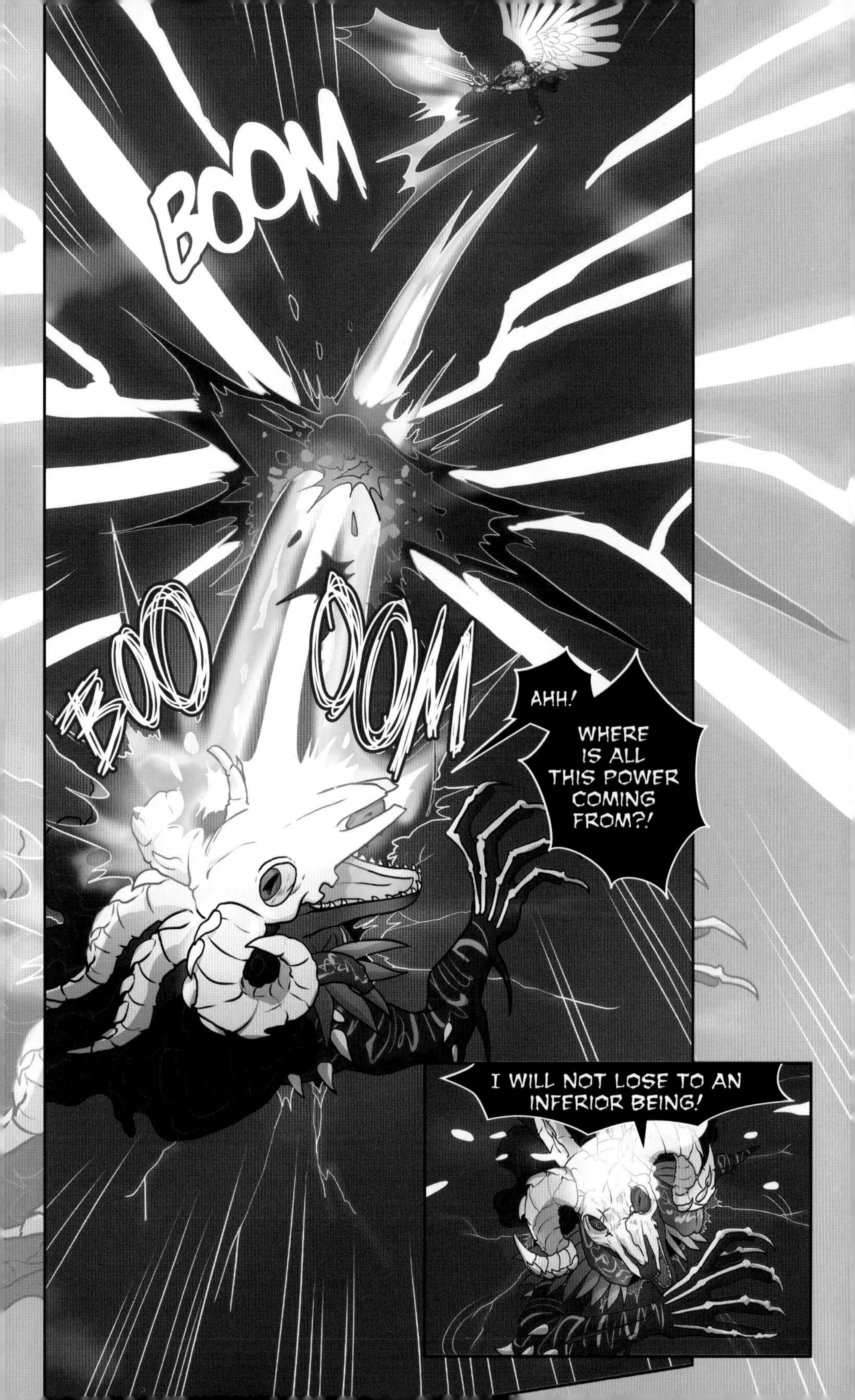
BOOM
BOOOOM
AHH!
WHERE IS ALL THIS POWER COMING FROM?!
I WILL NOT LOSE TO AN INFERIOR BEING!

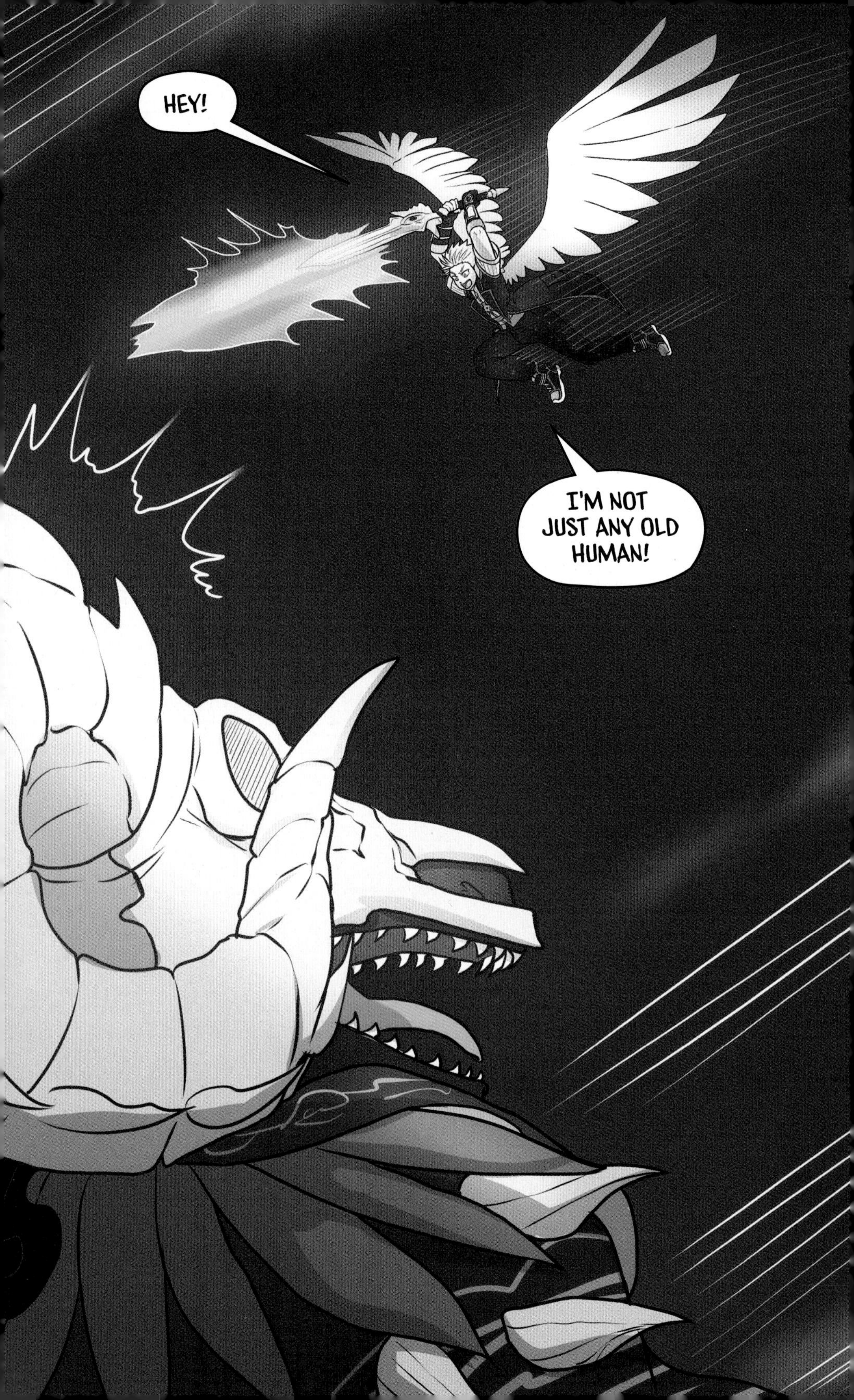
HEY!
I'M NOT JUST ANY OLD HUMAN!

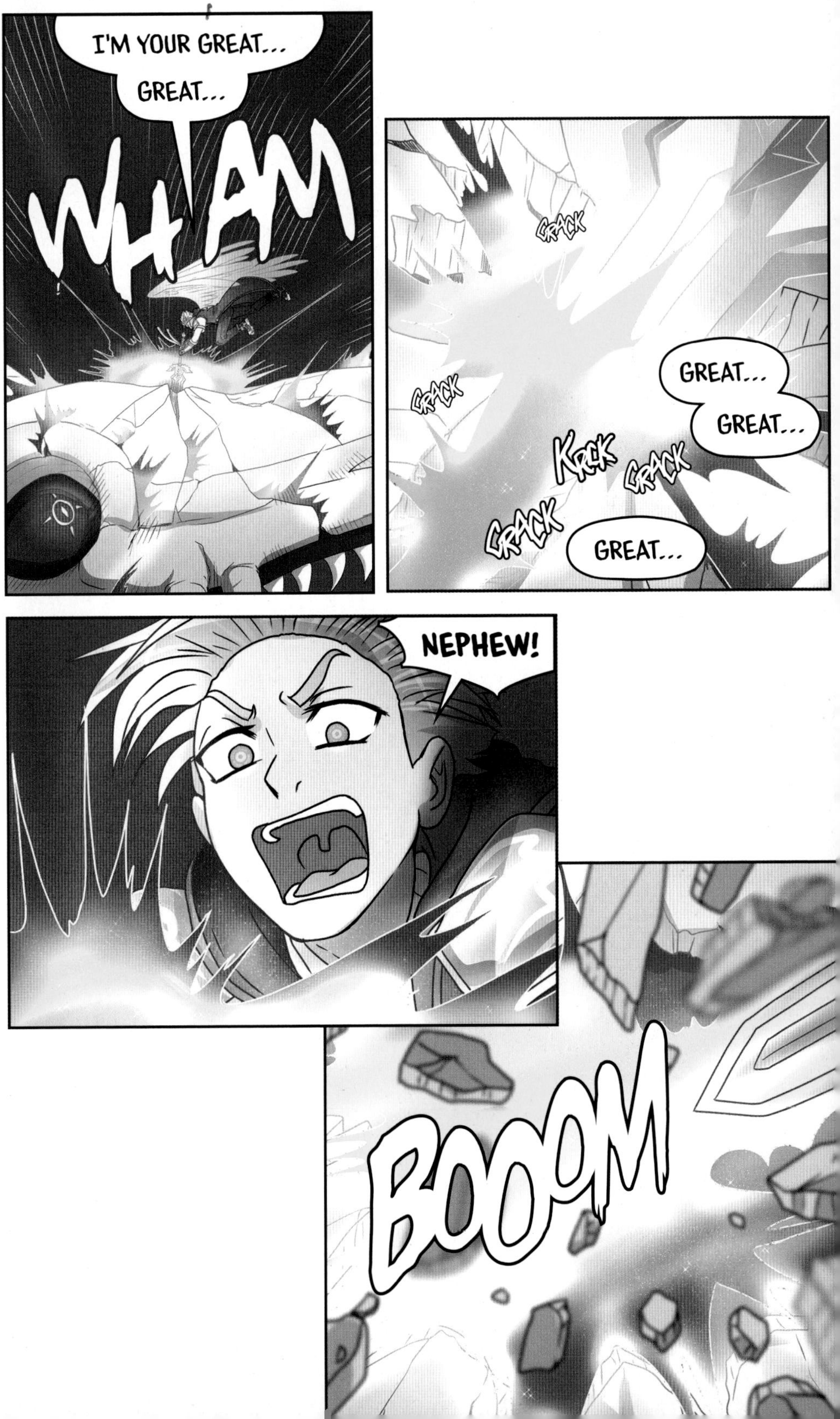
I'M YOUR GREAT... GREAT...
WHAM
CRACK
CRACK
GREAT...
GREAT...
KRCK
CRACK
CRACK
GREAT...
NEPHEW!
BOOOM

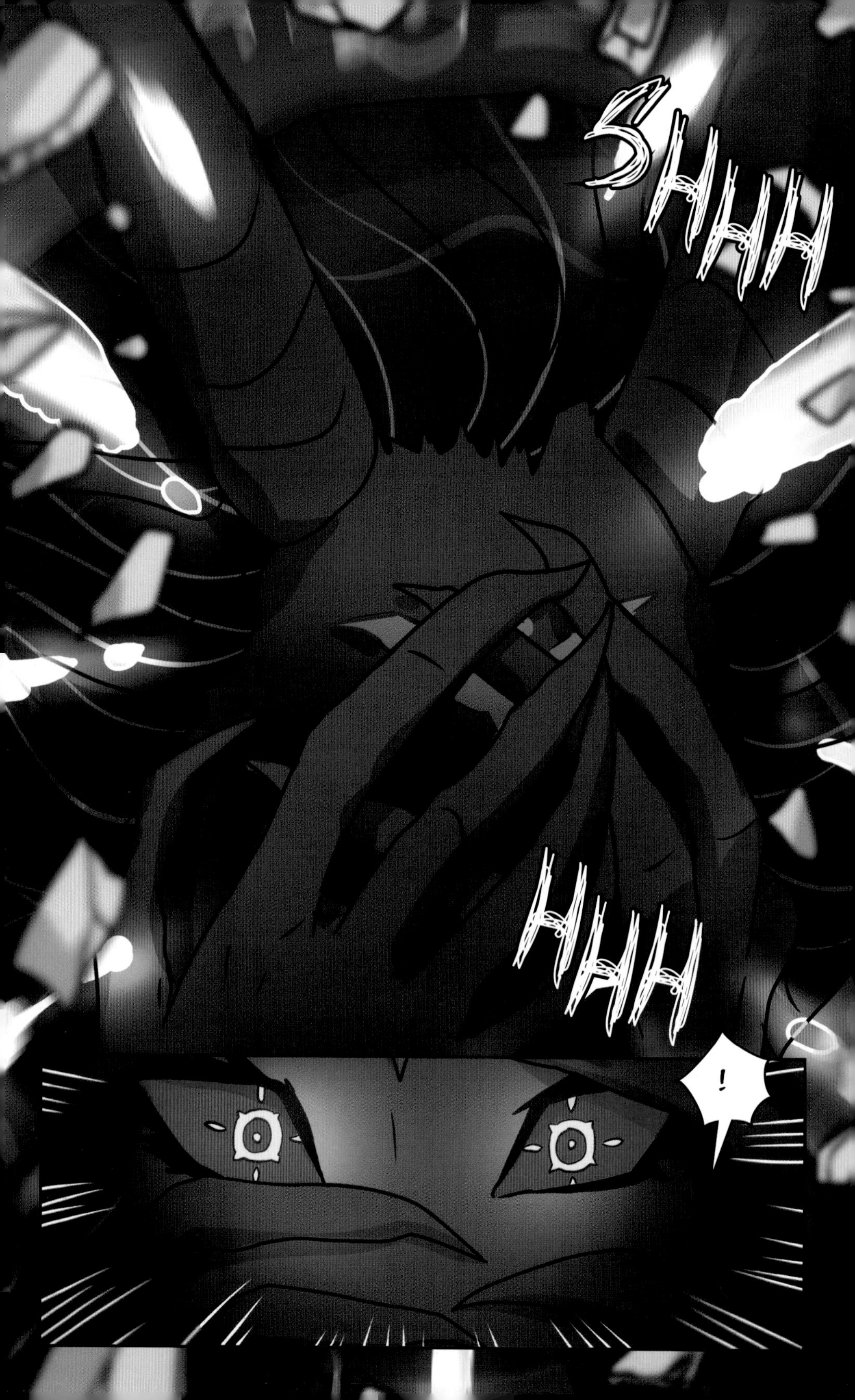
SHHHH
HHHH
!

EPISODE 29:

I AM MAGICAL BOY

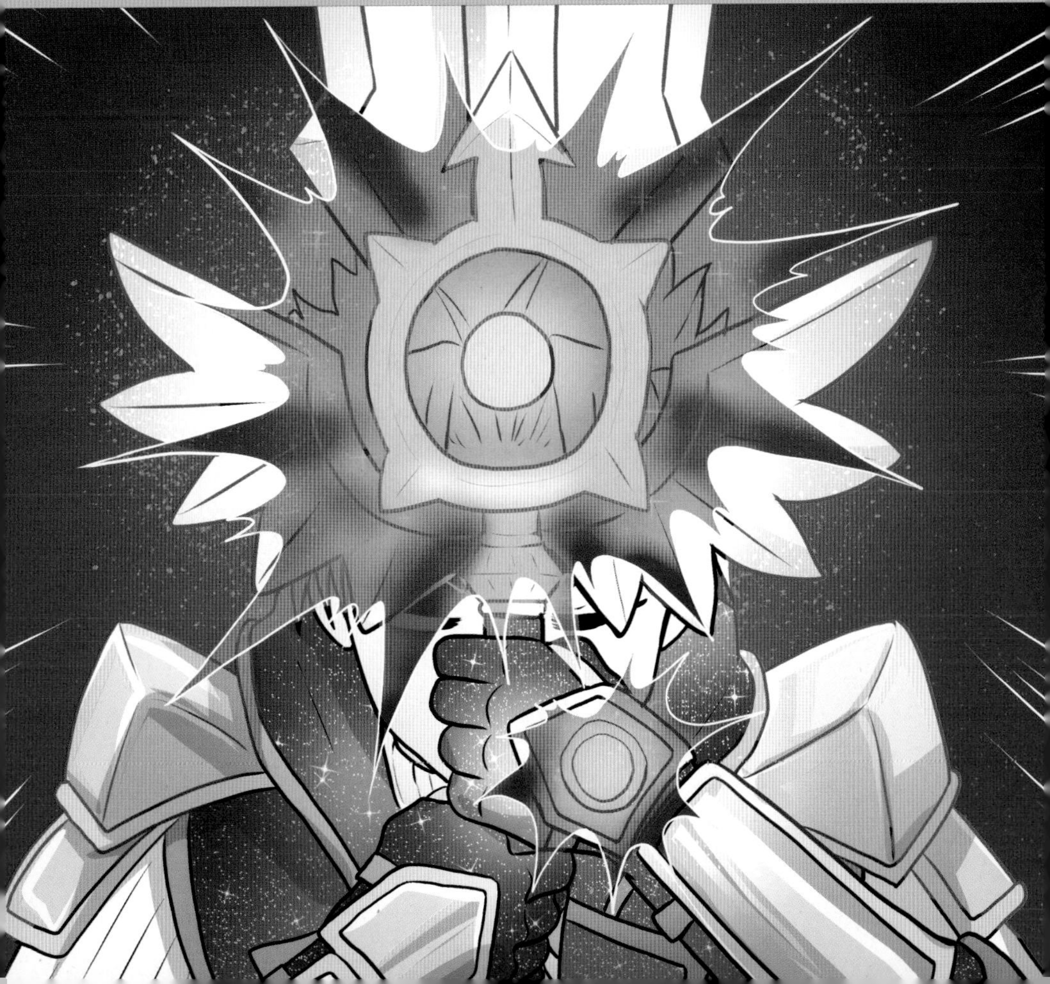

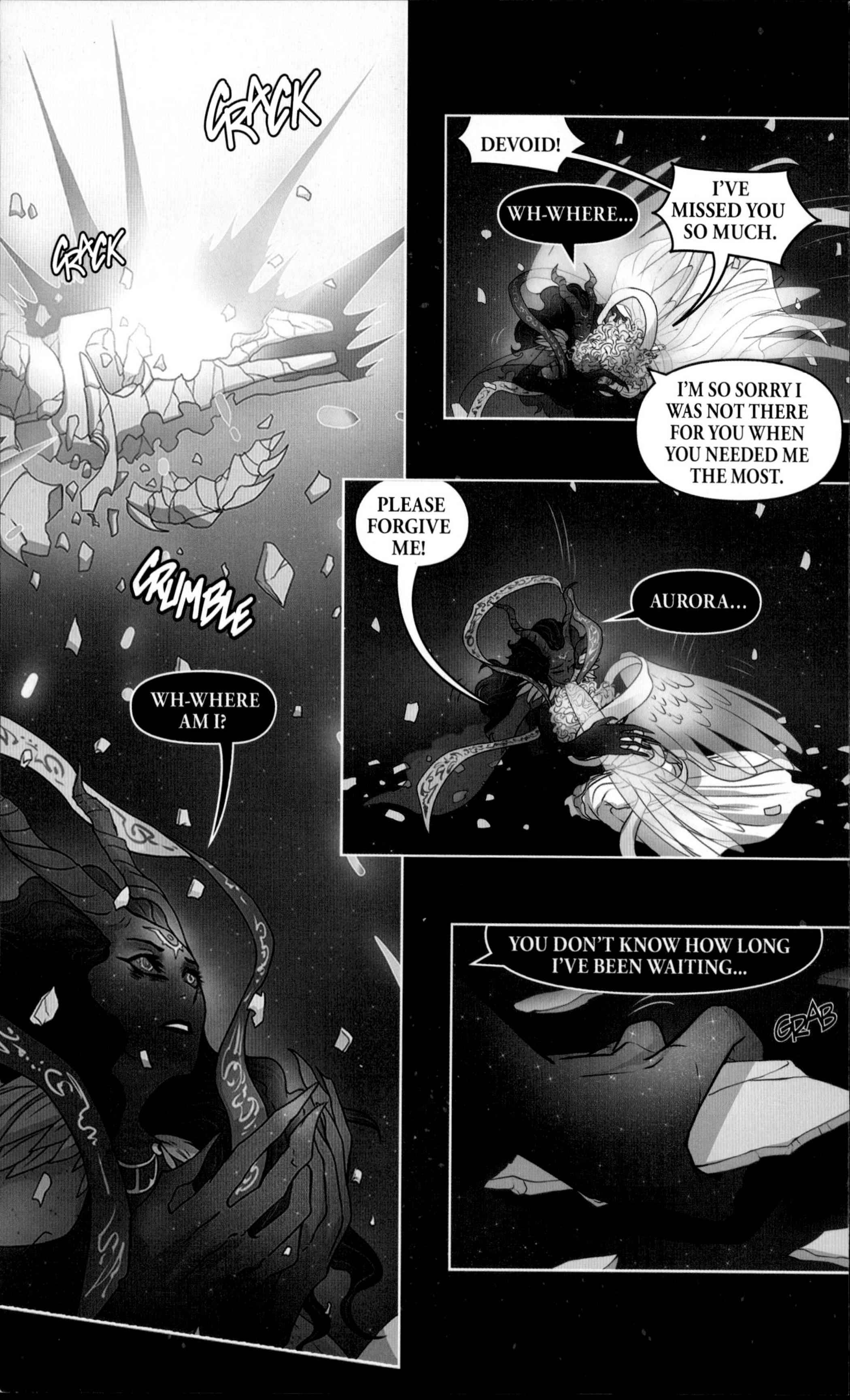
CRACK
CRACK
CRUMBLE
WH-WHERE AM I?
DEVOID!
WH-WHERE...
I'VE MISSED YOU SO MUCH.
I'M SO SORRY I WAS NOT THERE FOR YOU WHEN YOU NEEDED ME THE MOST.
PLEASE FORGIVE ME!
AURORA...
YOU DON'T KNOW HOW LONG I'VE BEEN WAITING...
GRAB

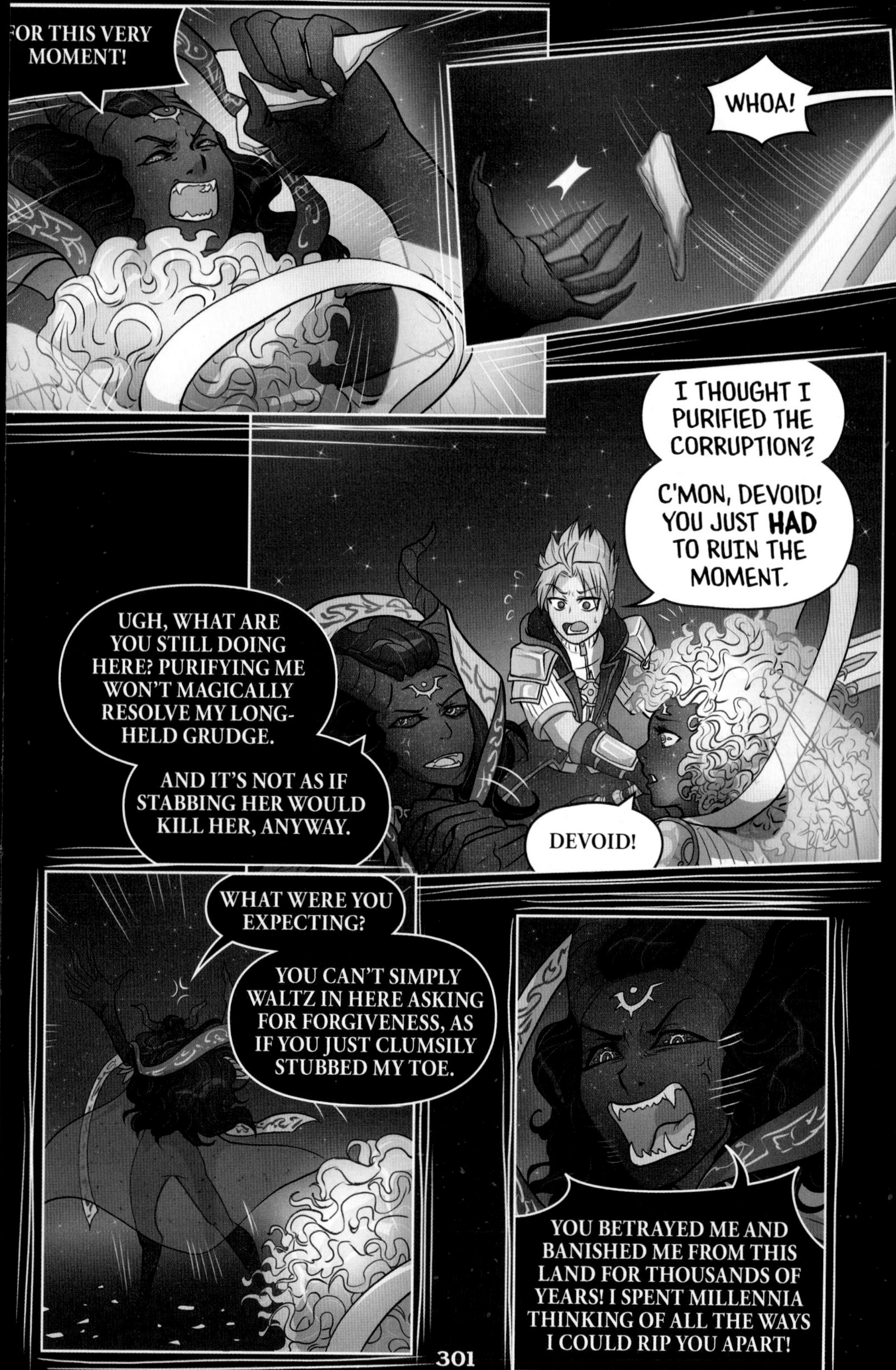
FOR THIS VERY MOMENT!
WHOA!
I THOUGHT I PURIFIED THE CORRUPTION?
C'MON, DEVOID! YOU JUST **HAD** TO RUIN THE MOMENT.
UGH, WHAT ARE YOU STILL DOING HERE? PURIFYING ME WON'T MAGICALLY RESOLVE MY LONG-HELD GRUDGE.
AND IT'S NOT AS IF STABBING HER WOULD KILL HER, ANYWAY.
DEVOID!
WHAT WERE YOU EXPECTING?
YOU CAN'T SIMPLY WALTZ IN HERE ASKING FOR FORGIVENESS, AS IF YOU JUST CLUMSILY STUBBED MY TOE.
YOU BETRAYED ME AND BANISHED ME FROM THIS LAND FOR THOUSANDS OF YEARS! I SPENT MILLENNIA THINKING OF ALL THE WAYS I COULD RIP YOU APART!

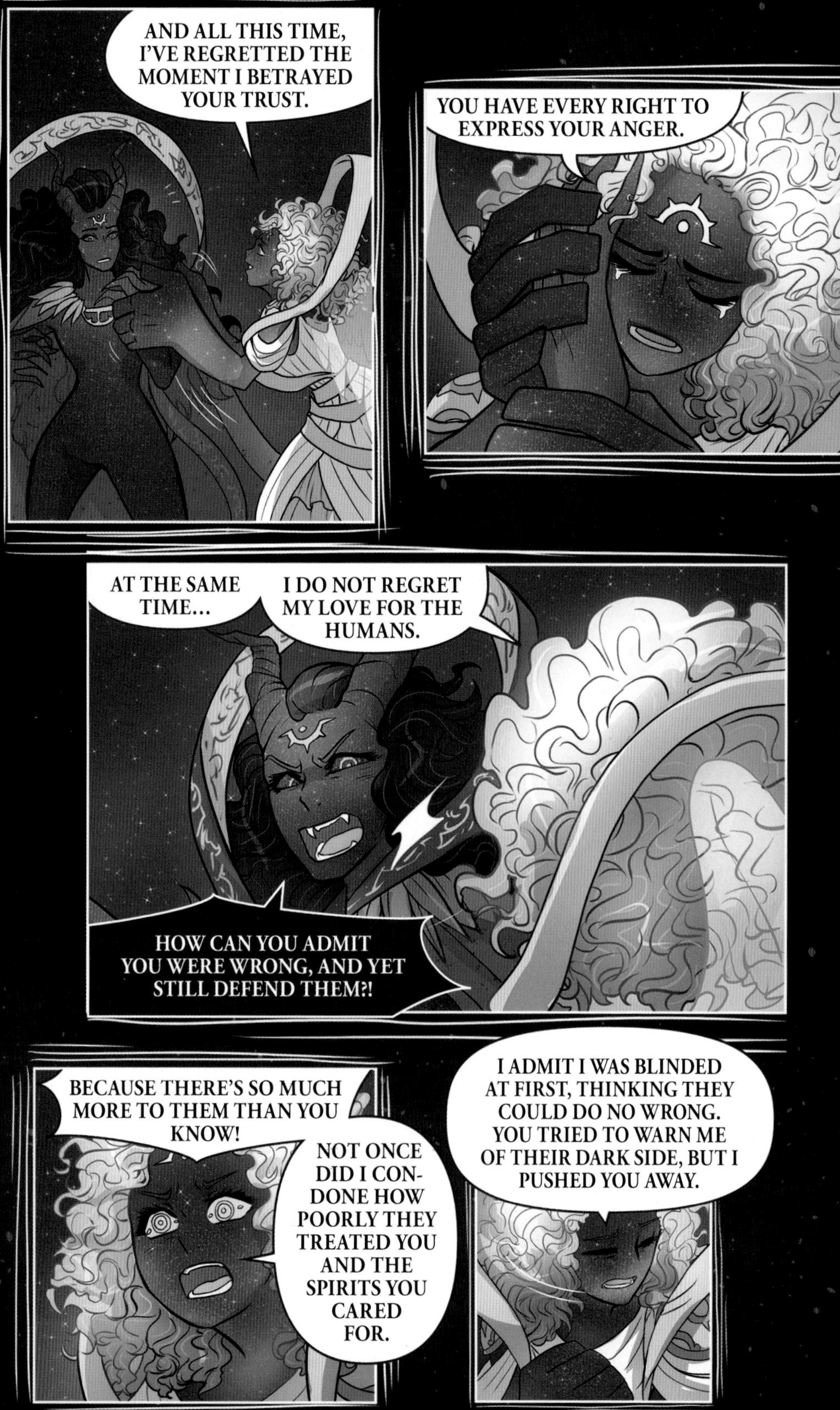
AND ALL THIS TIME, I'VE REGRETTED THE MOMENT I BETRAYED YOUR TRUST.
YOU HAVE EVERY RIGHT TO EXPRESS YOUR ANGER.
AT THE SAME TIME...
I DO NOT REGRET MY LOVE FOR THE HUMANS.
HOW CAN YOU ADMIT YOU WERE WRONG, AND YET STILL DEFEND THEM?!
BECAUSE THERE'S SO MUCH MORE TO THEM THAN YOU KNOW!
NOT ONCE DID I CON-DONE HOW POORLY THEY TREATED YOU AND THE SPIRITS YOU CARED FOR.
I ADMIT I WAS BLINDED AT FIRST, THINKING THEY COULD DO NO WRONG. YOU TRIED TO WARN ME OF THEIR DARK SIDE, BUT I PUSHED YOU AWAY.

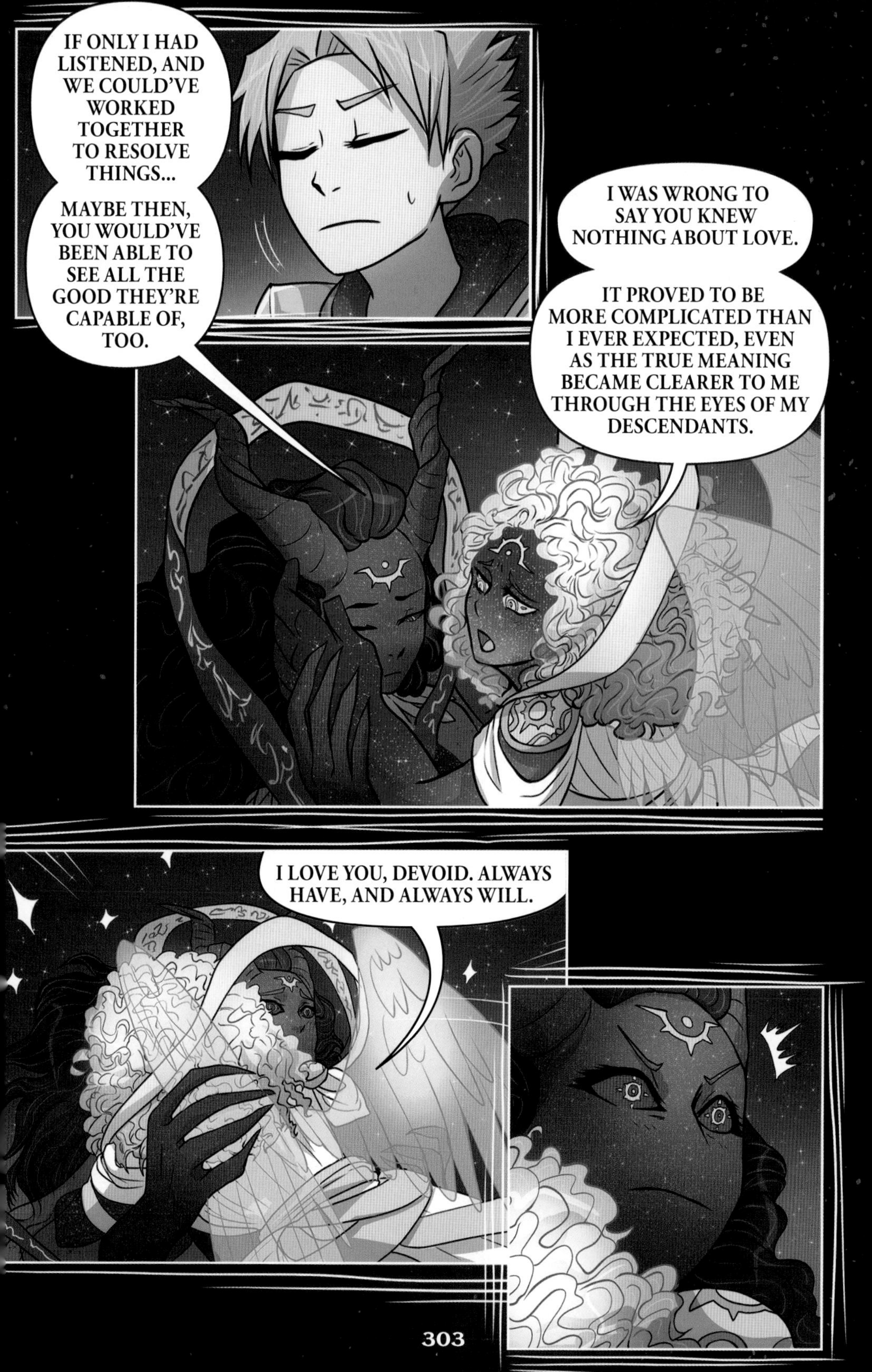
IF ONLY I HAD LISTENED, AND WE COULD'VE WORKED TOGETHER TO RESOLVE THINGS...
MAYBE THEN, YOU WOULD'VE BEEN ABLE TO SEE ALL THE GOOD THEY'RE CAPABLE OF, TOO.
I WAS WRONG TO SAY YOU KNEW NOTHING ABOUT LOVE.
IT PROVED TO BE MORE COMPLICATED THAN I EVER EXPECTED, EVEN AS THE TRUE MEANING BECAME CLEARER TO ME THROUGH THE EYES OF MY DESCENDANTS.
I LOVE YOU, DEVOID. ALWAYS HAVE, AND ALWAYS WILL.

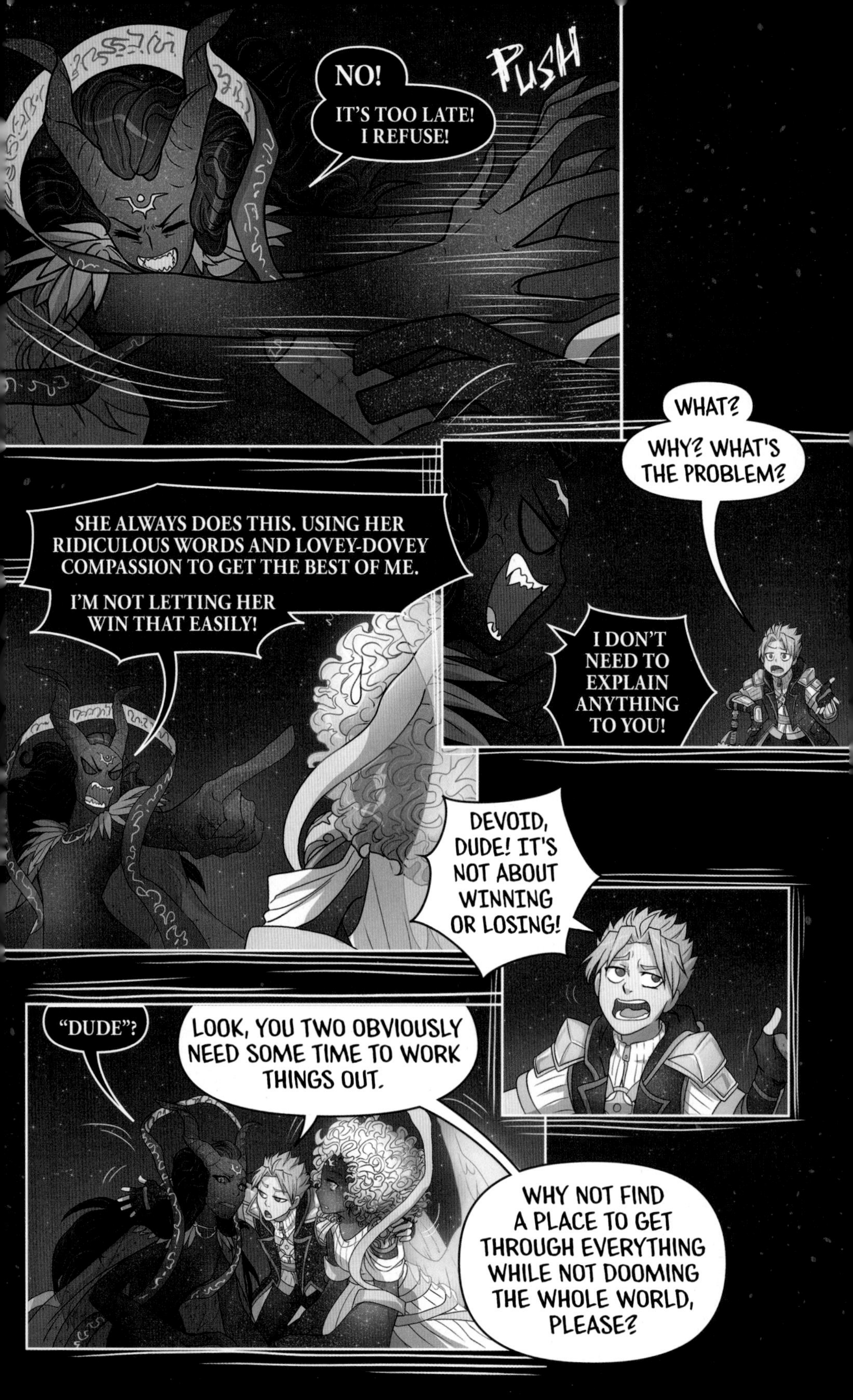
NO!
IT'S TOO LATE! I REFUSE!
PUSH
WHAT?
WHY? WHAT'S THE PROBLEM?
SHE ALWAYS DOES THIS. USING HER RIDICULOUS WORDS AND LOVEY-DOVEY COMPASSION TO GET THE BEST OF ME.
I'M NOT LETTING HER WIN THAT EASILY!
I DON'T NEED TO EXPLAIN ANYTHING TO YOU!
DEVOID, DUDE! IT'S NOT ABOUT WINNING OR LOSING!
"DUDE"?
LOOK, YOU TWO OBVIOUSLY NEED SOME TIME TO WORK THINGS OUT.
WHY NOT FIND A PLACE TO GET THROUGH EVERYTHING WHILE NOT DOOMING THE WHOLE WORLD, PLEASE?

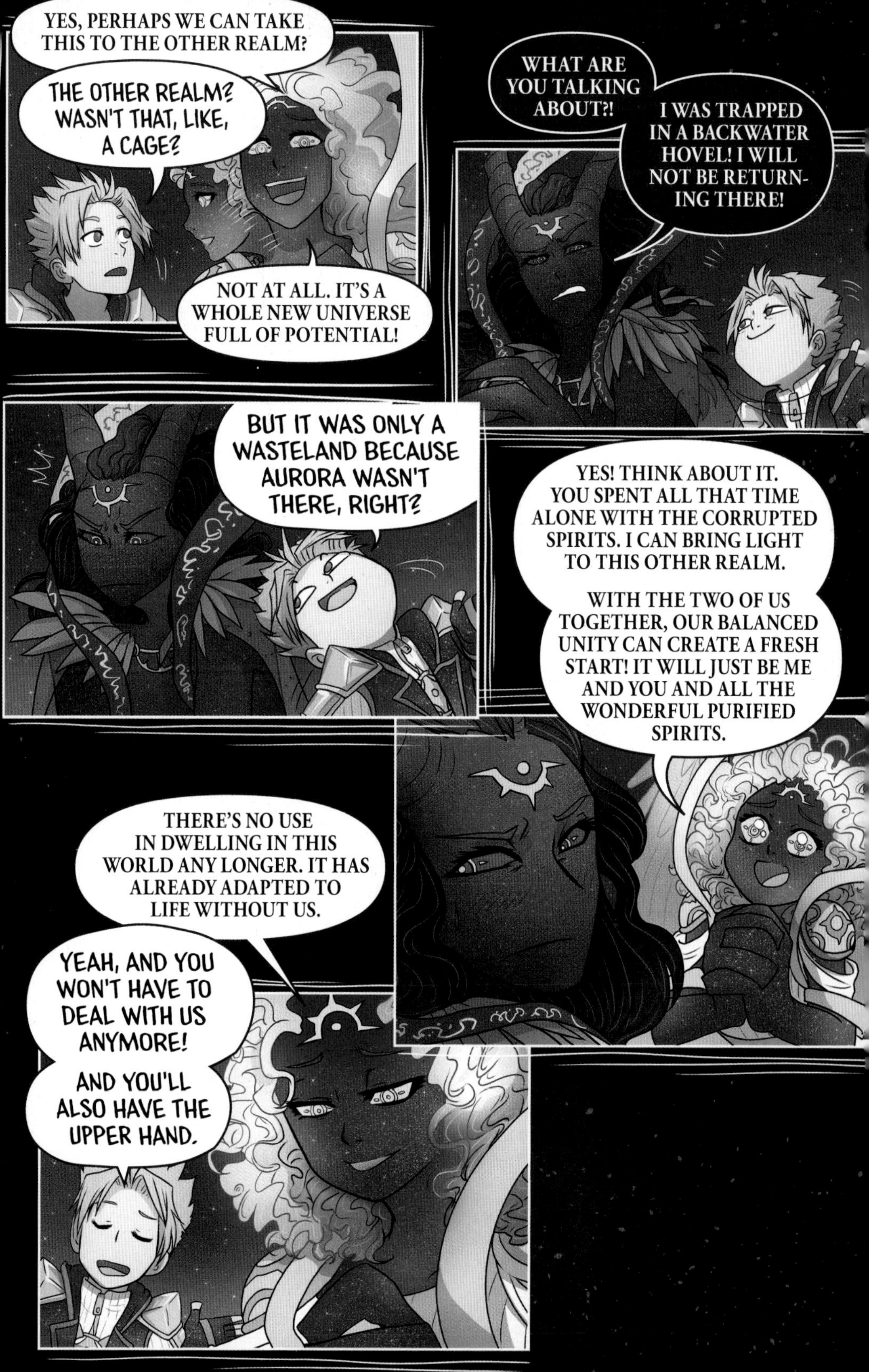
YES, PERHAPS WE CAN TAKE THIS TO THE OTHER REALM?
THE OTHER REALM? WASN'T THAT, LIKE, A CAGE?
NOT AT ALL. IT'S A WHOLE NEW UNIVERSE FULL OF POTENTIAL!
WHAT ARE YOU TALKING ABOUT?!
I WAS TRAPPED IN A BACKWATER HOVEL! I WILL NOT BE RETURNING THERE!
BUT IT WAS ONLY A WASTELAND BECAUSE AURORA WASN'T THERE, RIGHT?
YES! THINK ABOUT IT. YOU SPENT ALL THAT TIME ALONE WITH THE CORRUPTED SPIRITS. I CAN BRING LIGHT TO THIS OTHER REALM.
WITH THE TWO OF US TOGETHER, OUR BALANCED UNITY CAN CREATE A FRESH START! IT WILL JUST BE ME AND YOU AND ALL THE WONDERFUL PURIFIED SPIRITS.
THERE'S NO USE IN DWELLING IN THIS WORLD ANY LONGER. IT HAS ALREADY ADAPTED TO LIFE WITHOUT US.
YEAH, AND YOU WON'T HAVE TO DEAL WITH US ANYMORE!
AND YOU'LL ALSO HAVE THE UPPER HAND.

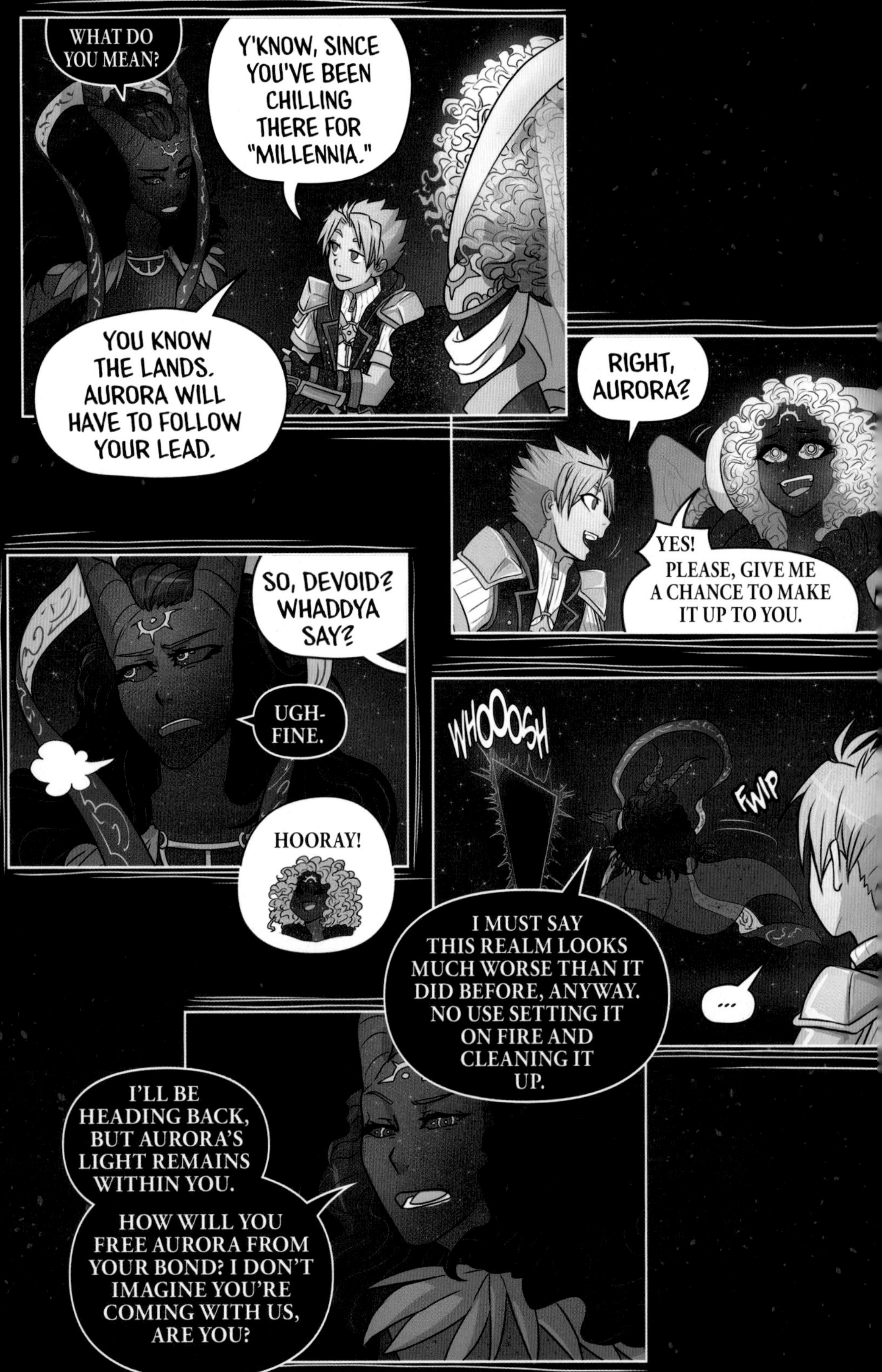
WHAT DO YOU MEAN?
Y'KNOW, SINCE YOU'VE BEEN CHILLING THERE FOR "MILLENNIA."
YOU KNOW THE LANDS. AURORA WILL HAVE TO FOLLOW YOUR LEAD.
RIGHT, AURORA?
YES! PLEASE, GIVE ME A CHANCE TO MAKE IT UP TO YOU.
SO, DEVOID? WHADDYA SAY?
UGH- FINE.
HOORAY!
WHOOOSH
FWIP
I MUST SAY THIS REALM LOOKS MUCH WORSE THAN IT DID BEFORE, ANYWAY. NO USE SETTING IT ON FIRE AND CLEANING IT UP.
...
I'LL BE HEADING BACK, BUT AURORA'S LIGHT REMAINS WITHIN YOU.
HOW WILL YOU FREE AURORA FROM YOUR BOND? I DON'T IMAGINE YOU'RE COMING WITH US, ARE YOU?

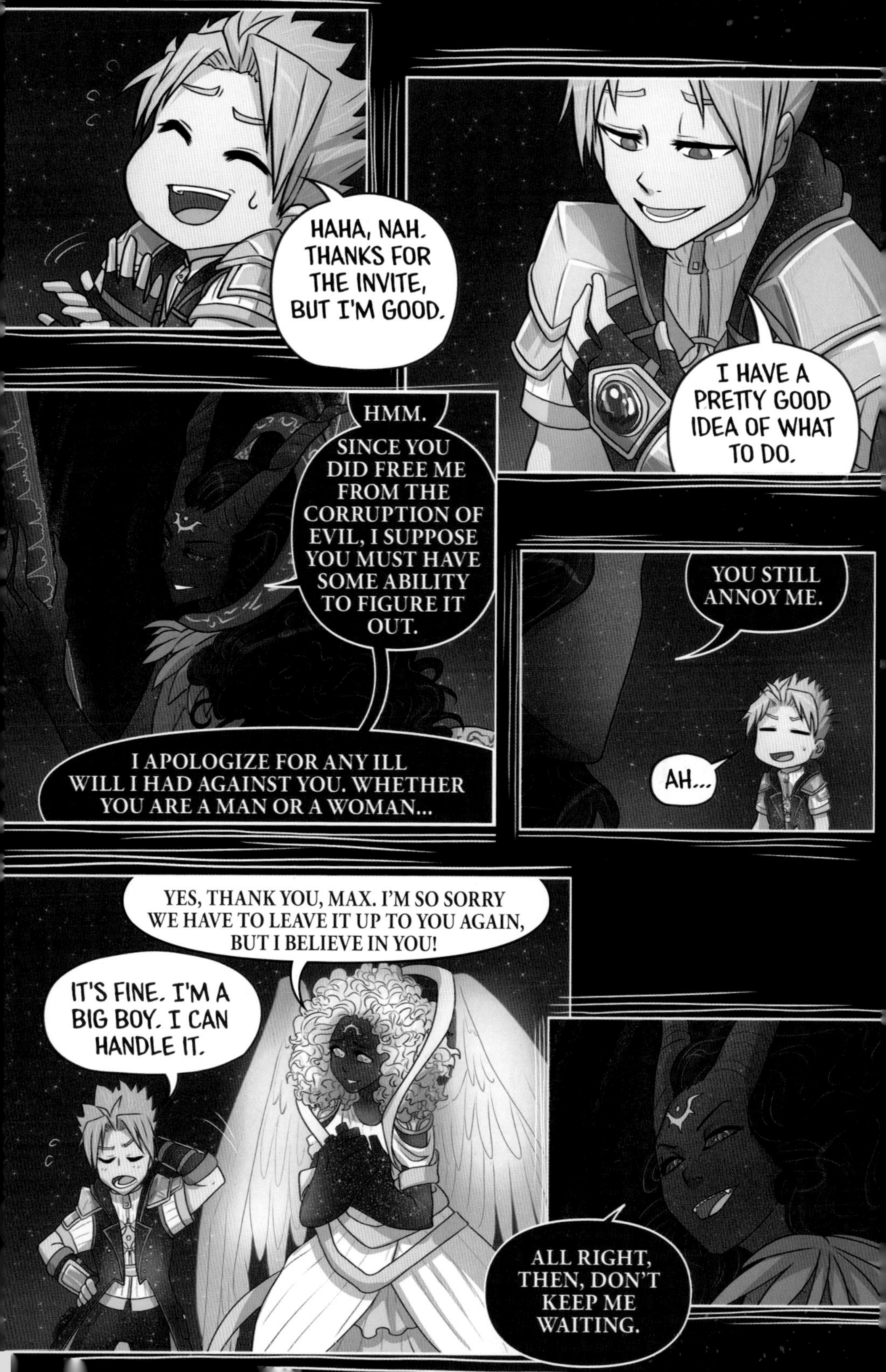
HAHA, NAH. THANKS FOR THE INVITE, BUT I'M GOOD.
I HAVE A PRETTY GOOD IDEA OF WHAT TO DO.
HMM.
SINCE YOU DID FREE ME FROM THE CORRUPTION OF EVIL, I SUPPOSE YOU MUST HAVE SOME ABILITY TO FIGURE IT OUT.
I APOLOGIZE FOR ANY ILL WILL I HAD AGAINST YOU. WHETHER YOU ARE A MAN OR A WOMAN...
YOU STILL ANNOY ME.
AH...
YES, THANK YOU, MAX. I'M SO SORRY WE HAVE TO LEAVE IT UP TO YOU AGAIN, BUT I BELIEVE IN YOU!
IT'S FINE. I'M A BIG BOY. I CAN HANDLE IT.
ALL RIGHT, THEN, DON'T KEEP ME WAITING.

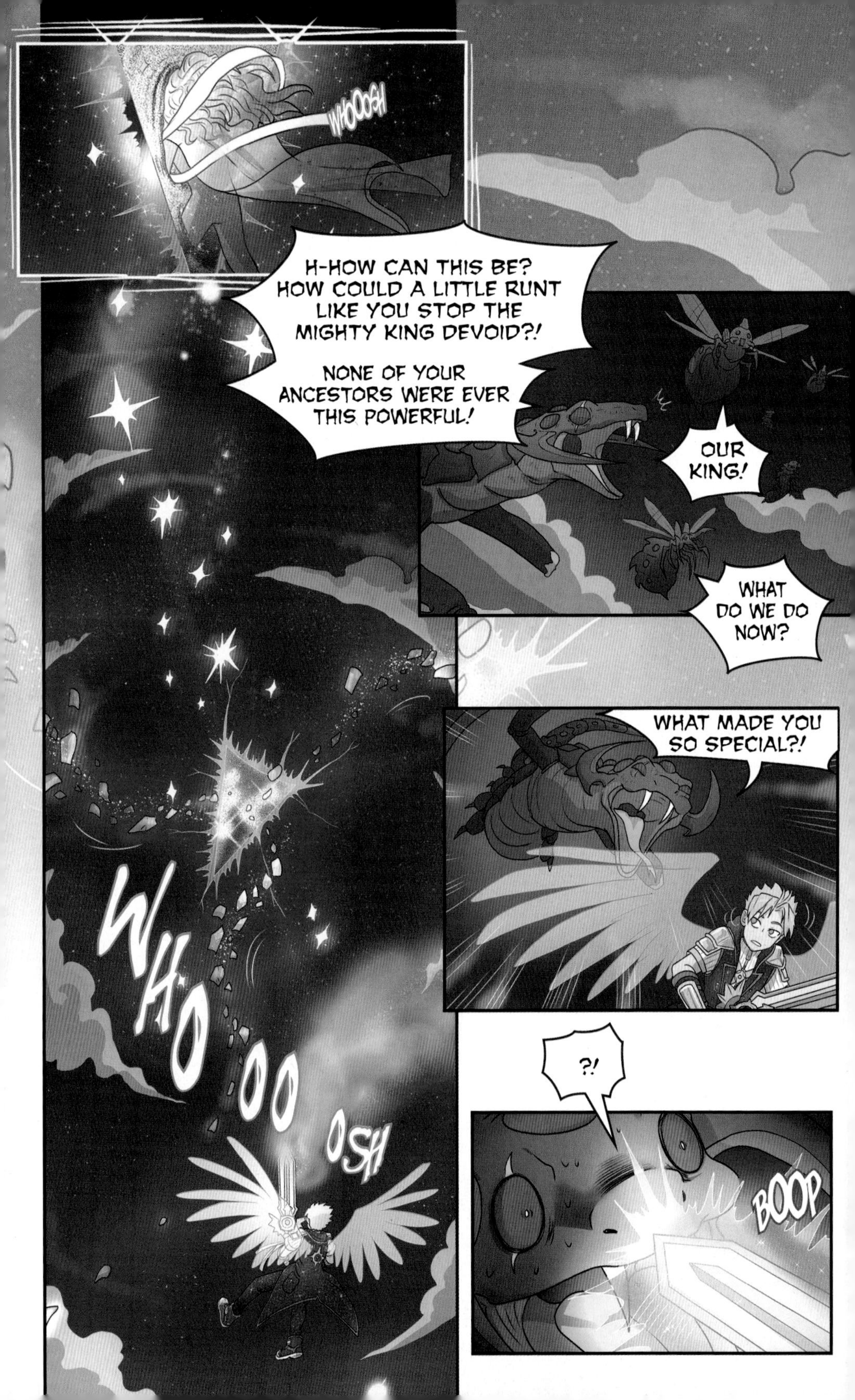
WHOOOSH
H-HOW CAN THIS BE? HOW COULD A LITTLE RUNT LIKE YOU STOP THE MIGHTY KING DEVOID?!
NONE OF YOUR ANCESTORS WERE EVER THIS POWERFUL!
OUR KING!
WHAT DO WE DO NOW?
WHOOOOSH
WHAT MADE YOU SO SPECIAL?!
?!
BOOP

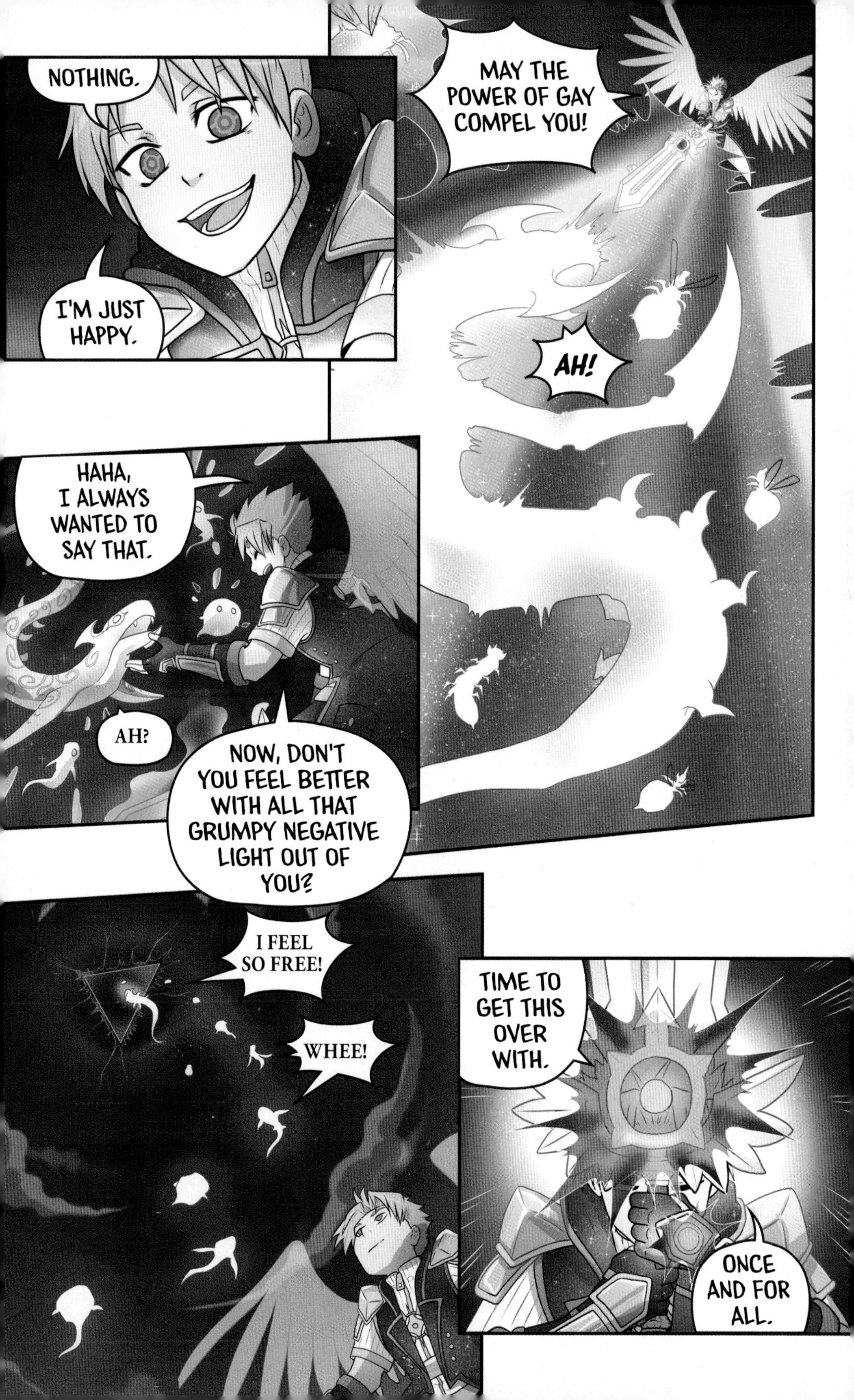
NOTHING.
I'M JUST HAPPY.
MAY THE POWER OF GAY COMPEL YOU!
AH!
HAHA, I ALWAYS WANTED TO SAY THAT.
AH?
NOW, DON'T YOU FEEL BETTER WITH ALL THAT GRUMPY NEGATIVE LIGHT OUT OF YOU?
I FEEL SO FREE!
WHEE!
TIME TO GET THIS OVER WITH.
ONCE AND FOR ALL.

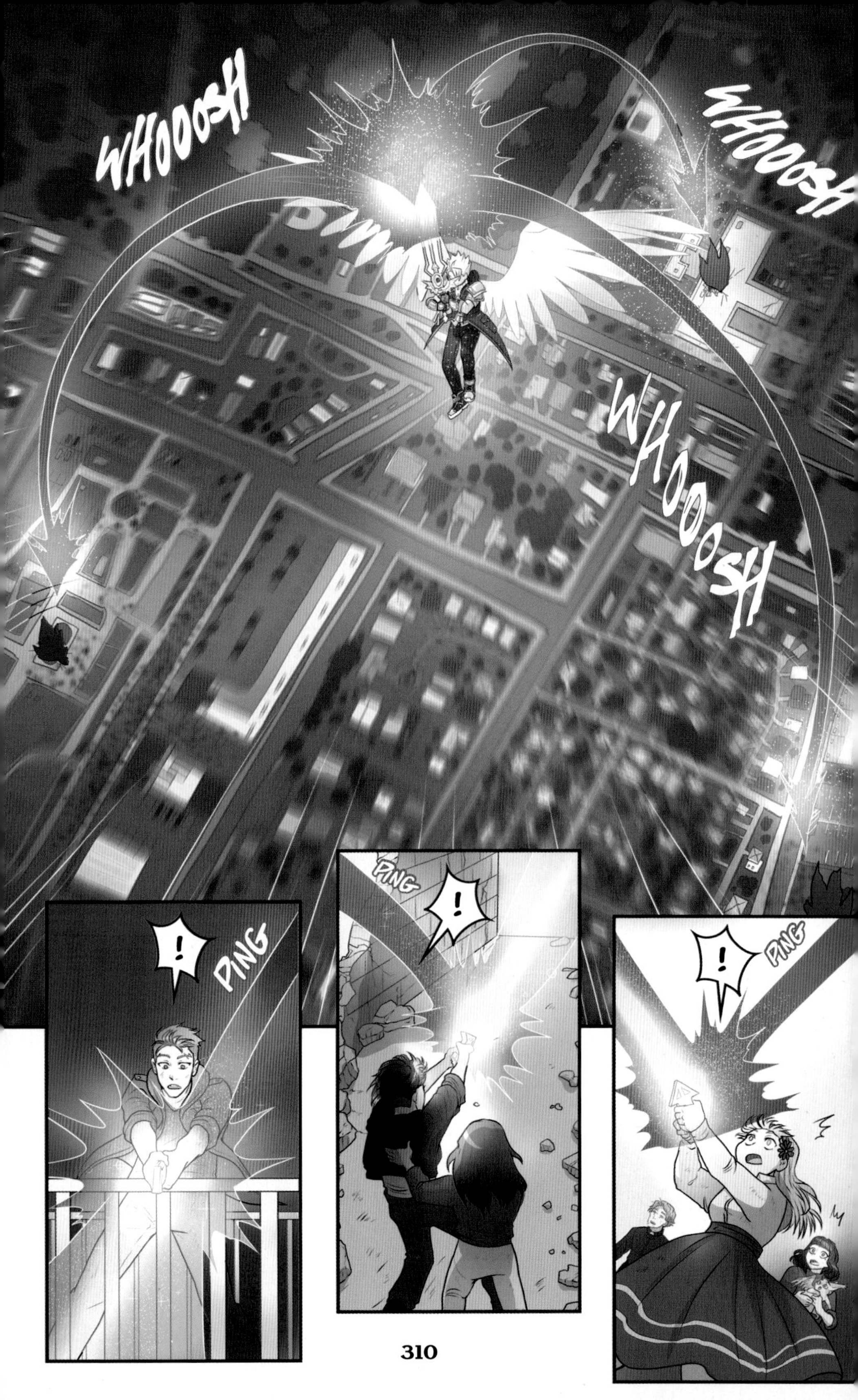
WHOOOSH
WHOOOSH
WHOOOSH
!
PING
PING
!
!
PING

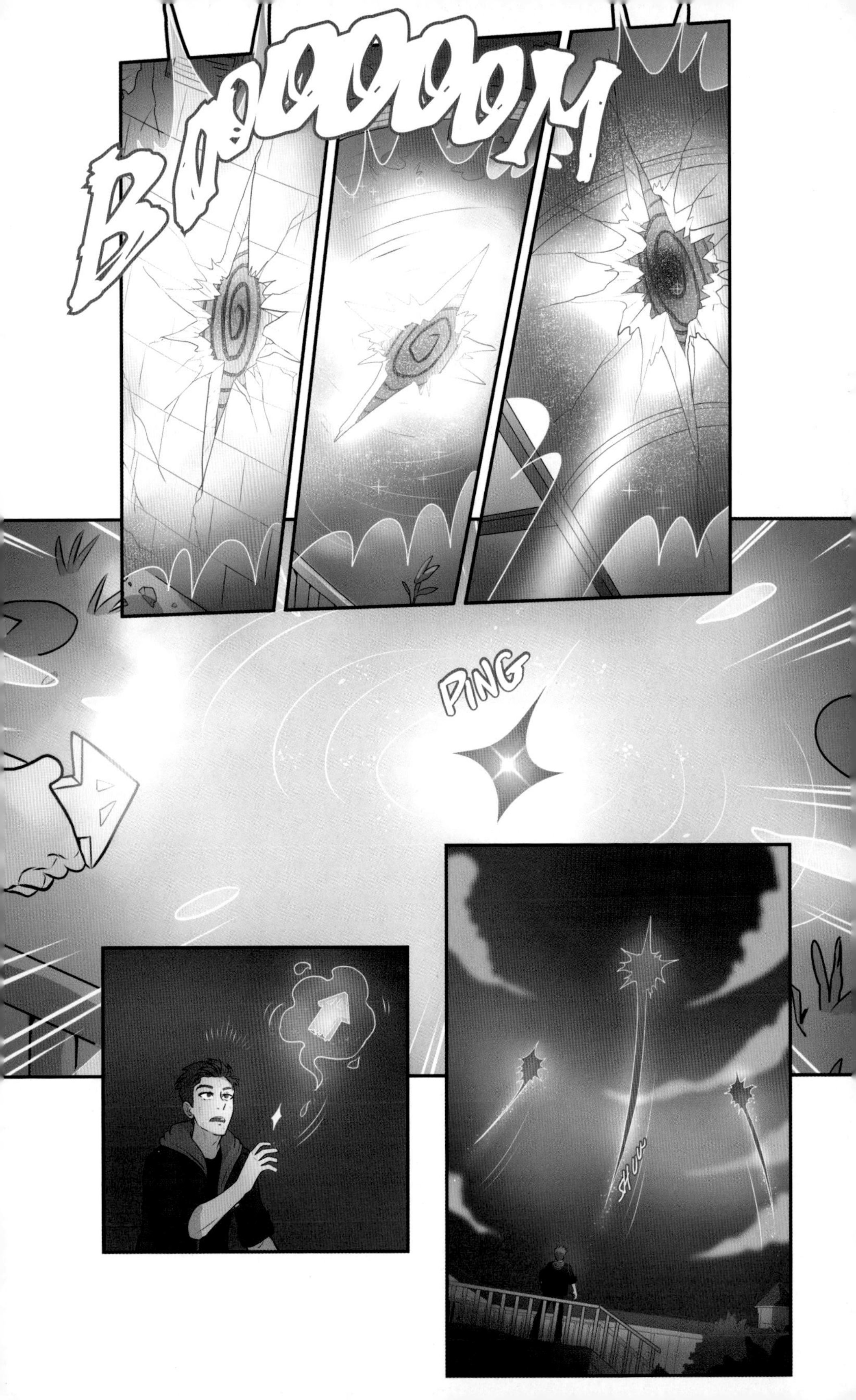
BOOOOOOOM
PING
SHUU

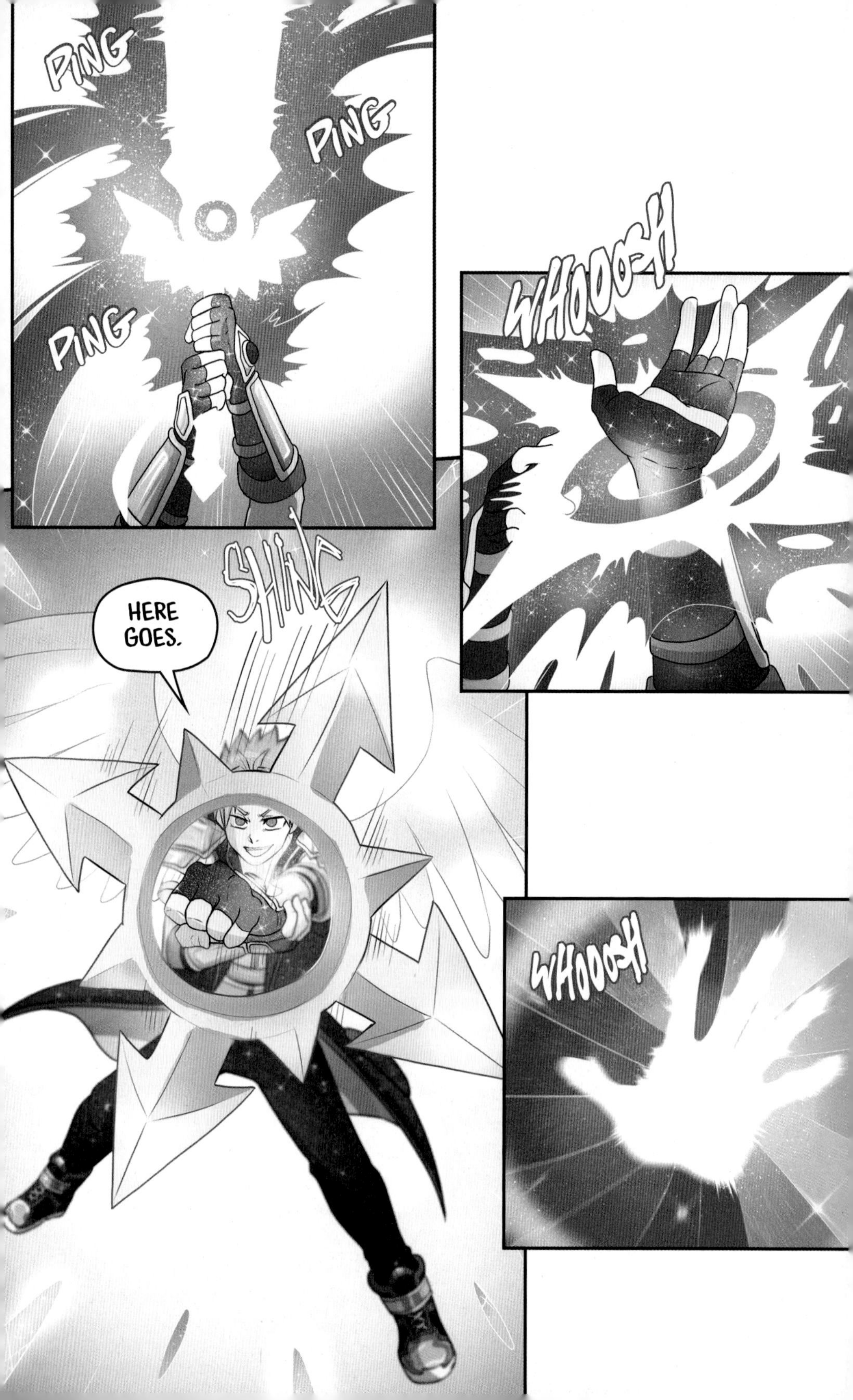
PING
PING
PING
WHOOOSH
SHING
HERE GOES.
WHOOOSH

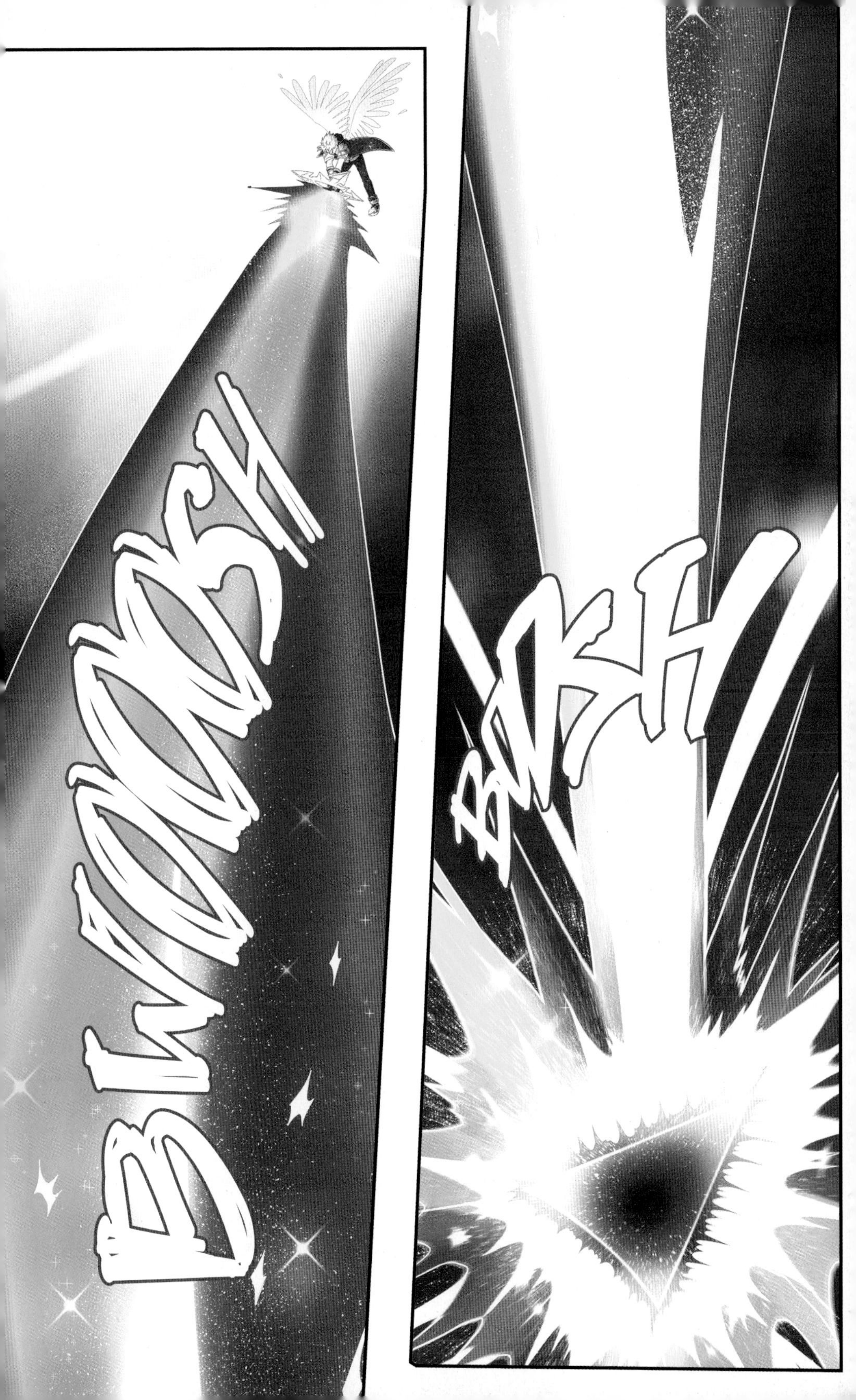
BWOOSH
BASH

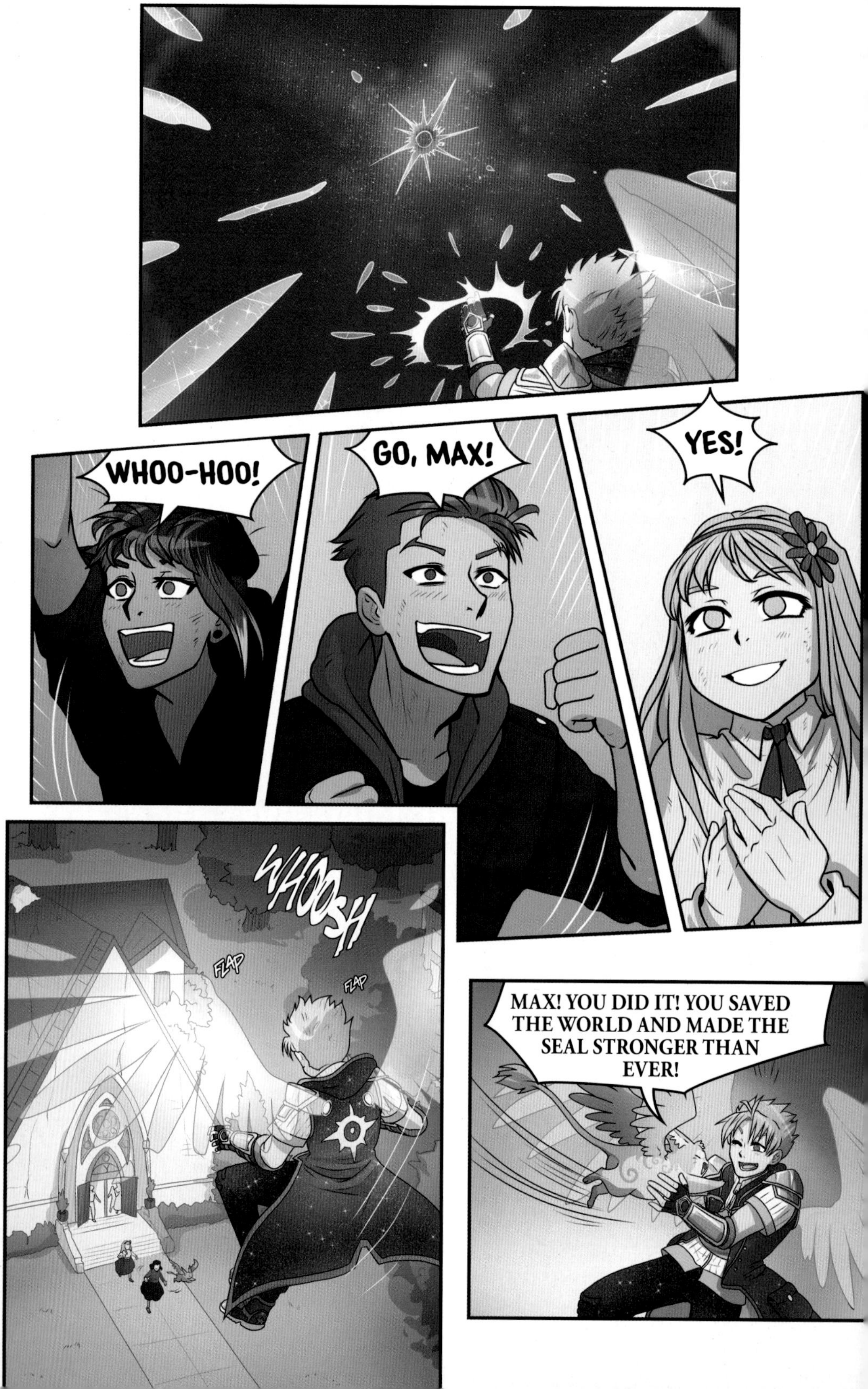
WHOO-HOO!
GO, MAX!
YES!
WHOOSH
FLAP
FLAP
MAX! YOU DID IT! YOU SAVED THE WORLD AND MADE THE SEAL STRONGER THAN EVER!

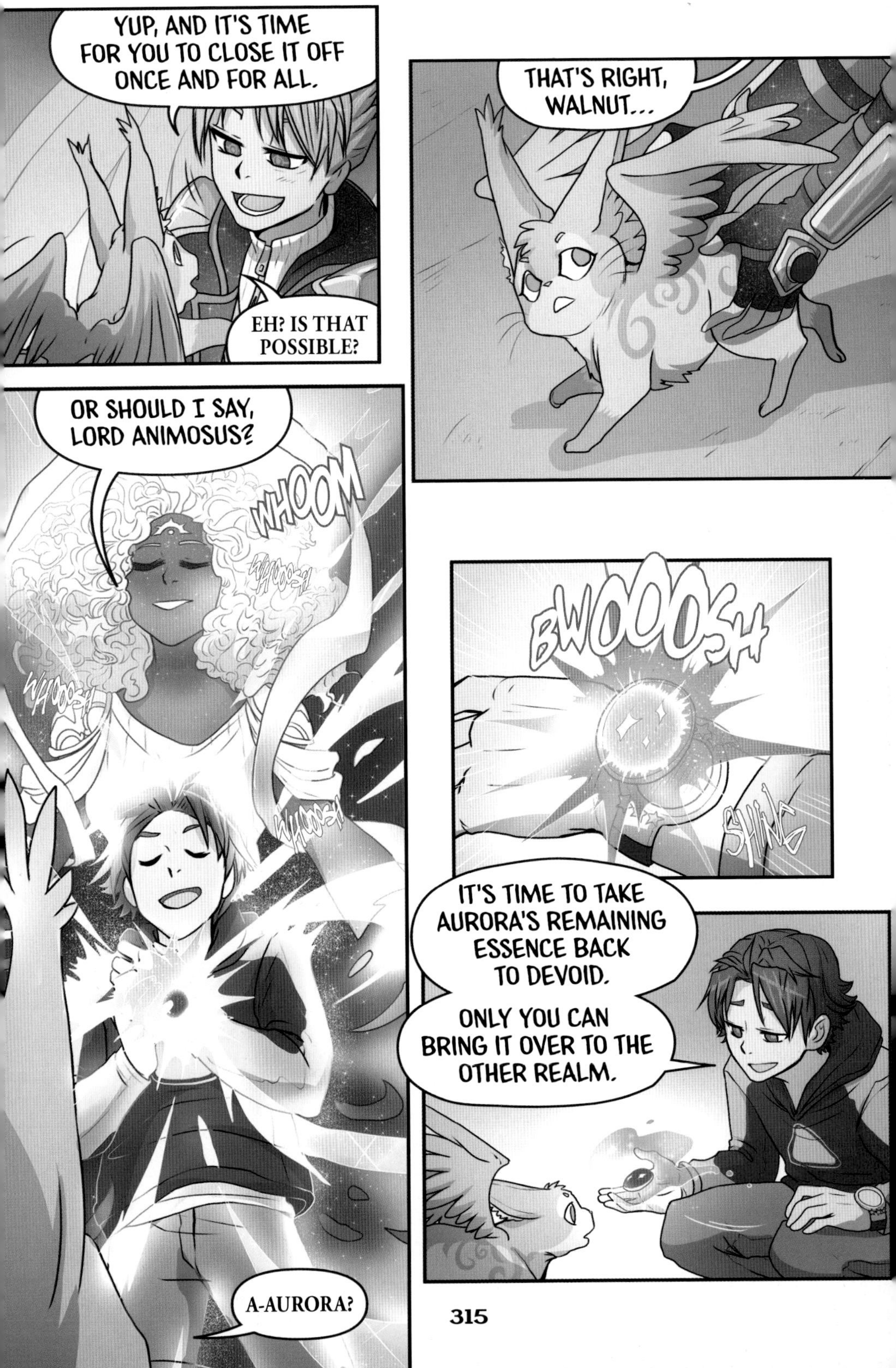
YUP, AND IT'S TIME FOR YOU TO CLOSE IT OFF ONCE AND FOR ALL.
EH? IS THAT POSSIBLE?
THAT'S RIGHT, WALNUT...
OR SHOULD I SAY, LORD ANIMOSUS?
WHOOM
A-AURORA?
BWOOOSH
SHING
IT'S TIME TO TAKE AURORA'S REMAINING ESSENCE BACK TO DEVOID.
ONLY YOU CAN BRING IT OVER TO THE OTHER REALM.

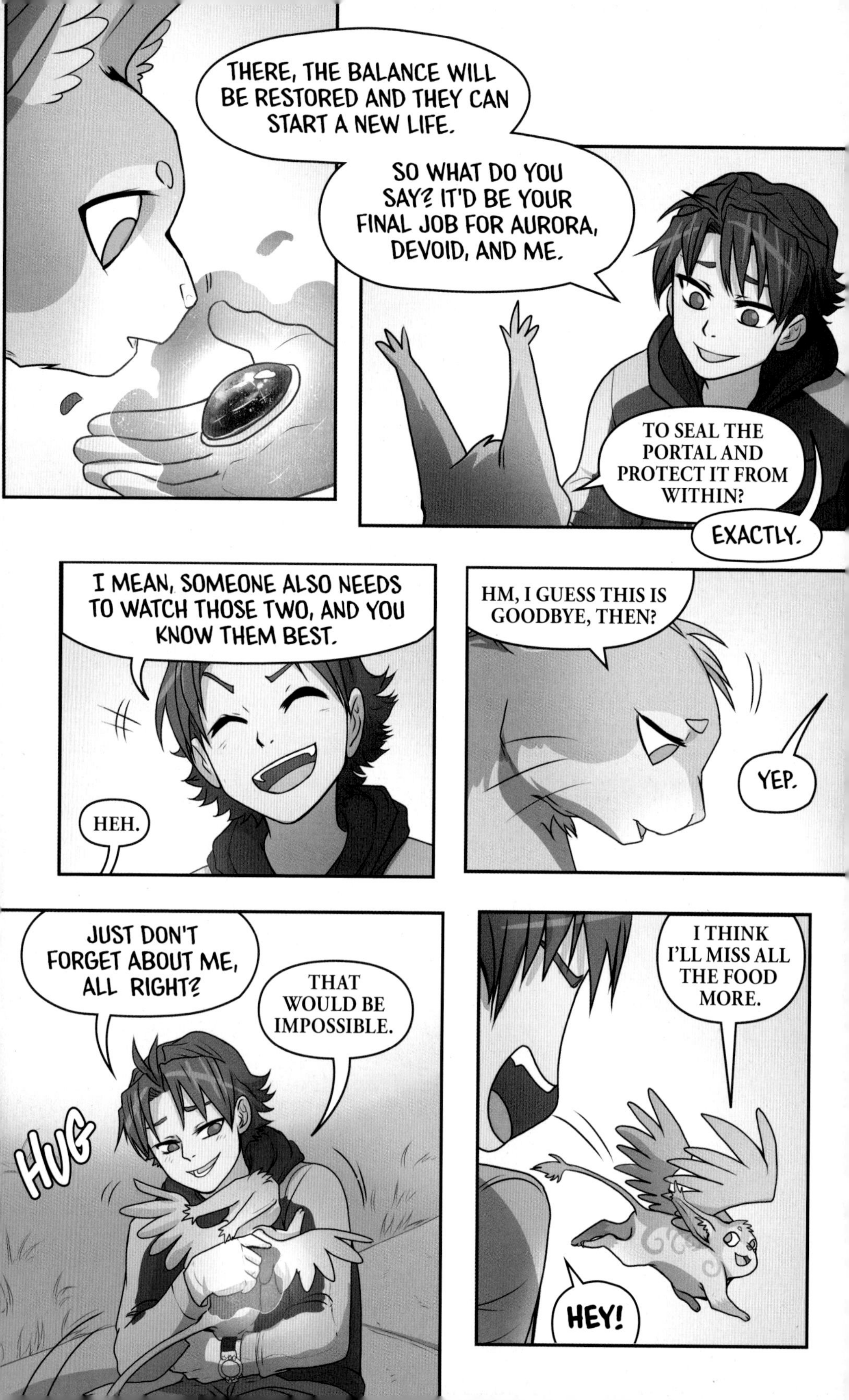
THERE, THE BALANCE WILL BE RESTORED AND THEY CAN START A NEW LIFE.
SO WHAT DO YOU SAY? IT'D BE YOUR FINAL JOB FOR AURORA, DEVOID, AND ME.
TO SEAL THE PORTAL AND PROTECT IT FROM WITHIN?
EXACTLY.
I MEAN, SOMEONE ALSO NEEDS TO WATCH THOSE TWO, AND YOU KNOW THEM BEST.
HEH.
HM, I GUESS THIS IS GOODBYE, THEN?
YEP.
JUST DON'T FORGET ABOUT ME, ALL RIGHT?
THAT WOULD BE IMPOSSIBLE.
HUG
I THINK I'LL MISS ALL THE FOOD MORE.
HEY!

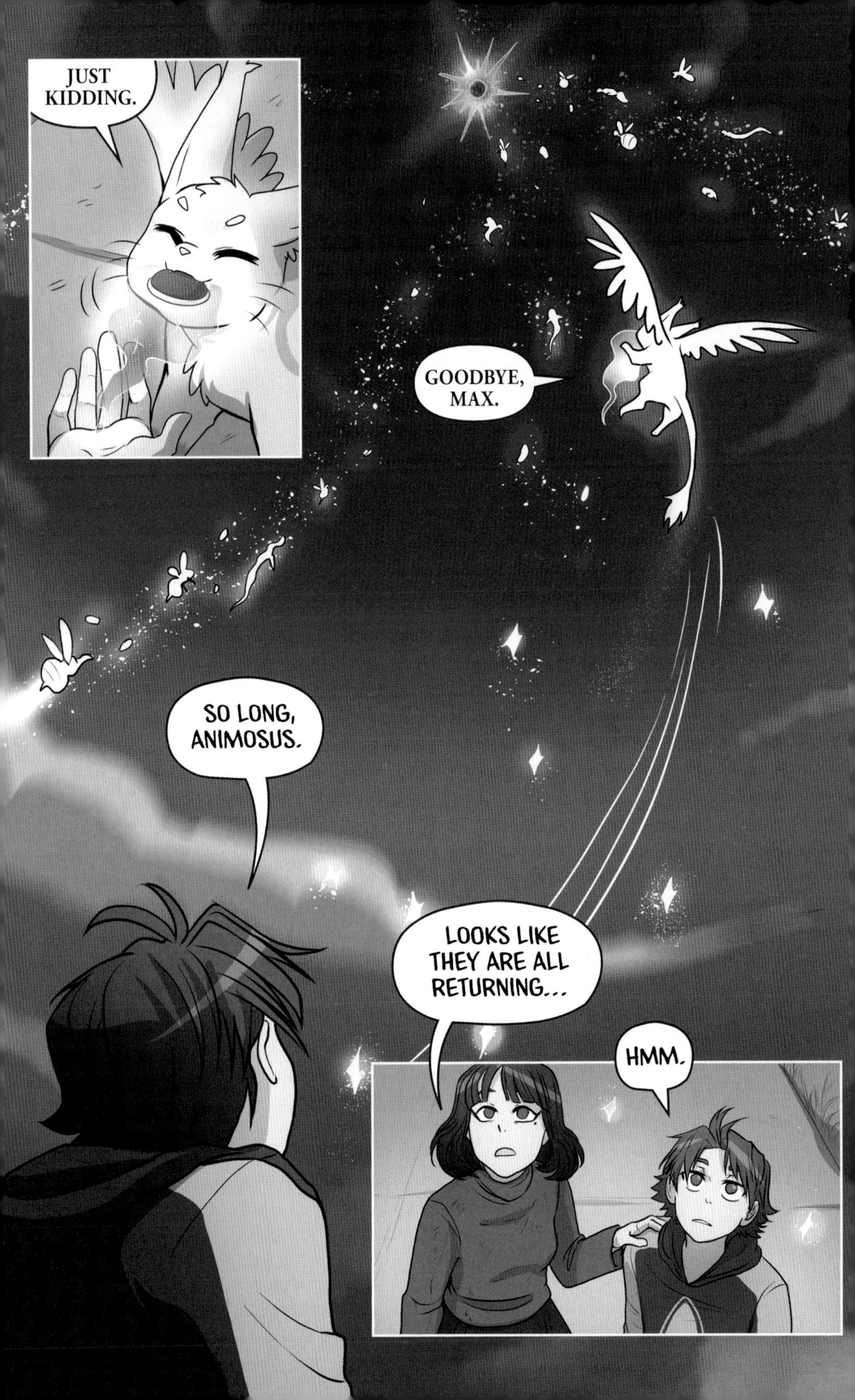
JUST KIDDING.
GOODBYE, MAX.
SO LONG, ANIMOSUS.
LOOKS LIKE THEY ARE ALL RETURNING...
HMM.

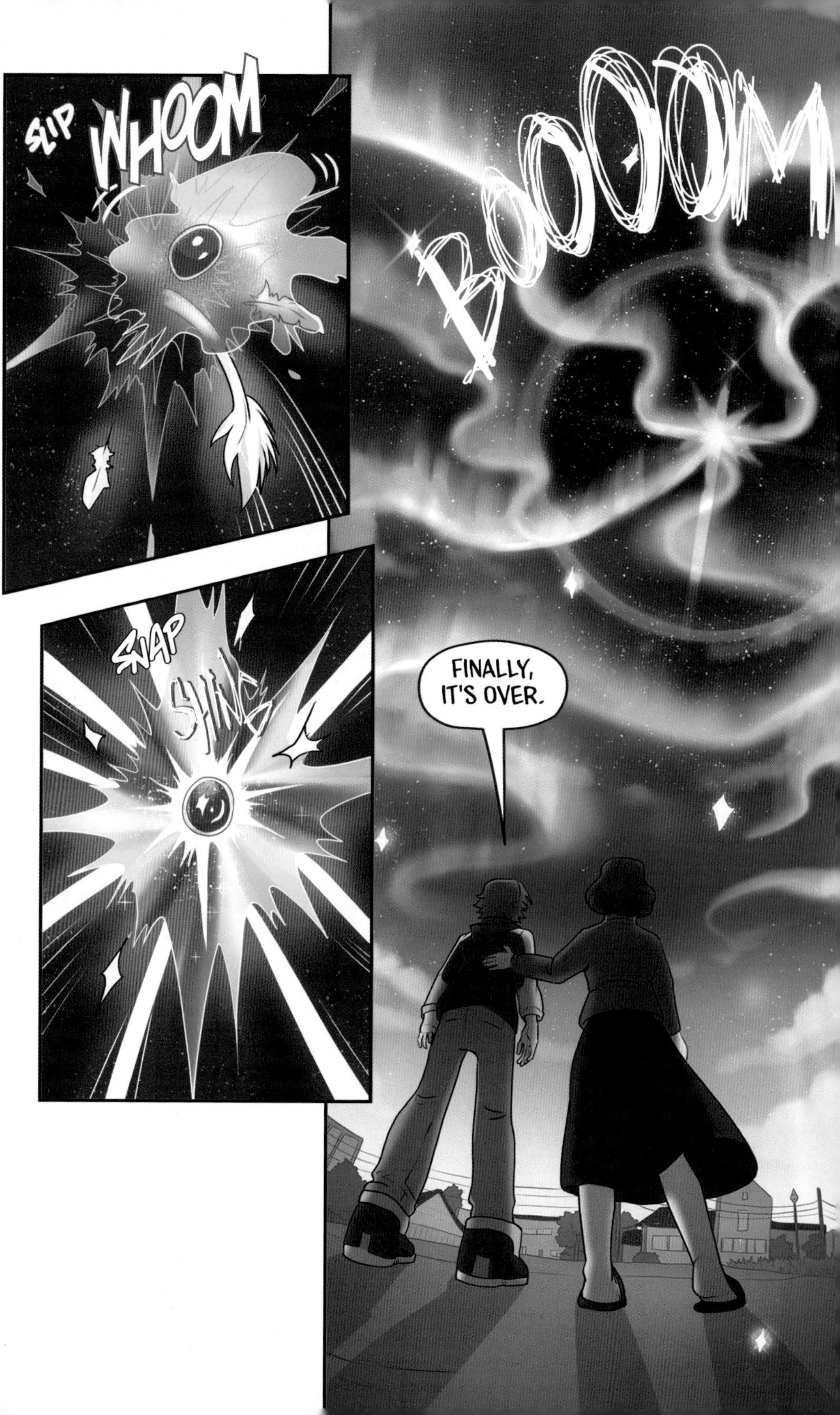
SLIP
WHOOM
SNAP
SHING
BOOOOOM
FINALLY, IT'S OVER.

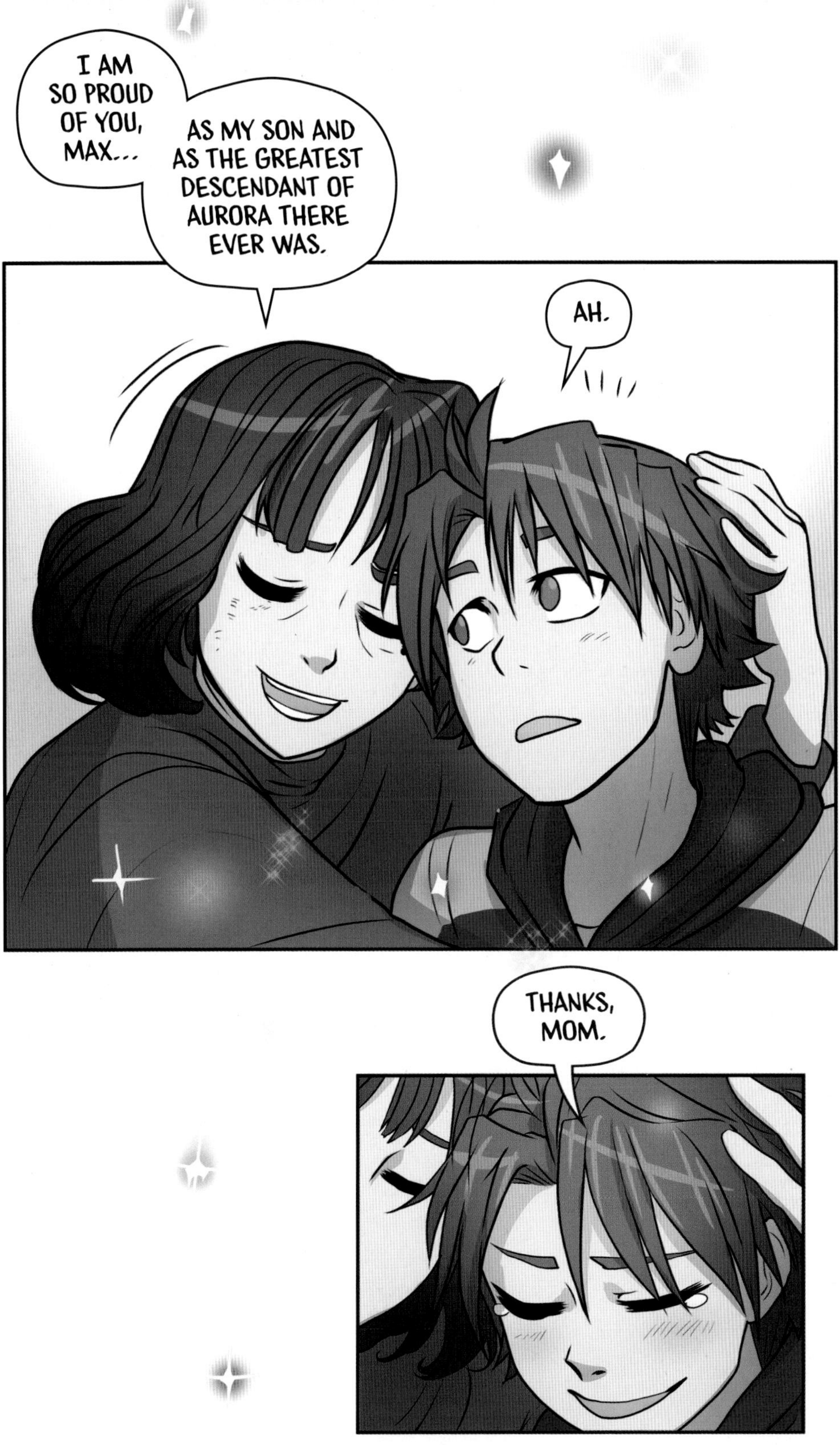
I AM SO PROUD OF YOU, MAX...
AS MY SON AND AS THE GREATEST DESCENDANT OF AURORA THERE EVER WAS.
AH.
THANKS, MOM.

EPISODE 30:
THIS IS MAX OWEN

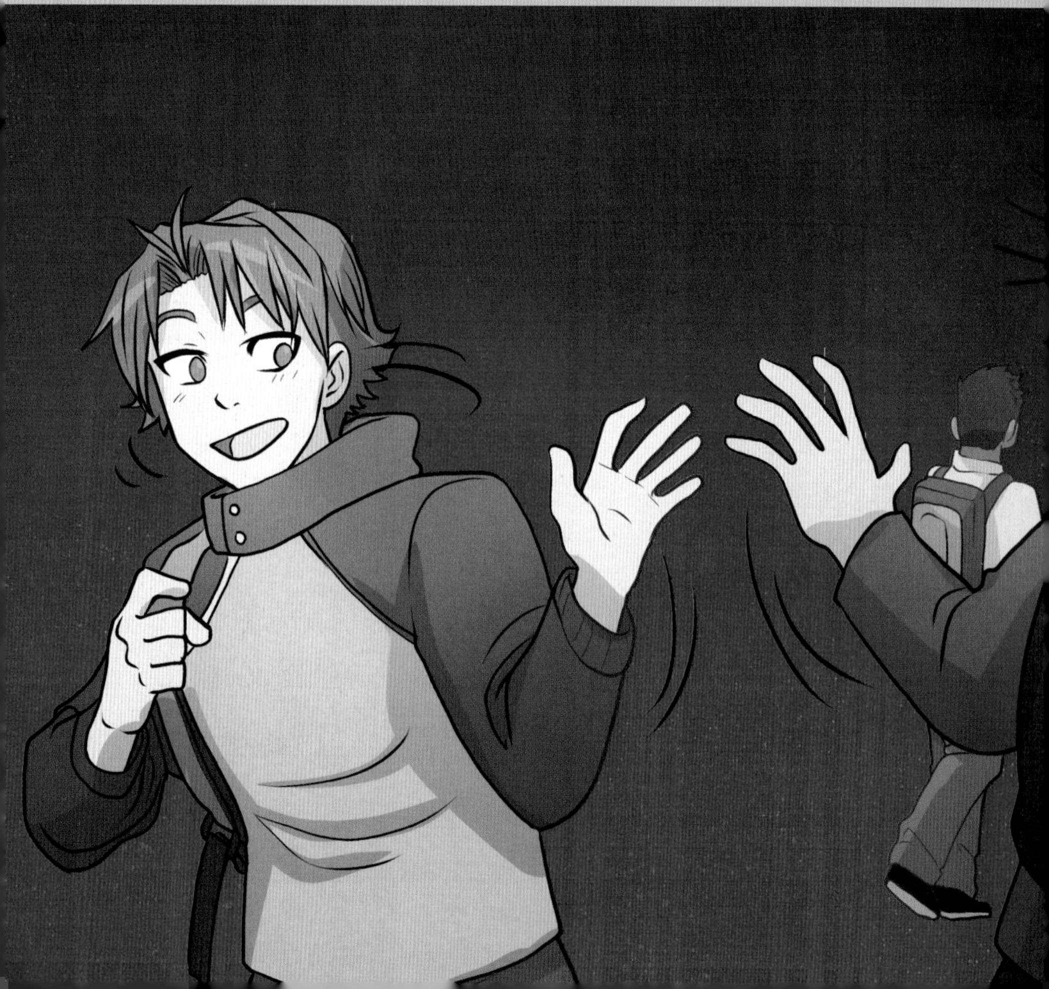

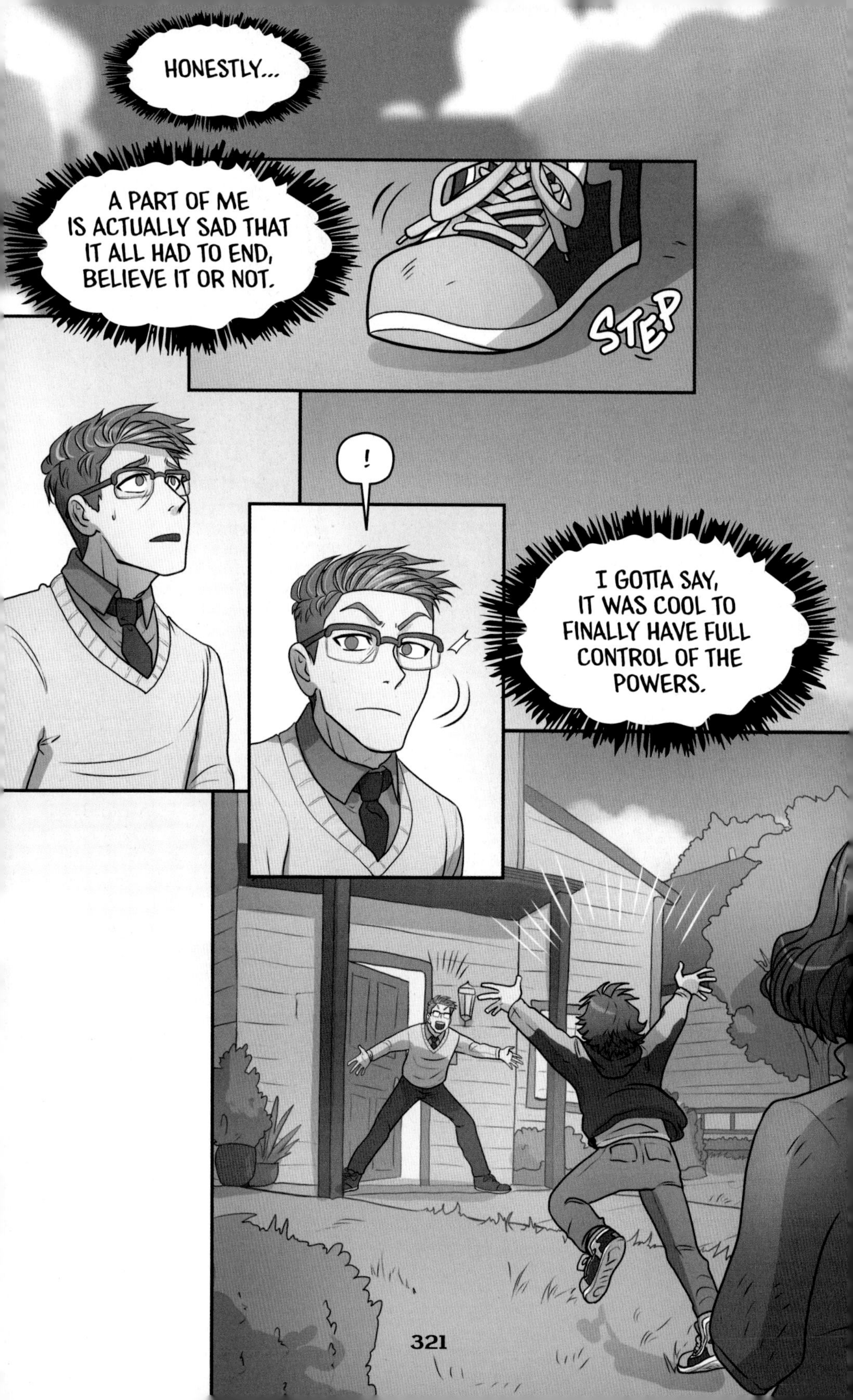
HONESTLY...
A PART OF ME IS ACTUALLY SAD THAT IT ALL HAD TO END, BELIEVE IT OR NOT.
STEP
!
I GOTTA SAY, IT WAS COOL TO FINALLY HAVE FULL CONTROL OF THE POWERS.

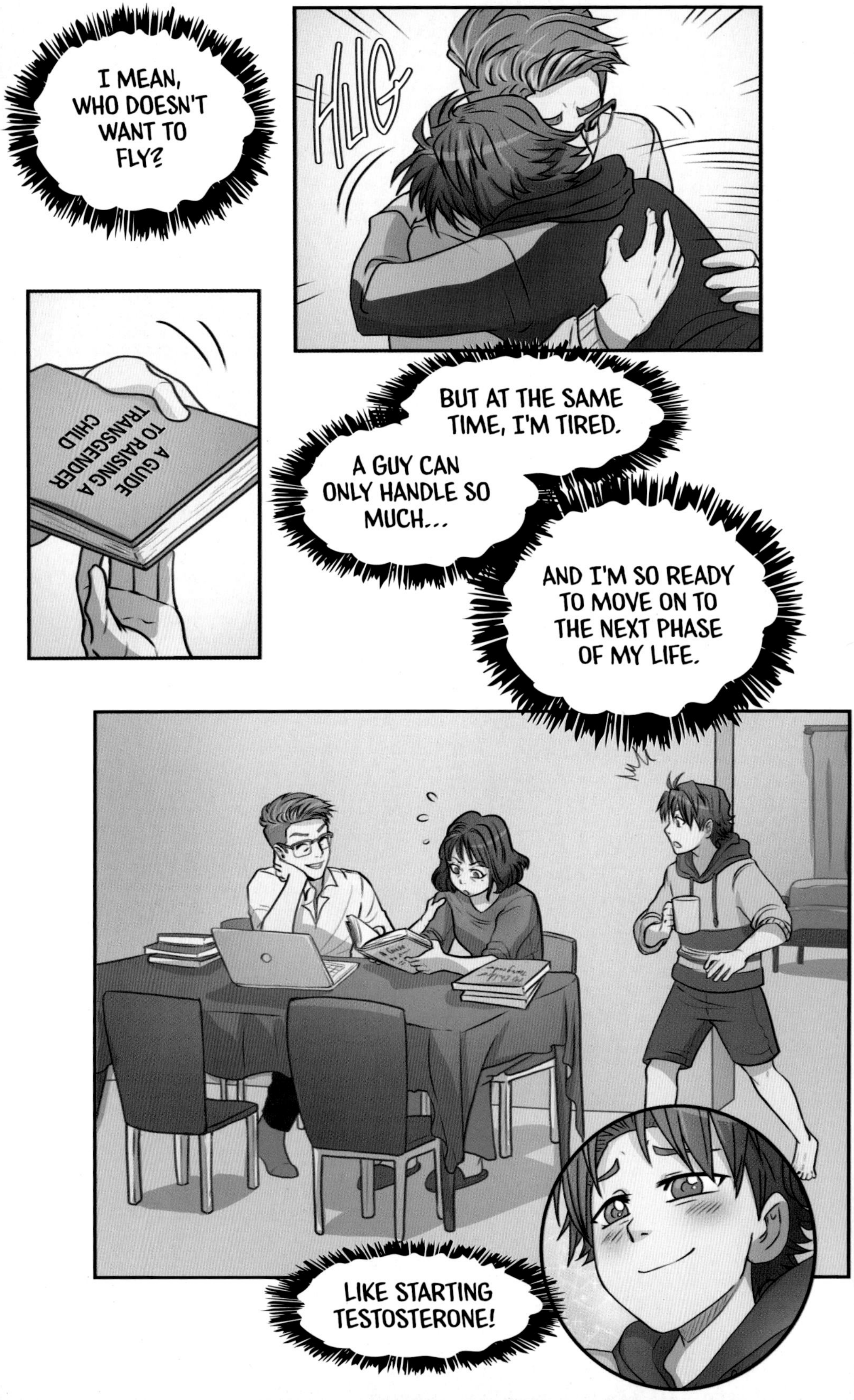
I MEAN, WHO DOESN'T WANT TO FLY?
HUG
A GUIDE TO RAISING A TRANSGENDER CHILD
BUT AT THE SAME TIME, I'M TIRED.
A GUY CAN ONLY HANDLE SO MUCH...
AND I'M SO READY TO MOVE ON TO THE NEXT PHASE OF MY LIFE.
LIKE STARTING TESTOSTERONE!

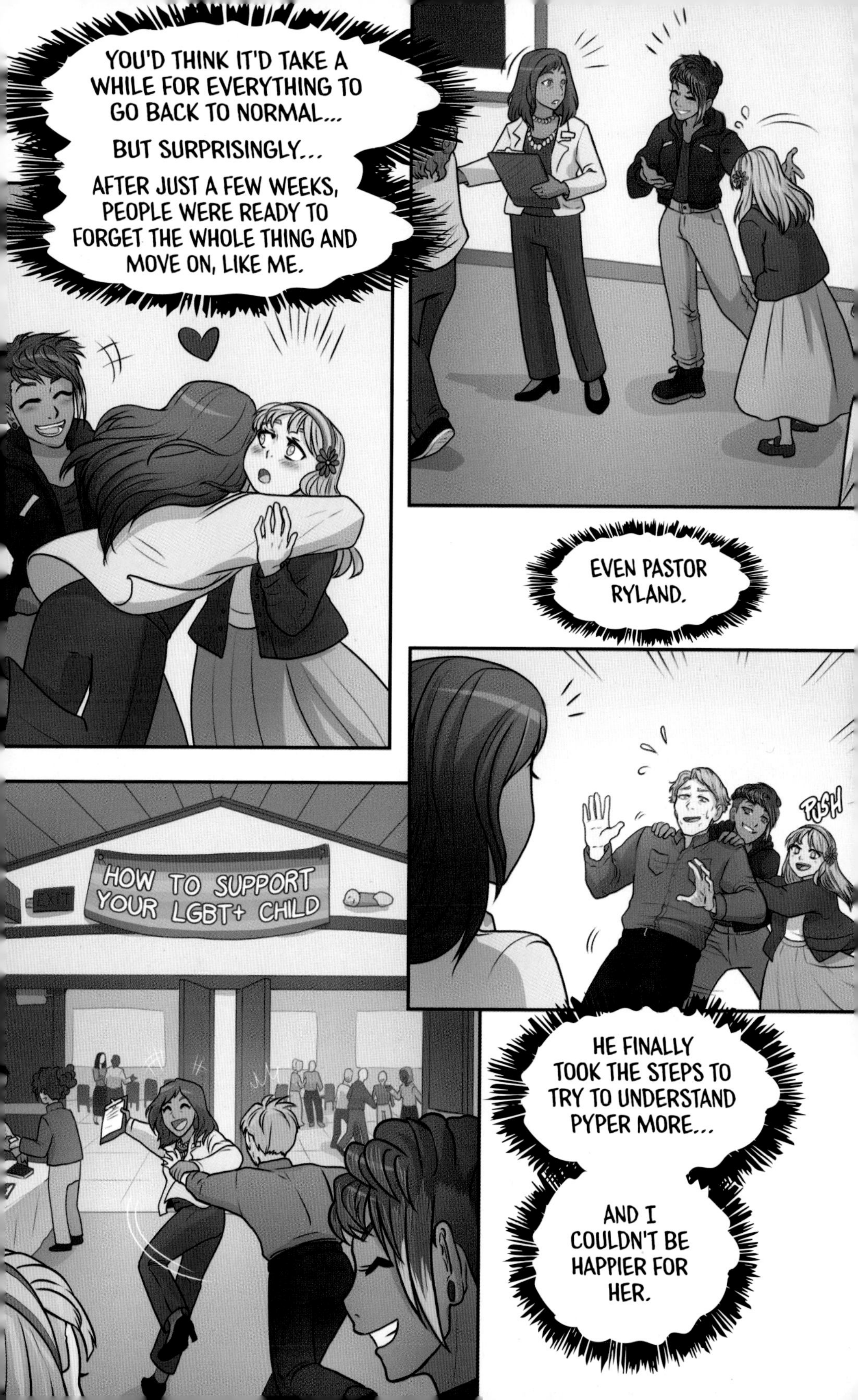
YOU'D THINK IT'D TAKE A WHILE FOR EVERYTHING TO GO BACK TO NORMAL...
BUT SURPRISINGLY...
AFTER JUST A FEW WEEKS, PEOPLE WERE READY TO FORGET THE WHOLE THING AND MOVE ON, LIKE ME.
HOW TO SUPPORT YOUR LGBT+ CHILD
EXIT
EVEN PASTOR RYLAND.
PUSH
HE FINALLY TOOK THE STEPS TO TRY TO UNDERSTAND PYPER MORE...
AND I COULDN'T BE HAPPIER FOR HER.

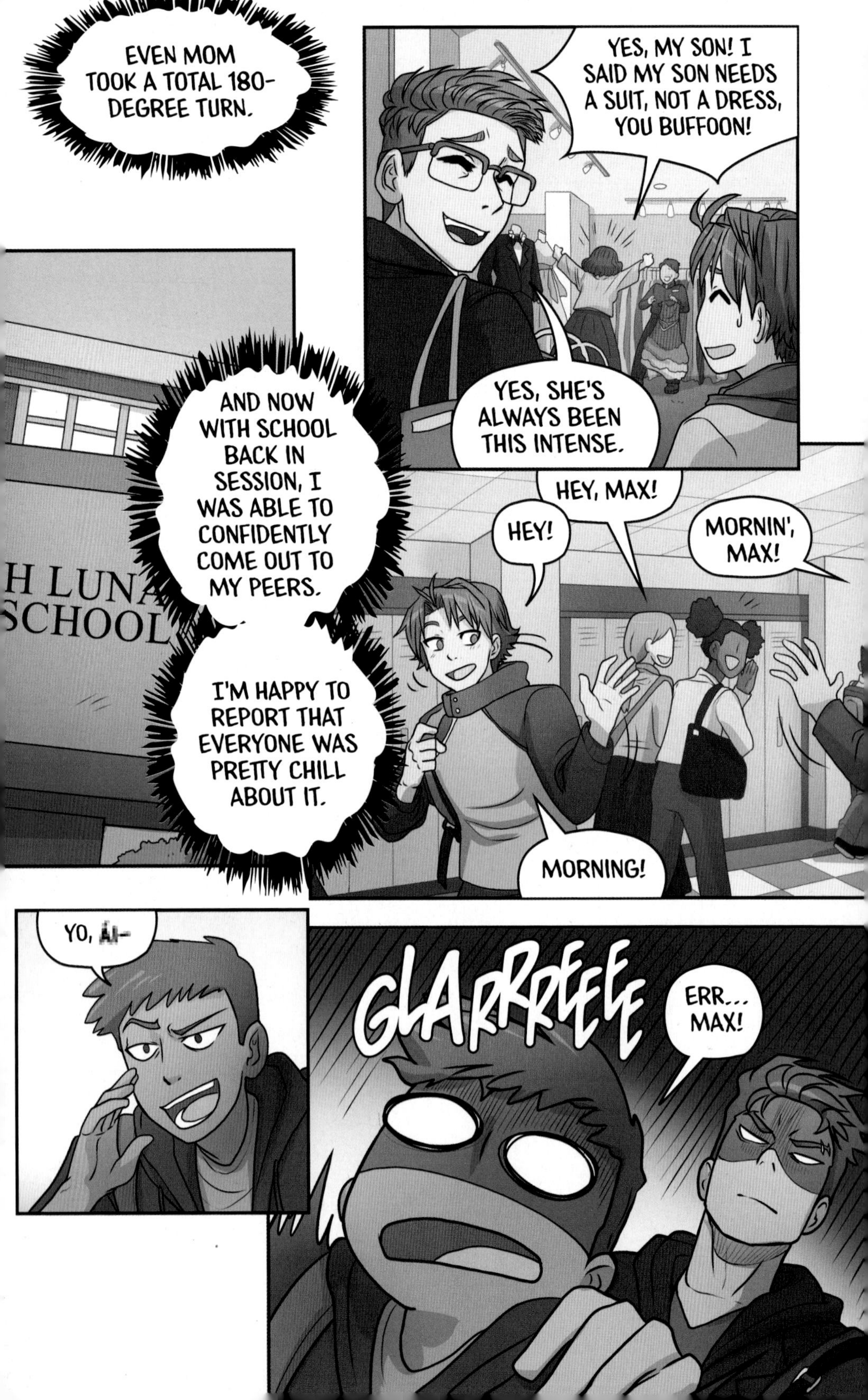
EVEN MOM TOOK A TOTAL 180-DEGREE TURN.
YES, MY SON! I SAID MY SON NEEDS A SUIT, NOT A DRESS, YOU BUFFOON!
YES, SHE'S ALWAYS BEEN THIS INTENSE.
AND NOW WITH SCHOOL BACK IN SESSION, I WAS ABLE TO CONFIDENTLY COME OUT TO MY PEERS.
I'M HAPPY TO REPORT THAT EVERYONE WAS PRETTY CHILL ABOUT IT.
H LUNA
SCHOOL
HEY!
HEY, MAX!
MORNIN', MAX!
MORNING!
YO, A-
GLARRREEEE
ERR... MAX!

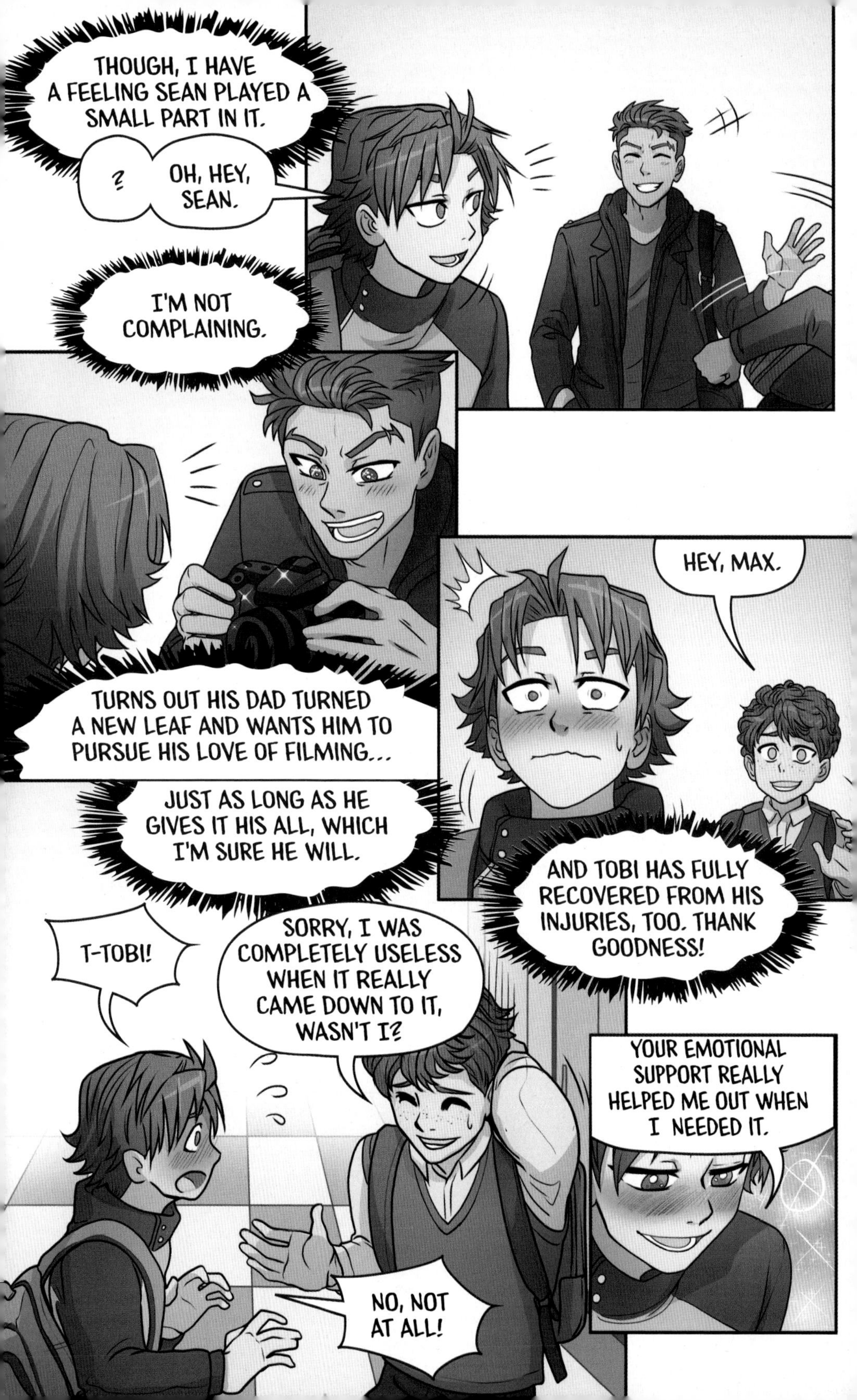

THOUGH, I HAVE A FEELING SEAN PLAYED A SMALL PART IN IT.
?
OH, HEY, SEAN.
I'M NOT COMPLAINING.
TURNS OUT HIS DAD TURNED A NEW LEAF AND WANTS HIM TO PURSUE HIS LOVE OF FILMING...
JUST AS LONG AS HE GIVES IT HIS ALL, WHICH I'M SURE HE WILL.
HEY, MAX.
AND TOBI HAS FULLY RECOVERED FROM HIS INJURIES, TOO. THANK GOODNESS!
T-TOBI!
SORRY, I WAS COMPLETELY USELESS WHEN IT REALLY CAME DOWN TO IT, WASN'T I?
NO, NOT AT ALL!
YOUR EMOTIONAL SUPPORT REALLY HELPED ME OUT WHEN I NEEDED IT.

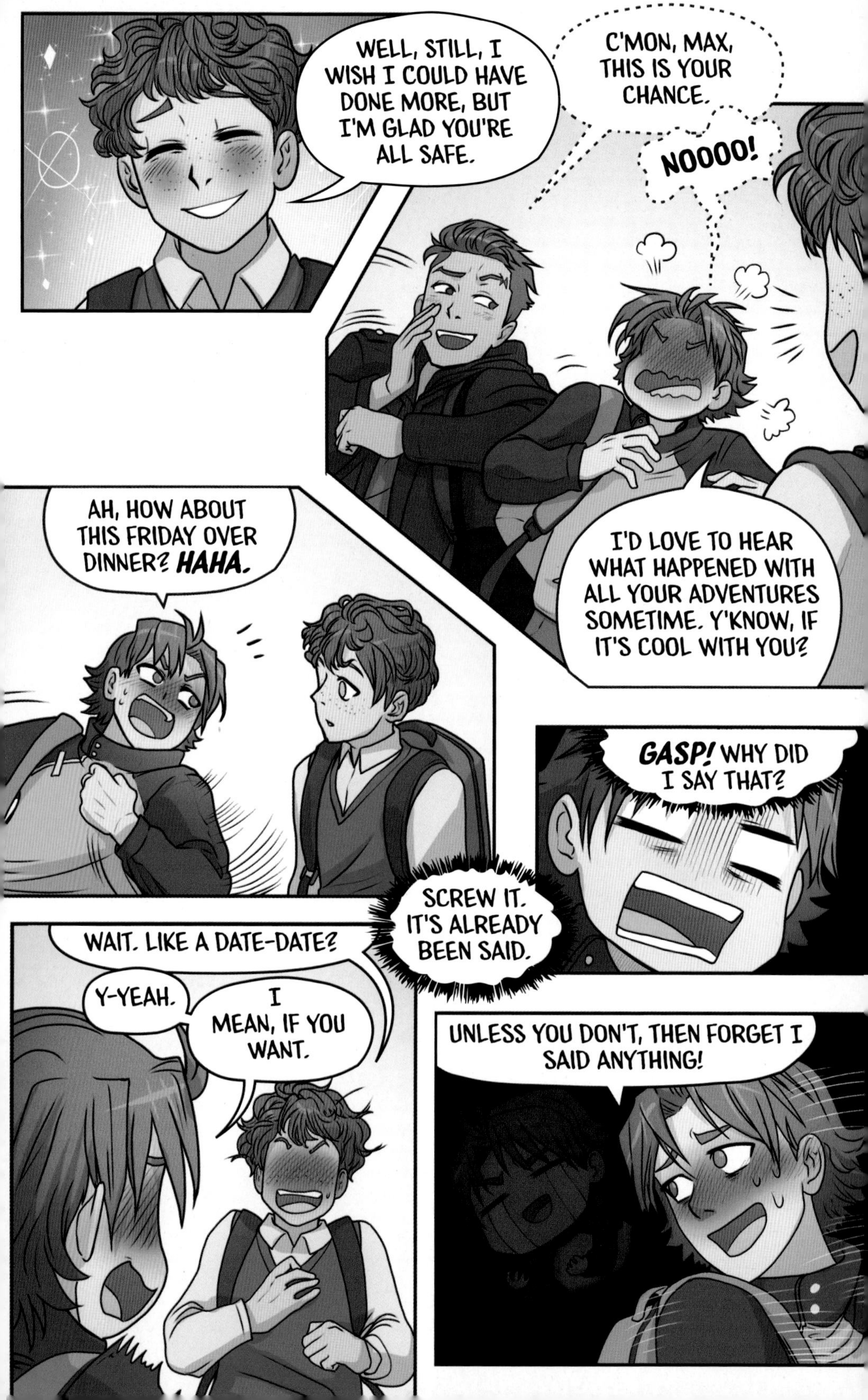
WELL, STILL, I WISH I COULD HAVE DONE MORE, BUT I'M GLAD YOU'RE ALL SAFE.
C'MON, MAX, THIS IS YOUR CHANCE.
NOOOO!
I'D LOVE TO HEAR WHAT HAPPENED WITH ALL YOUR ADVENTURES SOMETIME. Y'KNOW, IF IT'S COOL WITH YOU?
AH, HOW ABOUT THIS FRIDAY OVER DINNER? HAHA.
GASP! WHY DID I SAY THAT?
SCREW IT. IT'S ALREADY BEEN SAID.
WAIT. LIKE A DATE-DATE?
Y-YEAH.
I MEAN, IF YOU WANT.
UNLESS YOU DON'T, THEN FORGET I SAID ANYTHING!

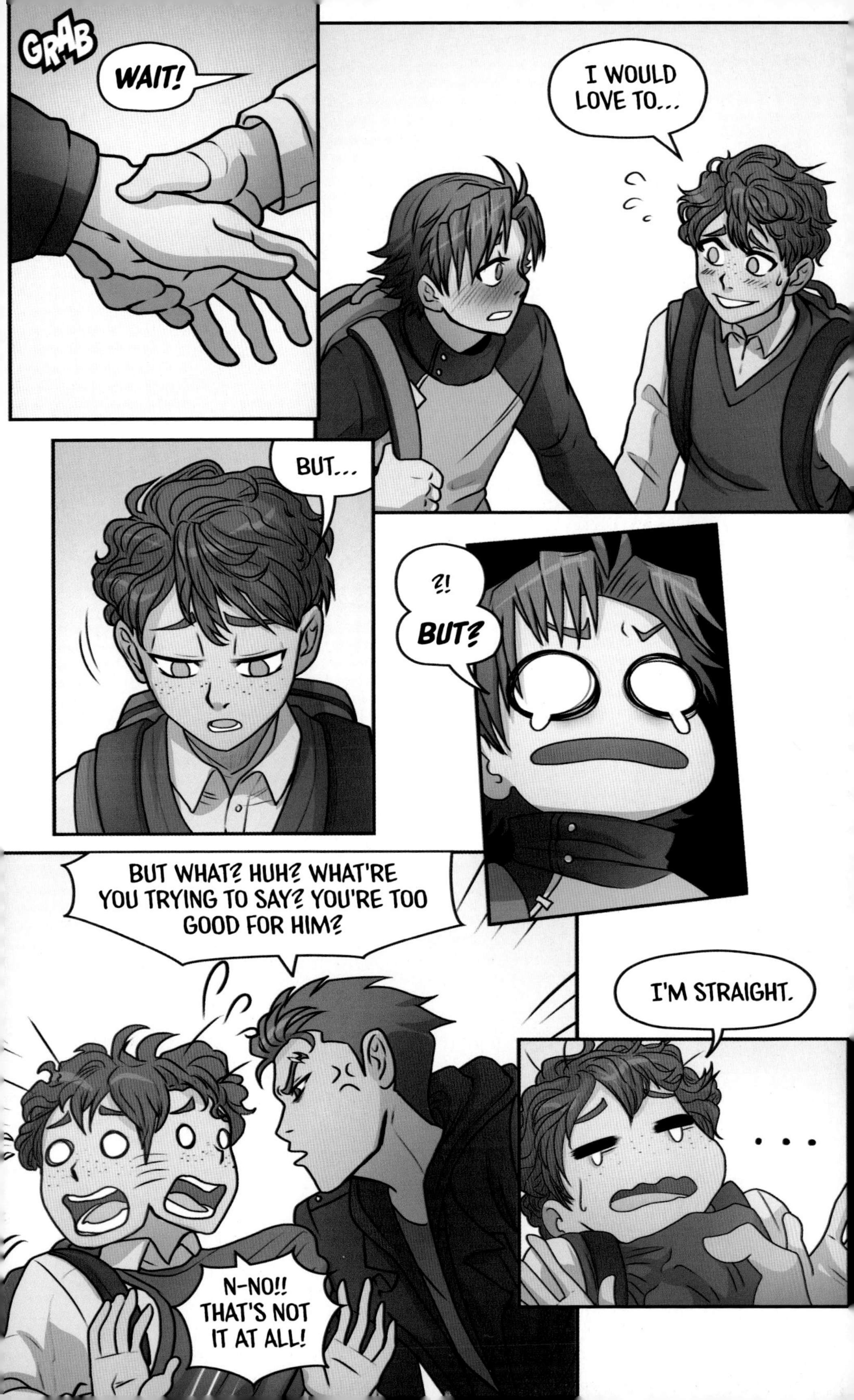

GRAB
WAIT!
I WOULD LOVE TO...
BUT...
?!
BUT?
BUT WHAT? HUH? WHAT'RE YOU TRYING TO SAY? YOU'RE TOO GOOD FOR HIM?
N-NO!! THAT'S NOT IT AT ALL!
I'M STRAIGHT.
. . .

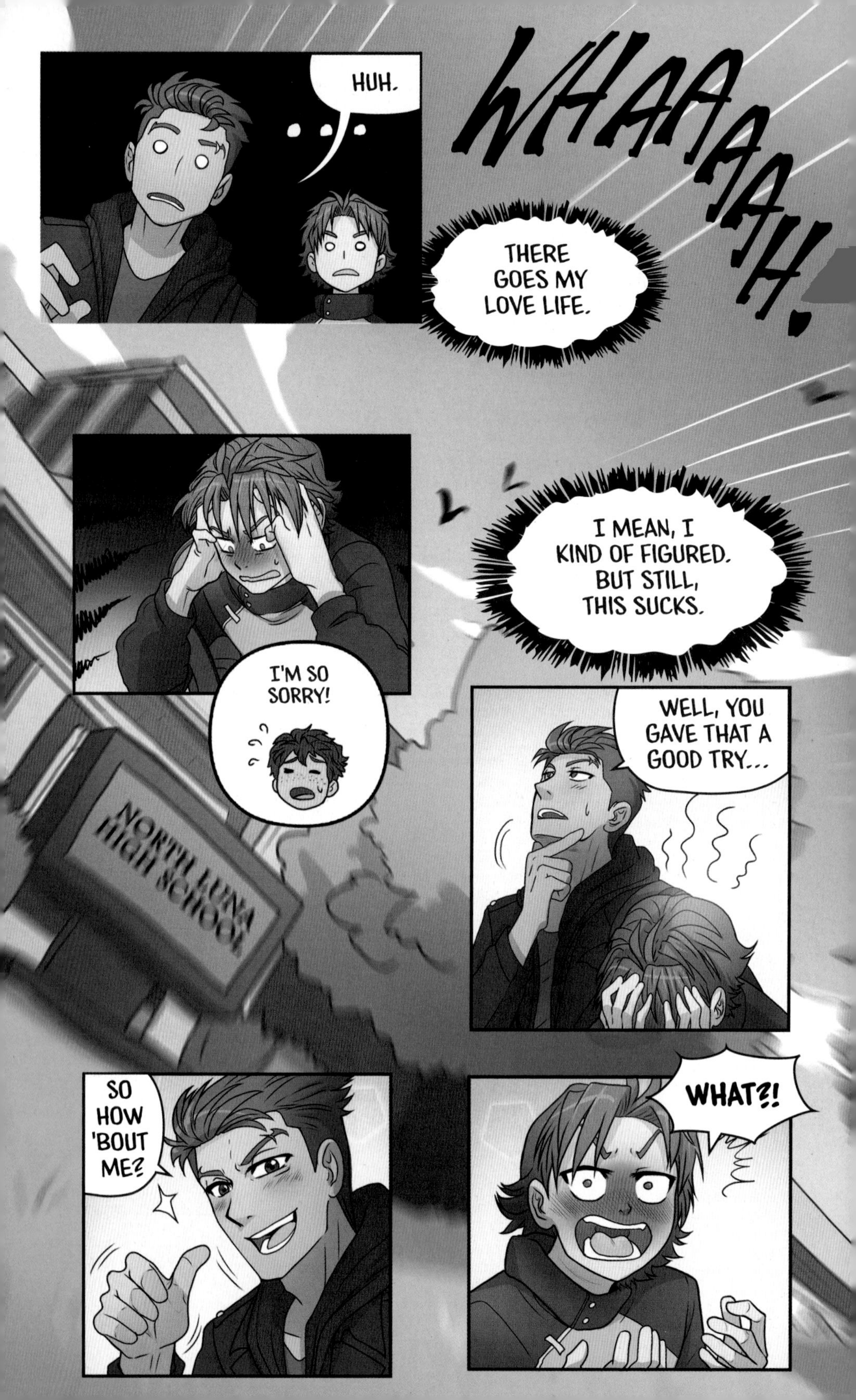
HUH.
...
WHAAAAAH!
THERE GOES MY LOVE LIFE.
I MEAN, I KIND OF FIGURED. BUT STILL, THIS SUCKS.
I'M SO SORRY!
NORTH LUNA HIGH SCHOOL
WELL, YOU GAVE THAT A GOOD TRY...
SO HOW 'BOUT ME?
WHAT?!

EPILOGUE

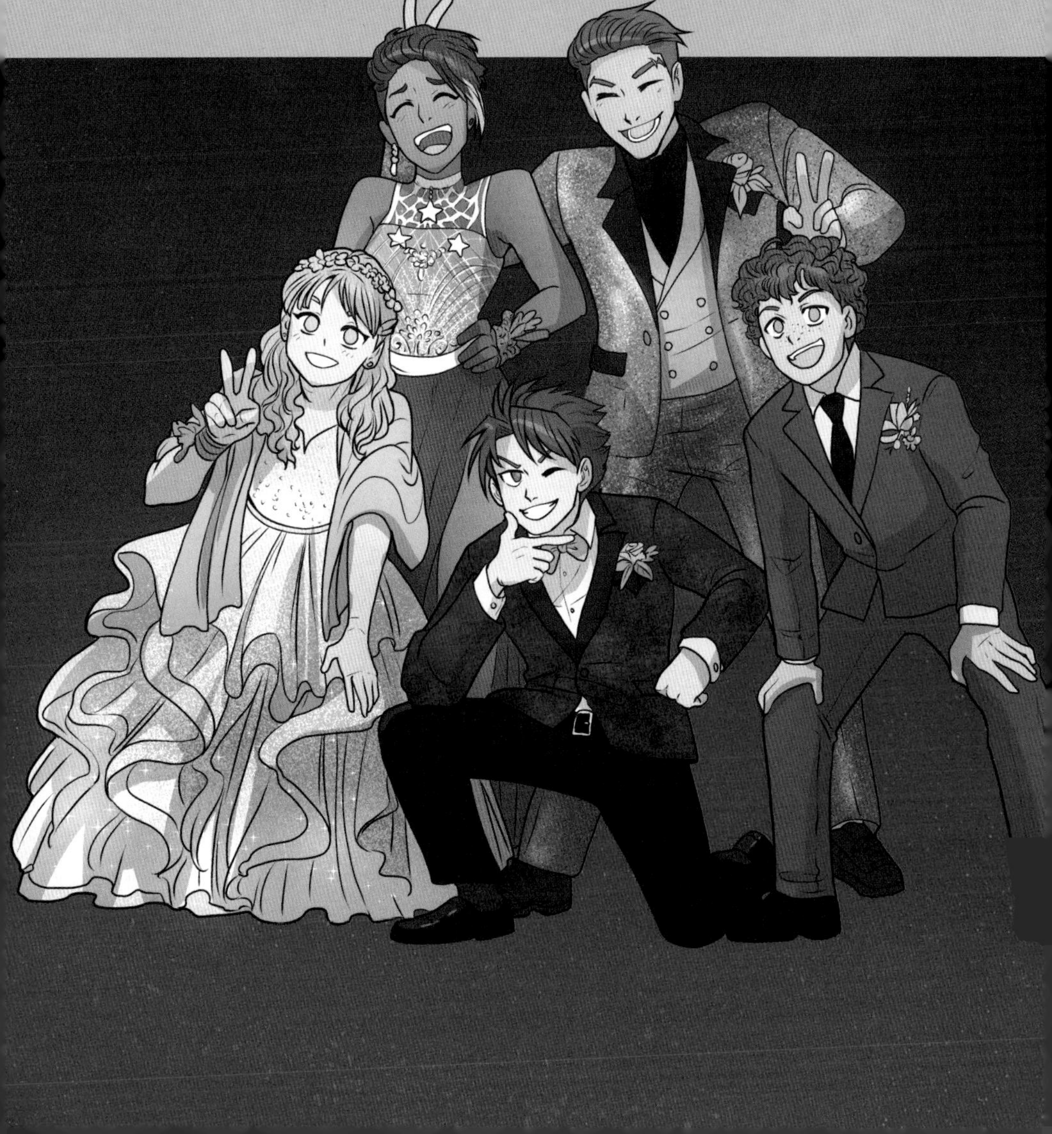

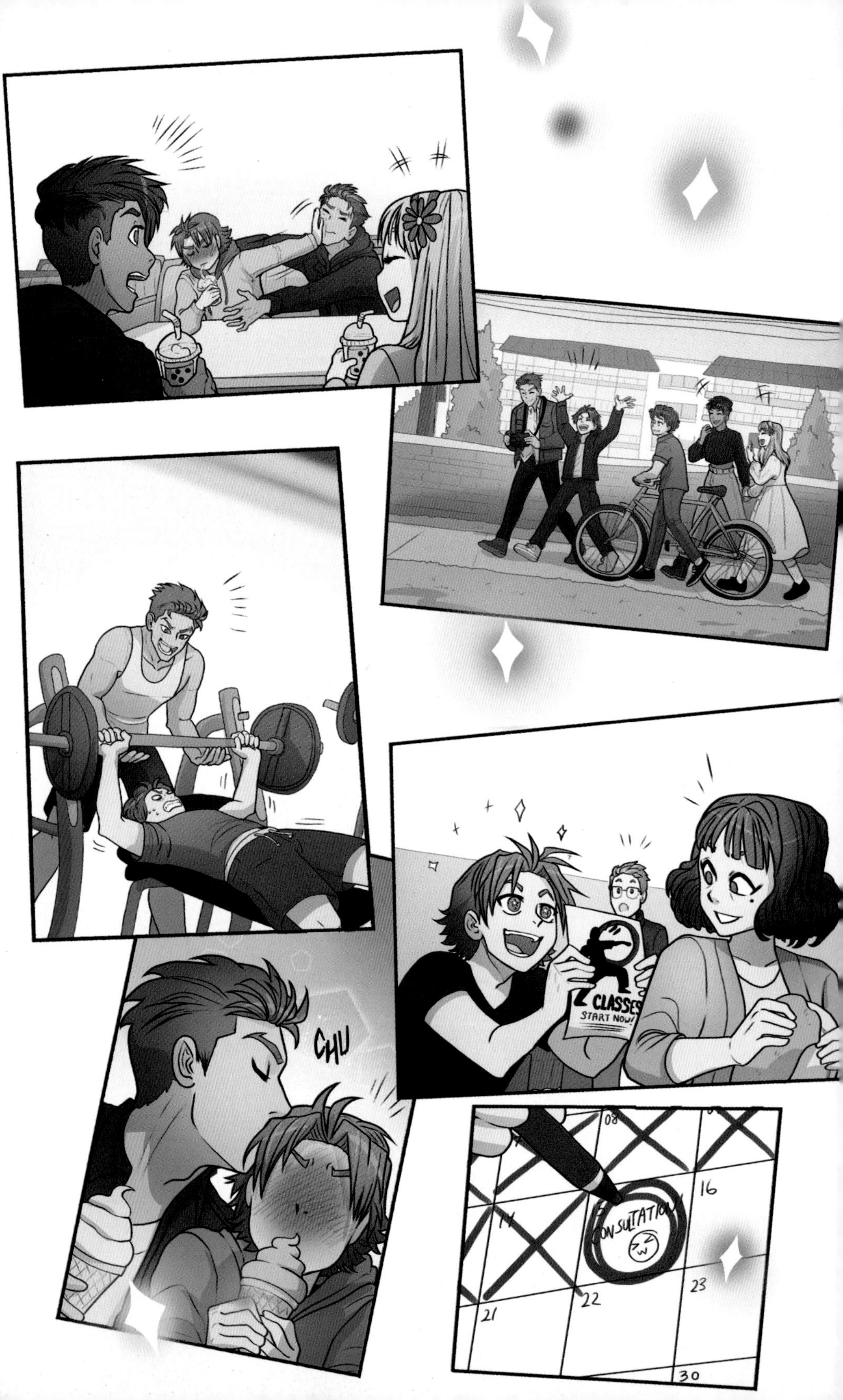

CLASSES
START NOW!
CHU
08
16
14
CONSULTATION
23
22
21
30

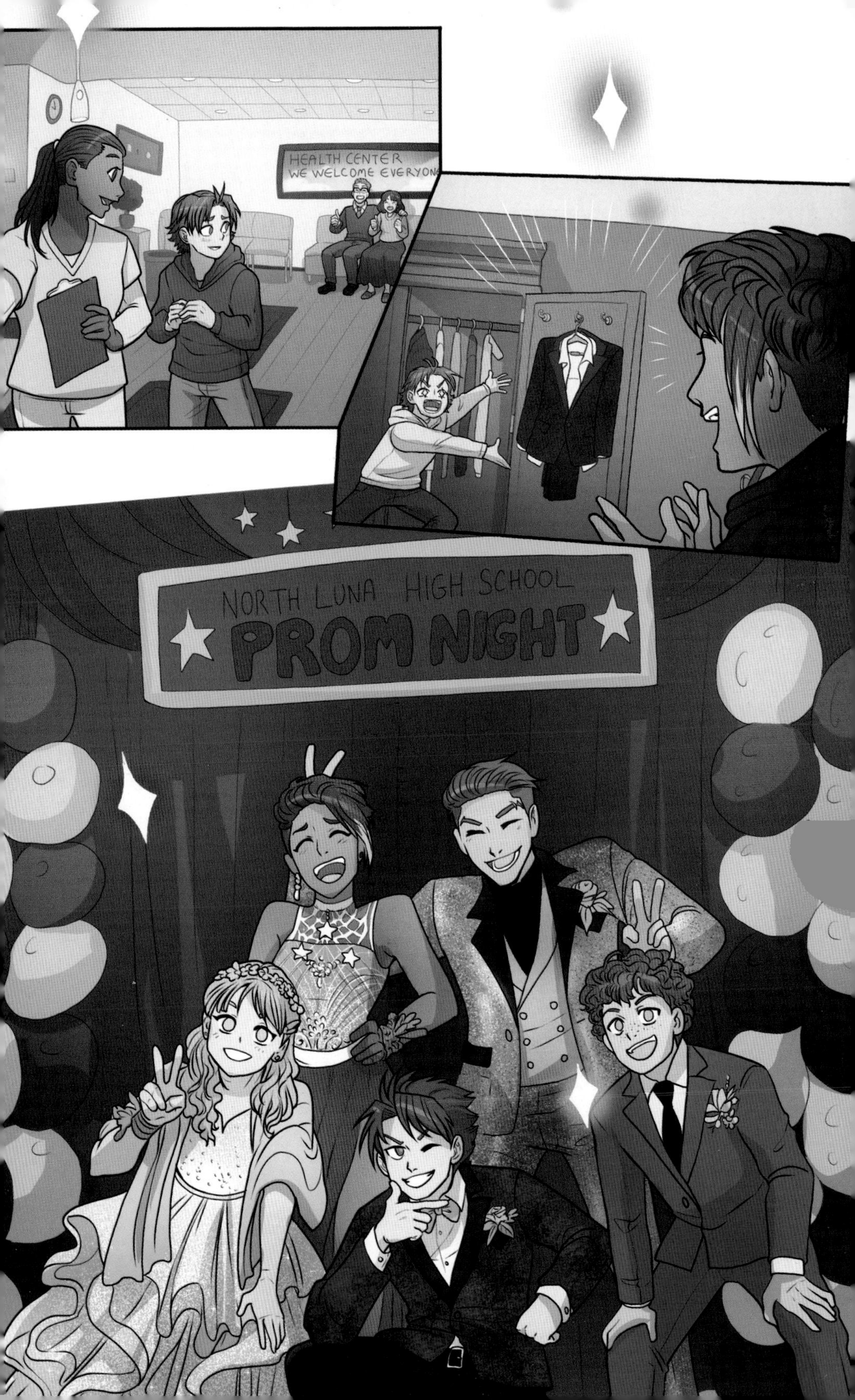
HEALTH CENTER
WE WELCOME EVERYONE
NORTH LUNA HIGH SCHOOL
PROM NIGHT

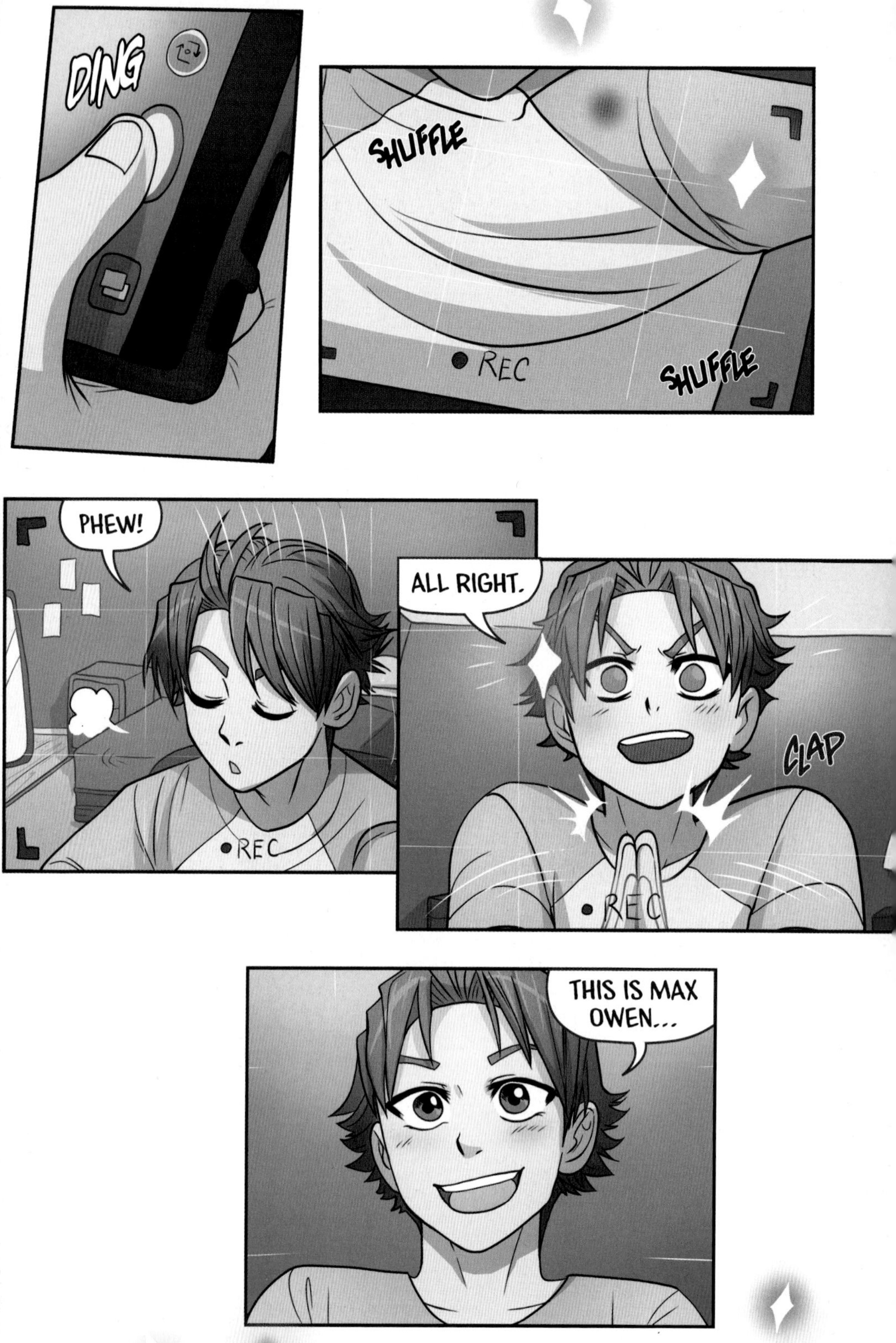
DING
SHUFFLE
REC
SHUFFLE
PHEW!
REC
ALL RIGHT.
CLAP
REC
THIS IS MAX OWEN...

AND THIS IS MY VOICE, ONE DAY ON T.

THANK YOU FOR
READING!

-THE KAO

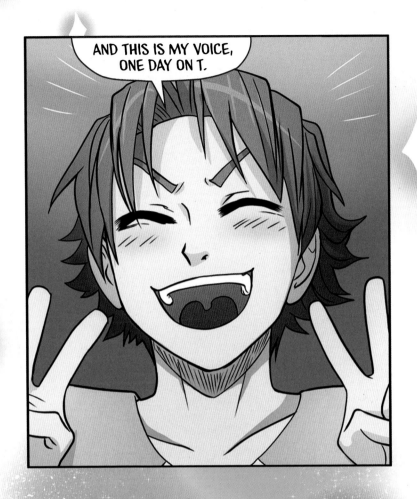

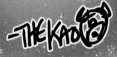